FIELDS OF WRATH

The Renshai Saga: Volume Two

Mickey Zucker Reichert

DAW BOOKS, INC.

DONALD A. WOLLHEIM, FOUNDER

375 Hudson Street, New York, NY 10014

ELIZABETH R. WOLLHEIM
SHEILA E. GILBERT
PUBLISHERS

www.dawbooks.com

First Paperback Printing, January 2016
1 2 3 4 5 6 7 8 9

DAW TRADEMARK REGISTERED
U.S. PAT. AND TM. OFF. AND FOREIGN COUNTRIES
—MARCA REGISTRADA
HECHO EN U.S.A.

PRINTED IN THE U.S.A.

To Koby Moore,

who defies explanation,
an enigma wrapped in riddles

ACKNOWLEDGMENTS

Sheila Gilbert, for her always invaluable assistance, Jody Lee, for her always invaluable cover art, and Mark Moore for his always invaluable invaluability.

Also Sandra Zucker, who never fails to ask, "How's the writing going?"

PROLOGUE

SUNLIGHT SEEPED THROUGH the thickly-bunched leaves of the towering *kirstal* trees, the clearing beneath them riddled with chaotic patches of brilliant light and gray shadow. Ensconced in play with his young mistress, Bobbin could never remember feeling so happy, so comfortable and secure. Then again, remembering was hardly his virtue. To his mind, the world began only nine months earlier, when he had awakened tucked firmly into what turned out to be a doll's bed.

Mistri toddled toward a wall of shale. Though only a head shorter than her playmate, her thick limbs and proportionately large head aptly demonstrated her youth. She was half his weight but seemed not to notice, dragging him around like a favorite stuffed toy. Bobbin did not quite understand his place in the world, but he never doubted his mistress' love. She clutched him more fiercely than she did her dolls and insisted on having him beside her every waking moment.

Bobbin glanced toward Mistri's nursemaid, who perched on the root ball of a fallen tree, alternately peering thoughtfully and writing feverishly on a scrap of parchment. She seemed gigantic compared to her charges, half again as tall and at least twice as broad as Bobbin, though well-proportioned and feminine. He knew humanity came in two distinct sizes: the Masters, like Mistri's nursemaid, and the Servants who resembled him in size and breadth. Bobbin, however, did not fit in with either.

A movement on a large rock over the shale slope caught Bobbin's attention. He peered through the checkered light, trying to make out a shape poised above Mistri. Only rocks, it seemed, yet Bobbin still thought he had seen a glimpse of motion. He had just decided to dismiss it as the flutter of loose leaves in wind, when he saw another movement. Gradually, his gaze carved out a dark creature crouched on a huge stone over Mistri's head.

Suddenly, it pounced.

"No!" Bobbin dove for Mistri. His hands struck her, driving her forward with a gasp of breath. The girl staggered a few steps, lost her balance, and crashed to the ground, wailing. The creature slammed into Bobbin with a force that rattled his teeth, hurling him to the ground. Enormous, curved claws ripped through his clothes to draw a line of blood along his spine. Teeth scored his scalp, and he sensed a jaw powerful enough to crush his skull if he allowed it to close.

Bobbin rolled, throwing off the creature. It dropped back to a crouch, utterly still. Rich brown hair covered its stocky muscular body, and stripes of creamy gold ran from each shoulder, along its flanks, to the base of its short bushy tail. It was smaller than its strength suggested, a quarter to a third of Bobbin's weight, its length perhaps half his height. Its tail was low, its back seemed slightly arched, its snout pointed and short, its head blunt, broad, and flattened. Widely-set eyes studied Bobbin as it snarled and hissed at him, otherwise unmoving.

Bobbin growled back at the creature, mock lunging with his arms spread wide to increase the appearance of his size. Rather than frighten it, the feigned attack seemed to enrage it, and it sprang at Bobbin again with a speed that belied its previous immobility.

"No, *jarfr*!" Mistri screamed through tears. "No hurt Bobbin!"

The nursemaid scooped up Mistri and carried her safely away.

This time, Bobbin ducked, and the animal sailed over him. Its scent filled his nostrils, chokingly musky, strong and horrible. The instant its short legs hit the ground, it bunched them again and flew toward him.

Bobbin dredged at the ground with his fingers. He caught up dirt clods and weeds, nothing solid enough to harm the creature. Nevertheless, as it careened toward him, he hurled both handfuls at its face. The debris proved enough to throw off the attack, and its sharp-nailed claws barely grazed his ear as it soared past him again. Wholly fearless, it gathered itself for another attack.

Blood trickled down Bobbin's back, and cold air seeped through the opening in his undertunic. His head ached. He knew he could not keep this up forever; the beast's endurance would last far longer than his, especially wounded as he was. He dug up more ground, this time rewarded by a fist-sized rock. He yanked it free, his hesitation nearly his downfall. The thing Mistri had called a *jarfr* flew at him again. This time, Bobbin had no choice but to catch it, to embrace it like a lover. The claws raked his sides. The teeth snapped wildly at his face. The foul odor emanating from it seemed to fill his head and made his eyes water. Struggling with its weight and momentum, Bobbin found himself hard-pressed to raise the rock. It slipped in his grip, forcing him to make a desperate choice. He could grapple fully with the creature while the stone fell or grab for the rock and risk losing track of the *jarfr* for the instant he did so.

Bobbin looked away just long enough to snag the rock out of the air. The beast took full advantage, seizing Bobbin's other wrist in its jaws. He could feel the teeth settling into place, prepared to shatter bone. He raised the stone, driving it against the *jarfr*'s skull between its small and wide-set eyes. The thing barely flinched, but the teeth did ease on his wrist in sudden surprise. Using all his strength, Bobbin slammed the rock against it again, in the same place. This time, something gave. Blood spurted from the wound, and the creature's hiss became a howling snarl.

Bobbin expected it to release him, but the jaws clamped tighter on his wrist. The claws flailed relentlessly, the hind ones tearing at his thighs, the forelimbs ripping through air to catch and tear his sleeve. Bobbin felt something collapse in his wrist, and agony speared through his entire arm. He could think of nothing except the pain; it consumed him fully. Yet his other hand acted with mindless instinct, hammering the rock repeatedly against the *jarfr*'s forehead until a hunk of skull detached, and the eyes drifted inward to touch in the center. The *jarfr* stiffened, then went limp in his arms.

Bobbin sank to the ground as well, focused entirely on his wrist, his vision an empty white plain. He barely heard Mistri's voice in his ear, sobbing, "Bobbin, Bobbin." The nursemaid tried to pull her off, then abandoned that job to free the *jarfr* from Bobbin's sagging arms with a broken branch. She poked the beast, apparently making certain it was dead. The blood of man and beast smeared all three of them.

The nursemaid did her duty. "Mistri, are you hurt?"

"No." The girl tightened her grip. "Bobbin hurt. Help Bobbin?" she pleaded, looking up at the woman, teary-eyed.

Bobbin rocked back and forth, trying to divert his attention from the pain. It was diminishing slightly, just enough so that he was becoming aware of the words and actions around him.

The nursemaid crouched beside them, sighing. She clearly saw little reason to assist the man, aside from the frantic entreaties of his mistress. "Where's he hurt?"

Bobbin held up his injured hand, wrist flopping.

"Ah." The nursemaid reached for Bobbin.

His first instinct, to pull away, passed quickly. He doubted she could make things much worse.

In fact, she cradled his wrist with such gentleness and warmth that the pain started to noticeably recede. Then, she made a few guttural noises, tossed her head, and normalcy slid quietly back into place. By the time she released him, Bobbin felt only a throbbing ache in a wrist that, only moments before, had felt on fire.

Bobbin stared at his wrist, moving it gingerly to assure himself it worked again. He had seen the Masters use magic before, and it never ceased to amaze him. He knew he had no such powers, nor did the Servants, and it seemed to him as if magic should not exist at all. Yet, clearly, it did. And now, he knew, it worked on him as well.

Mistri tore a piece off Bobbin's tattered tunic and awkwardly bound the wrist. Her sweet, childish touch felt as soft and harmless as butterfly wings, and a chill of delight fluttered through him. There was something inherently remarkable about a child's ministrations that made everything feel acutely sensitive and innocently special. He smiled at her, and she patted his head.

The nursemaid examined Bobbin's torn back, touching here and there, muttering a few syllables, and the pain faded. Bobbin had not worried about the scratches, despite their depth. Their sting had disappeared beneath the all-consuming agony of his wrist. Finally, she took Mistri's hand and rose, pulling the girl up with her. She brushed the dirt from her clothing, frowning at the blood smeared across her frock, but clearly realized the girl was not the source of any of it.

"Come, Mistri. Time to go home."

Mistri nodded, pulling free of her nursemaid's hand to take Bobbin's instead. She tugged at his arm.

Worried about the stress on his wrist, Bobbin rose quickly, using only his own power. He looked at the *jarfr*'s corpse.

Mistri followed his gaze with her own, and the nurse-maid looked as well. "Very well, Mistri. We'll take it with us." She ran a hand through the pelt, then sniffed her palm and grimaced. "We can wash out the scent, and it'll make warm scarves and gloves." She hefted the carcass and easily slung it over one shoulder. It looked small there, despite the wickedly curved claws drooping from its limp paws, its dead lips locked into a permanent snarl.

Thus far, the nursemaid had done everything with a calm manner that suggested nothing out of the ordinary, but a trembling in her fingers, a wobbliness to her steps told Bobbin the attack had shaken her at least as much as him. Only Mistri seemed unaffected, skipping along at his side, his hand clutched fiercely in her pudgy, sticky fist.

As they walked toward the massive, castlelike dwelling that served as home to Mistri's parents, the girl sang softly to herself, a repetitive tune that Bobbin had come to know well. Along with Mistri, he was learning to speak in stages, though he had not yet done so in the presence of Masters other than Mistri and, now, the single syllable "no" for her nursemaid when the *jarfr* had first attacked. He knew a slew of nouns and verbs, and even syntax was oozing slowly into his base of knowledge. He had a strange sense that he had once spoken fluently, oddly impossible; and in his dreams he had no trouble communicating freely in a language he did not recognize.

Yet, even as he learned, Bobbin often felt as if he were

missing huge parts of conversation, sometimes even the entire thing. Apparently, the language of both Masters and Servants contained a component he had not yet discovered: hand signals, perhaps, tone or timbre, inflection, or facial expression. Despite careful observation, he had not come close to unearthing the method. As a result, they classified him as animal rather than human.

And Bobbin knew he looked the part. Though he closely resembled the Servants in height and general shape, no one would mistake him for one of them. To a man, they had fine reddish hair and green eyes, their figures sleeker and more elegant than his. He had yet to meet one who stood quite as tall or broad as he did, though their size differential was barely noticeable compared to the enormous Masters. Coarse, black hair covered Bobbin's head in thick curls; and, though he believed himself quite young, he already had to scrape off facial hair every day. It seemed to grow faster and thicker than theirs as well, as though furry was his natural state. His chest sported clumps of inky hair, much darker and thicker than the Masters' or Servants', and it even coated his limbs. Mistri clearly liked his fur, grooming it with soft brushes and decorating it with ribbons that made him look silly but never failed to earn a smile from the Masters.

The tiny forest gave way to tightly packed cottages where the Servants lived, all huddled together like sticks in a bundle. Bobbin knew open places like the one they had just left were few and sparse, treasures to savor. Though he had little experience with wild animals, he knew they rarely attacked humans, especially in broad daylight as the *jarfr* had. He did not know how he knew this, but he suspected the dwindling woodland played a part, forcing the creatures onto smaller and smaller ranges with more competition for prey.

The villagers ceased their normal activities to bow to the nursemaid and her charge and stare curiously at Bobbin. He was a singularity or, at least, something quite rare. He had never met, or heard about, another of his kind. Mistri had discovered him on the shore, bedraggled and all but dead. She had insisted on bringing him home; and her parents had obliged her, as they usually did. The adults never hesitated to speculate in Bobbin's presence, but he had only recently managed to understand what they said about him. They seemed to place him in the category of relatively intelligent animal, a distant and primitive relation to the Servants.

The threesome soon reached the mansion, with its inordinately high latches and massive construction. Four Servants on the stoop snapped to attention as they arrived, and Bobbin wondered why his mind always conjured images of swords and spears where there were only rags and brooms. Struggling together, the tiny Servants managed to shove open the massive door for the burdened nursemaid, who nodded her thanks with a friendly smile. The moment they entered the entryway, voices emerged. Three women chatted over tea and honey bread.

Mistri's mother, Hortens, shared her daughter's straw-colored hair and bright blue eyes. The other two women wore their reddish locks in tight buns. One was speaking, "...one never knows when the tamest animal might turn on you. I wouldn't trust my precious daughter—"

Stunned by the words, Bobbin acted without thought. He ran to Mistri's mother, seizing the gigantic hand resting in her lap. "No! Love Mistri. Not hurt Mistri never never." Frustrated by the limitations of his vocabulary, Bobbin went silent. Only then, he realized he still wore tattered clothing steeped in blood.

Hortens leaped to her feet, screaming. The teacup dropped from her fingers, splashing its hot contents over both of them and smashing on the chair. Shards of crockery skidded across the floor.

Suddenly scalded, Bobbin sprang backward.

"Bobbin *save* me, Mummy!" Mistri said.

Every eye went suddenly to the child, then to the nursemaid. Apparently, the nursemaid had used that as yet undiscovered form of communication that always confounded Bobbin. Although no words emerged from her mouth, she did a swift acting out of the events, using the corpse to illustrate such points as the creature leaping at Mistri and whirling around Bobbin. Finally, she let it slip to the floor, dangling her wrist as if broken.

Bobbin found himself at Mistri's side, having apparently retreated there for comfort, without conscious intent. Mistri wrapped her arms around him.

Mistri's father, Kentt, came running into the room from one of the four doorways. Though not present for the nursemaid's playacting, he somehow seemed to know what she had communicated to the other women.

Kentt went straight to his daughter, ruffling Bobbin's hair before lifting Mistri in his arms. "Are you all right?"

Mistri beamed. "Not hurt, Poppy." She looked down at Bobbin. "Bobbin save me. Save me *jarfr*." She made a swooping gesture to indicate the animal's attempt to pounce on her. "It want *eat* me." She opened and closed her mouth, hands raised, fingers curved and separated to indicate claws.

Kentt stuck his face in hers. "Well, it's a good thing it didn't eat you." A mock snarl twisted his features. "Because then I wouldn't get *my* dinner." He feigned biting at Mistri, making exaggerated chewing noises.

She giggled, planting her hands on his face as if to stop him.

Kentt reached for Bobbin. Bobbin stiffened, uncertain what to expect; but the giant merely hefted him with his free hand, so that he now held them both aloft. "What a fine and loyal pet you have here, Mistri. Can I have him?"

"*My* Bobbin." Mistri grabbed him fiercely, arousing pain in his partially healed back. Fresh blood oozed along his spine.

One of the women, Bobbin could not see which, let out a noise of revulsion. "Kentt, please. It's hard enough to get blood out of clothing, you have to share it? If you're going to allow Mistri to romp with animals, at least have the decency to keep it a clean one."

Kentt lowered Mistri and Bobbin to the ground, only then looking at his tunic, now smeared with rust-colored lines. The freshly reopened wound had not touched him, but it currently dripped on the floor. "Your Aunt Floralyn's right, Mistri. Time you and Bobbin both got baths."

Mistri skipped happily toward the bathing room, the nursemaid chasing after her.

Hortens swept the crockery bits and tea from her chair. "Kentt, he spoke. Bobbin actually talked."

Bobbin turned his gaze to Kentt, worried. He had no idea whether revealing his ability to speak helped or harmed him.

To his relief, Kentt grinned. "Well, why not? His throat looks much the same as the Servants, so we always knew he had the capacity. What exactly did he say?"

"Well . . ." Hortens looked at her female companions for

assistance. "It was crude and broken, but I believe he essentially said he loved Mistri and would never hurt her."

The third woman glanced at the ceiling, then quoted Bobbin exactly, though in a dull monotone. "No. Love Mistri. Not hurt Mistri never never."

Kentt shrugged. "Well, that's clear enough. Discarding the double negative, which was surely spoken from ignorance, I think we can safely say he intends to continue protecting Mistri."

Though he did not understand every word, Bobbin caught the gist of Kentt's pronouncement and nodded.

Kentt's hand fell to Bobbin's head and tousled his hair fondly. "Every child should have a Bobbin."

Floralyn pursed her lips but gave some quarter. "Well, Bobbin does seem worth keeping. But I wouldn't trust something strong enough to do that . . ." She indicated the dead *jarfr*. ". . . with the life of my child, if I had one."

"Bobbin's safe," Hortens said firmly, sweeping the last bits of teacup into a pile. "I think that's abundantly clear. Now, if another one, another Bobbin, came along, it would have to prove itself. But I think Bobbin himself has done enough."

Kentt smiled at Bobbin. "Good ol' boy." He patted Bobbin's cheek. Though he clearly did not intend to harm him, a tap of that huge hand felt more like a slap. "Let's get you cleaned up and rested. Then we'll work on teaching you a few more words, eh?"

Bobbin returned the smile. He could not remember feeling so contented and right. Then, again, remembering was not his virtue.

CHAPTER 1

Involving oneself in the affairs of wizards should never be done in ignorance.

— *Colbey Calistinsson*

SAVIAR RA-KHIRSSON TOOK the castle stairs two at a time, rushing past servants and guardsmen, a sword on each hip. Strawberry-blond hair, still wet from his bath, streamed wildly around his young features. He had doffed his blood-soaked battle clothes for a fresh tunic and breeks, had slept off the exhaustion of a hard-fought war, and finally felt clean enough to face his darling.

In his haste, Saviar nearly skidded into two Béarnian guardsmen who stood, spears crossed, in front of Chymmerlee's door. To their credit, they remained firmly in place despite the muscular Renshai careening toward them, their expressions grim. Both wore standard blue and gold, with the rearing bear symbol of the high kingdom on their tabards. Saviar thought he saw a hint of fear in one's deep brown eyes.

An instant before collision, Saviar rescued himself with an agile sidestep. "Sorry," he said, smiling to put them at ease. "I just came to see Chymmerlee."

"We're under orders," the larger one said. "You cannot enter."

Saviar accepted the formality easily. As the son of a Knight of Erythane, he had become accustomed to much more extensive and oppressive decorum. Only the Knights knew how to turn even the most marvelous feast into tedium. "Tell her it's Saviar. She'll see me."

"Begging your pardon." Though smaller than his fellow, the other guard still had greater mass than Saviar and the majority of men in the Westlands. Most Béarnides did. "But you, specifically, cannot enter."

"Me? Specifically?" The words caught Saviar completely off his guard. The united armies of the continent had just won a massive war, in no small part because of Chymmerlee's magic and his own sword arm. She had doted on him since the moment his twin had led her to him, comatose, blood poisoned by a festering wound. She had saved his life and nursed him through his recovery. Later, they had held hands, laughed together, even kissed. She alone of her people had accompanied them to the war, the only mage who had assisted in a battle of epic proportions. It made no sense for Chymmerlee to turn her back on him now. "You must be mistaken. Can you please just tell her I'm here? She'll see me."

The Béarnides glanced at one another, the somberness of their expressions never changing. Their spears remained in place. The first speaker cleared his throat. "There is no reason to ask. It is by Chymmerlee's own orders that we are barring you . . . and your twin."

Saviar's hands drifted instinctively to his hilts. Renshai resolved most problems in a wild flurry of swordplay.

Apparently, the guardsmen had noticed Saviar's movement. Though they stayed in place, they clearly looked alarmed. The smaller one's voice cracked slightly as he explained, "We know you're Renshai, Saviar. You can probably gut both of us without breaking a sweat, but we hope you won't."

The first added, "We're only doing our jobs and protecting a woman you clearly care about."

Saviar deliberately took his hands from his hilts. Renshai trained to the sword from infancy, with both hands and in all conditions. Little mattered in their lives besides dying in glorious combat, thus earning the exquisite and violent afterlife of Valhalla. "I'm not going to attack you." Saviar saw little sense in doing so. He could kill them with a few lazy sword strokes, but he would bring the wrath of Béarn down upon him, make the Renshai even more hated, if possible, and dishonor his knightly father and grandfather. "I wouldn't do that."

Well-hidden relief barely changed the guards' stances, just a nearly imperceptible loosening of sinews.

To Saviar's surprise, tears pressed against his eyelids. He knew he had to leave as quickly as possible or risk embarrassing himself. Turning on his heel, keeping his head high, he went back down the steps and into the courtyard.

Once there, Saviar found himself more angry and confused than sad. He forced back the tears and pounded a fist on the natural granite wall of the castle. Pain flashed through his hand, but did little to distract him. He punched the wall again, harder.

A familiar voice wafted to him. "Not enough bruises from the war, Savi? You need to break a few fingers, too?"

Saviar spun, drawing his sword, glad for a target on which to sate his rage.

His twin, Subikahn, did not respond to the challenge. He stood near a neat hedgerow, watching Saviar curiously, his black hair in its usual disarray, his small wiry form a stark contrast to his brother's powerful one. Though born of the same pregnancy, each resembled his different father more than either of his brothers. "Sheathe it, Savi. We have no enemies in Béarn's courtyard."

Saviar blinked, suddenly realizing he stood in broad sunlight amid the numerous gardens that characterized Béarn's courtyard. So focused on his own problems, he had not noticed the myriad blossoms and shrubs, the neat rows of vegetables, or the many stone statues, with bears predominating. The sweet aromas of petals and pollen surrounded him. Feeling a smile edging onto his features, Saviar forced it down. "Renshai spar anywhere, anytime."

Subikahn could hardly deny it. "And Béarn supplies us with the best sparring room in existence. Don't we owe it to her not to trample her beautiful grounds and crops now that the war has ended?"

Saviar slammed his sword back into its sheath. Uncertain what to say or do, he spoke simple fact. "I'm angry."

"I noticed." Subikahn stepped around the hedge to sit on one of the whitestone benches. He patted the space beside him. "Besides having just fought the war of a lifetime, having slept what seemed like months, and attending myriad feasts, what's bothering you?"

Saviar did not move. "Chymmerlee refuses to see me."

Subikahn's grin wilted, and his brow furrowed. "Chym-merlee? Really?" He shook his head. "You were all over each other before the war."

Saviar made a wordless noise. It was not like Subikahn to repeat things they both already knew.

"Did she give you a reason?"

This time, Saviar twisted and slammed the bottom of his boot against the castle wall. "She wouldn't even see me. How could she give me a reason?"

Subikahn rose and walked to his brother. "You're strong, Savi; but I don't think even you can topple a castle formed from a mountain."

Saviar whirled. "What?"

Subikahn studied the muddy boot print on the wall. "If you're trying to shake her out the window, I don't think you can. Besides, someone else might get hurt."

Saviar was in no mood for humor. "You're not helping," he said through gritted teeth.

"Fine. Why didn't you ask whoever told you she wouldn't see you for the reason?"

"Because I—" Saviar had no good answer. He would never admit he had almost cried. "Because I didn't, that's all. I didn't." Something Subikahn had said stuck in his mind. . . . *shake her out the window* . . . Saviar glanced side-long at his swarthy brother. "Your father taught you how to climb buildings, didn't he?"

Subikahn chuckled, though it seemed a bit forced. He had reconciled with Tae Kahn, his father, only the previous day. The rift was still healing. "Your father teaches you man-ners and honor and responsibility, mine swinging on chan-deliers and slide-racing down banisters. King Tae and his courtly lessons on . . . the thrill of being shot by one's own guards breaking into one's own castle."

Saviar walked carefully around the subject. He knew the king of Stalmize from their family's once-a-year visits when they were children. Saviar had looked forward to it, eagerly, for months. The journey was grueling, but well worth it. Tae had always frolicked with the boys, more playmate than adult.

Now, however, it seemed wrong to joke about the childlike behavior of Subikahn's father. Tae had volunteered for a war-time spying mission that had left him so near death no one had expected him to survive. Though his recovery now seemed certain, he still suffered from the ordeal. "I'm just thinking . . . if someone climbed up to Chymmerlee's window . . ." He measured Subikahn's reaction as he spoke. For the moment, his twin half-brother seemed to be listening. ". . . he wouldn't have to deal with the guards . . ."

Still no sign from Subikahn.

". . . and she might talk?" Now, Saviar went silent, wishing Subikahn would give him something, some sign that he was listening.

Subikahn looked back, brow furrowed. "Sounds like a reasonable idea to me. Why don't you try it?"

Saviar took a backward step. "Me?" He made a grand gesture that outlined his large physique. "Do you really think I could climb a wall?"

Subikahn shrugged. "You're as competent as I am."

Saviar snorted. "At Renshai maneuvers, maybe." Then, worried he might have offended his brother, he added more forcefully, "Maybe." Saviar had lost some recent memory when he had awakened from his near-fatal injuries. Subikahn had once claimed Saviar had won a spar between them that he could not recall fighting. Saviar did not know the details of that battle, nor would Subikahn further enlighten him. Saviar assumed he had used a trick Subikahn did not want repeated. "But I'm clearly not built for climbing. My fingers and toes might just bear my weight, but I doubt I could find room for my massive hands and feet on tiny ledges. And the ledges would likely crumble beneath me."

"Ah." Subikahn's dark brows rose in increments. "So you really were trying to punch down the castle. You seriously believe solid granite can't hold you?"

Saviar studied his abraded fist. Tiny spots of blood had developed, but nothing worse. "I'm not applauding my own strength. I'm just saying the weakest part of stone is the tips of ledges. I weigh a lot more than you, and I don't move as quickly." The fact that he had to explain what seemed painfully evident further fueled his irritation. "I'm sick to death of discussing this. Will you do it for me, or not?"

"Not . . ." Subikahn said.

Saviar's hands balled to fists, though he had no intention of using them.

". . . for you. But I will do it for Chymmerlee."

Saviar breathed a sigh of relief and finally came over to sit beside his brother. Subikahn's reasons did not matter, so long as the job got done. "Thank you."

"Don't thank me yet." Subikahn's gaze rolled over the castle wall, measuring its height and its windows. "Just because I can climb doesn't mean I'll have the words to fix whatever blundering mistake you made that has her unwilling to even talk to you."

"To us," Saviar corrected, remembering the guard's words. "She won't see you, either." Few things could make less sense to Saviar. He, his father, and Subikahn had kept Chymmerlee safe, battling waves of attackers commanded by the enemy *Kjempemagiska* to kill her. The other side had had only this one user of magic while the allies of the continent had two: Chymmerlee and King Griff's second wife, the elf Tem'aree'ay, who had backed her up from the castle rooftop. The three men had worn themselves far past exhaustion protecting Chymmerlee.

Subikahn's brow furrowed. "So you got her mad at me, too, huh? Thanks."

Saviar wanted to punch the wall again, but he remained seated. "I didn't do anything. I haven't seen or spoken to her since the war. When the *Kjempemagiska* fell, our soldiers hustled her out." He shook his head. "There must be some mistake."

Subikahn looked thoughtful, still studying his route. "Must be." He rose and headed toward the castle wall, seemingly oblivious to everything else in front of him.

Saviar stood up and walked alongside his brother to steer him around obstacles, though he need not have bothered. Like all Renshai, Subikahn remained attentive to everything, even when he seemed incapable of noticing.

When he arrived at the base of the castle wall, Subikahn pointed upward. "It's that one, right? Fourth floor?"

Saviar looked in the indicated direction, shielding his eyes from the sun. He had irises so soft a blue they appeared nearly white, exactly like his grandfather's; and that pallor seemed to make him so much more vulnerable to light than his dark-eyed twin. "One over to the right."

Subikahn glanced from window to window. Both had

frilly curtains fluttering in the morning breeze. "One over to the right. You're sure?"

Irritation flared anew. "Of course I know Chymmerlee's window. Why wouldn't I know?" Then, remembering Subikahn was about to do him a huge favor, he moderated his tone. "I'm saying one over from directly above my head. That's not necessarily one over from what you're looking at, though."

"I've got it." Subikahn continued to stare upward. The sunlight did not seem to bother him at all. "I just don't want to get arrested for crawling into a princess' window. That might look very bad."

Saviar could not help smiling. Only a scant handful of people knew Subikahn preferred the company of men. Sodomy was a capital crime in the East, and Tae's fear for his son's life had resulted in the temporary rift between them. "True, but as a prince, you'd probably get little more than disdainful glances, a few whispers, and a rap on the knuckles."

Subikahn shrugged. "Maybe. But I could do without the scrutiny of my love life." He pressed his fingers into irregularities in the stone construction, kicked off his boots, and found similar notches for his toes.

"Careful," Saviar hissed, though he needn't have whispered. In open morning sunlight, anyone spying could see what they were doing farther away than they could hear it. Standing directly beneath Subikahn, prepared to support him if anything went wrong, Saviar glanced around the courtyard. Though he saw a few other people strolling through the pathways or sitting on benches beneath shading canopies, none were looking in their direction.

Subikahn scrambled upward with skill that belied his earlier protestations. Even dodging the easy windowsills for fear of discovery, he climbed like a spider, body tight to the stone, arms and legs reaching and pulling as if immune to the natural forces that held everything else to the ground. At times like this, Saviar felt proud of his brother's dexterity. Grace did not come as easily to him; he sometimes felt as floundering and awkward as a plow horse.

At length, Subikahn cautiously pulled himself up to the fourth-story window ledge of Chymmerlee's room. Several moments passed. Saviar's heart pounded as he tried to imagine the discovery, the meeting, and the conversation that followed. Then, suddenly, something flashed, as strong and sudden as lightning. An instant later, Subikahn plummeted from the window.

"Gods!" Saviar heard himself shouting. He clawed the air, as if to catch handholds for his twin. Subikahn, too, slashed crazily, his hands or feet skimming stone at intervals that barely slowed his fall. Saviar stood firm, bracing himself for the impact. Subikahn crashed into his arms with stunning force; and they both tumbled to the ground in a wheel of arms and legs. They tried to roll; but, knotted together, they thrashed around instead. Pain shot through Saviar's nose, chest, and both legs; and he tasted blood.

Subikahn unwound himself from Saviar and sprang to his feet.

Saviar also rose, wiping blood from his nose with the back of his hand. "What did she say?" he asked breathlessly.

Subikahn's eyes seemed unfocused. He looked around wildly. "She called us demons, deceivers, and liars. Then, she tried to kill me."

Shocked, Saviar could only find himself saying, "How?"

"Blast of magic in the face while I'm four stories in the air. I'm blind, by the way."

"Blind?" Concern shuddered through Saviar. A Renshai who lost his vision had little choice but *tåphresëlmordat*, deliberate suicide in battle. Saviar braced himself for his brother's attack, which never came. "Are you sure?"

Subikahn turned Saviar a look that might have withered, had it not focused several hands' lengths to his right.

Saviar seized Subikahn's arm, trying to hide the panic in his own voice. Blood continued to drip from his nose, unheeded. He guided Subikahn along a path and around a corner, thinking it best not to sit beneath the window of an angry sorceress. When they had traveled a reasonable distance, he pushed Subikahn onto a bench.

Subikahn scuttled into a defensive crouch on the whitestone.

Finding a sword-cleaning rag deep in his pocket, Saviar clapped it over his face, pinching his nose to stop the bleeding. "She's really mad."

Subikahn rolled his eyes, voice dripping sarcasm. "You think so?"

Focused on his own thoughts, Saviar failed to notice his brother's tone. "To try to kill you after all we—"

"All we what?" Subikahn's right hand clamped to his hilt. "She saved your life and revealed all the deepest secrets of herself and her people. People who, by the way, had kept themselves safely hidden for centuries. What, exactly, did we do for her?"

"We kept her alive through the war."

"A war we dragged her into." Subikahn squinted, blinking several times.

Saviar refused to accept that. "We didn't drag her anywhere. We sent her home; she chose to follow us."

"Because she knew we needed her. And she cared for you."

Saviar's chest squeezed. "I cared for her, too," he said, defensively. "I still do."

Subikahn blinked several more times in succession. "My vision's coming back."

Saviar breathed a sigh of relief. *Chymmerlee would never hurt us.* The reality belied the thought. If he had not broken Subikahn's fall, Subikahn would have been seriously injured, if not killed. As it happened, they were both lucky to have sustained nothing worse than bruises and a bloody nose. "I knew it would," he said, matter-of-factly.

"Well, I wish you would have told me. I was starting to panic." Subikahn studied his brother. "Ah, so that's why your voice sounded funny. I thought the magic affected my hearing, too."

Saviar finally dared to release the rag from his nose. Almost immediately, a trickle of blood flowed from it again. With a sigh, he replaced the rag and pinched his nostrils together. He looked up at the massive castle, tracing the route from the fourth floor to the ground. "Do you really think Chymmerlee wanted to . . . kill you?" He found it impossible to imagine the sweet-tempered, kind young woman intentionally harming anything.

Subikahn blinked a few more times, then measured his vision, turning his head this way and that. "By Hel's withered form, Saviar, she clouted me in the face with brutal magic and sent me plummeting four stories onto all kinds of stonework."

Guilt descended on Saviar. *The war ruined her. The war we essentially forced her to fight.* Despite harboring the only human magic, all the Mages of Myrcidë had shown themselves to be a peaceful, quiet people who wanted nothing more than to be left alone while they gradually regained their former numbers and power. More than three centuries earlier, they had suffered a great genocide at the hands of bored and exiled Renshai. Suddenly, as if awakening from a great blindness himself, Saviar understood. "Subikahn, she knows."

"Knows?"

"Knows we're Renshai. Someone's told her. She knows."

Subikahn made a gesture, half-nod, half-shrug. He finally looked at Saviar. "It was inevitable, I suppose. With your father commanding a platoon of exiled Renshai, and all their battle and death cries. I guess you should have told her before she found out on her own."

Saviar gritted his teeth and balled his fists, releasing his nose. If his brother had not just risked his life on Saviar's behalf, a serious spar would have been inevitable. "You're the one who made me promise not to! Now she thinks I'm a great, big *liar*!"

Subikahn's eyes widened as he stared down his twin. "At the time, you were awakening from a coma inside their compound. You had no idea of the extent of hatred the Mages of Myrcidë harbor for our kind. They would have slaughtered us."

Saviar turned away. He did not know how to reconcile his honor in these circumstances. At the time, weakened and confused, he would have done anything his brother told him, and Subikahn had demanded only that one thing. Later, Saviar had learned of a second deception. The mages had taken the twins in and healed Saviar only because they sensed an "aura," an indication that they carried magical blood. Saviar now knew the source of the magic the mages had sensed: his sword. Subikahn had been carrying it when he met Chymmerlee, and he had returned it to Saviar upon his awakening.

Subikahn knew the significance of honor to Saviar. The larger twin still had visions of joining the Knights of Erythane, like his father and grandfather. "I'm sorry, Savi. What choice did I have? You were helpless, and they had just saved your life. Was I supposed to say: 'Thanks for rescuing my brother's soul from Hel. Now you have to kill us'?"

Saviar had to admit the folly of such a thing, but he remained with his back to his brother, arms folded across his chest, bloody rag still clutched in his fist. "You could have let me die. Those were war wounds."

"Death from infection, even festering war wounds, would have damned your soul to Hel."

Saviar whirled on his brother, wishing he had retained some memory of the events surrounding his injuries. Subikahn's vagueness, and his own frustration, condensed to sudden anger. "I still don't understand that. If the battle wounds were not themselves fatal, then we had time. Why didn't you attack me when the wounds began to turn, while I could still fight and die with honor? Why didn't you let me find a hero's death, to earn the forever reward of Valhalla? You couldn't possibly have known Chymmerlee would happen along to save me."

As always, Subikahn changed the subject. "Think of this from Chymmerlee's viewpoint. She betrayed the secrets of her people to their bitterest enemies, then ran off with Renshai in ignorance."

Though he knew he had just been diverted, Saviar could not resist addressing the new tack. "But we're not enemies. That's what she needs to understand." Feeling a tickle of fluid sliding from his nose, Saviar again clamped the rag in place.

Subikahn made a broad gesture, using both hands. "Renshai murdered her people. All of them. The Myrcidians had to reconstitute from . . . from basically nothing. From a bit of scattered and diluted bloodline."

"Centuries-ago-Renshai murdered her people," Saviar reminded his brother. "Not us. Not the Renshai that Colbey Calistinsson presented to the world."

Subikahn's voice went soft. "Colbey Calistinsson was probably a member of those 'centuries-ago-Renshai'. He might have killed more than his share of mages. We know he had a hand in the downfall of the Cardinal Wizards, including the very last Myrcidian, the Eastern Wizard."

"That's not fair!" Though not loud, Saviar's tone sounded like a shout in comparison. "The Wizards brought about their own downfall when they banded against Colbey. He was in the right!"

Subikahn remained maddeningly calm. "Sometimes, Saviar, right depends on where you're standing."

Saviar started to reply, but the words died on his tongue. They had argued this point many times before; and, though he had always taken the side of absolute right, life and Subikahn had brought him too many logical points to the contrary. As Knights of Erythane, Saviar's father and grandfather had made peace with the concept of unconditional morality and honor, but Saviar had not yet formally done so.

Saviar had seen people on both sides of a conflict equally resolute, passionately asserting their viewpoints with the glib certainty of the righteous. Each believed, with every fiber of his being, that he had his feet firmly planted in honest and ethical truth. Somehow, the Knights of Erythane wound their way through such disagreements to find the kernel of shining, honorable accuracy that underlay everyone's beliefs. To the Knights of Erythane, justice was an absolute concept. And, while the Renshai and a few others mocked them, the rest of the world adored and revered them.

When Saviar did not reply, Subikahn added, "Fairness has nothing to do with it, Savi. I'm only trying to put myself in Chymmerlee's place. Right or wrong, she has grown up believing Renshai the ultimate enemies. We knew that, yet we chose not to reveal ourselves. Surely you can see why she'd consider that an enormous betrayal."

Saviar nodded grudgingly. Once again, he took the rag from his face. This time, the bleeding did not recur. He did not know what to say. Subikahn had made an inarguable point, but Saviar still felt quarrelsome and sullen. "She still didn't have to try to kill you."

Subikahn looked up at the castle wall, now safely distant. "I doubt she has the gall or desire to come after us; but, when I gave her the opportunity to help fix the problem she created, she seized it."

Saviar did not understand. "How would killing you accomplish that? It's me who should have told her what we are."

Subikahn rubbed his eyes, blinked a few more times, then smiled. Apparently, his vision had wholly returned.

"Had you climbed, I imagine she would have done the same to you. But the problem, in her mind, is that we know the secret of the mages."

Now, Saviar grasped Subikahn's point. "That they exist, and where they're hiding."

"Correct."

Murder seemed an excessive way to handle the problem. "But we vowed not to tell."

"Would you trust the word of liars?"

Again, Saviar chose not to argue. They had not actually lied, simply withheld the truth. "They could move. We would still know they exist, but we would have no way to find them."

"Except they think we're magical, because of the aura your sword gave us. Or they might not be able to move."

"Why not?"

Subikahn finally dared to rise, stretching each limb, apparently assessing himself for bumps and bruises. He seemed none the worse for a fall that should have killed him. "I'm not actually magical. I certainly don't know the rules. But Papa's library is extensive, and he's made me read everything, trying to get me to learn a bunch of different languages." Subikahn worked kinks from his shoulders and back. "Historically, items imbued with magic are exceptionally rare and users of it quite limited. The creation of an invisible city seems like the kind of incredibly difficult feat that would require the efforts of several magical beings working together as well as a receptive place."

Saviar blinked. For a man with little knowledge of magic, Subikahn seemed to know a lot. "A . . . receptive place?"

"A place where truly great magic had once been worked. A gods' battle, perhaps. An elfin gate." Subikahn shrugged. "Something."

Saviar placed a hand on his sword hilt, surprised to find that Subikahn's words made sense to him. His sword, *Motfrabelonning*, had come to him after their mother's death. An ancient Renshai *Einherjar*, a soul dwelling in Valhalla, had given it to her. The twins' younger brother wielded her other enchanted blade; its magic came from having belonged to Colbey Calistinsson when the immortal Renshai lived on Asgard, the world of gods.

So far, Saviar had noticed little special about those two

swords. They were both exquisitely crafted, but no more so than the Renshai demanded of any sword. He knew of only two things the so-called "magic" of the swords granted: they gave the wielder an "aura" and could cut beings that ordinary steel could not harm, like elves, *Kjempemagiska*, and demons.

Thinking while talking slowed Saviar's speech. "So . . . the mages might not be able . . . to move."

Subikahn shrugged.

"And . . . we know . . . their secrets . . ."

Subikahn bit his lower lip, and Saviar understood that "secrets" covered a lot of information: their existence, their magic, and their heritage as well as their location. The mages had expected the twins to remain with them forever; and their promises not to reveal any information had not proven enough for the mages to release them. They had had to take Chymmerlee as a willing hostage.

Suddenly needing to sit, Saviar placed his bottom on the whitestone bench. A lump formed in his throat. "There's no future for me and Chymmerlee, is there?" The words pounded in his head, and he felt tears sting his eyes again. His handsome face and muscular features had brought scores of young women flocking to him since he had barely entered his teens. This popularity had done nothing more than embarrass him. But Chymmerlee had come to him innocently, when he was at the brink of death, and she was the first with whom he had shared a mutual attraction.

Subikahn sighed, crouching beside his brother. "Once she gets back and tells her people about us, I'm not sure either of us has any kind of future."

Saviar's brows furrowed. He did not understand. "Their magic makes them unpredictably dangerous, but you don't think they'll come after us, do you? They didn't even follow Chymmerlee when she didn't return." He remembered the reason she had given, that she alone of her people ever left the compound. The others feared the perils outside and the possibility of someone discovering their secrets. "If someone kidnapped your great-granddaughter, you'd go after them, wouldn't you? No matter your fears. No matter what they threatened."

"I would," Subikahn admitted. "But I have a theory about that."

Saviar gave his brother his full attention.

"When they found us, they took us in for one reason only."

Saviar nodded. "They saw an aura around you and assumed you carried the blood of mages."

"Right. And their most significant issue, at the time, was reviving their line without destroying it with inbreeding."

Saviar shrugged. Early on, Subikahn had warned Saviar that the only relationship that could develop between him and Chymmerlee was one of breeding; but that was before Chymmerlee had chosen to accompany them home. "We don't have any actual magic, aside from the sword, so you assumed their only purpose for us would be . . ." Saviar flushed at the impropriety of what he was about to say, ". . . impregnating some of their women."

"Yes." Subikahn said nothing more, allowing Saviar to figure the rest out for himself.

Saviar did so, though the obvious extension of Subikahn's thought surprised him. "You think . . ." It seemed impossible. "You believe . . . they hoped . . . Chymmerlee and I . . ."

Tired of waiting for the euphemism, Subikahn went straight to the point. ". . . would romp like rutting rabbits."

Saviar's cheeks grew hot enough to draw attention from his throbbing nose. "That's obscene!"

"Nothing could be more so."

Saviar shook his head impatiently. "I mean no one would want a girl they love—"

"—to be buggered by a *gloik* like you?"

"Stop it!" Saviar had tired of Subikahn's deliberate attempts to shock. "I'm trying to make a serious point."

Subikahn went silent, brows ever so slightly arched.

Saviar spoke quickly, so as not to give his twin an entrance. "I just mean that no one wants a young woman they love to bear a child out of wedlock."

Subikahn stiffened, then lowered his right shoulder in a lazy shrug. "The mages seem more interested in silently growing their population and gaining magical power than worrying about other societies' mores."

Saviar looked toward the castle. From their new position, they could no longer view Chymmerlee's window. Subikahn had an undeniable point. Like elves, the mages clearly raised their offspring in packs, paying little heed to the rights and responsibilities of blood parents. For now, the survival of their kind mattered more to them than civilization's propriety and rules. He could not help imagining what might have been: Chymmerlee yielding to him, her breath warm in his ear, her arms winching tightly around him, begging for more.

Subikahn's voice jarred Saviar back to reality. "I know what you're thinking."

Saviar's flush went deeper. He imagined his face was as scarlet and glaring as a bonfire. "I wasn't thinking anything," he said defensively, which only made his brother's smile broaden.

"It's better this way," Subikahn assured. "Imagine what might happen if she came home . . . um . . ." Apparently, he sought a euphemism that wouldn't further embarrass his more honorable twin. ". . . short-skirted, and they discovered the 'lump' came courtesy of a Renshai warrior. How far would you go to save your child? Could you imprison a woman and snatch her infant from her bosom?"

Saviar bridled at the bare thought, yet he understood the dilemma. The Myrcidians might or might not feel obligated to slaughter the child. *The imaginary child*, he reminded himself. He and Chymmerlee had done nothing more than kiss. "There's no child to fight for. And I don't think the Myrcidians will come after us to protect their secrets, either. At least, not if we return Chymmerlee alive, as promised."

Subikahn gave his brother an ironic look. "I think you sorely underestimate the importance they place on their solitude."

Saviar wondered if he were missing something. Usually, Subikahn caught the subtleties better than he did. "If we return Chymmerlee unharmed, that makes us men of our words. They can hope we will keep their secrets as well."

"Or," Subikahn inserted, "they can murder us and assure the safety of their secrets."

"No." Saviar found Subikahn's miscalculation. "Because if they assume we're oathbreakers, they have to believe we already told the Renshai about them. They might worry our people will annihilate them again, but they know it is only a possibility. If they murder us, however, they will definitely raise the wrath of the Renshai. Their only real hope for their own security is to trust us."

"Would you?"

"Trust us?"

"Yes."

Saviar tried to look at the situation from a neutral viewpoint. The Mages of Myrcidë believed they had a common bond of magical blood. They knew Saviar was the son of a Knight of Erythane, that he cared deeply for Chymmerlee, and that Subikahn was his twin. That seemed enough for a reasonable expectation of trust. However, when Chymmerlee returned with the information that he and his brother were also unproclaimed Renshai, none of that would matter. "No," he admitted. "In their position, I wouldn't."

"There is one other option," Subikahn said with a softness that alerted Saviar. He would not like the suggestion. "We could prevent Chymmerlee from getting the information about our heritage back to her people."

"What are you saying? You want us to kill Chymmerlee?"

"That's one option." Subikahn responded with cool matter-of-factness. "Or, you could entice her to stay. Marry her, perhaps."

In less tense circumstances, Saviar would have laughed. "I can't even get her to talk to me."

"Find a way."

"I like her, but I'm not sure I love her. At least not yet."

"It wouldn't be the first loveless marriage."

Saviar gave his brother a scathing look. If Subikahn was joking, he gave no sign of it. "I gave my word I would see Chymmerlee home safe, and I have every intention of doing so. The facts are what they are; I can't change them. I'm going to do the honorable thing and let the consequences fall where they will."

Subikahn crooked one side of his face, bobbing his head from side to side. "A perfect example of why the good men die young. And why I hope you'll understand if I don't join you."

CHAPTER 2

It is an honor to die delivering a killing blow, but don't drop your guard just because you believe you did.
— Colbey Calistinsson

CALISTIN RA-KHIRSSON LIMPED into the practice room of Béarn Castle, marveling at its size. It could easily accommodate a small war. On either side of the entrance, racks held practice weapons of a variety beyond anything Calistin could have imagined. The Renshai used nothing but swords; and, though he could defend against anything, Calistin had never seen such an array of polearms, axes, swords, clubs, and hammers. Shields lay neatly piled in front of a shelf covered in wooden objects carved into the shapes of more familiar weapons. He wondered idly why someone might prefer a club in the shape of a sword rather than a solid stick.

The sparring room consisted of a wide variety of areas simulating everything from open terrain, to deep woodlands, to castle interiors. Calistin had heard that the men who designed it had done so for the convenience of the Renshai who served as bodyguards to the Béarnian princes and princesses. If so, they had done a stupendous job. Calistin could scarcely wait to try out every aspect of the room, other than the variety of shields and weapons.

Apparently, the same idea had occurred to every member of Calistin's tribe. Renshai scrambled up and down a spiraling staircase, steel flying at one another's faces. Renshai bandied back and forth over a field of simulated debris. Renshai fought wildly in an open area, in a boxed-in room full of battered old furniture, across a floor pocked with holes and cluttered with timbers. Hard-pressed to find a place to swing his sword, Calistin contented himself with watching, for the moment.

Once the others noticed him, they would make an opening for the most able Renshai warrior. With his broken left arm splinted and in a sling, Calistin would likely find more challengers than usual, people who believed they might actually best him. His battle with the enemy's only *Kjempe-magiska* had left him battered and aching all over his body. He wanted nothing more than to engage in *svergelse*, practicing sword forms quietly and utterly alone, but he doubted he would get the chance. He had not become the best by hiding from his injuries or coddling weakness. As a *torke*, he had forced his students to push themselves past exhaustion, past pain, and to focus most fervently on vulnerabilities.

At the moment, Calistin looked anything but menacing. Renshai had become more diverse over the centuries; but he typified the classic appearance of the ancient tribe. At eighteen, he looked some four to five years younger, his eyes a steely blue-gray, his hair golden, his skin as fair as that of any true Northman. Dark bruises and clotted gashes showed clearly where his tunic did not cover them. Renshai spurned armor, shields, and other unnatural defenses, relying only on their own quickness and skill.

When no one challenged him after several moments, Calistin headed for a position on the far edge of one of the practice areas, not caring whether he chose one with indoor or outdoor obstacles or none at all. It suddenly occurred to him why no one was demanding a spar with their war-weakened champion. They, too, suffered from battle wounds and exhaustion; they saw no advantage to sparring him in what would ultimately prove a match as uneven as usual. And, even if they did manage to defeat him, everyone would ascribe the victory to Calistin's injuries.

Calistin launched into his first *svergelse*, immediately cursing the splints that immobilized his left arm. He would have torn them off, but he was wise enough to realize that, if he did not give his arm the chance to heal, it never would. Four or five weeks of rest would bring it back nearly as good as new. Though it might seem more like twenty-eight days of wretched frustration, it was still preferable to his arm healing crookedly or not at all.

The room went suddenly silent. Ordinarily, Calistin would not have noticed such a thing while caught in something as all-consuming as swordwork, but only something of significant danger would distract Renshai from spar. Every eye had turned to the entrance, so Calistin looked there are well.

A large, well-built Northman had entered. Massive, handsome, and also war-bruised, Valr Magnus threw an enormous shadow over the myriad racks of weaponry. Seemingly oblivious to the Renshai's sudden change in demeanor, the general of the Aeri army examined the stack of practice shields.

The Renshai waited to see what Calistin would do. As the champion of the Northmen, Valr Magnus had planned to challenge Calistin in single combat. Through a combination of deft maneuvers by the Northmen, and pride from the Renshai, Magnus had wound up facing Calistin's mother instead. The battle had gone her way until skullduggery disguised as an accident had allowed Magnus a fatal stroke. Over the next several months, Calistin had chased Magnus halfway around the world with the intention of humiliating the brute before slaying him fairly in combat.

The war had disrupted Calistin's plans. Thrown uneasily together, the two warriors had found more common ground than anyone could have anticipated and, ultimately, became dedicated war partners and even unlikely friends. When the time finally came for their battle to the death, neither wished to fight it any longer. Valr Magnus had been the only one capable of assisting Calistin against the *Kjempemagiska* in the war. Side by side, they had fought the giant and nearly died together.

As visions of that battle swept down on Calistin, he forced them away. Usually, he savored war, its memories his pride and his joy. But he had lost another friend in that encounter, one whose loyalty he had never appreciated and whose courage he had never respected. He could not bear to think of Treysind, not now, maybe not ever.

Raised, like most Northmen, to despise Renshai, Valr Magnus now stood in a precarious position. Calistin knew the general could prove either a valuable ally or a bitter and dangerous enemy to the Renshai. Calistin's actions might well determine which.

Sheathing his weapon, Calistin stepped forward to acknowledge the Aeri general. "Valr." The word literally meant "Slayer," and the Northmen reserved it for their greatest swordsmen in history. The first Valr had earned his nickname as a prolific killer of Renshai.

Valr Magnus turned to face Calistin. His expression gave away nothing. Apparently, he also knew and cared how much lay at stake. That boded well, in Calistin's mind.

The room seemed to collectively hold its breath. All sparring and *svergelse* ceased. Every eye found the two men, one tall and broad, the other childlike in form but deadly as a pack of wolves.

"Calistin," Valr finally said, his tone as unrevealing as his expression. He selected a large, broad practice sword, its balance awkward and its edges blunted.

In a single movement, Calistin sprang up beside the general and placed a restraining hand on his wrist. "Not that one." He inclined his head toward the sheath at Magnus' hip.

Magnus looked startled. He spoke softly, barely above a whisper. "You've changed your mind again? You want that battle?"

"Just a spar," Calistin replied as softly. "But a good one: well-crafted sword to well-crafted sword." He gave the practice weapon a disdainful look. "That's a worthless lump of wood."

Magnus crooked a brow. "Most practice weapons are. That's what keeps friends from inadvertently injuring one another."

Calistin shrugged. "We can handle pain."

"What about accidentally killing one another?"

Calistin's jaw tensed, but he threw off anger. Magnus spoke from ignorance not any intention to offend. "That's a grave insult," he informed the general. "I'm a *torke*. If I can't control my practice strokes any better than that, then to what purpose do I serve my students?"

"I'm more concerned about me," Magnus grumbled, which only further irritated Calistin.

"If I can't keep you from killing me, I deserve to die."

"That's not what I . . ." Valr Magnus seemed to realize

that everything he said was only worsening the situation. "Very well. Real weapons . . . but . . . still a spar?"

Calistin nodded.

"And the end point?"

Calistin considered. He glanced around the room, noting the variety of terrain, the angle of the sun trickling toward the window, the many Renshai standing like statues, their attention gravely focused on the two men amid the racks of practice weapons. "First one to drive the other to the highest point of the room wins."

Magnus' brows flung upward. Clearly, he had never heard such a suggestion before. For that matter, neither had Calistin; he had made it up on the spur of the moment, with just a trickle of an idea in mind. He sometimes sparred a hundred times in a day and had often spiced up endpoints to keep them interesting. His own best *torke* had added knocking one's opponent on his ass in the dirt to his repertoire. For *ganim*, non-Renshai, there were three usual choices: first blood, first would-be fatal maneuver, and death.

Valr Magnus merely nodded. Likely, he felt questioning would only risk offending Calistin again. "Where do you want to start?"

Calistin knew the other Renshai had not heard their soft discussion. They had no way to know whether the fight was spar or genuine. To keep them guessing, Calistin roared, "Here! Now!"

Magnus' sword cleared its sheath in an instant. It seemed to gather the meager light from the windows, flashing vivid silver as it lunged for Calistin. Calistin sprang aside easily, certain Magnus had not used his full speed or strength. Apparently, the Aeri general still worried about sparring with live steel.

Without bothering to free his own weapon, Calistin hissed. "Stop playing and fight like a man."

"It's only . . . I don't want . . ."

Calistin glared, daring the Aeri to finish that sentence. "You couldn't hit me if I had two broken *legs*! And a blindfold!"

It was a challenge no warrior could stomach. Magnus lunged in earnest at his smaller foe. Calistin jumped, and Magnus' sword cut the air where Calistin had been. Calistin landed on a table, sending practice weapons sliding, smashing against one another, and slamming to the floor. Gaze fixed on Calistin, Magnus backstepped farther into the practice room. Clearly, he did not want to drag the fight into the castle or give Calistin the chance to pounce on him from above. "You don't have to prove it. Leave the leg breaking to your enemies."

Screaming a battle cry, Calistin charged the length of the table to hurl himself toward Magnus. Only then did he bother to draw his own sword.

Magnus seemed willing to stand back and wait, then abruptly seized the opening. Airborne, Calistin could not change his momentum. Magnus swept the flat of his blade into the path of the flying Renshai.

It took most of Calistin's strength to curl defensively beneath the sword, then fling out his legs and uninjured arm to backhand his blade against Magnus'. Harmlessly deflected, Magnus' blade circled back for another strike; but Calistin had already landed.

"Stop playing," Valr Magnus repeated Calistin's gibe verbatim. "And fight like a man."

Calistin grinned. Ordinarily, he would never have performed unnecessary acrobatics in combat. For once, he wanted something showy and wild to entertain the other Renshai and assure them that he would not allow his injuries to hamper him. "Fine," he said. With blinding quickness, he launched an attack at Magnus, his sword flickering in all directions.

Caught in the onslaught, Magnus retreated, parrying and dodging, nothing left for offense. He had just enough agility to avoid the floor debris and the other Renshai, most of whom skittered out of his way. No one wanted to bring down Calistin's ire by affecting the tide of battle; Calistin would win fairly or not at all. Anyone who made that victory suspect would pay dearly for the offense, possibly with his life.

Abruptly, Magnus turned a deft parry into a strong attack, thrusting viciously. The suddenness and uniqueness of the maneuver surprised even Calistin. He sprang aside cleanly but lost his attack advantage just long enough for Magnus to go on the offense. Blows battered down on Calistin with a speed that belied the Aeri general's bulk. Quick as a gnat, Calistin eluded every stroke, not daring to take one on his sword. He could not risk hurting his working hand.

Then, gradually Calistin took control again, body weaving through the flurry, sword darting in to put the Northman on the defensive again.

"Nice," Calistin could not help admitting. Calistin was the better swordsman; with one notable exception, he always was. Yet Magnus had a talent he had never witnessed from a *ganim* before. Others had given Calistin a real battle, but all of those had been Renshai or had come at him in such droves that the distraction had worked to their advantage. As an Outworld creature, the giant *Kjempemagiska* did not count as a human adversary any more than a god or demon would. Calistin suffered an uncharacteristic twinge of sadness at the accident of the Aeri general's birth. Started as a toddler, allowed to learn the secret maneuvers, Magnus would have made a highly competent Renshai.

Curious, Calistin guided the battle through all sorts of terrain and long into the morning. He did not want the battle to end. As time went on, Magnus seemed more antsy, his intention to force the battle onto the simulated spiral staircase more obvious. Calistin knew the older man could match his own endurance, if not his skill; but Magnus seemed less eager to spend the entire day engaged in a single spar.

Pity. With a blow to Magnus' side that would have been considered a would-be fatal one had they chosen a different end point, Calistin switched positions. They still headed toward the staircase, though now he had become the sheepdog instead of the ram. Magnus seemed not to mind the defensive position, so long as it drew them closer to their goal. The sooner they approached the highest point in the room, the less time until the contest finished.

Once both men's feet touched the staircase, the pace of the combat increased mightily. Swords blurred into flying webs of silver. Right arm hampered by the wall, Calistin again cursed the splints that immobilized his left. The perfect two-handed training of the Renshai failed him when he only had one available, but that did not stop Calistin. He threw himself into the spar as he would a battle, careful only not to harm his opponent with the same sharpened steel that had claimed the lives of so many. He fought in flawless arcs, using the wall as a springboard and the rail, at times, as a short-term perch. Gradually, at his own measured pace, he drove Magnus toward the landing.

As they approached, the frenzy of battle intensified even further. Magnus fought wildly to switch positions, even though this opened his defenses. Calistin instinctively charged for the hole. He slapped a would-be killing blow across Magnus' abdomen, as the general completed the circle. Now, Calistin's back pointed toward the landing, and a single driving step would lose him the battle.

Damn! The maneuver seemed utter madness. What good to win the spar if one forfeited one's life? Calistin's chosen end point allowed such a trick, without penalty; but the ability to drop survival instincts to accomplish it caught him utterly by surprise. As Magnus lunged in for one last backstep, Calistin did the only thing he could. He hurled himself at Magnus.

Calistin struck a form as solid as a brick wall, but momentum won out over bulk. Both men tumbled wildly down the stairs, a flailing ball of arms, legs, and swords. Magnus caught himself first, looping an arm through the railing while Calistin continued to fall, unwilling to release his sword and unable to stop himself without the use of his opposite arm.

Magnus waited patiently on the staircase for Calistin to collect himself. Even more bruised and battered, Calistin leaped to his feet and charged the general, his battle screams ringing through the room.

Once again, Magnus put all his effort into forcing Calistin's back to the landing, not worrying about defense, opening himself fully to Calistin's attacks. Calistin avoided Magnus' deadly strokes, uncertain whether to feel incensed or mightily impressed. He doubted Magnus meant to question Calistin's competence; they both knew the Renshai had promised not to land a real blow, had bragged that he would not allow the Aeri to do so, either. Simply by choosing such a strange end point, Calistin had obviated any purpose for simulated killing blows.

It was a galling strategy, brilliant in its own strange way. Calistin found himself drawn to Magnus' deliberate openings, expending effort just to ignore them, to avoid harming his opponent in spar. Emotions bubbled up and were discarded: anger gave way to irritation, then to wonder, admiration, and, finally, amusement. He had agreed not to kill Valr Magnus but never not to cause him pain.

Now, Calistin bore in to cover those holes, smacking

shins and anklebones with the flat of his blade. Like a dog at the heels of livestock, Calistin grew relentless, driving Magnus upward until the second of his large feet reached the landing. Only then did Calistin withdraw, looking up at his cornered foe, grinning at his timing. The sun had risen far enough to stream through the window, striking golden highlights from the Northman's hair. His raised sword made a grand contrast in silver.

Before Magnus could admit defeat, before he could even speak a word, Calistin joined him on the landing to address the staring crowd of Renshai. "Friends, fellow Renshai, I would like to introduce General Magnus Rognualdsson from the tribe of Aerin."

Scattered, confused applause followed the introduction. Clearly, no one wished to guess Calistin's next move. They knew him as ruthless, often cruel, and utterly humorless. They had no idea how much the events of the last few months had changed him, enough to stage a battle, to befriend his worst enemy. Without Treysind's sacrifice, Calistin realized, none of that would have happened.

Looking as uncertain as his audience, Magnus sheathed his sword and executed a polite bow.

Renshai fought wars without pattern or strategy, without commanders and titles. At Béarn's request, they had a leader, Thialnir, who represented them at the Council and in other foreign affairs. It was a flimsy hierarchy, more important to *ganim* than Renshai, so Calistin had no qualms about announcing vital information in his own time and manner. "We know General Magnus as the champion of the Northmen, the man who killed my mother and banished the Renshai from the West and their homes."

Rumbles rose from the Renshai. Other armies might have clashed weapons or shields, but they remained silent. They had no shields and respected their swords too much to risk notching them in anything less than spar or combat.

"Now, we know him, too, as a competent warrior and a man of honor. When my father found proof that deceit had played a role in winning that battle, Magnus retracted his victory, apologized, and nullified the agreement."

Murmurs suffused the crowd. Clearly, they needed more.

Calistin gave it, "Our banishment is lifted. The Fields of Wrath belong to the Renshai once more."

A great cry filled the practice room, echoing from the walls and funneling through the two high windows. Calistin suspected they could hear it throughout the entirety of Béarn Castle.

Calistin looked at Magnus, expecting a smile but getting, instead, a worried frown. Clearly, something troubled the Northman. Calistin waited until the cheers died down to speak again, "As if this were not enough to assure us the general is a fair man, worth trusting, look at his sword." Calistin gestured Magnus to unsheathe and raise the weapon again.

Valr Magnus did as Calistin bade, raising the blade to display its glimmering length, its perfect edge, the distinctive large, S-shaped guard a favorite of any Renshai, like Calistin's mother, who copied the ways of Colbey Calistinsson. Calistin drew and placed his own sword alongside Magnus'. They proved perfect twins, their lengths identical, their simple guards unwaveringly matched, their handgrips the same split-leather, and the pommels shaped like the nose of a cat. As they came alongside one another, Calistin's felt as if it trembled in his hand. Worried he had lost control of his nerves, Calistin studied the steel. Both swords wobbled ever so slightly, and the reflected light of the sun seemed to bounce perfectly between them.

The Renshai fell silent again, and every eye focused on the swords. Calistin need not have concerned himself. Whatever he saw, whether real or illusion, the entire group saw with him. "His sword, like mine, comes from the hand and sheath of Colbey. He gave this one to my mother, a miracle I never believed would get repeated. Yet, I saw with my own eyes as Colbey relinquished this weapon to Magnus."

Religious signs swept the crowd. Rare enough any Renshai would ever willingly give up a sword to anyone, but for the great immortal Renshai to do so, twice, seemed madness. The enormity of the tribute Colbey had bestowed upon Magnus could only truly be understood by Renshai.

Clearly uncomfortable with the intense scrutiny, Magnus sheathed the sword again. "Please," he started. "I appreciate your favor and your kindness, but it is more than I deserve. No man with a shred of integrity could have done anything less than I did."

Again, a cacophony of voices swept the crowd. One,

grumbled a trifle too loudly, came through, "Northmen aren't generally known for their integrity."

Valr Magnus' frown deepened. "I admit that not all of my ilk were convinced by the evidence nor pleased with my decision . . ."

It was gross understatement. Calistin had been present when Ra-khir presented the irrefutable evidence of fraud. At the time, the leader of the Northmen had demanded that either the results stand or another battle replace it. Magnus had refused to act as the North's champion a second time, had shed the ill-gotten title of Renshai-slayer, had insisted the contract become null and void. He had even apologized profusely to Ra-khir and the boys for killing their wife and mother.

". . . but I will not stand by while anyone denigrates my people." Magnus gave a stern look toward the crowd, as if seeking the speaker.

Never one to hide, the Renshai who had spoken stepped forward, revealing himself as Tygbiar. A veteran warrior with a deeply scarred face, he spoke words on the minds of many Renshai, "You can't deny that blatant Renshai-hating is rampant in the Northlands."

"I can't," Magnus admitted. "And much of it is ignorant and undeserved. But hatred is a two-way path."

"Eventually." Kristel, a contemporary of Kevral's spoke next in a strong feminine voice. "When someone is constantly trying to murder every member of your tribe, you do learn to dislike him. But Renshai do not teach our children to hate in organized schools. We do not have as a spoken and written goal to destroy all Northmen."

Kristel's closest friend Nisse added, "If the gods magically disarmed all of the Northmen simultaneously, we would remain at peace. But if they disarmed the Renshai, the Northmen would seize the opportunity to slaughter us all."

Magnus tipped his head and remained silent, clearly considering the words. Calistin knew the Renshai appreciated that the Aeri general did not dismiss their concerns out of hand. "I wouldn't, nor would thousands of other Northmen. To dismiss us all as monsters for the actions of a few is bias as unreasonable as that which you condemn."

Calistin did not point out that the "few" consisted of tens

of thousands. "We're not going to solve centuries of conflict by cornering a good man. Colbey finds him worthy, and so do I."

The Renshai could scarcely argue with the logic.

Magnus, however, had not finished, "I've been put in place as the new Western representative for the Northlands, so you're sure to see more of me over the coming months."

Though shocked, Calistin could not help smiling. He could not think of any Northman he would rather have representing them. At least, Magnus did not hate Renshai outright, like so many of his brethren.

"Whatever anti-Renshai prejudice school has drummed into me, I'll try to overcome; but I will always do what is right for my people. I warn you that may not always gibe with your preferences or needs. However, I'm not going to endorse anything whose sole purpose is to treat anyone, Renshai or otherwise, unkindly or unfairly." It was not a strong promise but the best Renshai could hope for from any Northman. As Magnus started down the faux castle stairs, Calistin at his side, the other Renshai returned to their spars and *svergelse*.

"Western representative for the Northmen?" Calistin could not help asking.

Valr Magnus made a deep-throated sound. "It's a ploy to keep me here, I think. Captain Erik of Nordmir wants to get home first to tell his version of the story."

Calistin could only nod. He had little understanding of diplomacy or titles, but one thing seemed certain. Erik was responsible for the battle and its original outcome. Erik was the one who had thrown a tantrum in the Council Room when the deception became clear and the contract negated. Compared to him, Magnus had to seem like a dewy-eyed lover of Renshai. "Do you think he'll lie?"

Magnus shrugged. "He'll guard his tongue, at least in regard to me. I'm as popular with Northmen as you are among Renshai, and for much the same reason."

Calistin did not allow himself a smile. His people loved him only because of his skill, while Magnus was not only the martial champion of his race but also a kind and generous man, intelligent, and a competent general. The Renshai revered Calistin as the best of their line, but they did not particularly like him.

It occurred to Calistin that, prior to the war, such thoughts would never have entered his mind. His people expected nothing from him but to improve his swordwork and, hopefully, teach some of them along the way. He could act as he pleased. He had no obligations, no chores, no need for social knowledge or proficiency. He could think what he liked, say what he liked, do as he chose to do without fear of retribution or even negative comment.

Two things had changed him. First, Calistin had been bested in battle by an elderly stranger who had then become his *torke*, only later revealing himself as Colbey Calistinsson and as Calistin's blood grandfather. Colbey had exposed an awful truth: Calistin's soul had been destroyed when his mother had suffered the bite of a spirit spider while pregnant with him.

Secondly, Treysind had died a hero. The Erythanian street urchin had annoyed Calistin for most of a year, trailing him like a puppy, insisting on protecting the Renshai despite having no combat training, infusing rudimentary social skills against Calistin's will.

For so long, Treysind had managed only to get under Calistin's feet and skin, gradually and irritatingly forcing the Renshai to reevaluate the way he had chosen to lead his existence. But Treysind's last act had not only saved Calistin's life, as he had so long promised, but had turned the tide of the war itself. Treysind had thrown himself between Calistin and a killing blow, causing the *Kjempemagiska* to slaughter the wrong target. A *Valkyrie* had come for Treysind's soul, as they did for all warriors who died in valorous combat. Then, Treysind had made the ultimate sacrifice, giving up his soul, which would have dwelt for eternity in Valhalla, to Calistin.

Calistin shook off consideration of a selfless act he had avoided thinking about for as long as possible. He had no idea how the *Valkyrie* had made the switch. If she had not told him, called him unworthy of the boy's incredible sacrifice, he would never have known it occurred at all. He certainly had no intention of becoming weakened by a decision in which he had had no choice, nor did he wish to belittle Treysind's heroic action.

Soulless, Calistin could never have found Valhalla, the final reward he had dedicated nearly every moment of every day to achieving. In the short time he had known he was soulless, he had suffered a torment beyond any he had known before, beyond any he could imagine. Yet he found himself as much burdened as rescued by Treysind's miraculous gift. Without it, his death would herald nothing. But, with it, he felt compelled to honor Treysind, to consider his own words and actions and their effects on those around him.

Still uncertain whether to deify or damn Treysind, Calistin simply watched Valr Magnus leave the practice room. He returned to his own *svergelse*.

CHAPTER 3

Achievement is no excuse for sloth. Past glory is for the dead. A true hero never rests, but always he drives on one deed further.

— *Colbey Calistinsson*

KING TAE KAHN OF STALMIZE, Eastlands, had never seen so many important people packed into one room. When it became clear the Council and Strategy Rooms would prove too cramped, and the library too delicate, Tae had volunteered his own enormous guestroom. It amazed him how swiftly and effortlessly the Béarnian castle servants had converted his sleeping quarters into a reasonably formal and not-too-uncomfortable meeting place. They had removed the bed, chest, and dressing table, replacing them with tables that did not quite fit together but still managed to create a large and mostly level surface. The myriad chairs surrounding it did not match but formed an eye-pleasing arrangement. Flowers and herbs covered the sickroom smell of healing injuries, and they had left Tae a plush seat in which to rest his battered frame.

Currently, Imorelda occupied the chair, her feline body stretched to fill it, her tail flopping leisurely back and forth across the stuffed armrests. Ignoring her, and the film of shed fur she left on his seat, Tae stared out the window and into the courtyard below. He had seen his son climb the castle walls, fighting an unexpected twinge of jealousy. Tae was the one who scaled walls for sport usually, a treat he sorely missed since his injuries had rendered even simple acrobatics impossible. It seemed absurd that only a week ago he had believed himself definitively dead.

Tae had also seen Subikahn fall, suffering desperate panic until Saviar caught his twin and the two, eventually, walked off under their own power. Awash in icy sweat, Tae had finally understood why the Eastern maid, Alneezah, had hovered around him when he did similarly dangerous and foolish things. For reasons he could not explain, she loved him. And, he was only starting to realize, he cared deeply for her as well.

Now, Tae hobbled to his chair, cursing the pain and stiffness that still assailed him. Slashed to the bone, his right shoulder ached. The healers kept it in a sling, reminding him not to overuse it so it could properly mend. Every breath brought a stab of pain, though it had lessened over time and the struggle became far less fierce since his arrow-shot lung had reinflated. He limped to protect his left thigh, where another enemy arrow had penetrated. A residual headache still distracted him periodically, a memento of his battle with a hungry shark.

Voices in the hall alerted Tae. *I need to sit,* he sent to the cat.

Imorelda stretched her sinewy body farther, driving each leg outward, extending every claw. It seemed impossible that an animal so small could take up so much room. *So sit.*

Under ordinary circumstances, Tae would have enjoyed bandying with the cat, but the seriousness of the current proceedings precluded it. He already faced an uphill battle to convince the allies that the massive war they had just won was only the beginning of the battle. Béarn had called up every alliance, every favor at its disposal, to win. The heady excitement of that victory would not be easily quelled.

With a brisk motion of his good arm, Tae scooped up the silver tabby, slipped beneath her, and dumped her into his lap just as the first members of Béarn's Council entered the room.

Hey! Imorelda hissed and fluffed up her fur in protest but did not swipe at him. She stood, ramrod stiff, in his lap. *How dare you!*

As a king, Tae was not required to rise at the entrance of

other nobility and chose not to do so. It would only further upset Imorelda if he dumped her on the floor.

Prime Minister Davian, Minister Saxanar of Courtroom Procedure and Affairs, Minister Aerean of Internal Affairs, and Minister Franstaine of Household Affairs entered together, bowed or curtsied to the foreign king, then claimed places around the makeshift table.

Tiny Minister of Local Affairs, Chaveeshia, appeared soon afterward, with her charges: Knight-Captain Kedrin, who represented nearby Erythane, and Thialnir Thrudazisson for the Renshai. After appropriate gestures of respect, the knight returned to quiet discussion with General Sutton from Santagithi. The two had spent much time together since the war had ended. Kedrin had a great historical interest in the ancient strategist for whom the general's city was named. Those four also took seats around the tables.

Imorelda paced across Tae's lap, complaining. *I'm a cat, gods damn you, and a friend. I deserve some decency and respect. Whatever possessed you to . . .* She continued in that vein, but Tae did not bother to listen. Soon enough, she settled into the crook of his lap, as if she had personally chosen the position.

Minister Richar of Foreign Affairs came next, overburdened with the representatives of hundreds of hamlets, villages, towns, and cities across the vast Westlands. Currently, he had no Northmen with him, which surprised Tae. Prior to the war, he had juggled delegates and generals from each of the nine tribes. That did not bode well for keeping them ready and waiting for the next wave of attack. Now, Richar brought sixteen Westland representatives to join General Sutton. Tae knew only one by name, the general of the West's largest city, Pudar, a massive soldier named Markanyin.

Minister Zaysharn, the overseer of Béarn's livestock, came in alone, then Valr Magnus, the Northern champion, soon followed by a larger group that contained Béarn's King Griff, Queen Matrinka, the captain of Béarn's guardsmen, Seiryn, Griff's primary bodyguard, Bard Darris, and, most surprisingly, Tem'aree'ay, Griff's second wife, who apparently accompanied him to represent the elves.

As the Westlands high king entered, everyone rose, except for Tae himself. Knight-Captain Kedrin made the most gracious and stately bow before Griff, then everyone else reclaimed their seats. King Humfreet of Erythane had apparently gone home, leaving the knight to represent his city as he did in peaceful times. That, too, bothered Tae.

King Griff accepted the burden of opening the meeting. Though massive, with coarse black hair and a full beard, he still projected a childlike naïveté at thirty-five years old. Nearly all of Béarn's ruling kings and queens through the centuries had displayed this odd balance of wisdom and simplicity. The ruler of Béarn was always the focal point of the world's equilibrium without which it would crumble into ruin. Currently, a magical gem determined the next successor through a grueling test that, more often than not, drove those who failed to madness. Because of that, the test was rarely invoked until the death of the current ruler, beginning with the royal most likely to succeed.

"Once again," Griff said in his slow-cadenced, deep voice, "I would like to thank all of you for your quickness, courage, and consideration at this most difficult time in our history."

As he had now thanked them each at least a dozen times, in groups and individually, no one bothered to reply.

"Without each and every one of you, the tide of this war could easily have changed. We know the enemy's intention: to overtake our lands and to murder each and every one of us. They took no prisoners and refused themselves to us through suicide. What little we do know of their strategies and plans comes from the efforts and sacrifices of King Tae Kahn of the Eastlands. It is to him I would like to turn over the floor."

Though staggeringly uncomfortable under scrutiny, Tae did appreciate the introduction. Everyone trusted King Griff, and the reminder of Tae's unique ability with languages could only help his cause.

As every eye turned to Tae, he steeled himself against inevitable discomfort. He had spent the first half of his life sneaking and hiding, doing whatever it took to remain unnoticed. Back then, catching any eye might mean a protracted and agonizing death. "I apologize for calling you here before the celebrations have finished, but I wanted to catch as many of you as possible before you leave Béarn."

The responses rumbled into one another, but Tae got a

general impression of tolerance. He had managed the only successful spying mission of the entire war and had returned, nearly dead, with valuable information. His status as king also accorded him respect.

Tae cleared his throat. He had prepared for this moment, trying to find the right words to convince without alarming. In the end, he chose the direct route. It would likely work best with men of action. "My concern is that the war is not finished, and the second wave will be much more deadly and dangerous."

Tae expected anything but the deep silence that followed. He tended to forget that men of action were also, mostly, men of patience who understood and valued procedure. They graced Tae's proclamation with an appropriate amount of deliberation. Then, suddenly, motions to take the floor appeared from every direction.

Griff first acknowledged General Sutton, to Tae's chagrin. A first-rate strategist, the Santagithian would also likely raise the most difficult arguments to counter. "I was led to believe our enemies chose to attack because they needed more land for a burdensome population."

Tae nodded once, noting the cautious phrasing of the question. As the only person currently capable of speaking the *alsona*'s language, Tae had personally relayed that message.

The Westland general continued, "They lost thousands to the war. It will take them decades to regroup and repopulate."

He has a good point. Imorelda walked a full circle in Tae's lap, then flopped down in the exact same spot.

Tae knew that and had anticipated it. "I agree that that would normally be true, General Sutton. But not in this case."

The silence recurred, with not even a whisper or chair movement to disrupt it. It seemed more fragile this time, so Tae continued carefully, "Aside from one notable example, we fought only the *alsona*, the little servants of the enemy. Apparently, they did not expect anything like the resistance we gave them, having made both intelligence-gathering and tactical mistakes." Tae tried to use phrases that made it clear he was neither ignorant nor foolish when it came to military matters. "They assumed our Northlands were uninhabitable from cold, thus overlooking the Northmen. They believed we had access to no magic whatsoever, so the little bit we did have surprised them. And I'm not sure even we believed we could bring together so many diverse countries in one cause so quickly and competently."

Tae threw in the last words to flatter the generals. It was a testament to the popularity of Griff, and previous rulers of Béarn, that everyone had rallied so spectacularly to his cause. But the generals, kings, and commanders of dozens of countries deserved the credit for moving so quickly and strongly against this common enemy.

"Magical giants, like the one who commanded those *alsona*, are in charge; and they care little for the comfort of their servants. They lost only one of their own, so their numbers have not appreciably changed, still too high for their land to sustain them." Tae had no idea how many *Kjempemagiska* might exist; but, judging only by what he had learned from the *alsona* he had mind-read with Imorelda's help, there could be several thousand. "That single giant nearly destroyed our massed armies. If a hundred of them came at us, we would stand little chance against them." Tae gave his words a few moments to sink in, concerned about the effect they might have. From the corner of his eye, he saw Griff wince. Matrinka's hand flew to her mouth in horror. Tae had already presented his case to them, but they still shuddered at the very thought of such a war.

The only Northman in the room, Valr Magnus took the floor. "Forgive my asking, Your Majesty, but how do you know this? Did you overhear this plan while spying on the enemy?"

It occurred to Tae to answer in the affirmative and obviate the need for more argument, but the lie refused to form on his tongue. *I'm too old to keep track of truths and mistruths.* He wondered if traveling too long with a Knight of Erythane had affected him as well. Ra-khir had often said, "One lie can undo a man forever," and he had a strong argument. The great men and women gathered in this room not only had skill in reading others' intentions, they also knew better than to believe things that made no sense. Once given reason to doubt Tae's honesty, they would believe nothing he said in the future.

Tae admitted, "I overheard no such plan." He smiled

crookedly. "It's not the way of fighting men to discuss strategies for . . . losing."

Apparently accepting that explanation, Magnus sat, only to be replaced by the captain of the Knights of Erythane. Age had only further distinguished Ra-khir's father, and he clearly saw authority as an honor rather than a burden. If anything, he had grown more handsome, more powerful-appearing, as he aged. "Won't it take time for the results of the war to even reach these giants? We know their servants came from across the sea, and none of their boats escaped us; as far as we know, they deliberately left no survivors of their own."

The knight spoke a truth Tae had considered; and, so, he had a ready answer. "I confess I know little about magic. I had hoped our elfin representative might help us." The moment the words left his lips, Tae suffered a pang of regret for putting Tem'aree'ay into the limelight without warning. He could not remember the elf ever deliberately drawing attention to herself.

All eyes fell instantly on the king of Béarn's second wife of three.

Tem'aree'ay seemed nonplussed by the sudden attention. Despite living with humans for nearly two decades, she still reacted in ways that seemed out-of-place and inconsistent, chaos incarnate. Her dainty face always bore a smile, surrounded by a swirl of golden curls with just a hint of elfin red. Unlike the humans who had grayed and wrinkled around her, she shed the years like water. Her sapphirine eyes still sparkled with youth and vigor, and she pressed her long-fingered, slender hands to the table. "Magic differs among those creatures who wield it." As she spoke, she revealed the small triangular tongue that reminded everyone of her alienness.

Humans collectively referred to the users of magic as Outworlders because they originated on other worlds. When the gods had fashioned mankind, they had meant for humans to have no contact with magical beings; and, for most of their history, it had remained so. To this day, many men still did not believe in the existence of magic nor creatures who wielded it. Some did not even acknowledge the gods.

"The elves have a silent form of communication called

khohlar." Tem'aree'ay pronounced the foreign term with an accent Tae envied. Because of their self-imposed seclusion, he knew little of the elves' language, and that bothered him. He made a mental note to learn as much as he could from Tem'aree'ay before leaving Béarn. "It's a direct mind-to-mind touch or a shout that radiates to any mind within reasonable distance. But our range is finite. We could never hurl *khohlar* across oceans."

Tae had experienced *khohlar*. It reminded him of the contact between himself and Imorelda except any elf could use *khohlar* to speak mentally to any single living being or to everyone within a circumscribed area. Elves could not modulate *khohlar* to include some and not others. Tae's telepathic ability was limited to Imorelda, although he had recently discovered he could participate in the *alsona*'s and *Kjempemagiska*'s mental communication by using the cat as an intermediary. Like every other human, Tae could hear *khohlar* but could not send it.

Nods swept the room. Tem'aree'ay seemed to be making Kedrin's point.

"The Cardinal Wizards, when they existed, lived great distances from one another. As I understand it, they used an *aristiri* hawk to carry messages to one another. They were considered some of the strongest users of magic to ever exist, and they could not communicate without this go-between."

Tae frowned. Tem'aree'ay's words seemed to clinch it, yet Tae could not believe the *Kjempemagiska* had no means to know how the battle had gone. He could understand that they had expected to easily conquer the peoples of the continent, that they never doubted General Firuz would return to them with news of the outcome. Yet, surely they had not waged a battle in total ignorance.

Tem'aree'ay looked at Tae as she added, "However, if an elf died, we would all know it at once." She did not elaborate; but Tae, and many others, knew their secret. The gods had given the elves no afterlife; instead, they had a specific and countable number of recyclable elfin souls. Elves conceived only after the death of an elder due to age, whose soul then entered the newly born elf. Since they never suffered illnesses or infections, the system had worked well for thousands of years. Their creator, Frey, had granted them an isolated world called Alfheim, without weather or need for work, where they could live in absolute peace.

Then, the *Ragnarok* had come, destroying Alfheim in a ball of fire. Only two hundred and forty elves escaped to Midgard, man's world, all others consumed, body and soul. The elves had lost forty more who had been so filled with hatred that the gods had named them *svartalf*, dark elves, and taken them to another world.

"It's possible," Tem'aree'ay elaborated, "that the death of the *Kjempemagiska* in battle was instantly known to his fellows."

Possible, Tae realized, *but not for the same reason.* Tae did not voice this thought aloud. He did not know how many people knew of the elves' plight. Every elf killed unnaturally meant the permanent loss of a soul, one less elf for all eternity. The *Kjempemagiska*, on the other hand, had come to conquer land because of a burgeoning population. Clearly, they did not suffer from the shared-soul issues that bound the elves together.

"The gods," Griff said.

All attention now went to the king of Béarn, who had probably not intended to speak the words aloud. For an instant, he seemed startled by the sudden attention, then covered awkwardly. "They can see and hear on all the worlds. Right?"

Gradually, all parts of the continent had come to accept the Northern gods as the real ones, but the detailed knowledge of the nature of the gods and their history was not as widespread. In large pockets, many in the East still worshiped their single deity. In the West, small groups still followed their own ancient pantheon. Even the Northmen, who had worshiped the proper gods and goddesses for as long as anyone could remember, still suffered significant lapses. A leader of the elves claimed he personally knew some existing Outworld sea gods. The Renshai had insisted for years that the *Ragnarok* had occurred, the worst of it diverted by Colbey Calistinsson; while Northmen still dreaded the coming of that world-ending destruction.

Though not a Northman, Minister of Foreign Affairs Richar had thoroughly studied the religious texts so as to know his visiting charges better. "The gods do not see us most times. That's why so many sins go unpunished. Only when they sit on Odin's high seat, *Hlidskjalf*, can they view the goings on from Asgard. Otherwise, they have to walk among us." Apparently more accustomed to discussing such matters with men prone to sin, he added, "Which they can take other forms to do, so one never knows when they're watching."

That last sent a shiver down Tae's spine, not so much because he worried for gods watching but for whether *Kjempemagiska* might also manage disguises and shape-changes.

"So," General Sutton said, and that one syllable gave him the floor. "I think we can agree it will take time for word of their defeat to get back to these giants. And, even when it does, they will need to create new strategies and update their knowledge about us. As magical beings, they probably have far longer lifespans, too. Like elves and gods. So, we probably have a few decades, at least."

"No!" Tae did not like the turn of the discussion. "They still have the same overcrowding problem they had yesterday. If they come at us quickly, they catch us weak from the war while they're at their strongest."

The intensity of Tae's tone stopped everyone cold. Though swift and decisive on the battlefield, most strategists tended to act with unhurried consideration in the Strategy Room.

King Griff finally broke the silence. "Both arguments seem . . . compelling."

Though utterly opposite, Tae realized. He glanced at Queen Matrinka who rubbed her hands repeatedly, a nervous gesture, and looked distraught. Usually, she shunned strategy sessions as frightening, preferring to leave such affairs to generals and kings. She had come only to support Tae. In all matters, she trusted his judgment, far more than he or Imorelda thought she probably should.

Valr Magnus reclaimed the floor. "Speaking only for the North, many of our people have already headed home. Our ground needs preparation for our short growing season. Much of our ore has gone to crafting weapons, and the world needs more. We can't all stay in Béarn indefinitely waiting for giants who might come tomorrow or in decades."

The ruler of a small Western conglomerate spoke next, one Tae did not know by name. Blocky and relatively short, he sported spiky, ash-blond hair and had a voice that seemed too deep for his figure. "And what if they choose another site of attack? They may come at us from a different angle, perhaps targeting the North or your own Eastlands. They could own the rest of the continent before they found our fighting men waiting in Béarn."

Who wants them here, anyway? Imorelda looked up at Tae, comfortably wedged into his lap and purring lightly. *They take up all the space, eat up all the food, and smell like toilets.*

Tae ignored the cat. "I'm not saying everyone should remain here. That's not practical or possible. I just pray you all keep your men prepared, don't allow them to slack off or become complacent in their victory. Be ready to assemble even more quickly as the *Kjempemagiska* will not harry our coasts and gather information before attacking as their *alsona* did. They may even have a magical means of faster travel. And one thing more." Tae's gaze strayed toward Tem'aree'ay before he could stop it. "If you know of any magical beings, you must use every means at your disposal to convince them to join us as well."

Tem'aree'ay's expression never changed; her smile persisted. But, beside her, King Griff frowned. They had tried to convince the elves to come, without success. "I'm afraid," the king started softly, "that without new words, without some proof of these giants' intentions, we have nothing new to motivate the elves."

"What about the girl?" someone called out.

Though bedridden through most of the war, Tae had heard tales of a young woman who had assisted in the defeat of the single *Kjempemagiska*. Details remained sketchy; but, from what Tae had gathered, Firuz had sent his surviving minions after her while he battled the Western armies on his own.

Knight-Captain Kedrin claimed the floor using an archaic gesture that few remembered and Tae never knew. "Several Knights are preparing to escort her safely home as we speak. We don't know who or what she is, but she clearly had some means of negating the giant's magic. Hopefully, my men will glean some information from her that we can use in any subsequent battle. They have been instructed to remain in her best graces and to enlist the support of her family and anyone else she might know with similar abilities."

General Sutton of Pudar cleared his throat. "Perhaps it would be better to keep her here."

Kedrin smiled indulgently. "I believe we all know that when it comes to beings of magic, wise men never choose to anger or detain them unnecessarily. The girl asked emphatically to go home. Hopefully, whatever induced her to help us will work again, and the Knights will endear themselves to her and her kind. Whatever they may be." He looked at Tem'aree'ay, brows rising.

Tem'aree'ay rose to the question. "She's human, Knight-Captain."

This time, startled voices rose into a rumble. To the best knowledge of the world's current scholars, no human had displayed even a trace of magical powers within the last several centuries. Even Tae felt his heart skip a beat. He had more experience than most, had read more history than even the princes and princesses of Béarn. The nearest thing to modern human magic that he knew of was his ability, and Matrinka's, to communicate with Imorelda and her departed mother, Mior.

"You're sure?" Kedrin said, politely, as always.

"We had to link magic to suppress the *Kjempemagiska's* magic. She's human. If I had to guess, I'd say a distant descendant of the Myrcidians, perhaps carried in her line since the time of the Cardinal Wizards. They're the only magical humans I've ever known."

Shocked silent, the assemblage did not seem to know what to say. Only Imorelda addressed Tae, *Is she saying she knew the Cardinal Wizards?*

Either that or Tem'aree'ay had used poor phrasing. While the common human trading tongue had a basis around the worlds, it was not the elves' first language. *She might have. It's rumored elves can live hundreds of years, even a thousand or longer. The one they call Captain earned his name ferrying about the Cardinal Wizards.*

"A descendant of Cardinal Wizards," General Markanyin said with equal measures of introspection and hope. "Her parents may have similar abilities? And others, too?"

Knight-Captain Kedrin sighed. "She's been polite but very secretive about her home and family. We're hoping she'll bond with some of the knights and become more talk-ative."

The regular ministers of Béarn normally spoke little when it came to matters of war; but, this time, Minister Franstaine said his piece. "She seemed rather close to your oldest grandson, Captain. Perhaps he can get her to tell us more."

Kedrin pursed his lips. "I'm afraid anything she told Saviar remains in confidence. And whatever closeness they had no longer exists. She wants nothing to do with him."

A Western leader Tae did not know spoke next. "Then what reason does he have for keeping her confidences?"

Tae winced, and the entire room seemed to join him. Kedrin turned his head slowly until he faced the speaker directly. "One's word is one's honor. Without it, a man is nothing."

The stranger persisted. "Even when not speaking could mean the destruction of your world? It seems to me that honor dictates a man must break his word to one when the lives of so many are at stake."

Kedrin's voice remained soft but commanding and full of building rage. "Do not preach honor to a Knight of Erythane. Integrity dictates that a man do the right thing even when it becomes inconvenient or will result in the loss of one's own life. My grandson will not break any vow he might have made."

Tae did not feel certain that the same held true for his own son. If Subikahn knew anything about Chymmerlee's background, he might be coaxed to tell it, in the right cir-cumstances, even against a promise. Clearly, however, now was not the time to mention it. "We have not gotten so des-perate we need to force a moral man to go against his prin-ciples. Let's see what the Knights of Erythane can do, first. Even if they fail, we have other options."

Queen Matrinka chose to skip most of the planning ses-sions, especially those regarding military matters. When she did attend, she said nothing. So when she opened her mouth, the room became like a tomb around her. "May I speak from a woman's perspective?"

Multiple gestures followed from every quarter, all en-couraging.

"Chymmerlee is at that age when a girl's fancy turns

to ... well ..." Matrinka's cheeks flushed. "... boys. She just lost one suitor, by her own choice, and she may be open to the attentions of another young man."

Matrinka and her mushy stuff, Imorelda complained. *If she's not trying to make me have kittens, she's trying to make some young girl have them.*

Tae could not help smiling ever so slightly. *I don't think she's talking about ... making kittens, Imorelda. I think she's just saying Chymmerlee might open up her thoughts to an attentive young man.*

Among other things.

Tae ignored the cat's crudeness. "It certainly couldn't hurt to have a well-mannered and reasonably handsome young man among the knights returning her home. One who might spare her some attention at a time when she might crave it."

Kedrin's growing frown forced Tae to add more.

"I'm not suggesting he lie to or mislead her, just show her the usual manners knights display. If he just happened to get assigned to her, well there's nothing inherently immoral about that, is there?"

"No," Kedrin had to admit. "We do have a trainee among those selected to bring her safely home. Since they are similar in age, they may drift together. Or she may feel so disgusted about her last attempt at romance she wants nothing to do with any young male. Either way, we will make her comfortable and respect her decision." The corner of his mouth twitched slightly, the only indication he had softened. "And if they do happen to drift together, no one will interfere."

"Thank you, Captain," Griff said. "No one could ask for more."

Sure they could. Imorelda lacked all of the king's subtlety.

You could, Tae admitted. *But it probably wouldn't work. You can't force love, and you can't rush it.*

The cat made a disgusted noise. *You humans attach too much sentiment to everything and analyze things to death. We can tell when you're in love. You have to be beaten over the head with a brick sometimes.*

Tae caught the reference. The cat had been trying to get him to marry Alneezah, the kind and quick-witted maid who watched over him, while he had repeatedly denied his affection for her. Tae had finally recognized that the cat was right, but he could not act on the knowledge until he returned home. Nor had he admitted his mistake to Imorelda. *You can't make people love on command. It has to happen naturally.*

Imorelda sent a mental laugh. *Men are poor dumb saps who don't even realize that women quietly, secretly make all your decisions. Including who you love.*

Tae did not have time to ponder the cat's words, other than to realize that one female did have great power over him: Imorelda herself.

King Griff summed up the proceedings. "So, it seems we have resolved to do several things today. First, we must prepare for a larger attack by giant magical beings. Second, we will shore up our communication systems, including leaving some representatives in Béarn and elsewhere to prepare for an attack in the near or distant future on any beachfront. Third, we will attempt to enlist the aid of magical beings, including the elves, Chymmerlee, and any others like Chymmerlee who might exist. Fourth, we need to learn the plans of these magical giants in order to thwart or prepare for them. We will meet back here in three days' time with specific ideas as to how to achieve those four objectives."

Tae sucked in a huge breath of air, knowing exactly which role would have to become his. He alone could speak the language of the enemy, and it required not only the use of voice but of mental speaking. He knew of only one other person capable of such a thing, and the idea of involving Matrinka in a spying mission like the one that had nearly killed him was revolting. Griff might even try to stop Tae himself from going. If he died spying, they lost the key to communication with the *Kjempemagiska*.

Tae had three days to make a decision.

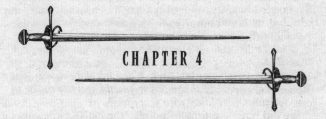

CHAPTER 4

*The Renshai will remain the finest swordsmen in the world,
but never again will we ravage lands at peace without cause.*
— Colbey Calistinsson

SAVIAR RA-KHIRSSON SLIPPED INTO the Renshai
encampment as the sun glided below the ocean, smearing
streaks of red across the waves. Voices carried over the
sand, and the dark figures of moving men filled the horizon
as they continued the job of sorting corpses. The Renshai
had already sent their own dead to the pyre. The *torke* challenged the mortally injured to combat, granting them the
death in valorous battle they all craved and required, humanely destroying those too weak to fight.

The rest of the cleanup fell to the companions of the
dead or to the noncombatants of Béarn. Healers worked
tirelessly on injured allies, while the dead and dying of the
enemy were piled unceremoniously or dragged into the surf
for the sharks to devour. Urchins and beggars ransacked
the heaps, seeking missed bits of copper or jewelry and
well-hidden weapons. Some groups fared better than others.
Where the Renshai had lost only a handful of warriors, men
and women alike, the untrained peasants of the central
West had fallen in numbers that required mass graves.

Saviar walked to the makeshift tent erected by his family, only to find his father's white charger saddled and ready,
Darby fussing over the last details of grooming his own
chestnut gelding. Though Saviar could not explain why, the

sight of the young squire diligently focused on the animals aggravated his already foul temper. He brushed aside the tent flap without bothering to ascertain that he did not expose his father.

Ra-khir looked up from his preparations, wearing the formal black breeks and long-sleeved silk undershirt of the Knights of Erythane. He looked out of place without his tabard and cape, his red-blond hair wild and his hands unclad. Although he smiled, the corners of his lips turned down ever so slightly. "Ah, Saviar." His tone did not express the usual joy at the sight of his son.

That bothered Saviar. Prior to his mother's death, he and his father had been close, much more so than the aloof, contemptuous Calistin or Subikahn, who had spent nearly as much time in the East with his father as on the Fields of Wrath with the rest of his family.

"Going somewhere?" Saviar stared into his father's face. Ra-khir should have told him; he should not have had to ask.

"On a mission for the knights," Ra-khir said matter-of-factly as he pulled on his tabard. Blue and gold in the front, it displayed the rearing grizzly of Béarn. On the back, it was black, with the orange sun and sword symbol of Erythane. Saviar knew it so well, he could draw every detail with his eyes closed.

"Where to?" Saviar asked innocently, wondering how long his father would remain evasive.

Ra-khir adjusted every seam and wrinkle. "North into the middle Westlands." He picked up his cape. "We're serving as an escort."

"We?"

"Me and three other knights." Ra-khir threw the golden fabric across his shoulders and reached for the clasp.

"Can I come along?"

Ra-khir did not miss a beat. He fastened the clasp, then set to adjusting every fold. "I'm sorry, Saviar. It's for knights only."

Saviar's ire rose further, and he fought it down. "You've taken me before."

"That was your grandfather's idea. And, at the time, you were contemplating becoming a Knight of Erythane."

Saviar studied his father, forever in awe of the splendid

figure cut by all of Erythane's knights. Even without the hat and the gloves, a Knight of Erythane inspired admiration and trust, especially in the son who used to worship them. "What makes you think I no longer am?"

Ra-khir stopped preening to study Saviar. "You've expressed no further interest. Joining the Knights of Erythane is not something you can do halfway. It requires commitment and intense dedication."

Saviar could only stare. "Since I expressed my interest, when have I had a chance to pursue anything? As soon as we returned home from that particular mission, Mother was killed in the Northmen's duel and the Renshai banished from the entire Westlands. We got back barely in time for the war, which has only just ended."

Ra-khir responded so softly even Saviar could scarcely hear him. "*You* were not banished."

"What?" Saviar could not believe what he had heard.

Dutifully, Ra-khir repeated, "You were not banished. I told you the Erythanian Council determined you and your brothers could stay, since your only living parent was Erythanian, not Renshai."

Ire flared to frank anger. "So you expected me to abandon my tribe?"

"I expected you," Ra-khir started just as softly, forcing Saviar to strain to hear, "to do exactly as you did. Aside from leaving in secret without telling me good-bye."

"So that's what this is all about."

Ra-khir looked all innocence. "What do you mean?"

"I abandoned you, so you're abandoning me." Saviar turned his back, the insult deliberate. "I suffered a lot of guilt for that bad decision. And I apologized. I can understand your being upset, but I can't understand your inability to forgive me."

Ra-khir put on his wide, yellow belt, fastening it from long habit. "I forgave you long before you apologized. Children do hurtful things sometimes, but you never stop loving them." He reached for his sword, long and broad. Saviar could never remember a time when he did not have a sword at his own hip or in his hand, but he had started with much thinner, shorter blades. He recalled hefting his father's mighty weapon in his youth and nearly falling on his face. "I'm not abandoning you, Saviar. I'm going on a short mission. I've been serving the Knights of Erythane your whole life, and I've gone many places without you. Why is this one so different?"

"Because—" Only one answer came, not the one Saviar had intended to shout, but the truth. Realizing his resentment had grown far out of proportion to the circumstances, Saviar let the words escape him softly. "—you're escorting Chymmerlee, aren't you?"

"Yes," Ra-khir admitted, attaching his sword to his belt and flicking it into the proper knightly angle.

"She hates me now, doesn't she?"

Ra-khir would never lie. "It would appear you are not among her favorites."

Saviar had to know. "Why? What did I do wrong?"

Ra-khir sighed. He sat on the deadfall that served as their only piece of furniture in the camp and gestured for Saviar to take a place beside him.

The Renshai complied.

"You lied to her, Saviar. About being Renshai."

Although he knew his only defense would not work with Ra-khir, or any Knight of Erythane, Saviar could not help trying. "I didn't lie. It just . . . never . . . came up."

Ra-khir gave Saviar a disapproving look, one he knew from his childhood but did not realize still worked so well on his conscience. "A lie of omission is still a lie, Saviar. You know that."

"Yes, but . . . Thialnir says we should not reveal ourselves as Renshai until people get to know us and like us. Otherwise, they might react badly to us just because of our tribe."

"Thialnir is a wise Renshai." Having defended the source, Ra-khir did not let Saviar off the hook. "However, I think you got well past the point where Chymmerlee got to know and like you without telling her. Yes?"

Saviar nodded and opened his mouth to explain.

But Ra-khir had not yet finished. "I don't expect you to act like a Knight of Erythane, but I do expect you to behave like the moral, decent man you are. Trust must be earned, and it shatters easily, with a single lie or betrayal. In the end, a man's word and his good name are the only things he truly owns. If he sacrifices those, he has nothing."

Saviar had heard those words before. "But, Papa, that's exactly what—"

Ra-khir still had a point to make. "Do you love her, Saviar?"

Saviar had not expected the sudden question. "I-I don't know. I suppose I eventually could. I like her a lot, but I'm not ready for marriage or anything." He could not help wondering, "Why does that matter?"

"Because, Saviar, if you truly care about someone, you would never violate her trust. Never. She must know, without any reason to ever consider doubting, that you would not harm her, that you would lay down your life for her."

Saviar screwed up his features, trying to fathom the new direction the conversation had taken.

"It is the ultimate measure of a man. Because, if his wife and children cannot trust him, those he professes to love most in the world, how can anyone? If he would be disloyal to his loved ones, how much quicker will he betray anyone of lesser importance? Most women, good women, do not need this explained to them; they know intuitively. But even usually-wise kings have made the mistake of putting men who deceive their wives in positions of power, then act surprised when the dog next turns on them."

Saviar shook his head. "I see your point. It's one I admit I never considered. But, in this case, it works against you."

Ra-khir's brows inched upward. "How so?"

"Because, when I awoke from my coma—"

Ra-khir interrupted, a discourtesy he rarely indulged in, "Coma?" Clear alarm came out in that solitary word.

"—having no idea where I was or what was happening, Subikahn made me swear I wouldn't tell anyone about us being Renshai. Having made that vow to a loved one, I could hardly break it."

"The loved one being Subikahn." Ra-khir shook his head repeatedly. "Coma?"

Clearly, they could not continue the discussion until Saviar answered the outstanding question. "Apparently, I took a bad hit and went septic. I lost a lot of remembered time, not only during and after the injury but even some before it. I'm told that happens a lot with bad accidents; the healers even have a name for it. Something long I can't pronounce. If you want more than that, you'll have to ask Subikahn."

"And when you woke up, you made a promise to your brother."

Saviar managed a weak grin. Ra-khir finally understood. "One I could not violate, although I wanted to several times. Vows, I'm told, are not situational; and a man is only as good as his word."

Ra-khir laughed. His very own words had come back to bite him. "I've heard you made vows to Chymmerlee as well. Ones she worries you won't keep."

Saviar felt his blood warming again and gritted his teeth to hold back rising anger. "And I am certain you assured her I would never break my word."

"I assured her you had always kept it before, and I would do my best to see you remained the upstanding and wonderful man I raised."

Saviar tried to find an underlying insult, seeking any reason to justify the irritation toward his father that he currently suffered. "Did you also tell her there must be some logical reason why I didn't tell her about being Renshai?"

Ra-khir gathered his hat and his gloves, pulling them into his lap. "I don't second-guess the motives of any man without speaking to him first."

Saviar snorted.

"Why didn't you tell her yourself?"

Saviar suspected Ra-khir knew the answer to his own question, at least in a general sense. He also had enough knowledge of his son's vows to Chymmerlee not to ask about her and her people. "I can't get near her. When Subikahn tried to help, she nearly killed him."

"She's not open to explanation."

That being self-evident, Saviar saw no reason to reply. Finally believing himself free from the mostly irrational anger, he asked softly, "You'll talk to her? Help her understand?"

Ra-khir sighed, winching his hands around the gloves in his lap. "I'm sure we'll talk; but, as I've already stated, she's clearly not open to explanation. I suspect that, in her case, the trust issue, while significant, is not what most bothers her."

Saviar cocked his head, not fully certain of his father's point. "So now that you've lectured me to death on trust, you're saying that's not even the problem?"

Ra-khir shook his head, face crinkled with dismay. "Oh, that's a significant transgression, one I'm glad to hear you didn't commit simply to save yourself discomfort. But, having listened to you and observed her, I suspect she hates you more for being Renshai than for neglecting to tell her." He peered intently at his son, obviously expecting a strong reaction.

Saviar only shrugged. Chymmerlee had never met a Renshai before he and his twin had come into her life. She knew them only as the bloodthirsty savages who had slaughtered all of her people more than three hundred years ago. Regaled with stories of cruelty and hatred since birth, she could feel no other way about them. She had cared deeply for Saviar once, before she knew what he was. Surely, he could make her see that he had not become a different person only because she had learned the race of his mother. "Then there's hope."

Ra-khir sat up. "Hope?"

"Prejudice stems from ignorance. If I educate her, she may not only come back to me but come also to understand Renshai."

Ra-khir remained frozen in place, clearly worried to display any sort of reaction. That, in and of itself, told Saviar that he had concerns about his son's words.

Saviar felt the old ire rising again. In the last day, it had become a familiar companion. "What's wrong with what I said?"

"Nothing," Ra-khir admitted. "It's a noble pursuit."

"But . . ." Saviar added questioningly.

Ra-khir hesitated, as if debating whether or not to continue. "I . . . know women, as much as a man can. And I know young men well. You will want to begin her schooling immediately. She will not wish to speak to or about you for weeks. Those two do not mesh well. Far better to give her the space and time to miss you."

"Except, you're about to take her away."

Ra-khir could hardly deny it. "If it's meant to be, she'll come back to you. I can't tell you the details of my mission, but you have to know all of us want her to like us, to return should we need her services again." He frowned deeply, warningly. "You also must know I'm bound to protect her against anything that might harm or upset her. Please, Saviar, don't place me in the position of having to defend her from you."

Truly Renshai, Saviar's thoughts went immediately to

prowess. *I'd beat you senseless, old man.* He kept the idea to himself. Ra-khir would not consider the danger. If he had to fight Saviar to complete his knight's mission, he would do so no matter the certainty of the outcome. Saviar had no doubt he could defeat his father, but to what purpose? It might impress someone who held the knights in high esteem, but it would mortify Chymmerlee, break his father's heart, imbue him with guilt, and accomplish nothing positive. The desperate turn of his thoughts fueled his irritability. This could not end well. "Can't I go with you?"

Ra-khir had already answered that question. "No."

"*He*'s going though, isn't he?" Saviar jabbed a finger in the general direction of the waiting horses.

Ra-khir looked genuinely puzzled. "Silver Warrior?"

Saviar rolled his eyes. "I mean the boy. The one who tags after you everywhere."

Ra-khir's lids widened. "You mean Darby? Of course he's coming with me. He's my squire, a knight-in-training. It's his job to tag after me everywhere, to observe and question, to anticipate my needs."

Unsure why he had taken such an instant and intense disliking to the youngster, Saviar merely grunted. He had only met Darby once, only long enough to exchange pleasantries. Not yet trained in the use of weapons, Darby had remained behind the lines during the war, though he had protested mightily.

Ra-khir seemed to have more insight. "Saviar, it's never too late to attempt to join the Knights of Erythane. We have no age requirement. If you're still interested and can make yourself available for the training, you're welcome to try."

"But you've already taken a squire." Saviar folded his arms across his chest.

"That was never an option."

Shocked by the words, Saviar stared.

"I'm not entirely sure I have the competence and control to impartially evaluate my own son, nor that you would display the same respect for me as you would for a stranger."

Saviar seemed incapable of seeing his father's words in any but the worst light. "So I'm a bad son."

"I didn't say that. I'm just letting you know that, if you chose to squire, you would be assigned to another knight than me."

That only further confused Saviar. "If I chose it?"

"It's not a requirement. It's normally reserved for those of less enlightened background, those who need more experience with the knights before attempting the actual training. I never squired, nor had the inclination to teach one."

"Hence Darby."

Ra-khir smiled. "Darby just sort of happened. We discovered one another while I was searching for you and your brothers, and he was looking for a better life for himself and his family. He's perfect knight material, and he wants it more than anything in the world."

As opposed to me, you mean. Saviar held his tongue again. Sometimes the desire to join his father and grandfather consumed him like a bonfire, while other times he barely gave it a thought. The life of a Renshai also required a dedication beyond that which most could give. Every moment not spent in spar or practice, in warfare or honoring one's sword was considered wholly wasted, including the time he had just spent conversing with his father. The added burden heaped upon him by agreeing to succeed Thialnir as titular leader of the Renshai only made things more difficult. "What if I squired to one of the knights accompanying you on your mission?"

Ra-khir rose, sweeping his hat to his head. "Not if you were Colbey Calistinsson himself." With that, he seized his gloves, left the tent, and headed toward his waiting charger.

Saviar also stood, watching from the flap as Ra-khir and Darby exchanged a few words, mounted their horses, and headed for Béarn. The suggestion that Saviar might feign interest in the Knights of Erythane for the sole purpose of attending this mission should have earned him a much heavier rebuke. Ra-khir had chosen that moment to leave as much to end the conversation as to meet up with his companions. Though a common Renshai brush-off, Ra-khir's last words were not something Saviar had ever heard him say; and Saviar could not help wondering if they contained more meaning than the mere syllables implied.

Colbey Calistinsson was the only Renshai to ever become a Knight of Erythane, too. True, he had only had to kill a knight in fair combat. At the time, the intensive training that included mock battles, protocol, drills, jousts, and ethical dilemmas already existed, but so did the loophole that granted Colbey his charger and his title. To Saviar's knowledge, no one had ever called on Colbey to fulfill any knightly duties. *Who would dare?* Perhaps Ra-khir intended to remind his son that even the immortal Renshai of legend had not managed to integrate the two worlds. Or, perhaps, he wished to point out to his son that the two worlds had collided once before and could again.

Saviar shook his head at the contradictory interpretations, then came full circle. *Or, perhaps, he was just trying to end a senseless conversation with a classic brush-off.*

In any case, it seemed, the point was lost on Saviar.

Nearly three hundred strong, all but a handful of the tribe of Renshai headed together toward the Fields of Wrath. Left arm still splinted, Calistin Ra-khirsson walked at the head, beside the massive, aging Thialnir. Most chatted as they strode, in happy tones, and laughter wafted on the foggy air. They had not looked upon their homes and land for several months, not since the now-retracted duel had sent them into exile.

Most of their conversations centered on favorite practice areas; the Renshai bore little attachment to objects other than their swords. A barren plain devoid of useful soil, the Fields of Wrath had never supported crops or livestock, even had the Renshai time or knowledge of how to tend them. They bought their necessities, went without most luxuries, and spent minimal effort on construction. Nevertheless, it was home, and they had missed it.

Calistin had always approached life boldly, without concern for emotions: his own or anyone else's. Now, strange doubts descended on him, raising memories he would rather ignore. He had spent most of his life on the Fields of Wrath, yet they had changed forever the day Captain Erik Leifsson had brought Valr Magnus and proposed the challenge. The Renshai had picked Calistin as their champion, but the Northmen had called foul, deeming it inherently unfair for anyone to have to fight the best of the Renshai.

The details and logic of that argument eluded Calistin. Only cowards would call a duel, then press their opponents to call forth a weaker contestant. Calistin had dismissed the

Northmen with the claim that it did not matter, even his mother could defeat the most skilled Northman in any duel. This sarcastic challenge they had taken in earnest, and Kevral had instantly agreed to the battle.

It was the only time in his life Calistin could remember feeling guilt or fear, both of which had swarmed down on him like an angry hive. The oddity of the emotions had only added to his discomfort. It was the one time he had turned to his older brother for assistance, though Saviar could offer little solace. When the battle commenced, Calistin could tell by their movements, their builds, their speed, knowledge, and dedication to the fight that Kevral should win. Magnus had the advantages of size and strength, but she had every other, especially the Renshai maneuvers. She got off the first attack. She took first blood. She scored the first serious wound.

Except that Calistin had not counted on the Northmen cheating to turn the tide. He could still envision the well-paid Erythanian leaping from a tree branch at Kevral. She had dodged him and Magnus' attack admirably, but the plummeting man had struck her a glancing blow that caused her to lose her balance and the fight. As the details returned too vividly to Calistin's mind's eye, he could practically feel the sharpened blade slicing through his mother's side.

Off-balanced by his own memories, Calistin veered left-ward and into Thialnir. Hard as rock, the elder did not budge, but he did glance toward his companion. Only then, Calistin noticed the anguished look on their leader's face. If even he could read it, anyone could. "What is it?"

"Where's your brother, Calistin?"

Calistin had two brothers. He knew Thialnir had to mean Saviar, but he answered for both. "I haven't seen either of them since yesterday at the practice room." He smiled at the memory. He had taken them both on at once and bested them, despite his broken arm. "Subikahn spends as much time with the Eastlanders as us, so I never expect to see him. Saviar did not sleep in our tent last night, either. I figured, with Father gone on his mission, he didn't want to spend the night alone with me."

Thialnir returned to his silent contemplations. Calistin saw no reason to further bother the old Renshai. He had opened the gates of conversation. If Thialnir wished to say more, he would. Instead, Calistin focused on creating a new Renshai maneuver, one the entire tribe would be clamoring to learn.

As the familiar outline of the Fields of Wrath came into view, memories pushed aside the necessary single-mindedness required to manufacture complicated sword-play. Calistin found himself staring at the foggy skyline of cottages that defined home: the slanting roof of Arsvid's home that had undergone so many temporary fixes it now consisted almost entirely of patches, the blocky common storage facility, the scraggly twisted trees that made up his favorite sparring grounds. Deeper inside, he would find his childhood dwelling, where they had lived as a family until the duel that had not only ended his mother's life, but began a new nomadic existence.

Worried a glimpse of the Fields of Wrath might raise bad feelings, Calistin relished the joy welling up inside him in its stead. His mother had died a valiant, hero's death, guided to Valhalla by a *Valkyrie* he had seen with his own eyes. He now wore one of her swords proudly at his hip. She did not want them to mourn, but to celebrate the glory of her life and her death. Though never the sentimental type, this time Calistin found himself drawn to the excitement of his peers. After months of uncertainty, the Renshai had come home.

Suddenly seized by a feeling of imminent threat, Calistin exchanged one form of excitement for another. His heart pounded with the slow, sure cadence that always preceded a battle. Only then, movement touched the corners of his vision. Gradually, figures appeared in the fog, between the Renshai and their village. They were not mounted, nor did they carry readied weapons. As the clot of Renshai drew closer, it became clear the others wore no swords at their belts. Most came barehanded, though a few clutched pitch-forks or hammers clearly balanced for forges rather than warfare.

Their builds seemed light, almost emaciated after dwelling among Béarnides and warriors for so long. Though most stood taller than Calistin, he saw children among the mass. Dressed frugally, mostly in patched homespun rimed with dirt, they presented a pitiful front that would give the Renshai swords no challenge. Disappointed, Calistin studied them, looking for some sign of competence. Though he noticed some possibilities in the contours of a few, even those had either not developed their potential or had already lived past their prime.

As the group did not give way, the Renshai stopped. Calistin did not recognize any of those who thought they could bar the Renshai's passage, but that did not surprise him. Anyone who could not give him at least a reasonable spar did not warrant his interest. Few enough *ganim* fulfilled that requirement. These might just as well be sheep.

When the Renshai said nothing, one of the strangers stepped forward. White and dark hair mingled into inseparable gray, receding from his forehead and temples. Veins ran like tortuous blue snakes through his thinning skin, and an artery throbbed at his temple. "You are not welcome here."

Uncertain what to make of the statement, Calistin looked behind him. Confusion knit across the Renshai faces.

Thialnir cleared his throat. Although Renshai paid little attention to formality and leadership, they had become accustomed to the old Renshai speaking for them. "The Fields of Wrath belong to us. You have no authority to welcome us or not. Step aside so we do not have to plow through you."

The old man did not budge, though his limbs trembled, betraying his fear. Those around him remained speechless, but Calistin could see a strange emotion taking form on their faces, similar to the expression his enemies wore as he cut them down in battle. Several stepped warily from foot to foot, and some of the children skittered behind the elders.

"The Paradise Plains belong to us," the man countered. "You took them from us once. We will not allow you to do so again."

Thialnir blinked, brows crushing inward in confusion. He glanced back, apparently still seeking Saviar, though he disguised the movement with a casual flick of his braids from his face. "You're talking nonsense. Our ancestors settled on barren land they called the Fields of Wrath. Never has this place borne any other name."

The elder snorted. "Perhaps according to history rewritten by Renshai. Our peaceful ancestors lived here before you savages destroyed them and took their land. We have reclaimed it, and we will not leave."

Calistin had little book learning, especially in regard to history. Once the tribe saw his potential, they encouraged him to dedicate himself solely to the sword. They supplied his needs and nearly all his desires, not wishing to distract him from the quest to become the ultimate warrior. He did not care about ancient history. Since long before his birth, his people had lived there. "Get out of the way or die. Either way, we will take back our homes." Calistin did not give the self-called Paradisians time to respond but raced toward them.

The rasping sounds of swords clearing sheaths came from behind and around him. The Renshai swept forward, as wild and fearless as a pack of hungry dogs. Calistin wished he could draw both weapons at once, to fall upon those who dared try to keep him from the homes that rightfully belonged to his people; but his splint allowed for only one. Screams rose from the line of Paradisians, no longer so bold and confident, and most broke from the line in ragged, crazed running. Only a few remained in place to face the certain death charging down on them.

Sudden as lightning, a figure appeared in front of Calistin. A sword like flickering silver wove through his defenses. It drove toward his hilt in a brilliant Renshai maneuver that defined speed and dexterity. An abrupt backward jerk saved Calistin from a disarming, but the discrepancy of movement disrupted his own grace and usually perfect balance. His opponent slammed a lithe shoulder into Calistin's chest. Stability lost, Calistin dropped to his bottom in the dirt.

Calistin's opponent shouted in the Renshai tongue, "Stop, friends! It's a trap."

Shocked, the Renshai halted their attack. All bravado lost, the last of the Paradisians fled back toward the Fields of Wrath.

Calistin sprang to his feet in an instant, but the damage was done. He knew only one man who could humiliate him in this manner, only one for whom dropping Calistin on his buttocks had become a standard of training.

Thialnir did not have the benefit of a prior meeting. "Who are you?" he demanded, also using the tribal tongue.

Behind him, the Renshai exchanged quiet conversation. Calistin heard his name bandied about. They had never seen anyone best their champion, even one-armed, and this man had done it quickly and without apparent difficulty.

The newcomer casually sheathed his sword and glanced through the Renshai. He looked ordinary in most respects: average in height, slender and sinewy, with blunt cheekbones and a gently arched chin. His hair was golden, speckled with glimmers of silver, his eyes an intense blue-gray. Four straight, deep scars scored the line of his cheek, just in front of his ear. He carried an aura of confidence that made him seem larger, stronger, and infinitely deadly.

As he seemed disinterested in introducing himself, Calistin did it for him. "That's Colbey, of course. Who else could it be?" He did not add that he knew the immortal Renshai well. Currently, only he and Ra-khir among the mortals knew Colbey was Calistin's blood grandfather.

The murmuring grew louder.

Thialnir only stared.

As Calistin seemed to be the only one wholly coherent, Colbey turned his attention to him. "Where's your brother?"

Now, Calistin found himself staring as well. "Why does everyone keep assuming I have any control over my two adult, older siblings?"

"It's not a matter of control." Colbey peered through the chaotic array of Renshai. His ageless eyes seemed to penetrate them to find anyone who might be hiding at the back. "It's a matter of Saviar agreeing to become Thialnir's successor, then disappearing when he's most needed."

Thialnir nodded broadly. Colbey clearly understood his discomfort in a way Calistin had not.

Colbey's lips pursed. "I should not have to intervene. It's dangerous when I do." The corners of his tightened lips twitched upward ever so slightly. "Trouble likes to follow me."

Thialnir finally found his tongue. "This time, the trouble came first. What did you mean by 'a trap'?"

Colbey glanced around the sparse and scraggly trees that managed to root in the sandy soil. "Let's find a less open place to discuss this." He gestured back the way they had come.

All talking at once, the Renshai opened a path for Colbey. They could have led the way, but every one wanted to see the legendary, greatest Renshai who had already proven himself with one sword stroke. In their hearts, Calistin

knew, they all wanted to match their swords against his.
They also wanted to touch him, to test the solid reality of
him, but no one risked losing his hands for the honor. Calistin found himself struck by a sudden, silly urge to hurl
himself upon Colbey just to shock them. He would pay for
the action with pain and a sharp lesson, but he knew Colbey
would not maim or kill him.

Colbey walked through the opening, with Calistin and
Thialnir at either hand. He showed no obvious concern surrounded by Renshai warriors, though whether because he
still considered them his people or because he felt competent
to handle any or all of them, Calistin did not bother to wonder. All of her life, Kevral had modeled herself on the Renshai of legend: quoting him, wearing her hair in his feathered
style, emulating his sword strokes in battle and *svergelse*. She
had reveled in the name the Renshai had bestowed upon
Calistin, which he shared with Colbey's deceased father, and
also in his muscular structure, natural dexterity, and skill.
Calistin might equal Colbey someday, but the Renshai of legend had nearly four hundred years of practice on him.

And, though it would have sounded beyond impossible
just a few short months ago, Calistin now realized he might
actually have the opportunity. Colbey had reached his
eighth decade before learning that his own blood father
was the thunder god, Thor. Colbey had married the goddess,
Freya, and produced Raska "Ravn" Colbeysson, Calistin's
blood sire. By Calistin's calculations, that made him 3/8ths
a god, by blood, though he knew it took more than bloodline to become immortal. Colbey had stated that Calistin
would have to earn the honor, though he either could not
or would not elaborate.

At the time, it had seemed desperately important. Soulless, Calistin had had no other option but an absolute and
dark death, without afterlife. Once Treysind had made his
great sacrifice, the possibility of immortality lost much of its
significance. Like every Renshai, Calistin wanted nothing so
much as to die in glorious battle and earn his new soul its
place in Valhalla, where the *Einherjar* battled all day, then
the fallen rose to join the victors in a night of feasting.

Colbey led the Renshai back toward the woodlands,
stopping short at the edge of a farm field. It took them far
enough away from the Fields of Wrath to discourage spies

yet near enough the Renshai would not feel as if they had taken the coward's path of retreat. Once every Renshai had gathered around him, Colbey explained, still in Renshai. "They wanted you to attack them, to slaughter their elders and children."

Thialnir bobbed his head sagely. "It would not take much for the world to call us savages unworthy of any homeland. Whatever the law might state, the sympathies of every nation would turn to these so-called Paradisians."

Calistin rarely bothered to consider other's intentions, but this one befuddled him. "They wanted us to kill their children? Their children? Why?"

Colbey turned his cold eyes on Calistin. "Because, Calistin, the Paradisians hate Renshai more than they love their children."

Though they learned swordwork from the moment their little hands could close around a small-sized hilt, Renshai offspring did not go to war until they passed the sequence of tests that proclaimed them competent adults. On average, this happened around age eighteen. No one had attained manhood at a younger age than Calistin, and even he had not done so until thirteen. Should a child die in combat, the Renshai celebrated rather than mourned him, as they did all brave warriors. But Renshai did not shove their children forward as fodder for more powerful enemies, and many Renshai had lost their lives fiercely protecting sons and daughters.

"What could be more savage than that?" a young woman named Alvida asked. Though she spoke softly, her voice carried over the silence. "Sending one's children to certain death to get the upper hand in a land dispute?"

"The world will not see it that way," Thialnir realized aloud. "No matter what we do, they will see us as bullies and the Paradisians as desperate victims making terrible sacrifices because they lack the means to fight an honorable battle against our warriors."

That made no sense to Calistin. "But it's as you said, isn't it? When the Renshai chose to live here, centuries ago, the land lay barren and unusable. No one called the Fields of Wrath anything else until . . ." He could not finish his own sentence. This was the first time he had heard of the Paradisians.

Thialnir made a gesture toward Colbey, the only one born before the Renshai had staked their claim to the land. "All true," the immortal confirmed. "The Fields of Wrath have remained under Renshai control until such time as some scheming Northmen convinced a handful of impoverished Erythanians they were the rightful heirs."

"But we have the truth on our side," said Gareth, an elder. "We can show them, in scrolls and texts."

Thialnir shook his head sadly. He, too, had started as an impetuous young Renshai; but the many decades of serving as leader, of interacting with diplomats, had taken their toll. "The truth will not matter. For most people, history begins at their own births and ends at their deaths. Between times, they believe what they wish to be truth. The majority cannot even read, and most of the world's most accurate history is contained in Béarn's library. Neighbors that we are, how many even among us read Béarnese?"

Calistin did not need to look to see how many Renshai responded. He had learned to speak Renshai, Erythanian, Common Trading, and Northern. Most of the Renshai could write those languages as well. But, when it came to the more obscure tongues and dialects, few were willing to take time from martial studies to learn.

Silence fell over the Renshai again. Nearly everyone had a hand clamped to at least one hilt. Combat was the one language they all embraced.

Gareth spoke the words on every mind. "So we should give our homes to thieves? When has what others think of us mattered to Renshai?"

Nods suffused the group, accompanied by cries of agreement.

Calistin would have joined them under ordinary circumstances, but Colbey's presence made him thoughtful. The consummate Renshai rarely appeared on Midgard. As Calistin understood it, any interference from gods on the worlds of men had massive and unpredictable ripples. Colbey's half-mortal bloodline gave him more leeway than the other inhabitants of Asgard, but even he rarely risked meddling. For him to appear and show himself to so many meant the situation had to have become dire. Calistin loosed a bitter laugh that drew every eye.

Kristel, who had trained with Calistin's mother and

questioned Magnus in Béarn's sparring room, demanded, "What's so funny?"

"You," Calistin spoke fighting words. "All of you. Are you questioning the wisdom of a Renshai who lives among the gods? Colbey has bested whole tribes of Northmen. Giants. Demons. The *Ragnarok* itself. If you believe you have the right to dismiss him, challenge him. I'll gladly stand by and watch you make fools of yourselves."

Colbey placed a hand on Calistin's shoulder, a plea for silence.

While Kristel glared, measuring Colbey and Calistin, a competent *torke* named Navali spoke up. "It's all a trick. That's not Colbey. It's a Northman hired by the Paradisians to undo us."

Calistin's brows rose nearly to his hairline. He could not believe any Renshai could say such a thing after the brilliant maneuver that had felled him. *Not everyone could see Colbey's attack. Others may have had their attention diverted elsewhere.* Still more, he realized, did not yet have the ability to fully judge a man by a single sword stroke. Colbey clearly wished him to remain quiet for the moment, so Calistin obliged.

"Don't let my fluent use of the Renshai tongue fool you." Colbey turned on Navali the fearless look of one already certain of the outcome. "Endpoint?"

Calistin could not help interrupting. "Drop him on his ass, same as you did me."

Navali frowned but did not contradict.

Colbey turned to Kristel, "And you?"

"First blood," Kristel said before Calistin could suggest anything.

A large, sandy-haired warrior named Tanvard added, "And I'll take first one to disarm the other." It was his specialty.

"Nothing more creative?" Calistin would not be left out of a competition against Colbey. He had ended every session with Colbey sore and exhausted, and he relished the opportunity to cross swords with the old man again. "Give me . . ." He tried to think of something absolutely original. ". . . first one to name the color of the other's underclothes."

Colbey looked over his various opponents with a seasoned eye. "Ready?"

Navali stepped forward. "Ready."

Quicker than a blink, Colbey lunged. As Navali drew, Colbey had already crossed inside his guard, inserted a foot behind his ankle. As Navali tried to avoid it, his own momentum took him down. An instant later, blood dribbled from a cut on Kristel's calf, and Tanvard's sword went flying through the air. Colbey caught it neatly, as any Renshai would do for an honored opponent. From the looks on their faces, Calistin knew they had expected Colbey to go at them one at a time. Calistin had readied his own sword the instant Colbey went for Navali.

Colbey sheathed his sword, not bothering to attack Calistin as he had the others.

Calistin crouched, waiting. "Have at me, old man."

"Blue," Colbey said.

Self-consciously, Calistin lifted an edge of his tunic to reveal the blue undergarments. Yet, he felt certain, Colbey had not touched him. "How?" he started, sheathing his sword as Navali sprang to his feet, Kristel swore, and Tanvard reclaimed his weapon from Colbey.

Colbey grinned mischievously. "I read minds."

The confession startled Calistin. Colbey had never mentioned it in the months they had traveled together, yet so many things now made sense. He had often bridged the seemingly unsurpassable yawning chasm between Calistin's ideas and Treysind's. He always seemed to know the mood, weaknesses, and strengths of his students. Some of that had to come from experience, but the more inscrutable parts had seemed magical.

Colbey bowed, then walked deeper into the forest. Many of the Renshai rushed to follow him, but the immortal soon became lost among the brush and shrubbery, disappearing like smoke from a campfire.

"Now what?" Kristel demanded of no one in particular.

No easy answers came. Despite his experiences with Colbey, Calistin had no better idea of their next course of action. He still preferred chopping down anyone who stood in the way of their goal, and he knew most of the Renshai would agree with him.

There was no Renshai wiser or more knowledgeable about the world than Thialnir, but he simply stood among the others, puzzling the matter.

Calistin knew his voice also commanded more authority than most. His sword skill spoke for him. Yet, at the moment, he had nothing clever to say. He was Renshai first and foremost, of the oldest school. So long as they could outfight their opponents, and they always could, Renshai never needed to compromise. "There are no good choices," he realized aloud. "So we might as well follow the one that makes sense to us."

Calistin's words jogged Thialnir. "Colbey Calistinsson did not come without reason."

"To warn us of a trap." Someone toward the back agreed. "So we didn't blunder into it in ignorance. But he never told us how we should handle it."

That set a few off, complaining about Colbey's methods. Chief among the questions was: "Why did he bother to come if he has no solutions or suggestions?"

A large group chimed in, claiming it a great honor to field a visit from Colbey, no matter the reason, and a sacrilege to complain. Through it all, Thialnir remained silent, thoughtful.

Then, the suggestions came pouring forth, most of them unwieldy, some of them silly, but they always came back to the same theme. The land belonged to the Renshai, historically and legally. Anyone who dared to stand in their way should die. And, though Calistin agreed wholeheartedly with the upshot of the discussion, he remained silent in deference to Colbey and Thialnir. Debating the matter seemed like a waste of time. Colbey should not have come. He should have let the Renshai attack and destroy the Paradisians come what may. Yet Colbey had come, and that changed everything.

Finally, as the sun sank toward the horizon and the situation, settled in most minds, gave way to other conversation, Thialnir finally spoke again. "I think . . ." he started, and everyone fell silent. ". . . that we do not fully understand the complexity of this matter. As much as the rest of you, I would like to slaughter these fakers and be done with it."

Calistin smiled. Had he not felt certain Thialnir's next word was going to be "but," he would have reveled in the certainty of a forthcoming battle.

Thialnir did not surprise him. "But I fear that may not be in our best interests at the present time. Currently, we have the governments of Béarn and Erythane on our side, if not their people. If we lose their favor, we may find ourselves banished again."

To Calistin's surprise, the other Renshai did not grumble or interrupt. They had exhausted their own ideas and wanted to hear Thialnir's, if only to see if he voiced anything they had already considered.

The massive Renshai looked old, his face wrinkled and tired. "We can always drive those Erythanian squatters away. That option remains even after we try other things. However, once we follow the course of violence, we cannot take it back. Better to start with the more peaceful solutions and increase the pressure if those don't work."

Calistin cocked his head, thinking. He trusted Thialnir but did not feel wholly certain the old man had it right this time. He personally preferred chopping up as many enemies as possible. Once a few died, the rest of the self-called Paradisians would get the message and leave.

"So we run like cowards?" someone called out.

The silence broken, many Renshai began talking at once. It became clear they would rather bring the wrath of the world down on them than consider such a strategy.

Thialnir glanced around the group with a patience Calistin did not share. The younger Renshai thumbed the edge of his pommel, needing to expel his discomfort in *svergelse* or spar, if not all-out war. It irked him he had lost a chance at Colbey because of a creativity Colbey usually encouraged and admired. Calistin could feel similar tension building through the tribe. They all needed to sate emotions.

Still, Thialnir waited until they stopped jabbering and turned their attention back to him. "I never suggested we run. Those homes belong to us, and we will retake them."

A cheer went up from the masses.

Again, Thialnir waited for quiet before speaking. "I'm not entirely certain what we should do, but I'd like to try something."

To indicate their willingness to listen, the Renshai found various places to crouch or perch. Only the youngest among them dared to sit. An unwary Renshai set himself up as a target for enemies, *torke*, and fellow Renshai seeking a challenge.

Thialnir explained. "We will return to our homes and live as we have done in the past."

Calistin watched looks of interest, followed by confusion, take shape on each face. He had no idea what Thialnir meant to propose, but he listened without showing any visible reaction.

"We will spar and train wherever we please, as always. We will eat as we have eaten, eliminate where we have eliminated, fix up our houses as we always have." Thialnir looked out over the group, perhaps to make sure he still had their attention. Mostly, they continued to look uncertain. Thialnir shrugged. "That's it."

"That's it?" Mumbles trickled through the group; but, this time, they did not break out in loud conversations. The same question blossomed in every mind, including Calistin's.

Gareth gave it voice. "What about the squatters?"

Thialnir's enormous shoulders rose and fell again. "What about them? They can't understand what we say in Renshai. They can't stop us from doing what we do. We need only learn to ignore anything they say to us."

Calistin finally caught on. "Without weapons, they can't harm us. And, if one does happen to attack, then it's within our rights to kill in self-defense, right?"

"Of course." Thialnir's smile still seemed strained. He had developed an interesting tactic that might or might not work in practice. "Don't let them goad you to do anything stupid. Interact with them, or ignore them, as you see fit. If it helps, pretend you don't speak a word of Common Trading or Erythanian. If they stand in your way, walk around them. If they lie in your beds, find something else to do—"

"—or join them!" someone called out, and the entire group laughed, including Thialnir.

"Why not?" Thialnir's face eased into its normal wrinkles as the other Renshai got into the spirit of his suggestion. "We certainly don't want to make children with these *wisules*." His words served as gentle warning. "But they might find our pallets uncomfortable with extra bodies on them. And our homes a trifle crowded."

"What about food?" someone Calistin could not see yelled out. "We don't have enough money to feed them *and* us, do we?"

Calistin had not given it much consideration. Renshai did not waste time or knowledge on hunting, fishing, or gardening. They bought what they needed, stored it commonly, and shared.

Thialnir spread his hands broadly. "I'm sure we'll find many small issues that we have to sort out in time. As far as food, I'm guessing they'll bring in more than we do. The Fields of Wrath won't support crops, but they've kept themselves alive this long. If someone chooses to cook a meal in my hearth, I'm going to have some. Won't you?"

Everyone seemed to agree that they would.

Calistin could see the possibilities in Thialnir's plan. No Westerner could possibly find it easy living with a group of people that consisted solely of warriors. A Northern saying went: "One need meet only one Renshai, man, woman, or child, to know them all." On general matters, they thought with one mind, focused blindly on swords and battle craft. He had a feeling it would not take long for the Paradisians to pack their gear and find a more welcome home.

CHAPTER 5

Families love each other, even when we can't stand each other.

— Calistin Ra-khirsson

SAVIAR HAD NO DIFFICULTY tracking the Knights of Erythane northward through the Western woodlands. They stuck to the main roads, their snow-white horses plainly visible even in moonless darkness. They moved slowly, hailed by every passerby, stopped multiple times to render assistance or petty judgments, always patient, always kind.

Saviar found his own tolerance perpetually pressed to the brink. He had brought a pack full of rations, keenly aware he had no skill at hunting, no particular competence distinguishing safe plants from deadly poison. The slow pace kept him constantly wondering if his provisions would hold, and he found himself rationing tightly. His growling stomach only increased his annoyance, especially when he saw the knights, their apprentice, and Chymmerlee feasting on roasted pheasants and conies that made his own hard, jerked pork smell like bark.

Erythane had a maximum of twenty-four full-fledged knights at any time, and most citizens of Erythane knew them all by name. The children made circle and rope-jumping games out of reciting the list without making a mistake. Saviar had watched his father's practices enough to know not only their names, but to recognize them all by sight as well. Not that he found it necessary, in this case. The

Knights of Erythane recited their full titles to everyone they met.

Sir Vincelin had the wiry figure of a Renshai, with quick brown eyes, darkly tanned skin, and mahogany hair that hung in a neat curtain to just below his ears. The quietest of the three, he led the way, consulting a map at intervals. The oldest, Sir Alquantae had traded a bit of his muscle mass for an abdominal bulge, but he still kept a strong hand on his mount's reins and he laughed easily. He kept his short hair plastered against his scalp, a perfect silver mix of black and white. The perfume he used had a distinctive smell that grew on Saviar. At least, he could follow them by scent when sight became too risky.

Chymmerlee rode a small, bay gelding, barely tall enough to qualify as a horse instead of a pony. Darby had his usual chestnut, and Saviar finally had a chance to assess it. He was no expert on horses, but even he could tell the gelding had a nice conformation and disposition, more than a widow's son should be able to afford. He suspected Ra-khir had purchased it for the boy from their own family funds.

Saviar had never concerned himself with matters of money, and the thought bothered him more than he expected. He did not know what his father saw in the lean, lanky teen. Darby had copied everything from Ra-khir, from the style of his hair to the blue-and-gold ribbons twined into his gelding's mane and tail. Saviar even thought he saw a hint of added red in the boy's previously mouse-brown hair. Although he had not yet earned his tunic and tabard, Darby wore only the kingdoms' colors: blue and gold, black and orange. He watched Saviar's father with the eyes of an *aristiri* hawk, copying his manner, his gestures, even the patterns of his speech.

Saviar looked at his own clothing, filthy and tattered. While the knights paused every night to wash their costumes, bathe, and brush the tangles and twigs from their hair and their mounts' manes, Saviar used that time to practice sword forms and work out his frustrations in the violence of his *svergelse*. To his bewilderment, his imagined enemies often took the form of Darby, though much quicker, more agile and deadly.

Exhaustion and hunger plagued Saviar, problems the mounted knights did not share. As a week dragged into two, he waited for his opportunity to catch Chymmerlee alone. The Knights hovered over her, attending her every need, plying her with questions he could not quite hear. Apparently they joked and told stories, because Saviar could pick her familiar, sweet laughter from the others at regular intervals. Over time, her guardians became less obsessive, though she spent increasing amounts of time alone with Darby. Saviar could not help noticing how they sat closer and closer as they talked and how her slender arm shot out occasionally to touch him lightly on the arm or shoulder.

One dark evening in the second week of their journey, Saviar practiced sword maneuvers a short distance from the clearing where the knights had set up camp. The sweet aroma of burning wood blended with the acrid odor of fire, and the first faint smells of sizzling meat twined through the mixture. Saviar concentrated on a small piece of a complicated maneuver, a two-sword attack that had the blades moving in different directions.

Saviar knew the general locations of the knights and their charge. Vincelin and Alquantae hunted game while Ra-khir dragged in wood to keep the fire going through the night. Chymmerlee and Darby sat on a barkless deadfall in the clearing, watching the fire, the packs, and the horses but—mostly—enjoying the warmth and the bright spray of stars across the sky. They pointed upward frequently, apparently tracing patterns in the heavens. At one point, Saviar saw them hold hands.

Saviar realized, with a sudden stab of anger, that Darby had stolen his life. He had always craved more of his father's attention, sneaking out after grueling Renshai practices to walk home with Ra-khir. Now, Darby had Ra-khir's favor, along with Saviar's chance to become a knight, and even his woman.

Chymmerlee left the clearing to relieve herself. As always, Saviar averted his gaze while she did so, accustomed to her immediately running back to join the knights. This time, however, she paused to study a plant growing near her chosen toilet. Her body language told him she had made a happy discovery, and he watched her curl up the bottom of her skirt with one hand and pluck berries into it with the other.

Silently, Saviar sheathed his swords and wiped sweat

from his brow. He ran through the positions of the knights in his mind. If he had calculated correctly, she would only need to take a few more steps to give him several moments of access before discovery. He crept closer, watching.

Chymmerlee continued to pull objects off the vine, following a line of plants that took her away from the clearing. Saviar drew near enough to see that she gathered green-and-orange–striped sugarberries, an awesome find indeed. He wondered how she had recognized them in the near-darkness.

When Saviar felt she had strayed as far as he could hope for, he slipped close enough to touch her with an outstretched sword. If she noticed his presence, she gave no sign. The Renshai maneuvers had initially come from combining the best techniques of all the world's warriors, including furtiveness from the barbarians living in the southwestern forests. Subikahn had always outdone Saviar in stealth classes; but, apparently, he had learned enough.

Saviar eased nearer, keeping his swords deliberately sheathed and his hands away from the pommels. He needed to remind her of the affection they had once shared without bringing to mind her image of Renshai: all swords and blood and violence. He had prepared his speech since that day in the courtyard when she had almost killed his brother; yet, now that the moment had come, words failed him. He managed only a soft hiss, "Chymmerlee."

The mage stiffened and whirled toward him. Berries tumbled from her makeshift carryall, and her skirt dropped back to her ankles. She was still beautiful, her hair a thick and honest mahogany that shimmered in the starlight, her features nearly as pale as a Northman's, her freckles hidden by the gloom. Light flared suddenly near her feet, blinding Saviar and revealing her. Before he could recover his vision, she screamed, high-pitched and deafeningly loud.

Brush rattled from all directions.

Torn between running and reasoning, Saviar chose the latter. He seized her arm, pulling her toward him. "Wait, Chymmerlee, please. Just hear me out."

A slap stung Saviar's face, followed by a knee slammed forcefully into his groin. Icy pain clutched his belly, and he staggered, unable to gasp out another word. It took all the mental training of the Renshai not to collapse; but, even though he kept his feet, he still felt helpless, vulnerable. Numb throbbing overcame his body, and agony shot up through his stomach and seemed to take over his brain. At that moment, it occurred to him he had to run, but his body refused to respond. It implored him to curl up in a fetal position and vomit out his guts.

Ra-khir arrived first. His expression turned from concerned surprise to scarlet rage in an instant. "Saviar!"

Chymmerlee raced back toward the clearing.

Vincelin arrived next, an arrow nocked, its shaft pinned to the handrest by a finger. Not recognizing Saviar as quickly as his father had, he drew and pointed the arrowhead directly at the Renshai.

As feeling rushed back into his body, Saviar ignored the weapon aimed at his heart. Even disarmed by Chymmerlee's attack, he knew he could move faster, dodging and drawing simultaneously, cutting through Vincelin's guard. But, for now, he waited in stalemate. Time would gain the knights another companion, but it would also give him a chance to recover fully. Facing three Knights of Erythane at his best seemed wiser than taking on two with his testicles on fire.

Alquantae arrived last, while Darby and Chymmerlee peeked at the group from the edge of the clearing. Darby kept a protective arm around Chymmerlee, which only upset Saviar more.

"What are you doing here?" Ra-khir demanded. If his green eyes had not blazed with anger, Saviar could still have read it from the tightness of his lips, the hand clenched around his sword hilt, or the darkening of his features. "I specifically commanded you not to come."

The pain and numbness faded enough for Saviar to demonstrate some anger of his own. "Commanded me? I'm not a knight-in-training. I'm a grown man by . . ." He trailed off. He was about to say, "by Renshai standards"; but, at the moment, that would only further alienate Chymmerlee. Frustration fueled his own rage. If only she would let him talk, he could fix things. She had fallen for him at first sight, nursing him through the months of fever fog and agony, even going so far as to chew up his food and administer it through a tube. It seemed nonsensical that one tiny piece of information could curdle that attraction into a forever hatred. "I'm a grown man, and I will do as my honor bids me."

"And I am your father," Ra-khir reminded him. "Do I deserve no respect at all?"

At the pronouncement, Vincelin lowered the bow and released the nock.

It took self-control for Saviar not to snort in answer. Ra-khir had earned his son's respect, as well as that of the knights and, through them, Erythane and the world. At the moment, however, Saviar did not feel particularly civil toward anyone or anything. He could not have wholly explained his exasperation, but it was as real as anything he had ever experienced. "With all respect due, Sir Ra-khir, you only stated I could not join you. You said nothing about . . ." Saviar hesitated, trying to find the right words.

Vincelin filled in different ones. ". . . sneaking around behind us like a thief."

Saviar gritted his teeth, taking a sudden disliking to Vincelin as well.

Ra-khir raised a hand to beg forbearance, and Vincelin lowered his head. "Would you like some privacy, Sir Ra-khir?"

Ra-khir bit his lower lip, still staring at Saviar. "No," he said slowly. "I want you all to witness this exchange, so no one . . . misremembers it."

Saviar made a wordless noise. His father had essentially just said he expected his son to lie.

Ra-khir continued, "And I don't want him slipping away before I finish, so he can claim he never heard me."

Saviar made a louder noise. Ra-khir no longer just walked the edges of insult. "So you don't trust me anymore?"

Ra-khir dodged the question. "I worry the adolescent intensity of your emotions might cloud your otherwise very sound judgment."

Saviar saw no reason to address his father when the person he needed to talk to had strayed within earshot. "Chymmerlee, please. I can explain everything."

Every man's gaze followed Saviar's to the young mage. She only shook her head, turned, and headed back into the clearing. Darby glanced at Saviar, his expression conveying something that looked like apology or understanding but which Saviar interpreted as withering disdain. Then, the boy followed Chymmerlee back into the clearing.

Ra-khir said softly, "She doesn't want to listen to you, Savi."

That being self-evident, Saviar saw no reason to reply. He tensed to follow her, but the knights moved between him and the clearing. Renshai instinct drove him to hack through all three men, then Darby, to face the object of his desire. He would enjoy every moment of the challenge. But reason overcame emotion, this time, at least. His body still felt tingly from the pounding his groin had taken, the anger throbbing through his skull seemed heavy as war drums, and forcing himself on Chymmerlee would not make her love him again.

Father and son had already discussed the matter, and Ra-khir did not seem eager to repeat his previous arguments. Instead, he took a resolute stance. "Savi, go home. Your people need you, and nothing good can come of following us. I'm fully bound to this mission, as are my companions."

Vincelin and Alquantae nodded in response.

"We do not want to brawl with you but will do so if you force our hands."

Fighting words Saviar understood, but he did not rise to the challenge. Ra-khir did have a point; nothing good could come of his slaughtering three Knights of Erythane, assuming he bested all of them. Most Renshai would win a fight against three equally matched *ganim*, but Saviar did not feel fully confident he could overcome these three. One at a time, certainly; but, all together, he had his doubts. He did not share Calistin's inhuman confidence, nor the godlike skill that inspired it. Most Renshai dismissed the knights as overly moral fools who learned too many weapon types to become competent at any of them. Saviar, though, had actually watched many of the knights' practices, spars, and challenges. Though not his best weapon, Ra-khir could handle a sword better than most *ganim*.

Saviar realized something he had never before considered: the limitation of the Knights of Erythane to two dozen active warriors had, shockingly, not resulted in a waiting list. Nearly every male child in Erythane, and through much of the other areas of the Westlands, dreamed of a chance to join them. Their name was legend throughout the world for their honesty, wisdom, weapons skills, and courage. Girls dreamed of marrying one, and nearly all Western boys hoped to become a knight someday.

Economic factors kept many away. Boys who needed to earn money for the household often did not have the opportunity to spend the necessary years training. Of those who did, few made the cut. The intensity of the training undid most of them. Others did not have the moral capability, the absoluteness of honor that allowed the knights to put justice not only above their own comfort, but above life itself. The protocol destroyed others, the depth and breadth of patience still more. Some simply did not have the quickness of thought, the natural intelligence to respond in dire or significant circumstances. The sheer enormity of the weapons training, though not as focused or complete as the Renshai's, was made up for in scope. For, while the sole focus of the Renshai universe was the sword, knights learned to wield pikes, staves, axes, shields, spears, bows, and other weapons Saviar could not name.

There was nothing more to say. Saviar had no intention of harming his father and the other knights, nor of returning home without confronting Chymmerlee. He would never make a promise to the contrary and besmirch his honor. Instead, he turned on his heel and calmly headed back into the forest. He could feel the knights' stares on him as he disappeared deeper into the foliage.

The effort of scaling the wall of Béarn Castle winded Tae, and that irritated him more than the pain that irregularities in the mortar slashed in his hands and feet. From the parapet above his head, a guard waved a friendly greeting that Tae did not dare to return. The guards' knowledge and approval of his climb took away most of the fun and all of the excitement; but, for now, it seemed necessary.

In Stalmize, Tae had skittered up and down the castle walls for exercise. He had climbed Béarn a few times in the past, always to secretly find Matrinka and without the knowledge of those on patrol. Gradually, he was working his way back to his former skill, but it seemed grindingly slow and frustrating. He had to keep reminding himself that just making the climb was a huge leap forward.

Tae had tried to make his choice of location seem casual, random; but he knew this spot well. Shortly before the war, he had climbed at this exact place and twenty years earlier as well. Tae pulled himself to the fourth-story window ledge, his first opportunity. Below that level, glass protected the windows from intruders.

Tae peeked into an empty bedroom, the bed tightly made, the furniture plain and utilitarian, without personal keepsakes and bric-a-brac. Apparently, it had served as guest quarters for someone who had left after the war, perhaps a general or captain. Tae glanced upward to the gauzy curtains fluttering from the window above him, Matrinka's room. Whispers of sound drifted to him on the wind, undecipherable.

Tae resumed his upward journey with slow caution, and the sounds gradually sorted themselves into the soft, familiar voices of Matrinka and Darris. Tae crept ever closer until he managed to discern actual words, currently Matrinka's.

". . . love each other. You know how strong that is."

Darris sounded exasperated. "They're sister and brother, Matrinka. By all the gods, that's . . . that's incest."

Tae froze, the topic too provocative to abandon. He knew he should announce himself, to let them know he was listening but found himself incapable. It was not weakness that held him in place; it took far more energy to cling to a vertical surface, unmoving, then to dive inside a window. He simply had to know.

"Not really."

"Really."

Matrinka did not give up. "Not by blood."

"Blood isn't everything. Sometimes, it is of no damned significance whatsoever. Do you really think Griff loved Arturo any less than I did?"

Tae cringed. The name of the late prince flowed easily off Darris' tongue, but that did not address the volcano seething below the surface. They had lost the blood son of Matrinka and Darris on a ship scuttled by *alsona*. The entire crew was believed to have lost their lives, though some of the bodies, including Arturo's, were never found. The sharks, it seemed, had made short work of them.

Matrinka's voice quivered; but, to her credit, she did not lapse into tears. "I know Griff loves all of his children. He shows no favoritism toward those who carry his blood. But sometimes . . . I mean . . . even Marisole knows you sired her."

Darris' tone became accusatory. "You *told* her?"

"I didn't tell her anything. She figured it out." There was

a short pause, the rustle of movement, then Matrinka continued, "It's not hard, Darris. The bardic curse is always passed to the firstborn child of the previous bard. She carries it, ergo . . ."

". . . ergo," Darris repeated with finality. Tae heard movement, perhaps pacing, then the bang of a fist against wood. "Damn it, Matrinka. I'm sure a lot of people have figured it out, but they don't say anything because they want to pretend. If they don't consider it too long, they can deny it."

"Well, Marisole thought about it. A lot. And why wouldn't she? It's her past and her future. It's who she is."

Tae knew the entire situation. Darris and Matrinka had loved one another for decades, but the statutes of Béarn were strict on whom royalty could marry. Darris did not meet the criteria, and they seemed doomed to remain apart. When the populace demanded that Matrinka and Griff marry, Griff had found the solution. She became the first of his wives, the official queen; but it was Darris who shared her bed, who sired her three children. Griff claimed them, and Béarn remained happy. Now, apparently, Marisole had fallen in love with one of Griff's other children. Tae ran their names quickly through his mind. Matrinka had borne Marisole, Arturo, and their younger sister, Halika. Griff's elfin bride, his true love, had born him only the hideously abnormal Ivana. Xoraida, the third of Griff's wives, was the mother of Barrindar, Calitha, and Eldorin. Of them all, Barrindar was the only living male.

"She is," Darris started slowly and distinctly, "a princess of Béarn and the next bard. Those titles come with enormous benefits and, also, responsibilities. She has to understand she will not always get her way."

"But they love each other." The conversation had come full circle. "You, of all people, know the agony of needing with all your heart someone you can never have."

More sounds of movement, this time solid. "She's a child. She doesn't know what she wants yet."

Matrinka snorted. "She's older than we were when I conceived her."

"Times have changed."

"Have they?"

"Situations have changed. Things have gotten more complicated. Matrinka, we can't just reveal our indiscretion to the world and expect no repercussions. When Griff agreed to the arrangement, he did us an enormous favor. We can't dishonor that sacrifice by divulging it." Darris paused, then ended decisively, "Marisole will have to live with that understanding."

Tae had heard more than enough. Morality had not featured strongly in his upbringing, his father an organizer of criminals and his mother murdered by Weile's enemies; but he still felt guilty eavesdropping for so long on friends. With deliberate awkwardness, Tae clamped a hand over the sill as if just arriving, drew up to the ledge, and crouched in the window. He found Matrinka perched on the edge of the bed, her features pale, her dark eyes moist, and her hair a thick and shaggy cascade. A simple shift covered her plump, ample curves; and two cats shared her lap.

Darris stood beside her, staring at Tae. He looked wan and thin, as if he had aged decades in the last few months. Bags dipped darkly below his eyes. "Tae? What are you doing here?"

Matrinka answered before Tae could. "Losing his touch, apparently." She turned her attention on the Easterner. "We heard you."

For once, Tae did not banter. He did not want them to figure out he had spied on them. "Hello." He clambered fully through the window, hopping to the floor.

Darris watched him without a hint of smile. "Tae, we're approaching forty. Don't you think it's time to quit scurrying around like a child? Especially so soon after you almost died? What if you had fallen climbing up here?"

Tae shrugged, pretending the thought had never occurred to him. Had he felt unstable, he would have scrambled back down or balanced on a sill. "Then I'd be almost dead again. And your sweetheart would have to pull me from the brink ... again."

Darris fairly growled. "Kindly refrain from referring to the queen of Béarn as my 'sweetheart'."

Given the recent topic of discussion, Darris' surliness made sense. Of them all, he had matured the most; circumstances had forced the change upon him more heavily than Tae or Kevral, Ra-khir or Matrinka.

"And just because she managed to keep you alive after a shooting ... stabbing ... drowning ... and ... and shark attack doesn't mean she can save you from your own stupidity."

"Well, I was rather counting on it." Tae gave Matrinka a smile. "After all, most would think the shooting, stabbing, drowning, shark attack was a perfect demonstration of my own stupidity."

Another cat slunk out from under the bed, gray and covered with cobwebs. It jumped onto the coverlet to join Matrinka and the purring felines in her lap. Paws appeared under the door, sweeping, and the gray leaped down to examine them.

Matrinka put a hand over her mouth to hide her own smile.

If Darris saw any humor in it, he gave no sign. "I'm serious, Tae. You're a king, now, with only one heir, and him a Renshai. You have to stop taking unnecessary chances."

What? And become boring, like you? Tae kept the thought to himself. Neither of them would appreciate it.

"Even if you still have the skill, why take a chance getting caught climbing in the queen's window? The guards of Béarn are competent and on high alert in the wake of the war."

Tae dismissed the danger with a wave. "Don't worry about the guards. I paid them off."

"What?" The word was startled from Darris, and a look of abject horror overtook his homely features.

Matrinka only laughed. "He's kidding, Darris."

Darris turned Tae a grave look. He had to know.

Tae suspected Darris could not withstand another jest, so he only nodded.

Darris continued staring at his old friend. "You're not funny."

Tae resisted the urge to point out Matrinka's laughter as evidence to the contrary. "Damn. And I had so wanted to become my own jester."

Darris only grunted and turned away. Tae thought he caught a ghost of a smile on the bard's large-lipped face.

"Actually, I came to talk to Matrinka. Do you mind terribly?"

Darris' stance relaxed. He seemed almost relieved as he turned back to Tae. "Not at all, old friend. I'm sure His Majesty misses me. When I'm not there . . ."

Tae cringed. Darris did not have to finish. "Rantire?"

"Who else?"

The overeager Renshai had made a promise to Colbey's son that she would always keep Griff safe, and she accepted her duty with a devotion that nearly drove the king to madness. It was the job of the bard through the centuries to serve as the king's personal bodyguard, and the two had made an uneasy agreement. When Darris was with King Griff, Rantire found other things to do, usually hovering nearby awaiting a lapse. And, when Darris was not with Griff, he was honor-bound to let Rantire take his place.

Still, Darris paused. The bardic curse inflicted him with insatiable curiosity and the unquenchable desire to know all the information in the universe. "May I ask why you wanted to see Matrinka?"

Tae could not help teasing. "I never properly thanked her for saving my life." He winked, as if plotting something lascivious.

Clearly in no mood for jokes, Darris scowled. "Fine, don't tell me."

The gray cat batted at the paws reaching from the other side of the door, and they retreated. The gray stalked closer. A paw shot out suddenly and hooked her foot. Startled, the gray leaped straight into the air.

Tae gave Darris a break. "Matrinka and I have had a brother/sister thing going for a long time. I just need a sister right now. I'm sure what we have to say will be far less interesting than whatever King Griff is doing with his foreign guests right now."

Although his interest was piqued by Tae's words, Darris could hardly remain. The curse forced him to consider what he was already missing. He finally managed a thin smile. "Fine. Behave yourselves. This is a queen's bedroom."

Tae saluted. "No wild pillow fights, I promise."

Pushing aside the gray cat with a booted foot, Darris opened the door. The gray ran around him to zip through the crack, and three more sidled in, including the silver-striped Imorelda. Darris stepped out and shut the door behind him, careful not to smash any tails or paws.

Imorelda raced for the bed, mewling a complaint the entire way. *What took you so long?* She sprang to the coverlet and quick-walked to Matrinka's arms.

The queen clutched Imorelda with evident love. One of the cats in her lap, a half-grown black kitten, flew under the bed in what looked like a single motion. The other, a fat orange tom, yowled a challenge at Imorelda. Tae gathered the tom into his own lap to rescue it from Imorelda's wrath and nearly suffered a scratch for his effort. Fluffed to twice its normal size, the ginger tabby joined the kitten under the bed. Its tail stuck out, lashing in angry bursts.

I'm still recovering, Tae sent in his own defense. *And I had to get rid of Darris.*

He's been in a snit since the war started.

War does that to people.

Matrinka looked enviously between man and cat. "Talk to me, Imorelda. Talk to *me*."

Remaining quiet in deference to any conversation cat and woman might exchange, Tae glanced around the room. The lovingly carved furniture, passed through royal generations, now bore scars and scratches. Clearly, unruly cats had used them as claw sharpeners and teething objects, rendering some of the detailed bears into shapeless lumps. Matrinka had lost many of her knickknacks to playful kittens and had stored the others away for safety. Now, the room seemed sparse, so much less an extension of Matrinka's sweet personality. The castle had far too many cats.

She has too many cats. Imorelda's announcement startled Tae, especially so close to his own thoughts. She pulled out of Matrinka's arms and headed toward Tae.

Tell her that. Tae wanted to encourage their communication. Matrinka desperately missed Mior, Imorelda's mother, and the once-unique bond they had shared.

Imorelda curled up in Tae's lap. *I have told her. But I don't want to talk to her any more.* Sullenness accompanied Imorelda's sending, and it surprised Tae. Usually, the females could find a lot of material just in their mutual disdain for him. The explanation came swiftly. *She wants me to have . . .* Disgust practically slammed Tae's mind. *. . . kittens.*

As much as he loved her, Tae could not take Imorelda's side. *You promised her you would.*

Imorelda let out an audible yowl. *Only because she tricked me!*

At the time, Tae had been locked in Béarn's prison learning the language of the enemy. He had not paid much attention, but the details he knew came back to him now. *You told her she had to clean them and feed them, and she took you up on your offer. That's not really a "trick".*

I don't want any nasty little brats. Imorelda turned her back on him, though she remained in his lap.

Matrinka shook her head. "She's mad at me." Her kind, brown eyes had gone moist.

Tae hated to see Matrinka sad, more than anyone in the world. "She doesn't understand."

I understand. She doesn't understand.

Tae ignored the cat to focus on Matrinka. "She's only thinking of herself and in the moment . . ."

Kittens are stinky, brutish, and demanding.

". . . She's giving no thought to our futures, nor the world's need for her and her kind."

Imorelda went suddenly silent. *What do you mean?*

Currently unable to hear Imorelda, Matrinka continued the conversation, "She's a cat, Tae. You can't expect her to think like we do."

Imorelda pinned the side of Tae's hand between her paws. *Was that an insult?*

No, dear one. Just a statement of fact. Tae turned his attention fully back to Matrinka. "Mior understood, didn't she? I mean, she knew she would . . . before you . . . ?" He hoped Matrinka could figure out what he meant.

Matrinka flushed. "I think we just got lucky that she had her litter when she did. I thought she was unique until Imorelda spoke to you, so I didn't encourage or discourage her."

Imorelda jumped back in. *She didn't pester my mother to make kittens. Why pick on me?*

Tae put a hand on Imorelda, urging restraint. He had not yet struck to the heart of his point, and he realized avoiding the significant word was not helping. "How did Mior . . . die?"

Matrinka gave Tae a curious look. "You know she died from old age." The moisture gave way to tears. Matrinka had never gotten over losing her best friend. "We never talked about the differences in lifespan between cats and humans. I didn't want to think about it, and if she did, she never told me."

Matrinka jerked her face toward Imorelda, and Tae felt certain she had suddenly realized she might have raised a topic he had deliberately kept from the cat.

Tae nodded encouragingly. He had never broached the subject with Imorelda but intended to do so now. It might be the only way to get her to bear those hated, but necessary, kittens.

Imorelda had gone uncharacteristically silent and still in his lap.

Apparently put at ease by Tae's gesture, Matrinka continued, "I always just secretly hoped the magical bond between us would extend her life as long as mine." She kept her gaze locked on Imorelda, surely alert to any signs of discomfort.

Imorelda remained in place, but her lengthy quiet, particularly when the conversation revolved around her, told Tae the words did affect her. He did not reveal his knowledge to Matrinka, however. If she thought she was causing Imorelda any distress, she would stop speaking; and Tae wanted Imorelda to hear the information from someone other than himself, someone she trusted. He knew Imorelda loved him, but she also knew he would not hesitate to lie if the situation warranted it.

Matrinka added swiftly, clearly as comfort, "She lived at least twice the lifespan of any cat I know of, so it did seem to have some effect." She reached cautiously toward Imorelda. "And Imorelda looks absolutely beautiful, as always. You'd never know she's almost eighteen."

Tae had to say it. "Already older than most cats ever live."

Matrinka cringed, but nodded. She stretched out a cautious hand to lay it on Imorelda's back.

Imorelda nearly spit. *So, I'm not a kitten anymore. I'm no crone, either. I'm in my prime.*

Matrinka snapped back her hand, though Imorelda made no attempt to scratch or bite, misinterpreting the cat's abrupt movement. "She's still mad at me?"

"No." Tae stroked Imorelda, though she seemed not to notice. She stood stiffly in his lap, her fur bristling. "She thinks we're calling her a withered old hag."

Imorelda whirled on Tae, eyes flashing. *I never said "withered"!*

Tae deliberately ignored her. "She thinks she's too old to make babies."

That's a lie! Imorelda fluffed her silver fur and arched her back. *I never said that! Tell her you're just lying!*

Tae considered it payback. When he had sprawled on the beach too weak to speak, he had tried to convey his dying words to Matrinka. Imorelda had deliberately twisted his wishes, making it impossible for him to die without assuring their defeat in the war. *You tell her.*

I will. Imorelda stepped gingerly from Tae's lap to flop onto Matrinka's. *I can too have babies. I just don't like them.*

A brief silence followed as Imorelda turned her complaints on Matrinka.

Apparently wanting to draw Tae into the full conversation, Matrinka responded aloud. "I promise I'll help you in every way possible." She ran her hands along Imorelda, scratching the places cats love best. "You won't have to do this alone." She put her face right up to Imorelda's ear, speaking softly, encouragingly. "Mior knew you would have her gift; that's why she gave you to Tae. If you have a kitten like you, will you . . ." Her words turned into a silent breath. Then, abruptly, she grinned. "Thank you, thank you, thank you, Imorelda." Matrinka hugged the cat, burying her face in the soft, stripy fur.

"She said 'okay'?" Tae guessed.

Matrinka laughed, "Not exactly." She lifted one eye over the cat, as if worried she might betray a confidence. Tae could hear Imorelda purring ever so slightly. "She said something like she certainly wouldn't trust anything precious and impressionable to you."

Tae said sarcastically, "How sweet."

I actually said I wouldn't trust anything of any value to a sorry excuse for a human like you. You're not even worth the skin you're printed on. The tabby rubbed against Matrinka's cheek. *Why does she always have to add sugar to everything?*

Because she's that rare person who really is nice and kind all the time. She's practically made of sugar.

Poor kitten.

Tae did not point out the obvious irony. Just a few moments ago, Imorelda had stated her avowed hatred for all things kitten.

Mior adored her. I think if she had had any idea of her own mortality, or that it would take you eighteen years to agree to start a family, she would have given you to Matrinka instead of me.

Gods save me.

Tae knew Imorelda did not mean it, that she reserved insults for those she cared for the most. He suspected she would have turned out much differently, probably much better, had Matrinka raised her. However, Tae had a feeling that raising two opinionated, communicating cats simultaneously would drive any human crazy, and Mior had known that when she gave Imorelda to Tae instead. She had also known he would have the capacity to form a bond with her, an ability few humans shared. As far as he knew, only he and Matrinka among the humans on the continent could do so.

Matrinka released Imorelda, who butted her hand for more petting. "She's telling me her conditions."

Tae nodded. Now that Imorelda had something Matrinka desperately wanted, she would use it to her advantage.

"She insists I castrate all the male cats in the palace except the one she chooses, then cast them all out of the castle." Matrinka went quiet for a few moments to commune with the cat before explaining aloud, "Then she wants me to work with the elves to find a way to permanently sterilize the females and send them out as well." Matrinka's brow furrowed, and she went silent again, her attention fixed on Imorelda.

Tae waited patiently. A scrawny, black-and-white tom crept closer, tale waving. Clearly, it wanted attention but was wary of Imorelda. Tae wriggled his fingers toward it, and it approached to investigate.

Matrinka spoke again, as if she had never paused. "I'm worried about cats raised in a castle surviving outside. Imorelda believes they'll do fine but gave me permission to build two large containment areas, one for males and one for females. She's promised to help me find all the cats."

Tae ran a hand along the young tom, and it snuggled against his leg. "How do you feel about Imorelda's demands?"

Matrinka sighed. "I love having them around, of course; but she's right. It's not fair to Griff or the servants." She lowered her head, still stroking Imorelda. "I've been selfish, Tae. I've always hoped that if I keep breeding Mior's offspring, eventually another Mior or Imorelda will emerge. Clearly, that's not going to happen by random chance. Imorelda's my only hope."

Tae pursed his lips, uncertain what to say. He wanted to comfort Matrinka, to promise her that everything would work out in the end. To do so, however, would be a lie she did not deserve. Matrinka hoped that whatever allowed Mior and Imorelda to communicate was passed like the bardic curse, in some fashion from parent to child; but they had no real proof that this was so. Matrinka's grandfather, King Kohleran, had discovered Mior as a grimy kitten in a sewage ditch. No one knew her origin and, as far as they knew, no previous cat had ever displayed her intelligence or talent.

"Of course, Imorelda has every right to pick the father of her children. She's asked for nothing unreasonable."

Yet. Tae gave Imorelda a stern look that she pretended not to see, becoming suddenly engrossed in cleaning a hind leg. "Imorelda knows better than to take advantage of a friend." He emphasized the last word. "Especially one who saved the life of her master."

Companion, Imorelda corrected without losing a beat in her cleaning.

"Companion," Matrinka said nearly simultaneously.

Tae thought he saw a catty smile behind Imorelda's busy tongue.

"And it's not as though you've never saved my life." Matrinka patted Tae's knee. "When we traveled together, I seem to remember some hairy encounters that would have ended badly for me if not for my competent companions, including you. I was the only one of us who had no ability with weapons."

Tae did not bother to mention that many of those dangerous clashes would never have occurred if not for him. He had initially joined Matrinka and her friends because he needed help battling his father's enemies, deadly men with a penchant for murder and a mission to destroy him. Matrinka's sojourn into memory brought him back to the real reason he had wanted to speak with her alone. "Matrinka, do you think we're too old for adventure now?"

The look Matrinka gave him was measured. "Why would you ask such a thing?"

Tae sighed. There was no easy way to broach the subject. "I'm supposed to start teaching spies the language of our enemies, but I know of only one other person who can actually learn it."

As Imorelda finished her bath, Matrinka went back to stroking her. "Who?"

"You."

Matrinka's hands stilled. "Me?" She frowned in deep consideration. "I'm not bad with languages, but I'm certainly no . . . you."

Tae flexed a hand in dismissal, nearly waking the tom who lay against his leg, purring steadily. The cat opened one eye, yawned, and stretched out for more access. Tae had never met anyone who picked up languages as swiftly and thoroughly as himself. Surrounded by his father's associates since birth, he had assimilated their many dialects and tongues. As a toddler, Tae had overheard and interpreted conversations for Weile Kahn. People spoke freely in front of the very young, who could also squeeze into small spaces unseen. "There's an important component to the *alsona*'s language that I haven't told anyone yet."

Matrinka caught on quickly. "It's similar to what we share with Imorelda, isn't it?"

Tae nodded.

"Like the elves' *khohlar*?"

"Not exactly." Tae considered the differences and how to put them into plain words. "As I understand it, *khohlar* has two forms. In the first, anyone within a certain range 'hears' the communication. It doesn't matter if the listeners are elfin, god, human, or animal. The second form can be directed at any individual, and only that one receiver 'hears' the *khohlar*."

Matrinka continued stroking Imorelda, though shed silver hairs now covered her dress and blanket.

Tae tried not to think too specifically of his encounters with the *alsona* and their language. None of them had turned out well for him. "The *alsona* and the *Kjempemagiska* have a common language: spoken, written, and mental. They have absolutely no experience with other languages or dialects. Their brains are so hardwired for a single tongue they have no concept whatsoever of linguistic differences. No slang. No local color. No intermingling or mangling of other culture's words."

Tae paused to give the concept time to sink in. It had taken him a long time to puzzle out the situation. The imprisoned *alsona* had actually believed the peoples of the continent were animals because they could not "speak" in any manner the *alsona* recognized as language. That allowed them to behave more ruthlessly than most people on the continent could comprehend.

Matrinka nodded thoughtfully. "Can they also choose whether to send their . . . mind-words to all or only one? Like the elves?"

Tae had the experience to answer. "When they want to converse in private, they have to use spoken language. Their mind-speech invariably goes to everyone who can receive it, that is, all *alsona* and *Kjempemagiska* within a certain distance. Without Imorelda's help, I can't 'hear' it; and, as far as I can tell, neither can anyone else who is not one of them. Apparently, that's another reason they consider us animals."

Matrinka nodded thoughtfully. "That explains something I heard some of the soldiers saying."

Lying on his deathbed through most of the war, Tae had never set foot on the actual battlefield. "What's that?"

"They said the pirates worked together extremely well, without needing to shout at one another. I heard someone suggest that acting unpredictably might foil them, since they clearly choreographed their battle plans."

"It didn't work, did it?"

Matrinka took her hands from Imorelda long enough to make an uncertain gesture. "You would know better than me." She had watched most of the war from the safety of the castle tower. "What does the pirate mind-language . . ." She groped for the proper word, ". . . feel like?"

"A lot like *khohlar* and our communication with Imorelda. The words get thrust into your mind, often with lots of surrounding emotion, impressions, and visuals that helped me decode their spoken language a lot more quickly."

Matrinka seemed deep in thought as she continued to stroke Imorelda absently. Finally, she asked, "If we can't hear it, how did you discover this mind-tongue?"

Tae sighed. He had difficulty explaining the concept, even to himself. "Remember how Imorelda discovered she could communicate with you on a different . . . mind-hearing level?"

Matrinka smiled and nodded. "One of the happiest moments of my life."

"It's like that. Apparently, all *alsona* and *Kjempemagiska* mindspeak on the same level. Imorelda discovered it shortly after she found your mind-hearing level and realized it was different from mine."

Clever cat, Imorelda inserted.

"Clever cat that she is." Tae worked in Imorelda's point, knowing he would find no peace until he did. "I can only hear and communicate with them when she carries my mind to their level."

"So . . ." Matrinka licked her lips, her hands stilling on the cat. ". . . it might be possible . . . for Imorelda to hook us together? With her help, we might be able to talk to each other . . . without talking?" She looked at Imorelda. "Would you try that for us?"

Tae waited for Imorelda's complaints. Instead, a touch of foreign curiosity entered his head, followed by Imorelda's full and silent presence.

It's probably easiest to take me to her, since I've made mind-level trips before.

The curiosity warped to disdain as Imorelda made it clear Tae had stated something so obvious that remarking on it would only make them both look stupid. The connection itself took effort, so Imorelda would not be able to speak to either of them while she made the attempt.

"Say something in your mind," Tae suggested.

Nothing happened.

Tae closed his eyes, concentrating, focused.

A faint flicker of excitement touched him, then a hopeful, tremulous, *Hello?*

Hello! Tae sent back with such vigor it had to seem like a shout.

I can hear you! Then, Matrinka spoke aloud, "It works. Tae, Imorelda, it works!"

You can just think that, Tae reminded Matrinka.

It works!

Apparently. Though fascinated, Tae had enough experience not to share Matrinka's runaway excitement. *Nice work, Imorelda.*

Matrinka's exhilaration disappeared from Tae's thoughts, replaced by Imorelda's voice, *Can I stop now?*

You already did. He turned his attention to Matrinka. "She's dropped the connection. I can't hear you anymore."

"I said, 'That's amazing!'"

"It is amazing." Tae grinned at Imorelda.

The black-and-white tom rolled to his feet, butting Tae's hand, then rubbing his slender body across it.

"Do you think," Matrinka started carefully, "that maybe everyone has a voice level? Perhaps it's only because we found ours that we could talk to Mior and, now, Imorelda."

Tae had considered many possibilities. "I've asked Imorelda to try to communicate with other people, but she's had no luck with anyone else from our continent."

Matrinka shifted her legs onto the bed, forcing Imorelda to move. "Do you suppose it's possible that, if we found the right levels, every cat could talk to every human?"

Imorelda got up delicately, yawned, stretched, and headed for Tae. *Other cats aren't like me. They're stupid.*

Imorelda doesn't mince words. Tae relayed the thought to Matrinka. "Imorelda believes she's unique."

The answer came nearly simultaneously again: *I am,* from Imorelda and "She is," from Matrinka.

Tae chuckled. "Well, yes. Every cat is special. I mean Imorelda believes she's the only one who can speak with humans."

They're stupid, Imorelda repeated. *They can't put words together or ponder the universes. Comparing them to me is like comparing you to Ivana.*

Tae understood but still knew Matrinka did not like the word "stupid" applied to anyone. "She thinks her ability has more to do with intelligence than . . ." *Than what? To what does Matrinka attribute this communication?*

"Magic?" Matrinka guessed.

"All right." It was as good an explanation as any, though not terribly useful for speculation. "It's pretty obvious most cats really don't understand more than a few words of our language. And while they obviously have ways of communicating with one another . . ."

Imorelda hissed at the tomcat snuggled against Tae, growling deep in her throat. The tom returned a higher-pitched growl, then clearly decided he was not up to the challenge. He sprang from the bed and darted beneath it, tail twitching wildly. Immediately calm again, Imorelda placed her front paws into Tae's lap and started kneading.

". . . it's not nearly as sophisticated."

Matrinka smiled as Imorelda and the black-and-white tom played out Tae's point. "But it's possible all humans could speak with their minds, if we could only find their . . . their voice level." She used Tae's awkward terminology.

Tae and Imorelda had already discussed this. "Possible. But I think there's more to it than that. I think a whole combination of features come into play, some innate and some learned. For example, I learned to speak with Mior by first knowing about and believing in your ability to do it. You didn't need convincing because you were a child who still believed in magic."

Matrinka looked stunned. "Magic is real. You've witnessed it."

"Obviously. But prior to the *Ragnarok*, before the elves came here, we had no magic and few people believed in it. The Cardinal Wizards lived centuries ago. Most considered them legendary creatures, their stories exaggerated to make a point. Even the *Kjempemagiska*, who watched us for decades, didn't think we had any magic."

"We didn't." Matrinka was quick to point out.

"We had enough." Tae knew they had been fortunate that the enemy had sent only one magic-wielding giant against them in the war, a mistake that would not be repeated. "We now know Chymmerlee and Tem'aree'ay worked together to negate the *Kjempemagiska*'s magic."

"I always suspected." Matrinka looked wistfully at Imorelda but did not attempt to move her. "Even before Tem'aree'ay confirmed it at the meeting. The pirates—"

"*Alsona*," Tae corrected. It made sense to call the enemy by the same name they used for themselves.

"The *alsona* massed against Chymmerlee during the battle, and she survived only because she had staunch protectors like your son and his twin. She didn't appear to actually do anything, yet she came out of it utterly exhausted."

Tae was impressed. "You noticed all that?"

One corner of Matrinka's mouth twitched upward. "When my friends are out risking their lives, and I'm helpless to assist, I try not to miss details. We had already lost Arturo and Kevral and possibly you, not to mention all the beloved guardsmen and soldiers, and our best admiral."

Tae found himself nodding absently. The mystery of Chymmerlee begged solving.

Matrinka returned to the original topic. "Believing communication can exist between cats and humans is not enough, Tae. Darris, Kevral, and Ra-khir also know about the link, and none of them ever managed it."

Before they had gotten sidetracked by a discussion of magic, Tae had intended to say more. "We also both happen to adore cats."

Imorelda's purring increased. *Who doesn't? We're irresistible.*

Tae did not rise to the bait. He suspected most of the servants in Béarn Castle had grown to hate cats, no matter their initial feelings about them. Others had no particular affinity, some were afraid of them, a few would as soon drown one as look at it, and some even became deathly ill in their presence. In Tae's experience, cats seemed to sense fear, loathing, and allergy, deliberately choosing to place themselves in the laps of those who least could stand them. "We share the ability to easily read people's personalities and moods. I think that helped. I kept imagining what Mior might be saying to you in various circumstances; and, by watching your reaction, and hers, the voice eventually came."

"I still think there's an aspect of love, too." Matrinka casually reached into Tae's lap to pet Imorelda.

The gesture embarrassed Tae. He considered Matrinka a close friend akin to a sister; yet, when she got so near, he could not help noticing her as a woman as well. She had generous curves, a more than ample bosom, and a hand that swept dangerously close to his manhood. "I think," he managed, "that others might be able to learn to use their minds like we do. Whether everyone has the potential, many people, or only a few, I can't guess. I'm not sure where to begin." Tae removed his hands from Imorelda so as not to bump into Matrinka and make things more awkward.

If Matrinka shared Tae's discomfort, she gave no sign of it. "It has to start by revealing your relationship with Imorelda. Are you all right with that?"

"No," Tae admitted.

"People will need convincing, so you'll have to prove it. Some will think it's a trick, others that you're insane—"

"—I know, Matrinka! I've thought the whole thing through."

Matrinka drew away, into a tense silence. Her expression mingled pain with surprise.

Immediately remorseful, Tae lowered his voice. "I'm sorry, Matrinka. I'm not mad at you; I'm mad at the situation."

"We don't have to tell anyone, Tae. The only people who ever knew about Mior were you, Darris, Kevral, and Rakhir."

Tae knew that as well, but he did not yell again. "Even if we do tell, we might not find anyone else who has the ability. Or we might find people who do but would take months or years to learn to use it." Tae did not mind revealing the secret to a few, but he guessed a multitude would be necessary. "Say one in ten people has the potential . . ."

Matrinka got the point. "We would have to recruit at least a hundred people just to find those ten. Of those ten, one might not believe strongly enough, a few more might not have what it takes to develop their potential."

"And even those who learned to communicate with Imorelda might not have enough affinity for languages or might not have the sense to use it wisely or it might just take too long."

"Too long for what?"

"Too long—" Tae caught himself. He had not yet decided to reveal his intentions to Matrinka.

Matrinka gave Tae a warning look. "I deserve to know everything."

Tae gave in. He had little choice. "It's nothing new. You know I don't think the *Kjempemagiska* will wait years to come after us again. The conditions that sent them against us the first time still exist, and the longer they wait, the more time we have to prepare."

"But the generals think . . ." Something in Tae's look made Matrinka change direction. ". . . I mean, they're experienced fighting men, so shouldn't they . . ." Again, she paused. "Tae, are you sure?"

"No, but I intend to become so."

"How?" Matrinka's tone contained a hint of caution that bordered on threat.

Tae met and held her dark gaze. "There's only one way."

"No!" It was a sharp bark, a royal command lost on one of the few people to outrank her.

"Someone has to sail to their land—"

"No!"

"—and spy on them. Someone who knows their language and has a way to listen in on it."

Matrinka rose and walked away, her back firmly toward Tae.

Dumping Imorelda, Tae followed her. "Matrinka, there is no other way."

Matrinka whirled suddenly, and Tae had to back-step to keep from getting knocked aside. A tear rolled down her cheek. "The last time you did that, you nearly died."

"I know." Tae had already resigned himself to his fate.

"And you were only spying on ships in our ocean. Carrying regular soldiers, not magical giants on their own lands."

"I know." Now Tae turned away. "I just need one more person, someone to keep Imorelda safe and to receive whatever information I can send."

"You mean me, Tae."

The roles had reversed. Tae spun around, though his eyes carried no tears. "No! It's too dangerous for you."

"More so for you."

"Your people need you. You're a queen, by all the gods."

Matrinka did not budge. "You're a king. Your people need you, too."

No they don't. Tae knew that argument would not fly. "Matrinka, you don't know how to defend yourself."

"Apparently, neither do you."

The insult stung. "At least I can use a sword."

"Passably." Matrinka gave that much. "Against a normal human or two. But the *Kjempe* . . ."

". . . *magiska*," Tae finished for her. He had taken to throwing around enemy terminology so that at least a few important words would become familiar to those who might have to stand against them.

Matrinka threw up her hands. She did not need to finish her obvious point. Against *Kjempemagiska*, Tae's fair ability with weapons would not help much.

The tears quickened, twisting down Matrinka's face. Knowing she needed him, Tae took her into his arms. She felt soft and massive there, pillowing his scrawny frame. "Matrinka, please. I appreciate your courage and sacrifice; I really do. But someone has to make it back with Imorelda and the information. Whoever that is will need far more skill than either of us has."

Matrinka calmed in Tae's arms. "All right," she finally whispered. "But how will we find this person who can commune with cats, move like a shadow, and fight like a Renshai?"

Tae had no idea. "Let's start with Tem'aree'ay."

Matrinka pulled free. "By convention, she's not the queen, but she is the king's most beloved wife. There's no way—"

Tae stopped her with a gesture. "Not as my companion, Matrinka. For help finding him. At least, she has some magic and mind-communication skills. How well do you know her?"

"She's reclusive, just less so than most elves. But if Griff loves her, she must be special."

"Do you trust her with our secret, if I need to tell?"

Matrinka nodded thoughtfully. "I do."

"Can you set up a meeting?"

Matrinka's head continued bobbing. "I think so. Where can I find you?"

Tae grinned. "I'm going to look for Subikahn. I haven't seen him in several days." That bothered Tae more than he would admit to Matrinka. He had finally made amends after banishing his only son, and he wanted nothing more than to rekindle their once close relationship. "Then, you know I'll find you."

Matrinka finally managed a smile through her tears. "If I don't hear from you by tomorrow, I'll look for your broken corpse under my window."

Grabbing Imorelda, Tae saluted. "Good plan."

CHAPTER 6

There is no such thing as half a Renshai.
　　　　　　　　　　　— *Thialnir Thurdazzisson*

RAIN SLAMMED THE WESTERN FORESTS with a
force that bowed the slimmer trees and sent seed pods and
petals pattering to the mushy ground. Huddled beneath his
sodden cloak, Saviar hugged his growling gut, cursing the
situation, the knights, and the weather. Once he recognized
Chymmerlee's error, he had lost the option of following his
fathers' command to return home. Saviar knew the way to
the magical mountain village that housed her people, and
Chymmerlee appeared to be lost.

At first, Saviar racked his mind for ways to subtly steer
the group without revealing his continuing presence. Before
he came up with a workable plan, however, he began to
wonder if Chymmerlee's misdirection of her escort might
be deliberate. She would never lead anyone, no matter how
honorable, to the precise location of the Mages of Myrcidë.
At least, not since she and Subikahn had carried Saviar's
comatose form there.

Saviar guessed Chymmerlee would part company with
the knights when she came near enough to find her own
way safely home without tipping off the Erythanians to the
actual location of the mages' compound. As he became
more convinced of her intentions, he grew more patient.
Soon enough, the knights would leave, and Chymmerlee
would have no choice but to listen.

Buoyed by the thought, Saviar threw off his cloak. The rain hammered him, but with his clothes already soaked through, it did not bother him the way it had when he was still partially dry and had hopes of staying that way. Exertion quickly drove away the icy prickles of the raindrops. Better than sweat, the rain bathed his limbs for the wind to carry away the excess heat generated by the intensity of his *svergelse*.

Saviar practiced hard, trying to revel in the hardship, as his many *torke* taught. Becoming the best meant practicing on every terrain, in every circumstance, the more difficult the better. Enemies did not wait for the sun to shine, for flat ground, for an injury to heal. If he gave his all, this practice would only make him more competent to battle in the pouring rain. *When any intelligent foe would know to stay indoors and not bother Renshai.*

A hilt in each hand, Saviar darted, lunged, and swept. Modeling his practice on the recent war, he charged enemies all around him, hampered by the closeness of allies and the sheer numbers and desperation of those who wished him dead. He charged the masses in front of him, mindful of those behind and, always, aware of the location of the Knights of Erythane and their charge. He spun to face a sword stroke from behind that nearly pierced him, flying back around to keep other imagined foes at bay.

Motfrabelonning sliced controlled zigzags through the air while his other weapon complemented its movements, now thrusting leftward to catch an enemy mid-sneak, then up to parry another's attack. For hours, Saviar immersed himself in *svergelse* and the created chaos of a fantasy war. Gradually, the rain ceased, leaving the ground a sea of ancient shed leaves and mud that sucked at his boots and threatened to steal them.

The sun poked out from behind the clouds, and the drip of rainwater off the leaves gradually slowed to occasional trickles. Saviar sheathed his swords and dragged out his waterskin, knowing no better time to fill it than immediately after a rain, when every crack and crevice gathered fresh water. He could hear movement and voices at the knights' camp. Quickly he topped off his waterskin, then capped it and put it away. He crept nearer, trying to catch as much as he could of the conversation.

Limited by his ability to move quietly, Saviar could only catch snippets of conversation. They clearly prepared to part company with Chymmerlee, and he sensed great reluctance. He heard each of the knights ask her, more than once, if she would allow them to escort her home. Earnestly, they implored her to let them meet her family, to no avail. Chymmerlee would tell them nothing of her people, would not permit a meeting, and insisted on walking the rest of the way alone.

Saviar had to smile. He knew she would never relent. He had used all of his own persuasive ability to beg the Mages of Myrcidë to assist the combined armies in the war. They had resisted him even when they had believed him one of them, a partial answer to the inbreeding problem. They would never listen to the knights.

At length, Ra-khir and the others acceded to Chymmerlee's demands. No longer needing to hear them, Saviar climbed a distant tree to watch the separation, to gain a clear idea of the routes they would take. While the knights gathered the last of their belongings and prepared their horses for the trip home, Darby and Chymmerlee embraced fondly.

Saviar's heart pounded as he watched them, and he bit his lower lip hard enough to taste blood.

Then, Ra-khir called so loudly his voice carried even up into the tree. "Savi."

Saviar froze. His heart rate quickened, like a drum beat in his ears. *He sees me.* He could not understand how. True, he was watching them, but only through a small hole in a cache of fully-leaved branches. And Ra-khir seemed so far away.

To Saviar's further surprise, his father walked away from his hiding place and into the clearing beneath an umbrella of trees. Darby and Chymmerlee pulled apart as Ra-khir approached and carried on a conversation with Darby. Faint laughter touched Saviar's ears, then Ra-khir put a fatherly hand on Darby's shoulder and walked with him back to the horses.

He meant Darby. Saviar's blood felt like fire in his veins. *He called that* kadlach *by my name.* His jaw ached, and he found his teeth clenched. Bark gouged the gripping fingers of his left hand, his right clamped to the hilt of Kevral's sword. It seemed impossible that a boy who had come from nowhere had so easily stepped into all the best parts of his life.

For a few moments, Chymmerlee watched the knights and squire ride back toward Béarn, their white horses and bright tabards clear despite the tightly clustered trunks and branches. A pack lay at her feet. She hefted it with clear effort, plopping it down on a deadfall. Opening it, she rummaged through, removing packets of food, multiple waterskins, two dry cloaks, a tinderbox, a knife, a faggot of kindling, and twine, a gift from the knights to get her safely home. Smiling, she shook her head and sorted the objects, leaving many behind, including the tinderbox and kindling, all but one skin of water, and the twine. Shedding her sodden cloak, she put on one of the dry ones and left the other two behind. She pulled the considerably lightened pack over one shoulder and headed eastward.

Saviar shinnied down from the tree and sneaked to the clearing, shoving everything she had left into his own pack. He followed at a safe distance. She still had a full day's journey to the village, and Saviar knew better than to accost her when the knights might still see her magic, might hear her scream. They would not go far. Likely, she had made them vow not to follow, and they would never dishonor their word. However, they would remain as near as their honor allowed, prepared to return to her in a crisis.

Chymmerlee seemed in no hurry. The sun dried her long chestnut-colored hair, but humidity left it curled and frizzy. There was a natural grace to her movements as she brushed gingerly through branches, trying to avoid wetting her fresh clothing, hopped over deadfalls, and looped around copses. She had none of the Renshai's sinewy poise nor the flowing dexterity of a dancer. It was a unique style, one that Saviar would recognize even from a distance; it simply defined Chymmerlee.

When the knights had been escorting her, Saviar had suffered from an anxious impatience. Now, it seemed to leave him entirely. He could, and did, watch her all day without interfering. At intervals, she paused to check landmarks or to pick leaves and berries from familiar bushes. Saviar grabbed one of the food packets at random, never taking his eyes from the mage. He tasted little of the jerked meat he shoved into his mouth and chewed only enough to safely swallow, but it did soothe the ache in his gut.

When Chymmerlee settled down for the night, she did not bother with a fire. She paced a circle around her sleeping spot, mumbling something Saviar could not fully hear or comprehend. When he touched his sword, he saw the glow of her aura and the steady light of some sort of magic surrounding her. She slept within its confines; and, still, Saviar waited. He had no idea what might happen if he disturbed the magic, but it seemed wiser to wait for morning than to risk setting off something he did not understand.

Worried Chymmerlee might sneak off during the night, Saviar slept little, while Chymmerlee seemed quite comfortable alone under the stars. By morning, the ring of magic had dwindled away, but Saviar did not bother the mage while she performed her morning toilet. He ate a bit more of her castaway food and tried to make himself look presentable. This proved more difficult as he had no dry change of clothing and only the extra cloak the knights had given her did not reek of travel and mold. His red-blond locks had gathered knots, twigs, and brush. He used most of his gathered water to wash the filth from his face and hands.

Finally, Chymmerlee prepared to leave. Still, Saviar waited, though he no longer understood why. It seemed so much easier to abandon his quest. Chymmerlee had already made her position clear, and it seemed dangerous and futile to continue. Still, his heart and mind urged him forward. He needed her to look him in the eyes and tell him she no longer wanted him in her life. If they could not rekindle the romance, at least, he hoped, he could revive the friendship. For the sake of every human and elf on the continent, he needed to talk to the Mages of Myrcidë, had to get them to at least agree to consider assisting in any further wars against the *alsona* and their masters.

Chymmerlee shoved into the woodlands once more. This time, Saviar set a collision course. When the young mage pushed through a clump of underbrush, she found Saviar standing in her way.

Chymmerlee hissed. She sprang backward, light flaring to life in her hands.

"No." Saviar grappled with her, catching both wrists in one hand. "Please. For once, just listen."

Chymmerlee screamed, kicking and twisting. Clutching tightly to her wrists, Saviar protected his privates this time. He spun around her, dragging one arm with him and pinned the back of her struggling body against him. He closed his arms around her, viselike.

"Chymmerlee, cut it out! I'm not going to hurt you. I just want to talk."

"Let me go, you demon, you Renshai!" Chymmerlee continued to fight wildly, long after it became obvious she could not break Saviar's hold. "Let . . . me . . . go!" Scream after scream wrenched from her throat.

Other than holding her securely, Saviar did not try to stop Chymmerlee. The knights could no longer hear her, and they were a long way from any open road or town. Quietly, he held her until her shouting ceased and she finally stopped squirming.

"Can we talk now?" Saviar asked, his voice gentle and soft as a breeze.

Chymmerlee let out a hoarse, angry noise and stomped a foot. "Let me go." Her voice sounded strained, husky.

Saviar took no pleasure from the warmth of her body against him. "I'd like to let you go, but you'll throw magic at me. Or kick me in the groin. Or run."

Chymmerlee could scarcely deny it. She had done all of those things.

"I just want to talk. Please, can we talk?"

Chymmerlee stiffened suddenly, raising her head.

Cued, Saviar glanced around the woodlands, seeing nothing but the trees and weeds, the striped shadows shifting with the wind. He tipped his head, trying to listen.

Chymmerlee talked over any sounds. "If I agree to hear you out, will you go away and leave me alone?"

Saviar hesitated. Once he released her, he might not manage to recapture her. "If you promise to stay right here, look at me while I'm talking, and hear all of what I have to say, I'll release you."

It was the best deal Chymmerlee would get, and she surely knew it. "All right. Let me go."

Reluctantly, Saviar released her, then tensed to give chase.

True to her word, Chymmerlee merely turned to face him. Her cheeks were reddened with exertion and anger, and her pale eyes narrowed in irritation.

Saviar tried to appear as earnest as he felt. Though anxiety always drove him to clutch a weapon, he kept his hands away from his hilts. Holding them would only remind her of his heritage. He opened his mouth to start his prepared speech, but three unexpected words slipped out instead. "I love you." It was the first time he had said it, aloud or to himself. "And I know you loved me, too, not long ago. I could read it in your eyes, your kiss . . ."

Saviar expected Chymmerlee to say something, anything, but she only stared at him, hands clenched to her hips.

"I'm the same Saviar, and you're the same Chymmerlee. What has changed to make you feel so bitter toward me?"

Chymmerlee had promised only to hear him, not to reply. Nevertheless, she gave him that much. "You're Renshai." She fairly spat the word.

"That hasn't changed." Saviar allowed a slight smile, careful not to let it become smirky or teasing. "I've always been Renshai. I was Renshai when you took me to your people, Renshai when I lay in a helpless coma, and Renshai when we held hands and ran together through the grass. I was Renshai when we threw mud balls at one another in the stream, Renshai when we kissed, and still Renshai when you held off the giant and saved so many lives in the war. You're a hero, Chymmerlee; and heroes don't judge people in stereotypes. I am the selfsame Saviar you loved."

Chymmerlee's stance did not soften. Her lips remained pursed in a tight frown.

He waited, every moment torture. Subikahn had told him that Chymmerlee had raved about Saviar's beauty from the moment she saw him, fevered and comatose. She had been attracted to him long before she knew anything about him but his appearance. Now, he hoped, that might work to his advantage.

Chymmerlee finally spoke. "Stereotypes are based on truths, and the stories of Renshai ferocity are not embellished. True, you have not harmed me. Yet. But your people murdered my people, not for any cause but for the thrill of battle. That savagery is in you."

Saviar could not deny it. "Channeled only against enemies, Chymmerlee. Centuries have passed since that massacre. The Renshai have changed. They've grown."

"No." Chymmerlee's reply fell like a stone. "When we

believed your aura meant you carried mage blood, you and I together worked. But now that we know it comes of demon seed—"

"No!" Saviar had to clear up that myth. "Renshai are not demons. We're human."

Chymmerlee fell silent. "Then why do you have an aura? How can you see ours?"

Saviar knew the answer but did not want to tell. His mind went back to the day of his mother's death. When he had first taken *Motfrabelonning* in hand, he had seen a *Valkyrie* come to take Kevral to Valhalla, had heard his mother's soul tell him to keep the sword. She had given her other one to Calistin and had only advice left for Subikahn.

Until the moment Saviar had touched the sword, he had seen neither the *Valkyrie* nor his mother's soul. Calistin, however, had experienced the same impossible things without a magical device. If any of them carried intrinsic magic, it was Calistin, the brother with whom Saviar had always believed he shared a full bloodline. *Although*, Saviar realized, *even other Renshai might suppose Calistin was a demon.*

The hesitation proved Saviar's undoing.

"Good-bye, Saviar." Chymmerlee turned on her heel. "I trust you have kept, and will continue to keep, your promise not to reveal us."

"Wait!" Saviar had not yet finished.

Chymmerlee continued walking.

"Wait!" Saviar shouted again. "I haven't told anyone. I've never broken my word, and I never will."

Chymmerlee whirled back. "What about your brother?"

Saviar's most recent brotherly thoughts had centered on Calistin. He froze, wondering how she knew, whether she might have the ability to read his unspoken mind. Only then, he realized she meant Subikahn. Saviar would not lie. "Subikahn is not as . . ." he struggled for words that would make his point without insulting his sibling. ". . . rigid as me about such things. But he's bound to keep quiet on my honor, and he would not undo me."

"Good." Chymmerlee started off again.

"Wait!" Saviar wished he did not have to keep shouting that. "I'm not done." He needed Chymmerlee to understand. "And you promised to hear all of what I had to say."

This time, Chymmerlee did not stop. "I've heard enough."

"Wait!" Saviar shouted. "Wait!" When that did not work, he chased after Chymmerlee. "You have to wait!"

She didn't, and she made that clear by ignoring his command.

Saviar broke into a run, swiftly gaining on Chymmerlee. His hand dropped instinctively to his hilt. Light flared around him, at least a dozen auras and a brilliant hedge of fully formed magic that must have served to muffle the mages' movements and hide their presence even from a wary Renshai. Abruptly alert to threat, Saviar drew his sword.

Pain slammed through Saviar, and his muscles twitched. Song filled his ears in a soft, gently pitched female voice. The ground under his feet became impossibly slippery.

Saviar clenched his sword, whirling on the mages. The spasms in his muscles intensified until it felt like every part of him rocked and clamped in rhythmical sequence. He pitched to the ground, slopping mud across his face and cloak. He rolled, trying to free himself from the magic, but it only clutched him harder. His muscles tightened and released, throwing him into seizure. He could feel his temperature rising, his cheeks violently hot, sweat pouring from him. It took all his concentration just to hang on to his sword. The voices around him became lost beneath that infernal singing. The pain in his muscles became an agony that scattered his thoughts. Helpless and vulnerable, detached from his logical mind by torture, he lashed out at anything that approached him. His sword thrust wildly, his other hand swept in manic circles, and he would have bitten anyone who came within reach of his gnashing teeth.

The uncontrollable thrashing became even worse, bending Saviar double, then throwing him backward until his feet and buttocks touched his head, then swinging him frantically back. Pain racked his entire body, from his spine to individual fingers and toes. Nothing worked as it should, and the mud filled his mouth, eyes, and nostrils. Incapable of coherent thought, far beyond speech, he surrendered to darkness.

Saviar awoke on a tightly knit blanket that barely cushioned a smooth, rock floor. Cold seeped from the ground to encompass him. His whole body ached dully, including his head. His hand went naturally to his belt, where he found his swords missing. An icy shock speared through him. He wanted to leap to his feet, to run in crazy circles, to hammer and kick at anything that might stand in his way. Instead, he remained as he was, aware any sudden movement would only intensify the agony throbbing through him.

Recognizing panic, Saviar battered it down. Cautiously, he sat up, muscles screaming even from that slow, deliberate movement. He was alone in a room with no obvious door. Two windows on adjacent walls afforded him different views of Western mountains and untamed forest. He knew from his previous time with the Mages of Myrcidë that, while he could see through them, the windows did not appear to exist from the outside. He would find no escape through them, only images of the real world brought to him in some odd, magical fashion.

Saviar wondered how the mages had gotten him into the room. His parents had insisted magic followed logical patterns, a fact they had learned by traveling with a pair of elves. It had limits and required proper constructs. Even Chymmerlee had once explained that magic did not allow the manufacture of real objects. For example, the mages could not summon food from air. Therefore, they could not have just plopped him down and created this room around him.

Or could they? Saviar had no idea how long he had lain unconscious. Perhaps they had had time to build it, stone by stone, without an exit. It seemed unnecessary and foolish. If they wished to kill him, they could have done so when they took his swords.

Saviar found his hands at his belt again, and his cheeks flushed with humiliation. He would have felt less violated had they stripped him naked but left a sword, any sword. Delicately, he rose to his feet, clinging to the wall to ease the riot of pain elicited by something as simple as movement. Many elders guarded their motions as carefully as he did now, and they clutched at backs or limbs with clear discomfort on their faces. Idly, he wondered if they suffered daily what he felt now. If they did, he never wanted to grow old. Valhalla could claim him any day. But to get to Valhalla, Saviar had to die in glorious battle. Locked in a box, swordless, he had no chance of doing so.

They're watching me. The thought intruded into Saviar's

head and refused to be banished. *I'm probably on the wrong side of several "windows."* If he had designed the structure, he would have put them on the other two walls. It explained why the mages needed no bars, no jailors. Saviar had no idea if and when others stood over him or who observed what he did. He wondered how long he could hold his bowels and bladder. Those bodily functions he wished to do entirely in private.

Once Saviar thought of them, the urge to go began growing on him. He immediately explored the room, before his impulse became need. He first discovered a dish and a decapitated gourd. The first held a cold mash that smelled of starch, probably some sort of roots for him to eat. Water filled the gourd, and it appeared fresh. At least, he saw nothing floating in it. He supposed those might do for toileting once he finished the contents, but he had no idea how, or even if, they intended to replace his sustenance or remove his waste.

The floor contained one other object, an oval opening that seemed barely wide enough to admit his wrist. He might cup his fingers to squeeze in his hand, but he doubted the muscles on his forearm would fit, at least not until he lost a lot of weight. Clambering back to hands and knees, he peered into the opening, seeing only darkness. No smell wafted up from it, not even the distinctive musk of a rat or *wisule*. No rodent had made this hole. It would take steel tools or, possibly, magic to create an opening through solid stone, particularly one so smooth-sided.

Though worried for his fingers, Saviar clenched his hand tightly enough to wedge it down the hole. As he suspected, he got hung up on the muscles of his forearm, but he did manage to grope a bit deeper into the opening. As far as he could reach, the sides remained solid stone, and he could not feel a bottom. He pushed harder, trying to gain as much distance as possible, until the sides of the opening abraded his skin and he had to stop before finding a bottom.

The answer came to Saviar in a rush. He had just stuffed his arm into his toilet. A faint smile slipped onto his lips, and he jerked back, only to find his arm securely wedged. The shock the sudden movement sent through his body set nearly every muscle screaming. Saviar went still, waiting for the agony to settle back into its normal, dull ache. Once it did, he twisted his arm gently. The rock cut into flesh, but it gave slightly. He continued to move it this way and that until he finally freed his arm.

That was stupid. Saviar wondered if the mages were watching him, laughing, but doubted it. In the months he and Subikahn had spent with them, they seemed an unusually serious and somber people, not given to mirth. Still mindful of his overtaxed muscles, he rose to check the only remaining part of his prison, the walls. He found them apparently solid, with no hint of hatches or openings. Again, he wondered how they had gotten him inside and how they intended to continue feeding him ... if they intended to continue feeding him.

Saviar considered the possibility that the gourd and the dish contained a self-filling magic. Perhaps no matter how much he ate or drank, they remained full. Then, he remembered something else Chymmerlee had told him: "Magic is a single event, a spectacle grand or small that lives only for a brief period of time. Permanent magic, imbued into an object, does exist; but it's countably rare and always ancient."

Saviar sank to the floor and picked up the gourd. For an instant, he wondered if it held poison instead of water. Ultimately, it did not matter. At some point, he had to drink or die. Tipping it back, he drank the contents: definitely water at a comfortably cool temperature. He continued to hold the gourd long after he emptied it, watching to see if anything changed. It did not refill itself. Only the remaining droplets clinging to the sides sank back into the bottom. Saviar put the gourd aside.

The deeper recesses of his mind brought more information from his studies. Renshai did not place much emphasis on schooling, but they did insist all of their children learn to read and write certain languages, know the history of the Renshai, and understand the underlying physical principles of swordcraft. Subikahn's father had also insisted that his son read as much as time allowed. Always one fact behind Subikahn, Saviar had developed a competitive interest in learning as well. On his occasional trips to Béarn Castle, Saviar had taken it upon himself to visit the library. After Subikahn's suggestion that "an invisible city seemed like the kind of incredibly difficult feat that would require the efforts of several magical beings working together as well as a receptive place," Saviar had taken another brief visit. Then, information about the defunct system of the Cardinal Wizards had seized his attention.

Saviar knew only a handful of items imbued with magic existed; the Pica Stone that tested the worth of Béarn's heirs to serve as its next ruler was most frequently cited. The Sword of Mitrian was a Renshai curiosity also rumored to have once contained magic in the gemstone eyes of its wolf-shaped pommel. It now sat, blind, in a place of honor, its eye sockets empty.

Saviar recalled from his reading that each of the Cardinal Wizards had lived in a magical dwelling that kept him safe from the others, for the four Cardinal Wizards, named for directions on the compass, had championed wholly opposite forces: law and chaos, good and evil. The world's balance now lay in the hands of Béarn's rulers, thus the Pica Test to assure whoever took the throne could rightly serve as fulcrum.

As Saviar thought, he idly reached for the bowl of mashed roots. It did not contain a spoon or other implement, and the memory of stuffing his hand down the toilet hole made him loath to use his fingers. So, he brought the bowl to his face and used his mouth and tongue like an animal. It had little taste, especially cold, but it would have to serve as fuel for a body that currently seemed to hate him. Renshai were supposed to practice hard enough every day to leave their muscles sore, but the agony caused by the full and repeated contraction of every sinew in his body went beyond anything he could inflict upon himself.

Saviar had the bowl licked clean sooner than he expected. The contents had had the consistency of paste and far less flavor; yet, when he finished, he missed it and wanted more. He put the bowl aside and looked at the gourd again. It was still empty. He sighed. Eating, drinking, toileting. The Mages of Myrcidë had addressed all of his basic needs but nothing more. He wondered how long they intended to keep him in this empty room with no company and nothing to do but simulated sword practices without a weapon.

Saviar curled up on the blanket, hoping to rest until something came to break up the monotony. Even had he felt tired, he doubted the shroud of pain that flared with every motion would allow him to sleep. His mind worked overtime. If magic could not be placed permanently, then how did the Mages of Myrcidë keep their village secret and in place? The building remained where no one who did not already know its location could see it. The windows did not move. It did not collapse during the night and get rebuilt each morning.

Uncomfortable in his current position, Saviar rolled to his other side, inciting the chorus of aches again. As he slipped closer toward sleep, more basic worries harried him. Would he ever see his father and brothers again? Would he hold a sword in his grip? Did he have any chance to die in battle and find Valhalla? Why had he undertaken this fool's mission when so many more important situations beckoned? Why did Chymmerlee's opinion of him matter so much?

Unable to sleep, Saviar sat up, put his head in his hands, and waited.

CHAPTER 7

War makes for the strangest of alliances, separates the incompetent from the skilled and the petty from the truly important.

— *Santagithi*

THE FIRST TWO TIMES Tae and Matrinka knocked on the bedroom door of Tem'aree'ay Donnev'ra Amal-yah Krish-anda Mal-satorian, they got no answer. As they stood in front of the teak panel a third time and Matrinka worked the bronze bear-shaped knocker, Tae could hear the thudding sound echoing through the room. Imorelda sniffed at the crack below the door, tentatively whisking her paws inside. *She's there.*

Imorelda had said the same thing the last two times they came, but Griff's elfin wife had not answered then, either. Tae tested the latch without fully lifting it. It moved easily. He eased it silently back into place.

"What are you doing?" Matrinka whispered.

"It's not locked." Tae's response did not address the question. He reached for the latch again.

"You can't go in there," Matrinka hissed. "What if she's not dressed?"

Tae doubted Tem'aree'ay would care. Elves had a carefree attitude beyond the ken of most humans. They whisked through lives devoid of responsibility, the passage of time meaningless, their dwellings nonexistent on a world that had no weather. They did not suffer from disease or infections and had magic to handle any form of injury. Though freely sexual, they did not have to worry about accidental conception. They used their magic most commonly for petty, playful purposes.

However, the longer Tem'aree'ay had remained among humans, the more like them she had become. She still took no clear notice of politics, yet she had learned to recognize Griff's discomfort and distract him when affairs of state furrowed his brow. Though she still relied on the servants to choose appropriate attire, at least she understood human modesty and never raced through the corridors naked. She still had a childlike wonder about her, and no one who knew about elves would mistake her for human, but she had changed dramatically in her nearly twenty years at Béarn Castle.

Ignoring Matrinka's warning, Tae gently and silently pushed open the door. The room seemed larger than Matrinka's own, which surprised Tae until he realized the appearance of space came from the paucity of furniture. The room had no bed, just a pile of earth-colored blankets in one corner. The furniture was simple: one wardrobe, one chest, one chair on which Princess Ivana currently perched.

Ivana's oddness never escaped Tae, nor anyone who looked upon her homely visage. She had a blocky body with short, thick legs, long fingers, and doll-like feet. Chubby cheeks nearly hid her small mouth and nose. She had elfin, canted eyes, an inhuman reddish-yellow in color. Her thick, straight hair fell, waveless, past her shoulders, blackish-blond with highlights of crimson and jade. White froth bubbled at the corners of her lips.

Tem'aree'ay crouched in front of her eighteen-year-old daughter. Her slender body revealed all the grace Ivana lacked, her golden curls a riot of contrast to the princess' limp and lifeless hair. She carried no bulk at all beneath a shift clearly not intended for crouching. It hugged her tiny buttocks, revealing the same boyish figure all of the elves shared. If not for the males' tendency to keep their locks shorn, Tae could not have distinguished most elves' gender.

Tae stepped inside, while Matrinka hung back, clearly uncomfortable with the intrusion. Inside, he noticed the wood composing the furniture remained true to its original form, still swathed in bark, mostly branches lashed together.

The window had no curtains. Sunlight beamed in, burning his eyes and forcing him to blink, though it did not seem to bother Tem'aree'ay at all.

Imorelda's voice speared into his thoughts. *You're acting rudely.*

Suddenly feeling like a voyeur, Tae cleared his throat.

Tem'aree'ay stiffened and turned. Tae had never seen her without a smile on her lips, and she did not disappoint him. Though small, it set off her dainty features and canted, sapphire eyes, bowing her heart-shaped lips. "Hello. I didn't expect company." Catching sight of Matrinka, she gestured for the queen of Béarn to enter. "Oh, Matrinka. Please, come in."

Matrinka complied, though she minced her steps as if the floor burned her feet. "I'm so sorry we bothered you when you obviously didn't want company." Her words were clearly intended for Tae's benefit. "We can come another time."

"Don't be silly." Tem'aree'ay's smile grew. "You're welcome any time." Her triangular tongue caught and held Tae's attention.

Ivana made a braying noise of welcome, so loud and abrupt it startled Tae. He felt his heart start pounding but covered his discomfort as well and quickly as he could.

More accustomed to the half-human, Matrinka only smiled and addressed her directly. "Hello, Ivana."

Ivana grinned at the attention and jumped down from the chair. Clumsily, she ran toward Matrinka. Imorelda rushed out of her path, and even Tae found himself recoiling. The girl threw her arms around Matrinka in a large, sticky hug.

Tem'aree'ay's smile grew wan, but it did not disappear. "Ivana, go out and find Nahnah, please. Matrinka and I would like to chat."

Ivana clung to Matrinka, and the queen returned the embrace with a genuine warmth Tae would have had to feign. He would endure a hug for the sake of propriety and his friends, but he much preferred that the strange and barely intelligent creature not touch him.

After longer than most would find proper, Ivana did release Matrinka. She looked around, as if trying to decide what to do next. Tae braced himself.

Tem'aree'ay glided in front of her daughter and made sure to catch her eyes. She enunciated each word clearly. "Ivana, go find Nahnah." She pointed out the door.

Ivana's gaze followed Tem'aree'ay's finger.

"Go find Nahnah."

Emitting loud, wordless noises, Ivana walked out of the room, and Tem'aree'ay closed the door behind her.

Imorelda had a guileless way of making difficult points. *Why do they keep that monstrosity?*

Tae winced. He wondered if he would have the strength and compassion necessary to care for a child so horribly crippled. *Humans love their offspring. No matter their . . . differences.*

Differences? Imorelda loosed a catty snort that sounded more like a sneeze. *She's not different. She's misshapen and almost mindless. If she were mine, I'd have eaten her at birth.*

Elves never acted hurried, and Tem'aree'ay seemed prepared to wait hours for Tae to explain his decision to enter her room unbidden. Matrinka, however, gave Tae a pointed stare. She had promised to let him do most of the talking, gathering as much information as possible and revealing as little as necessary. Matrinka had a tendency to simply lay out every truth and let things happen as they would.

Tae sighed. Now was not the time to get into a discussion of what constitutes humanity and proper human emotion with a cat.

Besides, the tabby continued, *her mother isn't human.*

Tae also did not wish to discuss elfin emotion with a cat, especially when he did not know much about it himself. "We're sorry to bother you, Tem'aree'ay. It's just that we're concerned about the *Kjempemagiska* returning."

Tem'aree'ay bobbed her head, guessing. "You want me to try to talk the elves into joining the battle against them."

Tae fell silent. It was not the prospect he had intended to raise, but it was at least equally as important. "Well, yes. That's one reason."

Tem'aree'ay pursed her heart-shaped lips. "I didn't have any luck convincing them to come for this last battle." She shook her head, finally losing the smile. "The only time elves went to war, it split us in two: the *svartalf* and the *lysalf.*"

Tae knew enough of their language and history to identify the terms: the dark elves and the light elves. The first group had tried to eliminate humans, blaming them for the *Ragnarok* and the ultimate destruction of Alfheim. The second group, to which Tem'aree'ay belonged, wished to live in peace with humans, though not necessarily among them.

"The *svartalf* would never help you, even if you could find the world to which they got banished. To the *lysalf*, war is . . . unconscionable. To many it's a . . ." Tem'aree'ay waved a hand, clearly seeking words that did not translate well. ". . . a nonconcept. A state of humankind beyond our understanding."

Tae spoke the elfin word she chose not to use: *vitanhvergi*. It translated literally as "understand a nowhere," and they used it to refer to ideas that did not translate from other cultures to their own.

Tem'aree'ay's eyes widened, and she stared at Tae. "You speak Elvish?"

Tae shrugged, accustomed to this reaction to his gift. "A few words."

Tem'aree'ay turned a critical eye on him, as steady a blue as a sapphire, without the star-shaped core so often seen in humans. "That's not exactly a basic, conversational word."

As always, Matrinka revealed more than she needed to, "He has an amazing ability with languages. Picks them up easily."

Tae did not reprimand her, not even with a raised brow. It was his own fault for casually inserting an elfin term into the conversation. He had done it hoping to win Tem'aree'ay over with his interest in things elfin. "I do all right, I guess. My current interest is *khohlar*."

"*Khohlar*?" Tem'aree'ay cocked her head. "Most humans just seem confused by it."

"I am, too," Tae admitted. "But I'd like to understand it."

"Why?" A hint of suspicion entered Tem'aree'ay's tone. Despite being of the *lysalf*, even though she had chosen to live among humans, she still clearly had doubts about humans' intentions toward elves. And if she worried about their motives, Tae had to imagine the other elves certainly did. And more so.

Imorelda's voice appeared in Tae's head. *Matrinka says you need to tell her.*

Tae did not need two females impeding his work. Matrinka had surely also noticed Tem'aree'ay's discomfort and worried Tae had missed it. *Tell her I'm as good with wordless communication as any other language. I work better when neither of you is interrupting me.*

Imorelda curled up on Tem'aree'ay's blankets. So long as they remained in the same room, with no doors or walls between them, she could continue to "talk" to him. *Well. Excuse me for relaying a message.*

Tae tried to address Tem'aree'ay's question as well as her underlying concerns. "Because the *Kjempemagiska*—"

Imorelda intruded, *I wouldn't want to interfere with your sparkling genius by sending a message I was—*

"—and the *alsona*—"

—asked to convey by a queen who is like a sister to you.

"—have a mind-language similar to *khohlar* that I—"

Tae felt sweat breaking out beneath his collar as he tried to hold together the threads of two separate conversations without revealing what he was doing to Tem'aree'ay or Matrinka. *Imorelda, please. Be quiet until I can finish, and I'll let you yowl at me the rest of the day.*

The cat broke contact, leaving a clear concept of righteous indignation.

"—have mostly figured out."

Tem'aree'ay stared. "You have 'mostly figured out' a mind-language?"

Tae glanced at Matrinka before nodding. She seemed relieved he had explained at least that much to the royal elf. Matrinka's main hope was to protect Imorelda's part in the translation, just as he did.

Tae nodded.

"Humans don't do mind-languages." Tem'aree'ay's long, slender fingers settled on either side of her dainty face. "They have no magic." The smile wholly vanished, leaving nothing but innocent question on her features. "Do they?"

"None that I know of," Tae said. "Except for this . . . this mind-language thing. Is it actually magic, or something else? I'm wondering how the *alsona/Kjempemagiska* mind-language relates to *khohlar*."

Apparently, even Imorelda had become interested enough in the conversation to neither interfere nor sulk; at least she did not barge into Tae's thoughts. The tips of Tem'aree'ay's fingers drummed gently against her temples. "The one *Kjempemagiska* I saw strongly radiated magic. The ones you call *alsona* had only a very faint aura. Perhaps it's this mind-language you speak of."

Tae knew too little of magic to add much speculation. "Or some means the *Kjempemagiska* have of controlling them."

Tem'aree'ay nodded with an all-too-human thoughtfulness that baffled Tae.

"You know, don't you?" Tae tried.

Tem'aree'ay swung her features around to him. They remained creased and curious. "I know what?"

"You have some idea of why the *alsona* radiate magic. Something you would not have thought of until we had this discussion."

Tem'aree'ay shook her head. The oddness of her expression vanished. "No. You've just triggered some new ideas about an old problem."

Tae suspected the elf had useful information he needed. "Perhaps we could help one another. I wonder if we don't have different pieces to the same puzzle. If we brought them together . . ."

Tem'aree'ay's head movement went from a slow shake to a slower bob. "The only human I've personally met with internal magic is Chymmerlee. I wish I had had a chance to talk to her about her abilities." She added thoughtfully, "To my knowledge, the only humans who ever possessed and shaped chaos were the Mages of Myrcidë, but they were annihilated before my birth, which was more than two hundred years ago. You know that Chymmerlee and I worked together to suppress the *Kjempemagiska*'s powers in the recent battle, but she left me with a conundrum. She claimed two elves assisted her from the rooftop of Béarn Castle."

Matrinka finally spoke. "So at least one of the other elves came to help! That's wonderful."

Tem'aree'ay's head moved more vigorously from side to side. "You were on the rooftop with me during the war. Was there another elf?"

"I just thought maybe . . . someone . . . I didn't see . . ." Matrinka shut her mouth tightly, then started over. "I thought maybe he or she remained hidden."

"No." Tem'aree'ay studied her small hands that looked so odd to Tae. The palms seemed doll-like, the fingers like overgrown stalks of fragile reeds. "I would have known if another elf had come, especially if he or she bonded with us; but I didn't." She wore an expression of dismay that went beyond what Tae thought logical.

Perhaps Chymmerlee miscounted. Maybe, in the excitement of the moment, Tem'aree'ay did.

"I thought Chymmerlee had made a mistake, but her insistence convinced me. Someone helped us contain the giant, someone who felt magically elfin to a human and human to an elf." Tem'aree'ay looked up at Tae as if she hoped he would connect the dots without her.

Matrinka had been there at the time. She knew exactly who had waited anxiously on that rooftop during the battle. Nevertheless, doubt tinged her voice so thickly, it seemed unlikely her guess could be correct. "Ivana?"

"It had to be."

Imorelda snorted again, another catty sneeze. *Impossible.*

Is it?

She's mindless.

Is she? Tae wondered if they both might learn a valuable lesson in not giving up on seemingly hopeless causes.

Would she act as she does if she weren't? Imorelda did not seek the most optimistic answer, as the humans and elf did. Whether this stemmed from her aversion to offspring or to more steady grounding in reality, Tae did not know.

Perhaps there is another answer.

Another snort.

It's worth looking.

Imorelda did not seem convinced, but she did drop the subject. Matrinka, however, rushed eagerly forward. She always gravitated to the happiest possibilities, whether or not they panned out. "Does Ivana have . . . the capacity . . . for magic?"

Tem'aree'ay tipped her head. "I don't know. She has some elfish blood, so I have to assume she carries chaos. Whether or not she has the ability to shape it into magic . . ." She lifted one shoulder until it nearly touched her cheek, then dropped it. "I would not have thought so if not for Chymmerlee's certainty that she had." Tem'aree'ay continued to talk, but her voice gradually lost volume. "Combining chaos to assist others is the most basic and easy form of magic, but it is magic nonetheless." By the time she finished, she was at a whisper. It obviously bothered her to share information about elfin methods with humans. That did not bode well for Tae.

At least, Tae seemed to have found Tem'aree'ay's weakness. If he could tie his need for knowledge with her concern for Ivana, he would have better luck than simply asking. "Can Ivana use *khohlar*?"

"What?" The question raised obvious discomfort.

Tae doubted Tem'aree'ay had misheard; elves had keen listening skills, and he had spoken clearly. For reasons he could not yet explain, his query had startled her. Dutifully, he repeated, "Can Ivana use *khohlar*?"

Tem'aree'ay hesitated, clearly torn between answering and dodging the question.

Tae glanced at Matrinka. She had more experience with Tem'aree'ay. They shared an interest in the healing arts and a husband.

Matrinka took the hint. "Tem'aree'ay, we're trying to help you and Ivana. Tae's a master of communication. If anyone can get through to your daughter, it's him."

Tem'aree'ay nodded ever so slightly, more to herself than Matrinka. "I'm just . . . When I came to live among you, I promised . . ."

Matrinka placed a gentle hand on the elf's arm, a plea to continue. It did not look like a soothing gesture to Tae, but Matrinka clearly knew better than him.

Tem'aree'ay's smile returned, if a bit lopsided, and she looked at Matrinka. "Dear Queen Matrinka, I know you mean me and my people no harm. I apologize for any mistrust I might have implied." She looked at Tae. "And King Tae Kahn. I know you're a good man with a good heart."

Tae could not help smiling. He had believed only Matrinka would describe him in such a way.

"It's only that I've grown adept at keeping the secrets of my people to myself." Tem'aree'ay gave Tae as pointed a look as she could manage with her delicate elfin features. "Is it true you intend to use this information only to help Ivana?"

Tae saw the trap. It seemed so easy to simply answer in the affirmative, but it would not achieve the desired effect. He and Matrinka had obviously come to Tem'aree'ay to learn about *khohlar* before the issue of Ivana had arisen. He chose his words with care. "We do intend to help you with Ivana, but it is not the only reason we want to know more about the elves."

Matrinka pursed her lips and nodded helpfully.

Tae realized that, had he chosen to lie, her expressions would have given him away. He had to remember the next time he entered into a negotiation: do not bring Matrinka. "I believe it's necessary for the survival of humans and elves to spy on the *Kjempemagiska*. Unfortunately, I can't do it by myself. I'm hoping elfin *khohlar* works enough like the enemy's mind-communication that someone might be able to assist me."

Tem'aree'ay did not move. She seemed to be considering his words, and Tae took that as a positive step. "Someone . . . meaning me?"

"No," Tae said immediately. "Someone who's not Béarnian royalty." He did not quite understand the titular conventions in Béarn. Only Matrinka bore the title queen. He did not exactly know what to call Griff's other two wives, except by their names. He appreciated that his own status as a king afforded him a lot of leeway with sloppiness and mistakes. "Someone careful and quiet who, perhaps, enjoys a bit of danger. My intention is to relay messages to a partner who stays out of harm's way. I'm hoping an elf might volunteer. Then, once we have proof of the *Kjempemagiska*'s intentions, we will have an easier time convincing the other elves, the humans, and even Chymmerlee of the danger. Having an elf involved in the initial spying can only help us."

Tem'aree'ay still had not moved or changed position, though she was clearly listening. Matrinka and Tae latched their gazes on her. It seemed like an hour passed before she finally spoke. "Elves do not have the luxury of 'enjoying a bit of danger.' Even should you find an elf willing to risk his life, I do not think the elders would allow it. As you already know, any life lost to violence means one less elf for all eternity."

Tae went to the heart of the matter. "But the *Kjempe-magiska* and their *alsona* puppets have shown no mercy at all. It seems worth risking one elfin soul to save two hundred."

Tem'aree'ay could scarcely argue. "You would have to prove there's danger to the two hundred first."

"I . . . think I can do that." Tae did not have to feign desperation. "Tem'aree'ay, I don't know if I can convince the other elves; but, before I try, I have to know if it's even possible our plan could work. Why waste my breath, and your people's time, talking them into a scheme without merit?"

Tem'aree'ay's smile remained, though still not whole-hearted or full. "What do you want me to do?"

Tae looked at Matrinka. The Béarnide wound her fingers through one another, her partial grin eerily similar to Tem'aree'ay's. "Help us figure out how well *khohlar* meshes with mind-communication."

"How?"

"By experimenting with me to see whether you and I can speak without words. By giving us enough information about magic, elves, and *khohlar* to at least try to figure out some way to use it."

Tem'aree'ay turned away.

Tae cringed. He thought he had convinced her, but her gesture suggested otherwise. He did not know how to proceed, so he waited for Tem'aree'ay to do something, anything, definitive.

At length, she turned back to face them. "I'm willing to work with you. With conditions."

Tae hid all trepidations, showing only an open expression.

"First, anything you learn about elves becomes our secret."

Tae did not like the phrasing of that condition, as it could hamper his ability to use the knowledge he gained. However, he assumed Tem'aree'ay would trust him to use his judgment and recognize her intention: to conceal any information someone could use to harm the elves. "Already assumed."

Matrinka nodded vigorously.

Tae did not give her a chance to add anything. He did

not want a long-winded debate about details. "What other conditions do you have?"

"That you find a way to reach Ivana."

That request caught Tae off his guard, though he supposed he should have anticipated it. He recalled Matrinka's claim: *Tae's a master of communication. If anyone can get through to your daughter, it's him.* "What exactly do you mean by 'reach' her?" He would never admit just how uncomfortable he felt around Béarn's half-human princess. Her strangeness repulsed him. He did not want to become attached to her in any way, particularly one that allowed her to touch him. Admitting this, even to himself, hurt. It made him feel stupid and evil, wrong-headed in every way. Ivana could not help the way she looked or acted, an innocent human/elf combination who deserved compassion and understanding. Still, the revulsion rose, unbidden and unwanted but altogether real.

"Find a way to communicate with her and to teach her to communicate with us."

Tae did not know what to say, so he only repeated stupidly, "Communicate."

Matrinka bumped him with her elbow. "When it comes to communication, Tae, you're the expert."

Tae had claimed to have superior skill when it came to reading nonverbal emotion, expression, and movement as well as verbal languages. He supposed that did all comprise communication. "But I've never . . . I mean, Ivana . . . it would be like—"

Imorelda interrupted, looking up sleepily from Tem'-aree'ay's makeshift bed. *—like communicating with an animal? A cat, perhaps?*

Tae caught the irony but gave it little quarter. *Like communicating with a nonintelligent cat.*

Now who's making assumptions about Ivana?

Imorelda had a point, and it irritated Tae. It appeared she intended to prove him wrong, even if it meant a full turnaround in her position on the matter.

Tem'aree'ay deserved an answer, and Tae gave the only one he could. "I can only try to communicate with Ivana. I can't guarantee it will work." Remembering his mental note from the strategy session, Tae seized the opportunity. "It will go easier if you teach me some basic elfin, too."

"Elvish," Tem'aree'ay corrected. "I'll do that." She went back to his original comment. "And it *will* work." She sounded infinitely more certain than Tae felt.

Matrinka looked from one to the other, then at Imorelda. "How do you know?"

"Because," Tem'aree'ay said, "I have faith in Ivana, in you, and in Tae. And I now think I know where we made our mistake."

"Mistake," Tae said carefully. Most elves and men believed the mistake came of lovemaking between an elf and a human. They considered Princess Ivana herself a mistake. Tae would never voice such a concept aloud, however, certainly not in the presence of her mother.

If Tem'aree'ay guessed at Tae's thoughts, she gave no indication. "We expected her to act human or elfin, to learn the way we do, to act the way we act. But she's neither human nor elfin. She's unique, without precedent. It's our duty, as parents and as a society, to figure out how to reach her."

It sounded like nonsense to Tae. He understood why Tem'aree'ay placed the burden on the community as well as herself and Griff. Because of the soul limitations and their long lives, elves seldom gave birth. At any given time, they might have no children or a single one among the entire race. So, they raised children communally, paying little heed to biology. But most human societies would have left a child like Ivana to die in the elements. "What makes you so sure that we and, in particular, I have the ability to reach Ivana at all?"

Tem'aree'ay's grin widened to its familiar proportions. "You learned to speak with the *alsona*, even though none of us had ever heard their language and they have a mental form of communication which humans do not share. You survived wounds pronounced fatal by every healer who saw you."

Tae gave Matrinka a pointed look. She had downplayed his injuries, making him feel like a histrionic coward for the bare thought that he might not survive them.

"I'm a healer," Matrinka reminded them. "And I knew from the moment I examined him that he would live." She had looked him over before any of the others, right on the shore; and Tae always suspected she had exploited his stubborn streak to shame him into recovering from the impossible. "Your point, however, remains valid. If anyone can reach Ivana, it's Tae."

Tae appreciated her support, though not necessarily her point. "As I said, I can only try." He would have promised the elf nearly anything to get the knowledge he wanted. "Now, tell me about *khohlar*."

Tem'aree'ay looked askance at Matrinka, who nodded. If Tae did not carry through on his promise to aid Ivana on his own, Matrinka would see to it he did. He, in turn, attended to Imorelda. *Are you ready?*

The cat yawned, stretching out her long body and striped legs. *Forever. I thought you'd never get around to tying yourself to that strange whelp so we could get on with this.*

Tae did not belabor her role. Imorelda knew what to do. Tem'aree'ay's voice entered Tae's head. *What do you want to know?*

Before replying, Tae addressed Imorelda. *Did you hear that?*

Sarcasm tinged Imorelda's mental voice. *Do you think I'm deaf? Of course I heard her.*

Tae ignored the radiating emotion to focus on the plan. *Where do you hear it? Is it near Matrinka's level? Mine? The* alsonas'?

Imorelda hesitated long enough that Tae raised a hand to stay Tem'aree'ay and Matrinka, who awaited his own answer. Finally, Imorelda spoke, *It's completely different. It doesn't seem to come from anywhere. It's just . . . there.*

Tae waited a moment in silence before realizing Imorelda had finished all she intended to say. "Can you *khohlar* again?"

Tem'aree'ay obliged. *What would you like to know, King Tae Kahn?*

Tae glanced at the cat, who shook her furry head, as if to dislodge something from her mouth. *Very different.* She expounded without really adding anything.

To Tae, the voices in his head, whether from Imorelda, elves, or *alsona* seemed the same. Imorelda had a far superior ability to discern, just as she could hear sounds he could not and pick out distinct variations in smells. *Can you elaborate?*

From the emotion leaching through their contact, Imorelda seemed more perplexed than annoyed. *If this elf-speak has a level, it's either so high or so low I can't sense it. Or else, it's just so different from our connection, I have nothing to compare it to. It's just . . .* She finished lamely, * . . . very different.*

Tae did not tease the cat. She was clearly struggling to explain a concept beyond her understanding. *Do you think you can carry me to her for a connection? Like you do with the* alsona?*

Imorelda walked toward Tae in that unhurried manner that felines perfected. *I can carry your voice, but I don't know where to take it so she can hear you.*

Tae could see the dilemma. *I'm going to try to send an unspoken message to her. If that doesn't work, I'd like you to try. If you connect, let her think you're me.* Saying nothing more, Tae thrust out his mental voice as he did when communicating with Imorelda. *Can you hear me?*

The reply came swiftly, *Of course, I can.*

Startled and thrilled, Tae grinned. *You can actually hear me?*

Why wouldn't I? We've been talking since I was a kitten.

Imorelda. Tae rolled his eyes. *Imorelda, I'm looking for a response from Tem'aree'ay, not you. I know you can hear me.*

Imorelda sat down in the middle of the floor. *Excuse me for answering your question.* Her tail twitched wildly. *I thought you were testing me.*

Tae tried again. *Tem'aree'ay, can you hear me?*

Matrinka elbowed Tae. "It's impolite not to answer."

Reluctantly, Tae abandoned his experiment. "I am replying. Mentally." He looked into Tem'aree'ay's gemlike eyes. "Could you hear me?"

"No." The elf shook her head. "Could you hear my *khohlar*?"

"Clearly." Tae sucked in a large breath, held it, then let it out slowly. "Let's try again." *Imorelda, please try to reach Tem'aree'ay.*

I've tried. No answer. The cat rose again and galloped to Tae's feet. She climbed his legs with her forepaws, leaving the hind ones on the floor and using no claws. *It's like talking to most humans.*

Tae reached down and lifted the cat absently, his hopes

sinking. If the elves could not hear him, even through Imorelda, he could not enlist their aid in his spying mission. Once again, he would have to do this thing alone, though he knew his chances for survival were bleak.

Imorelda snuggled into Tae's arms, purring.

Imorelda, try again. Keep trying.

It's useless. Like eating a mouse hoping you'll find a fine cheese in its belly. Even if it's there, and that's extremely unlikely, it's not likely to taste much like cheese anymore.

The analogy did not work for Tae. *Just keep trying.*

Imorelda continued to purr in his arms, but she did go conversationally quiet. Apparently, she was doing as he asked.

Hoping to assist Imorelda, Tae asked questions he thought might elaborate what made *khohlar* so unique. "How did you learn *khohlar*?"

"Learn it?" Tem'aree'ay placed her chin in her hands. She showed no discomfort standing so long in conversation. As Tae understood it, elves rarely remained still long enough to bother sitting. When they did, they perched on branches or stumps, rolled in the grass, or talked to one another in movement. "It's not taught. The knowledge for it exists in the soul. It simply is."

"Except," Tae said thoughtfully, trying to arrange his arms so he could hold and stroke Imorelda simultaneously. Ordinarily, standing so long would not have bothered him, either; but, so soon after near-fatal injuries, he felt tiredness pressing him. ". . . if you're an elfling without an elfin soul."

Tem'aree'ay nodded. She had clearly considered the situation much longer and harder than most elves would bother. "Even before Ivana's birth, I wondered about the effects of not receiving a soul filled with many millennia of the ghosts of elfin memory."

"What did the first elves do?" Matrinka sank to the carpet, folding her legs beneath her, then patted it, indicating Tae should also sit. "They didn't have a previously used soul to rely upon."

Tae appreciated the invitation. By sitting first, Matrinka had allowed him to do the same without looking weak. He carefully lowered himself to a crouch, the cat still clutched against him.

"And they thrived." Tem'aree'ay also lowered her bottom to the floor, leaving the single chair unoccupied. "The clean-wiping of elfin souls is not exact. Some elves have snippets of detailed, prior memory. Most have only a rare flicker of familiarity from time to time. Some seem to have none at all."

As Imorelda cozied into his lap, Tae used both hands to stroke her, sending loose hairs flying through the sunbeams. "The ones who have none. Do they need to learn *khohlar* differently?"

Tem'aree'ay closed her eyes, as if to draw mental images on the inner sides of her lids. "Not that I ever noticed." She opened her eyes and looked at Tae. "Elves don't analyze things the way humans do. We just do what seems right at the moment and deal with what goes wrong."

Tae found his head shaking and deliberately stilled it. They would get nowhere unless Tem'aree'ay made use of her two decades living among humans. "You're going to have to think like a human if you want to learn to communicate with Ivana." It was bluff. Tae doubted the princess had the thinking capacity for communication or learning much of anything. However, Tae knew of nothing else Tem'aree'ay wanted so much it might allow her to focus her thoughts.

Tae's words had the desired effect. Tem'aree'ay straightened, leaning slightly forward. "I'm young for an elf, about two hundred twenty-five years by your reckoning."

Tae forced himself not to smile. "What's the natural lifespan for elves?"

Tem'aree'ay hesitated, still hindered by her desire to keep her people safe. Then, apparently remembering whom she addressed and the promises they had made, she continued. "It varies widely. I saw one die of old age barely past her third century. The elder known as Captain claims to have lived for six millennia. He knew all of the Cardinal Wizards personally."

A wordless sound of awe escaped Matrinka, who clearly preferred listening to speaking in this situation.

The enormity of the potential elfin lifespan made it impossible for Tae to estimate. Assuming three hundred years, Tem'aree'ay would compare to a sixty-year-old human; but, given Captain's span, she would not yet be three. "Can you tell by the speed of maturity when an elf will likely . . . pass on his or her soul?"

Tem'aree'ay's brow furrowed. She obviously had never considered such a thing. "I . . . don't think so. We don't age in a certain progression, the way humans do. I mean, our hair sometimes flecks gray over time, but not so predictably as humans. It's not uncommon for an elf to have white hair from birth. Mostly, we judge age from eyes, and we don't count years per se. We do defer to the elders for positions on Council, but that only applies to our most aged. Not all elves survive millennia to take those seats."

The telling-age-from-eyes issue caught Tae's curiosity, but he did not delve. It would only divert him from the necessary information and make Tem'aree'ay suspicious. He did not need that knowledge to spy or to assist with Ivana. Wishing to keep the elf talking, he tried to make the conversation pertinent. "How long is an elf a child? Is it possible Ivana's . . . slowness . . . is related to the more gradual development of elves?"

"I've considered that." Tem'aree'ay went as serious as any human. "It might account for some of her physical awkwardness, assuming she got the worst of both parents when it comes to coordination." A hand flew to her lips, as if worried she had said something offensive. "By that, I mean the lengthier development of elves together with the . . . less fluid movement of humans."

I don't think I've even been called a clod more sweetly. Tae nodded encouragement.

But Tem'aree'ay only looked back, apparently having lost the thread of her intended point.

Tae reminded her. "Differences in human and elfin development might account for physical awkwardness." When a light did not flash in her sapphire eyes, Tae continued. "But not for intelligence?"

Nudged back to her previous explanation, Tem'aree'ay continued as if she had never stopped. "Elves start 'talking' about the same actual age as humans. *Khohlar* comes first. It's filled with pictures and concepts, and it only requires sending rudimentary thoughts. An elfin child radiates the basics: hunger, thirst, joy, discomfort."

The image flashed Tae back to an earlier point in the conversation, a question that never got answered. "Ivana can't use *khohlar*." This time, Tae did not ask. "She has never spoken to you that way."

Tem'aree'ay replied so softly, it took Tae a moment to decipher what she said. "It's worse."

Worse? Even after he figured it out, Tae did not know what to make of it. "Worse how?"

"In the last few days, I've come to wonder if Ivana can even receive *khohlar*."

Tae nodded, then stopped as full understanding overcame him. "How can that be? Even humans hear *khohlar*. And we have little understanding of the concept and no ability to use it ourselves."

"Worse," Matrinka repeated, reminding Tae of Tem'-aree'ay's description. "I can see why it might take someone eighteen years, or longer, to recognize such a unique problem." She clearly was trying to placate Tem'aree'ay, who had to feel like a failure as a mother.

Now, Tae appreciated Matrinka's presence. She could deal with the emotional issues while he pursued the facts. "What could cause such a thing?"

All eyes went to Tae, including Imorelda's. Tae got the sudden feeling he had asked the stupidest question in the history of the universe.

Even cats can hear it, you moron.

Tem'aree'ay explained more patiently, "Animals respond to *khohlar*, even ones who don't hear sounds. How can we know the cause when it's never happened before?"

Matrinka squirmed into a more comfortable position. "Are you sure about Ivana?"

"It's not difficult to test."

Attempting to redeem his intelligence, Tae guessed, "Just give her the same simple commands she already follows but deliver then as *khohlar*."

Tem'aree'ay made a gesture toward Tae to indicate the truth of what he said, then added, "The hardest part was thinking of the possibility. Every living thing can hear *khohlar*. Every living thing . . . except my daughter."

Tae tried to fathom what could cause such a defect but realized he could not even explain why he and Matrinka could communicate with Mior and Imorelda. Developing an understanding of mental languages was the exact reason they had come to Tem'aree'ay in the first place.

Tem'aree'ay remained stuck on maternal concerns. "It never occurred to me to worry about such a thing. She's the only hybrid in the world, so it didn't bother me when her development lagged more than a year behind Marisole's. I mean, elves don't come of age until they're about a century old. It wasn't until I saw a human imbecile that I realized how much Ivana resembled him. She seems less an amalgam of human and elf than a simpleton."

Matrinka cringed. She found it difficult to talk about anyone's deficiencies, no matter the purpose. "Even if she's . . . she's . . . a slow thinker, that might explain why she can't send *khohlar*. But she's obviously smarter than most animals, and you said even they could hear it."

"Yes."

Tae knew from raising Subikahn, and from watching other children develop, that babies surrounded by words became more gifted and earlier speakers. From the moment of birth, most elves experienced *khohlar* flying at them from every direction. Ivana had heard some from her mother but not the immersion she would have gotten had she been raised among elves. Yet, Tae realized, that should not matter. Humans grew up with no exposure to *khohlar*, and they had no trouble hearing it. Plagued with questions, Tae asked, "Tem'aree'ay, remember I said the *alsona* and *Kjempemagiska* had a mental language as well as a spoken one?"

The elf nodded. "Of course, I remember."

"During the war, did you hear them using it?"

"No." Tem'aree'ay added, "But I was never actually in the battle. I was on the roof."

Tae had not heard them from his sickbed, either; but walls appeared to block *alsona* mindspeak, just as they did his connection with Imorelda. When perched on the open windowsill, Imorelda had managed to relay some of their calls to him. "There's a limit to how far they carry, but I think you should have heard them from the rooftop."

Tem'aree'ay sprang to her feet, and her mouth flew open. "What are you saying? That I'm deficient at hearing unspoken languages, and I've passed that problem to my daughter?"

As Tae had intended nothing offensive, her reaction

took him by surprise. "Not at all. As far as I know, I'm the only human who can hear the enemy's mind-language."

You can't hear them, either. Imorelda reminded testily. *You need me.*

In more ways than you know, my pet, Tae sent back. *But I'm still trying to keep our connection to you a secret.* For now, he also wanted to protect Matrinka's ability.

Matrinka added, "I think Tae's trying to say that human-like creatures with mental forms of communication may not match up with elfin *khohlar.*"

Tem'aree'ay sank back to her haunches. "But humans can hear *khohlar.* Why wouldn't elves be able to hear . . . ?" She trailed off.

Tae realized they needed a simpler term for "humanlike creatures' mental form of communication." "For ease, let's call the enemies' spoken language '*Alsonese*' and their mental language '*Kjempese.*' I'm sure they have other names for it, but until we know, this will have to do." He addressed the actual question with a shrug. "The whole point of coming here was to find a common basis for unspoken languages. I think we're discovering there may not be one."

Tem'aree'ay put the details together. "Anyone can hear *khohlar,* but only elves can send it. With *Kjempese,* however, our enemies are the only ones who can send it or hear it. The exceptions to that rule being you, who can hear both, and Ivana who can't hear *khohlar.*"

The elf had summarized the situation well, except for two obvious gaps. "Under certain circumstances, I can also send *Kjempese,* but I can't do *khohlar.* And we don't know whether or not Ivana can hear or send *Kjempese.*"

Matrinka looked back and forth between them but added nothing.

The concepts worked easier for Outworlders, like elves and *Kjempemagiska,* because they had experience with magic and mental languages. For Tae, it seemed like a fourth dimension, the greatest challenge to his natural ability with languages. "Does this all make sense in the context of unspoken languages?"

Tem'aree'ay made a noncommittal gesture and reminded him, "Elves don't generally analyze things in this kind of detail." Clearly, she recognized the value of this particular knowledge to Ivana, and her time among humans had taught her to organize some bits of information logically. "The gods also have a mental language. It's impossible not to hear it if they want you to, and they can send it to as few or as many people as they choose."

Tem'aree'ay continued, "Demons are the physical embodiment of magic, and I've heard they literally penetrate minds. That would allow them to read, or even tamper with, thought and memory as well as communicate." She added carefully, "The gods can probably do that, too. It's possible the Cardinal Wizards had that power as well."

As Tem'aree'ay considered everything she had heard about various forms of mental communication, Tae did not interrupt. One bit of information seemed to jog the next.

"Those rare items imbued with significant chaos can be considered a type of demon as they possess a physical form that contains permanent magic. Legends abound about humans and Outworlders who could communicate with weapons, dwellings, or gemstones, often to their detriment. The one modern example is the Pica Stone. Only the heirs to Béarn's throne who have been tested know how it works, and the few not driven mad by it aren't talking. Clearly, the stone communicates with them in some manner that no one else can hear."

Tae looked at Matrinka. She had taken the tests, failed, yet somehow managed to maintain her sanity.

Matrinka's nostrils flared, but she added nothing. Clearly, she did not wish to talk about it with Tem'aree'ay or with him. Tae did not press. He had seen the various insanities inflicted on many of her cousins and siblings and refused to disrupt whatever internal defense mechanisms kept her sane.

Tae waited until he felt sure Tem'aree'ay had finished, but not long enough for Matrinka to feel as if she had to fill the subsequent silence with information about her experience with the Pica. "So, there definitely are several different forms of mind-communication."

Tem'aree'ay tented her inhumanly long fingers. "Yes. But until this week I thought they all had one thing in common: any living thing could hear them. Now, I know that's not true."

Suddenly, the intensity of Tem'aree'ay's previous focus and her new concern for her daughter made sense. Though disconcerted by the mere idea, Tae knew he had to help Ivana. Doing so might give him the understanding he needed to hone the bond with Imorelda, grant him the tools he wanted to unravel the *Kjempemagiska*'s language, and even help a previously hopeless princess. "When can I start working with Ivana?"

Tem'aree'ay's nearly ubiquitous grin grew radiant.

CHAPTER 8

The only way to become the best at something is to live it from sunup to sundown and into your dreams. Because every moment you're eating, sleeping, or engaging in unnecessary conversation or entertainment, you're missing a chance to improve your skills. And time is one thing you can never get back.

— *Calistin Ra-khirsson*

THE BLEAK, stone walls of his prison drove Saviar to a boredom deeper than he could ever remember. He wore himself to exhaustion with *svergelse*, though, without a sword, it seemed to lack all point and meaning. If not for the magical windows, he would have lost all track of time. Those gave him a view of the world outside his prison, sunup and sundown passing in perfect order, though it felt more like weeks than days.

On the second day, another tasteless bowl of roots poked through the wall at about head height. It penetrated the stone easily, without any evidence of physical might or violence. Saviar had taken hold of it, and the gourd that followed, and they had slid into his hands. Behind them they left no defect or opening, no hole that might serve as a weakness to aid escape, not even a slit through which he could pass back the empty dishes. To him, the wall seemed as solid as any other, and the dishes came through in some magical fashion he could not fathom.

By the third day, he learned that if he pushed his dish

against the wall, near the spot it had appeared and soon after he finished with its contents, it disappeared back the way it had come. The first set, however, had lost whatever property allowed it to pass through walls. He managed to get the second set back to the other side as well, though it took comparatively more force. He experimented with various parts of the wall; and, while it did not seem he had to find the exact same place the bowls and gourds had entered, they would not go through just anywhere, either. Apparently, the magic had a limited timespan and only worked near its source.

Other than the exchange of the dishes and gourds, Saviar had no interaction with his captors. During the day, he performed *svergelse*, imagining the weight of swords clutched in his fists. When he lay down, he considered speeches and words that might regain him the goodwill of the Mages of Myrcidë, if not that of Chymmerlee herself. The aftereffects of whatever magic had caused his spasms gradually faded until it mingled with the normal soreness that came from honing muscles with work. At times, Saviar simply stared out the window, watching rain pounding against stone and bowing the weeds, then rolling gaily down the mountainsides and off the stalks and leaves. He hummed songs to the rhythm of its silent falling.

Deep into the fourth night of his imprisonment, a sound awakened Saviar. He sat up, glancing around the room, instinctively seeking an enemy. Darkness filled the windowless half of his cell, and moonlight streaming in from the two adjacent sides with windows defined the shadows of his first bowl and gourd. He saw no movement, sensed no presence, and could no longer hear any noise. In the past, when he trod heavily or banged his dish against the floor, the enclosed room magnified the sounds, echoing them from the walls and ceiling. Nothing came from the outside. Surely, he must have made the sound that awakened him, a snore or a rustle of clothing or blanket. Saviar closed his eyes.

A hiss touched his hearing, and his eyes opened again. This time, he was not asleep, nor had he made any noise. Rising to a wary crouch, he studied the cell a second time, seeing nothing out of place. Still, the noise recurred, an airy sound, followed by a whirring foxlike call. Saviar recognized it instantly. *Subikahn?* He sprang to his feet.

Something flickered past one of the windows, a shadow in deeper darkness. Cautiously, Saviar headed toward it. As he did so, something sharp and metallic thrust through it, the bare tip of a sword. Subikahn's voice followed, through that tiny disruption. "Saviar, can you hear me?"

Saviar got as close to the sword tip as he dared, then whispered. "Subi?"

"Who else?"

"How did you find me?"

"It's not hard to follow someone who's following a bunch of noisy, overdressed men on white horses."

Saviar silently berated his incaution. The knights had no reputation to defend in this regard, but competent Renshai did not allow swordsmen to sneak around them unseen and unheard. "You followed me the whole way?"

"Someone had to."

Given his predicament, Saviar could scarcely deny it. He had to know. "How are you stabbing solid glass without breaking it?"

Subikahn's head finally appeared above the level of the window, showing a mop of black hair, an ear and cheek that blended into the night, and a single eye. The rest of his features remained safely below sight. "Don't you recognize your own weapon?"

Motfrabelonning. It's magical. Saviar reached for the tip, touching the familiar cold, oiled steel. "Push through the hilt."

"No."

"Why not?"

Subikahn's face disappeared, but the voice remained, a faint and careful whisper. "Because I don't want to earn the nickname 'No-Fingers' Taesson."

Saviar understood his twin's caution. If Subikahn did offer the hilt, Saviar could not resist pulling it through the window. Holding the sharpened blade at an angle Saviar could not see, Subikahn might well lose some digits in the transfer. "Just hold it on your palms. I'll be careful."

Even the tip all but disappeared. "What will you do with it if I give it to you?"

The question seemed beyond stupid. "Kill myself. What do you think I'd do with it? I'd practice *svergelse*, of course."

"*Svergelse?*" Subikahn sounded clearly surprised by an answer that seemed obvious to Saviar.

"Of course."

Subikahn's entire face appeared this time. "Wouldn't you use it to escape?"

"Eventually."

Silence followed, at least from Subikahn. The tip of the sword remained, and Saviar could hear the irregular chirp of night insects through the gap.

Saviar explained. "After I've talked things through with the mages, I'll escape."

"After."

"Yes."

"Do you think there's much chance they'll talk to you while you're holding a sword?"

Saviar doubted it. Thus far, the Myrcidians had not even deigned to talk with him while he remained safely imprisoned without one. "They have to talk to me sooner or later." He added for his own benefit, "Don't they?"

Subikahn raised his face just high enough to give Saviar a withering look. "They're clearly patient, Savi. Four days, and they're still just discussing what to do with you."

"They could have killed me."

"I would have stopped them."

Saviar massaged his arms, remembering the spells they had cast on him that left him helpless and twitching. He doubted Subikahn would have fared any better. "Obviously, then, they didn't try. They haven't starved or poisoned me, either." The mere thought of food sent Saviar's stomach growling in discontent. A large dish of roots did not satisfy a man his size for long. He suspected he had already dropped some weight.

"Don't think they're not discussing it." Subikahn had a way of finding the darker side of everything. "I heard it come up."

"And?"

Subikahn hesitated.

"Don't lie to me," Saviar warned. "I won't forgive you."

Subikahn sighed. "For the moment, they discarded the option. But it can come back into discussion at any time. Saviar, I think talking to them is worse than foolish."

Saviar gritted his teeth. He understood Subikahn's point, yet he could think of no better plan. The world had more persuasive speakers; but no one else could find the Mages of Myrcidë. Only he and Subikahn knew where they lived, and both of them had taken a vow of secrecy. No one had accidentally stumbled upon the mages in hundreds of years, and Saviar doubted such a thing could happen by chance. The magic of their city prevented it. "Perhaps. But without them, we can't win the war. And I'm the only one who might talk them into coming."

"And you've done so well so far."

Saviar did not bother to address Subikahn's sarcasm.

"Why don't I just cut through this wall and get you out?"

"No." Saviar could not allow it. "Not until I've exhausted my appeals. I'm not that desperate yet."

Subikahn disappeared again. "Let me make sure I have this right. You're forbidding me from rescuing you."

That summarized the situation well enough. "For now, yes. After I've had a chance to talk to them a few times, I might change my mind."

"And I'm just supposed to float around here until I'm either captured or you get more desperate."

Saviar would never inconvenience anyone to help himself. "You can leave whenever you wish. In fact, you should go home and let everyone know I'm all right."

"Why would I lie to our loved ones?"

The words seemed nonsensical to Saviar. "What?"

"Since when does 'all right' cover being trapped in a solid stone prison by enemies—"

"—they're not enemies," Saviar inserted quickly, but Subikahn finished his thought without responding to the interruption.

"—who despise Renshai?"

Saviar did not wish to argue. "Fine. Don't tell them anything. Let them worry and go searching for me in vain."

Subikahn ignored Saviar's point. "I'm not giving you your sword, Savi. Not until you're free."

Fighting words. Saviar grappled with anger. No Renshai would disrespect another by withholding something as important as his sword. He would sooner forgive a man for slicing off his ears. Saviar waited until he had full control over the volume of his voice, as well as his words, before speaking, "Why not?"

"Because, without it, I can't see magic and auras. I need it to find this city that, otherwise, blends perfectly into the mountains. I need it to outline the windows of your prison. Without the sword, they're just more stone to my sight. I can't talk to you without it, and I doubt I could steal it from the mages a second time, especially once they realize it must contain magic in order to penetrate the walls of your cell."

More insect noises.

Saviar wanted to know how Subikahn had gotten inside the magical dwelling, found, and recovered the sword, but that was a long story he could hear later. The longer they talked, the more likely the mages would capture Subikahn as well. "So . . . you're going to keep . . . my sword?" Even he knew it was the right thing to do, but the idea pained him deeply. Trained from birth to rely on his sword, he found it impossible not to argue, even when it had become pointless.

"Can you even hide a sword in there?"

Saviar knew of only one place that might hold *Motfrabe-lonning* out of sight, but he would never dishonor any sword by placing it where urine and excrement might foul it. Even then, the hilt would never fit. He could wrap it in his blankets, but it would leave a telltale shape. "No."

"Are you willing to use it to escape right now?"

Saviar wanted to leave, but no good would come of it. With him disarmed and contained, the mages might talk to him. They would not dare confront him armed, especially without knowing how it had happened. Once they discovered the magic in the sword, they would surely destroy it or, at least, guard it vigorously. "You're right. You need to keep it." The words came with difficulty. Subikahn better have heard because he did not think he could repeat them.

"Of course, I'm right." Subikahn did not give Saviar any wiggle room. "I had no intention of giving it to you. And now that you're admitting my superiority, why not let me cut you out of there and bring you home?"

"No!" Saviar managed to add vehemence to his whisper. "I'm not leaving until I've at least tried to make them understand."

"You're a fool."

"Someone has to be."

"You're going to die. Without glory and without reason."

"Maybe. But if someone doesn't convince the mages to join us, those magical giants will trample us; and we'll all die without glory or reason."

Subikahn did not show his face again. "*If* the magical giants attack, and *if* they don't just try to battle through their puppets again. And *if* we have no luck convincing the elves to help us, do you really think you're the best one to talk to these mages? Given that they hate all Renshai, and especially you, don't you think someone else could better serve that purpose?"

At least, this time, Saviar had already considered the questions his brother asked. "Unless you're volunteering, I'm the only one who can do it. No one else knows about the mages, and we're oath-bound not to reveal them."

"So?"

Expecting any other answer, Saviar fell silent. "What do you mean by 'so'?"

"I mean that the vow was broken when the mages attacked and imprisoned you. We're no longer under any obligation to keep our part of it."

The words horrified Saviar. He wished he could look his brother in the eyes, to let him know how important his word and his name were to him. He suspected Subikahn's desire to remain out of sight stemmed from more than just an avoidance of Saviar. He knew from prior experience that the mage's windows worked in only one direction. Just as the mages probably watched Saviar through windows on the opposite side of the room that looked like solid wall to him, Subikahn probably could not see inside Saviar's cell. That would explain why he needed the sword to find the outline of the windows from the backside. "Subi, I promised we would leave in peace, to release Chymmerlee unharmed, and to say nothing to anyone of the mages. I agreed to keep their whereabouts a secret and assure you did the same."

Subikahn did not quibble. "But, in return, they promised not to imprison, attack, or harass us. You, yourself, stated that your agreement to those terms hinged upon them allowing us to come and go freely from that time forth."

It amazed Saviar how Subikahn remembered every word verbatim. He wondered if Subikahn's father also possessed that skill. It might explain how he had learned so many languages. "You're right, and I'm going to mention that when I talk to them. But they only broke their vow because they thought we had."

Irritation tinged Subikahn's voice. "What are you talking about? We did everything we promised."

"Not exactly. When we promised to free Chymmerlee, we implied as soon as possible. Instead, we took her all the way to Béarn and risked her life in a war."

"That's not true!" Now Subikahn clearly struggled not to shout. "We did let her go right away, and she was never really a hostage, anyway. She chose to come with us and to help us."

"I know that, but the mages don't. At least, they didn't before Chymmerlee returned, and who knows what she might have told them since. She might be too angry to say anything nice about me."

"Nice things? Nice things?" Saviar heard a slap, as though Subikahn had just thrown his hands against the stone in frustration. "Saviar, you're acting totally idiotic. Chymmerlee tried to kill me. The mages tortured and forceably imprisoned you. And you're worried about what she says about you?" He hit the wall again. "You're insane, and you deserve to die. Now, one last chance: will you let me cut you out of there?"

"No." Saviar did not allow himself time to think. If he did, he might realize the wisdom of his brother's words and give up on something more important than either of them might realize. He could handle losing Chymmerlee, but the continent could not afford to suffer defeat in the coming war. "I can make them understand. You will not cut me out, and you will not give up the secrets of the mages. It's my honor at stake and not your right to sully it."

The tip of the sword jerked free of the window, and the glass sealed back in place as if the sword had never been there.

Saviar stared after it, wondering if he had just made a fatal mistake.

※

Calistin's swords wove deadly chaos through the air: swift, committed, unstoppable. After he had accidentally destroyed his fourth splint, the healers had relented, placing his left arm in a more pliable model that had allowed him the use of both. This was the first day he could use the arm the *Kjempemagiska* had broken without a support or any pain, and he intended to make the most of every lost moment.

Calistin made the most difficult *svergelse* look easy, creating new ones where his passion took him. As always, a crowd of Renshai gathered around him, watching and learning. Their gazes seemed to devour him, but Calistin paid them no heed. For now, he channeled excitement and rage into dexterous motions designed to slaughter imagined foes, every one of them Paradisian.

The Renshai had returned to their homes as the agreement specified, but nothing seemed the same. Everywhere he went, Paradisians intervened, performing no action that enhanced life on the Fields of Wrath. They stole food from the Renshai's purchased stores. They took over the homes of those Renshai who had not survived the Northmen's pursuit or the war. They gathered to loudly preach hatred of Renshai, creating fairytales of bullying Renshai who had stolen Paradise from them and teaching it to their children with the fervor of a religion.

Calistin swept the air to his right, felling two imaginary Paradisians with one blow, then spun abruptly leftward to skewer another. He dodged the rest deftly, parrying a high and incompetent stroke, before surging toward another horde.

Renshai barreled out of his way, and Calistin took some small satisfaction from their discomfort. The Paradisians had gone much farther, harrying Renshai whenever possible. A rash of "accidents" had claimed too many Renshai lives, and at least three infants had gone missing. Whenever the Renshai dared to retaliate, the Paradisians clogged the Erythanian court with their cases. Good Renshai rotted in cells for daring to avenge murder and mayhem, and the entire tribe had wearied of lectures. King Humfreet besieged them to act as good neighbors. They were warriors, he reminded, with well-honed weapons and skill. The Paradisians were weak civilians, fighting the only way they could hope to win.

By murdering babies and innocents. Anger fueled Calistin's *svergelse*, rendering it all the more violent, every sweep a deadly promise. His swords flickered through the air so swiftly, they became invisible, and his feet complemented their movements perfectly. No mortal could stand before such an assault, and Calistin wished, not for the first time, he could drive his blades through every Paradisian and the Erythanians who claimed to support their cause yet refused to take them into their own homes to live beside their own families.

A scream tore through the air, followed by several more in quick succession. In the same fluid motion as his *svergelse*, seamlessly, Calistin sheathed his swords and ran toward the noise. His audience trailed him.

As Calistin ran, he located the sound to the bathing pool. For an instant, his mind went to sharks, though the landlocked plains held only a small, freshwater lake. He glanced at the sky as he ran. It was still morning, which meant the pool belonged to the women and the men were banned. Calistin started to slow, then another screech rent the air. He heard the muted sounds of swords slamming wood, and unintelligible shouts among the screams. He quickened his pace, leaving most of his followers in the dust.

Nestled at the foot of the mountains, fed by a high stream, the pool remained mostly sheltered from view. Calistin had heard rumors that some of his adolescent companions occasionally sneaked to the edges to spy on the girls, but he had never done so. Now, he tore around the cliffs without worrying about rules.

A group of young Renshai women in the buff attacked two trees near the pool. Calistin could see Paradisians clinging to the branches, hurling rocks and sticks. More Renshai women, wet and wearing nothing but swords, clambered up the cliffs while Paradisians threw more stones or rolled boulders at them. Blood stained the pool water, and a blonde corpse floated near the bank. Another Renshai lay still on the beach.

"Bastards!" Calistin did not wait to see what his companions did. As he neared the trees, he could see that someone had sawed through all the lower branches. Apparently, the Paradisians had planned the attack well in advance and had tried to foil pursuit. The youths in the tree must have clambered up, leaving others to cut the branches and hand them up as weapons.

Carried by rage, Calistin did not need branches. He hurled himself at the trunk, caught it, and used his momentum to scurry up the bark to the lowest remaining branch. Three teen youths on the same limb watched incredulously as he came at them. Grabbing a leg, he unseated the first. Without bothering to watch him fall, Calistin shoved the next to the ground. The third lurched toward him, lost his own balance, and plummeted.

Calistin left the three to the women below. They deserved the right to finish their tormentors with swords. Calistin reached up, seized a leg, and jerked another Paradisian to his doom. Then, the attacks turned on him. By now, the Paradisians in the tree seemed to have run low on ammunition. Whatever stones they had gathered were gone, and they had only sticks to pummel him. These rained down on Calistin, scant blows compared to some of the sword strokes he had taken. They only made him laugh, and that clearly unnerved the Paradisians. One jumped on his own, preferring a controlled landing into frenzied warrior women to grappling with Calistin.

A feistier Paradisian clutching an enormous branch swung it at Calistin's head. Compared to a sword, it moved slowly, awkwardly. As it came toward him, Calistin judged speed and weight, catching it. He tried to toss it away, far enough that it would not harm any Renshai. Its wielder went with it, sailing toward the ground.

Calistin grabbed a limb, swinging himself up and over to face the last of the treed Paradisians. There were two, a long-haired, slender female who appeared close to his own age and a male in his twenties. She hid behind him, and her eyes looked dark and dead. The man rose to a cautious crouch, testing his balance as he freed his hands.

Calistin knew elevated combat well, having used rooftops, tree limbs, and even a crude rope strung between dwellings for *svergelse*. Many of the most competent Renshai preferred a makeshift log bridge suspended over a stream near the Road of Kings. Calistin had only had to slip once to know he never wanted to struggle through icy water again. He had spent the next month perfecting his footing before accepting challengers.

Now, Calistin balanced easily on the limb, watching the Paradisian male attempt to do the same. In ordinary circumstances, he would have waited for his opponent to prepare. Now, he worried more for time and the safety of the other Renshai. The Paradisians had attacked unarmed Renshai from the high security of crags and branches. They deserved to die for their cowardice and deceit. Without a word, Calistin drew his sword and slammed the flat against the man. The blow, and the Paradisian's own recoil, knocked him loose. This Paradisian, too, plummeted toward the ground.

The woman cowered behind an arm. "Please, spare me. I'll do anything. Anything."

Calistin knew no mercy. "Spare you like you spared them?" He gestured at the Renshai below.

The woman said nothing but continued holding her arms pitifully in front of her, hiding her face. "Please. I don't know how to fight. I have a brother and a mother and a father who love me."

Calistin did not understand her point. "So do I." He could not fathom why he had allowed her to say this much. Before he had incorporated Treysind's soul, he would never have hesitated. *Damn you, boy. You've softened me. And it's bound to be my downfall.* "If you can justify what you've done, I'll spare you."

"We . . ." she started, finally peering around her fingers to look at Calistin. She perched on the sturdy fork of two branches, her legs tucked under her. Her hair hung in a straight, dark cascade, except the fringe of bangs across her forehead. A spark had crept into her otherwise haunted eyes. "We're at war. We attacked only your warriors . . ."

"Which is every one of us."

". . . while you slaughter only our civilians."

"Civilians." The word had become meaningless. "Like you?"

She nodded and lowered her head, clearly trying to appear submissive and helpless.

Calistin could not respect either of those states of being. "When you made this plan, when you threw the first stone or stick, you ceased to be a civilian." With that, he kicked her off the branch. She screamed the whole way down.

Cursing the time he had wasted talking to the worthless

creature, Calistin measured the gap to the other tree. He could not leap to it from where he stood without risking the stability of his freshly-healed arm. A jump to the ground would probably break more bones. Looking higher, he noticed the trees flared outward at the tops and approached one another. Uncertain if it would work or only cost more time, he shinnied swiftly upward. The branch narrowed as it rose, the leaves bunched more tightly together. As his weight overcame its strength, the branch bowed toward its neighbor. He had to get higher before it snapped or bore him to the ground. He climbed swiftly, fingers barely touching one spot before moving on to the next. He raced the sagging branch until he drew near enough to try, then flung himself at the other tree.

Calistin managed to catch a slender branch, his weight bearing it instantly downward. He sprang for another, then another, seizing thicker and thicker foliage until he found an inner branch that could hold him. Loose sticks whizzed past his head, and a stone smacked against his cheek with bruising force. That only served to further enrage him. Locating four Paradisians in this tree, he slid deliberately toward them.

Two rushed toward the trunk, climbing down and away from this new threat. The other pair came toward him, flinging rocks and debris. It might have been leaves for all the effect it had on Calistin. As he reached the branch above them, they ran at him, fists swinging. Calistin grabbed the branch beneath his feet, threw his body backward, then swung forward, feet leading. His boots crashed into both Paradisians, sending them careening from the tree. Landing on the branch below, he chased after the two escapees. By the time he reached the ground, the Renshai women already had the Paradisians pinned on their swords.

Calistin hopped to the ground, watching the Renshai to avoid becoming a victim of an overzealous attack. No one menaced him. The bodies of the Paradisians lay bleeding on the ground. Renshai had gained the cliffs, and the Paradisians there had either died or run away. He saw only two Renshai bodies, the one in the water and the other on the bank. A few appeared injured, limping or cradling their heads in their hands.

Only then, Calistin realized he stood amidst a bunch of partially clothed or fully naked young women. Embarrassment overtook him in an instant, a wave of warmth that seemed to envelope his entire body. He shielded his eyes. As the rush of battle rage diminished, he worried about more embarrassing kinds of excitement.

One of the women caught his arm. "Thanks, Calistin."

He dared a peek. It was Valira, a muscular adolescent who had passed her Renshai tests of adulthood a few months before her seventeenth birthday. She had hair so blonde it looked nearly white, with wispy eyebrows and lashes to match. Though cut short in the front, it tumbled down her back. Despite the pallor of her hair, her skin bore the healthy hue of a woman accustomed to sun. She had sky-blue eyes, a nose that crooked to the left, and a delicate chin befitting a woman. He tried to lock his gaze on her face, but it wandered to her neckline where he found the collar of her shift. Breathing a sigh of relief, he allowed his gaze to sweep her clothed body, only to find himself pausing overly long at her breasts. He could make out the faint outline of a nipple through the wet fabric, and he found that surprisingly more sensual than the naked bodies behind him.

"Calistin?" Valira's voice brought Calistin's gaze back to her face. "I said 'thank you.'"

Calistin smiled awkwardly. "It was nothing." He liked the feel of her strong fingers wrapped around his upper arm. He could not remember the last time any Renshai dared to touch him. "The fools had no weapons and even less skill."

Valira chuckled. "How does one have less than none?"

Calistin shrugged a shoulder and smiled. He could hardly consider his confrontation with the Paradisians a battle, though he did feel the satisfying wash of victory. They had vanquished foes, though boring and unsatisfying ones, and he still felt the rush of both his practice and the exertion necessary to leap through trees. "Paradisians manage it. Sneaky, dishonorable bastards, all of them, without a thimbleful of actual talent between them."

"Well, it wasn't 'nothing' on your part. If you hadn't come, we'd have dulled all our blades hacking down those trees."

Calistin still saw little merit in his actions. "You would have had them in time. Once they ran out of ammunition, they were yours. They had to come down eventually."

"In two or three days, I suppose." Valira smiled at him.

Calistin's gaze traveled to her hand on his arm. "No one ever touches me."

Valira jerked away her fingers, as if burned. "I'm sorry."

Calistin cursed himself for mentioning it. "Me, too. I liked it."

"You did?" Cautiously, Valira reached for him again. This time, she touched his shoulder, but it felt less natural, more awkward. She dropped her hand to her side. "You know, a month ago, you'd have cut my arm off."

"I would?" Calistin could not remember slicing appendages off of Renshai. He had left a few battered, slashed, and bruised from practices and spars. He had killed those who came to him to die; Renshai suffering fatal wounds or illnesses usually chose him to bring about their ends in proper combat instead.

"You've changed, softened a bit."

Calistin stared, uncertain whether to take that as compliment or insult. "I'm as tough as ever."

"As competent as ever," she corrected. "More competent as a warrior. Just . . . more approachable. As a man, I mean."

More approachable. Calistin did not know what to do with that information. *As a man?* He thought he might like that. "Are you saying I'm weaker?"

Valira placed her hands on her hips. "Of course not. Stronger, if anything. More . . . well . . . desirable. More . . ." A ball of scarlet appeared on each cheek.

Calistin did not make her finish. "Women don't like me," he confessed. "I look like a child."

"No," Valira corrected. "We didn't like you because you acted like an unfriendly, unfeeling ass."

"Oh." Calistin did not know what else to say. He swallowed hard.

"Many Renshai look younger than their ages. You more so than most; but you're a man by Renshai standards. Chronologically, you're a bit older than me."

Calistin felt no need to clean up the aftermath of the battle, nor to examine it. He had no enemies at his back, only the terrifying sight of partially dressed women. He hoped they had attended to themselves and their swords while he talked. "Women have always preferred my brother."

Valira could hardly deny it. "That's because he's jaw-dropping gorgeous, funny, honest, and kind. The gods don't make nearly enough men like Saviar."

"Yeah." Calistin knew his oldest brother had the looks women preferred, but he had never considered the other aspects of Saviar's attraction.

"But I prefer a man who defines our tribe, an unparalleled swordsman who can keep me forever challenged. Sinewy as a lion, quicker than a striking snake, wholly committed to finding Valhalla and to the Renshai way of life. A throwback to the days when we looked like Northmen, blond and blue-eyed, like me."

"Do you?" Calistin wondered why she was telling him this. It made him weirdly uncomfortable.

"I do." Valira's pale eyes twinkled.

For a moment, Calistin thought she was going to laugh, but he doubted he was right. He had never read people well. He constantly misinterpreted their intentions. In give-and-take conversations, he missed the obvious. The games they played with one another confounded him. Jokes made no sense to the younger Calistin, and he tended to react literally to what others recognized as sarcasm. In the last few weeks, however, understanding had finally begun to dawn. Thanks to Treysind's living assistance, and now his soul, a whole new world was starting to open for Calistin. Thus far, he had tried to avoid its strange and scary newness; but Valira, at least, had noticed the change.

It was not that Calistin did not feel the stirrings that all adolescents do. He had watched a Renshai named Sitari from afar, often wishing he had the words to convince her to kiss him. Slaughtered by Northmen, she went to her pyre never knowing how he had felt about her. He had not given her the slightest clue, had never known how to act or what to say.

Calistin did realize it was his turn to speak. Emboldened, he reached over to touch Valira's shoulder. The fabric felt wet, the flesh beneath solidly muscled. For the first time in his life, he felt clumsy as a turtle and dropped his hand back to his side. "I hope you find him, Valira."

"Oh, I have." Valira turned with a knowing wink, the

picture of grace and dexterity. She deliberately brushed her hip against his as she walked away, and her hand patted his buttocks.

Stunned, Calistin whirled to watch her go, forgetting in his surprise to be concerned about the nakedness of the other Renshai. At the moment, he had eyes for only one.

Commanding Renshai is rather like taming volcanoes or herding butterflies.

— *Sir Ra-khir Kedrin's son*

CALISTIN WALKED AWAY from the bathing pool exhilarated, curiously excited, and—mostly—confused. Other than his mother, no woman had ever touched his bottom before. He wondered what it meant, why Valira had done it. He rarely made any human contact by hand; his sword did all the talking for him. He had slapped an opponent or two during combat, as a warning that they had done something so stupid he did not even need a sword to finish them. Other than that, he kept his hands to himself.

Before Calistin had become a man, his father had put an arm across his shoulders at times or tousled his hair. Occasionally, a *torke* had done the same as a sign of encouragement. Since he became a man, he could scarcely remember anyone even reaching in his general direction. Vigilance usually sent him dodging anything headed toward him, and he supposed he might have menaced someone who tried to touch him unexpectedly.

Finding a relatively isolated place, Calistin again launched into *svergelse*. Oddly, it felt more right and vigorous than the battle he had just fought. In the past, he would never have bothered to join such a ridiculous skirmish. The Paradisians clearly had no war sense. He saw no reason to begin an assault they had no way to finish. When they chose to rain sticks and stones on the Renshai women, they had surely known the conflict would result in their own deaths. Calistin understood desperation and flinging himself into an impossibly lopsided battle, fighting until he either won or he earned his honored place in Valhalla. Unarmed, untrained fools ambushing warriors who would not otherwise have bothered them seemed like inexplicable madness.

Calistin sliced and wove, his feet never still, his arms one with his swords. Even his antics in the tree, he realized, had not bothered his arm. For the first time in longer than a month, he felt whole, and that invoked an excitement that surpassed his encounter with Valira. It took too much mental effort to understand people. Only he and his swords had a perfect and utterly-comprehensible connection.

Hoofbeats interrupted Calistin's thoughts. Many Renshai became violent when someone dared to interfere with a practice. As Calistin often worked with his swords from sunup to sundown, he could hardly escape at least a few intrusions daily. It only bothered him when he focused on something so difficult it required every modicum of his attention. Currently, he was letting his thoughts wander anyway. Another break would harm nothing.

Calistin looked toward the sound, recognizing the white charger of a Knight of Erythane. Ra-khir was the only knight who lived on the Fields of Wrath, but he rarely made it home before nightfall. Most often, he stabled his horse at the knight's Bellenet Fields. Curious, Calistin sheathed his weapons and walked toward the approaching charger.

Ra-khir pulled up Silver Warrior in front of Calistin. Apparently still on duty, he wore his tabard, cloak, and sword, his hat perched at the proper rakish angle. Gold-and-blue ribbons were braided into the horse's mane and tail. "Where are your brothers?"

Calistin had no clue. "I haven't seen either of them since just after the war. They went off about the same time you did, and you're the first I've seen back."

An uncomfortable look spread across Ra-khir's face, but Calistin could not wholly identify it. "Saviar didn't come home?"

Calistin shrugged, tired of being asked about his brothers' whereabouts. "Not that I'm aware. My brothers don't normally confide in me."

"No, they wouldn't."

Calistin wondered what his father meant, but he did not bother to ask. It would only launch a discussion that would probably just confuse him more.

"Calistin, something happened here a short while ago."

"Something?" Violence defined the Fields of Wrath, where Renshai taught sword skills, drilled, and sparred all day. But, since the Paradisians had arrived, the Renshai seemed to have no peace at all.

"The Erythanians who live here claim Renshai slaughtered twenty-seven of their unarmed young men and women near the bathing pool."

"Oh, that." Calistin shrugged. If the Paradisians did one thing swiftly, it was complain. "What about it?"

"So, it's true?" Ra-khir seemed to be studying him.

Calistin saw no reason to lie. "I didn't count them. It could have been twenty-seven." From Ra-khir's expression, Calistin gathered his father wanted a different answer. He waited for the knight to clarify.

Ra-khir chewed his lower lip thoughtfully before finally speaking softly. "Calistin, did you have to kill them?"

Calistin knew his mannered father demanded honesty, not only when he served in his capacity as a Knight of Erythane, but at all times. "No. Our women did a fine job all on their own. I just shook a few out of the trees for them."

Ra-khir stared, as if trying to make sense of the words. "By 'you,' I didn't mean you personally. I meant 'you' as in the Renshai. Did 'you,' as a group, have to kill those young Paradisians?"

Calistin stared at his father, actually trying to read his intentions for the first time. In the past, he had simply dismissed Ra-khir as a well-meaning but overly honor-bound fool. "As opposed to allowing them to bludgeon more of us to death with limbs and boulders?"

Ra-khir winced. "As opposed to restraining them. As opposed to chasing them away. Could you have done that instead?"

Calistin found himself incapable of comprehending his father's suggestions. Uncertain what to say, he finally answered the only way that seemed honest, though more question than statement. "No."

"Why not?"

The query seemed no more sensible than a child expecting a parent to explain the blueness of the sky, the greenness of the grass, the deafening crash of thunder. Calistin shifted from foot to foot. "Papa, we recently fought a war in Béarn, correct?"

Ra-khir could scarcely deny it. "Yes, of course."

"How many enemies did you restrain? How many did you chase away?"

Ra-khir's brows furrowed. He leaned over his mount's arched neck to study Calistin with an intensity that might have bothered the young man, had he any experience with reading nonverbal cues. "That's an entirely different matter."

Calistin did not see it. "How?" he asked innocently.

Ra-khir straightened with a sigh. "We were fighting enemies who intended to kill every man, woman, and child on the continent. Foreign enemies, all warriors, hell-bent on destroying us and taking our land."

Calistin cocked a brow. He did not see the difference.

"Renshai live on Erythanian sovereign land by the grace of King Humfreet. That makes them de facto Erythanians. The Paradisians are also Erythanians. So we are allies."

"Allies don't murder bathing women by dropping rocks on their heads."

Ra-khir stiffened. Clearly, the Paradisians had not revealed their role in the conflict. However, he did not allow the newfound knowledge to interfere with his point. "I should have said 'neighbors.' Also, the Paradisians are civilians, while Renshai are all—"

"Warriors," Calistin filled in, ire rising. "I've heard that argument."

"And?"

"And nothing." Calistin refused to accept it. "Because they're lazy and dishonorable, we should allow them to murder us without retaliation?"

"You should understand that they're desperate and don't stand a chance against you in a face-to-face war. That's why they resort to underhanded tactics."

Calistin could not fathom why his father was telling him this. "And we're supposed to ... what? Let them? Because we work hard and train, we're not allowed to defend ourselves?"

Ra-khir sighed. Calistin could tell he wished he had not

started the conversation. Every line of his father's body suggested he would rather speak with Saviar or Subikahn and leave Calistin to his ignorance. "Of course, you can defend yourselves. I'm just saying you should respond with an appropriate level of force, not everything you have."

Calistin still did not get it. "Why?"

"Because it's the right thing to do, the fair thing."

Calistin could scarcely believe he had heard his father correctly. It went against every tenet of a warrior, something he knew better than anyone. "Papa, are you telling me a warrior has to modulate his battles? He has to hold back his strength, quickness, and ability to make every fight even?"

Ra-khir's features crinkled, and he shook his head vigorously. "That's not what I mean."

Calistin continued, "Because that would remove any reason to train, all purpose for becoming a warrior." Even as the words left his mouth, Calistin could not conceive of them holding even a grain of truth. To do so invalidated his entire existence.

Ra-khir sucked in a deep breath and loosed it slowly before speaking again. "Calistin, no. That's not what I believe, not the way you've phrased it, at least. You know how proud your mother and I have always been of your accomplishments, of your dedication and skill."

Calistin's anger dissipated in an instant, driven away by surprise. He could not recall his father ever saying such a thing. "You're proud of me?"

Now, Ra-khir looked as shocked as Calistin felt. "Of course, we're proud of you. Your entire tribe looks up to you, and the Renshai do not bestow admiration lightly. Throughout the world, the men who don't revere you, fear you. Parents always love their children, always believe them capable of accomplishing lofty goals. But, Calistin, you've achieved beyond any parent's wildest and most unrealistic dreams."

None of that mattered as much as Ra-khir's previous statement. *Your mother and I are proud of you.* Calistin wondered if this was the first time his father had spoken the words aloud or if he had simply never listened. When Kevral had trained him, as his *torke*, she had rarely used a word of praise, even as she drove him harder than any other student. It had never bothered him before; it was as things were meant to be.

Ra-khir glanced around the Fields of Wrath with obvious reluctance. He wasted a moment reading the sky as well. "Calistin, there's nothing I'd like more than to discuss this with you at length. I'll do so tonight, if you wish. But, for now, I'm on duty. I need to talk to others about what happened."

Calistin made a gesture of dismissal. Unlike Saviar and Subikahn, he had no idea what his father did and no particular desire to learn. He had noticed that Ra-khir spoke to Saviar differently than to him. The oldest of the brothers was expected to know how to handle himself around Ra-khir, his on- and off-duty personae and how to approach them. Ra-khir gave Calistin far more leeway, at least in this regard.

Ra-khir took a better grip on Silver Warrior's reins. Before he could signal the horse to move, Calistin spoke again.

"Papa?"

Ra-khir hesitated. A tolerant smile eased onto his features. Calistin rarely found him worthy of conversation. "Yes, son?"

The question tumbled out of Calistin's mouth, almost before he could stop it. "What does it mean when a young woman pats you on the bottom?"

A light flickered through Ra-khir's eyes, then disappeared. For an instant, Calistin thought his father would laugh at him, but Ra-khir maintained his composure. "It means she likes you."

"Likes . . . me?" Calistin supposed he knew that on some level. "Likes me . . . how?"

Clearly, Ra-khir considered his mission urgent and important, yet his hands eased on the reins, and he gave Calistin his full attention. "Did she say or do anything else?"

Calistin remembered clearly. "She winked. And brushed against me. She was talking about the type of man she wanted, and it sounded an awful lot like . . ." He trailed off, the connection suddenly clear. ". . . well, like me, I guess."

Ra-khir made a strange face. The corners of his lips twitched, as if trying to smile against his will, and he swallowed a laugh. "Does a cottage have to collapse around your ears before you realize it needs tending?"

Calistin supposed it would. He knew absolutely nothing about construction. "She wants to be my girlfriend," he realized.

"Do you want that?"

A smile eased across Calistin's features, beyond his control. "What should I do?"

Ra-khir remained silent. Calistin watched all amusement leave him. For an instant, he looked like he might actually cry, and the contrast with his recent amusement worried Calistin. "You really don't know?"

Calistin shook his head. "Should I . . . pat her bottom?"

"No," Ra-khir said, quickly. "Spend some time with her. Talk. Find things you both like to do."

"Like *svergelse*?"

"Sure. Why not?" Ra-khir added, "Just don't hurt or belittle her."

Calistin suspected Ra-khir would never have given such a warning to his brothers. They would instinctively know how to behave around a woman, how to treat a girlfriend.

"We can talk more about this tonight, too," Ra-khir promised. "If you want. When I'm off duty." Again he seized the reins, clucking for Silver Warrior to go.

"I'd like that," Calistin said, doubting his father had heard him. Emotions distracted warriors, and Calistin had long ago chosen to discard them. Yet, they had not, apparently, completely abandoned him. Treysind's soul had discovered them, determined to breathe new life into them; and Calistin did not feel wholly certain he wanted to escape. At least, not before he experienced romantic love.

Tae sprawled in a padded chair beside his bed, sweat dripping from his face and his arms limp on the rests. Imorelda purred in his lap, the sound shockingly loud in the hush, as if amplified. Ivana occupied Tae's bed, curled on the blanket like an animal, her broad thumb wedged into her mouth. Baby-fine hair lay in disarray across her cheek, and she snored erratically, just often enough to startle Tae each and every time. His mind glided back to Subikahn's youth, the boy lying still and innocent in sleep; but the analogy did not work. Watching his son rest had brought out every protective and loving instinct he had, while the girl evoked only sympathy and revulsion.

Had he not promised Tem'aree'ay, were she not the daughter of a respected friend, he would have avoided her altogether.

"What are you thinking?" Matrinka's voice came out of nowhere, startling Tae. He had forgotten she was there.

Well-trained to conceal discomfort, Tae hid his surprise behind a casual movement of his head in Matrinka's direction. He hoped she could not see the pulse hammering in his neck, the sudden stiffening of his fingers. "I'm trying to decide what I'm going to say to her parents." It was not true, but it was what he ought to be thinking. He deliberately turned his mind in that direction, interrupted by the squeak of the opening door. Tem'aree'ay floated through the crack, followed by the heavier bulk and tread of King Griff who scowled and examined the hinges. He had no way of knowing Tae preferred the noise; it warned him of visitors, wanted and unwanted.

Gently shifting Imorelda into his arms, Tae rose. "Come in. Sit." He waved Griff to his own chair.

The bearlike monarch of Béarn ignored the offering of the chair to seat himself, cross-legged, on the floor. Tem'aree'ay fluttered to the ground beside him. Never one for formality, Tae retook his seat without comment, and Imorelda settled back into his lap. Either she did not mind the movements, or she was too exhausted to complain.

Sitting on the only other chair in the room, a sturdy, high-backed seat with a pillow for a cushion, Matrinka looked nearly as tired as Tae.

Tae expected Ivana's parents to ply him with questions, forgetting elves rarely hurried and Griff displayed all the speed of a sleepy turtle. Tae had never met a more patient couple in his life. "As you both know, I spent the day working with Ivana."

Griff nodded solemnly, glancing at the sleeping child. Instinctively, his face broke into the fatherly grin Tae had not managed earlier. His dark eyes held all the charmed love Tae's lacked.

Tae tried to organize his findings. Though he and Ivana had performed few significant physical actions, the intensity of scrutiny and concentration had exhausted them both. "I did some reading, too, trying to learn as much as I could about . . ." He guarded his tongue, uncertain of the proper terminology. Parents had a way of blinding themselves to flaws in their own children. ". . . human imbeciles." He hesitated, judging their reactions.

The king and his second wife only watched Tae with proper focus, intent on his words.

"Ivana shows certain similar characteristics in her physical appearance as well as her actions." Tae did not think he was telling them anything they did not already know. He turned his attention fully on Tem'aree'ay. "Of course, there's nothing about elfin . . . defects in Béarn's library. Do elves suffer from . . . such abnormalities?"

Tem'aree'ay tipped her head. Gradually, her brow furrowed. She took longer than Tae would have thought necessary to consider the matter. Uncertain what to make of it, he glanced toward Matrinka, who shrugged.

Imorelda supplied the answer. *Remember? Elves don't spend a lot of time thinking about trends and details.*

For the first time, that seemed odd to Tae. Given centuries or millennia to live, he imagined he would consider every minuscule particular in the universe or risk utter boredom. He knew elves did not think like humans, however, and they mostly occupied themselves with play.

Tem'aree'ay answered eventually. "I can't recall any defective infants in my lifetime, nor any stories of such. We never become ill, per se, and our elders do not grow senile." She fell silent again but clearly had not finished.

Tae hesitated, allowing Tem'aree'ay to continue, although she had answered the question.

"I do know of one elfin imbecile, though he was not born that way. A powerful magical item rejected him. Explosively. So, apparently, it can happen."

Though intrigued by the story, Tae did not press. Likely, the thing this unfortunate elf had battled existed only on Alfheim. Its destruction at the *Ragnarok* was a sore subject with elves, Tae knew, and one he did not wish to raise at the moment. "I learned that, in some cases, a certain man or woman might produce imbeciles no matter who he or she coupled with. That's clearly not the case here. Griff has several normal children and, presumably, Tem'aree'ay, as an elf, cannot be the source of the problem. In other cases, the same couple can produce abnormal and normal children. The only thing for which we have no precedent at all is the coupling of elves with humans."

Tem'aree'ay answered more swiftly this time. Apparently, she did not have to give the matter much thought. "The elves believe it's the coupling itself. They think it's an unholy alliance and Ivana is an abomination." Her voice wavered, and Tae could not help looking for tears in her eyes. "They sequestered themselves so such a thing could never happen again, by chance or deliberation."

Tae did not want to press Tem'aree'ay but saw no way around it. "Do they know for certain the coupling is to blame? By some magical means? Or are they simply making assumptions?"

Tem'aree'ay sighed. "When I conceived Ivana, we thought we had found the answer to two problems." She gave Tae a searching look, hoping she did not have to explain.

Tae knew that, at the time of Ivana's conception, the *lysalf* and humans lived in grave predicaments. When killed unnaturally, elfin souls were forever lost. Whittled down by the *Ragnarok* and the division of the *svartalf*, they seemed doomed to disappear, slowly or suddenly. Meanwhile, the humans had suffered from an infertility plague inflicted upon them by the *svartalf*. Tem'aree'ay's pregnancy had seemed god-sent to rescue both groups from generational annihilation.

Over the years, Ivana's abnormalities had become more apparent. In the meantime, the sterility plague was lifted, allowing humans to procreate normally, and the elves had retreated to self-imposed isolation.

Tae raised his hand, rescuing Tem'aree'ay from explanation. Aside from Ivana herself, everyone in the room was familiar with the situation, including Imorelda. He repeated his question, which she had not yet answered. "Do the elves know for certain whether Ivana's condition occurred in spite of the pairing or because of it?"

Tem'aree'ay shook her head. "No one knows for certain, except perhaps the gods. And they aren't talking."

Tae realized she did not speak flippantly. In his youth, Griff had played with an "imaginary" companion/guardian, named Ravn, who had turned out to be the son of the goddess Freya and the immortal Renshai, Colbey Calistinson. Though exceedingly rare, the gods did, occasionally, interact with elves or humans.

The solution seemed obvious to Tae. "Why not make

another baby, then? If it's normal, we could put the contro-versy to rest. Those elves who wished to live among us could do so, and some humans might prefer to go to the elves. We could trade and communicate and intermingle freely." He smiled at the image. He would love to fully learn the elfin tongue, and he imagined they could teach others dancing, grace, quickness, perhaps even magic. They might find that a certain level of interbreeding brought strength and numbers to elves and humans alike. It still seemed like a winning scenario for both races.

King Griff buried his face in his hands. A look of horror stole over Tem'aree'ay's foreign features. "No," she said firmly. "No more children."

Clearly, the couple had discussed the matter on more than one occasion. Tae realized he had walked into a long-standing battle he might not wish to provoke, but the re-wards seemed too far-reaching to abandon. "How can it hurt to . . . just try?" Tae knew creating children was not a decision anyone should take lightly. Some couples felt it necessary to conceive as many as possible so a few might survive to continue their line. Others, like himself, found one difficult enough to handle. Some saw children as more hands to help, others as more mouths to feed. Griff consid-ered himself the father of seven children, including the de-ceased Arturo. Obviously, he had no particular desire to constrain himself to one, or even one per partner.

Griff's hand groped for Tem'aree'ay's. Her long, slender fingers disappeared into his enormous paw. Nevertheless, he made no attempt to take over the explanation.

Tem'aree'ay shifted closer to Béarn's king. Though she shared Griff as a husband, Matrinka smiled at their close-ness. The love between man and elf came through as clearly as her own for Darris. "People who don't have a child like Ivana can't ever really understand. We love our daughter, as all parents do; but we live in a fragile state, often running on exhaustion. Most of the time, I can't leave her side for an instant. When I do, I worry for her safety the entire time. The servants mean well, and they love their king, but they don't understand Ivana. Some fear her, some hate her, oth-ers she disgusts."

Tae forced his expression to a neutral state, concerned his own aversion to Ivana might become suddenly visible.

They trusted him to handle her appropriately, and he always would, but he had no idea how to get past the negative feelings she inspired in him. And he felt guilty for them, especially now that he had some understanding of her limitations.

Tem'aree'ay continued, and the fatigue now came out in her speech. "So, I rarely get a moment away from her. I'm worn out by the many battles. She can't express her frustration with words, so she throws tantrums. She doesn't understand what's safe or not, for herself or those around her. I have to constantly guard against her harming herself or others by accident. She can't handle her own . . . secretions and excretions. I'm always cleaning, always apologizing, always worrying that I'm not attending to her every need."

Tae felt more aware of a situation to which he had not given enough thought. Still, he saw a need he could not just release. "I get it, Tem'aree'ay. At least, as much as someone without a child like Ivana can." Tae could not help considering his own son. Subikahn had an affliction of sorts, a peculiarity that could result in his execution, at least in the Eastlands. Tae did not know how to explain it, but it was clearly not the simple choice he had once believed. He avoided the topic; Subikahn had a right to privacy. "But most people who have children have more than one, even those dealing with crippling abnormalities."

Griff finally spoke. "Tae, if solely up to me, I'd fill Béarn Castle with children."

Tae believed him. Fair and gracious, Griff had to make an excellent father. Aside from Ivana, every one of his children was well-liked and -mannered, even the ones sired by Darris.

The king continued, "Work grants me the time away that Tem'aree'ay can't take. By the time I take my shift with the children, I'm eager to interact with them all. I don't have a right to force her to care for another baby . . . like . . . Ivana."

Therein, Tae suspected, lay the real concern: the elves could be right. One Ivana proved difficult enough. Two would overwhelm Tem'aree'ay. "I don't think that's likely. I suspect a second baby would most likely be . . . normal."

Tem'aree'ay threw Tae's words back in his face. "Do you know that as a certain fact? Or are you simply making assumptions?"

Tae did not take offense, though he did smile at the clever turnaround. "Let's call it an educated assumption. After working with Ivana all day, I think I have some insight into what makes her the way she is and some ideas for how to improve her life." Tae pushed on, anxious to get his full point across before they forced him to focus on his findings. "If you gave birth to a relatively normal half-human child, it would prove the elves wrong. Even if you gave birth to another Ivana, it would not prove them right. Some families have more than one imperfect child and still make normal ones—"

The elf's sapphire eyes flashed. "You could never convince them. And they would condemn me for bringing another into the world, even if I believed I could handle two Ivanas."

Tae frowned but wisely kept silent. In most human cultures, including his own, defective children were humanely euthanized or abandoned to the elements, to the whim of the gods. Long ago, the Renshai had left every newborn outside overnight, believing only the strongest could survive the rigors of their training. Those born in winter were considered especially tough. The elves, however, found many human practices barbaric. This one, in particular, made no sense to them. Allowing an elfin baby to die meant losing a soul to oblivion, one less potential life for all eternity. Tem'aree'ay would parent any child she produced, even if it consisted of a disembodied lung and heart.

Tae sighed. Convincing Griff was not enough. Tem'aree'ay controlled her own fertility through magic. To her, eighteen years between children probably seemed a pittance. "Just promise me you'll think about it some more. To defeat the *Kjempemagiska*, we need magic as well as might. We need the elves. And, though they don't yet realize it, the elves need us in just as many ways. A normal coupling between an elf and a human would go a long way toward convincing them to return." It was a sore subject, and Tae knew it.

"Perhaps." Tem'aree'ay gave Tae the benefit of the doubt. "But another abnormal child would render your goal impossible. Better to try to convince them with words, once again, than risk alienating them forever."

Since the last Council meeting, Griff and others had held several discussions about ways to persuade the elves to join the forthcoming battle between humans and *Kjempe-magiska*. Until this moment, Tem'aree'ay had not given any indication she would assist, damning the attempt as futile. Without her, it seemed unlikely anyone could find the elves, let alone talk them into cooperating. "My lady, are you suggesting you would be willing to lead another expedition to your people?"

All heads flicked toward Tem'aree'ay. All eyes locked on her.

Tem'aree'ay looked carefully back at each of them in turn. Her triangular tongue flicked out to wet her lips, and she sighed deeply. "Lead it? No. Join it . . ." Tem'aree'ay's pause seemed to last a lifetime. ". . . maybe."

Tae found himself holding his breath and realized the other humans in the room were doing the same. No one wanted to miss Tem'aree'ay's explanation, no matter how softly spoken.

Tem'aree'ay continued to glance around the group. Apparently, she had considered herself finished, though her companions clearly wanted more. She added, "Don't look so surprised. I think every man, woman, and child currently in Béarn has requested, wheedled, cajoled, bullied, or begged me to join the expedition."

"Yes." Tae could not help but agree. "But, until now, you seemed . . . unwilling."

"Not so much unwilling as uncertain." Tem'aree'ay ran her long fingers across her forehead in a cross between an elfin gesture of understanding and human anxiety. "I personally know the power of one *Kjempemagiska*. It took three magical beings and two extraordinarily competent warriors to defeat him." She addressed the Easterner, "Tae, I believe you when you say these *Kjempemagiska* will return in force—"

Griff interrupted. "But will the rest of the elves believe us?"

Tem'aree'ay's brows rose. "I don't know," she admitted. "Proof would help, but we can try our best without it."

Tae had already received the Council's blessing to spy on the *Kjempemagiska*. He was waiting for Matrinka to clear him medically and for the promised "best sailor in Midgard" to arrive to assist. "If proof exists, I'll find it."

Matrinka cringed but said nothing. Tae suspected she would never clear him, always finding a reason why he had to become stronger before leaving Béarn. In the end, they both knew he would depart with or without her blessing. Reminded of the reason he had not yet departed, Tae rounded on Griff. "So, when is this mystery sailor arriving?"

"Any day now," Griff said, which only deepened Matrinka's grimace.

She could not help blurting, "I still think it's a bad idea. The last time Tae spied on the enemy, he came back . . ."

"Dead?" Tae inserted, deliberately antagonizing. She still would not admit she had tricked him into battling far longer than any human should have endured, had forced him to survive wounds that should have proved fatal.

"Nearly," Matrinka corrected. "And that was just against the nonmagical servants. Next time, I might not get to you quickly enough to save you."

"I let your husband choose my companions," Tae reminded, not at all sure what Griff had in mind. At the meeting, Tae had eventually agreed to take along a sailor and a bodyguard of Griff's choosing. Thus far, the king of Béarn refused to divulge their identities, revealing only that he had sent for the most competent sailor in Midgard and the bodyguard had to be Renshai.

Ivana loosed another loud snore that startled Tae. Once again, he had forgotten she was there.

Tem'aree'ay seized on the interruption. "We're here to discuss the future of my daughter."

Tae had not forgotten. He did have some positive news on that front. "As you told me, she's deaf to *khohlar*. That made me wonder if she had difficulty hearing regular speech as well. I've heard of cases where deaf people presented like imbeciles but responded swiftly to visual languages, even learning to read and write. If the deafness is incomplete, they can be taught to speak essentially normally with an ear horn."

Tem'aree'ay said simply, "Ivana is not deaf."

Tae had come to the same conclusion. "She isn't. But before I figured that out for certain, I taught her to communicate with signals. She learned seven consistently and strongly before I realized I got the same responses whether I used signals or words."

Tem'aree'ay and Griff leaned forward at precisely the same, interested angle. "Responses?" the elf said. "Ivana makes sounds: squeals, grunts, and screams. But she has never spoken."

Tae had also figured that out. "I don't know if she has mouth or throat issues, but she doesn't appear capable of forming words. She can, however, understand words and communicate them back using signals." Tae used information from his own life research. "All people understand many more words than they would ever think to use. It's most obvious with second and third languages. Many people can understand other languages but can't speak them, at least not fluently enough to carry on a conversation."

They all nodded. Even the elf was familiar with the concept.

"Animals can learn to understand hundreds of words of human speech, though it's rare for any of them to have a consistent sound to express something."

Imorelda bristled in his lap. *So we're stupid, are we?*

Tae realized his constant companion had remained unusually patient throughout the previous discussion. Usually, she felt compelled to add her opinion to everything. He chose an answer intended to fully appease her. *Present company excluded, of course, Imorelda. No cat, horse, or dog, and few humans, can match your brilliance.*

Imorelda's hair returned to normal, but she lashed her tail. *Which humans are these?*

Certainly not me, precious.

Imorelda made a sound that could pass for a sneeze but which Tae recognized as a snort. Arguing which of them was smarter could lead to nothing good. *But a few human geniuses do exist, and they might give you a challenge.*

The cat's tail continued to thrash. *Bring them on.*

Tae could do no such thing, and Imorelda knew it. He had no idea where Imorelda's intelligence would fall on a human scale, but she certainly knew enough to give him pause on a regular basis. Suddenly, he realized Tem'aree'ay, Griff, and Matrinka were staring at him. He tried to remember his last spoken words.

Apparently recognizing his dilemma, Imorelda cued him, *You were comparing their beloved child to a dog.*

Tae's cheeks turned warm. He hoped he had not offended them. "I knew Ivana had to be capable of much more than your standard animal, which means she probably has a receptive vocabulary of at least several hundred words. If we can get her to convey even a tenth of those, it should alleviate most of the frustration causing her to act out." He dared to meet Matrinka's gaze first. At least, she had no direct ties to Ivana. "The fact that I could do a full exam and teach her to communicate seven concepts in the same day suggests she has a lot of untapped potential." Finally, he braved the parents' eyes.

Griff wore a look of introspective glee. Tem'aree'ay showed less emotion, but the light did remain in her gemlike eyes. "What are the seven concepts?" asked the king of Béarn.

Tae demonstrated the proper hand movement as he named each one: "Yes, no, hungry, thirsty, sleepy, love, and chamber pot. If we can make up logical hand or movement signals, I believe she could easily pick up twenty new ideas per week without forgetting the old ones. Then, it's just a matter of teaching them to the staff to make Ivana mostly self-sufficient."

"Chamber pot?" Tem'aree'ay said hopefully. "Can you get her to properly use it?"

Tae gestured toward a pot in the far corner. "None of that's mine, and I didn't clean the floors. Once she learned the signal, she enjoyed making it. Every time she made the sign, I hauled out the pot and she tried to use it." Tae did not mention that the idea of changing a diaper or wiping up an accident for a grown woman revolted him. He doubted he had fully potty-trained Ivana in a single session, but she did seem interested in learning from him.

Griff practiced the gestures, mouthing them silently as he did so.

Tem'aree'ay went to the heart of the matter, the reason she had put daughter and friend together for the day. "Did you figure out why she's *khohlar*-deaf?"

Tae had initially spent a large amount of time exploring, relying mostly on Imorelda. He doubted he could say much now without the cat butting in. "I think there's some sort of barrier." He had difficulty translating the cat's ideas into logical human language, especially to those whose understanding of mental communication differed at best and had no basis at worst. "Usually, when I try to use my mind to talk to someone, I just concentrate on a thought and hope it goes where it needs to go. That's probably a lot less technical than *khohlar*, but it's all I have."

Tem'aree'ay only nodded.

Tae did not wish to reveal his connection to Imorelda, which limited his description even further. "It works for the *alsona*, but not for you or for any human I've ever tried. When we first came to you, I wanted to know if I could mentally communicate with elves and discovered I could not. At least, not with you."

Imorelda did not correct the fallacy, which Tae appreciated. Matrinka flinched. Had Griff and Tem'aree'ay not focused fully on Tae, she might have given his lie away. The truth was, he could only link with Imorelda and, through the cat, to *alsona* and Matrinka.

"With Ivana, it's not just sending a thought randomly into space. It's as if she has a . . . a . . ."

Imorelda supplied the same description she had the first time they tried to reach Ivana, *. . . pile of feces.**

Tae ignored her. ". . . barrier between her mind and the outside. Like a wall of . . . mud."

"Mud?" Tem'aree'ay's brows furrowed beneath her red-gold curls. "You mean, it's soft?"

"Sort of." Tae had as much trouble conveying the concept as Imorelda had had supplying it. "Softish. Brittle in spots, like drying . . ."

*. . . feces,** Imorelda contributed again.

". . . mud."

"Brittle," Tem'aree'ay repeated. "Like it could be broken?"

"Maybe." Tae hedged. Imorelda did not know, and he had nothing to go on but what she supplied him. "I don't think Ivana has any control over it. I can't help wondering if magic might . . . have . . . some way of dealing with it. Perhaps, if someone had the ability to physically enter her mind, the way you've described demons doing . . ." He looked askance at Tem'aree'ay. He had limited information about what magic could or could not do, but he suspected it had a better chance than anything mundane. He had no way of knowing whether breaking the barrier would heal Ivana, harm her, or kill her.

Tem'aree'ay's gaze flickered to the girl on the bed, still sound asleep. "It's not something I can explore by myself.

It's not my area; and, even if it were, it would probably require more than one participant." She pursed her lips into
a perfect heart. "But I don't know if the other elves would
help her, if they'd even dare to examine her. To them,
she's . . . anathema."

Tae raised his shoulders wearily to his ears, then dropped
them. He had nothing more to add.

Clearly sensing Tae's exhaustion, Griff clambered to his
feet. "Thank you, Tae. You've made an enormous difference."

Tae did not feel as if he had. "You know you're always
welcome."

Tem'aree'ay rose in one graceful movement, went to the
bed, and hefted Ivana. The girl flopped against her mother
without awakening. Griff made motions to take the burden,
but Tem'aree'ay shook him off. She had become accustomed to dealing with the girl who appeared to already outweigh her.

As the three moved toward the door, Griff promised.
"Get some sleep. I'll let you know when the sailor arrives."

Wearily, Tae nodded his agreement.

CHAPTER 10

*Bloodline and love are unrelated. To love someone only
because he shares your blood is as hollow and meaningless as loving someone only because he's young and beautiful. To a Northman, an unrelated blood brother becomes
more important than kin, since the bond is based on
honor and merit, not inescapable coincidence.*
— Colbey Calistinsson

SIR RA-KHIR KEDRIN'S SON sat attentively in his seat
in Béarn's sparsely furnished Strategy Room, relieved and
comfortable despite the forced rigidity of his posture. Anything seemed more attractive than his previous duty, attempting to keep peace between the Renshai and Paradisians,
investigating their accusations against one another, and
hauling in outraged combatants from both sides. Screamed
at by self-righteous bigots, pounded by belligerent drunk-
ards, besmirched by men deafened to reason by their own
one-sided certainties, Ra-khir had experienced more than
enough of the battle. Not for the first time, he found himself
questioning his fitness for his title, his dedication to the
Knights of Erythane.

In the chair to Ra-khir's right, his squire Darby perfectly
copied his pose. His brown hair combed to a sheen, his
clothing immaculate, the sword at the perfect angle on his
left hip, he looked the epitome of budding young knighthood. Yet, his eyes told a different story. The blue orbs had
lost their fiery gleam, now more quizzical and tired. Ra-khir

could never remember apologizing for the Knights of Erythane before; hard work and difficult moral dilemmas defined the order. Yet he seemed to do so every night since the Paradisians had claimed a stake in the Fields of Wrath.

To Ra-khir's left, Calistin sprawled in his chair, looking bored. The knight had gotten his youngest son to accompany him by proclaiming the possible dangers inherent in a journey to find the reclusive elves. Calistin could keep all of them safe, including King Griff's second wife, as well as serve as a representative for the Renshai. Ra-khir hated to admit he would have much preferred Saviar's company, Subikahn's, or, for that matter, almost any other Renshai.

Until after the war, Calistin had shown little interest in anything other than Renshai sword maneuvers. He displayed almost no affection for anyone; but, at least, he had clearly respected his mother for her competence and skill on the battlefield. Despite decades of effort, Ra-khir had never seemed to connect with his youngest. Their conversation the previous day, spurred by Valira's flirting, gave Ra-khir new hope. It would not prove easy, but he and Calistin might finally find common ground and experiences on a quest that took them far from the disputed Erythanian territory.

The door opened. Ra-khir rose from polite habit, Darby scrambling to do the same. Calistin merely rolled his eyes in the direction of the opening. He had scant experience with royalty, castle etiquette, and station.

Accompanied by his ever-present bard, King Griff ushered Tem'aree'ay into the room, empty except for the strategy table and its multiple, matching chairs. She wore a broad smile on her otherwise dainty face, and her gaze flitted over the room's occupants. Aside from the agelessness that accompanied every elf, and the canted eyes, she looked little different from a fine-boned, graceful human woman.

Griff looked ponderous in comparison, a stomping hairy beast with oversized features and massive hands. Ra-khir swiftly banished the image, replacing it with the grandeur befitting the West's high ruler. The knight bowed with a flourish that defined admiration and respect. Darby, as always, attempted to copy Ra-khir's movements, adding a gesture all his own.

The three newcomers took seats at the strategy table,

and Ra-khir and Darby sat only after assuring king and consort had done so comfortably. Calistin sighed, his boredom at the whole display evident. The Renshai glanced over the group. "Is this everyone?"

Ra-khir flinched, wishing he had managed to cram a few manners into his youngest.

Griff, however, took the rudeness in stride. He had become accustomed to Renshai abruptness, held little interest in formality, and rarely took offense at anything. "We have two more coming, representatives from the West and the North. The king of the Eastlands declined to add a delegate."

That did not surprise Ra-khir. Even after eighteen years, he had not grown accustomed to thinking of their sneaky, lowbrow friend as a king. Tae shunned decorum and ritual even more than Griff and Matrinka.

Griff added, "Darris and I are not going, of course. You'll have a party of six."

"Seven." The word seemed to float out of nowhere, remarkably soft and yet still strong and certain.

Griff stopped talking immediately and looked at Tem'aree'ay.

Cued by the king's gaze, Ra-khir also glanced toward the elf.

Tem'aree'ay explained, "I'm bringing Ivana." Her tone left no room for debate, but the shocked look snaking over Griff's face said otherwise.

"My darling," he started, an obvious attempt at diplomacy. "Don't you think we should have discussed this?"

"We're discussing it now." Tem'aree'ay's words left no opening for privacy. "Though I'm willing to wait until the last two representatives arrive."

As if on cue, Princess Marisole raced into the room, a long knife sheathed at her hip, a gittern across one shoulder, and a tooled leather quiver on the other. Ra-khir could see the top of a strung short bow sticking out of the center, with arrow-filled pockets on the side, their fletchings royal Béarnian blue with proper golden cock feathers. Every piece of equipment looked brand new, even the instrument, which she had surely played on more than one occasion.

Darris, her blood father, gave her only a stiff nod. Griff's mouth fell into a long oval, and his eyes widened to cow-like proportions. "What are you doing here, Marisole?"

Marisole took the seat beside Calistin, who eyed her gear critically. Ra-khir knew Renshai well enough to know they shunned ranged weapons as coward's toys and would see the musical instrument as nothing more than hindrance. Calistin might take some interest in the combat knife, however, as it fell somewhere between dagger and sword for length.

Marisole looked placidly at her father, as if he had asked the stupidest question in the history of the world. Then, sighing, she unslung the gittern and played a few resounding notes before singing in a youthful, confident tone. Though clearly improvised on the spot, the crudeness of the words disappeared beneath the perfect harmonics of voice and instrument:

> "The day has come for me to claim
> My rightful place as Béarn's bard's heir.
> As ingrained a part of the West's kingdom
> As the blue and the gold and the rearing bear.
>
> The bard's line is ineffably damned
> To a curse inescapable and lifelong.
> To acquire an unquenchable thirst for knowledge
> And the ability to impart it only in song.
>
> The bright part of this forever curse
> Is to serve as guardian to the great high king.
> I will proudly take my place
> When the dirge to brave Bard Darris we sing.
>
> Until that fateful day arrives
> I must gain knowledge, talent, and loyalty
> What better way to learn those things
> Then guarding important royalty.
>
> And so, I join the travelers six
> By land or over ocean's foam.
> Faithful to Tem'aree'ay
> I vow to bring her safely home."

When she finished, Ra-khir found tears in his eyes. Marisole had a stunningly beautiful voice, haunted by a depthless sorrow that had plagued her bloodline for centuries. The words themselves meant little, the rhymes clunky, yet understanding came clearly through the melody and rhythm. Marisole had come of age as a bard, inflicted with their boundless curiosity, their limited ability to communicate combined with an almost magical talent for swaying emotion with music.

When Ra-khir had first met Darris, at the age of seventeen, the curse had already embraced him. Marisole was nineteen. Apparently, whatever triggered the curse in the bard's heir had a timetable that had nothing to do with chronological age.

Ra-khir could not help pitying the girl. He had far more patience than most, but even he had found traveling with the bard's heir tedious. Tae used to roll his eyes, and Kevral would grow violent waiting for Darris to make a point. Bards could speak in normal conversation; but, when it came to divulging information, the curse forced them to sing. Now, Marisole, too, had apparently fallen prey to that scourge.

To an adolescent princess, it had to feel like a prison. She had to have to known this day would come, had prepared for it, at least in a musical way. Now, she would have to learn how to guard the king, whether Griff or his descendant, with an enthusiasm that would likely shorten her own life. She needed to learn weapons' skills with the proficiency of a man, a feat currently confined to Renshai and the bard, when female. Ra-khir masked a sniffle beneath a polite sneeze and unobtrusively brushed the tear from his eye.

Marisole played a few final notes as an ending, then placed the gittern on the table. Apparently, she anticipated the demand for further explanation.

King Griff's mouth had fallen so far open it appeared as if he planned to swallow her. He spoke so softly Ra-khir could not hear him, but he could read the words easily from the king's dry lips, "My daughters."

Ra-khir had no trouble understanding Griff's angst, either. Kevral had borne only sons, and Ra-khir appreciated that. His daughters would have had to undergo the same training as the boys; the Renshai made no clear distinctions.

Ra-khir had always known Kevral would die by the sword, but that had not eased the agony when it happened. He had found it almost impossible to continue without her, certain his heart would never heal. He doubted he could have survived the grief over losing a daughter in battle.

Ra-khir wished he could reassure the king. Whatever else happened, he would dedicate himself to making certain Tem'aree'ay, Ivana, and Marisole returned safely to Béarn. However, now was not the time to make promises he might not be able to keep. He had a feeling Griff would do what any father might and forbid his daughters from going. If so, whatever Ra-khir had to say would only sound foolish and as if he intended to dispute the king's decree.

Ra-khir felt lightheaded and, only then, realized he was holding his breath. Griff currently walked a fine line. If he forbade Ivana from going, Tem'aree'ay seemed unlikely to accompany them, either. Without her, they had no hope of finding and convincing the elves. At some point, Griff would also have to accept Marisole's god-granted position as the heir to the bard of Béarn and the dangers and responsibilities that came with the title. If he prohibited either daughter from going, then relented, he would appear hopelessly weak.

Ra-khir doubted the same options paraded through Griff's head. Simply, instinctively neutral, Griff had the luxury of following his impulses. Those rarely, if ever, steered him wrong. Ra-khir had seen the childlike king agonize over decisions, but he never seemed to make a mistake.

The arrival of the North's emissary put an end to those considerations. Valr Magnus stepped into the room, bowed dutifully to King Griff, then closed the door behind him. His sudden presence drew every eye, less because of his abrupt appearance than because he seemed to instantly fill the room. Large and well-muscled, he moved with a casual grace and seemed blissfully unaware of his remarkable good looks. Boyishly tousled hair fell in curls around chiseled, perfect features, his cheeks rugged and high-formed, his nose elegantly straight, and his honey-colored beard neatly trimmed.

Warmth suffused Ra-khir, and he suffered the image of Valr Magnus, huge and resplendent in his armor, thrusting a sword through Kevral's body. He knew the moment all too well. It had haunted his waking hours for months and plagued his nightmares to this day. The Northman had planted a foot on her abdomen to tear the blade free, spraying Kevral's lifeblood across the Fields of Wrath. So much had happened since that horrible day. Magnus had no hand in the deceit that won him that battle; when he learned of it, he had acted in an honorable fashion. Ra-khir wanted to forgive him, needed to for his own usually scrupulous integrity, but he could not banish the anger from his shattered heart.

"I sincerely apologize for my tardiness," Valr Magnus said in his Northern singsong. "I meant no disrespect, Your Majesty; but it was not fully decided until a moment ago who would represent us."

Griff finally found his tongue and his normal expression. "No apology necessary, General. You haven't missed anything."

The words were true enough, at least in regard to the quest.

To Ra-khir's surprise, Calistin demonstrated all of the enthusiasm his father lacked. "Valr!" The Renshai sprang from his seat and gave the huge Northman a brief but warm embrace. "I had no idea you were one of the choices."

Laughing, Valr Magnus caught Calistin, adding a hearty pat across the back. "It's mostly because of you that Erik picked me. When he thought Saviar was coming, he intended to send his son, Verdondi. But when he heard it was you, he demanded I go instead."

Calistin stepped back, challenge clear in his tone. "Ah. So he thinks you can handle me?"

"No one can handle you," Magnus assured him. "But at least I can *stand* you."

Calistin laughed and sat down again, and Magnus chose the chair beside him.

Stunned by the exchange, Ra-khir forced himself not to stare. He had never seen Calistin exchange friendly banter, let alone deliberately touch another human being. The grudging hugs he had managed to elicit as Calistin's father had ended the day the boy had passed his tests of manhood.

When Valr Magnus sat, Griff made a gesture to indicate the others should remain seated when he rose. "It seems everyone is here." He frowned. "Although, the Western representative is a member of my household, so I need to give the Western leaders the opportunity to add another."

"Done," Darris said, keeping his reply brief to avoid the need for song.

Ra-khir took that to mean the offer had been presented and declined; the Western leaders were content with Marisole serving as their delegate. Béarn was the high kingdom of the West and often stood in for the entire Westlands. Ra-khir knew Tae had also put his trust in the party as a whole, seeing no need to add anyone of Eastern background to the mix.

"Very well." King Griff gestured his bard toward the door. "Then we can leave our duly chosen representatives to their mission."

Darris rose dutifully but with obvious reluctance. Ra-khir understood his dilemma. The bardic curse plagued him with curiosity about the meeting he would miss but also obligated him to remain with Griff and keep him safe. They all watched the king and his escort leave and waited until the door clicked closed to speak.

Accustomed to command, General Valr Magnus took over the meeting, which, for reasons he could not explain, irked Ra-khir. "I believe we all know one another." He looked at each of them in turn.

Nods traversed the group.

"Do we know where we're going? Where we can find the elves?"

All attention shifted naturally to Tem'aree'ay, who studied Valr Magnus with patient, gemstone eyes. The silence that followed clearly did not bother her as much as it did the humans.

Knowing the answer, and feeling obligated to decrease the tension, Ra-khir answered. "Last we knew they lived on an island off the southern coast of the Western Plains."

The focus still remained on Tem'aree'ay.

Ra-khir continued, "However, the last time we sent an envoy there, we found no sign of them. We're not sure if they abandoned the island or hid themselves; but, unless Lady Tem'aree'ay has other ideas, it seems like the only logical place to start." Though he prodded gently by using her name, Ra-khir did not train his gaze on their only elf. It seemed rude to join the staring.

Finally, Tem'aree'ay seemed to realize she needed to say something. "I accompanied the previous envoy and did not see my people. Elves don't build permanent structures, though, and we can live in almost any environment. We leave little trace, even without using magic. My people could be hiding on the island, or even in Béarn's castle gardens, and no one might see them."

Those words did not bode well for their mission. Ra-khir frowned. "So they could be ... anywhere." He hoped Tem'aree'ay would put their minds at ease with some indication she had narrowed down the possibilities, that she had some inside information as to their location.

But Tem'aree'ay only confirmed the impression with a nod.

In his usual tactless manner, Calistin said the words that had to be on every mind. "What's the point of this? Wandering around aimlessly and hoping the elves take enough pity on us to come out of hiding?"

Tem'aree'ay sighed. Shrugged. Having dashed all hope, she finally added, "Some places are more likely than others; and, as I understand it, we need the elves desperately enough to make this trip necessary, if not worthwhile. Despite what I said about hiding in the castle garden, they wouldn't actually relocate near an established human city or town."

That information, though spare, gave Ra-khir an idea. "So, someplace humans would consider ... uninhabitable?"

Tem'aree'ay seemed to read his mind. "Inhospitable, maybe, but not uninhabitable. Even elves wouldn't consider the Western Plains, for example. The only water there is salty, and it's wide open. Elves prefer cold to heat, forest to barren land, and we would never consider living underground." She shivered at the very thought.

Ra-khir managed a smile. Humans might share the elves' aversion to darkness, but they nearly always chose warm over cold and farmland over forest. Apparently, the *Kjempemagiska* agreed. One of their largest miscalculations was assuming the Northlands were too cold for human habitation. Still, Tem'aree'ay's qualifications did not seem terribly helpful. It still left scattered pieces of the entire continent open for exploration, let alone islands and atolls.

They might search for years without finding any more

elves, especially if the elves did not want finding. With a population of only two hundred, a number that could only shrink over time, the elves did not require a lot of territory in which to hide. Still, a fruitless quest seemed more inviting to Ra-khir than the frustrating tedium of mediating between Paradisians and Renshai.

Darby cleared his throat gently. Thus far, he had not spoken, but the ensuing silence goaded even him. "I suppose if we started on Elves' Island, came to shore on the Western Plains, and worked our way outward in back-and-forth semicircles, we might just uncover signs of elves within a . . . few years." He spoke in even tones, with no hint of sarcasm.

Tem'aree'ay bobbed her head agreeably, as if he had made a cogent point.

For an instant, no one moved or spoke. The genius of the comment struck Ra-khir, and a new respect grew for his young apprentice. Darby had made several important points in a single statement, without presumption or insult. First, he had outlined the futility of the mission in its current form to the humans. He had also exposed the communication gap. To Tem'aree'ay, such a quest seemed reasonable because a few years, or even decades, meant little to her. Her mind grasped the quest as something to accomplish, and the idea of time constraints did not play into her logic.

Calistin stared, as if he thought all of them had gone mad.

Apparently also able to infer the purpose of Darby's comment, Valr Magnus said carefully, "True enough. But we have weeks, months at most. We'll have to greatly narrow our search." He directed his question to Tem'aree'ay. "Do you think we could pick out the two or three most likely places and concentrate on those? We may not find the elves; but, at least, we will have made the best faith effort given the constraints of time."

Tem'aree'ay cocked her head, clearly considering the point. By now, she must have some experience with human urgency. She might not fully understand it, but she should know of its existence and have some insight into its purpose. "Weeks or months?"

"Yes," Valr Magnus confirmed, pinching his honey-colored beard. "Enemies rarely offer a time schedule; but, it does us no good to recruit elves after we've already lost the war. In fact, were it not for the fact that we don't know from which direction the next attack will come, I'd insist that this many of our best warriors . . ." He made a gesture that encompassed every member of the group. ". . . remain in Béarn. Currently, Tem'aree'ay, you're all the reliable magic we have, and our world needs you more than anyone."

Though he despised agreeing with his wife's killer, Ra-khir nodded enthusiastically for the sake of the world. He felt certain Griff had already made clear how important Tem'aree'ay was to the continent as well as to this mission. "We're on a deadline, and we can't afford to fail. Please, Tem'aree'ay, help us narrow down our options."

Tem'aree'ay lowered her head, appearing as weary as an elderly human. She dropped any pretenses. "I've been praying daily to Frey, our creator, god of elves and sunshine, but he gives me no answers. It's said that when the elves lived on Alfheim, he walked freely among us, even joining our play. Since the *Ragnarok*, when our world, Alfheim, burned and some of us escaped to Midgard, we have seen too little of him. He did come to take the *svartalf* to Svartalfheim. At the time, the *lysalf* chose to stay on Midgard, hopeful for a new camaraderie with humans, our lives woven together. Ivana put an end to that. The elves worried her affliction was an omen, that the gods had punished us for becoming too interrelated."

Ra-khir finally understood. "You're worried they might be right, that Frey has abandoned you and Ivana because she wasn't meant to exist."

The smile that nearly always graced Tem'aree'ay's features disappeared, making her look strange and unwelcoming. For the first time, Ra-khir could see her as something not at all human. "My daughter is not a mistake, not some divine form of punishment." She spoke with the leaden emphasis reserved for those who need to convince themselves as much as anyone else. "Even if Frey, himself, abandons me, I will never believe it. I'm more concerned that the *lysalf* may have left Midgard entirely. They could have convinced Frey to take them to live with the *svartalf*."

Ra-khir bit his lower lip hard enough to hurt. He had never considered the possibility the elves had left their world entirely. If so, they could not be found, could not be coaxed. A single elf did not have the power to travel between worlds. It had taken a *jovinay arythanik*, the shared spell of dozens of elves, to transport Ra-khir and his companions between worlds when they had sought to end the infertility plague. Suddenly, Tem'aree'ay's reluctance to lead this mission became abundantly clear. If the elves had left Midgard, she would never see any of them again. And she would have to accept something no mother ever could: her child really was anathema, damned by her creator.

Now, the need to find the elves became even more necessary to Ra-khir. He could not allow Tem'aree'ay to lose faith in her daughter and her deity, could not accept that her people had forsaken her to such an extreme they chose to leave the world itself rather than risk bringing another Ivana into it. He tried to reassure. "My lady, I've been told that, on Midgard, gods rarely interact with mortals and only in the most dire of circumstances. Unlike Alfheim, our world requires neutrality to exist. That's why it's critical the right king or queen sits upon the throne of Béarn. Passing the Pica Test is impossibly grueling in order to assure that only a pure and worthy bastion of balance rules the West."

Ra-khir had learned what he knew from the gods-charged keeper of that neutrality, the immortal Renshai, Colbey. "Unlike elves, humans have no magic." Ra-khir frowned, realizing Chymmerlee had disproven a statement he had long considered fact. "Well, very little, anyway. Because of that, even small acts of magical beings have enormous effects on our balance. When gods interfere, even with the best of intentions, they risk destroying us. Perhaps Frey has not answered your prayers because he believes it safer for you to find the way without his assistance."

Tem'aree'ay sat back. She could take hours or days to mull the matter.

Calistin lacked her elfin patience. "Colbey has been known to interact with humans, and his son has done so on at least one occasion." He looked pointedly at Ra-khir.

Ra-khir's blood seemed to freeze in his veins. *What does he know?* A vow on his honor kept him from revealing Calistin's blood origins, but he had never liked the situation. Misleading anyone bothered him, most especially his son, particularly since Ra-khir had come to hate his own mother and stepfather for a similar deception. They had changed his name from Rawlins to Khirwithson and attempted to convince everyone that Khirwith was the only father he had ever had. They had treated his blood father, Kedrin, cruelly and denied him any sort of interaction with his son. But young Ra-khir had remembered his father, enough to innocently turn his own name into a hyphenated amalgam. And when his mother forced him to choose between parents, he had selected the father who loved him rather than the mother who loved only herself.

Despite their similarities, the situations were vastly different. Ra-khir had vowed to keep his silence to protect the kingdom of Pudar as well as Colbey's family. The king had extracted the promise in exchange for allowing Kevral and Ra-khir to raise her son rather than the Pudarian king. In a misguided attempt to prevent the termination of the royal bloodline during the sterility plague, King Cymion had imprisoned Kevral and forced his only living son upon her.

Colbey's son, Ravn, had given Kevral the option of conceiving with him instead, and Kevral had chosen what she considered the lesser of evils. At Colbey's direct request, Ra-khir had raised Calistin as his own, the only father Calistin had ever known. Doing so protected not only Calistin, but the royal family from its embarrassing misdeed as well as Colbey and Ravn who could not significantly intervene in Calistin's upbringing without threatening the world's balance.

Ra-khir had never appreciated any kind of deception, but especially one that forced him to lie daily to his own sons. However, it had been the only way to assuage Kevral, prevent a deadly war, and rescue Calistin from life as the heir to a royal rapist. Again, it had required a choice between evils, and Ra-khir had taken the most honorable of several ignominious paths. Now, it seemed, Calistin had obtained information that might drastically change their relationship. Ra-khir only hoped for good, not ill.

All of these thoughts flashed through Ra-khir's mind in an instant, never far from the surface. He addressed Calistin's remark rather than his intimation. "Colbey has interacted with humans, even with me; but Colbey is not an actual god."

Valr Magnus cocked his head, examining Ra-khir quizzically. "Forgive my ignorance, but I was taught that a belief in the divinity of Colbey Calistinson was the major contention between Northern religion and that of the Renshai."

Ra-khir appreciated the opportunity to explain because it also addressed the potential new problem threatening his relationship with his youngest son. "Actually, Magnus, the major contention between Northern and Renshai religions is whether the *Ragnarok* is imminent or has already occurred. If the gods responded to prayers on Midgard, we would know the answer. The Renshai believe only a handful of them survived the *Ragnarok*, while the North feels equally certain it has not yet happened so the entire pantheon still exists. If Odin or Thor or Ullr, all dead by Renshai reckoning, revealed their presences to mankind, we would have to favor the explanation of the North. If, however, only Frey and Vidar and a handful of others did, we would have to favor the Renshai's version."

Heads bobbed around the table, some with wordless resignation, others with boredom. Ra-khir had not yet gotten to the point he wished to make and realized others did not share his patience. "That Colbey still lives some four hundred years after his birth is not in contention." He turned his gaze on Valr Magnus, "Is it?"

The Northern warrior's hand fell to his hilt, not in anger but memory. "Not to me," he admitted.

Ra-khir continued, "Colbey carries the blood of Thor and a mortal Renshai. The woman died in combat during her pregnancy, and Thor rescued the fetal Colbey to implant him in another Renshai womb. Neither Colbey, nor his mortal parents, knew his bloodline was not theirs growing up. Even long after Colbey learned the truth, he forever considered himself Calistin and Ranilda's son." Ra-khir did not add that they had raised and loved and taught him. Blood might be thicker than water, but love and availability trumped everything. Overdoing the point, making the comparison too obvious, might have the opposite of its intended effect on a man of Calistin's age.

Valr Magnus cocked his head. "So . . . Renshai believe Colbey is half-god. But . . . not divine?"

Ra-khir realized, in his eagerness to make a secret point to his son, he had not fully made the obvious one. "Colbey does not consider himself a god, merely an immortal. The gods tolerate his presence, some may even like him, but they do not accept him as one of them. The preferred terminology is 'the immortal Renshai.'"

Valr Magnus stroked his beard. "Interesting."

"And yet," Ra-khir realized aloud. "Of no significance to our current task." It occurred to him that the mix of people assigned to this undertaking might undo it. Tem'aree'ay was too patient to interfere when conversations went off on tangents. Marisole's need to sing would only prolong them. Darby would never consider interrupting his master or others he considered his superiors. Ivana could barely communicate, and Calistin took little interest in matters outside of swordplay and practice. It would fall to him and General Magnus to keep the party focused and on task. And Ra-khir could barely stand the Northman.

CHAPTER 11

*To have one's son finally surpass him is the secret dream
of every father.*

— *Talamir Edminsson*

A BRILLIANT ORANGE SUN hovered over the western
horizon, and the first hint of evening gray stole color from
the gardens. Outside the compound, Tae peeked over
Béarn's castle wall, watching three guards amble through
the flower and vegetable beds, poking their heads behind
benches and into every gazebo. Tae had spent most of his
day watching them, confused by changes in their usual patterns and procedures. He had seen Ra-khir and Darby
enter, the knight insisting on stabling his own white charger
and Darby his gelded chestnut. Valr Magnus had arrived
soon after, but Tae doubted their presences had anything to
do with the oddities of the day and the changes in the duties
of Béarn's guardsmen.

The need to understand had become an obsession. Tae
could not quite creep near enough to hear the guards without them spotting him as well. In the last hour, he had determined they seemed to be looking for something, but he
could not figure out the objective of their search. He had
not intended to engage in spying games, but he had risen to
the bait throughout the day, testing his limits and honing his
skills simultaneously.

Tae lowered himself to the ground with a silent sigh.
When he rated his performance, he deserved high praise for

avoiding detection and visualizing the targets. However, he considered the mission a failure because he still could not surmise the purpose of their actions. He would need to work on his listening skills prior to studying the *Kjempe-magiska*. While counting them, gaining a feel for their activities, and glimpsing what they could do with their magic would all help their cause, absorbing their strategies and intentions would prove far more useful.

It occurred to Tae that the enemy's methods of communication would work to his advantage. While they also tended to resort to speech for quiet conversation and covert operations, they did not hesitate to mentally broadcast commands and the less private portions of their life. While some of their assumptions about the continental peoples had caused them to underestimate numbers and come mostly unprepared for answering magic, they still had no reason to believe anyone from Tae's part of the world could "hear" their mind speech or understand their language. *Of course, there, I'll have to sneak around with a flabby tabby on my shoulders.* Tae was careful not to broadcast that thought. He had no idea where Imorelda had gone, but she would surely take offense.

Prepared to peer over the wall again, Tae looked up, only to find a furry face staring down at him from the pinnacle. Imorelda perched on the walltop, her silver fur nearly disappearing into the grayness of twilight, the white tip at the end of her tail curling and flopping in turns. He had no idea how long she had been sitting there watching him. She waited for him to meet her amber gaze before she finally addressed him. *I know what they've been looking for.* A catty smugness accompanied the sending.

Though intensely curious, Tae feigned indifference. *So do I.*

Imorelda called his bluff. *Do you? Because I don't think you do.* Her haughty complacency grew to the level of provocation.

Tae tried one more gambit. *I don't think you know. You're just trying to taunt me into telling you.*

Imorelda snorted. Tae had heard that sound before and always suspected it took the place of a human chuckle. *Fine, then. I won't tell you.* She hiked up her tail, flipping it over her nose to hide her entire face.

They had come to a stalemate Tae could only lose. He drew in a deep breath, though he did not intend to make a sound. *All right, you win. What are Béarn's guards looking for?*

Imorelda lowered her tail enough to reveal a catty grin. *You.*

All of the gathered breath left Tae in a rush.

I knew you didn't know.

Tae could hardly deny it. *They're looking for me personally? Or they're looking for someone sneaking around Béarn Castle?* The answer mattered; Tae hated to think his practice scouting had taken security from more important matters, nor that he had grown clumsy enough for them to worry about a breach in security.

They're looking for Tae, the irritating, disappearing king of the Eastlands.

"Damn," Tae said, though secretly pleased. He had managed to evade Béarn's entire security force while never leaving the city.

His pleasure must have leaked through to Imorelda. Her tail lashed, and her gaze intensified. *You know, you wasted a lot of their time. Griff's getting concerned about what happened to you.*

Tae hid his pleasure behind an appropriate air of chastisement. *You're right. I need to put them out of their misery.*

I'm always right, Imorelda reminded him. *And you're going to have to do a better job of hiding your glee from Griff and his men. You don't want to insult them, do you?*

Tae did not, but he felt certain they could not read him the way Imorelda did. *Do you know what they want?*

The long-awaited sailor has arrived. Griff wanted you down at the docks.

Tae gestured for Imorelda to come down from the wall. She crouched, then launched herself toward him. Tae barely had time to brace himself before she slammed into his arms and against his chest. He staggered backward a step, righted himself, and took a more dignified hold on the cat. *I didn't necessarily mean for you to land on top of me.*

Imorelda ruffled her fur. *Is that a snide way of calling me fat?*

Tae dodged his earlier, silent characterization of Imorelda

as a "flabby tabby." *It's a direct way of asking you not to fling yourself at my still-recovering body suddenly and at great speed.* Tae hugged Imorelda's warm mass against him.

Imorelda licked her striped fur back into place. *So, I'm supposed to fling myself at the cold, hard ground?*

If you can climb up something, you should be able to climb down it. Yes?

Imorelda unsheathed her claws abruptly and sank them into Tae's flesh.

Pain flashed through Tae's forearm. It was all he could do not to drop her, though when he managed to keep her in his arms, he wished he had followed his instincts instead. She deserved to fall. "Ow, damn it!"

Imorelda retracted her claws immediately. *Do those feel like they're designed for upside down use? They're curved, you silly two legs.*

Tae examined his arm. He could see the individual impressions of the claws, but not one had broken skin. *When I climb down, I never go head first.*

Well, unless you have eyes in places I don't care to know about, it's a good way to wind up with a stick or a sword up your ass.

Tae realized Imorelda had a point. Cats did prefer high places, and they climbed effortlessly. Designed for pouncing from above, they often appeared to have trouble descending. He had watched cats pace elevated branches for hours, even days. It was a wonder the world's trees were not festooned with feline skeletons. Tae also realized the conversation served no purpose other than delay. Apparently, some piece of him worried more for the mission, and his life, than he let on even to himself. *Imorelda, do you think they're still waiting for me? At the docks?* Still carrying the cat, he headed toward the ocean.

To Tae's relief, Imorelda took his hasty change of topic in stride. *I've seen Griff and Darris come and go. The sailor's probably carousing in a tavern, but I think we can count on whatever ship he sailed in on still being there.* She clambered onto his shoulders for the ride.

Tae nodded. Although his only sailing experience came from being a passenger, he had read enough to recognize construction. The type of ship the sailor had used could, at least, pinpoint his origin. Thus far, Griff had refused to identify Tae's companions, stating that he worried about making a promise on which he could not deliver. Tae had made it clear he wanted the smallest, least obtrusive ship that could still make it safely across a vast stretch of ocean. Anticipating an enormous crew, he planned to anchor just beyond view of the *Kjempemagiska's* island and take a smaller boat to shore alone. He already knew they would have to use great caution. Magical seeing might far outdistance his own.

Tae thought it best to remain hidden as he worked his way to the docks. He did not want people stopping him every few steps to inform him that others were seeking him or that he needed to go where he was already headed. Though slinking through shadows lengthened his walk, he still arrived much more quickly than he would have had he conversed with several people along the way. Soon enough, he arrived at Béarn's shore, still littered with hunks of smashed and burned planking from the *alsona's* once-massed ships. The warships sat, quiet, in the harbor; the flimsier lower docks contained only a handful of Northern longboats, flying the colors of their tribal origins. The *alsona* had quashed ocean trading, and no merchant ships had come to Béarn in the weeks leading up to, and during, the war.

Only one ship appeared out of place, a relatively tiny clinker-constructed lateen with two masts and a jib. Built with an angular elegance that made the other ships appear clunky, it did not seem sturdy enough to survive on the open sea. It had lines composed of a substance Tae had seen only once before, on the magical ship piloted by the oldest of all the elves who named himself Captain. *Captain?* Tae shook his head in disbelief. *Can't be. If Griff had connections with the elves, Tem'aree'ay would not be so concerned about finding them.* Yet no other possibility presented itself. Only the millennia-old elf could safely pilot such a craft in the vastness of the ocean.

As Tae drew closer, he made out a figure on the deck. Lean and wiry, it moved with the confidence and grace that characterized the most talented dancers. Every slat and line, every clamp and spar underwent repeated, minute inspection. Soon, Tae recognized the red-brown hair, randomly sprinkled with silver and knotted at the nape of the neck, the sun-baked skin, and the androgynous figure. *Definitely*

Captain. Tae broke into a run, and Imorelda's claws sank into his shoulders.

Leaping onto the dock, Tae raced to the lateen-rigged ship and sprang aboard. He landed neatly on the deck, hollow footfalls revealing the presence of a cabin in the hull. Captain had always favored below-deck quarters over castles. Armed with new information about ships, Tae suspected the elf looked upon his rare passengers as ballast and at above-deck constructions as interfering with the precious balance of his ship and the tiny nuances of its piloting. He was as fastidious about his seacraft as Renshai about swords, and Tae did not fault him. After thousands of years on the sea, Captain had to know just about everything; and, when it came to ships, Tae could think of no one in whose hands he would rather place his life.

Before Captain could do more than face the threat of a sudden boarding, Tae caught him up in a welcoming embrace. "Captain, you old sea dog. I had no idea Griff could find you, let alone convince you to come."

Captain laced his arms around Tae as well, without the boisterous enthusiasm Tae had displayed. His amber gaze locked on Imorelda, and he seemed worried to bring his face too near her. "Tae Kahn Weile's son. You look—"

"—old?" Tae inserted. Eighteen years passed like nothing for elves, especially one as ancient as Captain. To them, humans probably appeared to wither as swiftly as fruit on a vine.

"I was going to say 'great.'" Captain unwrapped himself from Tae. "I'm hardly one to judge another's age."

Tae could scarcely argue. Captain claimed to have long forgotten the number of years that had passed since his birth, along with his given name. "True, but you never look a day older, gods damn you."

Captain studied Imorelda from all sides. "I thought your companion was the one with the cat."

Tae saw no reason to delve into details. They would have more than enough time for small talk on the voyage. "Matrinka's infected me with her craziness, and Imorelda's no ordinary cat."

So now it's crazy to associate with a cat?

Tae had known Imorelda would take offense, the reason he had added the second part of his comment. *It's a bit crazy to carry one on a ship. Would you even agree to come if I didn't need you?*★

 ★*You always need me. You're helpless without me.*★

Tae chose not to argue. He could not risk upsetting her when his life, and so many others, relied upon her bridging the gap between his mental abilities and those of the enemy.

Captain reached a tentative hand toward Imorelda. "Nothing about you is ordinary, Tae Kahn. Like arriving without escort when the whole of Béarn is out looking for you. And jumping onto a captain's ship without requesting permission to board and not getting yourself incidentally skewered."

Tae looked over Captain, for show rather than any necessary reason. Other than a utility knife, Captain never carried a weapon. "Were you planning to 'skewer' me with your bare hands?"

"No," Captain admitted. "I thought I'd leave that to the rampant Renshai that King Griff chose to accompany us."

Tae stiffened involuntarily and dropped to a wary crouch. He could not believe he had missed someone else on board, especially one quick enough to kill him. Imorelda's claws penetrated deeper.

A sinewy figure stepped from the shadows of the mast. "I'm not rampant enough to kill the charge I'm here to protect." Bronze-colored braids dangled around a circular, female face; and gray eyes studied Tae fiercely.

Tae recognized Rantire immediately. Appointed by Ravn to keep Griff safe prior to the day he took the throne, Rantire took her work seriously. Rigidly dedicated, she guarded him so tightly he could scarcely move. Had any king other than Griff assigned her to him, Tae would have believed he did so from selfish reasons, to rid himself of her overbearing presence. But Tae would never ascribe such motives to innocent, kind-hearted Griff. More likely, he had wanted Tae to have the most devoted guardian he could find, just as he had insisted on the most competent sailor.

The captain placed a loving hand on the foremast. "Shipmaster, when do you wish to set sail?"

Tae laughed. "You're the shipmaster, Captain." He stopped himself from adding that the elf should determine the time of launching. Though Captain had spent the majority of his millennia on Midgard and had the most human mannerisms of his kind, he still might not recognize the urgency of this quest. Tae would have preferred an immediate departure, if only to forestall the teasing he deserved for spying on those openly seeking him without recognizing their goal. "Did you know there's another group of us preparing to meet with the elves?"

Captain nodded. "King Griff mentioned it."

"Have you spoken with them? I'm sure they could use your guidance."

Captain's features turned pensive, more alien. "Really?" He chuckled. "Then they truly are desperate."

"Would you mind trying to help them, at least?" Tae gestured toward the castle built into the mountain. "I'm sure they would appreciate anything you might know." He added casually, "And I'm sure Rantire would like one more night to prepare. We'll meet back here in the morning and cast off before lunch."

Imorelda saw through him. *You sneak. You're looking for a way to ditch the bodyguard.*

It bothered Tae that Imorelda knew him better than he knew himself. He had not yet considered his motives in such detail. *Do you want to travel with her? Let alone try to spy in secret while she's all over us? At the first sign of trouble, she'll want to fight, six hundred to two. I work much better when no one knows I'm around.*

Imorelda shook out her fur. *You don't have to justify it to me. I hate her.*

Tae kept himself from frowning. He always tried not to allow his mental conversations to leech into physical expression. Imorelda could read his moods through the process and did not require it, and she could not see his face while perched on his shoulders anyway. *Hatred's not fair or reasonable. She's only doing her job; and she's expert at it.* Trying to play both sides did not suit Tae. *It's just, I'm not an heir to Béarn's throne, so her job doesn't include me. Even if her master ordered it.*

Tae clambered back onto the dock. Captain sprang up after him. He offered a hand to Rantire, who refused it with a glare, then leaped to the dock with a dexterity that rivaled his own.

You know, you promised Griff you'd take his sailor and bodyguard.

Tae remembered his exact phrasing. *Actually, I prom-

*ised I would take his sailor and a Renshai bodyguard. All I have to do is find one a bit less . . . impassioned.**

Imorelda made a sound like a single, tamped purr. **A restrained Renshai? Good luck.**

I know just the one. Tae could think of no Renshai he would prefer to have accompany him more than Saviar, though he recognized the irony. When they had traveled together, Ra-khir's rigid honor had driven Tae to insanity; yet it was the manners Ra-khir had instilled in his son that made Saviar the most contemplative and easygoing of the Renshai. Tae only wished the twins had not disappeared shortly after the war. **Unfortunately, I don't know if I can find him.**

You'd have had a lot better chance if you hadn't wasted the day playing hide-and-seek with Béarn's guardsmen.

Tae could hardly argue. **You're right, as usual, my love.**

They headed in silence toward Béarn Castle, each, apparently, lost in his or her own thoughts. Tae realized he did not have enough time to travel all the way to the Fields of Wrath to choose the best Renshai to accompany him. He would have to content himself with one already at the palace, which might prove difficult. Most, if not all, of the Renshai remaining in Béarn had been assigned to guard a particular heir who they would not abandon. In fact, Griff had probably chosen Rantire because she was redundant, free to leave on the quest whether or not she wanted to do so.

Tae's thoughts next went to the only Renshai in his command. Subikahn's lover, Talamir, led a phalanx of the Eastern army by a strange twist of fate. Tae had condemned the Renshai to death before being called to Béarn. In Tae's absence, Weile Kahn had stayed the execution and elevated Talamir to his current position. Tae now appreciated his father's interference. A skilled and good man would have died, and Subikahn would never have forgiven him.

Tae contemplated the thought of traveling with Talamir as his bodyguard. Though initially uncomfortable, the trip might give the two an opportunity to bond, to use their mutual love of Subikahn to become uneasy friends. Tae had grown up with the understanding that sodomy was repellent, shameful and loathsome, a capital crime without excuse or reason. Changing lifelong thought patterns did not come easily to anyone, and shifting his perceptions from Talamir as corruptor of his son to treasured by his son was a slow and painful process for Tae.

The troops had come to appreciate Talamir's intelligence and competence with a sword. Quick-thinking and -acting, he had won them over, as well as Weile Kahn, Subikahn, and even, grudgingly, Tae himself. Tae supposed weeks trapped on a ship with Talamir might force him to gain new insights, perhaps even teach him to value the Renshai as a general and a future son-in-law.

Though logical, Tae discarded the thought. He preferred Talamir to Rantire as a traveling companion, but his army needed all of its lieutenants to guide them in Béarn and bring them safely home. Tae required his wits about him on this mission, and he did not know if dealing with an issue fraught with emotional peril might distract him. Even the in-laws of arranged marriages did not always get along with one another, and he still had serious conflicting feelings about the entire situation.

While Captain and Rantire went directly to Béarn Castle, Tae found himself avoiding it without intention, instinctively choosing a path that took him to the outskirts of Béarn. For some time, he meandered along the edges of the mountain city, no attention given to location or goal, lost in thoughts of the upcoming mission. He did not want to talk to anyone at the palace, not to Matrinka, not to Darris, not to Griff, not to anyone who might mention Rantire.

Tae did not know how long he had wandered aimlessly, but his shoulders ached from the weight of the cat, his gut growled from missing dinner, and he suddenly realized he had no clear idea where he was. The sun was slipping below the western horizon. The world around him had become shrouded in gray, premature dusk created by the confluence of trees, and the stony city streets had given way to dirt pathways lined with brush. Just to Tae's left, something moved, an inky shadow slightly denser than the surrounding darkness. Wariness seized him. His heart quickened, and he trained his gaze fanatically on the figure, even as it disappeared into silent immobility.

For a long time, Tae remained in place, trying to visually carve the figure from the darkness again. Human, he believed, or perhaps elfin, it moved with a natural grace and a well-trained ability to lose itself in shadow. Patiently, he watched the spot where he had last seen it, eventually re-warded by another movement as it glided deeper into the trees. Tae hesitated, wondering why he felt compelled to follow it. While in the woods, it posed him no threat, and he had no wish to face a bear or even a large deer so far from anyone who could assist him. However, with thoughts of spying on the *Kjempemagiska* foremost in Tae's mind, it occurred to him that he had to worry for the enemy having the same idea. They had not come to the war wholly ignorant.

The idea that he might have discovered an enemy spy be-came an obsession. Worried to lose track of the other, Tae followed the slithering figure soundlessly through the wood-lands, taking care not to snap a twig, rattle brush or shuffle a pile of old leaves. The longer he followed, the more certain he became that it was human or, at least, humanoid. It moved with a wary caution that suggested it, too, fretted over making a revealing noise, and its pauses seemed more deliberate and well-timed than an animal. Then, abruptly, it disappeared.

Damn. Tae shuffled cautiously forward, parsing shadows, seeking anything out-of-place as the setting sun made his job progressively more difficult. At length, he discovered something small, glinting red in the gathering dusk. Tae ap-proached it cautiously, inching toward it with a slow steadi-ness intended to hide his movement. As he edged forward, he suffered an internal buzz of warning, a sensation of twice-seeing, as if he had lived this precise moment before. It reminded him of a maneuver he had invented: leaving a small, metallic object, usually a coin, in the path he had been following, as a distraction, before doubling straight back behind his pursuers. Tae froze in place.

Above! Imorelda shouted suddenly in his head. She leaped from his shoulders.

Tae dodged sideways. The weight intended to land fully atop him caught him a glancing blow instead. That proved enough to drive him off his balance. He toppled, attempted to roll, to catch his feet under him. The other was faster, more agile. It scrambled on top of him. In an instant, cold steel touched his throat. Tae went utterly still.

Images flashed into Tae's mind. It shocked him how many times he had found himself in similar situations. He reached for the solace of knowing he had escaped all of them, though never unscathed. This time, he had a hidden partner, Imorelda, who could change the odds. *Imorelda, stay out of sight.*

The cat gave him nothing in return, only an insolent silence laced with something he could not quite identify.

A familiar voice hissed into Tae's ear. "You move, you're dead."

Suddenly, Tae recognized the emotion in Imorelda's sending. The cat was strangely amused by the situation. Obeying the order, he rolled an eye toward the man pinning him to the ground. "Subikahn? Is that you?"

"Papa?" The sword retreated from Tae's throat. The weight left him.

Tae scrambled to his feet and whirled to face his only son. Subikahn looked thinner even than usual, his black hair a snarl, his dark eyes haunted, and his clothing covered in filth and burrs of every variety. He threw himself at the boy, this time wrapping him into a joyous embrace. "Have you taken up purse-snatching and ambush?"

Subikahn hugged his father, stepped back, and sheathed his ever-present sword. "I was just coming home. *You* came skulking after *me*." He grinned. "By the way, that distract and double-back trick really works."

Tae brushed dirt off his front and grumbled, "Yeah, it's a gem."

Imorelda stepped into view. *Normal families just exchange greetings, hugs, and kisses.*

Torn between appreciating his son's competence and concern for his own, Tae did not feel much like bantering. *Is this the first you've noticed we're not a 'normal family'? Because the mother living halfway across the world and married to another man should have given you a hunch.*

Gingerly, Subikahn hefted Imorelda, petting her in all the right places while she purred contentedly. She seemed happy to disengage from the conversation.

Tae tried to make his question sound casual. "So, is Saviar with you?"

"No." Subikahn frowned so forcefully, Tae could see it through the gloom.

That surprised Tae, who suspected he was not getting the entire story. "No? When you both disappeared at the same time, I figured you'd gone off together. Ra-khir said he saw Saviar when he took Chymmerlee home."

"Saw Saviar?" Subikahn studied his father. "Is that what he said?"

Tae had no trouble remembering. "Exactly."

"Did he mention the shouting match? The threats?"

"No." Tae realized Subikahn had just answered his first concern. "So you *were* with Saviar."

"Only if you consider sneaking around behind him without his knowledge to see what he's up to being *with* him."

Tae had done the same thing to Ra-khir, Darris, Matrinka, and Kevral so many times he had lost count. "As a matter of fact, I do."

"Oh." That seemed to catch Subikahn off guard. "Then I was with Saviar. And the Knights of Erythane, too."

"Hmmm. I can't help but notice the knights have returned, you have returned, and Saviar has not . . . returned."

Subikahn's hands balled to fists at his sides. "Saviar . . . is a moron."

"And Calistin?"

"A bully . . . and a moron."

Tae could not resist trying, "And Subikahn?"

Subikahn hesitated. "A *bonta*." He used the Eastern vulgar term for a homosexual, a word he knew his father despised.

Tae ignored the impropriety in an attempt to mend the relationship with his son. ". . . and a moron?"

Subikahn sighed. "Probably. But not as big a moron as either of my brothers."

"Ah." Tae feigned sudden understanding. "So the size of the moronicism is significant. And the lesser of morons gets a pass."

Subikahn managed a chuckle.

Tae wrapped an arm around his son's shoulder and steered him toward Béarn. "You don't usually put Saviar in the same category as Calistin when it comes to acting stupidly."

Subikahn walked along with his father, still clutching Imorelda. "Trust me, Papa. This time, he deserves it."

"What did he do?"

Subikahn shook his head. "I promised not to tell."

Tae groaned but did not press. "Never make a vow to a Knight of Erythane or any of his offspring. Haven't I taught you that yet?"

"Over and over again, but I don't seem to get the

message." Subikahn sighed again. "His heart's in the right place. He's just lucky no one's shoved a dagger through it."

Tae shivered involuntarily. Such phrasing always took him back to his own childhood, when enemies of his father had murdered his mother, stabbed Tae sixteen times, and left him for dead. He still had vicious scars, including one directly over his heart. Thus far, he had refused to explain them to his son, so he knew Subikahn had not deliberately baited him. "Saviar's just like his father, you know."

"Yeah, well. I can hardly hold that against him. I resemble mine quite a bit, too."

Tae nodded. Not only did Subikahn resemble him physically, the younger man had used his own trick against him to great effect. Whenever Tae doubled back, he either found a better hiding place or put as much distance between himself and his pursuers as he could. Trained as a warrior, Subikahn chose a more confrontational approach.

"Including some of his idiotic ideas."

"Idioticisms," Tae corrected, deliberately wrongly. Playing with words came as naturally to him as swords did to Renshai.

Tae stopped suddenly. He could not recruit Saviar, apparently; but he did have a shot at another Renshai, a better choice than Rantire or Talamir, at least. "Subikahn, would you be interested in helping out your dear old Papa?"

Subikahn came to a halt so fluidly anyone watching might not know who had initiated it. "I don't have a 'dear, old' Papa. I have a hardheaded, obnoxious, young Papa. You were my age when I was born."

Tae never liked it when the conversation went in this direction, although it bothered him less since learning of his son's sexual orientation. The one clear advantage to a male lover was the impossibility of accidental pregnancy. "But now I'm your age plus your age and feeling every year. I'll be starting my fifth decade soon."

"You're thirty-eight, Papa. You're hardly a swaybacked old nag ready for pasture."

Tae resumed walking, and Subikahn, again, joined him seamlessly. "I can't kick your ass anymore."

"In your prime, you couldn't kick my *mother's* ass, and you couldn't kick mine since I turned nine. We'd have been worthless Renshai if you could."

Tae had to smile. If Kevral had needed more than six sword strokes to kill him, she would have taken her own life instead. He also realized they had gotten far off-subject. He steered the conversation back to topic. "Speaking of Renshai, I'm going on a spying mission. I promised King Griff I'd bring a Renshai with me." He stopped there, hoping Subikahn would take the responsibility onto himself without needing to be asked.

"Which explains your interest in Saviar's whereabouts."

Slowly, Tae turned his head toward his son, feigning incredulity. Although he would never reveal the truth of that statement, it bothered him that his son had struck so close to home. "I asked about Saviar because I thought you had run off together. Twins have a tendency to do that." He modulated his voice to make it clear he meant his next utterance to be taken seriously, "I'm trying to ask you to accompany me without—"

"—actually asking?" Subikahn supplied.

Tae knew what he had to do. "Subikahn, would you please accompany me on my mission? It will be grueling and dangerous. One or both of us may not survive." He added facetiously, "On the downside, it will take you away from home for at least a week or two."

Subikahn's smile finally faded as he clearly considered the offer. They had reached the edge of the city before he finally said, "No."

Tae had not expected that. "What?"

"I don't think I can go."

Tae heaved an exasperated sigh. "I get it." He dropped to one knee and adopted a wheedling tone. "Please, Subikahn, please. I'm begging."

Subikahn grabbed Tae's wrist and hoisted him to his feet. "No, Papa. I'm not joking around to make you beg. I just have to spend some time with Tally. I promised."

Tae examined the sky. Red-and-orange bands still colored the horizon where the sun had fully disappeared. The last rays of dusk would soon fade. "I can give you a few hours for . . ." As Tae considered how they might use the time, the words died on his lips. Despite his new acceptance, he could not say what he was thinking.

Subikahn did not make him finish. "No, Papa. It's not just about saying 'good-bye.'" Finally, he seemed to have given up on teasing. "I really wanted to go back East with your army and Talamir. I have things I need to discuss with Grandpapa."

Tae clamped his back teeth together. Weile's charisma had become legendary, the only man who had ever organized criminals en masse and gotten the better part of bargains with the most unreasonable of kings. A need to meet with Weile Kahn never boded well for anyone. "Do you want to talk about it . . . with me?"

"It wouldn't do any good. It's one of those things that requires . . . his . . . expertise."

Tae heard the squeak of his teeth grinding, and forced himself to relax. "I can keep the army in Béarn until we return from our mission, or we can meet up with them later. I need to send a message to my father as well. We could . . . combine notes?"

Subikahn pursed his lips, looking sideways at his father. "You really want me to come with you."

"More than anything." The words were true enough, if not exactly for the reasons Subikahn assumed. Without him, Tae would find himself stuck with Rantire.

Subikahn shuffled his feet, looked up at the fading dusk, then back at Tae. "I'll talk to Tally. If he's all right with me going, I'll meet you . . ." His expression turned puzzled.

"There's a double-masted, lateen-rigged—"

Subikahn interrupted. "You mean a ship?"

Tae smiled. His son knew little to nothing about sailing. "A ship, yes. Moored at the lower dock with the Northern longboats. It's the smallest one there. Get there as soon as you can, definitely before sunup."

"You mean, I don't even get a night—"

"Sorry." Tae hoped he sounded sincere.

"What would you have done if I hadn't arrived when I did?"

Tae did not have an answer.

CHAPTER 12

To the immortal, centuries pass like months; but the shortest-lived see every moment's glory.
— Colbey Calistinsson

BY THE TIME CAPTAIN REACHED Béarn's Strategy Room, the guards had left their posts, indicating the meeting had concluded. Captain lowered his head, trying to decide how to proceed. More than anything, he wanted to return to his ship, the only place he ever felt truly comfortable, but he had a duty to Tem'aree'ay and Midgard. He could not leave before doing what he could to assist her and her mission, however doomed it seemed. Not expecting an answer, Captain knocked softly on the Strategy Room door.

A muffled voice wafted through the panel. "Come in."

Captain tripped the latch and allowed the door to swing slowly open. In stages, the crack revealed the barren walls, the simple wooden chairs, and the table holding only a map of the continent and nearest islands. King Griff and his elfin wife sat in chairs facing away from both door and table, studying their half-breed daughter. Ivana seemed to be trying to do something with her awkward, oversized fingers.

A smile wreathed Griff's features. He looked pleased and relieved to see the oldest elf. "Come in, Captain. Please, join us."

Captain stepped inside the room, closing the door behind him. Ivana sprang from her chair with an ear-splitting shriek of welcome.

Tem'aree'ay winced at the sound but also grinned at Captain's entrance. "Arak'bar Tulamii Dhor, what a wonderful surprise. My husband told me you had come, but he didn't seem to think you would honor us with your presence." She chose to address him in Common Trading speech, presumably in deference to Griff and Ivana, neither of whom would understand the Elvish tongue.

"Tem'aree'ay Donnnev'ra Amal-yah Krish-anda Malsatorian." The elfin name flowed effortlessly off Captain's tongue, and her grin wreathed most of her face. She probably had not heard the entirety of it in years. He considered doing Ivana the same justice, but it seemed unnecessary. To the child, it would sound like a string of random syllables. However, he did nod a greeting toward her, more for the sake of the parents than Ivana. They would want him to acknowledge her as normally as possible. "Your husband need only speak a request, and I would gladly assist him if it is within my power." He gave Griff a pointed look.

Like the king of Béarn, Captain had dedicated himself to neutrality. In his original capacity, he had served the Cardinal Wizards, the embodiments of the world's forces, equally, never favoring good or evil, law or chaos. That, he suspected, was the sole reason he still existed long after the system, itself, had expired. Though he addressed Tem'aree'ay, Captain deliberately stared at Griff.

Griff flushed under the scrutiny. "I didn't wish to presume. I thought it daring enough to request one favor from an immortal."

"I'm not an immortal." Captain had no idea whether or not he spoke the truth. Just because he had not died of natural causes yet did not mean he never would. "I'm merely the longest-lived elf. I sometimes think Frey assumes I died with the Cardinal Wizards. Or, perhaps, he has forgotten me."

"More likely," Tem'aree'ay said, "he still has a purpose for you."

Captain saw no reason to argue. No good could come of challenging the judgment of the gods, particularly when it pertained to one's own lifespan. "So, how can I help the king of Béarn and his queen consort today? King Tae Kahn Weile's son says you can use my advice."

"Tae?" Griff's expression revealed a mixture of simultaneous surprise and pleasure. Captain had become adept at reading human faces, better even than elfin ones. "You found him?"

"Actually, he found me." Captain also smiled, the natural state of his face. Over the years, he had developed permanent facial lines in a happy pattern, akin to human wrinkles aside from their location. "That's usually the best approach with King Tae Kahn Weile's son."

Ivana let out another squeal and hurled herself at her father. Griff caught her easily, hauling her into his lap with a grin of genuine pleasure. "Good advice, Captain. I'm going to remember that."

"But it's not the advice you wanted from me."

"No." Tem'aree'ay took over with an all-too-human sigh that made Captain wince. Elves who spent too many years among humans tended to develop similar mannerisms and gestures. He did not know if the reverse might also prove true, as the elves had never encouraged or accepted humans among them. "I'm charged with leading another expedition to implore the elves to assist humanity in battle. The first time we tried it, they refused. The second time, no one could find them." Her beautiful sapphire eyes found his yellow ones and held them. "Can you help us . . . find them?"

Captain disengaged from her examination, resting his gaze on every item in the spare room in turn. "I can help you find them, but that's probably the most you can hope for from me."

Upon receiving disappointed looks, he continued. "It's true the current elves abandoned Dh'arlo'mé'aftris'ter Te'meer Braylth'ryn Amareth Fel-Krin and his *svartalf* to follow me, but it had far more to do with Frey's interference than my charm. Until our creator arrived, only one elf chose to follow me, a child. The rest had named themselves *dwar'freytii*, claiming to follow the will of Frey. When he branded them 'unworthy' and explained his plan to relocate them to a dark, quiet place where they could simmer in their hatred, most finally realized that anger and vengeance do not suit elves. Those who subsequently joined me were spared, and he took the rest to Svartalfheim, where their decisions could no longer destroy us."

Captain had voiced the only vote against sowing chaos in Béarn through assassination and had gone renegade over the decision to allow Rantire to live when the other elves had condemned her to death. "I've lived on Midgard for thousands of years. I was the only elf not on Alfheim when the fires destroyed it. Most of the others consider me *menneskelik*." He searched for the translation. "Humanized."

Tem'aree'ay unconsciously rubbed her arms and torso, reminded of her own agony. Captain knew it had taken years of magical healing to abolish the physical scars; and, for some, the emotional ones remained, though most of the worst cases had become *svartalf*.

"They worried I put the best interests of men over those of elves. In a situation such as the current one, I would prove less than useless to you."

Tem'aree'ay shook her head, clearly disagreeing. "So it might seem, but they always listen to you in the end."

Though Captain could not wholly deny the truth of that statement, it did not change the facts. "Eventually. They see the light on their own and take the proper course despite my counsel. But I often think they do so much quicker when I'm not involved in the decision."

Tem'aree'ay clearly realized that arguing the point would not change Captain's mind. "Where will we find the elves?"

Captain considered. He tended to lose track of time, and years often slipped by without his notice. Much could happen in that span. "I sailed some of them ..." He gave Tem'aree'ay a nod, "... including you, from Nualfheim to Béarn." He explained for Griff. "Nualfheim is our name for Elves' Island."

Griff nodded his understanding. Likely, Tem'aree'ay had mentioned it over the years.

"Later, I took them back to the island in groups. For at least the last decade, you're the only elf I didn't return to Nualfheim. I haven't sailed a single one anywhere since that time, so I have to assume they're still on the island."

Griff clamped his lips shut. Clearly, Captain had added nothing helpful. They must have already considered the island and discarded it. "The last time we sailed to Elves' Island, we saw no sign of them at all."

The words did not surprise Captain. "That means they did not wish to be found, not necessarily that they have gone away."

Griff clutched Ivana in front of him, rocking gently. "But if we can sail to them, they could sail to the continent, right?

I mean, Elves' Island is due south of the Western Plains and not far out to sea. The only ones who might have seen them land are barbarians, and even they prefer the forests to the open plains."

The king had applied human logic to elves. "Elves don't routinely build structures, Your Majesty. That includes ships."

"What about magically?"

"Chaos must be shaped by law to become magic, so it works within boundaries. Since the destruction of the Cardinal Wizards, I'm not sure even the gods have the power to create solid objects from magic."

Griff nodded brusquely. Humans had a different attitude toward gods than elves did, seeing them as dangerous supreme beings that required constant reverence and worship. "But couldn't the elves build something shiplike and use magic to patch any errors in construction?"

Captain cocked his head, considering. "They could potentially build a ship, join in *jovinay arythanik*, and wind up with something reasonably seaworthy." He was stretching the definition of worthy. "But they would have to start with an object that more than just vaguely resembled a boat. I believe if you talk to your shipwrights, Your Majesty, you'll find it requires a long and arduous apprenticeship as well as many years of calculation and practice, a keen eye for proportion, an imagination that can take into account the effect on every part of his construction from windlessness to puffs to gales."

Realizing he could talk for days about the details of shipbuilding, Captain forced himself to take another tack. "Elves cannot risk a single life. To place a significant number on the open sea would seem to them like madness. If they wished to leave the island, they would simply contact me or hire human sailors."

Griff shook his shaggy head, and Captain took that to mean he would know if human ships had transported the elves. Captain did not know exactly how the king would know but assumed the humans would find it noteworthy enough that word would reach him. "Tem'aree'ay says there's no magical way for them to travel from Elves' Island to the mainland."

It was not strictly true. With enough chaos present at

both ends, the elves could magically transport themselves from one place on Midgard to another. However, they would first have to relocate a significant number of elves to the endpoint by mundane means. "I think we can say with reasonable confidence that the elves still occupy Nualfheim, whether or not your people found them on their last visit."

Tem'aree'ay broke her lengthy silence. "Unless they left Midgard entirely."

Captain hesitated. It would require a large number of elves working together, but they could create a portal to an Outworld site. "Why?"

Tem'aree'ay lowered her head. "To get away from . . . us."

Captain immediately assumed she meant the humans, not him and her, then another thought seized him. "You and Ivana Shorith'na Cha-tella Tir Hya'sellirian Albar?"

She nodded glumly.

Captain did not understand. "Are you chasing them? Do you pose them some lethal threat?"

"Of course not!"

Captain shook his head. "Then there's little reason to assume they escaped off-world. First, it would require at least thirty banded together in *jovinay arythanik*. And where would they go?"

"Svartalfheim?" Tem'aree'ay suggested.

Captain gave her a glare that he hoped suggested she had taken leave of her senses.

"Asgard?"

"The gods would not allow it. Do you think they would risk the wrath of our creator? Again?"

Now Tem'aree'ay shook her head. "Jotunheim and Alfheim were destroyed." She named the worlds of giants and elves. "Niflheim." She bared her teeth at her own mention of the world harboring Hel. "No chance." Her features relaxed a bit, then stiffened again. "Of course, there are all the smaller worlds."

Captain discarded the theory. "They exist, but their access is random. We hopped a group around some of them by focusing on the shards of the Pica Stone. Without something on which to center their magic, they could wind up anywhere."

"Which would make them even harder to find," Tem'aree'ay pointed out.

Captain had meant something entirely different. He used a real-life example. "Like on a world of spirit spiders."

Tem'aree'ay shuddered. Spirit spiders consumed the souls of those they bit, and elves could not risk losing a single one.

"Or one of utter chaos, underwater or eternally burning. A world ruled by elf-eating wolves or humans at constant war."

"All right." Tem'aree'ay had clearly gotten the point.

"So, unless your elf-seeking humans threatened to destroy them, body and soul, I don't see the elves magicking off to some arbitrary place to hide."

Ivana let out another squeal of excitement.

Griff's brow furrowed. "I sent the group to win over the elves, not harm them. You don't think we might have spooked them into . . . jumping worlds?"

Captain could not entirely rule it out. Elves did things capriciously, on whims. They could spend a decade mulling a fine point of one specific aspect of the appearance of the moon, then waste every evening in random procreation. "Not likely." He wished he could say "impossible." He glanced at Tem'aree'ay. She shifted from foot to foot, clearly agitated, a state more suited to humans than elves. "Tem'aree'ay Donn-nev'ra Amal-yah Krish-anda Mal-satorian."

She stopped moving to study Captain.

"Surely you don't believe the elves would skip worlds to avoid you and your half-human offspring."

Tem'aree'ay responded slowly, carefully. "There . . . was a time, albeit a short one . . . when our people considered living freely . . . near and in human cities. With humans." She studied him, an all-too-human gesture through all-too-elfin eyes. "When it . . . became clear that . . . Ivana was not . . ." She paused a long time. Accustomed to lengthy silences between thoughts, Captain felt no need to finish her sentence, but Griff apparently did.

". . . normal?"

". . . appreciably elfin," Tem'aree'ay corrected. "They fled from us until none remained."

Captain defended his own. "Elves have more reason than most to fear the unknown. The few things they cannot fathom represent possible danger."

Tem'aree'ay's lips pressed firmly together and her

fingers curled, both elfin signs of significant anger. "But they've made no attempt to fathom Ivana, given her no chance to prove herself . . . fathomable."

Captain's amber gaze whipped to Ivana. Outwardly, she appeared too simple to even have fathoms, a drooling, animalistic creature doomed to act solely by instinct. He understood why the elves would want no claim on her. "I do not believe they fear her existence so much as the possibility of populating the world with more of her."

Doubting he had made himself clear, he elaborated. "Elves are spontaneous, capricious, and free with sexuality. If they remained among humans, interspecies copulation would certainly occur. Elves have a natural way to control their population: the need for a freed soul. Humans do not, and elves who breed with humans can produce unlimited offspring. How soon before the . . ." Captain stopped himself from using the current elfin term for half-breeds: *ivanas*. ". . . human/elfin children outnumber the elves? What happens when elfin wombs fill with them and leave no room for the rare elfin soul? How long before the humans come to despise these creatures and blame us for them? Any imperfect human child will be assumed to have elfin blood. Accusations of rape, of coercion, of corruption will fly."

Captain stopped there, worried to offend Griff. He had lived long enough to foreseè the dangerous inequities that might occur: people declaring themselves superior by virtue of blood, accusing those they considered inferior of carrying various amounts of elfin "contamination," whether half or only a drop. Elves had pinkish blood compared to the rose-petal red of humans. Some might see that as physical evidence of inferiority.

Apparently, Captain had not quit soon enough. A frown deeply scored the king's rugged features. "I think you give both humans and elves too little credit for intelligent and ethical thought. Surely, the elves understand that humans sometimes have imperfect children, no matter the race of their spouses."

Captain pointed out what seemed obvious to him. "With other humans, it's uncommon. With elves, it's certain. Even with the best of intentions, assumptions will be made." Captain had enough experience to realize every eye in the room had riveted upon him, suggesting he had said something untoward. "What?" he demanded.

Griff pointed out the problem. "You've just said every coupling between humans and elves will result in imperfect children. As if it were fact."

"Isn't it?"

Tem'aree'ay put it in terms Captain could not help but understand. "Suppose you awakened one morning to a blizzard. Would you assume you'll suffer through ice storms every morning?"

Captain could see the analogy she wished to make, but it did not fit. "Of course not. Because I've lived on Midgard for thousands of years, and time has proven blizzards relatively infrequent. On the other hand, we have a single human/elf combination, and she is ..." Captain finished cautiously. "... what she is."

"And what is that?" Tem'aree'ay demanded, anger clear in her voice.

Captain would not be baited. "A less than ideal representative of either race. And all we have to go on for what happens when elves and humans procreate together."

Tem'aree'ay turned away, arms clenched to her chest.

Captain turned his attention to Griff. "With your permission, Your Majesty, I'd like to leave."

Griff grimaced. "You are free to come and go as you please, Captain. You are not a prisoner. But I wish you would stay. I want very much to understand this situation from the viewpoint of the elves. I think you know you can always speak freely here. I would never punish anyone for stating facts or beliefs, even if they're painful to me and those I love." He walked around Tem'aree'ay to force her to look at him. "My lovely wife may certainly leave, if she finds the topic offensive."

Tem'aree'ay stiffened, then turned back to face Captain. All signs of anger had fled her features, though she looked close to tears. "My good husband is right, Arak'bar Tulamii Dhor. We both need to hear this. I'll handle meeting with our people better if I have an idea what they think and feel." She took a seat and gestured at Captain. "Please continue."

Captain had finished his piece, but he elaborated to

accommodate the request. "I'm merely saying that if a man eats an unknown berry and dies, it's safest to presume it's poisonous." He believed his analogy more apt.

Tem'aree'ay's brow furrowed, probably in response to the equating of her daughter to poison. "Unless it's all you have to eat."

"In which case," Captain said smoothly, "there's no significant risk to trying again, is there? It's simply a matter of choosing a quick death over a slow, prolonged one." He could not help adding. "Of course, one could always argue that other food could be found prior to starvation, so it's still better not to eat the berries." His mind went naturally to people who, trapped on the sea, resorted to drinking sea water. And, invariably, died. Those who held out for rain usually survived.

Griff took a different tack. "Tae was right. We need to have more children, to prove Ivana was an anomaly."

"Or not an anomaly." The words needed saying, so Captain did so. "There exist only three possibilities when it comes to children produced by the coupling of elves and humans: they are all . . . defective, many are defective, or abnormalities are as rare as when humans breed without elves. I'm not certain elves could accept any of those states, but the best case scenario at least has a chance of convincing them to interact, at some level, with humans."

Griff grunted. "You mean, if abnormalities are as rare with elf/human pairs as with human/human pairings."

"Yes."

Tem'aree'ay slumped in her seat. Quite possibly for the first time in eighteen years, she had allowed herself to look at the world from the vantage of an elf who was not Ivana's mother. "So Tae is right."

Captain chuckled. "I find that, ultimately, he usually is." He added, "Damn it."

Tem'aree'ay ignored Captain. "We do need to . . . make more . . . children." She studied Ivana with a mixture of love and tolerance. She clasped her long-fingered hands, squeezing until they whitened.

Griff shrugged. "I'm game." The look he gave Tem'aree'ay could have defined human lust.

She shoved him, and the expression disappeared. "It's not a joke, beloved. What if the elves are right? What if we just make more . . . imperfect children? What if it's not an elf/human thing but a me/you thing? What if every child we produce is . . . defective but other elves and humans could safely couple?"

"All valid questions," Captain had to admit.

"And all surmountable," Griff added. "Let's take it one step at a time. First, we decide what we're going to do if our second child is like Ivana. If we can come to a satisfactory agreement on that, we produce the child. If he or she is relatively normal, we can eliminate the worst of the possibilities Captain presented. If not, then we can probably reasonably conclude that either all, or an unacceptable proportion, of elf/human combinations are . . . not ideal. Or, at the very least, that the two of us . . ." He weighed each word, "do not . . . create . . . ideal . . . offspring."

Clearly oblivious to her role in the conversation, Ivana curled up on the floor for a nap.

Tem'aree'ay pinched her heart-shaped lips, clearly wavering.

Captain wondered if he should even bring up his next thought, then decided to do so. The couple had a difficult enough decision without hearing all the facts. "You may want to consider one other thing." As both looked interested in hearing what he had to say, Captain continued, "You know about mules, don't you?"

Tem'aree'ay looked at Griff, who nodded. "We've had a few donkey and horse crosses here, but there's a region in the East that specializes in them. We've traded in the past to get certain colors and features."

"The ones with more horselike features cost more: smaller, rounder ears, hairier manes and tails, thicker limbs. The larger-sized, horsey ones are the most expensive of all. Do you know why that is?"

Griff shrugged. "I'd always assumed people preferred them." He cited simple economics. "More demand, higher price."

Captain shook his head. "In this case, it's less supply, higher price."

Griff's brows twitched downward. "You mean donkey features come out more commonly."

"I mean mules are easier to make than hinnies."

Griff shook his head. Captain had fully lost him.

"It's much simpler to get a jack to breed with a mare than a stallion to breed with a jenny. And fewer breedings result in foals."

Griff blinked several times in succession. He seemed eager to speak but could not find his words.

Ever patient, Captain waited.

"So," Griff finally managed. "When the donkey is male and the horse female, you get a mule. When the donkey is female and the horse male, you get a . . . hinny."

"Correct." Captain waited for Griff to take the evident leap.

"Hinnies are smaller and more . . . horselike."

"Yes," Captain encouraged.

The expression dawning across Griff's coarse features suggested he had finally taken the plunge. "You're saying even if the offspring of a male human and a female elf are all abnormal, it is possible the offspring of a male elf and a female human . . . are normal."

That came close enough to Captain's point. "Normal is a relative term, of course, but it's worth consideration."

Tem'aree'ay shook her head, hair flying, with obvious outrage. "Donkeys, mules, and horses are one thing. But you're talking about experimenting with intelligent lives here. Ivana is not an object of study; she is a person."

Captain sucked in a deep breath, releasing it slowly. "She's a person. And an object of study." He took another cleansing breath. Taking Griff at his word, he went on long after he entered foolish and dangerous territory. "Elves see each and every life as sacred. To do otherwise would condemn us to oblivion. If we allow even one life to end short, we lose that soul for all eternity. We can only decrease in number over time, never increase. With humans, it's not the same." Not wanting the wrong conclusion drawn, Captain continued, "The loss of a single human, while tragic to those who loved him, does not pose a threat to the survival of the entire race."

Tem'aree'ay tipped her head, looking at Ivana. "Are you trying to say . . . that human life . . . isn't as valuable . . . as ours?"

Captain could not help smiling. "I'm trying *not* to say it."

Griff nodded his appreciation. "Thanks for that, but your

point is valid and important. It puts several things in perspective that I hadn't considered before." He did not elaborate. Captain suspected it clarified Tem'aree'ay's handling of Ivana. "Another way to think of it is that humans deal far better with issues of death because we have to. If an infant dies, we suffer terrible grief, but we can ease it with the knowledge that we can make another child. We also know, when we conceive, that a certain large number of infants do die." He shuddered at a realization that must have struck him at that moment. "To elves it must seem impossibly callous, but most people do not keep children like Ivana."

Tem'aree'ay's head jerked so suddenly to Griff it looked like the movement must hurt. "What does that mean? What does it mean not to keep them?" The only realistic explanation dawned on her. "They don't feed and shelter them? They leave them to . . . die?"

Griff shuffled his feet, avoiding his favored wife's gaze. "More often, they . . . humanely end the suffering of the child, thus allowing the other children, and the families, to lead normal lives."

Tem'aree'ay stared at Ivana. "That's disgusting! It's barbaric!"

At her mother's sudden outcry, Ivana stirred in her sleep.

Captain seized Tem'aree'ay's arm. "It's not fair to judge others by our frame of reference. We live exceptionally long lives free of illnesses and, for the most part, of imperfections. Occasionally, someone loses a finger, a foot, an eye, but these are not the kind of issues for which humans euthanize their own. I've spent time with Khy'barreth Y'vrintae Shabeerah El-borin Morbonos." He named the one feeble-minded elf, his brain damaged by taking two repelling magical items in hand at once. "We care for him because not doing so means he dies of something other than age, which utterly destroys the soul that future elves can use. But that care comes at a price. It's demanding, difficult, distracting, and a constant reminder of a costly mistake. If I had to choose between saving Khy'barreth and any other elf, I would have no difficulty. Would you?"

Tem'aree'ay turned away. Captain could only guess at her thoughts. Although she would never consider allowing anyone to harm Ivana, she had to understand why others felt differently about such matters. "No one chooses to have a child like . . . ours. But one is responsible for the lives one creates. For the problems one causes to others."

Griff said softly, "Which is why so many choose to end them. Because human lives and resources are finite. Whether it's time, money, food or even just sanity, how does a poor tradesman justify spending it on an imbecile rather than those children who can assist him with his work, who can help provide for the family, who can marry and contribute to future generations?"

Tem'aree'ay rounded on him. "Are you suggesting we should euthanize Ivana?"

Griff backpedaled fiercely. "Of course not. We have the resources and inclination to take care of her. We don't have to choose between love and necessity."

"But if we made a second . . . abnormal child?"

"Let's talk about that possibility and our options now, while I'm still young enough to make children and enjoy them. I don't want to wait another eighteen years, and I'm sure we can come to an agreement we can both live with."

Griff's pronouncement got Captain thinking in a direction he never had in all of his centuries. He wondered if elves ever became too old to make children. The random mating habits of elves rendered paternity a nonissue. No one kept track of timing or partners. Any male could have fathered any child. Although maternity was never in question, no one cared whose womb had carried a child. They raised their rare offspring communally; every young elf belonged to all of them. No one looked for his own height or facial features or coloring in the offspring. The only inheritance that mattered to elves was the reborn soul of the last elf to die of age.

Now that Captain had brought up the point of mules and hinnies, he could not help wondering if the product of an elfin male and a human female might prove more stable than its opposite. If so, he might be the only elf willing to prove it. He wondered what the world would make of a six-thousand-year-old father.

As the couple had much to discuss, Captain tried to take his leave again. "Rantire, Tae, and I plan to leave by noon tomorrow." He did not mention the fourth passenger; Griff would not approve and Captain had promised to keep the secret. "I'll need a few hours to get the ship in peak condition."

Griff nodded, smiling. "I doubt your ship is ever out of peak condition, but you're free to go."

"No," Tem'aree'ay said unexpectedly but without vehemence. "Before you go, I'd like to try a scrying spell."

Captain understood the words, but Tem'aree'ay knew as well as he that such magic was currently impossible. "That's not a specialty for either of us. We'd need a good-sized *jovinay arythanik*." Despite having declared it impossible, he could not help asking, "Who are we trying to see?" He did not believe all the elves together could scry a site none of them had seen, such as the *Kjempemagiska*'s lands.

Tem'aree'ay clearly had considered the matter longer than Captain. "Just the elves, for a single moment, without sound. Using a powerful magical device, we could do it with a minimal *jovinay arythanik*."

Captain knew exactly the artifact she meant: the Pica Stone. Even if Griff allowed them to use it, they would need more elves. "A *jovinay arythanik* requires a minimum of three elves."

Tem'aree'ay did not miss a beat. "And, luckily, that is what we have."

Captain paused, uncertain what she meant. He licked his lips tentatively. He might have taken all night to work out the answer, without noticing the passage of time.

Tem'aree'ay saved him the trouble. "You, me, and Ivana."

Captain cocked his head, assuming she had access to information he did not rather than that she had lost her mind. "Ivana can ... ?"

"It would appear so. When it came to repelling the magic of the single *Kjempemagiska* who attended the war, she linked with me and Chymmerlee."

That intrigued Captain, both for Ivana's ability and the mention of an elf whose name he had never heard. "Chymmerlee?"

Tem'aree'ay continued as if he had not interrupted. "Of course, it wasn't a true *jovinay arythanik* with Chymmerlee being human."

"Human," Captain could not help repeating. "Wait! A

magical human?" The description raised ancient memories of those long ago days when Myrcidians walked the continent and Cardinal Wizards kept the balance. "You linked with a magical human?"

Tem'aree'ay tossed her head. "Linked isn't the right word. She tapped the *Kjempemagiska*. Ivana and I fed her raw chaos. It wasn't a well-coordinated effort, but it did the job."

Captain did not know which question to ask first, which only further delayed speaking.

Griff finally returned to the conversation. "I told you we had help from a woman with magic."

"Yes," Captain concurred, "but I thought you meant Tem'aree'ay." At the time, it had seemed the logical conclusion. Griff would certainly think of Tem'aree'ay as a woman, regardless of her elfin race. "Raw chaos is raw chaos. What makes you so sure Ivana played a role in this?"

Tem'aree'ay nodded vigorously, indicating she understood his thought processes, had followed them herself. "At first, I didn't. Chymmerlee told me she could feel two elves assisting her, and Ivana was the only possibility."

Captain mulled the matter, fascinated by the many implications. Even in the days when human users of magic existed, he knew of only one circumstance where one might have combined her power with an elf's. The Northern Sorceress, Trilless, had chosen an elf as her successor, the first time any wizard had done so. Unfortunately, the line of Northern Wizards had ended with her, and the elf, Dh'arlo'mé, had led the *svartalf* before Odin took over his body and both had died at the *Ragnarok*. Captain had no idea whether sorceress and apprentice had managed to find a magical means of linking. Even if they had, it might not prove anything. Cardinal Wizards had always developed a direct connection to their successors. "This is . . . significant."

Though Tem'aree'ay nodded, she seemed more confused than in agreement. "To which event are you referring? Ivana's ability to channel chaos? Locating a human user of magic? Or the fact that we found a way to work together?"

"All three." Captain looked at Griff, who needed to know. "This is all very significant."

"Yes," Griff said, as if the point were so obvious it did not need speaking. "That's why we have various groups working on Chymmerlee and on the elves. It took three users of magic and our two best warriors to defeat one of the *Kjempemagiska*. If Tae is correct, and—as you pointed out—he usually is, we will need to entice every user of magic to assist us. If not, we will lose this war and all of our lives: magical or otherwise."

That point, Griff had already made very clear to Captain. The elf suddenly realized that getting the king's permission to use the Pica Stone for scrying would prove no obstacle at all.

CHAPTER 13

There may well come a time, Captain, when you need to choose between what's right for your people and your loyalty to them. When that time comes, the world may rest on your decision.

— *Rantire Ulfinsdatter*

WELL AFTER MIDNIGHT, yet hours before sunrise, Tae, Imorelda, and Subikahn reached the lateen-rigged sailboat that Captain had dubbed the *Sea Skimmer*. It looked even less sturdy in the dark than in the dawn, a tiny craft with no business navigating the open ocean. Yet, Tae did not worry for that. No one knew the many aspects of the sea like Captain. If he felt comfortable with the vessel, Tae had no doubt it could do what the elf claimed it could.

Subikahn studied the ship impassively, showing no more concern than his father. That, Tae believed, stemmed from ignorance. Subikahn knew nothing about sailing or their captain. Clearly, he trusted his father's instincts on this one. He knew better than anyone that, for all his risky behavior, Tae rarely took chances that relied on something other than his own competence.

Captain met them at the starboard bulwark, nearest the docks. He looked refreshed, though Tae knew the elf had spent much of the night in conversation with Griff and Tem'aree'ay. When he and Subikahn had sent their separate messages to Weile Kahn, the guards had informed them of Captain's whereabouts. Tae knew different elves needed varying amounts of sleep; and, from their previous voyage together, he had discovered that Captain required little or none. "Welcome, welcome."

Subikahn froze on the dock, staring. "Papa," he said softly. "That's an elf, isn't it?"

"Yes." Tae replied, equally softly. While most of the elves could pass for human in a pinch, particularly to those like Subikahn who had seen no elves besides Tem'aree'ay, others never could. Tae had interacted with several elves, as individuals and in a large group, and he could spot the differences more easily. They were generally androgynous, lean, and unhurried. Their faces were more angular, sometimes more animal than human in appearance. Their eyes were canted, singularly colored and uniform, lacking the stellate cores around the pupils that most humans displayed.

Elfin hair spanned the gamut from elder white to inky black, with every shade of brown and yellow between and a propensity toward reddish hues and highlights. They sported eye colors that did not exist for humans: yellows and oranges, purples and reds, and even their greens and blues held the brightness and consistency of gemstones. Tae had never seen a brown-eyed elf. Their bodies had a gawky adolescent quality, even the elders, that defied gender; yet they wielded their long limbs and fingers with astounding grace.

Captain stepped aside as his charges, including the cat, scampered over the gunwhale. Imorelda set to work sniffing lines and planking, leaping onto every perch as if testing its worthiness to serve as her personal seat.

"Good to have you back, Tae Kahn. And this young man must be your brother."

From almost anyone else, Tae would have taken the words as a deliberate attempt to flatter him. Captain, he suspected, simply had some difficulties keeping track of time. "This is my son, Subikahn. Subikahn, this is our captain."

Subikahn bowed and raised his head. "Nice to meet you, Captain . . ." He paused, clearly waiting for the elf to fill in the missing name.

Captain politely returned the nod. "Just Captain, if you please. I've long forgotten my original name, and others keep hanging new ones on me." He winked. "I collect names like a hull collects barnacles."

Subikahn laughed. "Well, I, for one, appreciate just Captain. I'd heard elves had names that would take an entire sea voyage to learn. In the East, it's considered an insult to shorten a man's name. I'm hoping elves don't feel the same way."

Tae made short work of the query. "I think we can assume from his request that it doesn't bother him." He winked at Captain. Subikahn's time spent with Ra-khir and Saviar made him more formal than necessary on occasion. "You don't think Tem'aree'ay, a mere four syllables, is a full elfin name, do you? And that's how we address the high king's second wife."

Subikahn gave his father a sour look. "Well, maybe I'd rather hear that from him . . . Tae."

Tae chuckled. His son made a good point. His father, Weile, had deliberately given him a one syllable name to prevent anyone from shortening it. He had added the family name "Kahn" but only as a separate appendage. The Renshai had a limited pool of names, as they greatly preferred to name children after heroes who had earned their places in Valhalla. This *Einherjar* supposedly protected his or her namesake, so only one living Renshai could use a specific name.

Subikahn, originally spelled Pseubicon, was the only available Renshai name with the "kahn" sound at the time of Subikahn's birth. To a man, the Easterners called the young prince Subikahn, though his closest, non-Eastern friends frequently referred to the twins as Savi and Subi. Talamir sometimes called his lover Kahn.

"Shortening a name is not, in and of itself, an insult," Captain assured Subikahn before addressing Tae. "You're early. I figured you wouldn't come back until you'd had a full night's sleep in a soft and steady bed."

Tae snorted. "Soft and steady," he grumbled. "Are you calling me a princess?"

Captain smiled his perfect smile. "If the diamond-encrusted slippers fit . . ."

Tae merely shook his head. They could banter all day, and that would defeat the purpose entirely. "I'd like to cast off as soon as possible."

Captain leaned against a cleat to which the mainsail had been belayed. "We can cast off the moment our last passenger arrives."

Tae had known they would have to have this conversation, and he had no idea what the elf might have promised King Griff. "I agreed to bring a captain and a Renshai."

And a cat, Imorelda added unnecessarily.

"That particular Renshai was not mentioned by name. I would have objected. Strenuously."

Subikahn studied his father, head cocked. "So I'm a last-moment substitution."

Tae would not lie. "Yes."

"For who? Calistin?"

"Rantire," Tae supplied.

Apparently, Captain had not made the vow Tae had not. The Easterner hoped that, after so many millennia, Captain would have learned not to throw promises around freely. "Rantire's a competent and resilient bodyguard with a wise head. I'd trust anyone to her."

"Even me?" Tae knew Rantire and Griff had ridden on Captain's last ship, the one destroyed by the demon. He had witnessed the over-the-top dedication she displayed toward her charges. Or, at least, to the one who mattered.

"She could keep anyone alive," Captain insisted.

"Alive is not the concern in this case." Tae met Captain's gaze, not put off by the oddness of those canted, steady eyes. "There is also the issue of sanity."

"Ah." Captain straightened. "I see your point, but I want you to understand something." He lowered his volume, "I like Rantire very much. More even than you, if you wish to know, though I consider you an ally, too."

Tae's heart sank.

Imorelda looked smugly down from the forecastle. *You're in trouble. About time someone took measure of your relative worth.*

Too irritated for witty repartee, Tae sent only, *Shut up.*

Captain explained, "When I first met Rantire, she was a prisoner of my people, treated savagely by those who became the *svartalf.* She told me the sagest words I'd heard from a Renshai since Colbey Calistinsson stood against the other Cardinal Wizards."

Not that Renshai are known for their brains.

Tae phrased it more diplomatically. "Excuse me for pointing out such a thing, but when one thinks of Renshai, sage words do not automatically come to mind." He looked at Subikahn to ascertain he had not insulted his son. "Not that there aren't plenty of intelligent Renshai, it's just not usually their best known quality."

Captain shrugged, then made a throwaway gesture. "These particular words from that particular Renshai literally saved Midgard and the life of every human and, probably, most of the elves as well." He turned his attention to Subikahn. "So your son is also Renshai, then?"

"Kevral was his mother."

Captain bobbed his head. "They don't come more Renshai than Kevralyn Tainharsdatter."

Tae could scarcely deny it, although he found Rantire just as dedicated and far more irritating. Grief invaded his thoughts, and the deck blurred. He closed his eyes to stop the tears. Even after so many months, Kevral's death still plagued him. The lack of control bothered him, and his tone grew terse. "Subikahn can keep me safe. Can we leave now?"

Captain hesitated only an instant before turning his attention to the lines. "Agreed. But only because doing so will, ultimately, make Rantire happy. She was going at Griff's command, but she despised the thought of leaving him." He dashed off to prepare the ship.

Tae looked after the elf, shaking his head. He wondered if the suicidal nature of the mission had anything to do with the decision as well. Captain would never say it, but he might consider Rantire's life more significant than Subikahn's or Tae's.

The elf took over immediately, indicating a dock line for each of them to manage. "Release on one." He pointed at Subikahn. "And two." He nodded toward Tae. "Then prepare to fend off." Without explaining the nautical terms, he trotted off to tend the rudder.

Clouds overcast the moon, lending the sails a ghostly glow against a backdrop of gloomy gray-black. Exhausted, Tae leaned against the forecastle, scratching Imorelda while she quietly purred. The night wind felt cold against drying sweat, and the honest exertion that accompanied casting off a ship, even one this small, brought him a sense of deep pleasure that had kept tiredness at bay until this moment. Now, his eyelids felt as heavy as anchors, and he wondered if he had the energy to crawl down the hatch. It seemed so much easier to curl up on the forecastle with the cat.

Subikahn caught Tae's arm. "Come on, Papa. Captain says he's finished with us. Time to get some sleep."

Tae did not argue. He stumbled through the darkness with his son, too foggy to wonder why Captain had worked them so hard. He did not recall the elf needing much help the last time they had sailed together, at least not until the summoned demon had assaulted and destroyed the ship. Tae had no idea whether or not the *Kjempemagiska* had the ability to do something similar, at the moment did not even care, but he filed the thought in the back of his mind. Eventually, he would want and need to know.

Tae had no idea how he got midship, but found himself confronting the hatch sooner than he expected. Wearily, he reached for it, and Subikahn did the same. Together, they pried it open and descended belowdeck into a small compartment that contained only a wooden desk and chair, three pallets, an empty chamber pot, and an oil lamp hanging from a peg. Apparently, Captain stowed the edible supplies elsewhere. As Subikahn closed the hatch, Imorelda slipped through the receding crack to join them.

Without bothering to undress, Tae flopped onto the nearest pallet, intending to fall asleep en route. To his surprise, he found the blankets bulky, oddly shaped, and they seemed to jerk. A startled scream emerged from beneath him. Instantly awake, Tae rolled off the pallet, only to find himself confronting a larger human being he had lain on in his haste.

Splayed out awkwardly on the floor, Tae studied the figure in front of him, now sitting up on the pallet, expression as shocked as his own. No longer numbed by sleep, his mind awakened in an instant, and he recognized the person who had, apparently, been sleeping until he had casually tossed himself on top of her. "Matrinka?"

"Tae?" Matrinka folded her arms across her ample chest. "You're like a brother to me, but I still think it's frowned upon to share a bed with a man who is not one's husband."

Imorelda rushed to Matrinka, rubbing herself all over the queen and purring loudly.

Although fully dressed, Tae attempted to cover himself up with his arms as well. "Matrinka." Her presence refused to register. He shook his head, trying to understand where dream ended and reality began. *Am I still in Béarn Castle? How did I get to Matrinka's room?* He had no history of sleepwalking, and the vividness of preparing Captain's ship for launching seemed unshakeable. "What are you doing here?"

"Well, I was sleeping, if you must know. Then a man hurled his sweaty body on top of me, waking me . . . rather abruptly."

"Sorry." Tae could think of nothing else to say. "I . . . didn't know anyone . . . I thought only me, Captain, and Subikahn . . ."

And Imorelda, the cat reminded insistently. *You keep forgetting me.*

Tae could not take his gaze off Matrinka. Her thick, dark hair was wild with sleep, and sheets that covered the pallet straw had left impressions on her cheek. "Subikahn?" Matrinka's attention shifted until it fell on the young Renshai who studied another pallet before sitting on it. She smiled. "I hope instead of . . ."

"Instead of," Tae confirmed, without bothering to name Rantire. "But what are you doing here?" He realized abruptly the significance of Matrinka's presence. She did not have the skills or training for a spying mission, and she was far too important to risk. "We have to take you back."

Imorelda butted Matrinka's hand, demanding more attention.

Matrinka obliged by increasing the petting, using both hands to stroke the cat. "You can't. You need me."

Tae did not understand. "What?"

Matrinka curled her legs under her substantial body. She was a large and handsome woman, full-figured and well-endowed. Though she wore heavy woolens, they did little to disguise her womanly curves, and Tae felt like a voyeur. He could still feel her softness pressed against him, from when he had accidentally lain down on her. He could not help wondering how he had missed her, realizing how exhausted he must have become to allow himself to do such a reckless thing. Usually, his instincts kicked in sooner, his natural wariness protected him from foolish mistakes that could, in other circumstances, kill him.

"You need me," Matrinka repeated, emphasizing each word as if she believed he had misheard her rather than questioned her decision. "Remember why we went to Tem'aree'ay? You were searching for someone with whom you could communicate by mind. Someone to whom you could send information, in case you didn't survive this mission."

At the moment, Tae could barely remember his own name. The shot of excitement that had infused him at Matrinka's scream was rapidly waning as his mind and body realized he did not face true danger. "Well, yes, but ... not ... you."

"Oh, so now I'm not good enough for the great King Tae Kahn."

She's good enough for me. Tell her that.

Irritated by the situation, Tae balled his fists. *You tell her that. You're the reason we can communicate by mind.*

Fine. I'll go to her level. She pets better anyway, and she's always glad to hear from me.

Tae appreciated the cat would interrupt Matrinka instead of him for a while. He did not rise to the bait. "Matrinka, I distinctly told you *not* to come. This is an extremely dangerous mission."

"Of course it's extremely dangerous," Matrinka shot back, clearly not hampered by Imorelda. "You're involved in it."

Tae knew it was pointless to mention her status. His was equally royal. "You're not trained for danger, and you don't ... exactly ... thrive on it."

"I'm not helpless."

"I didn't say 'helpless,'" Tae pointed out. He had deliberately avoided such disparaging terms. At the least, they were not true. Matrinka was a highly competent healer, a clear thinker, and no one could match her empathy and compassion. "You're a beautiful woman with some tremendous skills, but not one of them is spying. Or combat."

Tae expected her to argue his point, but she grinned instead. "You think I'm beautiful?"

To his surprise, Tae found his face growing noticeably

warm. From the moment he had met her, he tried not to think of Matrinka in those terms. She had a lover, and, eventually, also a husband. She was like a sister to him, special and adored, but never in a romantic sense. "It's a simple fact, Matrinka. The bard of Béarn himself sings arias to the loveliness of Béarn's queen."

Matrinka rolled her eyes. "The bard of Béarn is Darris." She did not have to add that they had loved one another since childhood, that Darris had fathered her children.

"Which doesn't change any of the stated facts. You are beautiful. But, more to the point, you're not trained to spy, and I'm not sure you know which end of a sword to hold."

"Give me some credit. I did travel with a knight and a Renshai."

"And me," Tae reminded. "Which is how I know you the way I do." He grabbed her hand and opened it. It looked soft and supple beside his filthy, callused palm. "Missions like this one aren't for people like you."

Matrinka jerked her hand from his grip. "Except you need me. And I'm going. I don't have to know how to spy or fight, because you and Subikahn do. My job is to remain on the ship and gather the information you send me."

Matrinka had a good point, but the idea of her in harm's way bothered Tae too much to consider the use or necessity. "Does Captain know he has a stowaway?"

"Of course. Why do you think he distracted you until we were underway?"

That bastard! Tae suddenly understood why Captain had required so much assistance to launch the ship this time. "Here I thought I'd gotten away with something by switching Subikahn for Rantire." Realization struck hard; she had outclevered him. "That was the plan all along, wasn't it? Captain never had any intention of bringing Rantire."

Matrinka's grin broadened. "And you thought I wasn't a capable spy."

Tae felt like he just took a kick to the head. "So it was all your idea?"

Subikahn loosed a snort, ruining his pretense of having fallen asleep.

"Who knows you better than I do?"

Tae shook his head. "Well, if you're half as crafty with the *Kjempemagiska*, they don't stand a chance."

Matrinka lay down, seized Imorelda, and rolled to her side to leave her back toward Tae.

Tae threw himself down on the only empty pallet, glad to find it unoccupied. Within moments, he was asleep.

Saviar imagined some people thrived on consistency, on knowing exactly what would happen every moment of every day, the same thing, day in and day out, through eternity. For him, it was torment of the worst kind. Each morning, the same breakfast arrived, thrust through the invisible opening: a shapeless lump of meat surrounded by barley gruel and a bowl of crushed berries, more pulp than juice. These he always ate, then shoved back through the magic portal before it disappeared. At midday, a bowl of water came. Then, in the evening, scraps of whatever dinner the Mages of Myrcidë had enjoyed: gray wads more gristle than meat, unidentifiable roots, and cold vegetables, usually too mushy to classify.

Saviar tried to ignore the bite marks on the foodstuffs, the evidence of cutting, the wateriness suggesting he got whatever remained on others' plates after their meals. If he contemplated what he put into his mouth too long, he might not allow himself to swallow it or might do so, then vomit it. He needed the energy, whatever its source; and, if the mages chose to treat him like a dog, he had little recourse. It was still an improvement over the once a day bowl of tasteless roots they had inflicted upon him for the first week. Hating them for it would not serve anyone.

Between meals, Saviar practiced *svergelse* as well as he could without a weapon. Body and mind needed the exercise, even if it contributed little to enhancing his skill. Without it, his muscles would wither, his circulation might congeal. Even with it, his thoughts turned in strange directions. Initially, he found himself obsessing, so he focused instead on rehearsing spelling or language details, creating math problems to solve, devising new techniques for battle, or contemplating the questions of the universe. Later, he found his mind strangely empty, thoughtless, utterly devoid of emotion or drive. It felt as if his consciousness descended into a pit and, if he reached its bottom, he would simply die. Despite the regularity of his meals, he tried to vary his toileting, worried to fall into a rut so deep his mind escaped only into madness.

Though not usually taken by regret, Saviar found himself desperately wishing he had allowed Subikahn to rescue him. When it came to interacting with other people, Saviar had always considered himself a bit on the shy side. Yet, now, he desperately craved human company of any sort. Even debating with a Renshai-hating Northman who considered him a gods-damned demon would be preferable to the silence to which the Myrcidians had condemned him for far too long.

Despite the regularity of his meals, and his view of the outside through the one-way windows, Saviar had no idea how long he languished in his tiny world of granite. Time lost all meaning, and minutes passed like years. He pleaded with the walls, uncertain when, who, or even if anyone could hear him.

One morning, when his gruel came through the wall, Saviar did not take it. Instead, he leaned his mouth against the spot where the dish penetrated, floating in rock. "Please." His voice emerged as a dry croak, unfamiliar to his own ears. "Let me die with honor rather than steeped in insanity." The misery in his tone brought tears to his eyes. He could never eat food he knew was poisoned; to die in such an ignoble way would doom him to Hel. Yet he could not help secretly hoping they did it without his knowledge. There seemed no reason to drag out the end. "No man can live this way."

Saviar did not expect an answer. He had never gotten one before. But, this time, a thin voice replied. "Are you ... ill?"

Saviar blinked, frozen in position, his right ear steeped in barley gruel. It was not the first time he had imagined voices; yet, this time, he did not sense the fog of delusion closing in around him. He did not feel as if he had to shake madness off before it fully engulfed him. "Isolation is the worst form of torture. I can handle bodily pain. This ... this destroys a man's mind."

This time, Saviar received no answer. "Imaginary." He slumped, not caring that it drenched the side of his face in warm mash, that he had clumps of gruel in his hair and bodily filth in his breakfast. "Again."

The thready voice returned. "I'm real. I just paused to think."

Saviar could not remember the last time anything had made him this happy. "Talk to me. Please."

"What ... What ... ?" The person on the other side seemed confused but clearly did not want to leave Saviar in silence again. "What ... do you want ... to talk about?"

"Anything," Saviar croaked. "The weather. The dietary habits of insects. The current price of Pudarian tea. I just want to hear a human voice."

"All ... right." The voice sounded vaguely familiar, as it should. Saviar had met all of the Mages of Myrcidë, had lived among them for several months while recuperating from his injuries. Then, they had considered him one of them and treated him like a friend. As they numbered only twenty-six, he knew them by name, although he had not spoken to most of them individually. "Um ... are you all ... right?"

The question seemed patently ridiculous, but Saviar did not judge. At the moment, hearing speech seemed like a lifeline he could not risk. "I've suffered a festering wound that would have been fatal had you not brought me around with magic. I've been smacked in the head with a sword's broadside so hard it knocked me out. I was in a coma for months. This is worse than all of those. Please ..." Saviar started to ask for terms of freedom, then decided not to overreach. At the moment, he would take any dispensation. "Do you think ... someone could talk to me every day? Even if it's just ... telling me a story? You can torture me at the same time, with magic or knives or hunks of wood, so long as you talk to me. Otherwise, at least let me die quickly and with dignity."

Again, silence fell. Saviar's neck was developing a cramp from the unusual position. His fingers trembled, entirely against his will, and nausea bubbled in his gut.

Apparently realizing what he had done, the other abruptly filled the hush. "I'm still here. I'm just pondering what you said."

Relief flooded Saviar. The quivering increased.

"It's really ... that bad?" The tone suggested genuine amazement. "Worse than ... torture?"

Saviar was desperate enough to tell the truth. "Much

worse. It's like my mind . . . is turning to dust. I'm trapped in a dark and eternal misery where even my thoughts don't work. It's . . ." Words came from Saviar's mouth that he never thought any Renshai would say, "It's worse than a coward's death."

"We . . . had no idea." The man drifted off again, much to Saviar's chagrin. "Saviar, my name is Dilphin. I'd like to discuss this with the others, but I'll have to leave you to do that."

Saviar wanted to say he understood, that Dilphin could go, but the words would not leave his mouth. *What if the others chastise him for speaking to me at all? What if he never returns? What if I never hear another real human voice again?* It bothered him that these thoughts even mattered, but they did. And more than he would ever have guessed. He wondered how Griff had survived as a prisoner of the elves and gained new appreciation and insight into Rantire. She had endured both isolation and terrible, daily torture. "Dilphin . . . don't go."

Dilphin's hesitation, though minuscule, seemed to stretch into an eternity. "Saviar, listen. I'm trying to help you, but I can't if you don't let me talk to the others. Whatever is decided, I promise to come back."

"What if they decide you can't?"

"It makes no difference. I'm a man of my word." There was a spare hint of malice in his tone, as though he had found others wanting in the same department. "I have promised, and I will return."

Saviar knew it did not truly matter. He had no way of keeping Dilphin against his will. He also worried to ruin what little he had already gained. "Should I stay where I am? What happens to our ability to talk if I lose hold of the tray?"

Now, Dilphin sounded amused. "Take your breakfast, eat it, and return the tray as you have in the past. We can reopen the way for communication."

"All right." For the first time reluctantly, Saviar pulled his breakfast into the cell. With talk came hope, not only for his sanity but for his mission that had, until that morning, seemed hopeless.

Ra-khir had worried Tem'aree'ay would stall the mission until it became pointless, rendering any assistance too late. Yet, to his surprise, she beat him to the meeting site. By the time he and Darby had their horses packed and prepared, it was too late to assist Griff's second wife and daughter. Tem'aree'ay had selected a sleek dark brown mare for herself, while Ivana sat astride a fat, cream-colored pony with a flaxen mane and tail. Three groomsmen had assisted the women, and they tacked up three more horses for the remaining members of the group.

Silver Warrior stood out from the others. Gleaming white from nose to fetlocks, his hooves buffed to a sheen, his mane and tail festooned with ribbons of blue and gold, he was the unmistakable symbol of a knight's steed. The bridle, reins, and saddle blanket were Erythanian black and orange. Alone or in a group, Knights of Erythane never rode incognito.

Marisole arrived next. Ra-khir attempted to assist her, but she politely waved him away. "On this mission, I'm the bard's heir first and a princess second."

Ra-khir backed off with a convivial salute. Marisole would need to toughen up to properly do her job. He found watching her juggle her property, weapon, and instrument too painful, so he turned his attention to the last two members of the team.

Calistin and Valr Magnus arrived together, laughing at some joke they did not share with the others. Again, Ra-khir felt a spike of annoyance, though he hid it behind a mask of knightly sobriety. He did not know which bothered him more: the need to interact competently and coolly with his wife's slayer or the fact that Calistin seemed to do it easily. Ra-khir could not remember Calistin ever chuckling so freely over anything and never believed the boy had a sense of humor. The only things that had amused Calistin in the past were other's frailties and misfortunes. He wondered if the Northman's champion had a similar cruel streak that attracted Calistin, and that bothered Ra-khir all the more.

Tem'aree'ay waited until everyone had mounted and she had the pony's lead rope tethered to her own saddle. "I can now state with assurance that the elves are still on Nualfheim, also called Elves' Island. King Griff sent a ship to meet us, with rowing boats, on the beach of the Western Plains. They will also watch our horses until we return."

Even with only one open passage through the Southern Weathered Mountains, overland travel to the southmost tip of the Western Plains was quicker than a sea voyage. Ra-khir knew the ship would have to have departed days earlier to arrive before or at the same time as them. More likely, Béarn had initiated regular navy patrols off the coastline since the "pirate" incursions had started. It would be easy enough to add a rowboat rotation at the proper location for when the elf-finding party finally arrived.

The route to the Western Plains remained fresh in Ra-khir's mind. He had recently traveled that way, following the path of the exiled Renshai toward the Eastlands. He had never actually reached the mountain passes separating the settled Westlands from the barren sand that comprised the Western Plains. He had caught up to the Renshai and was diverted northward into the central areas of the Westlands where his sons had gone. Soon thereafter, the Knights of Erythane had called him back to Béarn for the war.

And, now, it all seemed for naught. All three boys had survived the war, yet two had disappeared soon after. The third was with him but might as well be missing, too, for all the heed he paid his father. Calistin seemed to prefer the company of his mother's killer, and that bothered Ra-khir even more than the way he had left things with Saviar. Only Darby appeared interested in anything he had to say or do, in any aspect of knowledge he might impart.

As they headed toward the Road of Kings and the first leg of their journey, Ra-khir had a feeling he was in for a difficult ride.

CHAPTER 14

*Whenever faith is involved, whenever men believe some-
thing so intensely that they know in their hearts the gods
share their convictions, they lose their compassion for
disparity and grow blind and deaf to others.*
— *Knight-Captain Kedrin of Erythane*

WHEN SAVIAR LEANED BACK in his padded chair,
stretched out his feet, and closed his eyes, he could imagine
himself free to walk among the Mages of Myrcidë. Though
still small, the room little resembled the squalid prison in
which he had spent the last few weeks. Pillowed chairs and
benches lined the walls, and a table occupied most of the
middle. At the moment, it contained only a covering cloth;
but Jeremilan, the leader of the Myrcidians, had assured
Saviar it would soon contain fresh foodstuffs, the like of
which he had not seen for many days.

Currently, six of the mages shared the room with Saviar,
all male and most sitting bolt upright, certain they would be
called upon to contain a rush of violence. Saviar did his best
to put them at ease. He had no intention of attacking. Without a sword, he felt naked and vulnerable. Even unarmed,
he suspected he could handle all of them, if not for the
magic they could cast upon him in an instant. That, Saviar
did not understand, though he felt certain it would undo
him. Again.

Jeremilan cleared his throat. He was clearly old, with
skin like wrinkled parchment, his thinning hair snowy white

and receding. Still, Saviar found it difficult to believe any human had survived for over two hundred years, as Subikahn claimed. "Dilphin tells me you prefer death to imprisonment."

Saviar did not want the old mage to misunderstand. "I prefer death to the type of solitary and changeless imprisonment you inflicted on me. I was becoming . . . unhinged."

Jeremilan pondered the words as if tasting a fine wine. He had the slow deliberateness of an elf. "Are you usually . . . of a claustrophobic nature?"

Saviar shrugged. "Not to my knowledge." He tried to explain; this went far beyond a feeling of entrapment. "I've never been confined before, but I don't mind solitude as a rule. I think . . . isolation can damage any man's mind if it goes on long enough." He tried to recall anything he had read on the topic, but his thoughts felt thick as pudding and it was not a subject on which he had had previous reason to focus. "I . . . recall some mention of societies using solitary confinements as a form of torture. People rescued after spending days trapped in buildings or under fallen trees often report incalculable rages, depthless sadness, as well as seeing and hearing things that did not actually exist."

"Really." Jeremilan seemed more pensive than his companions, whose faces displayed everything from shock to thoughtful discomfort. When he finally spoke, his words surprised Saviar. "I'm sorry."

Saviar blinked, expecting anything but an apology. "You . . . are?"

"Of course we are." Jeremilan seemed almost offended by Saviar's question. "Our only intention was to keep us safe while we decided what to do with you. We had no intention of driving anyone to madness."

Saviar almost expected him to add, "That was just a lucky consequence."

"We're not like any other people you know. We don't wish to harm anyone. Ever. Only to repopulate ourselves and live in peace."

Saviar closed his eyes and sighed. He tried not to think about the fact that the freedom he currently experienced was illusory and transient. At any moment, the mages could corner him and place him back into the solitary madness of his previous prison. At a time when he struggled to think,

he had to watch his every word. "Sir, I know you won't believe me, but I think you're mischaracterizing people outside of Myrcidë. Most civilizations have no intention of
harming anyone; they, too, only wish to live in peace."

A murmur suffused the group.

By the time Saviar opened his eyes and looked around,
he had missed the reaction to his statement.

Jeremilan's brows rose into a sea of wrinkles. "You're
Renshai."

Saviar would not deny it, though he tried to hide any
vestiges of pride. "I am."

Another murmur passed through the men, although Saviar felt certain they already knew what he acknowledged to
be the truth.

"And you wish us to believe Renshai don't want to harm
anyone. That they want only to live . . . in peace."

Saviar glanced around the room, suspecting many other,
possibly all, of the Myrcidians watched him either directly
or through their magical, one-way windows. "Sometimes,
sir, war is the only true way to peace."

Jeremilan shook his head, rolled his eyes. "That's nonsense. Given that peace is, in fact, the absence of war, how
could this be so?"

Saviar had a ready answer. "Because the absence of war,
in and of itself, is not always a desirable thing."

Jeremilan's white eyebrows disappeared beneath his
bangs, and the other Myrcidians shook their heads dubiously. "I disagree. Peace is always good and always the objective of a civilized world." He rose and turned away. "A
person of your background can never understand that."

Though it irritated him, Saviar ignored the final, grumbled comment. "In theory, peace is always good and always
the objective of a civilized world. And if evil did not exist,
we could, theoretically, live in a world of unadulterated
bliss." Saviar shook his head, finding it difficult to imagine
any group of people this naïve. "But pretending there is no
such thing as evil doesn't make it disappear."

Jeremilan whirled back to face Saviar. "We know all
about evil," he said pointedly. "Everyone has the propensity
for evil . . . and also for good. We need to bring out the good
in everyone and suppress the evil." He reclaimed his seat.
"For example, Saviar, when we debated what to do with

you. Some suggested we kill you, but we did not because it would have been an act of evil."

Saviar could not help adding, "Instead, you nearly drove me permanently insane, an act of . . ." He cocked his head in question. ". . . goodness?"

Jeremilan flinched. His fingers curled. "We merely meant to contain you. We didn't know doing so would cause you any damage. Once we discovered that, we released you from the situation and apologized."

Saviar realized he did not want to lose his sanity to make a point. "And words cannot fully express my appreciation for that, sir. Thank you."

Jeremilan accepted the gratitude with a single nod. "As I said, we would have found a different solution had we known isolation could induce such discomfort. In fact, our wisest heads are considering alternatives even as we have this conversation."

"Much appreciated."

"Much deserved." The patness of the response made it clearly a standard exchange in their society.

Saviar did not dwell too long on his current situation. At the moment, any alternative to isolating confinement seemed tolerable. "But good and evil are not always so obvious or well-defined. There are times when the same action can be considered good by one group of people and evil by another."

"Only if one side deludes itself. Considering something good does not make it so."

Saviar could hardly disagree with the latter statement, though he did have issue with the former. "So, you're saying good and evil are absolutes."

Jeremilan did not hesitate. "Within the context of a particular situation, yes."

Now, it was Saviar's turn to find his eyebrows so raised they tangled with his hair. Even the Knights of Erythane wrestled with the ambiguity of right versus wrong at times. They always chose the honorable path, but they did occasionally have to consider which road fit that ethical description. "Then, Jeremilan, you should be able to perfectly define them."

Jeremilan pursed his lips and threw a glance around the room. He clearly suspected a trap. "When an action causes death or suffering, it is evil. When it alleviates or avoids causing suffering, it is good."

Saviar stared. He could drive a merchant's wagon through the holes in that definition, without scratching the sides. He used a familiar situation, clearly decided in Renshai culture long before his birth. "Let's say a friend is dying from a slow, horribly painful injury. Is it evil to kill the friend or good to alleviate his suffering? Is it good to keep him alive as long as possible or evil to force him to remain in pain longer than necessary?"

Jeremilan had an easy answer. And a smile. "I seem to recall a pair of brothers who came to us in that precise predicament. Chymmerlee kept the wound in stasis, so it didn't worsen, and you asleep so you didn't feel the pain. When she got you here, we worked together to heal you."

Saviar sighed. He had not intended to use himself as an example. "But you have options the rest of us don't. For us, a lethal wound is invariably fatal. We do have herbs and healers, but their uses and skills have limits far smaller than your magic."

"You can still keep them as comfortable as your herbs allow until they die naturally."

Saviar did not like the direction the conversation had gone. To all Renshai, Valhalla was the ultimate goal. To die outside of battle condemned a warrior's soul to Hel, and no Renshai could permit another Renshai to die a natural death. Saviar still did not understand why Subikahn had allowed Chymmerlee to bring him to Myrcidë rather than granting Saviar a proper death before the infection stole his consciousness. Of course, if Subikahn had done so, Saviar would not be sitting here trying to talk sense into Myrcidians. "Healers are rarely nearby precisely when you need one, and knowing the proper herbs and amounts requires training most people don't have."

Jeremilan refused to concede the point. "Then you should train more healers. No one should have to suffer needlessly."

Saviar realized Jeremilan could never truly envision himself living in a nonmagical culture, and continuing to argue this particular point would get him nowhere. Saviar had faced the Myrcidians in debate before, when he had tried to convince them to assist in the previous war. Then, he had told them the continent could not survive without their assistance, while Jeremilan felt certain they could. As the Myrcidian had clearly won their original argument, Saviar suspected convincing the Myrcidians had only become more difficult. At least, it now seemed he would have the opportunity.

Rain poured from the cloud-darkened sky, pattering musically against the leafy canopy. Curling, autumn leaves held water like cups until it became too heavy. Then they detached, dropping their sodden contents always onto Ra-khir's head, or so it seemed to the Knight of Erythane. Protocol dictated he keep himself as tidy and clean as circumstances allowed, but nature seemed hell-bent on leaving him dripping and out-of-sorts. Remaining immaculate had never been Ra-khir's forte; but, now, he felt particularly incompetent. Some unseen force dragged mud onto his stallion's white coat, and the wind seemed singularly bent on untying the ribbons bedecking his mane and tail, in stealing Ra-khir's hat, and in instantly undoing any small rearrangement he made to maintain some semblance of knightly dignity.

At his side, Darby actually seemed to enjoy the weather. His cloak hood shed the rain and neatly covered any untidiness in the rest of his clothing. His calm chestnut plodded through the mud as if made for it; if any clung to the gelding's dark legs, Ra-khir could not see it. Water made its red-brown coat shine.

Ra-khir found some solace in remembering his own time in training. Knight-Captain Kedrin had worked him harder than any of the others, demanding a perfection he could never quite achieve. Day after day, he collapsed from exhaustion. Day after day, he improved. Despite the effort, or perhaps because of it, he had only positive memories of his education. He had cherished the time spent with an amazing father stolen from him in his youth. The more he had learned about Kedrin, the more he had come to admire and love him, the more he tried to emulate him.

Ra-khir glanced over the other members of the party. Tem'aree'ay looked about in wonder, her hands alternately outstretched and a smile etched on her features, allowing the rainwater to flow down her face and neck into her sodden clothing. He knew Alfheim had had no weather; the temperature stayed essentially constant and precipitation never fell from the sky. Elves also seemed impervious to cold, so he supposed the uncomfortable sensations that kept humans indoors during rainstorms might not bother elves. Ivana, too, seemed to enjoy the rain, bouncing on her pony and making repetitive noises with each movement. After a week, even the horses had become accustomed to her sudden squeals, twitching back an ear but otherwise unresponsive.

Marisole huddled so deeply into her hooded cloak, Rakhir could not have recognized her had he not already known who rode the steadfast, bay mare. The rain did not seem to concern Calistin, either. He remained alert, as always, without allowing any part of his clothing to interfere with his sword arms. Valr Magnus looked as confident and handsome disheveled as he did in his usual state. At least, he had stopped chatting with Calistin to cast glances around the forest and their route.

Reminded of his own adolescence, Ra-khir felt empty and uncomfortable. For him, it had been a period of getting to know and learning to respect his father in a way that had only grown with time. In contrast, his own sons seemed to have abandoned him. He had tried his hardest to always put them and Kevral first in his life, teaching them morality and respect, serving as an ever-loving and courageous example of the way a man should live his life. Though Ra-khir had never treated them differently for their varying paternity, he had found Saviar the closest to him in every way. Not only did they bear a striking resemblance, they had similar personalities and tastes, and Saviar had seemed as instinctively drawn to knighthood as Ra-khir.

Though it made a certain amount of sense, it had often bothered Ra-khir that the son with whom he felt the closest bond was also the one who shared his bloodline. Such trivial things as ancestry should not matter. He had always tried hardest to reach Calistin, the one everyone believed shared his bloodline, the one who, he had been given to understand, would never know about his blood father.

The more Ra-khir tried, the less Calistin seemed to appreciate his efforts. The boy had mostly ignored him and openly maligned the Knights of Erythane. And now, at the time of life when Ra-khir had become closest to his own father, Calistin appeared to have rejected him entirely for the company of the man who had gleefully killed his mother. The situation felt all the more painful for the brief glimpse of humanity Calistin had revealed on the Fields of Wrath and during their longer discussion of women that had followed at home.

Valr Magnus rode up beside Ra-khir. At the moment, Ra-khir had no interest in speaking with anyone, but no one less so than that particular Northman.

When the knight ignored him, Magnus trotted ahead, then veered toward Ra-khir, forcing Silver Warrior to slide to a stop on the muddy trail. Slop churned up by the stallion's hooves peppered his usually snowy white sides and belly. Forced to confront the last person in the world he wished to speak with, Ra-khir flicked his gaze to the Aeri general.

Magnus did not seem to notice the hostility in Ra-khir's expression. "According to the map, I think we would make better time if we took the south fork." He gestured toward a path that currently ran essentially parallel to the one Ra-khir had taken.

Ra-khir frowned. His training would not allow for sarcasm or rudeness, especially while on duty, which he essentially was at all times on this particular mission. He licked lips wet with rainwater and studied the Northman carefully. "Are you familiar with this part of the world?" Though asked benignly, the question was loaded with unspoken malice. Any Northman would have only one reason for having come to this remote area, as part of the group that had chased the Renshai during their exile with the hope of slaughtering all of them at a time of relative weakness.

"Well, no," Magnus said. "But I have studied the map." He clamped a hand to his left chest, and Ra-khir could make out the shape of rolled parchment beneath his cloak. "The Western Plains lies at the southernmost tip of the continent, so it only makes sense the shortest distance would . . ." Apparently sensing some discomfort, Valr Magnus slowed his explanation to focus on the knight. ". . . be . . . southward."

Ra-khir said nothing.

Apparently feeling obligated to fill the silence, Magnus

continued, "According to the map, this path leads straight to the passes, while this other route . . . curves northward first." His gaze swept Ra-khir's face, apparently trying to tease out some indication of the knight's emotional state.

Trained to hold his features neutral for hours, Ra-khir deliberately kept Valr Magnus guessing. Though not terribly polite, it could scarcely be considered outright rude to do so. "I've traveled this way quite recently, and I can assure you I've chosen a suitable route."

"Oh." Magnus backed his horse toward the center of the road, until it no longer blocked Ra-khir's way. "Sorry. I just thought—"

Calistin rode up. He had, apparently, heard enough of the conversation to join it. "Papa, it's true you recently passed this way, on this route, but you were tracking us then. The Renshai chose this path because we wanted to avoid the towns and villages along the way. Thialnir worried a mass of Renshai might frighten them or drive them to attack us. With this small group, and a Knight of Erythane among us, we shouldn't have any difficulty taking the shorter route, even if it is more . . . civilized."

Calistin had an undeniable point and, for reasons Ra-khir could not explain, that only irked him more. "Thank you, son." He emphasized the final word, for Magnus' benefit. "I appreciate you've given the matter good thought, and your observations are well-reasoned. However, while having a Knight of Erythane along will ease the minds of the villagers, they will insist on feeding us, provisioning us, tending to our horses—"

Valr Magnus interrupted, "Those all sound like great arguments for the south fork."

Ra-khir tried not to relish drawing the Northern general into his trap. "—finding as many ways as possible to delay us. Every town will insist we spend the night, regale them with heroes' stories, judge their every small dispute."

Darby and the others gathered around to listen to the conversation without adding to it.

Valr Magnus' brow crinkled. "Can't you brush such things aside? Surely, they'll understand we're on an important mission, in a hurry."

"If I had the manners of a barbarian." Ra-khir deliberately stopped short of directing the insult, of accusing

Magnus of exactly that. "I'm honor-bound to assist those in need, important missions notwithstanding."

Valr Magnus used a flat tone indicative of building rage. Ra-khir's manner, though never obviously provocative, still served its purpose. "So, if you're on your way to an active war, and some fiend nicked a baby's rattle, you would have to track down the thief first?"

Ra-khir sighed. An enormous part of knightly training included tackling the trickiest moral dilemmas of the universe. Etiquette required him to answer the question, though it clearly mocked him and his ilk. "Not necessarily. How I responded would depend on the details of the circumstances."

"What if you were heading for the wazz-jar?" Calistin used a vulgar euphemism for a chamber pot.

Ra-khir expressed his displeasure at his youngest son with a single, crooked brow, though subtlety had never worked on Calistin in the past.

This time, however, Calistin shut his mouth.

Ra-khir was in no mood for humor. "If you're done maligning what I am and do, I'll leave the decision in your hands. We could gain a few days taking the southern fork, but we'll probably lose even more to the need to socialize. I'm happy either way, but I'll leave it up to the rest of you." Ra-khir dismounted, handed the reins to Darby, and wandered into the forest for private ablutions.

When Ra-khir returned, he found the others circled up, using their cloaks like great wings to shield the map. At the sight of him, Valr Magnus rolled up the parchment and stuffed it beneath his cloak, while the others separated.

Ra-khir mounted swiftly, trying not to look at the mud splattering Silver Warrior's hide. Ordinarily, decisions regarding the route did not concern him. This time, oddly, he found himself anxious to hear the others take his side.

Valr Magnus did so. "I believe we're all agreed to stay on our current path. We can consider the shorter, more populous route home, when we're more concerned about supplies than speed." He looked at Ra-khir. "Does that work for you, Sir Knight?"

Ra-khir accepted the earnestly spoken honorific in lieu of an apology. "That sounds like a fine plan." From the corner of his eye, he could see Darby fidgeting and worked out the boy's issue without much contemplation. "If no one minds, I'd like us to ride through Keatoville on the return trip. We need to check up on Darby's family."

Everyone responded at once. Ra-khir heard a couple "not at all's" and at least one "absolutely." That, and the happy grin stealing over Darby's face, made him certain he had made the right decision. Appeased by the confirmation of his route, his apprentice's joy, and the promise of seeing Darby's attractive and intelligent, widowed mother again, Ra-khir continued through the pouring rain in a much improved mood.

Saviar paced the sitting room floor from corner to corner in mindless patterns while the five male Myrcidians who shared the room watched his every movement. He appreciated the improvement in his conditions. At least now he had company in a rotating arrangement, fresher food, and furniture. But, as a week went by without a change of scenery, Saviar found himself feeling nearly as trapped and crazed as he had during his solitary imprisonment. The Mages of Myrcidë decided nothing quickly.

Saviar tossed himself into a plush chair with a bored sigh, focusing on the pressure of the chair against his clothing, the odor of his too-long-unwashed body, the grain of the weave. These details failed to distract him any longer. An instant later, he found himself standing again, swept into the same senseless movement he had abandoned moments earlier.

The Myrcidians continued to watch Saviar. At length, one man, named Giddion, spoke. "Young man, what's the purpose of this roaming?"

Saviar froze in position. Slowly, he turned to face the speaker who appeared middle-aged, his skin nearly as pale as Saviar's, his eyes dark, and his hair a russet brown. He wore the standard, loose-fitting Myrcidian garment and perched in his chair like a predatory bird. "Purpose?" Saviar shook his head, trying to clear a fog that grew denser every passing day. "There's no purpose. I can't control it anymore. It's . . . madness."

The Myrcidians glanced amongst themselves before Giddion spoke again, "You're still . . . suffering?"

Saviar forced himself to sit again, curling his legs against his chest and clasping them to remind himself not to pace. "I'm still a prisoner." He did not wish to sound ungrateful for what they had done to try to accommodate him. "Thank you for providing me with better food, for the company; but I'm afraid it's just not enough to keep me ... healthy. I'm used to sky and sun and fresh air. To working my body until it aches. To the randomness that comes naturally from interactions with other people."

"We're people," said a short, round man named Archille defensively.

"Of course you are." Saviar fought his instinct to rise again, to pace restlessly. "But our interactions aren't ... conventional. Aren't casual." He had trouble forming coherent thought, and that bothered him. He had always considered himself intelligent and facile, at least with the Common Trading tongue. "For me, it's the same room moment to moment, hour after hour, day after day. I'm having trouble keeping my thoughts in line, my body from aimless motion." He shook his head. "I can't explain it. I don't think it's possible to understand unless you've experienced it."

A small blond seated on a hard chair in the corner spoke softly, "I understand it."

Every eye went to him. Saviar had never spoken to this man before, but had heard others call him Paultan.

"Some of us have taken turns in your previous cell, trying to recreate this madness you spoke of." Paultan drew in his shoulders and clasped his hands, clearly uncomfortable with the memory. "I lasted almost a day and a half." He shivered. "It's horrible."

"Torture," Saviar agreed. He concentrated on the spoken words, unwilling to allow his mind to drift back to those terrible days of near-total isolation. "But I'm afraid this isn't much better. I'm not sure if it's the quiet or simply the lack of freedom."

Paultan nodded. "Some time alone with one's thoughts is a good thing. Too long, and they do nothing but condemn."

Saviar had deliberately avoided mentioning that phase, concerned the mages would see it as apt punishment for his demonic Renshai sins. "You can feel your body withering and your thoughts grow distant, numb. You start to question everything you see and hear, some of it real, some of it only in your imagination."

Every man in the room winced. Paultan fixed hazel eyes on Saviar. "I didn't get to that stage. I demanded they let me out."

Saviar was on his feet before he could stop himself. He took three steps before he realized he had resumed pacing and forced himself to sit down again. "Maybe if I had a window? More talkative company?"

The nods of the group told Saviar he had not asked for anything unreasonable yet.

"Even a little bit of freedom would make all the difference."

Now, several of the men's lips bowed downward into budding frowns. Giddion spoke the words on every mind. "As it is, some worry we're risking lives by remaining in the same room with you."

Though Saviar suspected he should have anticipated the comment, it struck him as wholly nonsensical. A laugh emerged before he could stop it. "You're holding *me* hostage, remember? There are a couple dozen of you and only one of me. I'm disarmed, weakened, and half-crazy. What do you worry I'm going to do? Think you to death?"

Archille piped up, as if simply reminding Saviar of something obvious. "You're a demon."

Saviar jerked his head toward the squat man who perched in a chair similar to his own. "I'm a what?"

"A demon," Archille repeated. "A Renshai."

Saviar would not lie, even if doing so might actually help him. "I am Renshai. And, like all Renshai but one, I'm distinctly and entirely human."

A tall willowy man with a wispy gray beard, Netheron spoke next. "Then why do you have an aura? And your brother, too? You're certainly not Myrcidian."

Saviar knew where the aura came from, the sword now in Subikahn's possession; but he doubted they would believe him given the rarity of items imbued with magic. It also might compromise Subikahn's safety. "I don't know enough about magic to speculate, but it's not impossible we carry some Myrcidian blood."

Archille snorted. "How could that be? The Renshai slaughtered all of us, leaving no Myrcidian alive aside from the Eastern Wizard."

The evidence against Archille's statement stood directly in front of Saviar. "And yet, men and women exist with the blood of Myrcidë flowing through their *living* veins." Saviar did not pause to allow Archille to explain. He already knew the wizard blood of those who had imprisoned him was greatly diluted. "Not long after the destruction of your people, the tribe of Renshai met a similar fate, vastly outnumbered by the other Northern tribes and assaulted in the middle of the night." It was the bitterest moment in all Renshai history, tempered through the centuries until Saviar could recite it without discomfort. "But, no matter how cohesive the tribe, it's made up of individuals. Some Renshai had interbred with other peoples."

"Raped them, you mean," Netheron groused.

Saviar frowned and shook his head. "I can't say it never happened; history records the deeds of individuals only when they have an effect on the world, or a society, as a whole. However, there are many known cases where Renshai legally married tribal outsiders. My parents, for a recent example. My brother was named for a half-barbarian child raised as a full-fledged member of the tribe. His Renshai mother was reportedly raped herself."

The evidence was scanty and poorly recorded; Saviar had always wondered how anyone could force a Renshai woman to do anything she did not wish to do. Only very recently he had learned his own fierce mother might have suffered a similar, terrible fate. "It's also known that some full-blooded Renshai had chosen to remain in the West rather than return to Renshi. Our current tribe descends from those half-breeds and traitors." He looked Archille fully in the eyes. "How Myrcidë was recreated is very similar, isn't it?"

Archille grunted. The Myrcidians had reconstituted only because Jeremilan had discovered his powers and sought out others with auras, binding them in secrecy. All of them descended from whatever traces of Myrcidian blood remained in the world after the indiscretions of sorcerers introduced their magical bloodline into common humans.

A deep silence followed. The expressions on the mages'

faces varied considerably. Netheron wore a ruddy guise of outrage, Archille's eyes had gone round as coins, Giddion's features screwed up until he seemed close to tears, Paultan looked away, and the other man, who had not yet spoken, tipped his head and dipped his lids, in clear contemplation.

Jeremilan stepped through the wall, into the room behind the other mages. Apparently, some sort of magical door existed in that precise location, one that refused to yield to Saviar, because the mages always entered and exited from the same place. There could be no mistaking the anger Jeremilan dragged into the room with him. His dark eyes flashed, his cheeks bore a flush, his fists balled at his sides. He embodied all the warmth and calm of a raging blizzard. "Stop that at once."

Every eye went to him. As no one was moving or speaking, his words seemed nonsensical.

"Do not compare Renshai to Myrcidians, not ever. They bear nothing in common but magic. Where the Myrcidians' originates in light and decency, the Renshai's is evil and raw, demon-play."

Saviar could not let that claim pass unchallenged. "Magic is one of the few things we don't share with Myrcidë. In fact, it's the main reason we have a population of a few hundred, despite our many enemies, while you have only twenty-six, even though no one knows you exist."

Apparently, Archille did not make the connection. "What's that supposed to mean? Are you saying magic makes us more vulnerable?"

Saviar never took his attention from Jeremilan. In spite of his age, the leader of the mages was the most powerful and dangerous creature in the room. "Unlike us, recruiting is barely an option for you. You can only attempt to bring in those with an aura, those with magical blood. That also greatly hampers your ability to breed." Saviar knew the Renshai, too, preferred to keep their bloodline pure, mostly because centuries of war had weeded out the weakest members and bolstered the strong, the quick, the competent. However, they remained open to permanently adding outside blood, so long as it enhanced the tribe in some respect. His father, and Subikahn's, had proven their offspring worthy of the training in very different ways. "Despite what you might believe, Renshai are wholly human. Our abilities come from dedication and training, not blood. Therefore, we can interbreed more freely, less carefully, than you and not have to worry about diluting our power."

"That's not right," Netheron said. "Renshai abilities stem from foul rites and consummation of human blood. From demon magic."

Saviar found himself incapable of allowing this misconception to pass. "Renshai abilities come from hard work and a dedication to the art of the sword. We begin studying it as infants and devote our entire lives to becoming the most competent swordmasters in existence. The pinnacle of Renshai existence is to have no responsibilities other than swordcraft, to die in a blaze of glory and be found godworthy of Valhalla."

Jeremilan waved off the description. "It's the goal of all Northmen to earn Valhalla, yet none of the other tribes bears the Renshai's dreadful reputation." He clamped his hands to his hips. "You see elders among the other Northern tribes, those who do not maintain their youth with demon magic."

Saviar tipped his head. "We have many elders who look their age. My wrinkled, gray-haired grandmother can still give me a worthy spar, though she can't always remember the names of the maneuvers she uses against me. No one would mistake her for my mother, let alone my sister."

Jeremilan scoffed. "I've never seen an old Renshai."

Saviar could not believe he had to argue this point. "With all due respect, when's the last time you've seen any human outside the walls of your own village? Chymmerlee met my grandmother and many other older Renshai. Ask her."

All the rage returned to Jeremilan's ancient features. "Leave Chymmerlee out of this!" he barked.

Saviar could think of no Myrcidian he would prefer to discuss, but he could tell pursuing the matter against Jeremilan's objections would only result in more isolation. He knew the historical basis for the blood libel that still existed centuries after its disproval. "In your day, Renshai spent nearly all their time in battle. We spurn armor and shields, so we tended to die in our teens and twenties. Back then, a thirty-year-old Renshai was considered quite aged. Traditionally, we name our infants after a Renshai who died in battle and, presumably, reached Valhalla. So, you can see how it might seem as if one Renshai lived long and appeared youthful rather than that several Renshai of successive generations had used the same name."

Saviar did not mention the additional detail that the Renshai bloodline seemed to carry a propensity to appear a few years or a decade younger than chronological age. Its contribution seemed minuscule in comparison and only brought the discussion back to the possibility of magic in the blood. Overworked people, especially women, grew into adulthood more slowly. Many Renshai women never menstruated, never bore children, never even attained the proper curvaceous proportions of other women. But it had nothing to do with rites or demons.

Jeremilan cleared his throat. "I know the truth, Saviar. Your words will not convince me otherwise."

It was a non-argument. "And where did this so-called truth arise? Can you prove I'm any older than the nineteen years I claim? Have you ever witnessed a Renshai drinking any kind of blood, human or otherwise?"

Jeremilan rolled his eyes. "I don't need to touch the sun to know it's hot. Or be bitten by a *jeconia* snake to know it carries poison."

Now it was Saviar's turn to consider another's statement foolish. "But we could easily find men who have seen the results of a *jeconia* bite. And we feel the heat of the distant sun on our skin." He shrugged at the ease with which he had felled Jeremilan's point. "It's true we believe some things on faith alone, but one man's point of faith often contradicts another's. Clearly, then, one of them must be wrong."

"I'm not wrong about the Renshai." Jeremilan sounded as certain as any priest.

Saviar sighed. "I've lived among the Renshai all my life and never saw one use magic, fail to grow older, or consume human bodily fluids." *At least not on purpose.* It seemed unnecessary to mention that, during battle, blood could fly anywhere, and a splatter on an open mouth or lips could happen to any warrior. "How can you explain that?"

Jeremilan had an easy answer. "You haven't come to the age when those secret practices are introduced to you. Or you're simply lying."

"Ah." Saviar feigned comprehension of the ludicrous.

"So you determine what's truth and what's fiction. And anyone who disagrees is lying."

Saviar had meant it sarcastically, but Jeremilan played it perfectly straight. "Or ignorant."

"Lying or ignorant," Saviar repeated. "Which must mean you're never wrong."

"Rarely."

"So, you are . . . sometimes wrong."

"Rarely," Jeremilan said again, stressing the word. "A man doesn't get to be my age without learning things about the world that you will probably never understand." He took a seat beside Giddion and gave Saviar a pointed look. "I'm older even than I look."

Saviar had no idea what a two-hundred-year-old man should look like. "So . . . the older the man, the more right he is?"

"In general."

"Making no allowances for intelligence, wisdom, experience? No accounting for a bent toward deceit?"

Jeremilan leaned toward Saviar. "I did say 'in general.' Would you not agree the gods have more knowledge than you?"

"Of course. But gods are divine and immortal. I'm willing to bet elves who have lived for hundreds or thousands of years still make mistakes. That their faith can be shaken, perhaps even broken, in the right circumstances."

Jeremilan hunched farther forward until Saviar worried the brittle old man might fall off his seat and break some bones. "The right circumstances meaning . . . proof?"

"Proof, fine." Saviar surrendered the point, at least superficially. "But how does one disprove a lie that another man takes on faith? Especially when that man dismisses the only eyewitnesses as liars based on nothing but his own beliefs. It's impossible to prove a negative, that a group of people does *not* do a particular thing. That's why rumors and gossip spread so wildly and, once in place, become difficult to dislodge, no matter how false they are."

"But the truth comes out eventually. Why would the legends of Renshai blood magic still exist if they had no basis in fact?"

Saviar had a ready answer. "Because faith is a tricky thing. It requires no proof, no truth, no basis other than belief. It allows people to ignore, avoid, or discard facts to cling to ideas based solely on personal considerations and biases. In this case, prejudicial hatred of Renshai, which is rampant in many cultures."

Jeremilan's eyes narrowed to a mass of wrinkles. His lips puckered. His clenched fists whitened. "Dislike for Renshai can hardly be called baseless or prejudicial. Without cause or reason, those demons wiped out our people, stealing all magic from the human world."

Saviar winced and considered. He could defend the actions of ancient Renshai in a much different time, under circumstances current-day people could barely comprehend. However, better arguments came to mind. "Jeremilan, I'm not going to try to justify or excuse the behavior of my long-ago ancestors. Correct or not, I'll grant you the premise that they behaved inhumanely, that their intentions were nothing but evil, that they slaughtered innocents in the name of sport. Certainly, I could argue that others of their era performed acts equally barbarous, if only because we know the other tribes of the North banded together and all but obliterated the Renshai, too."

The Myrcidians studied Saviar, clearly waiting for the moment when he would make a viable point. No one interrupted, allowing him to continue.

Saviar knew he had to say something clever now that he had gotten them to listen. "Some three hundred years and more have passed. The Renshai from that era died during the battle of Renshi, only scant years later." Saviar deliberately left out Colbey for the moment, worried the discussion might take a tangent and he would lose an opportunity when he still had their attention. "The current tribe of Renshai lives in Erythane, works for Béarn, and has never slaughtered indiscriminately. We don't even share a direct bloodline with the slayers of Myrcidë." As the final words left his mouth, Saviar suffered mild stirrings of guilt. He did not know whether the so-called Western Renshai split from the main tribe before or after the destruction of Myrcidë, so he added, "Even if we did, we're the children's children's children of their children. What crime have we committed?"

Jeremilan looked away. "A few centuries are nothing for demons and their spawn. For all we know, you're one of the golden-haired devils who murdered our own."

Saviar clamped his mouth shut. There was no arguing
with one so firm in his convictions, so steadfast in his faith.
When one's arguments had no basis in logic, they had no
boundaries. The most obvious proof could not dislodge
them. He wondered how so much ignorance could reside in
one so old, so powerful. As he considered what he faced,
Saviar came to a realization that now seemed so obvious he
wondered how he had missed it. *These are magical beings.*
"If I'm a demon . . ." Saviar captured Jeremilan's gaze with
his own. "Summon me."

A murmur traversed the room.

Unable to escape Saviar's ice-blue stare, he met it with
an angry glare of his own. "Why would we summon you?
You're here."

Saviar reached back into memory, to his father's description of the elves' demon summoning. "Then bind me." He
held out his hands. "With the type of magic that only holds
demons. I can prove I'm a man."

Jeremilan's eyes narrowed to slits. "And how does one
who professes to know nothing about magic say so much
about summonings and bindings? How would you know
that if you're not actually—"

"—a demon?" Saviar inserted, shaking his head. "I'm
not a woman, but I know menstruation happens once a
month. I'm not a healer, but I know *sarvenna* leaf can ease
the sting of minor wounds. I'm not a cat, but I know they
purr when they're contented." He clasped his hands, holding out his wrists. "Bind me." Though he said it with confidence, he hoped they would not take him up on the offer.
The idea of less freedom than he already had rankled. He
knew nothing that held only demons could harm him, yet
he had no real understanding of what the mages could do
with their magic.

The mages in the room huddled together, exchanging
whispers. Saviar deliberately looked away, lest he accidentally glean some information by lip-reading. He had no particular skill at it, but it seemed dishonorable to intrude
upon what was clearly intended to be private conversation.
Knowing the mages tended to long discussions, he did attempt to persuade. "You asked me for proof. Now that I
found a way to provide it, how can you deny me the opportunity?"

Giddion looked at Jeremilan, who nodded. Only then, the younger mage addressed Saviar. "It's not a matter of denying you the opportunity to provide proof but of denying you the opportunity to weaken us before attacking."

"Attack you?" Saviar did not understand on several levels. If he wished to attack someone, he would do it while they were at their full strength; anything less would cheapen his victory. He doubted the mages would appreciate that particular point, though. "Do you really not understand why I'm here?"

"You're obsessed with my great-granddaughter," Jeremilan supplied. "You kidnapped her, you damaged her, and you followed her back here."

Saviar's lower jaw sagged. Surprise and indignation carried his voice up half an octave, to his dismay. "I did none of those things." He amended swiftly, "Well, I did follow her, and I am enamored of her, but I'm not obsessed. I certainly didn't kidnap or damage her in any way."

The mages simply stared. They seemed just as shocked by his words as he did by theirs. Netheron found his tongue first. "How can you say you didn't kidnap her? You took her from us at knifepoint and dragged her off to Béarn."

"After promising," Giddion added, "to release her as soon as you had gotten safely past our magic."

"Which we did," Saviar said firmly. "I ordered her home, but she insisted on accompanying us." He added proudly, "And it's a lucky thing she did. Without her, we would have lost the war. The peoples of every country would lie dead at the feet of pirates, including all of you." Saviar saw horror stealing across the men's faces. "King Griff gave her a suite in the palace, treated her like a princess, and our bards would laud her as a hero if she would allow it. Is that what you mean by 'damaging'?"

Archille snarled out, "We're referring to the rape, demon."

The venom in the comment might have shocked Saviar had the words not already done the trick. "What rape?"

They all stared at him, accusation in every expression.

"Me?" Saviar could barely comprehend it. "You think I raped Chymmerlee?" Incredulity swiftly turned to rage. "That's obscene and ridiculous. I would never harm any woman in such a ghastly fashion, especially Chymmerlee.

I . . . love her." It was only the second time Saviar had spoken the words, and he was not wholly certain he meant them.

"Perhaps," Giddeon suggested carefully, "you convinced yourself she was a willing partner."

Saviar did not know where to put his gaze. The very idea that he would rape anyone humiliated and appalled him. "I've never slept with any woman, willingly or otherwise. I'm a virgin." A thought occurred to him. "Chymmerlee must be also. Why don't you check?" Even nonmagical healers had ways of determining such things, Saviar thought.

Uncomfortable looks passed between the mages. Only two possibilities seemed plausible: either someone had previously raped her or Chymmerlee had slept with one of the mages.

Saviar did not know how to deal with that. At the moment, he did not want to think about it. "Well . . . you're free to check me. If you think you can learn anything from it."

Jeremilan's features turned bland, showing no trace of his previous anger. "You mean, you would willingly allow us to . . . examine you?"

Saviar found his hand slipping toward his privates and halted it. "Could I stop you?" He glanced around the group, wondering why they found his cooperation so odd. A horrible thought struck him then, "You don't have to . . . cut it off or anything?"

The quietest of the mages loosed a snort of amusement, and a smile touched at least one other face. Even Jeremilan seemed ever-so-slightly amused. "No. We don't need to cut . . . anything . . . off. We're just surprised by your willingness to oblige us. Resistance makes our spells more difficult, sometimes impossible. When we cast them on a willing subject, we have much more freedom and leeway."

Saviar wondered if it were possible for two people to misunderstand one another more. He saw no reason to remind them he could not prevent them from casting anything they wanted on him. He did not want to open the door to every random idea they might have. "I'm fine with you using magic to test my purity, so long as it doesn't do me any permanent harm. I have nothing to fear from binding." A better use of their talents came to him then. "Do you have a means to test whether or not I'm telling the truth?

I'm all right with that, too; and it would obviate those other spells. That way, I could just tell you I'm not a demon, that I did not and would never harm Chymmerlee, that the Renshai are inarguably human."

"That would work," Archille said.

Jeremilan frowned at him, and they all leaned in for another whispered discussion. Saviar wondered if they could bathe and dress themselves without advisement. If they had the ability to differentiate truth from lies, or confine him to honest answers, there seemed no need for discussion. If they could not, they would fare as well telling him they could and pretending to cast such a spell on him. He would never know the difference.

The mages did not confer long. They all sat up straight and looked toward Saviar while Jeremilan explained. "On a willing human subject, we could cast a spell that differentiated truth from lies. It's not the same with demons. By Odin's laws, once summoned and properly bound, a demon must answer a single question honestly and perform one service."

Saviar knew the rest from Ra-khir's description, but he feigned ignorance. He did not want them thinking his information came from firsthand knowledge. "Fine. Attempt to bind me. If it fails, you'll know I'm human, as I claim. If it succeeds, I'll have to answer you honestly anyway."

"The problem," Giddion explained, examining Saviar intently, as if to judge whether he already knew, "is that once a demon fulfills his promise, he gains power. Eventually, he can break the bindings, and he always claims payment in blood."

Saviar stared back. "So now you're worried I'm going to use my demon magic to maim or kill one of you?"

No one spoke, but their expressions gave up the truth of that fear. "I'm not bound now. If I were a demon, and I wanted to attack you, what's currently stopping me?"

Paultan chewed a fingernail, then bobbed his head. "He does have a valid point. The magics on the room might keep even a demon confined, but it could not stop him from harming those of us already inside it."

"Unless," Giddion suggested, "he's biding his time, waiting for us to take the barrier down so he can slaughter all of us at once."

The quiet Myrcidian, a young man who had originally introduced himself as Lycros, finally spoke, "Is it your experience that demons can devise such elaborate plans? I'd always thought of them as shapeless, vicious globs of untamed chaos, wholly lacking order or the contemplation of such. Impulsivity incarnate."

Archille turned him a withering look that might explain why he had not spoken up sooner. "It's clear enough Renshai are not demons in the classical sense. I suspect from his eagerness to get us to try it that binding would not affect him, regardless."

"I'd hardly call myself eager," Saviar grumbled. These mages seemed willing to consider anything that might justify their faith, no matter how senseless it seemed to an outsider like himself. "If I understand you correctly, even proof will not convince you I'm not a demon. You'll just revise your conception of reality to conform with what you already believe." As soon as the words left his mouth, Saviar wished he had not spoken them aloud. He had made a bit of progress and did not wish to jeopardize that by angering the mages.

But they seemed to take his words in stride. And Lycros, at least, considered them. "There's sense to his argument. You tell him to prove he's not a demon, yet even before you take him up on it, you've come up with reasons why you won't believe the results."

Archille shook his head. "That's not exactly fair, either. We've always known Renshai are a unique type of demon simply by their ability and desire to pass for human. Perhaps it's better to describe them as humans who use demonic forms of magic. In that case, binding would not affect them any more than you or me."

Lycros stroked his chin, as if in deep contemplation, though a sparkle in his eye gave away some impulsiveness of his own. "Well, he certainly hasn't had a chance to indulge in demonic forms of magic for the last few months." He addressed Saviar, "You're all right with me casting a spell on you that will differentiate truths from lies?"

At the moment, Saviar would have agreed to anything Lycros had to say. "Of course."

Lycros muttered some harsh, sibilant sounds, waved his arms, and ended with all of his fingers stiffly pointed at

Saviar. He pinned his gaze on Saviar's eyes. "What's your name?"

"Saviar Ra-khirsson of the tribe of Renshai."

The mages studied Saviar even more intently, then bobbed their heads and mumbled amongst themselves.

"Tell us you have two sisters," Lycros commanded.

"But I don't." Saviar did not know what might happen if he lied. "I have only brothers."

Lycros' gaze bored into Saviar's. Either the spell demanded that he maintain direct eye contact or he chose to do it for other reasons. Either way, Saviar dared not look away. "Say it."

"I have . . . two sisters," Saviar lied. He winced, anticipating pain that never came.

The mages only bobbed their heads more intently and muttered longer sentences.

Saviar did not know how long the spell would last, but he wanted to get out as much information as he could while it did. "Actually, I have brothers, no sisters. I'm wholly human and know absolutely nothing about demon magic. Everything I've told you about the Renshai is true. I have never deliberately hurt Chymmerlee, and I cannot conceive of any circumstance where I would. I came here with exactly two intentions: to get back into Chymmerlee's good graces and to try to talk all of you into helping us defeat our common enemy." Saviar halted, running out of things he felt he needed to say.

"Stop." Jeremilan held up a hand. "All of your statements ring true, but one. When you said, everything you've told us about the Renshai is true, the magic tagged it as falsehood." His dry lips twisted in suspicion. "What is the lie?"

Saviar's heart rate quickened, and he felt as if it had suddenly become encased in ice. He forced his thoughts backward, over the previous conversation, surprised to swiftly find the answer. "Forgive me, I did state one falsehood, though not intentionally. When I said all of the Renshai who took part in the purging of Myrcidë had perished, I was simplifying. One, and only one, Renshai from that time still lives. Everything else I stated about my people was absolute truth." Saviar took his gaze from Lycros to pin it on Jeremilan. He wanted to convey to the old man he had nothing to hide.

Apparently no longer doubting Saviar's words, Jeremilan went off on the tangent Saviar had tried to avoid. "There is a Renshai older than myself?" His lids narrowed. "Now I know demon magic is involved."

Archille shook his head. "Can't be. You saw the results of the spell." He made a vague gesture that encompassed Saviar and Lycros.

Rarely did Renshai sacrifice a chance to talk about the immortal hero of their people. By now, Saviar thought everyone knew about Colbey.

Though they clearly did not know he still lived, the mages were not altogether ignorant of the situation. Netheron nodded sagely, "The last Western Wizard, right? The process of becoming a Cardinal Wizard would have granted him a significantly extended lifespan." The nodding stopped mid-movement. "Except all the Cardinal Wizards died at once, and you said this Renshai still lived."

Saviar did not have a complete grasp of history, and the information about Colbey fell into the realm of religion. Not everyone agreed with the Renshai version, though Saviar believed his father when Ra-khir had said he personally met Colbey, alive, on more than one occasion. "I know for certain he did not die with the rest of the Cardinal Wizards and that he still lived when I was an infant. I have no idea if anything has happened to him since that time. We believe him to be immortal and that the blood of Thor runs through his veins."

Saviar knew many stories of gods cavorting with humans existed; more then a few peoples proclaimed their past and present heroes or rulers demigods. But Colbey Calistinsson was the only one who had reappeared through history with enough frequency to ascertain the claims. "It's ascribed in the historical texts of Béarn that, at the end of the first Great War, Colbey and the Eastern Wizard, Shadimar, quibbled over the Pica Stone. Each of them believed himself the last of his people, Renshai and Myrcidian, and thus entitled to claim the enormous sapphire as his own. It is said that another huge battle might have ensued had Colbey not offered a sincere apology for the prior actions of the Renshai and renounced all claim to the Pica Stone, insisting Shadimar keep it."

Saviar glanced around the room to see if he still had the

mages' attention and discovered every eye on him, waiting for him to finish. "The texts clearly state that Shadimar forgave Colbey, and they became blood brothers. Because of that eternal bond, there isn't a Renshai living who would not consider himself a loyal friend to the Mages of Myrcidë." Saviar added hastily, "Assuming any other than Subikahn and I knew you still existed."

Again, the mages in the room went utterly silent. Saviar wondered how long they had remained isolated from the rest of the world, how much history they had missed, even of their own people. He knew they had an enormous library filled with ancient and decaying tomes, most written in languages long dead. A group with so much time and inclination to study would revel in the sage of Béarn's collection.

Jeremilan broke the hush first, and the focus of his question surprised Saviar. He had expected the next inquiry to have something to do with Colbey or the promised brotherhood between men who believed themselves the last Renshai and the last Myrcidian. "What happened to the Pica Stone?"

At one time, Chymmerlee had asked the same question. "While in Shadimar's care, it was . . . shattered."

A collective intake of breath followed, and Saviar saw several of the mages wince. Jeremilan turned Saviar a look of withering disdain, which had become familiar. "The Pica Stone is the most magical item ever to exist. Do you know the power it would take to destroy such a thing?"

Saviar had no idea. He could only shrug in ignorance.

"He's not lying," Netheron pointed out.

Archille's entire face seemed to pucker, as if he had eaten something sour. "There are weaknesses to the truth detection spell."

Now, Netheron turned the same look Jeremilan gave Saviar on Archille. "Fine. He wholeheartedly believes it to be the truth. Perhaps he can enlighten us as to why."

Saviar did so. "Because my parents, Subikahn's father, some elves, and a few others went on a successful mission to gather up the pieces from multiple worlds. We were infants then, and our mother was carrying our youngest brother in her womb." Saviar's own words gave him pause. For the first time, he dared to wonder if that strange and exotic adventure had affected Calistin. At the least, it had exposed him to Outworldly magic during his early development and might account for some of his peculiarities. "As I understand it, combined elfin magic put the Pica Stone back together, and it's currently used as the means to determine the fitness of future Béarnian royalty."

If anything, Jeremilan's expression grew more judgmental. "The Pica Stone . . ." He shook his head and snorted. ". . . an object of ridicule?"

Saviar did not understand how Jeremilan had drawn such a conclusion. "I think most would consider it the most significant job in human history. The ruler of Béarn is the focal point of the world's neutrality. Selected wrong, Midgard would drift into oblivion."

Jeremilan only grunted.

Saviar looked over the mages, each lost in deep thoughts of his own, and felt a sense of accomplishment, the type that usually only accompanied a long, rugged, and seamless sword practice. At least now, they believed him, perhaps even understood that the Renshai and Myrcidians were not so different. At long last, he had moved them a step closer to reconciliation, and he only hoped he could continue the momentum.

CHAPTER 15

Don't you want the chance to guide your son on different paths than just the one his mother chose for him? You lose that if you decide only to play with him, to avoid the difficult events and discussions in his presence.
　　　　　　　　　— *Knight-Captain Kedrin of Erythane*

RAIN POURED from a turbulent ebony sky, and lightning flashed ragged zigzags through the clouds. Sodden from the crown of his head to the tips of his boots, Calistin Ra-khirsson sliced sword forms that cleaved fog and lines of water, sent armies of soggy leaves pattering from the branches, and strained his limbs as well as his temper. He was used to practicing in all terrains, through any type of weather, yet it seemed as if the gods had banded together to keep the elf-finding party eternally wet and uncomfortable.

Mud sucked at Calistin's feet, slowing his perfect and delicate timing. Irritated by his myriad minute mistakes, he pushed himself beyond his usual intense dedication while the others sought the cover of a nearby cave. For once, the water dripping into his eyes and mouth contained little salt, and his imagined enemies spent more time laughing at his technique than falling to the brilliance and timing of his sword strokes.

With a growl of rage, Calistin drove into another *svergelse*, feet mired in muck, sword heavy with rainwater, arms aching from repetitive effort. Sick to death of cold and damp, of sticky clothing, of slogging through putrid puddles by day and splashing himself with mire and muck by night, Calistin launched into his maneuver with all the intensity of the demons others named the Renshai and all the finesse of a landed fish, at least in his own mind.

A lanky youth blundered into the clearing where Calistin practiced, glanced upward, then wildly attempted to lunge out of his way.

Desperate for a target for his rage, Calistin lashed out at the young man. He barely managed to turn his blade to the flat before it cut the legs out from under the other, spilling him to the ground. In a flash, Calistin was on top of the youngster, the point of his sword pressed to the bared throat and ready for a fatal cut.

Darby screamed. "Calistin, it's me! Don't kill me!"

It took every bit of Calistin's self-control to keep from thrusting the blade through Darby's neck. "You out-and-out simpleton! Have you no appreciation for your own life? How dare you interrupt my practice!"

Fear opened the boy's face: nostrils flared, eyes bulging, brow arched to his hairline. Deep in his pale eyes, a flame flickered, then started to flare. Before Darby could say another word, Calistin sensed danger at his back.

The Renshai whirled, sword slicing, and his blade slammed against steel so hard the contact thrummed into his hands and rang through his ears. Instantly, he withdrew, cutting again. The other backstepped, catching Calistin's second strike on his blade as well. Again, the impact ached against Calistin's hands, vibrating to his elbows. He recognized his opponent an instant later: Ra-khir. His father's features were screwed in concentration, anger smoldering in his eyes. Calistin would not allow even this surprise to upset his timing. Once more, he lunged in attack, sword cutting air with a speed few could match. Ra-khir parried the attack harmlessly aside, even managed a thrust of his own before Calistin's superior speed forced him back on the defensive.

Calistin had sparred with his mother on many occasions. A highly competent Renshai, she had bested him consistently until he reached his early teens. For a couple of years after, the battle could go either way, before he became the assured victor. He had never previously crossed swords with his father. The Renshai deemed the knights' skill unworthy of their acknowledgment, and sword had never been Ra-khir's best weapon. To Calistin's surprise, Ra-khir made no effort to rein in his attacks, going at his youngest son with all the severity and strength he might show the bitterest enemy. Calistin appreciated that; he would have found anything lesser a deliberate insult to his skill.

Within six strokes, Calistin had the upper hand, forcing Ra-khir to tend solely to defense. A sudden jab sent the knight reeling backward. A jutting tree root snagged his heel; and, as he stumbled, Calistin disarmed him. In an instant, he held both weapons. One more drive opened Ra-khir's leg to a quick trip and shove. Ra-khir tumbled to the ground, both swords at his throat.

Unlike Darby, no fear showed on Ra-khir's face. His cheeks reddened, and rage clearly strained the boundaries of his courtly and mannered training. He surely realized Calistin could kill him in an instant, might do so purely from instinct; but he gave no notice of the danger. With a careless toss of his hand, he batted the blades aside, rose with impressive agility for a man of his size, and glared into Calistin's eyes. If he felt any shame for his defeat, he gave no sign of it. His rage clearly stemmed from other sources, ones Calistin could not yet identify. He had become more adept at reading people, but he still lacked the skill that came so naturally to most.

Without a word, Calistin handed Ra-khir back his sword.

The Knight accepted the weapon. Then, his hand lashed out.

Quick as he was, oriented to survival, Calistin never thought to move. Ra-khir's hand caught him a sharp blow across the cheek that surprised more than stung. In all of his eighteen years, Calistin could never remember his father striking any of the boys. His own rage building, he ran a hand along the offended cheek and dodged his father's intense, green-eyed gaze. Though clearly boiling, Ra-khir spoke in a calm, deadpan voice, "You can't behave like that any longer."

Calistin had no idea what his father meant.

Ra-khir's massive hands seized Calistin's shoulders, simultaneously gentle and firm. "Your mother and I, your brothers, your entire tribe had lofty goals for you. In helping you to achieve them, I failed you as a father."

Now, Calistin could not help meeting Ra-khir's gaze. The

mix of emotion forming in them was unfathomable to Calistin, but the passion was obvious. Whatever lesson he intended to convey, Ra-khir believed it with all his heart, needed for Calistin to understand.

"You received support without discipline, patience without sternness, love without responsibility."

Calistin did not agree. He felt his own anger building, even as Ra-khir's seemed to disperse. "You know nothing of Renshai training. It's all discipline, sternness, and self-responsibility. No maneuver in the history of the world was ever performed well enough to please Mama."

"I'm not talking about your mother or your weapons training." Ra-khir did not bend a bit. His grip on Calistin's shoulders tightened, though he surely did not believe he could restrain the Renshai. "I'm talking about life, about you as a human being."

Calistin still could not fathom his father's point. He was Renshai first and foremost. Swordcraft and Valhalla were the only things in life that truly mattered.

"A good father does what's best for his child, regardless of others' plans for him. I modeled decency, kindness, and honesty in the hope you would learn them, but allowed you to treat me with disrespect and derision. The Renshai expected nothing but the best swordsmanship from you—no manners, no chores, no humility, no . . . humanity. And you never disappointed them." Ra-khir lowered himself to Calistin's level, eye-to-eye, head-to-head. "But I never said a word when you disappointed me."

Until a few months ago, Calistin had never concerned himself with what others thought of him. A tirade like this one would have left him laughing in contempt. Then, Treysind had opened his eyes to a previously hidden world with a lecture not so different from Ra-khir's. Since the boy's soul had come to inhabit him, Calistin had seen things he never noticed before, had come to recognize emotions, occasionally even to empathize. His father's words cut as deeply as any sword stroke. *I never said a word when you disappointed me.* For the first time in Calistin's life, he realized his father's opinion of him mattered. A lot.

Shame came first, a wash of acid that burned Calistin in every part. Irritation followed swiftly, directed less at

Ra-khir and more at the boy who had ruined his life. Trey-sind's sacrifice, inconceivable to most, had finally granted Calistin a soul; yet with that gift had come more baggage then he could bear. Calistin had loved life inside his selfish shell. Unburdened by the cares of others, or the effect he had on them, he had maintained a perfect existence, admitting only that which made him more skillful, more powerful. Treysind had ruined that utopia forever. No matter how Calistin closed himself off, Ra-khir's words would follow him. Calistin had achieved so much, yet it all came tumbling down with a single slap and his father's verbalized regret.

Trained to answer anger with killing, Calistin did the only safe thing he could. He walked away. Intent on venting his fury on imaginary enemies to keep him from doing so on all-too-real friends, he moved as far as he could before launching into *svergelse* of his own making. The standard techniques of the Renshai no longer required the concentration he currently needed; yet even his inventions did not fully distract him this time. Wholly against his will, Calistin overheard the conversation that followed.

Valr Magnus spoke first, in a commanding voice that brooked no nonsense or rebuke. "You were out of line, Ra-khir."

"Oh, was I?" The tone revealed a tense jaw and gritted teeth. It was more challenge than question.

"Calistin didn't do anything that any Renshai, some might argue any truly dedicated warrior, wouldn't have done in the same situation."

Calistin drove harder into his practice, trying to distract himself from a discussion he did not mean to overhear. He knew he could move farther away, that he ought to do so, but he had to hear Ra-khir's reply.

"So . . . I should just allow him to slaughter innocent companions?" Ra-khir's voice sounded flat, toneless, unrevealing. Calistin had the feeling his father was leading the general into a trap.

Magnus either did not notice or did not care. "If Calistin had wanted Darby dead, he had ample time to kill him. He was merely teaching the boy an important lesson."

"Is that so?" Ra-khir was still holding back. Calistin had grown accustomed to his father's patience, his ability to hold his tongue when any normal person would launch into a verbal, if not physical, attack. But the slap and tongue-lashing he had inflicted on his son already proved that even a Knight of Erythane had limits. As unschooled in human emotion and reaction as Calistin was, even he knew now was not the time to push Ra-khir.

"You're a lucky man." Valr Magnus sounded genuinely wistful. "I would be proud to call Calistin my son."

Warmth suffused Calistin. The words should have made him happy, but he took no pleasure in them for reasons he could not explain. He drove himself to more intricate maneuvers in the hope the voices would disappear from conscious thought. It enraged him that such a thing could distract him from total immersion in his *svergelse*. Until recently, he had never cared a bit about what others thought of him, what they said when they spoke of him.

"I'm proud of all of my sons," Ra-khir proclaimed, without a hint of self-satisfaction and clearly including Subikahn. "But that doesn't mean I allow them to do dangerous, obnoxious, or inappropriate things without comment."

"When you chase a bird, you expect it to fly. When you disturb a Renshai—"

Ra-khir did not allow Magnus to finish. "What you rightly know of Renshai couldn't fill the eye of a needle."

Calistin nearly lost his timing. He had never heard his father hurl a deliberate insult, even one so mild. The point was not lost even on him. From infancy, Northmen learned little but lies and exaggeration about the Renshai, trained to despise them as something less than human.

Magnus rose to the bait. "That's not fair, Ra-khir. By Northern standards, I'm a Renshai lover. I ..."

The general lapsed into a silence that seemed inappropriately long. Calistin had little understanding of nonverbal communication, had no basis on which to imagine the scathing look Ra-khir conferred upon Magnus. The Renshai did pause to glance in their direction, wanting to assure himself that Ra-khir had not silenced Valr Magnus by force. He could not picture the Knight of Erythane losing enough control to leap bodily on another person outside of a formal duel or warfare.

On the other hand, Calistin could still scarcely believe Ra-khir had struck him. The blow ached on his cheek the way no previous injury ever had. He had taken his share of the sides of blades to his head, nicks, slashes, tumbles, bruising hits during teaching and spar, yet none had ever pierced him so deeply. His father's comment brought back memories that had meant little to Calistin in the past. Ra-khir was a good father, quite possibly the only non-Renshai capable of raising three Renshai boys without descending into madness. Their welfare, their happiness had always meant more to him than to themselves, including Kevral's. Ra-khir had seen to it they wanted for nothing, even as they treated him like an inferior, incapable of understanding what drove them. Instead, he knew it most of all and loved them all in spite of it.

Magnus began again, "I'm not downplaying your accomplishments or minimizing your marriage, Ra-khir. I just mean I acknowledge the humanity of Renshai, understand their passions and ambitions, recognize that they're not so different from any other fully dedicated Northern-based warrior. Calistin and I are as alike as brothers. Our skills and abilities were recognized early and cultivated, at the expense of others. We have a kinship based on—"

Ra-khir's tone was ice. "I am Calistin's father. You are the murderer of his mother in an unjust duel."

Mama. Something snapped inside Calistin. The fury he had held in check since finding Valr Magnus in Aerin burst to the fore. No longer in control, Calistin turned from spar to battle in an instant. Charging back to the clearing, he hurled himself on Magnus.

The general managed a dodge, more instinct than skill. His own sword was instantly grasped in his hand, as if by magic. The two crashed together, ringing like the aftermath of deafening thunder. Strong and quick, Valr Magnus set to his defense, meeting Calistin's lightning attacks with deft weaves, evasions, and parries. Swift as a weasel, Calistin came at the Northman from every direction at once, never bothering to tend his own defense. He did not need it. Wherever the other sword cleaved, he was not there: swiftness incarnate, never still, as unpredictable as raw chaos.

Calistin had no idea how long the battle lasted. Driven by a hot frenzy of assault, he knew nothing but the deadly motion of their dance. Bigger, stronger, more experienced, Valr Magnus had all the classic advantages; but Calistin had the one that mattered, the maneuvers of the Renshai. In the last several years, no mortal had ever bested Calistin, and Magnus would not prove the exception. It only took one mistake, one tiny opening, and Calistin seized upon it. He cut through Magnus' defense, between his fingers, and the sword flew from his hand.

In his current state of mind, Calistin would have preferred to let the sword fall, to dishonor his opponent by stomping it into the mud; but doing so would disgrace the man who had given it to Magnus, Colbey himself. Instead, Calistin caught the hilt in midair, the moment it took to do so allowing Magnus time to draw another weapon.

"No!" Ra-khir's command cleaved the fog of Calistin's rage as nothing else had done. Though spoken as if to a wayward dog, it had the proper effect. Calistin and his opponent froze in position.

Ra-khir stepped directly into Calistin's path, without producing a weapon of his own. He displayed no fear, fully confident Calistin would not harm him. Calistin caught the message inherent in his choices. Valr Magnus got Ra-khir's back, a symbol of disdain. In Renshai culture, doing so implied that the other was unworthy of attention. Either Ra-khir believed himself a better swordsman than the general or he fully trusted Calistin to protect him.

Not wanting to disappoint his father again, Calistin lowered his arm and sheathed his sword. Still clutching Magnus' weapon, he waited. Behind Ra-khir, Magnus put away his second sword.

Reserving his concentration solely for Calistin, Ra-khir spoke softly. "I'm sorry."

Calistin stared, uncertain what to say or do.

Ra-khir continued, "Not for what I said to you, because you needed to hear it. I'm sorry for what I said to General Magnus that set you against him. It was unchivalrous and inappropriate. I should not have let my emotions overtake my honor."

At the moment, Ra-khir little resembled a Knight of Erythane, his hat missing, his face and tabard smeared with mud, his hair a tangle of filth. Never in his life had Calistin seen his father this disheveled, not even immediately following the war. Suddenly struck by an urge to laugh, Calistin felt his unreasoning anger dissipating. With no idea what to do or say, he returned Magnus' sword and wandered back into the rain for *svergelse*, this time making absolutely certain he could not hear what anyone else was saying.

The *Sea Skimmer* scudded westward across an ocean Captain named the Mahajian. Tae had never sailed so far, had never heard these waters called anything at all. It was generally believed that traveling westward from the continent would soon send a ship tumbling over the edge of the universe to a dark, depthless void that would erase its victim from the world. Despite these dire warnings, from the moment he stepped aboard the *Sea Skimmer*, Tae never concerned himself with this possibility. He trusted Captain more than anyone to know the boundaries of the universe, especially by sea.

Aside from Imorelda, sprawled across Tae's pallet and sound asleep, everyone aboard the ship now sat around the rickety table that served as the only real piece of furniture in the cabin. Half-cut barrels were their seats, and they slept on makeshift pallets of straw and blankets. They kept their clothing and other belongings in piles: Matrinka's always neat, Tae's tucked away behind his pallet, and Subikahn's wildly scattered.

Captain had dumped his own belongings to provide them with their seats. His things consisted of a few changes of clothing and an odd assortment of metal clamps and cleats, fine rope, wooden pins, and other sailor's bric-a-brac. He kept a few books neatly under the table, topped by a strange box with curved glass windows that Tae could not identify.

As Captain had gathered them, Tae deferred to him to speak first. He could not help wondering how the ship steered itself in Captain's absence. The elf spent most of his time at the rudder and, as far as Tae could tell, never slept. Even those nights when Tae's own restlessness drove him to study the dark horizon and absorb the noises that defined the sea, he found Captain steadily maintaining his course, gemlike eyes open and aware. The elf seemed content to stand in silence, or to converse, at any time of the day or night.

Now, Captain leaned forward, placing his mysterious box

on the table without explanation. "How do you want to approach the island?"

Tae had given the matter a lot of thought over the past several days. He had discussed some of his ideas with Captain but had not yet given the elf a coherent plan. As the others were not privy to those conversations, he thought it best to start with the basics. "I'd prefer to catch as many as possible sleeping. Fewer eyes to see me."

"Us," Matrinka interjected, but Tae ignored her. He had no intention of allowing her to disembark.

Subikahn bobbed his head thoughtfully. Although they would never consider a sneak attack, Renshai did learn stealth techniques as part of their training. "Although, we might run into more security at night. These are magical beings, you know."

Tae only nodded. He had considered that possibility and discarded it. No matter what sort of magical alarms they set, he doubted they would prove as deadly as scores of wide-awake users of that magic. He looked at Captain. "You've been to this island before?"

A slight smile appeared on Captain's face, more in the canted, gemlike eyes than the mouth. "I'm thousands of years old and an inveterate sailor. I think it's safe to assume I've been everywhere you can get to by sea."

Subikahn could not help jumping in. "Have you seen . . . the Edge?"

Captain's head swiveled toward the young Renshai, his movement more catlike than human. "The . . . Edge?"

"The edge of the world. The place where it all ends." Subikahn assumed the intonation of a storyteller intending to frighten naughty children. "The dark, horrible hole from which nothing . . . *ever* . . . *returns*."

Tae feigned good-natured patience, but he really wanted to know the answer, too. To his knowledge, no one had ever come close to seeing the infamous Edge, but he could think of no one more likely than an elf who had sailed the world's seas for millennia.

A mischievous smile teased Captain's face. "I'm still here, aren't I?" It was a nonanswer Tae hoped would not satisfy his curious son.

Subikahn did not disappoint his father. "That just means you didn't fall into it. I asked if you'd *seen* it."

Captain met Subikahn's interested gaze deeply and directly. An involuntary shiver traversed Tae. He had never dared to stare into elfin eyes with such focus. They always seemed so venerably ancient, so inexplicably icy, as depthless as the Edge itself. "I've sailed everywhere the ocean goes and never found such a place. If you travel in one direction long enough, you wind up right back where you started."

For several silent moments, Subikahn stared back at the ancient elf, brows raised. Then, abruptly, he sat back with a strained laugh. "Fine. If you want to keep it a secret, I won't ask again."

Once more, a smile tugged at the corners of Captain's lips but never fully materialized. Tae could not help wondering, but now was not the time to grill their host. If Captain had spoken the truth, no logical explanation existed. Tae could only assume that, when Captain sailed over the Edge, the gods chose to scoop him up and drop him back in the place he had begun. Tae doubted they would show the same consideration for foolish humans who sailed too far.

Tae returned to his original question. "You've sailed to this island before. Can you tell us what you saw?"

Captain rummaged through his things for several moments, returning with a quill, ink, and a curled hunk of blank parchment. He drew a lumpy, enclosed shape with blunted outreaches and lacking any flat edges. "This is the general shape." He raised the quill, using it only to gesture. "We're currently coming toward it from this side. Here . . ." He indicated an inlet. ". . . is where the natural pull of the current carries a floating object."

"What's there?" Tae asked.

All eyes went to him, and no answer was immediately forthcoming.

Tae pointed toward the spot Captain had indicated. "I mean, on the shore. Besides a bunch of flotsam. What do they use that area for?"

Captain shook his head. "Nothing, as far as I can tell. It's too near the ocean to build on and too cluttered for a port. Last time I came here, it looked overgrown and rocky." He glanced up. "I couldn't tell you exactly when that was, but I'd say at least ten years by your reckoning."

Matrinka cocked her head. She had shared her husband

with an elf long enough to know Tem'aree'ay calculated years along with the Béarnides. "And by your reckoning?"

Captain grinned. "A moment?" He chuckled. "On their own, elves don't measure time. We understand the concept but don't see it as significant enough to quantify."

The endless interruptions wore on Tae. He fidgeted in his seat, trying to reclaim the conversation, to keep it targeted. "Can you give us a full description of the island as you know it?"

Captain tapped his crude map with the end of the quill. "Here." He outlined about two-thirds of the island with a finger. "Large buildings that house the giants. As far as I can tell, they live in groups that may represent tribes or families. If I had to categorize them, I'd say somewhere between humans and elves."

Clearly Captain did not refer to height.

"How so?" Tae pressed.

Captain sighed and glanced at the ceiling, clearly gathering his thoughts. "Attitude and approach to life, I mean. To elves, magic comes as naturally as breathing. It's a part of us to which we don't give much thought. We're impervious to heat and cold on a natural level, and most of us don't sleep, so we don't place much emphasis on structure and rules—"

Subikahn could not help interrupting. "No sleep? How lucky is that?"

"Most of us," Captain reiterated. "A few elves have always required it. Since we've come to Midgard, that percentage has grown. I may not even be correct when I use the term 'most' anymore."

"Why?" Subikahn pressed. "Why more sleep?"

Captain merely shrugged. "Some believe it's because we have more responsibility, more concerns, more cares. Others ascribe less innocent reasons, usually when they want to condemn mankind as a whole. It's all supposition."

Again, Tae had to take control of the conversation. He tried to guess Captain's point to forestall a long discussion off their topic. "So, the *Kjempemagiska* exist in a state somewhere between elfin anarchy and human order."

Captain confirmed Tae's statement by turning his attention to the Eastern king. "I can't say exactly where on that spectrum because I've never interacted with them. I'm going only by what I've observed from a distance."

That boded well, in Tae's mind. If Captain had managed to sail close enough to observe them, without them bothering him, scouting was not impossible. Of course, Captain had made his observations before the war, and the *Kjempe-magiska* might have increased their security. "Like their structures."

Captain nodded. "They live in buildings. Apparently, the weather is not immaterial to them."

"What kind of buildings?" Tae already knew their enemy had a high level of technology. The *alsona* ships had seemed larger and sturdier than their own, their swords and armor well-crafted, their arrows more slender and metal-shafted. They had considered the continental architecture primitive copies of their own.

Captain popped out of his seat, tucked the box under his right arm, and seized Tae's sleeve with his left. "Come and see."

Terror clutched at Tae's chest, and it was all he could do to follow numbly. "You mean . . . we're close enough . . . to see them?"

Matrinka and Subikahn trailed them to the hatch, the Renshai stating the more important point, "We're close enough for them to see us?"

As they emerged, a gust of wind buffeted Tae's face, and the luffing of the sails snapped through his ears. Apparently, Captain had anchored them. Tae still managed to hear the elf say, "Of course not." He came to a halt near the starboard rail, facing southward; and, still clutching Tae, handed the box to Matrinka. "Put it up to your eyes."

Matrinka examined the object in her hands. She turned it over several times. "Like this?" She placed it near her face.

Captain released Tae to gently guide Matrinka's movements.

As the box came up to eye level, Matrinka gasped, fumbled it, and might have dropped it had Captain not been there to steady it in her hands. "I see it."

"You do?" Tae scanned the horizon, seeing only sea, sky, and a distant blob that could pass for a resting sea bird. "How can you?"

Matrinka brought the box back to her eyes, this time eagerly. Tentatively, she reached out a hand toward the ocean. "It's like it's . . . right there."

Tae could scarcely wait to get Captain's magic box to his own face. "Let me see."

Matrinka ignored him, either consciously or spellbound, Tae could not tell. "This is . . . amazing."

As selfish behavior and rudeness were not in Matrinka's nature, Tae gave her the benefit of the doubt; but impatience was driving him wild. "Give it to me." He reached to take it from her.

Captain watched, a bemused expression on his face. He almost seemed to be enjoying Tae's consternation.

As if awakening from a trance, Matrinka slowly handed the box to Tae, who nearly smashed it into his brow in his excitement. The world turned fuzzy, and he wondered what Matrinka had seen that he could not. Then, his mind reoriented the image, and he realized what had, to his naked eyes, appeared to be a sea bird now took the form of distant land.

It little resembled the Béarnian coastline they had left behind some three weeks earlier. No mountains crowned the *Kjempemagiska's* empire, at least not on the side Tae was viewing. Instead, he saw smooth, constructed rectangles reflecting sunlight with the blinding intensity of steel. Blurry figures moved through what appeared to be wide-open spaces, surprisingly ill-detailed for as near as they appeared.

Sandy flatlands stretched from the ocean, the landscape as desolate as the uninhabited Western Plains but the area oddly teeming with people. He thought he could make out living beings splashing through the ocean, as if insanity had overtaken them all simultaneously. To the left, a fleet of enormous warships bobbed in strangely peaceful waters, their sails strapped tightly to their beams.

Wordlessly, Tae handed the box to Subikahn. Surely, curiosity stabbed the boy as intensely as his father, but he had not spoken a word nor demanded a turn. Immediately, the scene returned to the vastness of ocean and a blob of undefined darkness toward the horizon. "Amazing," he said. Then, a worrisome thought struck him. "Captain, they have magic, too. They might have created something like your . . ." Captain had not yet given it a name, at least not that he had shared with Tae. ". . . Box of Farseeing. Perhaps they're looking at us right now."

Captain's gaze followed his so-called Box of Farseeing, now in Subikahn's steady hands. The bobbing of his head, though slight, did not reassure. "Only gods have the power of creation. That's why the world has so few solid objects endowed with magic."

Tae noticed he did not exactly say the Box of Farseeing had no magical properties, and certain aspects of Captain's ship defied logic as well. The ocean swells should have crushed it to matchsticks, yet they had weathered squalls with little to no damage. Captain's extraordinary seamanship could not account for all of it.

Captain seemed to read Tae's mind, not for the first time. Though a clear extension of the conversation, Captain's explanation sent a chill through Tae. "Elfin magic is little more focused than the chaos it's composed of, but many of us have a particular talent or niche. For some it's healing or summoning. For others, it's self-directed or other-directed magic. Helping things grow, detecting abnormalities, finding balance . . . the possibilities are limitless." He stopped abruptly, as if worrying he had said too much.

Tae pressed forward. Captain had to know his present company meant him no harm. He tried not to think about the fact that information, once revealed, could not be withdrawn and alliances, at least among mankind, changed nearly as swiftly as the weather. Sometimes, a little knowledge proved more dangerous than too much. Tae needed to make it clear he had heard and deduced enough that Captain might just as well finish his thought. "Your talent is . . . stabilizing constructs."

Captain gave the announcement ample thought. "That's near enough correct. *Hervani arwawn telis braiforn.*" He slipped into the musical elfin language, using a phrase Tae had never heard yet which fit easily into the comprehension his minimal contact with its speakers provided. "It doesn't translate into languages that have no real concept of magic. Nothing human can truly encompass it."

Tae sifted the phrase through his mind, combining his own rare talent with languages with the "otherness" they helped him understand and the words he had picked up when he and his friends had traveled with a pair of elves. It conjured an image of joining together that which normally had no true focus, a magical strengthening of concepts that existed without need for explanation. His experiences with Captain filled in the rest. Captain's talent allowed him to add magical strength to solid objects.

Tae also realized he should have deduced this particular ability long ago, from direct observation. With the power of elfin *jovinay arythanik*, Captain had located every piece of the broken Pica Stone, scattered through many worlds, eventually reassembling them. His ship demonstrated stability far beyond its materials and even its expert craftsmanship. Then, the box came to his mind, and Tae lost what had seemed like a clear train of thought. "So, the Box of Farseeing has an innate ability to bring things closer even without the use of magic. Your magic only strengthens the basic structure and . . ." Tae was not wholly sure if he had deduced this properly. ". . . enhances its properties."

A hint of fear flitted through Captain's gemlike eyes, replaced immediately by their usual ancient glow. He managed a laugh. "I forget how quickly your mind works, Tae Kahn Weile's son. The box has hunks of glass ground more finely than our current technology allows. And your fears are quite reasonable."

Tae tried to think back on the conversation to when he had expressed a fear.

"I got these bits of glass from a similar contraption lost in the ocean by the *Kjempemagiska*."

That clinched it for Tae. Initially, he had surmised the possibility that the *Kjempemagiska* might be observing them from the same distance.

Captain continued, "But you needn't worry. I refined this device both creatively and magically."

Tae nodded, though not wholly reassured. The *Kjempemagiska* also had cleverness and magic to enhance things, especially an object they had created. It seemed unlikely, however, that Captain had not considered this possibility. Surely, he left unspoken the fact that his particular magical ability, honed over millennia, was more powerful than anything the *Kjempemagiska* could muster. This only made the mission to recruit the elves to war more critical. Without intention, Tae's subconscious mind worried the idea that this odd ability of Captain's might somehow prove invaluable to the continental warriors.

At some point, Subikahn had passed the Box of Farseeing back to Matrinka, because she held it firmly to her face as she made a sound of wistful awe. "They could teach us so much. If only we could be—"

Tae sprang to her side, clamping a hand over her mouth before she could finish. "Don't say it! Don't *ever* say it!"

Startled, Matrinka dropped her arm, the box still clutched tightly in it.

Tae released her just as swiftly. "Don't even think it."

Matrinka glared at Tae, reaching around him to hand the Box of Farseeing safely to its owner. "What's wrong with you, Tae? I was only going to say—"

Tae silenced her with an angry gesture. "The moment, Matrinka . . . The moment our warriors start to think of the enemy as human, the war is over."

Subikahn developed a sudden interest in cleaning his always pristine sword.

She thrust her hands to her hips. "That's crazy!"

Tae shook his head abruptly. "I've been in their heads, Matrinka. To a man, they see us as animals, no more significant than cattle and, in some ways, inferior. That belief is central to their philosophy, essential to allow them to slaughter us wholesale, which—believe me—is their intention."

"Maybe if they saw us as . . ."

Tae's vigorous head shake silenced Matrinka again. "Maybe, but they don't. And, until we can convince them otherwise, we can't afford to see them as human or human equivalents." He added, for Captain's benefit. "The laws of Béarn and the Eastlands already include elves in their definition of human, although I think the elves themselves mostly prefer 'equivalent by law.' But we aren't at war with the elves." He did not bother to add "anymore." It would only complicate a simple point. "And, hopefully, we never will be." *Again.* "Once our warriors see the *Kjempemagiska* as humanlike, they will hesitate to kill."

Matrinka could not remain silent. "I consider that a good thing, Tae. I don't want anyone to become so callous he can kill a human being . . ." Apparently realizing the flaw in her own description, Matrinka added, ". . . or other similar being without compunction."

Subikahn finally stepped in, quoting an old Renshai proverb, "The uncertain warrior is dead, and he who hesitates might just as well kill himself."

Matrinka looked over her shoulder at the younger man before turning back to Tae. "But isn't it better . . . I mean don't you think it's . . ."

Tae gave her time to gather her thoughts. It seemed only fair when she had to argue against two.

"Don't you believe peace is preferable to war?"

"Of course I do," Tae said. "Who wants a life lived in terror, where any breath could be his last? Who could enjoy a long or happy life knowing his friends, companions, and loved ones might disappear the moment he closed an eye or turned his back? That they could be tortured, stolen, raped? Surely, you've seen enough to know wishing war did not exist will not make it go away."

Matrinka rolled her eyes. "I'm not totally naïve, Tae. You know that. I just think, if we could get both sides to see one another as useful and intelligent beings in their own right, it might make the war unnecessary or at least . . . more civil."

"A *civil* war." Tae laughed at the oxymoron. He imagined every soldier as neatly primped and pressed as a Knight of Erythane, bowing to his enemy and relating: *If you'll pardon my rudeness, kind sir. I'm going to have to attempt to kill you now.* Realizing the incivility of his own behavior, Tae sobered almost immediately. "A marvelous idea in theory and impossible in practice, at least not with lives and property at stake. Most men would stoop to any level to protect themselves, their families, and their land."

Subikahn added softly, "And that's the way it should be."

Tae ignored his son, taking Matrinka's hand. "Matrinka, I've heard their conversations, mental and spoken. I've been inside their heads." He hesitated a moment, expecting Imorelda's interruption, a reminder that he could not have done it without her expertise. Then, he remembered they had left the cat sound asleep belowdecks. "They have a single language, always have, and they can't conceive of the idea that the noises we make might represent sophisticated communication. Apparently, their constructions and technology far exceed our own, and they think we have only cheap imitations, brought to us by the tides and occasional visits by their people. To them, we are barely intelligent animals, and they see no reason to allow any of us to live. If they ran low on provisions, they would think nothing of butchering and roasting us."

Matrinka made a gesture that indicated Tae had made her point for her. "And that was their downfall, wasn't it? They undercounted and underestimated us. Perhaps if they had recognized us as humans equal to them—"

Subikahn interrupted, "They would have attacked harder and in greater numbers, assuring our slaughter to the man, woman, and child."

Matrinka whirled to face the young Renshai. "No. That's not what I was going to say."

Subikahn backstepped, which amused Tae. No Renshai would withdraw from a physical battle; but, in a war of words, Matrinka intimidated him.

Matrinka also moved, clearly seeking a position where she could face both men simultaneously. Captain appeared to have withdrawn from the conversation, calmly leaning on the taffrail and looking out over the ocean.

Tae had the answers Subikahn did not. "Matrinka, I'm sorry, but the lad is right."

Matrinka did not back down at all. "He's not right, Tae. Their inability to see us as human is what lost them that war. We believed them to be as human as us. And we triumphed."

Tae sighed. He had a choice to either withdraw from the argument without compromise or enter the realm of complication and detail. He decided it was worth a try. "We saw them as human, Matrinka, but only barely. To us, they were murderous, savage humanlike . . ." He sought a better word, realizing it might also define elves and not wanting to offend Captain. He avoided his previous term for elves, "human equivalents." "Humanish beings . . . humanides . . . without compassion or control, unworthy of anything but death. Not equals. Never equals. Aside from general shape and size, nothing like us."

Matrinka hesitated. She clearly saw the point but did not want to concede what had seemed, moments before, her stunning victory. "But if we did see them as fully human . . . if they could see us that way . . ."

"If we could eat 'ifs,' we'd have no need for food." Tae would not back down. "They see us only as unworthy obstacles to their goal. They intend to slaughter each and every one of us and would rather kill themselves than let us take them prisoner. It's hard . . ." Not wanting to leave her an enormous hole, he amended, ". . . nay, impossible to reason with people . . ." He caught himself, ". . . ish . . . beings of that mentality."

Matrinka had one last argument. "That was the *alsona*, the servants. These Keyempay . . ." She shook her head. "These giant masters may better know us for what we are. They may consider their own lives more valuable."

With that, Tae could only agree. "Which is, of course, the purpose for this mission of ours. To find out what's in the minds and hearts of our true enemies. To discover all their strengths and figure out ways to counter them. To find any weaknesses and exploit them." He tossed her a crumb. "Including the possibility that they see us as human, despite what they told their servants, and might be willing to parley."

When Matrinka was not watching, Subikahn rolled his eyes and shook his head. He clearly did not believe such a thing possible, though he did, apparently, understand Tae's reason for expressing it.

Tae reached for the Box of Farseeing again, and Captain handed it over without a word. Tae pressed it against his face, seeking details his previous, quick inspection had missed. That time, he had become caught up in the magic and construction of the box itself, its ability to bring the distant things to his vision, the strangeness of the island. Now, he scanned the area more carefully. The huge ships bobbed between the landed arms of a harbor. He counted forty, each of which could have held a hundred normal-sized men but no more than half that number of giants. Tae could not see all the way into the harbor; more ships might nestle there. He guessed from the curvature of the island he might be seeing a quarter of it. More ships could also be waiting on the other sides.

Tae could not help doing the math. At least two thousand *Kjempemagiska* could make it to the continent, more than enough to destroy their entire world. He lowered the box to his side. Grossly understating the problem, he murmured, "This is not good." He turned to Captain, speaking necessary words he would rather have kept to himself. His mind told him they had best turn around, disappear as quickly as possible, and return to Béarn. Instead, he said what he had to say, "We need to get closer."

CHAPTER 16

A man who can't keep himself alive is not worthy of that life.

— *Colbey Calistinsson*

A LITHE SHADOW under the cover of darkness, Tae Kahn slid back into the *Sea Skimmer* with barely a rock and without a sound. His companions met him on the deck, except for Imorelda who he wore, like a high-back collar, around his neck. His shoulders ached from her weight, essentially dead as she had napped most of the time. His need to have her always scanning the natives' mental wavelength did not allow conversation to pass between them, which left her bored and restless.

While Captain glided the craft away from the massed warships and beyond sight of the island nation the *alsona* and *Kjempemagiska* called Heimstadr, Tae's companions gathered around him to learn what he had discovered.

Originally, Tae had planned to put everything back on the ships exactly as he had found it, but he had discovered something too interesting to leave behind. He lowered half of his booty to the deck, a thin coil of white rope that did not seem sturdy enough to serve as ship lines yet, somehow, miraculously did. He looked around for Captain, though he knew he would find the elf at the helm. "What do you think of this?"

Dutifully, Matrinka and Subikahn inspected the prize, running it through their fingers and opening the coil until most of it rested on the deck like a dead snake. Laid end to end, it would wrap around the ship several times, at least the length of ten tall men, possibly twenty. Tae knew it did not contain a single splice. Even the great city of Pudar did not contain a ropeworks big enough to craft such an object.

Imorelda made the first comment, hopping from his shoulders to the gunwale, threading across the narrow prominence, then dropping to the deck with no more noise than her master. *It's a rope. Amazing.*

Matrinka and Subikahn glanced at Tae curiously, apparently little more impressed than the impassive feline. As Tae clearly seemed to expect something from her, Matrinka said carefully, "It's certainly well-crafted." She pulled a hank between her hands. "And it has a coldness to it, almost as if it had woven metal inside."

"Try cutting it," Tae suggested. Now that the excitement of exploring a *Kjempemagiska* ship had passed, he felt chilled to the bone. He pulled his cloak more tightly around him.

Dutifully, Matrinka found her utility knife and set the edge against the rope. She sliced at it, first gently, then with more force, then by wrapping it around the blade and sawing. The motion did not dislodge so much as a dust mote.

Subikahn watched her for a few moments. Then, apparently needing to test it himself, he drew his own utility blade and hacked at the high tensile fibers. Tae knew neither of them would have any success.

Matrinka returned her utility knife and examined the rope. "Not a mark on it," she said, this time with clear awe. "I couldn't even scratch it."

Subikahn frowned, but sheathed his blade as well.

Tae drew the rest of his booty from his pocket, half a dozen knives, large as short swords, confiscated from several different *Kjempemagiska* ships. "Try using this. Stick to an end, please. I'd like to preserve as much of this rope as possible. It could be useful."

Subikahn took one of the knives, hefted it, and frowned. "Judging only from its balance, it's nothing special." He examined the blade critically, shrugged, and ran it along the rope. It did not split the strands like butter, as he clearly expected, but it did cause a neat scar along it as the other knives had failed to do. Immediately, Subikahn dropped the rope to study the knife more closely. Matrinka took the rope end, giving it a similar scrutiny.

A wave of amusement passed through Tae's mind. Imorelda explained, *Have you ever seen two people more defined by their actions?*

The sophistication of the comment surprised Tae, even after so many years of interacting with the cat. She never ceased to amaze him. He, too, had noticed that the Renshai found fascination with the blade while the healer turned her attention to the injury. He had not expected Imorelda to notice or, even if she did, to sum up the situation so succinctly. *Very observant,* he sent back. "I think it's related to another phenomenon I've observed. Kevral's sword could cleave a demon, while mine and Ra-khir's chopped right through it without leaving a scratch."

Matrinka nodded thoughtfully. She and Captain had been present at that battle as well.

"And Magnus couldn't draw blood from the *Kjempemagiska* until Colbey Calistinsson supplied him with a different weapon. Calistin could, already possessing a sword from the same source." Tae considered his own words carefully. "It seems to have something to do with —"

"Magic." Captain supplied the important word.

They all swung toward the elf. Even Tae had not heard him approach. Though the sudden appearance of Captain surprised Tae, the explanation did not. "Clearly magic, but I'm not exactly sure I get it. Is the magic from the being? Or the weapon?"

"Technically both." Captain's eyes lighted on the rope, and he seized a loop to study it with the same fanatical attention Subikahn had given the utility knife. Apparently distracted, he spoke maddeningly slowly. "A being . . . imbued with enough . . . magic . . ." Captain trailed off completely, and the humans all hung on words that did not follow.

Tae tried to take over. ". . . is innately protected from normal bumps, scrapes, and bruises? Has immunity to the normal mortal tools and weapons we craft?"

Captain dragged his gaze from the rope reluctantly to turn it on Tae. He took a moment to consider words he had, apparently, heard but not immediately processed. "Something like that."

"So we need magical weapons to fight the *Kjempe-magiska*." Tae looked down at the rope. "Or even to cut their lines." The magnitude of that realization seemed overwhelming, yet another one shouldered through. "And these . . ." He pointed to the utility knives he had purloined from the ships. ". . . are magical weapons?"

Captain finally picked up one of the knives, studied it, then shook his head. "Not magical. Not the way you're thinking."

Tae allowed his brows to inch upward. "You know what I'm thinking?"

★*Please,*★ Imorelda sent. ★*Even I know what you're thinking.*★

Captain returned his attention to the rope, running its length through his hand a bit at a time as he spoke. "Don't be getting paranoid now. I've lived on Midgard long enough to know how humans think about magic, at least in a general sense. To you, it's all or nothing, but magic doesn't work like that."

Tae bobbed his head back and forth, encouraging Captain to continue. The elf did not need to look at the rope, using only his sense of touch to evaluate it fully.

"I've already explained the rarity of permanent magic, but perhaps I haven't made that entirely clear. To my knowledge, only four swords actively imbued with magic have ever existed. The three Swords of Power were crafted by the Cardinal Wizards and, because of their danger, had to be stored on the plain of chaos. Each Wizard line, one representing good, one evil, and two neutrality, had the option of calling forth its Sword in a time of desperation to place it in the hands of a champion. Their power was so great, it was prophesied all the worlds would end if the three Swords were called out of chaos at the same time."

Tae put together all the information he had gathered in his life, from written and spoken sources. "That happened, didn't it? Centuries ago."

"It heralded the *Ragnarok*," Captain admitted, the rope still twisting through his hands to rise from one side and land in a heap on the planking beside him. "The three Swords eventually became fused into one, still in Colbey's hands, if I'm not mistaken."

Matrinka piped up, "And the fourth?"

For a moment uncertain to what she referred, Tae glanced at her. Dark circles had formed under her large, beautiful eyes, and a few creases marred the areas around her lips and eyes. She was starting to show her age, especially when she had not gotten enough sleep. He had always thought of her as a younger sister, and the urge to protect her stirred in him now. Only after Matrinka's question did it occur to Tae that Captain had originally said four swords imbued with magic had existed, then referred to the three Swords of Power.

Captain did not miss a beat. "The fourth wasn't actually magic, but it contained a jewel in its hilt that was."

Subikahn blurted out, "The Sword of Mitrian." It was a Renshai artifact that still maintained a place of honor in their society and minds.

Captain gestured at Subikahn to indicate he had guessed correctly. "The gem was broken in the same battle that brought the Swords of Power together. It's no longer a sword imbued with magic, though it shares one thing with the knives you recovered from the *Kjempemagiska* warships."

Tae looked at the piled weapons. "It could cut the rope. And magical creatures."

"It can, assuming it hasn't been rendered unusable over the centuries for some other reason: broken, dulled, softened."

Subikahn scoffed, apparently taking the comment as a personal affront to the Renshai. "Certainly not."

Imorelda reached her paws up along the left leg of Tae's trousers, as if to sharpen her claws on it. Instead, she merely stood as tall as possible against him. *Ask him what makes the knives work. You're going to need a lot of them to fight a war against those giants.*

The thought had already occurred to Tae, but he did not want to discourage Imorelda from sharing strategic thoughts. She had a unique viewpoint and might see things they missed. *Excellent idea.* He gave her words a spoken voice, "Captain, what's special about these blades . . ." He indicated the utility knives. ". . . Calistin's sword and the weapon Valr Magnus got from Colbey? What gives them the ability to cut demons and other creatures of magic that standard steel does not?"

Captain continued running the rope through his hands, but Tae thought he detected a slight trembling in the elfin fingers. Otherwise, Captain seemed unperturbed by the question. He sighed and rolled his gaze upward, though it seemed more to do with finding the right words to provide a coherent description. "We call it *skyggefrodleikr*." The elfin word flowed musically off his tongue. "It literally means 'shadow of magic.' It's essentially an impression, an echo, that comes from an object's long and close proximity to powerful beings or raw chaos."

Everyone considered Captain's words in silence. Before anyone could comment, he added, "I know what you're thinking, but it's a bit more complicated than that. It takes time, and not just anything in the presence of magical creatures becomes *skyggefrodleikr*. For example, a sword freely handed to someone after its use by an immortal Renshai is surely *skyggefrodleikr* because of the strong connection between the Renshai and his sword as well as the sacrifice it requires for him to release it. A sword handed to you from me, even if I carried one, would not be *skyggefrodleikr* because I would have no use for it anyway."

Tae cleared his throat. "However, a piece of your ship would have *skyggefrodleikr*." He pronounced the foreign word perfectly, exactly as Captain had done, and the other humans on the ship jerked their heads in his direction. Tae wondered why his ability with languages still amazed them.

Captain also brought his attention fully to the Easterner, though for different reasons. "That sounded a bit too certain for assumption."

Tae explained, "When the demon destroyed your last ship, I used a hunk of the debris to whack it. That blow landed, where all of my sword strokes had failed." He did not allow his thoughts to wander to the incident. The destruction had separated him from his friends; and, in the end, set the scene for Kevral marrying Ra-khir instead of him. The wounds he had sustained had haunted him, but none so much as the loss of the woman he had loved.

"That's *reipfrodleikr*, trace magic. Those rare items endowed with true magic, like the Swords of Power, we call *sannrfrodleikr*. *Reipfrodleikr* is a side benefit to my 'stabilizing constructs' ability."

With a grin that might pass for evil, Tae deliberately threw the words the elfin Captain had used back at him, *"Hervani arwawn telis braiforn."*

Captain's nostrils flared, and his canted eyes opened a bit wider. "You really do have a talent with languages or, at least, remembering long names. Are you sure you're not an elf?"

Tae laughed. He could not imagine anyone mistaking his criminal father as anything but human. "As sure as the morning sun in a cloudless sky. I just pay close attention, especially to anything spoken, and it sticks."

Matrinka hefted one of the utility knives. "So why do these particular knives contain 'shadow magic'?"

Captain touched one but did not bother to heft it. "Elucidating magical sources is not a forte of mine, so I'd only be guessing, same as you. If they looked older, I'd guess they just picked it up by being in the presence of magical beings who relied on them for many decades."

Subikahn shook his head. He knew a fresh blade from an antique.

Captain did not miss a beat. "It's barely possible they place the same significance on these knives as Renshai do on swords."

Now, Tae frowned. If so, he had surely alerted them to his presence by taking them, although the suggestion seemed unlikely. A Renshai's valued weapon never left his side, and these knives did not seemed particularly well-tended. Most showed signs of weathering, and several contained the remnants of fish guts or mud.

Captain still continued, "It's possible they war amongst themselves and require blades that can draw blood, or they may need the blades to hunt or protect themselves from some sort of naturally magical animal."

Subikahn added another thought, "Perhaps they think all their weapons need this shadow magic in order to strike at us. They may not realize they can bludgeon us to death with simple rocks and tree limbs."

The young warrior's words made Matrinka cringe.

Captain shrugged, not addressing Subikahn's point either, the first made aloud. "But, most likely, they are surfaced with magic, either stabilized or blessed or something foreign to me, to negate the need for sharpening or merely so they can cut line in the course of their sailorly duties." He finally dropped the last bit of rope to the deck.

Unable to resist, Imorelda batted at the falling end like a kitten.

Although Captain had felt every part of the rope from one end to the other, he still seemed incapable of taking his eyes from it.

Tae addressed the unspoken question. "You can keep that line, if you have a use for it. They have plenty; I don't think they'll miss a bit."

The corners of Captain's broad mouth twitched upward. He did not show emotion precisely as humans did, but Tae recognized it as a smile. "Thanks. I definitely can use this." He hefted the rope again and started winding it into a delicate coil with a speed that revealed he had made the same motion untold times in the past. "I do have one other thought that just comes to me now." He glanced around.

That clued Tae to do the same. He had known they were moving from the moment he returned to the ship, but he only now realized they had gone far enough to leave the island and the moored ships beyond naked sight. The moon hung, waning, in the eastern sky. Midnight had clearly come and gone, yet he still had a few hours left of night, if he needed them.

"The *Kjempemagiska* have crafted objects technologically beyond our own, like the lens in my box, this rope, and the construction materials they use for their dwellings."

Tae noticed Captain did not mention the *alsona*'s weapons, which had included thin metal projectiles, similar to arrows, but with built-in heads and no feathers. Somehow, they flew true and straight, often not only piercing but passing through their targets to hit another behind it. Béarn's top fletchers were studying the curious objects, along with the bows that shot them.

"I imagine the process they use to craft their special items requires a form of magic unique to them. Or, at least, a type elves don't know or practice."

"Imagine," Matrinka said breathlessly, but Tae stopped her with a brisk gesture. He knew exactly where she was going. The idea of trading goods with others of such knowledge and ability would appeal to anyone, but such considerations would only make their defense more difficult.

These were not allies with whom they could barter. These were cold-blooded killers who wanted all humans dead.

So far, Tae realized, he had learned more from Captain than from his own spying. He hoped the elf seekers were finding their magical neighbors and convincing them to help the cause, if only by supplying information and understanding of magic and the beings who used it. For now, Tae needed some sleep. Tomorrow night, he would begin scouting Heimstadr in earnest.

Tae awakened to a dinner of raw fish and dried fruit, feeling strangely feral. Fires were too dangerous on shipboard even when they did not have an enemy they dared not attract, but he craved the soft texture and warmth of cooked foodstuffs. He had eaten enough fish that the mere smell of it stole his appetite, and he had to force himself to consume enough to retain his strength.

Now, he watched the golden ball of sunlight slip over the horizon, leaving a wake of clouds tinted in shades of blue, pink, and violet. Orange-yellow streaks rose in a semicircular array from the departing sun, and the deep indigo sky began to take its place around the stars and moon. At Tae's request, the *Sea Skimmer* drifted quietly in the natural pathway of all flotsam around Heimstadr. By now, the *Kjempemagiska* would have become accustomed to debris floating in, at the lazy pace of the current, in this particular direction. Tae intended to allow the craft to come as near to land as Captain felt was safe, then to swim the remaining distance with a complaining cat perched on his shoulders.

Subikahn sat with his back against the forward bulkhead, methodically cleaning and sharpening blades that did not need the attention. Captain quietly handled the postmeal cleanup, not needing to steer the coasting craft. Imorelda lay curled in Tae's lap, and Matrinka scanned the island with the Box of Far Seeing.

Tae also kept his attention on the shore. As it gradually grew more visible, he realized they also became more conspicuous to those on Heimstadr. He considered asking Captain to toss the anchor, to swim the rest of the way to keep his companions safer, but it seemed foolish in too many ways. First, they would appear more suspicious moored in place while the remaining flotsam drifted toward the cove. Second, the long swim would use up much of his scouting time and energy, as well as put his own life in unnecessary danger from sharks and other creatures he did not care to contemplate. Third, he did not think he could weather Imorelda's strenuous objections, let alone Matrinka's. So he remained in thoughtful silence, contemplating his mission, until an odd, squeaking noise captured his attention.

The Box of Farseeing dropped from Matrinka's hands, and Tae dove to rescue it, even as Captain did the same. Only after he had committed to that particular movement did Tae realize Matrinka, herself, was collapsing to the deck.

Subikahn was on his feet in an instant, sword brandished. Dumped unceremoniously from Tae's lap, Imorelda yowled. Tae collided with Captain, sending both into an ungainly heap, and the Box of Farseeing slammed to the planking. Whatever sound it made was swallowed into the crack and shudder of Matrinka's body striking at the same time.

Tae freed himself from the elf and ran to Matrinka's side, while the others scrambled to the gunwale to get a better view of the island. Tae's first thought was that someone had shot the queen of Béarn, and he looked her over for some sign of a penetrating wound. The fletchless *Kjempemagiska* arrows tended to punch right through a body, leaving nothing to protrude.

Matrinka groaned, turned her head, and looked at him. She said something Tae did not understand.

Tae scooted to her face. "Where are you hurt?"

Matrinka shook her head and cleared her throat. It sounded raw, as if she suffered from a sore throat and raging fever. Somehow, her mouth had gone from normal to utterly dry in an instant. "Arturo," she croaked. She sat up, clearly uninjured. "My son is alive."

Tae could only blink silently. Arturo was dead, killed by *alsona* pirates before the war began. There was nothing ambiguous about the report of the killing. Everyone on board the Béarnian warship had been slaughtered: every sailor, every warrior, every Renshai. Most of the bodies had been recovered, with gruesome injuries from weapons or teeth. No one could have survived that tragedy. "Matrinka, what's wrong with you? Were you shot?" Tae had little healing experience or knowledge of toxic substances, but he knew some sentient beings used poison on their weapons. Some of those poisons could cause delusions.

Captain scurried up beside them. "Are you all right, my lady?"

Matrinka blinked several times in rapid succession, then felt around her for something. "Arturo's alive. I saw him."

Tae did not know what to say. "Prince Arturo?" He gave Captain a questioning look. "She's seeing spirits."

Matrinka pushed Tae aside and rose to her feet. Spotting the cracked Box of Far-Seeking, she snatched it up and snapped it to her face. She pointed a shaky arm toward the island.

Tae and Captain exchanged looks. Clearly, she had not sustained a physical blow, or she would not have been able to move so swiftly. They stepped to either side of her. Tae reminded, "Matrinka, we can't see what you're seeing."

Matrinka lowered the box, finally noticing the damage to the casing. Scarlet crept from her neck and along her cheeks. "Oh, Captain, I'm so sorry." Her expression wilted; she looked about to cry. "I've broken it."

Tae tried to gain control of the situation. "Matrinka, are you trying to say you saw a living, breathing Prince Arturo through that box?" He looked at Captain as he spoke. Only the elf knew whether magic could explain the situation and whether or not it posed a significant danger.

Captain took the box from Matrinka's hand, holding her fingers for a moment as he did so. "It's all right." A human would have continued, mentioning that the object still apparently worked and rationalizing that no one could keep hold of something while he fainted, but Captain did not. Apparently, despite all his time with and study of humans, he had not wholly adopted their ways. He also did not ask after Matrinka's welfare, something Tae knew he, himself, ought to do were he not utterly intrigued with what she might have seen.

As he clearly would not get an answer from Captain, Tae took the box and put it to his own face. Uncertain exactly where to point it, he scanned the shoreline. Many figures still graced the stretch of sand. Most appeared to be standing and facing toward the setting sun, though they did not take a formation nor a particularly attentive stance. He saw some smaller beings that appeared to be giant children rather than *alsona* based on their proportionately large heads and the way they romped between the standing figures. He saw no one who could pass for a prince of Béarn.

Tae then swept past the buildings and wild tangles of growth to settle on the outcropping housing the flotsam cove. Two figures, noticeably smaller than the hordes on the shore, capered around one another, apparently more *Kjempemagiska* children. He lowered the box, head shaking. "Matrinka, I don't see him." Again, he glanced at Captain. "I wonder if it has something to do with the magic used to carve the glass."

Captain tipped his head, brow furrowed. He clearly had no idea what Tae meant.

"Over there." Matrinka pointed impatiently, though her stabbing finger did not help to clarify the situation much. "Near the cove. There's a giant child playing with Arturo."

Tae arched an eyebrow, wondering if Matrinka had gone fully insane. He put the box back to his face, pointing it toward the figures near the cove again. He saw the same two creatures dashing about as before; but, now, he also spotted a third figure, much larger than the other two, sitting on the nearby sand. "I see a giant and two others." To Tae's eyes, both of them could pass for *Kjempemagiska* younglings. "What makes you think one of them is Arturo?" He lowered the box again.

Matrinka slowly turned her head toward Tae in the ultimate gesture of disdain. Her expression only reinforced the motion. "A mother always knows her child."

Tae did not understand her offense. "A father, too." He glanced at Subikahn. "But I can't make out enough to judge gender, let alone race. How are you seeing details?"

"I don't need details." Matrinka gingerly took the box from his hands. She had now dropped it twice and seemed reticent to touch it. She put it up to her eyes. "It's in the way he moves, the general form of him. And, now, I can even make out some features. That's Arturo."

Madness. Tae did not speak his opinion out loud, though Imorelda clearly received it.

Water everywhere. Weeks of pitching and tossing. It could drive anyone crazy.

Agreed. Still, Tae found it difficult to wholly condemn Matrinka. He had traveled with her, admired and trusted her. She had a naïve side, even now, but her observations had always seemed sound. "Matrinka, do you think...?" Tae was not sure how to finish what he started.

Matrinka did not allow it anyway. "I'm not moon-mad, Tae, nor under the spell of an evil giant. I've watched Arturo through the years, and I know every bit of him. He's dead, I know. There's no question he was on the ship when it went down. The bodies of his Renshai guards were found, covered in wounds no man could survive and savaged by sharks. Unlike my youngest daughter, I've never harbored a shred of doubt that Arturo died with them. And yet, Halika may prove to be the wisest of all of us. For the moment, at least, Arturo is alive."

Tae reached for the box again, and Matrinka passed it to him carefully, watching closely to assure he held it firmly before she let it go. Tae put the box to his face again. They had drawn near enough to discern more details. The *Kjempemagiska* child appeared quite young, a solid head shorter than her companion. Though blond as a Northman, she lacked their pallor, more yellowish than pink. She had the oversized head and pudgy limbs of a toddler, her hands swaddled in furry mittens and a matching cap pulled over her forehead.

Tae focused on her playmate, clearly male. Despite his size, barely taller than the toddler, he had the proportions of an adult. Unlike all of the *alsona* Tae had seen, every one of them ginger, he had hair as black as Tae's or Matrinka's, thick and curly. If Tae had seen him on the continent and had to guess his origins, he would have said Béarnide. The third member of the trio remained seated, making it difficult to judge height, but was clearly an enormous adult. Long hair hung from its head, suggesting a female, and it clearly looked down at something in its hands. Tae lowered the box again. He did not resist when Subikahn slid it from his fingers.

A frown scored Tae's features so deeply he could feel its impression on his face. "Matrinka, I admit he does look Béarnese, but are you absolutely certain it's Arturo?"

Matrinka hesitated for the first time since she had collapsed on the deck. "I'm not sure it's possible to be absolutely certain. But I believe that's him. With all my heart."

Tae supposed he could get no better assurance than her

reaction to the first sight of him. Then, she had recognized him solely by form and movement. Closer observation had only made her identification more likely. "This changes everything."

Subikahn studied Heimstadr. "Indeed."

This is no longer a scouting mission; it's a rescue mission. Tae had a harder time than he expected letting go. Once they turned their attention to this new project, they lost the element of surprise and any chance to spy on the *Kjempemagiska*. He mulled the options. He could insist on secretive exploring that night, with the option to rescue Arturo, if it was indeed Arturo, at a later time. The logical argument could be made that, if the man had survived here for the past year, the *Kjempemagiska* had no intention of immediately slaughtering him. There was time to scout first and rescue later.

On the other hand, Tae realized, if he got caught spying, they would lose any chance of rescuing the missing prince of Béarn. Or, probably, himself. He had never truly expected to survive this mission. He had only hoped to relay information to Imorelda who would then send it on to Matrinka. Now, he realized, more than his own life lay in the balance. The entirety of his strategy needed to change.

Even if Tae never got caught, he had no way of knowing whether or not they would find Arturo later. Anything he left amiss might fall on Arturo, including the stolen knives and line from the warships. For the moment, the *Kjempemagiska* seemed to be tolerating the man, for whatever reason, but Tae knew from overhearing *alsona* that the *Kjempemagiska* temper was as horrible and deadly as any volcano. He had seen images of the giants tearing their mannish servants to pieces or using their heads like balls in children's games.

Tae knew the decision would ultimately fall to him. Matrinka would want to save Arturo while they could, as swiftly as possible. Nevertheless, even she would yield to his opinion on the matter. Unless directly questioned, Captain confined his advice to issues of sailing. Subikahn had a good head on his shoulders, but he still deferred to his father in matters of strategy and espionage. Tae sighed deeply.

Imorelda's suggestion went straight to the point. *If it is Arturo, or any human, you have to save him.* She pawed his hand with retracted claws.

Of course, Tae reassured his friend and pet. *I'm just considering timing.* He glanced at Matrinka.

The queen of Béarn stood in silence, but her fingers wound nervously through and around one another. She wanted to speak, almost certainly to convince him to turn his focus wholly on Arturo, but she allowed him the privacy of his thoughts.

It was the final realization that made the decision for Tae. *You know, once we have Arturo, assuming it is Arturo, he can probably tell us far more about the* Kjempemagiska *than I would learn from one night of scouting.* Fully convinced, he did not wait for a response from the cat. "This is now a rescue mission."

Matrinka clamped her hands to her mouth but could not fully hide the grin. "Thank you, Tae. Please let me help."

Captain had, apparently, also been waiting for Tae's decision before speaking. "This is as close as we can safely come." He did not tend to modulate his voice much, but Tae had become accustomed enough to the elf to read beneath the spoken words. They had already drawn nearer than they should have.

Subikahn handed Captain the Box of Farseeing. "I'm going with you." It was not a request.

Had they still focused on the initial mission, Tae would have argued. Now, he needed Subikahn's sword arm. He hefted one of the huge, *Kjempemagiska* utility knives and shoved it through his belt. He indicated Subikahn should take one as well. "You're going to need something that can cut magical beings." For the first time, he wondered if elves might also count as creatures needing a *skyggefrodleikr* object to harm. If so, Captain had put himself, his entire race, in great danger in order to help them. Clearly, he had faith in Tae, Matrinka, and Subikahn; Tae intended to fully earn that trust.

"I already have something." Subikahn patted the hilt of his sword.

That stopped Tae cold. "You do?" At the time of Kevral's death, her swords had gone to the two sons present at the duel. Calistin received the one handed to her by Colbey and Saviar the one from Rache Kalmirsson, one of the *Einherjar* in Valhalla. There had been nothing left for Subikahn except advice.

Subikahn froze, a hint of guilt flashing through his dark eyes.

Tae's gaze instinctively went to the sword at his son's hip. His attention on his mission, he had not noticed the familiar hilt, usually with Saviar, now at his son's hand. "That's *Motfrabelonning*!"

Subikahn didn't reply, simply thrusting one of the utility blades through the right side of his belt. Many Renshai maneuvers required two weapons. "Let's go."

Tae wanted to ask more. A Renshai sharing any sword was rare enough to warrant comment, and a sword this special all but impossible. Yet, now did not seem like the time to press Subikahn. If they both survived, he would demand his answers later. "Matrinka, you stay here."

She opened her mouth, as if to object, but she really could not have much to say. In a combat situation, she would more likely get in the way than assist.

Tae turned his attention to the remaining companion aboard the *Sea Skimmer*. Tae had no authority to command an elf, particularly one so ancient. "Captain, do you have any idea what sort of magic we might be facing?"

Captain shook his head, broad lips tightly pursed. "It depends on how the *Kjempemagiska* learned to shape chaos over the millennia and how much they vary individually."

Subikahn fidgeted with clear impatience, and Tae understood. It seemed unlikely the child would remain outside long after sundown. When she left, the others might go with her, including Arturo. That would render any rescue mission much more difficult, if not impossible.

As usual, Captain seemed oblivious to the constraints of time. "Elves vary vastly in ability, but—"

Tae raised a hand to stem the tide of words he had requested. In ideal circumstances, he would have considered every possibility; but they did not have the luxury of time. He and Captain had discussed the possibilities of *Kjempemagiska* magic many times on the voyage, and he doubted the elf could add anything significant now. "Sorry, Captain. I know I asked, but I just realized we need to move before it's too late." He gestured at Subikahn to head out.

To his surprise, the Renshai clambered into the water immediately, without bothering to swaddle his swords to protect them from the sea. Tae realized it probably did not matter. Renshai always tended their swords meticulously, so they did not remain wet or salt-rimed for long. The *Kjem-pemagiska* ship knife probably had magical protection from the elements, and Tae doubted *Motfrabelonning* would fare any worse. He worried more for his own weapons, especially at a time when iron ore had become scarce and mostly came from the province of the North.

"Wait, one thing." Captain handed Tae the carefully coiled rope. "You may need this."

Tae doubted it but accepted the object without argument, avoiding the inevitable delay and discussion. He could not imagine a circumstance in which they would have the opportunity to bind the *Kjempemagiska* woman. Since she could broadcast a shout long distances in an instant, Subikahn would probably be forced to kill her as swiftly as possible. The child, Tae hoped, they could ignore.

Imorelda leaped from the gunwale to Tae's shoulders. *Unfortunately, you're going to need me, too.*

Tae had considered leaving Imorelda behind, had even planned to do so had she not volunteered so forcefully, but he knew she was right. *I'll do my best to keep you dry if you do your best to stay on task. If one of the giants alerts the rest, we'll need to know immediately.*

Imorelda dug her claws through his tunic and lightly into flesh. *I know that. How stupid do you think I am?*

Smarter than me, my love. Tae did not know if she got the message before switching to the level of the *Kjempe-magiska*'s communication, but she did not reply. He followed his son into the ocean, and they swam toward shore, buoyed by a tide that seemed determined to drag them to the proper destination. He could not help wondering why the *Kjempemagiska* had chosen such an unlikely pair to travel with a prisoner, perhaps because one giant sorceress, even distracted by young offspring, was all it took to keep even a large and battle-trained man of the continent in line. *And why there?* He supposed they might check that particular shore regularly to see what presents the tide had brought them.

Tae spoke softly to Subikahn, "I'd like you to keep the giantess busy while I explain the situation to Arturo. I don't know if he'll recognize me. I've only met him a few times, but he should realize anyone from his native land could lead him home. These giants aren't known for treating their servants well." It surprised him they even kept Arturo alive. Perhaps, he had cooperatively supplied them with enough information, whether true or false, to convince them to spare his life.

Subikahn only nodded. Hidden in the shadows of the cove, they both easily timed their movements to lose splashes and footfalls beneath the natural sounds of the tide. This close, Tae could make out more details. The adult *Kjempemagiska* was working with a piece of fabric, her attention fixed on the knotwork, though she glanced up at intervals to watch the child with Arturo.

Definitely a girl, the little one was blonde and fair, with brilliant blue eyes. Based solely on proportions and movements, Tae judged her age between three and four years old. She was chattering at Arturo as if to a friend, waving around a rag doll at least twice the size of any similar toy Tae had seen in the hands of Eastern children. He whispered one last instruction to Subikahn, "Don't hurt the child."

Subikahn rolled an eye toward his father, brow cocked. Clearly, he thought Tae was making a dangerous mistake.

"She's too young to master magic or the mental language." Tae had no idea whether or not he spoke the truth, but Subikahn would not know that. Though inappropriately tenderhearted, and probably foolish, he did not want to bear the responsibility for murdering a helpless little girl, no matter her bloodline.

The shadows swallowed Subikahn. Burdened by the weight of cat and rope, in addition to his normal accouterments, Tae crept quietly toward Arturo. He watched the girl wedge the rag doll in front of a large, flat rock. "Heffy, sit." She looked at Arturo, motioning to the opposite side of the makeshift table. "Bobbin, sit."

Tae did not know if "bobbin" was her name for Arturo or a word he had not yet encountered; but Arturo dutifully dropped to a crouch across from the rag doll.

The girl frowned. "No, no, Bobbin! No . . ." Words apparently failed her, so she imitated his squatting position. ". . . like this." She plopped her well-cushioned bottom onto the rocks. "Like this. Sit."

With exaggerated motions, Arturo flopped into his makeshift seat. "Like this?" He used the verbal tongue of the Heimstadr folks, with the same uncertain pidgin quality as his companion.

The girl clapped her hands and laughed. "Good, Bobbin. Good, boy."

Startled by the interaction, Tae found himself staring. As he tried to process the situation, he missed Subikahn's signal, cued only by the child's sudden cry, "Nahna!" She ran up the cove, toward the position Tae had last seen the giant woman.

Arturo sprang from his poorly defensible position, hurling his bulk in front of the girl. Unable to check her speed, she somersaulted over him, landing in a breathless heap in front of him, suddenly wailing. She sent a mind-call, filled with outrage, pain, and need. From the corner of his eye, Tae saw the grown giant's crumpled form, Subikahn beside her, his sword striped scarlet.

Arturo stepped in front of the girl, teeth bared, like an animal. Tae stepped from the shadows, using the Common Trading tongue of the continent. "Arturo, it's me, Tae. Your mother's with us on the ship. Come quickly."

Arturo did so, but not the way Tae expected. The Béarnide charged Tae with the ferocity of an angry bull, hands out, face protected. It was all Tae could do to scramble out of the way.

"Arturo, stop! We're trying to rescue you." Sudden doubt rushed down upon him. Matrinka had to be wrong. This furious, manlike creature could not be a missing prince of Béarn.

Arturo overran Tae, then whirled to face him again. Tae seized the moment to hurl himself bodily onto the larger man. "Stop fighting, Arturo. We're friends. Friends."

Something slammed against Tae with enough force to knock him off of Arturo and send him sprawling. Pain lanced through his head, and nausea overtook him. A second hammering blow stole all tone from his limbs. Against his will, he collapsed to the ground, prone and helpless. Words crawled through his dizzied mind in the voice of a child, "No hurt Bobbin!" Unable to move his limbs, Tae rolled his eyes upward to see his attacker. The child had nearly brained him with a sand-filled rag doll. Her arm rose to strike him again. Tae felt control returning, but not fast enough. He could not dodge the blow.

Suddenly, Subikahn was there. His sword sliced through the doll, showering Tae in a mixture of blood and released sand. His shoulder struck the child, who tumbled to the ground again. Tae rolled awkwardly to his feet, looking for Arturo. He still felt oddly disconnected from his body, out of control, head aching. He barely managed to huff out, "Don't hurt the child." Then, he remembered her mind-call. "Grab him and get out of here!"

Arturo rushed Subikahn with a roar of fury. Shoving the child aside so hard she stumbled, Subikahn met the charge with a quicksilver weaving of steel and all but invisible footwork. Unscathed, at least by the blade, Arturo careened wildly. It required several stomping steps to keep his feet. The maneuver took him to the *Kjempemagiska* child. Already off-balanced, he swerved to avoid crushing her, forced to dive and roll over her instead. As he came up, Subikahn put his blade to the man's throat. "No more trouble. Come with us, or you both die."

Just in case, Tae repeated the words in Heimstadr's verbal language.

Arturo clambered to his feet, and Subikahn's sword followed his every movement. "Tie him up," he instructed Tae.

Tae cursed his weakness. He felt like a toddler, still regaining his coordination and wits. He could scarcely believe a child's toy, even one owned by a giant child, could do so much damage. Carefully but swiftly, Tae bound Arturo's wrists, then his ankles, mindful of the fact that they would have to drag him through the water without drowning him. The *Kjempemagiska* child rose, staring from the remaining tatters of her doll to the trussed Béarnide, tears streaming from her enormous eyes.

Suddenly, Subikahn's head jerked up, and he looked inland. An instant later, Tae heard what had caught his son's attention: shouts and heavy footfalls heading their way.

"Go, go, go!" Tae shouted, waving for Subikahn to take the lead.

The Renshai ignored him. "Papa, get Arturo safe. I'll handle what's coming."

There was no time for argument. Tae grabbed the end of the rope, dragging Arturo down the beach, cringing at every pause, every need to tug harder. Not only did it probably indicate a rock in the prince's back, but they could not afford to let the *Kjempemagiska* catch them. He tried to empty his mind of the images the *alsona* had put there: limbs ripped from screaming bodies, torsos torn in half or baked alive, organs tossed around like playthings. If the *Kjempemagiska* could do these things to their servants, an enemy stood little chance. He shouted to Subikahn as he moved. "Just get me the time to haul Arturo. Don't stay and fight. You're Renshai, not stupid."

With Subikahn behind her, the child turned her wrath back on Tae. She pounded him with her enormous fists, screaming into his mind and ears. "Let go! Give back Bobbin. No hurt Bobbin."

Tae did not have the wherewithal to handle her and the weight of a struggling Arturo. So, he ignored her, hauling the Béarnide to the water with a singularity of purpose. He found himself panting, unable to speak. Water sloshed under his feet. Then, the burden eased as water swelled beneath Arturo's body, floating it. "No!" Tae finally managed in the Island tongue. "We're not going to hurt him. Stay back!" As the bottom fell away beneath his feet, Tae managed to plant one hand in the girl's chest and shove her toward the land. She fell on her bottom on the sand, still clutching half of the tattered, empty rag doll.

Tae heard Subikahn splash up beside him, to his relief. With the Renshai's help, he managed to buoy Arturo quite easily, keeping him face upward so he would not drown as they rushed him toward the *Sea Skimmer*. Then, something heavy slammed onto Tae's shoulders, submerging him. Sharp objects slashed his face in a frenzy; then, as he clawed his way back to the surface, the bulk settled across his shoulders. Tiny lines of blood trickled across the water, and the salt stung fresh gouges in his face. Imorelda's voice filled his mind, *Quit trying to drown me!*

Tae could have made the same demand, but he found himself too desperate to converse. *Stay on their level,* he commanded, needing to know what the *Kjempemagiska* were doing. He could hear them shouting to one another but could not make out individual words. A cluster of their metal bolts struck the water all around him, and pain sliced through his upper back to lodge near his spine. Tae bit his lip to keep from screaming, losing his hold on Arturo.

"I got him," Subikahn shouted.

Tae took the younger man at his word, his own will to swim subsuming him. Scarlet stained the water all around him. Then, something enormous churned the ocean with an all-too-familiar violence. *Not a shark. Please all the gods, not another shark.* Tae had grappled with one the last time a spying mission had gone sour, and it had all but killed him. He did not have the stamina to face another one, even to save the beloved animal clinging to his back.

The frenzied object bumped him, feeling sleek and soft, trailing hair, nothing like the rough and cutting scales of the shark. A desperate voice slashed into his mind, *Can't breathe. Help me! HELP!* That mental communication was replaced by a more familiar one, Imorelda again. *Grab her. She's really drowning.*

Her? Tae lunged for the flailing object as it went limp in his arms. Imorelda disappeared from his shoulders as he dragged the drowning creature to the surface, dead weight buoyed by ocean. *The* Kjempemagiska *child.* Fear gave way to abject panic. Tae did not want a toddler to die, but he doubted the giant sorcerers would let her go without a fight. He clung to her, treading water viciously with his injured arm, every movement spearing him with agony. The pain battered at his consciousness, and he knew loss of blood was not helping. He doubted he could keep his grip much longer.

Then, massive hands seized his arms, drawing him upward. Nearer, Subikahn once again relieved him of his burden. He suddenly realized the voices in his head had gone silent. "Imorelda!" Tae cast about wildly for the cat. He could not bear to lose her. "Imorelda!"

"I've got her," Matrinka said, closer than Tae expected. It was, apparently, she who was holding him, adjusting her grasp to pull him over the gunwale.

The tugging strained at Tae's injury. "Imorelda," he gasped against pain. "I need to hear them." Through a blur of salt, water, and discomfort, Tae could barely see Subikahn helping the girl to the deck, then leaping up beside her.

The mind-voices of the *Kjempemagiska* came back to him, mostly indecipherable magical exhortations, assorted cries for attack, and words whose vehemence suggested swearing. Then, abruptly, one cut over the others, *No ve-thrleikr!* Tae got an image of weather-related magic, tearing storms, and crashing waves. *My little girl is out there!* The mental voice added in clear desperation, *Somewhere.*

With Matrinka's assistance, Tae flopped over the side of the ship, the gunwale driving air and a dribble of water from his chest. The young giantess huddled, shivering from fear or cold, her clothing soaked, her golden hair a snarl. Clearly disoriented by her near-drowning, her head bobbed strangely and she seemed unable to process the presence of the sword-wielding Renshai at her side. On the deck, Arturo writhed in his bonds, howling and fighting like a trussed and feral animal.

Captain stared out over the sea, his mouth moving soundlessly, his eyes rolled upward and blazing like living citrine.

Tae rolled onto the deck, regained his feet, and seized the elf's arm. "Captain," he gasped. "You've got to get us out of here! Fast."

Captain turned his gaze on Tae, as if in a daze.

Tae shook the elf, though the movement triggered his own pain. "Captain, move!" He tipped his head, listening for the *Kjempemagiska* voices. He could still hear them, which meant Imorelda was doing her best, but they had grown softer, more distant. It took him a moment to sort the conversation and realize what they were planning. As soon as he did so, he explained. "They're headed for their warships. They're coming after us. We have to cast off immediately." He shook the elf again. "Captain, do you hear me?"

The elf shoved Tae away, sending him stumbling. A gentle hum filled his head, and a fog of black and white spots replaced his vision. Dizziness drove him to one knee.

"Tae!" Matrinka's voice sounded a million nautical miles away.

Tae ignored her, concentrating on maintaining consciousness. The *Kjempemagiska* voices disappeared, but he could still feel emotion pulsing through a single, remaining mental connection. It was filled with an agony worse than his own, a deep primal throbbing far beyond physical pain. Desperate, the owner of the voice called out repeatedly, a single word that Tae had never previously encountered: *Mistri, mistri, mistri!*

Gradually, as Tae recovered his own equilibrium, the word gained context. He saw the familiar image of the *Kjempemagiska* child, laughing and running, her long yellow hair streaming behind her. Mistri, apparently, was the girl's name. He could feel the ship lurching under Captain's command. Matrinka's physical voice in his ear could not compete with the mental pounding of a grieving and despairing parent, though he could not tell if the mind reaching out to the ocean came from a male or female giant. Apparently, the girl either could not hear it or was too shocked or confounded to respond. Uncertain why, Tae sent a message in the language of the enemy, *She was drowning, but she's safe now. Alive and being tended.*

Shock chopped through the overbearing mantle of grief, and the call for Mistri disappeared. *Mistri . . . is alive? She's safe?* As the ship ripped free of the dragging tide and headed out to the ocean, the voice faded into the distance.

Yes. Tae glanced at Mistri who fell back against the bulkhead, attention firmly on Arturo. *No harm will come to her. I'll see to it.*

One last question floated over the sea. *Who are you?* As the ship pulled away, the words brushed Tae's mind like a whisper.

Tae saw no reason not to answer, *My name is Tae.* He did not bother to add more, uncertain whether even those words could reach the island.

Taut with wind, the sails dragged the *Sea Skimmer* briskly into the ocean. Matrinka held pressure against the top of Tae's shoulder with one hand, the other tracing the course of the metal bolt along his back. She was speaking, apparently had been doing so for some time, ". . . have a gods-be-damned target on your forehead? There's no exit wound, Tae. It's still in there."

Tae could have told her that. He could feel the thing against his spine, shifting whenever he moved. He started to rise, but Matrinka held him in place. "Tae, hold still, damn it! How many times do I have to tell you that movement could paralyze or kill you?"

That finally seized his attention. "What?" He looked at Matrinka.

The queen of Béarn stared him down, anger and tears filling her gaze simultaneously. "Now, you're listening?"

"I'm listening," Tae promised, freezing like a statue. "Did you just say movement could paralyze me?"

"Or kill you," Matrinka added. "Or is that of much lesser significance to you?"

Tae did not bother to consider. He was not fond of either possibility but imagined finding himself immobile but alive might be the worse fate. "You've got my attention. Why is movement so dangerous?"

Arturo continued to holler and jerk on the deck, but Matrinka wholly ignored him. That brought her warning to a new level. If she felt compelled to ignore her long-lost, believed dead, and clearly distressed son to minister to Tae, he had to be in imminent and serious danger. Tae could think of one other possibility. "Is that ... in fact ... Arturo?" He did not want to contemplate the prospect that they had sacrificed the mission and put all their lives in serious danger to kidnap an *alsona*.

"Of course, that's Arturo." Matrinka snapped, clearly frustrated by her need to ignore her son at a time when he desperately needed her. "I know my own child, Tae Kahn. Now, hold still."

Tae did not think he could get any more motionless without losing consciousness. "You still haven't explained why."

"I didn't think I had to." Matrinka continued to clamp cloth to his shoulder. "You have a hunk of metal in your body. It came in here ..." She squeezed the hand already clutching the wound, adding little to the already fiery agony. "It appears to have dissected a straight line between your skin and muscle, which is odd but relatively fortunate. Without penetrating muscle, it can't poke holes in any vital structures, like organs or large vessels."

That sounded like good news to Tae, but he let her finish.

"It's wedged in the plane between muscle and skin. So long as you remain still, you're fine. When you move, you shift its position somewhat randomly, and it could penetrate into the muscle or, worse, the spine or could rupture blood vessels and cause severe bleeding."

Tae rolled his gaze to Subikahn to make certain the Renshai kept his attention focused on their unintended hostage as well as the bound man flopping on the deck. He did not speak of it, however. It would insult Subikahn to suggest he

might not be entirely devoted to their safety. "So . . ." Tae
did not fully understand what Matrinka had said but
enough to know he preferred not to move until the object
in his back was dealt with. ". . . you're going to . . ."

"Well, you obviously can't spend your life in one position; you might as well be paralyzed." Matrinka pursed her
lips, and Tae knew her well enough to realize she did not
like any of her options. "I'm going to have to remove it."

Tae swallowed hard, uncertain if he wished to know the
answer to his next question. "Is that . . . dangerous?"

"Not really." Matrinka's answer surprised him, though
he knew she was not above lying to him when it came to
matters of his health. "At least not under normal circumstances. I have only a limited supply of herbs with me, and
I wasn't expecting to have to make someone sleep through
a serious procedure."

"Sleep," Tae repeated. He suppressed the urge to shake
his head. "I can't sleep now. We're going to need every brain
and sword arm to keep ahead of the warships."

A mental voice brushed Tae's mind, but it was not Imorelda. Startled, he flinched but managed to keep himself
from leaping to a more defensible position.

Tae?

Matrinka put her hand on Tae to steady him. "If you
can't even hold still now, how are you going to do it while
I'm cutting?"

Cutting? Tae appreciated that his attention to the mind-
call allowed him to disregard the word. He knew Imorelda's
contact intimately. Whoever had called his name was not
her or elfin *khohlar*. Only one other had the ability to speak
to him in this manner. *Mistri?* he tried.

Am I going to die?

Tae turned his gaze to the young giantess as much as he
dared, wishing he could look into her eyes. *No, Mistri.
You're not going to die. You're going to be fine.*

Are you going to die?

No, Tae assured her, though he was not at all sure.
Not me, either. He addressed Matrinka. "Is it going to
hurt?"

Matrinka attempted to show no emotion, but a twitch in
her left eye gave her away. Apparently deciding there was
no easier way to say it, she blurted out, "Hell, yes, it's going

to hurt, Tae. What do you think? It's going to hurt a lot. That's why I'd prefer you asleep, if only so you're not biting me. Or leaping around like a fish."

Subikahn snickered.

Tae wished he did not have to move to give Subikahn an evil look. It would almost be worth it. Almost.

Unable to make sense of the verbal conversation, Mistri addressed Tae again. *Cause you're the only one who can talk to me, yes?*

Yes, Tae returned. Accustomed to two nonoverlapping conversations simultaneously, he switched back and forth easily. He appreciated that Imorelda could not hold the mental exchange at Mistri's level and also communicate. Tae doubted he could maintain three separate discussions, even at the peak of health. *But it's easier for me if you talk out loud.* Matrinka was the only one who knew he required the cat's aid to converse in this manner, and he intended to keep it that way.

Mistri continued speaking to his mind. *But I'm only little. I can't say much, yet.*

Mistri's words confused Tae, but only momentarily. He had heard the pidgin language she had used when addressing Arturo. This mental form of communication allowed images, emotion, and intention to flow along with words, filling in the gaps. He imagined much of what he gleaned from their current conversation had little to do with actual vocabulary and everything to do with basic ideas, feelings, and other nonverbal cues.

Nausea bubbled up inside Tae, presumably from the injury, though the rapid movement of the ship might have exacerbated his queasiness. He had never suffered from seasickness, but he had also never moved so fast across the ocean as they did now. Elf or not, Captain had clearly understood the urgency of the situation.

Tae supposed they had little to worry about. The *Kjempe-magiska* might have weather magic, but so, he felt certain, did Captain, at least when it came to moving his ship. Without it, the tinier craft already held the advantage, particularly manned by someone who had spent thousands of years learning the sea. "All right," he finally said. "Use whatever herbs you brought, then." He sighed, though the depth of that breath aggravated his wound. "If you, Subikahn, and

Captain together can't handle whatever comes, I doubt I'd add much anyway."

Matrinka scurried off immediately, without giving Tae a chance to change his mind again. Tae rolled his gaze back toward his son. "Her name is Mistri. Be gentle with her, please. She's very young, and she doesn't understand what's happening."

Subikahn responded with obvious sarcasm. "I think I can control myself."

The little girl's mental voice touched Tae again. *You'll help Bobbin?*

An image accompanied the question, and Tae knew she was talking about Arturo. *No harm will come to him. The lady who's helping me is his mother, and she loves him dearly.* He could hear Matrinka's footfalls approaching, and knew he had to swiftly tell Mistri what was about to happen to him. With a heavy sigh, he set out to explain to a young child what he did not wish to contemplate himself.

CHAPTER 17

The three of you mock what you claim to represent. If you constitute Balance, then I am the counter-Balance. All forces must have opposition to exist.

— Colbey Calistinsson

AN INDEFINABLE SOUND awakened Saviar Rakhirsson, and he found himself dodging an attack purely from instinct. Jeremilan stumbled into empty air, lost his balance, and sprawled onto the floor beside the chair that had, an instant earlier, held Saviar's sleeping form. The old man rolled stiffly. Ignoring Saviar's proffered hand, he clambered to his feet, glaring at the now wide-awake Renshai. "What have you done with her!"

Saviar blinked, brow furrowing. "Wh-what?" he finally managed, utterly confused. He drove aside blurry thoughts to the memory of what he had been doing prior to falling asleep that evening. He recalled a bland meal, a strange dice game with seven male Myrcidians that he had lost badly, and a routine practice with a pretend weapon. Nothing further came to mind.

Jeremilan balled his fists but did not lunge at Saviar again. "What have you done with her, you bastard spawn of demons?" His head lowered like a wolf preparing to bite, and he spat out each word, "Where . . . is . . . my . . . great-granddaughter?"

Alarm warred with Saviar's confusion. "Chymmerlee? She's . . . missing?"

Jeremilan's fists turned white with strain, and his face seemed to acquire all the color they lost. "Of course, she's missing. You know she's missing." His dark eyes glared into Saviar's, though he had to look upward to meet them. "What have you done with her?"

Bothered he had to defend himself with time better spent finding the missing sorceress, Saviar huffed out an incensed breath. "I'm a prisoner, remember? I haven't seen Chymmerlee, or any female Myrcidian, since you captured me. How could I?"

Apparently, the logic of Saviar's words calmed at least some of Jeremilan's rage. He hesitated. In that moment, another Myrcidian, a lanky white-haired man called Eldebar, stepped through the invisible doorway. "Paultan's gone, too, sir. And Janecos."

"What!" The flush drained abruptly from Jeremilan's face. "Are you sure?" As he whirled to face Eldebar, he seemed to have forgotten about Saviar.

Too concerned for Chymmerlee to worry about whether Jeremilan meant him insult by turning his back, Saviar stepped up beside the Myrcidians' leader.

Eldebar glanced behind him, as if he wished he were anywhere else at the moment. "We're all in and locked up tight now. We've accounted for everyone but those three. There's no indication they went anywhere together, and they didn't leave word they intended to go outside."

Saviar had become accustomed to the Myrcidian paranoia. Not for the first time, he wondered how they could lead any kind of contented life cooped up in their joint dwelling. "I can find them," he said softly.

Both men whirled on Saviar. "Find them!" Apparently, circulation returned to Jeremilan's face severalfold, turning it a dark shade of reddish lavender. "You? You're the one who did this. You have to be the one."

Eldebar shook his head. "Please, sir. That's just not possible."

Jeremilan continued to stare viciously at Saviar, but he did not speak, which encouraged Eldebar to finish.

"We've had guards on him all night. He hasn't moved." Eldebar added conclusively, "Jeremilan, there's no possible way this man could have had a direct role in their disappearance."

"Demon magic," Jeremilan said, though Saviar could tell even he did not believe his own words.

"Sir," Saviar started, trying to sound as logical and reasonable as Jeremilan did not. "The issue of whether I'm man or demon has already been settled, and I have assured you I have no magical abilities at all. Now, if you have some kind of magic that will find Chymmerlee and the others, please use it. If not, let me find them."

Jeremilan only stared, his demeanor thoughtful but his facial features dark and hostile.

"The longer we wait to start, the less likely we can find them." Saviar knew the Myrcidians could spend days discussing the situation and weeks coordinating a plan. Whether the missing Myrcidians had fallen into unexpected danger or had willingly and deliberately left the fold, they would likely blunder into danger without someone to protect or rescue them. Chymmerlee had more experience and thus more cunning and knowledge than the others, but she still had many of the limitations that accompanied an overprotective environment. "What if they've fallen into a pit or gotten lost in a cave? What if they've run into highwaymen intending to sell them into slavery?"

Jeremilan focused on the wrong word. "Slavery? What countries still practice—"

Not wishing to get into a tangential discussion, Saviar cut him off. "No countries legally. But there's an underground trade, and women in particular . . ." Saviar changed the subject, refusing to get sidetracked. Some considered arranged marriages a form of subjugation, while others simply saw it as a normal way of life. "Look, we can talk about this later. Right now, we need to work quickly if we're going to have any chance of saving your missing mages."

Jeremilan started to speak, then stopped, started again, and finally clamped his jaw shut.

Eldebar stood quietly, awaiting his leader's decision.

With a sigh, Saviar returned to his chair. It did him no good to continue arguing. The more Saviar pushed, the more it would convince Jeremilan he had ulterior motives for volunteering for the mission.

Jeremilan sucked in a long breath, then let it out just as slowly. "What assurance do we have that you'll even help us, that you won't just run away?"

It was a reasonable question. Saviar supposed even a true Knight of Erythane would have difficulty suppressing the urge to do exactly that in his situation. "If you're still not satisfied with my word, surely you trust your magic. When Subikahn and I left you, we agreed we would release Chymmerlee as well as keep your existence and presence a secret. You wanted to seal that oath with magic, but my brother would not allow it. Clearly, such promise-binding magic exists."

"It exists," Jeremilan said, without elaboration. "You would have to agree to bring our missing Myrcidians back alive and well. Also that you would return to our captivity."

Saviar considered the words carefully. "I can't do that, sir."

Jeremilan's silver brows shot up.

Saviar explained, "How can I promise to deliver safely people whose current status isn't known? They could already be dead or maimed or injured. I could spend my life looking and never find them."

Jeremilan continued to stare, clearly unhappy with the answer.

When neither of the others spoke, Saviar continued, "I can promise to do everything within my power to bring them back alive and well. I can also promise to return to your captivity, though I can't agree to remain there indefinitely." Saviar supposed a more savvy man would not have mentioned the latter part of the agreement. He would simply have returned, then found a way to escape. However, he had no intention of entering an agreement through trickery or bad faith. "I can't remain here, inactive, while the many other peoples of this world fight for their existence against a terrible enemy."

Again, Saviar stopped short of the full argument. The Myrcidians might not realize that others would, eventually, come for him. It might take them a while to locate the magical settlement, but it could not remain hidden forever. At the very least, Subikahn knew exactly how to find him, and his twin did not espouse the same tight honor as Saviar and Ra-khir. It was not in the Myrcidians' best interests to hold him too long against his will. "So my part of the agreement would be to do everything within my power to locate your three missing companions and bring them back alive and well. At that time, I will also return to captivity."

Jeremilan rubbed his chin, apparently finding a loophole Saviar did not consider. "You need to add that you'll accomplish this as quickly as possible. Otherwise, you could wait until your eightieth birthday to start looking."

Saviar did not see how that jibed with attempting to bring them home alive and well, but—again—he did not see a reason to waste time arguing. Adding a time limit would make things more equitable, and as he had no intention of cheating them, he saw no reason not to comply. He also wondered if ancient Jeremilan really understood normal human lifetimes. *Eighty, indeed. Why not a hundred?* "Fine, put a time limit on it. Just don't make it impossible."

Jeremilan studied Saviar so intently it made the Renshai uncomfortable, as if the ancient eyes could see through his tissues to his very soul and marrow. Saviar tried to keep his own expression mild. Despite the old man's rampant paranoia, Saviar had nothing whatsoever to hide. Finally, the elder's lips parted. Words emerged, sounding rusty and hesitant. "And for our part of the agreement?"

Saviar hesitated nearly as long as Jeremilan. What emerged surprised even him, "I can do that?"

Jeremilan sighed, as if worried he was giving away another precious secret. "The strength of the binding lies in the equity of the agreement."

Saviar wondered if Jeremilan realized that he would never have surmised such a thing on his own. He would not even know whether or not the spell was cast, let alone its power to constrain him. The Myrcidians could simply pretend to cast the spell and tell him any violation would result in slow, agonizing death with no chance to obtain an afterlife in Valhalla. He would have no way to discern the truth of the claim, and his honor would hold him to the task with or without active magic. He could not help noticing how isolation had shaped Myrcidian society. Their suspicion of outsiders, especially Renshai, seemed to know no bounds; yet they often came across as blindingly naïve, perhaps from the way they had learned to rely on one another.

Realizing Jeremilan was still awaiting an answer, Saviar attempted to craft one. "I'd like a promise that, if I try my best but fail at this mission through no fault of my own, no punishment or blame will ensue. I'd also like some assurance you won't hold me indefinitely: that, if you won't assist in the war, you at least won't prevent me from doing so."

Jeremilan waited patiently, clearly expecting more.

Saviar could think of only one other thing to demand, and he already knew he would not get it. Simply asking would result in an argument that would only waste time and put Jeremilan back on the defensive. There was no possible way the ancient leader would agree to be magically bound to force any of his people to assist in the war. However, Saviar realized, accomplishing the mission might gain him far more goodwill and put him closer to that goal.

Saviar also considered asking for his weapons, but he knew such a request was folly. He could probably convince Jeremilan that he would have a far better chance of getting the three missing Myrcidians back with a weapon. However, if the ancient leader went to retrieve Saviar's swords, he would discover the missing one that Subikahn had taken, which would surely cause further delays and problems. Though he felt naked without a sword, Saviar knew his Renshai training would prevail.

It was a well-known proverb: "If there is a sword and a Renshai in the same room, no matter who wields it, the sword will find its way into the hand of the Renshai." If Saviar wound up in a combat situation—and he doubted he would—he felt certain he could win whether or not he started with a weapon. It seemed far more likely the missing Myrcidians had simply wandered off and become trapped by some natural phenomenon: a landslide, an unexpected hole, a falling tree.

When Jeremilan still waited expectantly, Saviar shrugged. "That's it."

Jeremilan raised a silver eyebrow.

Saviar felt obligated to explain. "This may seem like a difficult task to you, but I'm looking forward to it. I'm bored to death sitting here waiting for you to decide my fate. I'd rather die rescuing people I scarcely know than sit here wasting away physically and mentally." He added truthfully, "Anything I want from you would have to come willingly and because someone convinced you it was the right thing to do. I'm not going to obligate anyone, through magic, to something he or she would not choose to do."

Jeremilan's other brow rose beside the first. He tipped his head, clearly contemplating Saviar's words. At first, Saviar dared to hope the ancient leader was finding the wisdom in them, realizing Saviar's point was so morally correct that the Renshai knew the Myrcidians would, eventually, see its necessity. Then, it occurred to Saviar he had probably insulted the old man, albeit backhandedly. His words could also be interpreted as suggesting that what Jeremilan intended to do, by forcing Saviar to comply through magic, was ethically repugnant. Also, it could be seen as condemning the very art of magic, the process on which the Myrcidians based their worth and their lives.

Jeremilan frowned, but he did not rise to the bait. Either he believed Saviar's insult was unintended, or he saw it as more trickery. Either way, he neither chastised nor relented. He made a sharp, strong gesture toward the invisible opening, and three male Myrcidians came through it.

Braced for the inevitable promise-binding, Saviar focused on the individual words of the agreement. He suspected exact phraseology would take precedent over intent, and he needed to make certain he had not committed himself to something impossible, unethical, or just plain stupid.

The whole process took nearly half an hour, and Saviar felt as if he had suffered through one of the knights' extensive procedural affairs. The magic required the use of a language he did not understand, and he suspected the Myrcidians also switched to their own tongue to communicate issues they did not want him to hear. But the wording of the promise came through clearly enough. Saviar agreed to doing everything in his power to bring the three missing Myrcidians back to their home alive and well. When he returned them, he would surrender himself back into their custody. He also promised to return the missing Myrcidians as swiftly as possible, no matter the condition in which he found them; and, if he could not locate them, he was to return without them within one week's time. In return, Jeremilan agreed to release Saviar from his captivity in time to assist in any hostilities that threatened the peoples living within the rulership of Béarn.

There followed a lot of words Saviar did not understand,

the tingle of magic that did not appear to harm him or leave any lasting effects. In the end, he remained in the room, facing eight Myrcidians, some male, some female.

"Finished?" Saviar asked calmly, though he could barely contain his excitement. He could scarcely wait to feel the kiss of cold air against his skin, to see the natural light of the sun, to smell loam and rain and leaf mold. If he found nothing better, he could fashion a stick into a sword; its weight in his hand, no matter how unbalanced or bulky, would bring the lost reality back to his practices.

Jeremilan nodded. "I assume you want to know what happens if you violate your oath." He added carefully, "Or if we do."

Saviar shrugged with a nonchalance he did not have to feign. "What for? I've never broken a promise in my life, and I don't intend to start now. If I died horribly for doing so, it would be nothing less than what I deserve."

Murmurs swept the group, and even Jeremilan turned pale, utterly speechless.

Saviar headed toward the invisible exit, knowing he could not pass through it without the aid of magic. "May I start now?" He felt driven but not, as far as he could tell, because of any unnatural source. It was the familiar eagerness of a man too long in one unwelcome place, of a warrior who felt as if his strength, stamina, and cunning were withering.

A woman standing near the entrance glanced at Jeremilan, who nodded. She uttered more of the strange, guttural syllables that had come to symbolize magic in Saviar's mind, then gestured for him to walk through it.

Though a bit skeptical, Saviar walked into the space, fully expecting to slam his face against a solid wall as he had so many times before. This time, however, he swept right through it as if the boundaries had never existed. He found himself in a familiar drawing room that he recalled from his first, friendlier visit to the Myrcidians' communal dwelling, when Chymmerlee had tended his festering wound, his blood poisoning, his fatal fever. It all seemed so long ago, another world and another lifetime.

Once there, Saviar had no difficulty finding his way through the adjoining rooms to the world outside the compound. He fairly ran, ignoring the furnishings and the stares that followed him. He could scarcely wait to plow through the doorway and into the fresh air. He imagined the sun beaming down on him, dew drops sparkling amidst slender-bladed fang grass and fields of wildflowers, broken by the squat shapes of bushes and the taller, more slender trees swaying in a gentle breeze.

Instead, Saviar found himself enveloped in swathes of fog, penetrated only by an icy drizzle and anemic patches of sunlight. The trees bowed in an intermittently howling wind, leaves rattling and trunks groaning. Heavy with gathered rain, the bushes sagged. Mud interrupted the fang grass in rain-battered patches, and the wildflowers were closed tightly into well-protected buds. Saviar laughed and fairly danced in the rain, enjoying the cold droplets, the dim light, the ripple of the breeze against his face and funneling through the sleeves of his cloak to encase him in a chilly blast. What once might have seemed a discomfort felt like an old friend. *Weather! How I've missed you.*

Knowing the eye of every mage was trained on him, Saviar reined in his excitement, pulled up his hood, and trudged into the cold, damp terrain. Within a few steps, he discovered a sturdy branch, broke it down to proper size, and jammed it into his too-long empty sheath. At any other time, it would have seemed a poor substitute for a sword. Now, Saviar reveled in carrying it, so much so that he left it in place only a moment before drawing it repeatedly as he walked, accustoming himself to the feel of it, adjusting his draw to its weight and balance. In his mind's eye, it was a sword, albeit a poorly made one. He would trade it in when he could; for now, it was better than the nothing at all that had plagued his days and nights for longer than he would have thought he could stand.

The Myrcidian's magical dwelling disappeared the moment Saviar left it. He did not bother to look behind him; he had previously experienced the phenomenon, and he had no wish nor reason to do so again. He knew the Myrcidians would continue to watch him until he passed beyond their sight, perhaps enhanced by magic. So he waited until he had traveled far beyond that point before bothering to get his bearings. Only then, it occurred to him he might need to find the missing Myrcidians alive just to fulfill his promise to return. He did not know for certain if he could find the essentially invisible dwelling without their assistance.

The Myrcidians rarely left their dwelling for any reason. Even if they did, they would not have paths or roadways that could lead a traveler randomly to their home. The ground beneath Saviar's feet ranged from marshy to rocky, from sloppy to rife with roots and deadfalls. Forest closed in all around him, a mixture of old and new-growth trees entangled with vines. The shade of the trees discouraged undergrowth, except where the branches opened to reveal dappled sunlight. Copses flourished in places, disappeared in others, and some held terrible thorns as large as daggers.

Saviar came to a halt. In theory, the mission had seemed relatively simple. He imagined he could thwart any natural or human enemy that threatened the missing Myrcidians. He had focused on his forthcoming freedom, on the sheer delight of leaving the dank walls that had imprisoned him for so long. He had even looked forward to the rescue, whether as simple as lifting them from an entrapping hole, helping the injured limp home, or as complex as forcing robbers to release them, complete with a few rousing battles. He had refused to dwell on the difficulty he might have just locating the missing people, not because he had never considered it, but simply because it seemed the least of his concerns. Now, it became the all-encompassing problem.

Where to look. Where to look. Saviar truly had no idea how to start. Without pathways or roads, they could have walked in an infinite number of directions, stopped only by the natural phenomena that fully blocked movement. Except, Saviar realized, they could have used some sort of magic to penetrate prickly barriers or overgrown plant materials or to ford any stream. They had gone missing, which meant they had probably done something foolish, something a man more experienced with woodlands and the outdoors would never consider doing. Chymmerlee had once told the twins she was the only Myrcidian who routinely left their dwelling, and only a few did so even occasionally. He had to hope she had enough forest wisdom not to do something so inexplicable that someone like Saviar, who had spent most of his time outside since infancy, would never even imagine it.

A branch snapped. Though muffled by the howl of wind

and the rattling dance of the trees, it alerted Saviar. In an instant, he had his makeshift sword in hand, his posture crouched, his eyes scanning the misty brush. They were on him in an instant, three swarthy men dressed entirely in black, even their swords dully colored to resist the glints of sunlight.

Always hyperalert, Saviar got in the first strike, his branch hammering the fingers of one attacker. The man swore, losing his grip. Saviar barreled in, head slamming the other's chest, free hand snatching the real sword from its reeling owner. He dodged the anticipated attacks of the other two, then spun to face the three again. Low and ready, with a sword in his left hand a stick in his right, Saviar got his first close look at the swordsmen. The one he had overpowered scrambled for purchase on the slippery ground, face contorted in pain and rage. The other two stared at Saviar but did not press.

Patient as a snake, Saviar waited for them to make the next move, which they did not. All four stood in position, as if some whimsical god of winter had frozen them solid.

Another figure glided from the brush, and Saviar pivoted to keep all of them in his field of vision. "Saviar," the newcomer said in a vaguely familiar voice. "It's all right. We're allies."

As if to demonstrate, the two men still holding swords sheathed them, and the fourth clamped his injured hand in the other, pain obvious on his face.

Saviar kept all of the figures in his peripheral vision to focus fully on the newcomer. His first impression, of size, vanished under scrutiny. The man was not large, though he gave the impression of it in the confidence of his stance and the command in his voice. He had straight but short jet-black hair, liberally sprinkled with silver and wholly white at the temples. The eyes were dark, almost black, large, and hard as diamonds. The features were craggy, those of a man well into mid-life or even beyond, and Saviar felt certain he knew those features, though he could not quite place them.

The leader did not wait for Saviar to recognize him. "Saviar, it's Weile Kahn, Subikahn's grandfather."

Saviar's jaw sagged, and he found the captured sword in his sheath without remembering placing it there. He let the stick fall from his hand. "What . . . what . . . are you doing here?"

Weile snorted. "We came to save you, of course. Did you think I'd leave you at the mercy of a band of ignorant mages?"

"But how did you even know—" There was only one answer, and Saviar did not like it. Clearly, Subikahn had betrayed his honor. Saviar clamped his mouth shut. He did not want to hear the answer spoken aloud.

"Come," Weile said. Keeping a wary distance from Saviar, watching him as they moved, Weile's followers approached their leader.

Even Saviar took two steps forward before catching himself. "I can't go with you. I'm on a mission, and I'm magically bound to complete it."

"I know your mission," Weile said. "And we can help you." He turned on his heel and melted into the brush. "Come, Saviar. Keep the sword."

"How . . ." Saviar started, then kept the thought to himself. *How could he possibly know?* Yet, he did not doubt the Eastern leader of the elite palace guards. Weile had means of knowing things that went far beyond logic. He was a terrifying man, with terrible enemies, yet Saviar could think of no one he would rather have on his side. More accurately, he could think of no one he would rather not have as an adversary.

Saviar followed.

CHAPTER 18

I prefer to face a Renshai armed than angry.
          —Prince Leondis of Pudar

THE ELITE EASTERN PALACE GUARDS spoke little as they led Saviar to their campsite, which suited him. The route they took required him to crawl through copses that seemed impenetrable, to clamber over massive deadfalls towering over his head, and to scamper through tiny openings he would not have noticed without the help of his wiry leaders. Nevertheless, they reached their goal quickly, stopping at a clearing that seemed far too small to comfortably fit even the four men who accompanied Saviar.

One man brushed aside a tangle of vines to reveal a hole that ran deep into the ground. The dark-clothed men skittered inside, two in front of Saviar, including Weile Kahn, and two held back, gesturing for him to enter.

Doubtfully, Saviar pressed forward. He was naturally tall and well-muscled, easily the largest man of the group, and the idea of pressing into an opening that hampered his sword arm rankled. Trusting Weile, however, he hesitated only a moment before following them. The agility trained into him since infancy allowed him to maneuver through the relatively tight space without as much effort as he expected. He did not have to wriggle, as he had first suspected, and managed to crawl through without falling behind.

The tunnel swiftly opened into a large room carved from the dirt and lit with lanterns. Weile was already explaining

Saviar's presence to a group of six men when Saviar spilled into the space behind him. The other two men quickly followed, and the eleven total occupants of the room fit comfortably, leaving plenty of space for packs of traveling gear and makeshift sleeping quarters. A long, heavy curtain spiked into the earthen wall hid a portion of the wall about the size of a doorway. The fabric was heavy enough to dampen sound, and Saviar suspected this simple abode had a second room behind it.

Weile gestured at the floor, and Saviar quickly dropped to a crouch in the indicated space. The other men sat around him in various stages of readiness, much as Renshai would have done in the same situation. The man whose sword Saviar had taken hunkered down nearest the exit, studying his injury in the guttering light of one of the lanterns.

Saviar tried to catch the man's eye. "Sorry about your fingers. I didn't know you were allies." He added reluctantly, "Would you like your sword back?"

The swarthy Easterner looked away from his hand long enough to give Saviar a wan smile. "Keep it, Renshai," he said magnanimously. "I'm not mad at you; I'm mad at myself. We're better off with you armed, and I have another."

A few nods followed that pronouncement, and Saviar accepted the gift with a sincere nod. Renshai were never so generous with weapons, mostly because they carried only the best.

Weile Kahn remained standing when the others sat, looking exceptionally spry for his age. "Your mission, Saviar. Would it involve finding three missing mages?"

Saviar tried his best not to appear stunned, though he found his head bobbing without intention. "Well, yes, in fact." He tried to stay a step ahead. Weile had a way of off-balancing others, whether warriors, paupers, or kings. "And you know this because . . ." Saviar did not give Weile time to answer before venturing his own guess. ". . . you captured them. Didn't you?"

Weile grinned at Saviar's quick wit, apparently more used to people asking rather than seeking the answers on their own. "My men did, yes."

Saviar tried to catch some sign of smugness from the men, some indication they took pride in a difficult job done well, but he saw nothing. These elite guards kept their thoughts nearly as well-hidden as their leader did. He ventured another prediction. "And you're holding them on the other side of this curtain."

"Indeed," Weile said. "They're trussed and gagged to keep them from using magic against us, but they're otherwise well-kept."

Saviar supposed the Myrcidians should appreciate the absence of torture, but he found it difficult to reconcile "well-kept" with "trussed and gagged." "And ... you're going to let me return them without a fight." He glanced around at the guardsmen. He could battle them all on open terrain and feel reasonably confident of success. Here, hampered by the closeness of the quarters, he felt less so, especially when he realized that, whatever they lacked in sword ability compared to a Renshai, they more than made up for in guile and stealthy training.

Weile chuckled. "Saviar, I pick my battles carefully, and I don't make unnecessary enemies, especially powerful ones. When you return with them, I intend to accompany you."

Saviar drew breath to protest. Bringing outsiders to the Myrcidians' compound would violate his vow. *Or would it?* Saviar suddenly realized he had made no such promise, at least not this time. He tried to recall the explicit details of his original agreement with the Myrcidians, the one he had made before the war. "I ... don't think I can do that." He wished he could remember exactly what he had said the first time he and Subikahn had left the mages. They had done so under duress, with Chymmerlee as a captive. So much time had passed, so many things had happened; and, at the time, Saviar had not yet fully recovered from near-death injuries he could not even remember receiving.

Weile Kahn grinned wickedly. He had the words Saviar did not. "You agreed to ..." Clearly, he quoted Jeremilan word-for-word: "'Release my great-granddaughter unhurt, keep our existence and whereabouts a secret, return to us, and assure that your brother ...'" Weile broke out of direct reference to clarify, "... meaning Subikahn ..." He returned to Jeremilan's voice, "'does the same.' According to Subikahn, who has an irritatingly excellent memory, like his father, you replied, and I quote you: 'I so vow, but only with the reassurance that we are free to come and go as we please from this time onward.'"

Saviar nodded, certain the leader of the Eastlands' elite guards had recited the conversation verbatim. "Yes, that sounds right, sir. And that 'irritatingly excellent memory' clearly runs in the family farther back than Tae Kahn."

Weile's tight-lipped grin revealed little. "It's clear the Myrcidians violated their part of the agreement first, thereby fully negating the contract."

Saviar sucked in a deep breath, shook his head. "I only asked for his reassurance. Just because Jeremilan was not true to his word doesn't give me the right to breach my promise."

Weile remained in position. Saviar expected him to sigh or roll his eyes at the rigid stupidity of Saviar's position, but he did not. His expression never changed. "It's your right to see things the way you wish, Saviar, but you must also understand that most men would view that exchange as a contract. Once the mages dishonored it, it ceased to exist."

Saviar held his ground. He respected his father, his grandfather, and the Knights of Erythane too much to back down. Though he had not joined the knighthood, at least not yet, he saw no reason not to honor its tenets. "I am not most men."

"Indeed." Weile made no attempt to argue. "But, at least on this issue, Subikahn is. Though he made no similar vow, he valued your promise, obeying it until the mages broke the contract. He then felt free to entrust me with their secrets. Surely, you can see that Subikahn violated no one's honor by doing so."

Saviar wondered why such a thing mattered to a man infamous for organizing the basest criminals in the world. Yet, he had to admit, Weile had never done anything directly dishonorable to his personal knowledge. "I have no malice toward my twin. I understand, and appreciate, his decision." Saviar had never tried to force his personal code of honor onto anyone else, and he understood Weile's and Subikahn's position. "But you have to understand that I must . . ." He sought the exact words Weile had used to quote Jeremilan, ". . . keep their existence and whereabouts a secret."

Weile finally chuckled. "A secret from whom, Saviar? Everyone in this camp knows about the existence and whereabouts of the Mages of Myrcidë. I am merely asking to walk with you into the compound, not show me its location."

Saviar blinked. He could hardly argue with the point. He would not be revealing any secrets to Weile Kahn, who had already approached, or even entered, the hidden fortress to purloin three of its inhabitants. "You make an undeniable point. Fine, we'll go together." He glanced around the room, at the dark-swathed men in positions around their leader. "But I think it's best if it's the two of us and the captives. Any more than that, and they're likely to attack."

"Agreed," Weile said, though Saviar doubted Subikahn's grandfather wanted it any other way. Weile had a crafty ability to arrange situations to get exactly what he desired, even when it seemed otherwise. "It'll be you and me and two Myrcidian captives."

Saviar stiffened. "Did you say two? Jeremilan's under the impression he's missing three."

"And he is," Weile said.

Saviar's heart rate quickened. If a Myrcidian had died, it would make any negotiation Weile planned more difficult. The mages had only twenty-six members and had suffered great hardship attempting to find or create more. It was the sole reason they had insisted Saviar and Subikahn return, when they had still believed the twins' auras indicated Myrcidian heritage.

Weile put that fear to rest with his next statement. "We're holding one back. As leverage."

Saviar wanted to argue but knew it would prove pointless. He would eventually reunite all three mages with their people, but he would have to do it Weile's way. Only then, when he stopped thinking of the captured Myrcidians as a single group did it occur to Saviar the situation gave him an opportunity he had sought since before his capture. "Sir, would it be all right if I spoke with one of the captives in private?"

Weile tipped his head but otherwise gave no sign he needed to consider the request. "If you'll stop calling me 'sir.' I'm not titled."

The comment seemed ludicrous. Weile had used his influence with the criminal element of the East to usurp the kingdom and install himself as its ruler. Since then, he had passed the throne to his son, turned his followers into elite guardsmen, and, apparently, disclaimed any right to an official position or designation.

"Very well." Saviar did not use the man's name, either. It felt odd not to use an honorific when addressing his twin's grandfather, especially one who had once sat on the throne of the Eastlands. "I'm going to need to ungag her. Will that bother anyone?"

Weile glanced around the group. Saviar did not hear or see a reply, but Weile must have received something because he nodded. "Just remind Chymmerlee we can make her captivity easy or more difficult, depending on her actions."

Saviar stiffened at the name. He should have assumed Weile would know it, as well as to which prisoner he referred.

"If she uses magic, we'll have no choice but to stop her. And see it doesn't happen again."

The vague threat troubled Saviar. He felt certain the type of men surrounding Weile could imagine ways of silencing a woman that would never occur to him. He could not allow them to harm her no matter what she did. Not wishing to raise trouble where none yet existed, Saviar kept his mouth shut on the matter. "May I?" He pointed toward the curtain.

Weile was at the entry before Saviar saw him prepare to move. He gave no indication of what he had intended to do. "Let me talk to the guards first, let them know what to expect. We'll move the others away from her. We don't have enough space to give you an unoccupied chamber; but, if you keep your voices down, no one will hear you." He did not wait for a reply before ducking through the curtain, as swift and soundless as a shadow.

Saviar glanced around the room, avoiding the dark, Eastern eyes of his new companions, instead focusing on their swords. They appeared reasonably made and welltended, similar to the one he had taken from its owner.

Shortly, Weile returned and made a motion toward the curtain. Saviar lifted it, finding it even heavier than he had expected. No sound had emerged from Weile's conversation with his guards, and Saviar suspected the heavy cloth had everything to do with it. He ducked through the opening he had created and let it fall back in place behind him.

The room reeked of sweat and fear, mingled with the damp odor of fresh earth and a faint hint of a recent lightning storm. Saviar recognized the smell of Myrcidian, a unique neutral scent he could not have described, that permeated the Myrcidians' compound. On one side of the room, a dark-clothed Easterner sat watching a bound man and woman. On the other side, Chymmerlee sat alone, hands tied behind her back, ankles wrapped together, a gag thrust into her mouth and tied behind her head. It hid her mouth, but the rage in her blue-gray eyes came through clearly. She glared at Saviar.

Saviar glided over to Chymmerlee and crouched in front of her. "Chymmerlee, I've been trying to speak to you for months, but you wouldn't listen."

Chymmerlee made a muffled noise. Her eyes narrowed.

Saviar hated to speak under these circumstances. He longed to remove the gag and the bindings, but he dared not do so. If she behaved the way she had the last few times he had attempted to speak with her, she might get herself tortured or killed. "Chymmerlee, you know how I feel about you."

Chymmerlee rolled her eyes toward the ceiling, dodging his gaze. Saviar expected tears to follow, but they did not.

Saviar sighed and continued. He had once considered himself a competent speaker. His current series of failures with Chymmerlee and her great-grandfather convinced him otherwise. "Maybe I'm stupid, but I don't understand why you don't . . ." He hesitated, seeking the right word. He knew she had once loved him; but, as she had never spoken the word aloud in his conscious presence, it did not seem fair to use it. ". . . like me anymore."

Chymmerlee's gaze shifted suddenly, meeting his full on. There was raw hatred in those eyes; and, suddenly, Saviar wished she had continued to avoid his stare. Now, he found his eyes locked with hers, unable to look away.

Saviar continued, "I know I didn't tell you I'm Renshai, and I should have. That was a betrayal I deeply regret, but I didn't do it to hurt you in any way. You see, I had already sworn an oath to my brother, before I even knew you existed, that I wouldn't tell any Myrcidian." Saviar gave her an attentive look, certain that piece of information, the one he had waited so long to deliver, would appease her. "You know I'd never violate a promise. Not to you. Not to anyone."

Chymmerlee's eyes remained fixed. He could not tell whether or not any of what he said had gotten through to her. "Other than that, I've done nothing but good to you. You know that, Chymmerlee."

Chymmerlee continued to stare.

Saviar smiled, though only slightly. He wanted to let her know he had the best of intentions, without taunting in any way. "I'm going to remove the gag, now. These men . . ." He indicated the elite Eastern guardsmen with a jerk of his head. "I have little to no influence with them. I'm trying to convince them to return you home." He looked over his shoulder at the two men still standing with the other Myrcidians, then returned his attention to Chymmerlee. "If they attempt to harm you, I'll do my best to stop them. Short of that, I can't help you. So, please, don't try to use magic." Believing himself prepared for anything, Saviar removed the gag.

Immediately, Chymmerlee spat in his face.

That, Saviar had not expected. He backstepped instinctively, releasing a small whimper. Though physically painless, the attack felt like a dagger thrust into his chest. He looked at Chymmerlee in open surprise, and she appeared slightly blurred. Apparently, tears had formed in his eyes. He fisted them away, along with the glob of spittle. "If you have something to say, say it now. Otherwise, the gag goes back in, and we're finished here."

Chymmerlee's jaw set. She seemed about to spit at him again, but the step backward had taken him out of easy range. Instead, she swallowed hard, and her glare grew even more intrusive. "You demon bastard! Spawn of Hel herself! You raped me!"

The words made even less sense from Chymmerlee's mouth than they had from the other Myrcidians'. Shocked and humiliated, Saviar did not know what to say. "I . . . I did nothing of the kind, and you know it! I've never laid a violent hand on you. Aside from not telling you I'm Renshai, I've treated you with nothing but kindness."

Each word was a deadly snarl. "You . . . raped . . . me."

As they had both practically shouted, Saviar knew the others in the room had heard her accusation as well as his denial. He dared not look behind him. It would mortify him to find them all staring. "When did I supposedly do this heinous thing? I've never even been fully alone with you."

"While I slept, I suppose. I don't know!"

A nervous chuckle escaped Saviar.

Chymmerlee's expression hardened more, if possible. "So you think rape is funny, you barbarous devil!"

"Of course not." Saviar ignored the insults to focus on the significant points. "Rape is a monstrous evil. It's never humorous. But, if someone actually raped you, don't you think you'd be the first to know?"

"Magic can erase the memory," Chymmerlee said. "But I still know it happened."

Saviar shook his head. "How?"

Chymmerlee spat out her next words so forcefully, Saviar expected more gobbets of spittle to accompany them. "I'm pregnant, you monster! Explain that!"

Saviar could not, at least not without besmirching her honor. "Are you . . . sure?"

"Of course, I'm sure. I'm sure." For the first time, tears marred her eyes as well, turning them into gray puddles. Unlike Saviar, she did not have fists to blot them.

"I had nothing to do with it," Saviar insisted. "I swear it."

"Then it was your brother. And you must have allowed it."

Saviar had to bite his lower lip to keep from laughing. "It wasn't Subikahn, either. He . . . doesn't . . ." Saviar did not know how to phrase the situation. "He's not . . ." Though not a secret, Subikahn's sexual orientation was his own business. "Let's just say he couldn't have done it." As he contemplated his own words, Saviar grimaced. They were not technically correct. When Subikahn had told Saviar, he had admitted to having tried sleeping with women. Saviar's use of the word "couldn't" might imply that Subikahn had undergone accidental or deliberate castration.

Chymmerlee did not give Saviar a chance to explain. Screams ripped from her throat, as if every man in the room was assaulting her at that moment.

The elite guardsman in the room darted to her side and

thrust the gag back into place in one smooth motion. As he tied it, Saviar backed away, then turned, and ducked through the curtain. He found the Easterners in various stages of repose, some eating, some tending weapons, others talking in small groups. Weile chatted with two of his men, the slight smile playing across his face the only indication he had heard anything coming from the other room.

Certain they had all heard Chymmerlee's screams, Saviar waited for someone to demand an explanation. No one did. They all remained calm, as if such things happened regularly, and they did not appear to stare at him.

Saviar walked through their silent ranks to hunker down in a corner, an arm across his face. *Chymmerlee's pregnant.* The claim refused to take shape in his mind. *And she believes I raped her.* His thoughts wandered back to his discussion with the Mages of Myrcidë. They had also accused him of rape, and Jeremilan's hostility toward him suggested their leader believed it; but the aged leader of the Myrcidians had likely gotten the conviction from Chymmerlee herself.

Perhaps she's wrong about the pregnancy. Saviar had heard some weird stories: babies happened when men and women stared lovingly into each other's eyes, when they held hands, when she swallowed a "baby seed." The ignorance of youth, the discomfort of parents, the shame and secrecy of an unplanned birth planted interesting ideas in children's heads. Perhaps a stray tale or thought had lodged in Chymmerlee's mind and caused her to believe in a pregnancy that did not exist.

The more he considered it, the more sense it made. Chymmerlee was the youngest of the mages; she had never seen a child born. The mages kept no pets or animals, so Chymmerlee would have had no chance to watch a bull or billy perform his job in a pasture or watch a cow or nanny squeeze out the results of their mating. Chymmerlee might have no real idea of how procreation worked, only the stories of her elders.

Saviar shook his head. The hatred in Chymmerlee's eyes, in her entire demeanor, had made it clear she understood the concept of rape. That it went beyond the myth of the implanting of an infant in her womb by virtue of a loving stare. For whatever reason, by whatever misconception,

Chymmerlee truly believed someone, most likely Saviar, had forced himself upon her in a way that had resulted in the creation of a new life inside of her.

Saviar's headshake grew more violent. He could not bear to consider the possibility. He sprang to his feet, this time drawing many an Eastern eye, though he had interest in only one of them. He turned his attention wholly on Weile Kahn. "Would you mind if I went outside for a bit? I need to practice." It was nothing but truth. Saviar did his best thinking with a sword in hand and a battle, even a contrived one, at the fore. He wanted nothing more in the world than to train.

Weile Kahn gave no indication he found the request unexpected or untoward. "An excellent idea, grandson's twin. I could use a spar myself, if you'll go easy on an old man."

Saviar suspected the "old man" would prove spry enough, and he would have a few tricks the young Renshai had not yet encountered. The opportunity intrigued him, though the Easterners did not seem as keen. A couple of them edged toward their leader, and worried frowns scored features usually well-schooled at hiding expression. It seemed an odd time for them to worry for Weile's well-being. Surely, they knew Saviar meant him no harm, and Renshai never killed by accident.

Already impressed with Subikahn's grandfather, Saviar's appreciation rose further. Organizing dozens of men who had little regard for law or order, many imbued with streaks of cruelty and raging bitterness, seemed an impossible feat in and of itself. Saviar could scarcely imagine not only successfully employing them, but creating loyal attachments with genuine fealty. Clearly, these men honestly worried for the welfare of their leader.

"Of course you may accompany me." Saviar added, as warning more than information, "I'm sure you're aware of the intensity of Renshai practices." During his youth, Subikahn had spent many months with his father in the Eastern kingdom, accompanied by a Renshai *torke*. Even if he hadn't watched the daylong training sessions, Weile had surely seen Subikahn practicing for hours afterward. He would know Renshai sparred only with live steel and that Saviar would have enough control to handle any situation without harming his partner. To suggest otherwise was grave insult.

As they headed through the tunnels and back outside, nausea bubbled in Saviar's gut. His imprisonment had left his skills rusty and his confidence shaky. He had no idea of Weile's prowess or lack or what wiles he might throw into his repertoire. Saviar did not worry for his own life; if he could not defeat an aging *ganim* who had no true designs against him, he deserved to die. His concern involved a faint thought that he might accidentally harm or kill Subikahn's grandfather. And, while that would leave him horrified and guilt-riddled, it would also turn him into the most hunted man in every kingdom.

Saviar emerged into the forest and turned. To his surprise, he found no one behind him, not even the great Weile Kahn, let alone his wary bodyguards. Saviar waited a polite moment; but, seeing no sign of the Easterners, he launched into a complicated *svergelse*.

Immediately, joy rushed over Saviar, so intense he nearly lost his timing. The sword in his hand felt so natural, so right, as if some magical being had reattached a missing limb. It seemed as if he existed only for this precise moment: the perfect weight of the sword in his hand, every precise movement bringing the *svergelse* to proper life, his arms and legs entwined in a lethal dance of ecstasy. The sword sped around him like a live thing; he controlled it with the same certainty and power as his own legs. It went where he commanded, no matter the seeming impossibility of the pattern, the need for ultimate strength, a speed that rivaled lightning.

Nothing else in the world mattered, not the hardheaded Myrcidians nor their magical demands on him, not the prisoners, and only the upcoming war held any other meaning. He moved with a peerless and fatal precision, driving through faceless enemies by the score, taking down imaginary phalanxes despite their well-trained and commanded exactitude. He pictured them as the best militia he had ever faced, competent warriors with deadly speed and accuracy, enormous in numbers and fortitude.

Saviar had no idea how long he practiced before a real sword joined the myriad imagined ones. Though deep into his fantasy, he still had the presence of mind not to thrust his blade into the real flesh of his living opponent, even while he took down the others around him in bloody splendor. Soon, it was just the two of them exchanging thrust and parry, dodge and strike. The other was good, though no match for a strong, young Renshai, at least not one-on-one, face-to-face. Several times, Saviar drove in, then retreated before dealing the killing blow, even as a nonlethal touch. At last, he found an opening too good to pass up, weaving the tip of his blade through the other's fingers to cut the sword from his hand. An instant later, Saviar held both weapons while Weile Kahn skittered safely backward, all the while examining his now-empty hand.

Though Saviar had followed the man's every movement, he lost track of Weile in the shadows. He blinked trying to figure out how that had happened, when the Eastern's voice emerged from behind a copse of nettles. "I'll never figure out how you do that." He shook his hand, as if restoring feeling to sleeping fingers. "Wouldn't it be easier just to take the whole hand?"

Saviar had to admit Weile had a point. It did require a lot more control to carve a weapon harmlessly from a warrior's grip. "We reserve that for opponents who don't deserve hands . . . or a clean death."

Weile finally lowered his arm. "Well, I appreciate the compliment." Though unnecessary, he explained. "That you find me worthy of life and of keeping my body parts connected."

Saviar merely nodded respectfully. He tossed the sword toward Weile.

Weile snatched it from the air with a quickness and finesse even a Renshai would appreciate. He replaced it in its sheath. "Saviar, we need to talk."

Saviar appreciated that, though he longed to return to his *svergelse*. In truth, he suspected he could practice for three days straight, without stopping to eat or sleep, and still not satisfy his need to practice. "All right."

Weile continued, "I apologize if I'm violating Renshai protocol or manners by asking. We can talk and spar or we can talk, then spar. I know your people consider it foolish to do both at once, but you also consider it important to prepare for all eventualities, so you might look at it as an obstacle to be overcome."

It was the longest speech Weile had ever given Saviar; he seemed to be a man who saved words until he needed them.

Saviar had a feeling he was about to tell Subikahn's grand-father anything the Easterner wanted to know. Oddly, Saviar suspected that having his wits about him for the conversation was more important than for the spar. "Let's talk first." He sheathed his weapon as well.

Weile headed into the overgrowth, with Saviar at his heels. They were alone as far as Saviar's well-trained senses could detect, but he realized he had not heard Weile's arrival, either. The Easterner led him deep into the underbrush, and Saviar knew that, if anyone had followed them, they could not have negotiated the way without considerable noise. Finally, Weile found a reasonably comfortable perch on a gnarled and rotting deadfall. He waited until Saviar took a seat as well before speaking.

"So," Weile said. "Tell me everything you know about the Mages of Myrcidë."

CHAPTER 19

Rely on only a few maneuvers, and one of those will cause your death. Deliver every blow with the confidence that it will kill, yet always assume your opponent can deflect you. For every attack, there're multiple dodges, parries, and counterattacks. Draw him into patterns, then catch him off guard with change.

— Colbey Calistinsson

WEILE KAHN AND SAVIAR approached the residence of the Mages of Myrcidë, one male and one female prisoner sandwiched between them. They had left Chymmerlee at the bunker, a situation that worried Saviar. He had promised to return all three prisoners, and he had no idea what effect the magical sealing of that agreement might have on him when he brought back only two.

Uncertain how the magic worked, Saviar tried to console himself with the knowledge that he would return the youngest of the mages, too, as soon as the Easterners allowed it. As Weile had already agreed to release her later that same day, Saviar was not overly concerned. Apparently, neither was the magic, because, not only was he not exploding into flame, he felt nothing untoward at all, except for a fluttering in his stomach that he knew had everything to do with anticipation.

Saviar had seen great men at work before. His Knight-Captain grandfather embraced morality with a violence most men reserved for warfare. He had watched Kedrin negotiate with ministers and kings, and the leader of the Renshai had chosen Saviar as his successor. Though he had personally bargained with men of great import, Saviar suspected he had never seen anything like the confrontation that would take place between ancient Jeremilan and aging Weile Kahn. If he survived it, he would learn a lot about the ways and means of great leaders.

Usually, the common house of the mages disappeared into the mountains, a blurry image against a backdrop of forest. Without the aid of his magical weapon, Saviar doubted he would be able to see it at all; the combined magics of its inhabitants had kept it secret for too long. Yet, now, it seemed to jump out at him, a simple construct interrupting the otherwise wild and overgrown plain at the base of the Weathered Mountains. Perhaps it was due to the presence of the captive mages who shuffled at his heels, heads low, mouths still gagged to protect him from their magic, hands bound at the small of their backs. Weile brought up the rear.

There was no sign of Weile's men, though Saviar assumed they trailed the group at a respectable distance. The fact that he could not hear or see them did not deter this thought; they could move as soundlessly as any forest hunter on the prowl. They would not accompany Saviar and Weile the entire way. Weile had seen to that with a series of commands in a language, presumably Eastern, that Saviar did not understand. Whatever his sword skill, or lack, Weile clearly trusted his ability to escape from a difficult situation alone. Either that, or he was so unaccustomed to failure the thought of it did not occur to him.

Trailing the prisoners, Weile gave no indication he had difficulty visualizing the Myrcidian compound either, though he also had Saviar and his captives to guide him. He carried himself with an alert dignity that suggested nothing in the world could harm or upset him. Calm incarnate, he strode toward twenty-three hostile mages as if he did such things every day. Saviar suspected he just might.

A single figure exited the compound and headed toward Saviar. A study in contrasts, he looked exquisitely nervous, his steps mincing and hesitant, his stride faltering, his head flicking in all directions, as if he expected to be attacked from every side. As he stepped from a patch of shadow into the early morning sunlight, silver glimmers appeared in his beard. Saviar identified Netheron by his mannerisms and movements before he could make out any facial features. Moments later, those became clear as well. The willowy old mage approached cautiously, clearly prepared to cast a spell with the slightest provocation.

Saviar stopped to allow Netheron to make the first move. Netheron took only one more step before coming to a halt as well, a bit too far for comfortable conversation. That forced him to fairly shout to the group. "Why have you brought a stranger here?" He clearly intended to sound guardlike, but it came out more like dithering.

Saviar did not bother to look behind him. The others must have stopped as well, or they would have shoved into his back. "I've brought no strangers, Netheron. You know Janecos and Paultan. The man at the rear is Weile Kahn, leader of the elite guardsmen of the Eastern kingdom and my brother's grandfather."

Netheron hesitated a moment, calculating words that should not have required much thought. Generally, one's brother's anything bore the same relationship to oneself. "Your brother's grandfather is a stranger to us. You're oath- and honor-bound not to reveal us to him."

"I have broken no promises," Saviar said, hoping he successfully hid the irritation that Netheron would even think such a thing, let alone suggest it aloud. Under the circumstances, it had to appear as if he had done so. "Weile already knew of your existence and the location of your residence while I was still held prisoner there, incapable of telling anyone. Otherwise, how could he have taken Janecos, Paultan, and Chymmerlee?"

"Chymmerlee," Netheron repeated, his features turning frantic. "Where is Chymmerlee?" He peered around the bound figures as if expecting her to suddenly appear among them.

Weile stepped up beside Paultan and spoke his first word of the conversation. "Insurance."

Netheron jerked his attention to the Easterner. "What?"

"She's unharmed, and we will return her when the time is right."

"When's that?" Netheron demanded.

"The time is right," Weile explained, "when I say it's right."

Netheron stood there a moment in speechless silence. He rubbed at his beard. When he finally spoke, the words seemed too weak to have taken so long to think of them. "She's unharmed?"

Weile's face took on a self-indulgent smile. "I assure you we haven't harmed her nor will we, so long as you don't give us just cause."

Netheron studied Weile for several moments in another prolonged hush. Then, he glanced at the captives. He cleared his throat. "Please wait here a moment." He turned on his heel and rushed unceremoniously back into the compound.

The smile still plastered on his face, Weile turned Saviar a quizzical look.

Saviar merely shrugged. Nothing needed saying. Jeremilan would not prove nearly as easy to intimidate as Netheron.

Quicker than Saviar expected, Netheron returned and ushered them toward the compound. "Please come along. Jeremilan will speak with you."

Netheron led the group into a familiar front room filled with numerous pieces of matching wooden furniture, all couches, benches, and chairs swathed in pillows. Two additional doors stood at the far end of the room, and Saviar knew how easily those came and went with the mages. One moment, a man could walk into a room, the next, it became an inescapable prison.

"Please take a seat."

Saviar glanced at Weile. He had warned the Easterner about the disappearing doors.

Apparently unperturbed, Weile chose a sturdy chair heaped with pillows and perched atop them as if accustomed to such seating. Saviar chose the closest place to his right, the farthest corner of a long bench.

"We'd like some time to examine these two." Netheron gestured at the captives. "Then, Jeremilan will come speak with you."

Weile nodded his assent without, apparently, bothering to consider the ramifications of becoming separated from all of the mages. Either he did not consider the fact that the recovered prisoners would talk and that the mages could now contain Saviar and Weile, or those things did not worry him. He barely bothered to watch Netheron walk through one of the back doors, with Janecos and Paultan in tow, and close it behind him.

Saviar opened his mouth to remind Weile of the disappearing doors and the mages' ability to cast spells through invisible portals; but Weile shook his head ever so slightly, a clear instruction for silence. Saviar closed his mouth. Apparently, the elder believed the mages would spy, and he intended to give them absolutely nothing. He did not even bother to survey the room for possible danger. He simply sat, high in his seat, waiting patiently.

Saviar pursed his lips and sat quietly as well, though every nerve and muscle felt tensed to bursting. He preferred motion to stillness, violence to ignorance.

A moment later, all three of the doors shimmered slightly, but they remained in place, much to Saviar's surprise. It appeared he and Weile could leave at any time, and the mages would make no move to stop them. The strategy made no sense to him, and he pondered it during what seemed like an interminable delay.

Saviar found himself studying Weile, the only truly interesting object in the room and the one that ceaselessly drew his eye. More regal than any king, the Easterner seemed as comfortable in his chair as he had in the catacombs. As in all parts of the mages' compound, the lighting in the room was a constant magical glow, yet it still seemed to gather around Weile, as if drawn to him. When Saviar looked away, he found all parts of the room equally visible, as if the effect only occurred with direct observation, apparently an illusion.

Saviar knew more than his share of charismatic people. To a man, the Knights of Erythane kept themselves meticulous in every way, used a posture that made them seem bigger than life, and followed an honor so intense and vast it fascinated. Weile, on the other hand, radiated an allure that seemed entirely effortless. He had the same silky, black hair as most Easterners, carelessly tousled and liberally flecked with white. He wore standard travel clothing, nothing special or fancy, dusty and stained, a far cry from the impeccable uniforms of the knights. His dark eyes were unfathomable, reflecting a deep intelligence and nothing more. His spry movements seemed more suitable to a man half his age, yet he had seemingly infinite patience that others twice his age never learned.

From experience, Saviar knew the man preferred silence, but never from lack of understanding or eloquence. Weile could say more with a well-placed word than most could with a paragraph, but Saviar had also heard him speak long passages with an articulateness that rivaled the king's best advisers. He seemed to know everything and everyone, inside and out. Saviar wondered what sort of upbringing he must have had and also gained a new appreciation for Tae Kahn. It must have been arduous to be such a man's only son.

Tired of speculating about his companion, Saviar turned his thoughts to the Mages of Myrcidë. If anyone could barter his freedom from them, Weile could. Saviar had no doubt the two of them would leave together, with little effort expended on the part of Weile Kahn. The previous night, Weile had plied Saviar for information and got plenty of it, but Saviar's own questions had gone mostly unanswered. He had given Weile puzzles to ponder: how to convince the mages to assist with the war, how to make them tolerate—if not appreciate—Renshai, how to handle the tricky question of Chymmerlee's pregnancy, real or imagined. The Easterner had offered nothing useful, and Saviar wondered why he had not demanded more in exchange for the information he had given.

It seemed like hours before the mages appeared, gliding through the doors in the same manner they had used to enter the walls during Saviar's captivity. This appeared stranger, however, because it seemed easy enough to open the doors without bothering to waste magic. Saviar named them silently as they entered: Hevnard, a quiet beefy man with a balding head who had seemed intelligent and reasonable to Saviar during his first stay. A frail and wrinkled woman who appeared closest to Jeremilan's age, Arinosta entered on the arm of Roby, another elder who leaned on a staff when he walked. Saviar had observed the man moving easily enough without it, on occasion, suggesting it was more affectation than necessity. Each of the mages spoke his or her name before taking a seat on a bench in front of Weile Kahn.

Hevnard nodded politely as he sat; Arinosta fussed over the arrangement of the pillows. Roby fixed his gaze on

Weile Kahn so intently he seemed not to notice he had leaned his staff against Arinosta's leg rather than the bench. Weile glanced at them each in turn, his features expressionless, his demeanor oddly casual, as if he had nothing to fear from three mages in their own home. If he noticed the oddity of their entrance, and he surely must have, he gave no sign.

As those three settled into place, another trio of mages entered without opening the door. Blenford had hair as orange as a well-washed root, worn halfway down his back, and a matching spray of freckles. Saviar knew his clownish appearance hid a quick wit. He looked younger than nearly all of the other mages, mid-thirties perhaps, and as ivory-skinned as any Northman. It occurred to Saviar that most of the Myrcidians suffered from the unhealthy pallor of men and women who rarely ventured outside.

Recently returned from captivity, Paultan followed Blenford, gaze dodging Weile while the others chose to study him. Beside the small, blond man walked Chestinar. Saviar had never conversed with the last man but knew him on sight by his skeletal figure and sickly countenance. He had brittle, colorless hair so thin it revealed patches of greasy scalp. His eyes were a watery beige, his cheekbones jutted from a gaunt face, and his lips were cracked and scabby. He sniffled almost constantly, and the heel of his hand rose frequently to brush the tip of his nose. Saviar suspected the man had left the womb with a nasal discharge, had probably never known a healthy day in his life.

These three settled into places on either side of the first group, Chestinar and Paultan on a couch to their right hand and Blenford on a well-pillowed chair to the left. The best seat remained open, a comfortable-looking chair at the front and center of their group. As they settled into position, Jeremilan floated through the doors using the same magical method as the others. Stiffness affected his walk, and age thinned and colored his skin in blotches. Nevertheless, he managed to convey a stately bearing nearly as impressive as Weile's own, if not quite as effortless. Silence reigned as Jeremilan took his seat, broken only by a haphazard cough from Chestinar.

Saviar chewed his lower lip. He had no intention of saying anything; he had spoken his piece multiple times and had nothing more to add. Jeremilan might well have been a stone for all Saviar's prior words had moved him. He wondered what possible arguments Weile Kahn had that he did not and if they would leave this room alive. Suddenly, he appreciated Weile's decision to hold Chymmerlee back. She might be the only reason the mages had not already blasted them to pieces.

Abruptly, Saviar realized Jeremilan's attention was riveted not on Weile, but on him. He froze, lip caught between his teeth, mid-squirm, and followed the direction of the elder's stare to the sword at his hip. It was the only obvious weapon in the room. Surely Weile carried something sharp as well, but he kept it hidden.

Jeremilan's snarl broke the hush. "I knew you would betray us."

Weile responded before Saviar could. "He didn't betray you." Jeremilan's gaze flicked to the Easterner as he continued, "*You* betrayed *him*."

Jeremilan stiffened, and his eyes blazed. "How dare you!"

"Speak the truth?" Weile added, as if finishing Jeremilan's thought. "You promised those boys they could come and go freely, yet you locked this one up like an animal."

Jeremilan glared at Weile, as if he had forgotten Saviar and his newly acquired sword. "That was on the condition that they release my great-granddaughter."

"Which they did."

"Which they *didn't*!" Jeremilan countered forcefully. His features darkened noticeably, and spittle flew from his mouth as he spoke. "They kept her, forced her to help in a . . . a war." The last word fell from his tongue like lead, viler than any blasphemy. "Then the demons raped her."

Something flickered through Weile's eyes, then disappeared. For an instant, Saviar thought Subikahn's grandfather would leap to his feet and wave his arms, would become as verbally violent as his opponent. But, as usual, Weile did none of those things. He remained as calm as ever, the only sign he took offense at Jeremilan's accusations the quirking of a dark eyebrow. "None of that is true, Jeremilan. And everyone in this room knows it."

Jeremilan snorted. "Because of a truth detection spell?" He snorted again. "Anyone with an inkling of magic knows it doesn't work the same on . . . demons."

Saviar glanced around the room, at each mage in turn. Chestinar bobbed his head in agreement, but the others remained in place, utterly still, as if some artist had quietly replaced them with perfectly replicated statues.

Weile tipped his head. "Saviar is as human as . . . me."

Saviar had expected him to use the common phrase "you or me," and the missing pronoun was conspicuously absent. Apparently, the mages had anticipated the same because a murmur swept through them. Even Jeremilan contemplated the lapse, then responded to it. "Are you saying he's only as human as yourself, not us? Are you also Renshai?"

Weile laughed, the sound strangely joyful in an otherwise tense situation. "I'm Eastern to the core: born, bred, and raised. No blood is more common than mine, and I'm no more Renshai than you are."

Jeremilan settled back into his chair, apparently willing to play the game, at least for the moment. "Then why did you not claim Saviar as human as everyone in the room rather than only as human as yourself?"

Weile kept his gaze on the ancient, though he gave no other sign of his thoughts. "Because I'm not convinced you're human."

"Ah." Jeremilan sat back, tenting his fingers. "Prejudice, I understand. Because we use magic, we're something other than human, something Outworld. Elves or giants or demons, perhaps. Something . . . not you."

Weile leaned toward Jeremilan. "What I question is not your powers; I consider elves people. It's your humanity."

That led to total silence. No one seemed to know how to answer that claim or even whether or not it needed answering. When Jeremilan finally did respond, it was with something totally inadequate. "What?"

Weile dutifully repeated. "I question your humanity, your ability to empathize, your understanding of what it means to care about those who are not yourself, to see value in other intelligent beings."

Jeremilan leaped to his feet. "What nonsense is this! We're the most peaceful people in the world, the ones most dedicated to the prevention of suffering and the only ones who have never deliberately harmed another."

Weile laughed again, this time with a contagious mirth

that left Saviar grinning for reasons he could not wholly explain.

The mocking only further angered Jeremilan, whose features turned nearly scarlet with fury. "How dare you laugh at me? There's nothing funny about what I said."

Weile stopped immediately, as if moved by Jeremilan's words. "I'm sorry," he said, though without a hint of apology in his tone. "Weren't you joking?" He glanced about as if everyone in the room surely understood and sided with him, although none of the mages had joined the laughter. He swiped the back of his hand across his eyes, as if the immensity of the jest had brought him nearly to tears. "I'm always amazed at how those who commit the most monstrous crimes can unabashedly label themselves pure. How the most vicious of the intolerant dare to call themselves victims of the selfsame prejudice."

As if his jaw had suddenly grown too heavy to close, Jeremilan let his mouth fall open. "What are you suggesting?" The words sounded strangled. His fingers twitched, as if they intended to cast magic of their own accord.

"Sit down," Weile commanded. He added softly, "I know what you did."

To Saviar's surprise, Jeremilan obeyed. For an instant, the Renshai considered magic, until he remembered which one of them was the mage.

A sharp intake of breath came from the direction of the Myrcidians, but Saviar did not try to discern which one had made the sound. He was too fascinated by the events unfolding in front of him. He had no idea to what Weile referred, but Jeremilan surely did.

Weile had everyone's full attention now. He spoke barely above a whisper, and as every person in the room clung to his words, the quiet around them grew as deep as death. Arinosta leaned forward, tipping her ear in his direction, clearly not fully trusting her aging hearing. "You justify your seclusion with the claim that humans would harm you if we knew of your existence. You simply assume we're evil."

"No." Jeremilan would not accept the statement. "We don't assume all humans are evil. There will come a time when we live among them again, when we're strong enough to defend ourselves, when our numbers have swelled to a tolerable level. Until then, we must protect ourselves from the few who might wish to destroy us for no better reason than our differentness, our power."

For the moment, Weile conceded the point to present another. "You call all Renshai demons. You believe in a blood libel long dispelled as myth. Even when your own magic proves you wrong, you find reason to dismiss the results in favor of your prejudice."

"It's not prejudice to hate avowed enemies!" Jeremilan found his temper again. "The Renshai nearly destroyed us entirely. No other group of humans is expected to embrace a mortal foe, one that nearly caused their extinction for no better reason than sport."

Weile hesitated just long enough that Saviar worried he had lost the upper hand. "It does not give you the right to spout falsehoods as facts nor to hide behind a war that ended centuries ago. The gods, in their infinite wisdom, gave mankind a finite lifespan for a reason. Hatreds have a limited time to fester. Old enemies pass away, and their offsprings' offspring become friends, even lovers, with or without apologies. Hundreds of years ago, the Renshai and Myrcidians battled for reasons we can never truly know. We can only surmise based on historical references and old tales laced with, and colored by, our own biases and those of our ancestors. Since the demise of the Cardinal Wizards, evil and good, law and chaos are no longer such clear and absolute things. So long as you hold tight to the fallacy that all Renshai are demons, you can believe yourselves wholly pure, utterly right, and condemn those you dislike as monsters in human guise." He looked into the eyes of the leader of Myrcidë. "Isn't that the very definition of bigotry?"

Jeremilan blinked, very slowly, very deliberately. "Are you actually trying to say there's ambiguity in the Renshai destruction of Myrcidë? That anyone could look at what happened there and find fault and righteousness on both sides?"

"I'm saying that's true of any conflict. No one rushes into war, or even an argument, believing he holds the moral low ground. The enemy is always to blame. Only a traitor would stand against his own people, at which point, his people cease to be his own."

Jeremilan's brow crinkled. Weile's point clearly was not as obvious to him as it was to Saviar. "But one only need look at the outcome to see who was right and who was wrong."

Weile's expression remained mild. "So, the loser of any conflict is, by definition, right?"

"Well . . ."

Weile continued, "So, if my men assaulted your compound, and you repelled us, we would be good and you evil merely by virtue of our loss?"

Jeremilan rolled his eyes, waved a dismissive hand. "Of course not. The instigators of the war are always the ones who are evil. Good people never start wars."

"Never?" Weile kneaded the arms of his chair, still focused on Jeremilan.

Saviar fought down a smile; the master was back in control.

"Two adjoining cities exist. One is stricken by a flood, losing all its crops, while the other is spared. The flooded city asks for assistance from its neighbor, but is rebuffed, leaving them with the choice of whether to let its citizenry starve or force the spared city to share its bounty by force. If they choose to attack, which side is good and which is evil?"

Jeremilan had no answer. "That's an artificial situation."

"Hypothetical situation," Weile corrected. "But one that has occurred often throughout history, with varying responses, solutions, and outcomes. Surely, one could argue the spared city is the evil one for not being willing to share. Others might point out that, if the spared city did share, its own citizens would suffer for a tragedy that does not belong to them." He tipped his head, his expression inviting. "Indulge me for a moment, if you would, please. What's your solution to the problem?"

Jeremilan's eyes narrowed in clear suspicion. Apparently, he suspected a trap. "There's always a way to stretch scarce resources. Everyone might endure hunger, but no one would have to die."

"Stretch resources." Weile mulled the words far longer than they required. The suggested solution seemed straightforward, even simplistic, to Saviar. It might not take into account the fundamental nature of human beings or alliances between different villages, but it was an obvious theoretical resolution to the presented scenario. He added contemplatively, "Like with magic?"

Jeremilan shrugged. "If necessary."

If Weile was about to pounce, he gave no sign. He still seemed intrigued by Jeremilan's counsel. "So, you would agree that, if someone had the magical means to assist in a dire situation, he should do so? I mean, if his not assisting could result in unnecessary deaths?"

Several of the mages behind Jeremilan held their breath. The silence deepened, tangible. The eldest face in the room screwed into a fabulous display of wrinkles. "Nice try. It's one thing for us to help increase the food supply so people don't starve. It's another to put our own lives in danger by taking part in a war that doesn't involve us."

Weile nodded, as if in understanding. "So . . . death by starvation . . . is bad and worth rescue. Death by war . . . good?"

"No." Jeremilan shook his head, as if trying to explain something obvious to an imbecile. "It's just that saving someone from starvation causes us no harm. Saving him from war puts our lives at risk as well."

Saviar wanted to break in but decided against it. Weile was doing fine on his own.

Weile tipped his head still farther, as if even more confused. "But I thought you'd been promised that anyone you sent would remain a safe distance from the front. You'd be protected."

Jeremilan sighed heavily. For the first time, Saviar got the idea he wanted to help but felt incapable. Previously, it had seemed more as if the mages had no interest in assisting, only in remaining hidden. "We're safest here, a great distance from any violence. We can't afford to risk a single Myrcidian life. There are too few of us to lose even one."

Weile bobbed his head, as if finally understanding. "Your lives are more valuable than ours."

Jeremilan's expression combined apology with a hint of pride. "I'm afraid so. There's extensive value to the rare ability to use magic, and it's not something easily found, created, or even bred."

"Clearly." Weile's tone held a hint of something withheld.

Jeremilan turned him a look Saviar could not quite read.

The emotions seemed mixed, jumbled, but he thought he saw at least a trace of annoyance and, maybe, fear.

If Weile noticed Jeremilan's additional discomfort, he did not show it. He remained as unreadable and implacable as ever. "I've spent some time among royalty, so I'm familiar with the concept of differential value among human lives."

It was gross understatement. Saviar knew Weile had served as king of the entire Eastlands for many years before passing the job to his son.

Weile continued, "I can't deny agreeing with the underlying concept, though, admittedly, my notion of ranking and priority would be unorthodox. I judge the value of a human life by competence, intelligence, and strength of character rather than bloodline. A wise man is useless if he uses his wisdom in ways that benefit only himself. Competence of any kind is valuable only when it's channeled for intelligent and useful purposes. Benevolence is misused by a fool."

Weile turned his gaze to the Myrcidians behind Jeremilan, as if worried his words would be wasted on their irrational leader. "Having the propensity for magic might make a man special, but it doesn't make his life valuable unless he uses it in a shrewd and compassionate fashion. The best swordsman in the world is worthless if he's also a coward."

Saviar did not like that word. It was a terrible insult in his culture, worse than any swear word. He knew others did not consider it so severe, yet he could not shake the feeling that Weile had insulted the Myrcidians deeply and subtly, in a way that might leave them wondering why they felt so offended.

Jeremilan tipped his head, studying Weile through half-slitted eyes. Clearly, he did not know how to respond. "What are you trying to say? That our magic is useless because we're too afraid to use it to defend a bunch of savage strangers who would as soon kill us as look at us?"

Weile did not miss a beat. "I'm looking at you, and I haven't killed anyone. You can't deny I've had the opportunity. I won't go into who's savage and who's civilized except to say that we're the ones cultivating vegetables and fruit, creating works of art and architecture, tending livestock, educating our children, traveling, and dwelling in diverse communities interconnected with a common language. You're the ones huddled in a hidden cave, sharing nothing, consorting only with yourselves and clinging to ignorance under the guise of our presumed savagery or demonic possession."

Jeremilan rose, pulling himself to his full height which, even had Weile been standing, would have towered over the Easterner. His obvious age took any real menace from his posture. "Are you finished insulting us?"

"Insulting?" Weile's brow crushed down further, as if he made no sense whatsoever of Jeremilan's distress. "I meant no offense."

"Didn't you?" Sarcasm coarsened Jeremilan's tone. "You've essentially called us worthless and selfish because we won't share our power, cowards for avoiding war, and barbarians for the way we choose to live."

"Did I?" Weile glanced at Saviar, pretending to read whether or not the Renshai was also confused by Jeremilan's claim. He rolled his gaze to the ceiling as if in deep consideration, then beamed like he had come to a great epiphany. "And here I thought the name-calling had come from your side." He tapped the words off on his fingers. "Savages, demons, inferior beings." He considered further. "Thousands of our lives not worth risking even one of yours." He nodded sagely. "I wonder if this is how wars start? Each side sees the other as less than human, thereby justifying inhumane treatment, even extermination." He continued to speak as if having just discovered a concept never before considered. "Yes, I'll bet that's it." He shrugged to suggest what followed was a foregone conclusion. "Come, Saviar. Apparently, we have another war to fight."

Saviar shook his head slightly. His vows, whether reinforced with magic or not, kept him from leaving. "I'm sorry, sir. I've promised to stay. A man is no better than his word."

"Ah." Weile scratched his chin. "Well, then. I guess this session is finished." He stood up; and, though a head shorter, he seemed to tower over the leader of the mages.

"Wait." Jeremilan stepped between Weile and the exit. "You can't leave."

Weile gave no indication he took the words as a threat. Saviar's heart rate quickened enough for both of them, and it was all he could do to keep his fingers off his hilt. "Can't I?" the Easterner asked. "What's stopping me?"

"Do you see any exits?" Jeremilan made a gesture with both arms to indicate the entire room.

The approach surprised even Saviar, who had no trouble visualizing the doors and even a single window behind Chestinar that he had not noticed earlier.

"Three," Weile said calmly. "Four if you count the window, though it seems a bit of a squeeze."

A loud murmur swept the mages, cut off by an abrupt gesture from Jeremilan. "You can see the doors?"

Weile's gaze traveled from one to the next to the next, then back to Jeremilan. "Can't you?"

"Well of course I can," Jeremilan said impatiently. "But I'm a ..." He broke off suddenly. "You *are* Renshai, aren't you? You must be demon seed."

"Must I?" Weile snorted. "Because I'm neither."

"Then how ... ?"

"Did it ever occur to you that I carry mage blood, too? Or, maybe, I'm carrying something powerfully magical."

The mages stared at him, and the hum of myriad conversations filled the room. Nothing Jeremilan said or did would stop that now, but their leader did not seem to care. He was fully focused on Weile. "Are you?"

"Mage-blooded?"

"Or carrying something powerfully magical?"

"Yes," Weile replied.

Jeremilan realized his mistake. "Which of those?"

Weile shrugged and headed for the door through which they had entered. "Does it matter? I thought we'd finished our negotiations and decided to remain enemies."

"I never said that," Jeremilan insisted. He retook his seat and gestured for Weile to do the same. "You have my full attention."

Weile returned to his chair and sat on the edge, as if ready to leave at any moment. "I returned two of your mages in good faith. Now, I'd like to barter for the third." He spoke as if kidnapping was the most natural thing in the world, its victims a commodity for trade.

Jeremilan leaned forward, his expression skeptical. "Let me guess: you wish to trade one mage for our promise to risk all the mages by assisting in your war."

Put that way, it certainly seemed like a lopsided bargain,

made all the more ludicrous by the fact that Chymmerlee had never truly belonged to Weile.

"I prefer my proposal." Weile's tone and phrasing suggested he found the previous proposition unfair on his end instead of Jeremilan's. "I trade your great-granddaughter, and your unborn son or daughter, for Saviar."

Saviar contributed to the gasp that filled the room. Weile had said more in thirteen words than most men did in entire conversations. He had immediately shot down any complaints of unfairness twofold. The mages could scarcely claim Weile was only giving back something he had stolen when they had done the same to Saviar. Weile offered a two-for-one exchange and added a piece of information that the Renshai, at least, did not know. And that bit of news held him spellbound.

Unborn son or daughter? What did he mean by that? Saviar did not want to contemplate it, but his mind ran with the information. *Is he accusing Jeremilan of rape and incest?* Abruptly, outrage exploded through Saviar. He felt himself leaving his chair, and only Weile's piercing gaze kept him from leaping upon the leader of the Myrcidians. Instead, he lowered his head to hide his expression, clenching and unclenching his hands but keeping them away from his hilt. Despite the easy tone of the conversation, it would not take much to spark a battle they could not win. Saviar knew from experience that the mages' magic would undo him. No matter how enraged he got, he needed to let Weile take charge. He had a feeling the Easterner was always four steps ahead of the conversation, his strategy more detailed and targeted than any general's.

All of that dashed through Saviar's mind in an instant; and, for all their inherent wisdom, the mages did not seem to process the information any quicker than he did.

The eyes of every mage swept to Jeremilan. If Weile's quiet accusation was true, they gave no sign they knew about it.

Jeremilan's face purpled, but his lack of other evidence of indignation implied the truth, or near-truth, of Weile's accusation. Suddenly, everything fit together in Saviar's mind. The mages had initially claimed the baby his. However, when he had suggested testing Chymmerlee's virginity, they had seemed uncomfortable. They had known she would not pass, whether or not Saviar had raped her, which meant they knew she had slept with someone. Given the secrecy of their society, it had to be a mage, and only another Myrcidian could have done such a thing without her knowledge.

Saviar wondered why he had not considered the situation more carefully before; it should have been obvious to him. Jeremilan had lamented the difficulty inherent in creating more mages multiple times; and, when she still liked him, Chymmerlee had suggested the mages secretly wished they would sleep together. At the time, they had believed him mage-blooded because of the aura, and they had not known of his Renshai background.

Another wave of blistering resentment boiled inside Saviar. *How many times did the males of the tribe defile Chymmerlee and clear her memory of the assault? How young was she when the process started? Did she have any idea what they had done to her?* Abhorrence overtook Saviar, and nausea bubbled through him. Driven to sate his rage and revulsion with swordplay, he envisioned hacking his way through the Mages of Myrcidë, mangling their bloody corpses, and wondered how many he could strike down before they subdued him with magic.

"We will trade Chymmerlee for Saviar, so long as she is alive and unharmed." Jeremilan's gaze had fallen to the floor, and he seemed to have difficulty looking at Weile. "And you must let us bind you both to secrecy."

"No," Weile said.

Jeremilan managed to raise his head ever so slightly. "Are you refusing to carry through on your own barter?"

Weile fastened his attention on Jeremilan, granting no quarter. "We will not submit to magical constraints of any kind. Too many people now know of your existence to silence them all. Saviar and I are the least of your worries."

Jeremilan clamped his jaw shut. He seemed even older, if that were possible, long past his time. He no longer looked strong to Saviar, just a tired and ancient ruler of a people long forgotten. "Fine, then. We can always move."

Weile did not dwell on the point, but Saviar had a feeling he knew something he was not saying.

"Are we finished?" Jeremilan demanded.

Weile started to rise. "I suppose we are. You need only remove your magic from Saviar so he can leave as well."

Jeremilan glanced behind him. "Only after we have Chymmerlee back safely."

"Very well." Weile finished standing.

Saviar looked quickly from one man to the other, his own business still outstanding. He had not come this far, not suffered through this much, to leave without obtaining magical allies in the war against the *Kjempemagiska*. Thus far, he had let Weile do all the negotiating. Now, he needed to say something before he lost all opportunity. "Wait, sir, please. We still haven't settled the most important detail."

Weile turned Saviar a mild look. His expression evinced curiosity, but a twinkle in his dark eyes suggested even his grandson's twin had played into his hands. For the first time, Saviar found himself irritated by the Easterner's smug assurance. It was one thing to watch him handle others, quite another to be handled.

A bit shaken, Saviar continued. "I came here for a purpose, one that imprisonment, torture, and suspicion could not shake. I will not abandon my mission." He attempted to stare down Weile. "I am no distressed damsel waiting helplessly for rescue."

Weile made a palm-up gesture clearly intended to encourage Saviar. Jeremilan sighed and shuffled his feet, apparently weary of Saviar's repeated request.

Neither swayed Saviar. "As everyone knows by now, our world is under siege by a magical band of giants bent on destroying everything human for the apparent purpose of taking our land. For the first battle, they sent their nonmagical, human servants and only one of their own kind. We were able to defeat them, at the loss of many brave lives, but only with the magical aid of Chymmerlee and our elfin queen." Saviar lowered his head and blew out a savage breath. He had explained this before, without much success, but he hoped the change in circumstances brought about by Weile and his gang might aid him. "It's expected their next attack will feature many more giants, perhaps thousands. Without magical assistance, we have little to no chance for success. They will sweep across our continent and, being magical, will not miss this compound." He directed his last comment at those who sat behind Jeremilan. Perhaps they would see the logic that the eldest of them did not.

The group studied Saviar in silence, most with arms

crossed over their chests. They were waiting for something, perhaps for him to restate his request. "As you know, I came to convince the Mages of Myrcidë to assist us with this battle."

As before, Jeremilan shook his head, without any obvious consideration. Before he could speak, however, Weile chuckled. "Surely, there's no need to barter for such a thing. Why anyone with common decency would—"

Jeremilan interrupted as if Weile had not spoken, "And, as you know, we have refused your request time and again. In that regard, nothing has changed. Nothing can change."

Weile rolled his eyes. "I forgot we are not dealing with a group that practices common decency. Men who would rape their own daughters and granddaughters and great-granddaughters cannot be expected to consider the needs of others, to understand even the grossest morality and ethics."

Several of the mages behind Jeremilan leaped to their feet. Others stared at their sandals. Jeremilan looked defeated, near tears. Saviar worried someone would lose control, hurling magic that started a fight that would surely end in several deaths.

But, apparently taking their cues from Jeremilan, the mages did nothing worse than clench jaws and fists.

Jeremilan's voice was small, barely audible and childlike. "I can't expect others to understand the desperate measures to which we must resort to keep the magic alive. It is not a course of action we embarked on without many years of agonized discussion. It is easy to judge what you do not understand, actions others have undertaken for which you were not present for the decision-making process. We proceeded with enormous misgivings and in a method designed to shield Chymmerlee as much as possible from any negative effects. No one took any but the necessary liberties. She doesn't even know." He turned Saviar a sincere look that beggared explanation. Saviar could not imagine any situation, any amount of desperation, any possibility in which he would ever allow such an atrocity to occur.

Apparently, Jeremilan believed he had made his point, because he stopped attempting to defend what was, to Saviar, wholly indefensible. "So, you can surely see, we cannot risk even one of our members. We have too few and no reasonable means to create more."

Acid crawled up Saviar's throat, and he had to fight to keep from vomiting. His oath compelled him to return Chymmerlee to the mages, and Weile had also agreed to do so. Yet, the idea of placing her back into the situation Jeremilan described left him painfully ill. He tried to think like a Knight of Erythane but found it impossible to reconcile the dilemma. What did an honorable man do when his word clashed so horribly with his ethics? Never had he wished more fervently for the counsel of his father and grandfather. "Surely." The word emerged hoarsely, and he cleared his throat. The effort made it feel raw and uncomfortable. "There must be another way . . . than this . . . this . . ." He could not finish. No word seemed suitably horrible; and, even if he found the right one, would only offend.

Up until that moment, the other mages had remained silent. Now, Arinosta, the ancient female, spoke up. "Of course, there's a simpler and kinder way. The collective intelligence of all the world's mages, using all the forms of magic available to them, can't see it; but a naïve young man can. Don't you think if there were another way, we'd try it? We're talking about the sole means for survival of our people. I'd willingly donate my body, as many times as necessary, if I was still capable of bearing babies."

Jeremilan looked relieved to have the pressure taken off him for a moment, especially by a woman.

Silence followed her pronouncement. Saviar could think of many things to say, but none of them would do anything other than incite them to violence. They would have an answer for any question he asked, one that would only irritate him. Any condemnation he made would only prolong the conversation, only make them more defensive.

With a casual air more suitable to a courtroom than a standoff, Weile flicked back an edge of his cloak to reveal a round object the size of a woman's head. Brilliant azure, it seemed to color the entire room, as if the ceiling had melted away to admit the open sky. Every stray beam of light rushed to the stone, as if pulled, and the mages drifted toward it as unconsciously as moths to a flame. Every one of their mouths fell open. In tandem, their eyes widened. Wordless sounds escaped, too random and short to be coherent magic, at least in Saviar's meager experience.

Weile closed his cloak, and the enormous gemstone disappeared from sight, but clearly not from mind. Still acting as one, the Mages of Myrcidë stared at the air, exactly where the stone had been exposed.

Jeremilan found his voice first. "That's the Pica." He seemed incapable of dragging his gaze from the spot, not even to meet Weile's eyes. "The Pica Stone. That's ..." An inappropriately long silence ensued again, before he spat out the last word, "... ours." His fingers twitched into fists, and he finally managed to look into Weile's face.

"No." Though softly spoken, the word was solid and sincere. Weile had no doubts about the proper dispensation of the item. "Once, long ago, it belonged to the Mages of Myrcidë. History shows the Renshai took it as a spoil of war and venerated it as a symbol of their own tribe for many years."

A frown formed on Jeremilan's features, but he did not interrupt. Apparently, he wanted to know what happened next, perhaps even needed to hear it. He made a gesture for Weile to continue.

"In time, the Renshai were also defeated and, presumably, extinguished by the combined forces of the North. The Pica was sold several times, its trail lost to antiquity. It's said a steep and imprudent bet on a gladiator battle put the Pica in the hands of General Santagithi. He passed it off as a bauble to his only daughter. She, in turn, used it as payment for a magical sword crafted by the Eastern Wizard, putting the Pica, once again, in Myrcidian hands."

"Which makes it ours," Jeremilan pointed out. "Because there's no way any Myrcidian, especially one as powerful as a Cardinal Wizard, released it."

Saviar realized Weile had come to the part of the story he had already elucidated to the mages and hoped the repetition would encourage them to see it as truth.

"Right." Weile seemed to be contradicting himself. "But Shadimar did do something unexpected. It's well documented that the last Myrcidian and the last Renshai ..." He let out a friendly snort as he glanced over the current assemblage, now all standing. "Let's change that to what was believed to be the last Myrcidian and the last of the Renshai. In any case, the two met on the battlefield after the Great War, having served on the same side."

Saviar knew enough military history to realize Weile's Eastern ancestors had lost that war to the West, while Shadimar and Colbey had fought for the winning side.

"Colbey Calistinsson recorded the following exchange: He reportedly said, 'If we both claim the Pica Stone for our peoples, then our peoples must become one and you my brother. You may keep the Pica.' To which, the last Myrcidian responded, 'I'll join this union and consider it an honor.' They then clasped hands to seal the bargain." Weile pursed his lips. "Now, it seems to me that it serves no purpose for the last Renshai to lie about this matter, especially since he admits to giving up any rights to the most valuable object in the history of Midgard."

Saviar did not know what to consider first: Weile's knowledge, his ability to quote details verbatim, or the sudden realization that the Renshai shared not only a truce, but a tribe, with these mages. Most people considered a blood brotherhood stronger than any accidental kinship of birth, and the decision to combine peoples made it all the more significant. It rendered every Myrcidian a blood brother to every Renshai.

Several of the mages seemed stuck on the same realization, muttering amongst themselves, but Jeremilan stayed on point. "All interesting and worthy of consideration, but the point remains. The Pica Stone belongs to the Mages of Myrcidë."

Weile raised a hand. "I'm not finished. History is not wholly clear on what happened next, but the Cardinal Wizards recorded that, while using the Pica Stone to test one of their own, it shattered beyond repair. It would appear this is an accurate chronicling, vague as it is, because the Pica does not return to the annals of history until centuries later when, at the direction of the elves, a group that included both of Saviar's parents retrieved the largest pieces of the Pica Stone. The combined magic of the elves restored it and, after using it for a worthy purpose, the elves presented the Pica to the king of Béarn for use as the deciding factor in who becomes his heir."

Every eye remained on Weile. Several of the Myrcidians retook their seats, and the others hovered on the verge. "The Cardinal Wizards, including the last known Myrcidian, declared the Pica Stone a total loss. And, as the elves went to extraordinary lengths to find and repair it, no one could possibly dispute that it became their possession to keep or bestow on whomever they pleased."

Though clearly unhappy, Jeremilan did not try to argue. To do so would not disprove Weile, only display the ignorance of the mages' leader. "Assuming you're telling the truth, the Pica Stone currently belongs to Béarn. How did it come into your hands?"

"I'm borrowing it by the grace of King Griff. Without it, I might never have found this place, built, as it is, on the ruins of the Western Wizard's lair."

Jeremilan reeled back as if struck, then tried to convert the movement into an awkward attempt to sit. He settled back onto his chair, though he clearly would have preferred to stand. "Is there nothing you don't know, Weile Kahn?"

Weile ignored the hypothetical question. "Without the Pica, I would have had difficulty finding you, but mark my words, I would have found you. I knew where to look, and so do all my men. You, on the other hand, have a limited number of places to hide. The lair of the Northern Wizard was on Alfheim and no longer exists. That of the Southern Wizard was unknowingly incorporated into the bustling Eastland cities. And the Eastern Wizard's lair . . ." He shrugged. ". . . a possibility but not nearly as well-situated as this." He made a gesture to indicate the compound.

Saviar wondered if Weile had even needed the information he had supplied about the mages. The man had already done more extensive research than Saviar would have known existed. He had always admired Weile Kahn, had always known him to be a man of power and influence, but his respect for the Easterner grew at that moment. It was not just inexplicable charisma that made Subikahn's grandfather special; he probably worked a lot harder at it than anyone would have suspected. Saviar realized that leadership had less to do with prowess or appearance, less to do with flowery vocabulary or a booming voice or presence and everything to do with intelligence, wisdom, and the ability to read and anticipate others. At least, that seemed so in Weile's case.

Jeremilan, too, appeared to realize he had been outplayed. His voice went quiet, almost meek. "Is there any way . . . we could see it . . . again? Touch it? Know it?"

Though long past its antecedent, even Saviar knew Jeremilan referred to the Pica Stone.

"I'm sorry." Weile sounded truly apologetic, though nothing obvious kept him from revealing the sapphire again. "If you study it, you will want it. Enough that you may resort to tactics I can't stop. If you touch it, you may draw power from it that Saviar and I cannot resist." He added carefully, "However . . ."

Saviar had a feeling that no matter how it seemed, everything had led up to this precise moment.

No one spoke or moved, sifting the hush for Weile's next words.

"If you came to Béarn, if you helped to save the kingdom and its people, even if only from a safe distance, King Griff would be truly grateful. He was chosen by the Pica Stone itself as the worthy successor to the previous king, and by definition he's the essence of neutrality. He's also a benevolent and generous man, in my experience. I can't help but think he would understand your attachment to the Pica and would find a reasonable way to reward you, as well as ascertain that the Pica was used to its best and fullest potential."

Saviar could almost visualize Jeremilan's brain swirling, racing, wheeling with considerations, with images of what might be. Saviar had appealed to Jeremilan's humanity, morality, even to his greed. He had tried to wheedle, to barter, to convince. Weile, however, had trapped the Mages of Myrcidë in a way Saviar never could have done. He had cornered them with his knowledge and resources. Subikahn had guessed the mages chose their compound's location for a magical reason, and even Saviar had considered the possibility it sat on the site of a previous Wizard's fortress. But Weile had taken it one step further. He had done the necessary research.

Exposed to the world, the mages had only three real choices. They could attempt to hide in a much less comfortable location, remain forever on the run to avoid interacting with the other peoples of the continent, or they could find their place in the current society. As heroes of the war, their magic would be venerated rather than reviled, hopefully enough so that the king of Béarn would give them special status and access to the greatest treasure of their people and the world. As allies or wards of Béarn, the Mages of Myrcidë would be safe, at least until they rebuilt their numbers and power.

There was still the matter of Chymmerlee's rape, of the innocent life growing inside her, of the misconceptions she still carried about Saviar and Subikahn. Saviar no longer saw her as a potential mate, not because the mages had despoiled her, but because she had so quickly come to hate him. If she truly had loved him, as she claimed to Subikahn, if they had ever had a chance of building a life together, she could never have believed he would harm her in any way. She would not have trusted ancient superstition over his word. Things could not have gone so wholly wrong. Still, she did not deserve the fate her fellow mages had inflicted upon her; no one did. She had every right to know the truth and to make her own informed decisions based upon it.

Now, however, was not the time to insist.

CHAPTER 20

Those who appease our enemies cannot remain our friends.
— *Thialnir Thrudazisson*

THE BEACHES OF THE TINY ELVES' ISLAND gave way to a single tangled forest that took up the entirety of the central area and expanded as far as the sandy edges allowed. The trees looked strange to Ra-khir: some had long bumpy trunks and enormous drooping leaves like withered crowns, others stood squat with serrated fringes of foliage, while a few resembled the more familiar trees of the southern westlands. Between them, plants of myriad varieties grew in thick copses, and vines twined through the foliage, enwrapping the many trunks like lines on a ship. It did not appear as if anyone had come through this area in years, perhaps decades.

Ra-khir looked askance at Tem'aree'ay, only to find nearly every member of the party doing the same. Marisole proved the only exception. The bard's heir seemed more captivated by the scenery than who might, or might not, dwell within it. Even the Béarnian sailors were attentive to the one elf among them, although the details of tending the ship should have wholly consumed them. Ivana clutched her mother's hand, mercifully silent. Darby stood quietly beside Ra-khir. Calistin crouched at the edge of the forest, a hand resting on each hilt. Though every other member of the party stood between them, Valr Magnus struck a re-

markably similar pose to Calistin's, watching Tem'aree'ay
and the area behind her simultaneously.

Tem'aree'ay did not seem to notice the scrutiny. She
looked into the trees and brush, head cocked in a gesture
that appeared more curious than concerned or puzzled. In
no clear hurry to make her thoughts known, she remained
silent, and Ra-khir found his mind wandering to the same
concerns that plagued him during the day and even disrupted sleep. He knew he had not handled every situation
with appropriate aplomb since leaving Béarn. He worried
he had allowed too much of his own emotions to taint his
dealings with Magnus and Calistin, not wholly maintaining
the professional dignity and distance appropriate for a
Knight of Erythane.

Magnus spoke the words on every mind. "There's no sign
of life. Is it even possible the elves are still here?"

"There's life everywhere," Tem'aree'ay whispered, though
Ra-khir, standing right beside her, heard her clearly. He
knew she meant the trees and plants, the animals that inhabited them, the birds quietly perched in the branches. She
seemed awed beyond conversation, and Ra-khir thought he
understood. After so many years in the company of humans,
she enjoyed the simple pleasures of wind in her hair, the
mingled aromas of budding plants and pollen, the faint lingering musk of animals. They had blundered into elfin bliss,
and he supposed that boded well for finding the elves here.

Ra-khir shook his head, divesting it of his last wishful
thought. Unrestricted natural growth might please elves,
but it also defined the absence of them. With or without the
elves, the island flora would continue to grow unfettered,
and the wildness of the land bore no relation to the presence or absence of Tem'aree'ay's people.

Ivana let out a bray of excitement that startled Ra-khir,
sent a nearby bird fluttering into the air, and seemed to
echo across the island.

Calistin stood up. "Well, they definitely know we're here
now." He said it with no intonation, stating a simple fact.

Tem'aree'ay finally spoke, "If they're here, they already
knew. They could sense our approach disrupting the water."

Valr Magnus also rose to his full height, towering over
everyone except Ra-khir himself. The similarities between

his son and the Northern warrior still grated on Ra-khir, though far less now that he had self-analyzed his irritation. "So what do we do now? Look for them in there?" Magnus pointed into the forest.

Though willing, Ra-khir hoped they would not have to negotiate the dense growth. He did not relish the stuffy confines, nettles stinging exposed flesh, sticks stabbing his limbs and eyes, tearing his clothing, and the crush of leaves and vines tripping and grasping, filling his mouth with bits of greenery and bugs.

Tem'aree'ay turned to answer the general, then stiffened. Apparently, she had finally realized the intensity of her companions' concentration on her. "We're not going to find them by searching randomly, if that's what you're asking. I do think we should move away from the ships. The fewer humans, the less intimidating."

"You want us to split up?" Calistin guessed.

Ra-khir frowned. That was rarely the correct action, especially when the propensity of the ones they sought was not certain.

"I'm not leaving my charge," Marisole announced with unusual fortitude. "The rest of you can do whatever damn fool thing men do in dangerous situations." She did not elaborate. To do so, she would have to switch to song, and that gave Ra-khir an idea.

"Come." Ra-khir led the group along the shore, away from the waiting Béarnian ship and its crew. Still outside the thickly grown forest, but beyond sight or sound of the Béarnides, he addressed Marisole. "Can you play something . . ." He did not know how to put it. He had heard Darris play so many times, so sweetly and evocatively it could bring tears to the hardest eyes, smiles to the dourest faces. ". . . something . . . that might draw them to us? Something irresistible?"

Tem'aree'ay caught Marisole's arm before she could unsling the gittern. "Wait, let me try first." The elf lowered her head and sent out a *khohlar* every one of them could hear.

More concept than words, it floated out over the forest like a shout, silencing the birds and filling Ra-khir's mind with images he could not quite compartmentalize. They spoke of loyalty, but in a looser sense than what he knew for the knights or for his family. They evoked images of group morality that did not allow for individuality, a need so raw

it required an answer, and a plea for tolerance if not understanding. Other ideas came with it as well, ones Ra-khir did
not understand well enough to qualify, sketches of notions
for which he had no basis for comprehension. Then, the
khohlar died away, leaving silence in its wake.

Ra-khir waited for a response that never came. Gradually, the birdsong returned, but nothing more. If anyone replied to Tem'aree'ay's plea, they did so with direct *khohlar*
sent to her and no one else. "Well?" he asked carefully.

Tem'aree'ay shook her head in sad frustration. "Nothing
yet. Perhaps in time."

Ra-khir sighed. Time for elves had little meaning. For
warriors such as Magnus and Calistin, patience came with
great difficulty. He did not want to deal with flaring tempers
again, including his own. The knight had spent the last several nights considering his behavior and felt justified in
every action except one. Pitting Calistin against Magnus,
even unintentionally, had not been wise. The Renshai desperately needed a strong Northern ally, no matter his history, and Ra-khir had no right to jeopardize that relationship.
"Would you mind if Marisole tries now?"

Tem'aree'ay made a graceful gesture that Ra-khir could
not fathom.

Marisole strummed a few full, sweet chords on the gittern, then gradually added melodic riffs. Her voice became
a third layer, woven magnificently between the chords and
individual notes, complementing them without taking anything from their splendor. Darris' playing had dragged Ra-
khir's emotions in every direction, driving him to tears or
fury or elation at a whim. Yet, Marisole's dulcet tones had a
natural beauty that threatened to surpass her father's once
she mastered the more complicated music, memorized the
ancient songs.

The bard's heir sang of objects intertwining, of the value
of ancient bonds and brand-new alliances, of morals and
ethics and the primal virtue inherent in assisting neighbors
in need. She sang of the necessity of combating evil, even at
the risk of good men's lives, the age-old concept of preparing for war for the sole purpose of assuring peace, of remaining stronger than enemies to deter them from causing
harm.

Ra-khir had no idea if such concepts existed in the

strange and alien minds of elves, but they struck deep to his own core. He felt himself drawn to Marisole. Apparently, he was not alone. By the time the last notes of the gittern echoed across the forest, he discovered all of the humans in a loose circle around her. He could not recall having taken a step.

The faint rattle of brush sent Calistin and Magnus into identical crouches. Instinctively, they faced different directions, as if they had started back-to-back and pivoted toward the forest in perfect synchrony. Ra-khir suppressed his own self-preservation instincts. The elves meant them no harm and might see fighting stances as a threat.

Marisole restrung the gittern across her back but did not reach for a weapon. She did glide a bit closer to Tem'aree'ay and Ivana.

Tem'aree'ay sent out a *khohlar* greeting in words Ra-khir did not understand, though the accompanying emotion and context made it clear she welcomed her fellows joyfully and appreciated their time and attention.

The response came in *khohlar* common tongue, and it seemed hesitant and lacking the excitement of Tem'aree'ay's sending. *Why have you brought this abomination to us?*

Calistin's gaze rolled to Ra-khir. "Which abomination is he talking about?"

It was all Ra-khir could do to keep a straight face. He supposed most Renshai became accustomed to name calling, especially Calistin.

Though still out of sight, the elves must have heard him. *We're referring to the* muldyrein, *the* vesell argalfr.* He substituted elfin terms where human terminology failed him, then qualified once more. *This* ivana.* He used it more like a common noun than a name.

The mundane parts of the elfin language nearly approximated the northern tongue. Keeping his voice much lower than Calistin's, Valr Magnus explained, "I think he referred to her as some kind of animal, then as a combination of woman and elf."

"A mule," Tem'aree'ay clarified. "And a wretched woman-elf hybrid." She returned to *khohlar.* *So, you reject my daughter, the fruit of my womb?*

Ra-khir continued to study the woods, making out an occasional subtle movement or a flash of sun from a gemlike eye. He could not tell if the same elf or a different one spoke next. In *khohlar*, they all sounded the same, and he did not know enough about the differentiation of gender to tell the difference, at least from the mental voice.

We have no problem with your womb. But, apparently, when you intermingle our seed with pollen from human loins, you create something as abominable as the creature before us. Why would you bring it here?

Tem'aree'ay explained, *She needs your help, intervention beyond the ken of the human healers.*

The answer came swiftly, *We cannot help her.*

Marisole replied equally as fast, "Cannot? Or will not?"

Calistin shifted in position, clearly losing patience. Ra-khir slipped around the others to stand within reach of his son. He did not need an edgy Renshai interfering. Dealing with elves often required near-infinite forbearance, and it seemed far better to allow Tem'aree'ay to deal with the matter, as much as possible, alone.

An aura of disdain leaked through the mental contact, as if the elf found Marisole's question beneath notice. Nevertheless, someone answered. *Magic has limits, including healing magic. Tem'aree'ay Donnev'ra Amal-yah Krishanda Mal-satorian knows this well.*

Ra-khir suspected Tem'aree'ay was getting additional information in the form of individual *khohlar*. Her usual smile had vanished, and the corners of her lips sank deeper with every passing moment.

Tem'aree'ay sent out another group *khohlar*. *So you will not even examine her? Will not even listen to what I have to say?*

Ra-khir pursed his lips, not liking the direction of the conversation. They needed the elves' assistance against the *Kjempemagiska*. While a worthy cause, securing help for an individual, even a princess, paled in comparison. Even if the elves could make Ivana flawless, which seemed highly unlikely, she would die with the rest of them in the upcoming battle. Still, he did not interfere and hoped the other humans would not either. Only Tem'aree'ay had a chance of talking the elves into assisting. He could not wholly blame her for putting her motherly interests over all others.

Tem'aree'ay received no direct response, which was, in itself, an answer. *Very well,* she sent. *It's clear I have no

choice.★ The emotion accompanying the sending confused
Ra-khir. It seemed simultaneously resigned and determined, grief-stricken and highly dangerous. She spoke
aloud. "Sir Ra-khir, your dagger, please."

Ra-khir was attentive and at her side in a moment. He
had taken vows to serve the sovereigns of Béarn and
Erythane. Only the first wife of the king of Béarn held the
title queen, the others queen consort; but they were still
royalty. Without hesitation, he drew his dagger, offering the
hilt to Tem'aree'ay with a grand bow and flourish.

Tem'aree'ay stiffened a bit, clearly trying not to look
put-off by Ra-khir's display. She did not usually take part in
affairs of state, leaving them to Matrinka or, more rarely,
Xoraida, the king's third wife. Gently, she tugged the proffered dagger from his hand. Leaning toward Ivana, she
whispered something into the young half-breed's ear, accompanied by an elaborate hand gesture.

Apparently thinking it a game, Ivana screeched excitedly
and lay on the ground at her mother's feet.

Ra-khir's heart rate quickened. His nostrils flared. He
spoke almost as softly, "My lady, please forgive me for
asking . . ." He waited for Tem'aree'ay to glance in his direction, which she did not.

Tem'aree'ay raised the dagger. Tears filled her eyes.

Khohlar burst from the woods in several voices, all demanding or curious, every one wishing to know what she
was planning.

Tem'aree'ay explained, her sending heavy with grief, *★I
can't suffer Ivana Shorith'na Cha-tella Tir Hya'sellirian
Albar to live this way, not while I know we can make her life
so much better.★*

A dense silence followed as every human, every elf, considered those words. No one tried to stop her.

Tem'aree'ay waited until the perfect moment, when the
hush became a painful crescendo. *★And when I'm finished
with this horrible deed, I will have no choice but to take my
own life as well.★*

From the dark depths of the forest, figures appeared, as
if formed from the leafy darkness. Almost human, they
moved with a flowing grace, their eyes canted and gemlike,
their features angular. Their expressions ranged from oddly
unreadable to concerned to outright angry. Apparently,

they chose direct *khohlar* aimed only at Tem'aree'ay. She tipped her head, as if listening to several conversations at once, and she did not move. She held the dagger aloft in a steady hand while Ivana twisted to watch the newcomers.

Ra-khir had a good idea what messages they sent, searing reminders of what her simple words truly entailed. If Tem'aree'ay died of self-inflicted wounds, her elfin soul would perish with her, leaving a permanent hole. The elves could not allow that.

Tem'aree'ay answered so everyone could hear. *If I took the life of my own daughter, I could not continue living, no matter the cost. It is what needs to be done.* The dagger descended toward Ivana's throat.

Ra-khir knew Marisole also would not allow it. He stepped directly into her path, trying to make his positioning appear casual and accidental.

The bard's heir sprang forward, crashing into Ra-khir's solid form. Impact barely budged the well-muscled knight, but it sent Marisole staggering wildly backward. By the time she regained her balance, an elf had slipped in to catch Tem'aree'ay's wrist. Sporting short red hair and blazing amber eyes, the male elf placed his body between Tem'aree'ay and her offspring. He spoke aloud, in common tongue, "You can't do that!"

Tem'aree'ay looked all innocence. "What choice do I have?"

The elf plucked the dagger from Tem'aree'ay's fingers. "Let one of the humans handle the abomination." He glanced around, then tossed the knife toward Ra-khir.

There was no malice in the gesture. The knife sailed in a harmless arc, and Ra-khir backstepped to avoid an accidental stabbing. Quick as poured water, Calistin was there, snatching the weapon from the air.

"Humans don't take the lives of innocent young women." The Renshai fairly growled. His head lowered in threat, and he focused intently on the elf. "And if you insist on hurling weapons, you had best prepare for battle."

Ra-khir touched Calistin's arm, a plea for restraint.

"Even the king of Béarn could not command me to murder a princess of the realm." It was not entirely true, but he did not want to go into a long-winded, detailed explanation. Ra-khir could never imagine a king chosen by the Pica

Stone demanding such a thing. If it ever happened, it would pit his sworn devotion to the crown against his internal morality. Ultimately, such a thing would never happen by his hand.

Neither, he knew, would the elves do it, which was why he had prevented Marisole from interfering. Te'maree'ay, he felt certain, would never harm a hair on Ivana's bulbous head. Living among humans had taught her how to bluff, and she was playing her own people with a competence only an elf experienced with human tactics could.

Marisole picked herself off the ground, rearranging her gear.

Ivana swung her legs around to a sitting position. She seemed not to notice the drama unfolding around her, oblivious to the discussion of her fate. She studied the edge of the forest, pointing toward where the elves had appeared.

"Elves," Tem'aree'ay explained patiently, tapping her fists together in an exaggerated gesture. "Elves." She repeated the gesture.

Ivana tapped her own fists, then pointed again.

Tem'aree'ay had the elves' attention, and she took advantage of it. *Ivana Shorith'na Cha-tella Tir Hya'sellirian Albar is not the abomination you name her. She has done no harm to anyone; cruelty is not in her nature. She learns slowly, yes; but she advances. She can and does achieve, has skills she can contribute.*

A different elf stepped from the shadows, far more human in appearance than the one who had stopped the sacrifice. Softer-featured with auburn ringlets falling around a dress of leaves, she studied Tem'aree'ay through nearly level blue-green eyes. She asked the question on almost every mind, whether elfin or human. *What can this thing possibly contribute?*

Tem'aree'ay almost smiled. "She has joined two *jovinay arythanik*, for starters. I believe her capable of so much more, once we cure her *khohlar* deafness."

Another elf stepped up beside the first.

Ivana made a gurgling sound, raised her hands, and banged her fisted fingers together.

Tem'aree'ay patted her head. "Yes, Ivana, elves." She copied the gesture Ivana had made.

More elves poked their heads out, as they had once before.

Ra-khir moved away, drawing Calistin with him. With the ocean behind him, he could not afford to retreat much farther, but he wanted to give the elves as much space as possible. Calistin handed Ra-khir his dagger, which the knight quickly sheathed.

Tem'aree'ay responded to something sent to her alone. *Jovinay arythanik does require at least three elves. Our third was a magical human.*

Ivana seized her mother's skirts and rose awkwardly to her feet.

Again, Tem'aree'ay gave an answer to an unheard question. *Apparently, at least one exists. She's secretive; but there is precedent. Some rare humans did have the capacity to shape chaos.*

And you managed a jovinay arythanik *together?* The elfin voice sounded intrigued. He used indirect *khohlar*, as Tem'aree'ay was doing, so, this time, everyone could hear.

We bound our magic in order to negate the chaos of a hostile giant. It required all three of us. Not a classical jovinay arythanik, *but I've since discovered Ivana Shorith'na Chatella Tir Hya'sellirian Albar can join one of those as well. Arak'bar Tulamii Dhor came to Béarn for other business, and we managed to scry Nualfheim with her help and the Pica Stone.*

Murmurs swept the elves. More made themselves visible, dappled by the shadows of trees and brush.

What about this deafness you speak of? Even animals hear khohlar.*

There appears to be a blockage of some sort. Flimsy according to one who knows these things.

Who? The query came from many directions at once, and even Ra-khir might have sent it if humans had any ability to do so.

Tem'aree'ay dodged the question. *I'm asking you to examine her, to heal what can be fixed, and to understand what she is and what she can become.*

No! The response came almost too quickly, with emphasis that made it feel like shouting. *We know what she is: Frey's penance for interbreeding with humans. She's an* *abomination, anathema, and can do nothing other than bring the gods' wrath down upon us.**

Ra-khir cringed. He doubted any human mother would put up with similar attacks against her offspring. Tem'aree'ay seemed to have boundless tolerance.

If that's so, Tem'aree'ay sent, *then what harm can it do to examine her? Surely, the gods would want us to look upon what they have wrought, to learn from it.**

Go away, the elf said. *And take that thing with you.**

Tem'aree'ay raised her head. *So, it's come to this? I'm no longer welcome among my own people?**

A different mind-voice said, *You're always welcome, Tem'aree'ay Donnev'ra Amal'yah Krish-anda Mal-satorian. Just, please, don't bring the* ivana *with you.**

Tem'aree'ay turned away and spoke to Ra-khir. "My people have become fools."

Ra-khir acknowledged the words with a masterful bow. "My lady, would you mind if I raised the king's business while we still have their attention?"

Tem'aree'ay gestured toward the forest. "I only wish you better luck than I have had."

Ra-khir doubted it, but he had to try. He cleared his throat and faced the elves, catching the twinkling green-eyed gaze of the middlemost one. "Good neighbors, we have called upon you for another reason. I hope you will find it in your hearts to listen."

The elves murmured amongst themselves, probably sent some direct *khohlar*, but they did not leave.

Encouraged, Ra-khir continued. "Something enormous threatens our entire world and every intelligent creature in it. Magical warrior giants are coming from across the sea with the intent of killing us all and taking our land for themselves."

Silence followed Ra-khir's proclamation. The elves stared, obviously waiting for more.

Realizing he had not yet asked anything of them, Ra-khir continued, "We have already fought a battle against their much smaller, nonmagical servants led by a single giant. It took the massed armies of all human societies to repel these servants, and we defeated the giant only because of the *jovinay arythanik* of Tem'aree'ay, Ivana, and the magical human combined with the skill of our finest swordsmen."

Still, the elves remained in a hush. This was not the first time humans had requested the elves' support in this matter. They had to know what Ra-khir wanted. Still, they waited for him to direct a question.

Ra-khir obliged. "The next wave will surely consist of multiple giants, perhaps a vast army of magical warriors. It took all the skills of our three wielders of magic to defeat one of these giants. To have any chance against this new army, we need your assistance. Without it, all of humankind is doomed."

Even then, the elves stared, seeming to see no reason to speak.

Finally, Ra-khir asked the necessary question. "Will you help us?"

Several elfin mind-voices popped in then. Though in nothing close to unison, they all gave the same answer. *No!*

The finality of their responses surprised Ra-khir into silence, which opened the way for Valr Magnus to speak.

"So you would watch us all die. And feel nothing for our plight."

One elf took over for the group, *We would feel badly for you. We're not made of stone.*

Still speechless, Ra-khir allowed Magnus to take over. "But you would not come to our aid. You would allow these giants to slaughter us?"

We would not assist them, one elf pointed out.

"And when they come for you next," Magnus said. "Would you let them slaughter all of you as well?"

More murmurs, then, *Of course not. We would create a portal and leave for another world.*

"So you would run?" Calistin said incredulously.

Ra-khir grabbed his son's arm before he could condemn their cowardice. "I've been to some of those other worlds. I've yet to find one nearly as welcoming as the one we currently inhabit. In fact, most are downright dangerous: spirit spiders, monsters, demons, fire, and ice. Worlds ruled by gods intolerant of intrusion. Even the ones that, at first, seem safe hide dangers that would destroy the unwary. I'm sure benign worlds do exist, but you'll lose a few elves finding them, their souls gone for eternity."

The elves took a few moments to digest Ra-khir's words.

They knew he had traveled; their magic had sent him to and from those worlds, accompanied by two of their own.

"We've worked together before. Successfully." Ra-khir searched the mob for Chan'rék'ril and El-brinith, the elves who had assisted gathering pieces of the shattered Pica Stone. "We can do it again." The elves seemed to be listening, so he pointed out the significant factor. "Alone, the humans can meet these giants sword to sword, and they will defeat us with their magic. Then, they only need to draw their weapons to cut down the elves. If we unite, it's sword against sword, magic against magic."

And we would risk all of our lives. We would lose many elves.

No! Tem'aree'ay rejoined the conversation. *Chymmerlee, Ivana, and I were never at any risk. We didn't hurl chaos back and forth. Ivana and I stayed far beyond the battle lines, then bonded to disable the giant's magic so the warriors could fight them, weapon to weapon. The humans kept Chymmerlee safe.*

This Chymmerlee is human. The only one with magic. Of course, they protected her.

Ra-khir tried not to take offense. "And we would protect you with at least equal vigor. You have the word of a Knight of Erythane."

The word of a human.

Ra-khir refused to become riled. "A human whose vows are as solid as any magic. I would sooner kill myself than violate a promise."

More elves appeared at the edge of the forest. *Elves may die.*

"Humans *will* die," Valr Magnus said. "Are our lives worth nothing?"

You can make more. At will.

"Not if we're all dead." Magnus sighed. "We understand the elfin recycling of souls. You do not show the same comprehension of humanity, so I will explain it." Magnus glanced at Ra-khir, who nodded for him to continue. He had no idea which argument might sway the elves. "Because we each receive a fresh soul, we're all wholly different in a way elves can never be. We're not a unit, and we don't act as one; but we do come together when it's the right thing to do, when necessity requires it. You see us as replaceable, but nothing could be further from the truth. Each human death is a tragedy to be mourned; every one of our souls, whether lost to age or illness or accident is utterly irretrievable."

Ra-khir was as caught up in the argument as the elves themselves. He had never considered the differences that way, had never thought to present it in such a manner.

Tem'aree'ay seized the moment. *The humans did nothing wrong. They don't deserve extermination. How can we allow that to happen?*

A new mind-voice joined the others. *Where were the humans when we lost most of our own to Ragnarok's fire? Why didn't they help us?*

They were here, Tem'aree'ay pinned her gaze on an individual elf. Apparently, she could tell who had spoken, while it all seemed nebulous to Ra-khir. *On Midgard, where they live. Even if they had had any knowledge of our plight, they don't have any ability to jump worlds to help us.*

Ra-khir knew more. "If not for a human, you would not have gained the time to jump to our world; and even if you still managed it, you would have found Midgard in flames as well. If not for a human, Frey would have died, as long prophesied, in the *Ragnarok*. All elves would have perished, and all but two humans as well, leaving only a scant handful of lesser gods. It was the immortal *human* Renshai, Colbey Calistinsson, who thwarted Odin and turned the tide of that long-ago decided battle." He found himself adding for his son's benefit, "*Sir* Colbey Calistinsson, the world's only Renshai Knight of Erythane."

Calistin swiveled his head to his father, clearly startled by the proclamation, though his brothers had known for at least a year. Ra-khir only hoped the information might earn them some elfin dispensation.

We lost a lot of elves.

Ra-khir would not allow them to shunt any of the blame to humanity. "Through no fault of ours. The fire giants set the world ablaze, as foretold. We have done you no harm at all, even after elves cursed us and took over our high kingdom."

Defensiveness entered the next sending, and Ra-khir also thought he sensed a hint of guilt. *That was the* svartalf, *and they were punished.*

Though he hated to do it, Ra-khir had to capitalize on

whatever remorse the elves might suffer. "At the time, there were no *svartalf* or *lysalf*. There were simply elves. We know only that you invaded our world, stole our fertility, caused our women untold misery. An elfin imposter took over our high kingdom, condemning our finest ministers to death." He made a gesture that encompassed the group. "Every one of us here now, requesting your assistance, endured direct and terrible pain as a result of the *svartalf's* actions; but we still come peacefully, without a shred of anger or bitterness."

Ra-khir seized Marisole's shoulders. "This young woman's grandmother, Béarn's one true bard, was murdered in the purge." He pointed at Calistin. "That young man's mother, also my wife, was imprisoned and raped under the guise of maintaining her fertility. Calistin lost his soul when she got bitten by spirit spiders in the quest to restore what the elves had stolen from us. He was in her womb at the time."

That pronouncement sent a shiver through the elves. They understood the significance of lost souls, at least.

Still touching Marisole, Ra-khir drew Tem'aree'ay into the same embrace. "This beautiful elf created a child in the hope it might solve two problems: elf-inflicted human infertility and the shortage of elfin souls. For her sacrifice, you shun her child and make her feel as if her life no longer has meaning." Ra-khir released the females and shook his head. "And you dare to call us cruel and warlike, ponderous and set in our ways. It's you who refuse to open yourselves to new experiences, who condemn without knowledge, who turn your backs on those in need."

Heavy silence greeted Ra-khir's words. He could hear the faint hum of insects, the gentle lap of surf upon the beach.

Ra-khir shook his head. "I know you don't believe it, but there will come a time, another time, when elves need our help. And we will be there for you because that is what we are, who we are. An alliance with the king of Béarn would do you nothing but good, yet you reject him just as you do this lost young woman who carries half your blood." This time, he indicated Ivana with a tip of his head. "And, soon enough, you will have no one to call upon in your time of need. We will all be dead, and the giants will come after you with their swords already soaked in our entrails."

Without another word, Ra-khir turned on his heel and headed back toward the waiting ships. He could hear footsteps behind him and knew at least some of the others were following him.

One elfin voice tickled Ra-khir's mind. *Your son has a soul.*

Ra-khir stumbled. A root caught his foot, and it took a sidestep and a sweep of his arm to regain his balance. Calistin had to draw up to keep from walking into his teetering father, and even Magnus stared at the knight with obvious curiosity.

Ra-khir looked for the source of the information, not wishing to send anything aloud. He felt certain he alone had received the message. Otherwise, Calistin, at least, would have reacted in some fashion.

The elf appeared to understand Ra-khir's need. *It's Chan'rék'ril, Ra-khir.* He used the shortened form of his elfin name, the only one Ra-khir had ever known. *Look farther left, and you'll see me near El-brinith.*

Ra-khir turned his head leftward, seeking familiar faces among the many elves. Finally, he found them. Chan'rék'ril looked the same as he had eighteen years ago, with shaggy bronze hair and amber eyes. Beside him, El-brinith waved. She was slight, even for an elf, with red-blonde hair that nearly matched his own. Ra-khir smiled and returned a subtle greeting.

El-brinith spoke into Ra-khir's mind. *Calistin Rakhirsson has clear ejenlyåndel. Nod if you understand.*

Ra-khir remembered the elfin concept. They had discussed it after the spirit spider had bitten Kevral. At the time, they had assumed her soul was lost; but, using that same word, Captain had stated Kevral gave off an "immortality echo," a sense of infinality that represented the elfin magical concept of the spirit. Diverting his thoughts from the cause of Kevral's death, Ra-khir had learned a *Valkyrie* had guided Kevral to Valhalla, proving her soul did, indeed, exist. Only later, he discovered the victim of the spirit spider's attack had been the infant in her womb at the time: Calistin.

The elves had suffered a similar tragedy. Another spirit spider had bitten Chan'rék'ril. Given the necessary recycling, it had to seem a far worse fate to them, another soul forever lost from the elfin pool. Ra-khir studied Chan'rék'ril, too far to discern emotion in his eyes. Only the silent wringing of hands told him what he had only just surmised. The elf had an enormous stake in their discovery. If Calistin had retrieved his spirit, there was still hope for Chan'rék'ril and the past and future owners of his elfin soul.

Ra-khir nodded carefully. He wanted to make sure the elves knew he understood without revealing the private conversation they clearly did not want the other elves and humans to hear. Only then, Ra-khir thought to look for his companions, all of whom had followed him toward the ship. He pointed surreptitiously at Ivana, hating to admit that, if he had a choice of which mission the elves accepted, it would have little or nothing to do with her.

Chan'rék'ril apparently understood the gesture. *Don't leave yet. Give us some time to talk.* Having traveled with humans, he had a better grasp of how they functioned. For an elf, two decades was not so long ago. *Can you find something to keep you here until tomorrow?*

Ra-khir nodded. As little as he liked the delay, he knew it could have been a lot worse. "Wait here," he said softly to the other members of the party. He needed to talk to the captain and did not want the others to follow him onto the ship. Once they all came aboard, he would have a difficult time explaining why they all needed to disembark.

Ra-khir had no idea how much influence El-brinith and Chan'rék'ril might hold in the elfin community, if such things even mattered. Worried to get his hopes up, worried not to, Ra-khir hurried onto the ship.

CHAPTER 21

When so many conflicting people clash, each believing themselves utterly correct, I don't see how any of them possibly could be.

— *Knight-Captain Kedrin of Erythane*

TAE KAHN AWAKENED to a world consisting almost entirely of pain. It rushed down on him with a suddenness that disoriented, filling his mind, overwhelming his senses. Eyes tightly closed, he tried to orient himself, to remember the circumstances that had brought him to this loathsome plane of existence. Gradually, the agony became circumscribed, limited almost completely to the length of his spine. He could feel smooth, fast movement beneath him, and Imorelda's presence pounded relentlessly at his at mind. *Wakeupwakeupwakeup!*

Tae responded dizzily, *I'm up . . . I think.* He forced his eyes open and found the cat so close he could see nothing but a sea of darkish fur.

Talk to the girl. She's desperately scared.

Tae could not believe everything hinged on him when he felt this bad. *Why didn't you keep her calm?* His memory plowed through fog. He could not recall what allowed him to sleep in a desperate situation. *Why didn't someone wake me up?*

Imorelda fairly yowled into his head. *I've been trying forever.* She added, answering his questions in reverse order. *And I don't speak gibberish.*

The prior events finally returned to Tae in a rush: the capture of Arturo and, incidentally, the young giantess; the arrow in his back that might paralyze him; the certain pursuit of a magical armada. Afraid to move, he closed his eyes again. *Imorelda, is Matrinka finished with me? Can I sit up without risking paralyzation?*

Ask her yourself. The cat's tail lashed into and out of his limited vision. *Mistri needs you. Arturo, too. Subikahn keeps knocking him down.*

"Matrinka," Tae attempted. His dry mouth emitted the name as a croak. He tried again. "Matrinka!"

The queen of Béarn was at his side in an instant. "Are you all right?"

Tae addressed Imorelda first. *Why's Subikahn knocking Arturo down?* Then to Matrinka, "I feel like about twenty large men with spiked clubs were beating me in my sleep." He finally took in his surroundings. He had awakened on the deck at the base of the main mast. The sail bulged above his head. Sea air and salt spray whipped past at a dangerously fast pace.

Mental responses nearly always beat physical ones. *Because Arturo is acting crazy.*

"I'm sorry." Matrinka crouched at Tae's head and stroked his tangled hair. "Do you want me to help you up?"

"No, I can do it." Tae tensed, sending a stab of pain through his back. "I just wasn't sure it was safe yet." Accustomed to his usual grace, he moved too quickly. Vertigo crushed down on him, his vision washed to a plain of whirling spots, and he had to clutch the mast and go absolutely still to avoid losing consciousness again.

Matrinka steadied him. "Are you sure you're all right?"

For a moment, Tae could not answer. When he finally considered himself capable of speaking without descending into oblivion, he succumbed to irritation. "I'm fine." He shook her off, still holding the mast. "Stop babying me." Determined to stand, he did, though much more slowly.

Matrinka stepped back. "Tae, I drugged you, remember? Then performed some surgery. It's going to take time for the effects to wear off."

Tae knew he was angry at himself, not Matrinka. She was one of his closest friends and the queen of Béarn. He had been lucky to have a highly experienced healer on board; if

Matrinka had not come, he would be paralyzed or dead. "I'm sorry. I meant to say thank you. Again."

"You're welcome," Matrinka said as graciously as if those had been the first words out of Tae's mouth.

★*Arturo is acting crazy,*★ Imorelda reminded.

"Matrinka, Imorelda says Arturo's acting crazy."

Matrinka looked away. Her shoulders heaved.

This time, Tae took her into his arms. "Matrinka?"

"He doesn't remember." Matrinka hid her eyes, but Tae could hear the tears in her tone. "He doesn't remember me. I don't think he remembers anything."

Tae did not know what to say. "You're ... sure it's Arturo?"

Matrinka turned him a look that withered even through welling tears. "I know my son."

★*It's Arturo,*★ Imorelda confirmed. ★*I know his smell.*★

★*His smell?*★

★*All humans have a unique smell. I've told you that.*★

Tae needed to shut the cat down to converse with Matrinka. ★*You've told me I stink.*★

★*You all stink. Just in different ways.*★

Tae did not take the bait. "Matrinka, how does something like that happen? Does it mean his brain got ... damaged?"

Matrinka sighed deeply. "Quite possibly, but not necessarily. Sometimes, when something traumatic happens, something too horrible to remember, a person blocks out all thought of it. Rarely, they do such a good job, they lose all memory: past, present, or both."

Surprised, Tae stared. "You've seen that?"

"On a much smaller scale." Matrinka nodded, tears abating as she considered her own experiences. "I've had patients who couldn't remember what happened to them or even how they ended up at a particular location. It was as if their memories just stopped at a certain point, and everything after that moment was ... erased." She gave him a pointed look. "I think you've been there at least once."

Tae supposed he probably had but preferred not to consider his many injuries at the moment.

Matrinka continued. "Often, they forget a lot of what happens later, too, including my treatments."

Tae realized something. "You don't get a lot of gratitude for all the work you do."

"That's not why I do it, Tae."

Tae knew she spoke the truth.

Imorelda slammed her furry head into Tae's shin. *The little girl!*

Combined with the swiftness of the ship's glide, the bump nearly took his feet out from under him. Tae gripped the main mast again. He would never describe Mistri as little, but he understood the significance of the cat's words. "Where is Arturo?"

"In the hold." Matrinka indicated the ring to the under decks with one outstretched foot. "I'd have preferred to treat you there, but it was too dangerous to have you unconscious with them stumbling around, and Subikahn worried they might leap overboard."

"I'm fine," Tae said, seizing the ring. Dizziness surged through him again, and his stomach threatened to disgorge its contents. He tried to hide his weakness but had no choice. He paused long enough to control his roiling gut as well as his steps. When he recovered, he pulled it open carefully.

Imorelda slid past to glide silently downward. Light poured into the hold, illuminating a darkness barely held at bay by a single lantern. Before Tae could fully get his bearings, Subikahn called up. "Come on down, if you want. It's safe for the moment."

Tae accepted the invitation, and Matrinka pounded down after him. Subikahn sat on a chair in the middle of the room, facing a corner where Mistri cowered behind a glaring Arturo. All of the remaining furniture, including all of the pallets, were shoved into an untidy heap at Subikahn's back.

I'll take you to her, Imorelda said, and Tae understood she meant to the mental level of Mistri's communication.

Tae! The giant girl greeted him with a burst of enthusiasm. She clearly would have hugged him had Subikahn not sat between them.

Tae dropped to a sitting position beside Subikahn. He would have preferred to crouch but suspected the pooling of blood into his lower extremities would send his senses reeling. He responded verbally in the Heimstadr language. Not only did this obviate the need to rely on his pounding head, it was the only way Arturo could hear him. "Hello, Mistri. Hello, Arturo."

When Tae switched to verbal, Mistri did as well, though she clearly preferred the mental language. It allowed her more fluency. "He name's Bobbin."

"No, Mistri." Tae kept his tone gentle. "You call him Bobbin, but his name is Prince Arturo."

Mistri's gaze went suddenly to her companion. "Bobbin prince?" She shook her head doubtfully, then made a noise of disbelief. She started to laugh.

Tae could not join her mirth. "He is a prince, Mistri. Prince Arturo of Béarn. Béarn's our high kingdom."

Mistri shook her head again, more forcefully. "No it not."

Tae tried again. "*Our* high kingdom." He made a gesture that encompassed Subikahn, Matrinka, and himself. "Not your high kingdom."

Mistri tipped her head. She clearly did not understand.

Tae lowered his head and sighed. He had to remember that, despite her size, Mistri was quite young.

"What's wrong?" Matrinka came to Tae's side. Mistri shrank away, and Arturo put his hands out to widen his protective shield. It was almost comical to watch a human attempting to hide a giant behind his back.

Tae addressed Matrinka in the common tongue. "She's practically a toddler. I don't know what to say or how to say it."

Matrinka snickered, which drew Tae's attention fully. She explained, "Tae, I saw you with Subikahn as a child. You're the best father I've ever known, the kind everyone wishes he had."

Tae had no idea. "Really?"

"Really." Matrinka's tone left no room for doubt. "You were always romping on the floor. Don't say anything to Ra-khir, but he always seemed a bit miffed by how excited Saviar would get whenever the time came for him and Kevral to visit you."

Tae could not help smiling. He had always considered the Knight of Erythane superior to him in almost every way. "But the twins were boys. I don't know how to entertain girls."

"Until they hit double digits, there's not a whole lot of difference."

Tae was not sure he agreed with that, but he did not argue. Unlike him, Matrinka had raised a son and daughters.

"Well, I gave a lot of horseback rides." He looked doubtfully at the enormous child. "I don't think that would be wise here."

Matrinka appeared almost scandalized by the suggestion. "Don't you dare put anything on your back! I just got done fixing it."

Tae turned his head slowly to rest his gaze entirely on Matrinka. "She could give *me* horseback rides. She might outweigh me." At full height, she probably matched him almost perfectly. He had more muscle mass than she did, he supposed, but she still had quite a bit of baby fat.

Mistri poked her head around Arturo. "What you saying?" she demanded.

Tae did remember young children had short attention spans. He switched back to the island tongue. "This woman is Queen Matrinka. She's Art . . . Bobbin's mother."

Mistri's blue eyes widened until she looked more owl than human. "Bobbin has mummy?"

Tae smiled but suppressed a laugh. "Everyone has a mother, Mistri."

"Even *alsona?*"

"Even *alsona.* Even your parents. Even intelligent beings like me and Bobbin who are neither *Kjempemagiska* nor *alsona.*" Tae found the concept almost impossible to convey with words. The Heimstadr language had no overarching concept of people, only *alsona* and *Kjempemagiska* as separate beings. Everything else living fell into plant or animal categories.

Mistri tipped her head farther, clearly considering.

Tae suspected she had enough to think about for the moment. "I'm going to try to talk to Bobbin now."

Mistri ignored the pronouncement. "I scared." Tears filled her oversized eyes. "Want go home, Tae. You take home?"

Tae sighed deeply, uncertain how to explain the situation to someone so young. "I wish I could." He sought the proper words. "We didn't mean to steal you. We just wanted . . ." He suspected that would not prove a strong enough word to justify kidnapping. ". . . we *needed* to bring Bobbin home. Just like your family will want to bring you back home." A shiver traversed him at the realization of what those simple words implied. "Bobbin is lost. We're taking him back to his family."

Mistri put her arms around Arturo and spoke into the side of his head. "You lost Bobbin? This you family?"

Arturo shook his head. "Not . . ." he said clumsily. ". . . not."

Mistri looked at Tae. "He say 'not.' He mean not he mummy. Not he family. Right, Bobbin?"

Arturo nodded.

Tae saw no use in arguing the point. "Bobbin was hurt very badly. He was on a warship fighting a battle against . . ." He thought it best not to get specific, ". . . pirates. We're not sure how he wound up with you." He opened the way for Mistri to tell her story.

"Find Bobbin beach. Same one you come to."

It made sense the tide would wash a body onto the same shore it did most flotsam. "He was badly injured when you found him, wasn't he?"

Mistri's tone turned grave. "He very very hurt." She brightened. "We make better. He friend."

Tae looked at Arturo, hoping the prince would answer even though he addressed Mistri. "He doesn't talk, does he?"

"He animal." She sounded almost proud. "Smart animal. He learn talk. A little."

"He learned to talk like this." Tae hoped Imorelda's silence meant she still maintained the proper mental level to allow him to communicate with Mistri. *But not like this, right?*

Mistri bobbed her head excitedly, still clutching Arturo. *That right! Have to* usaro. *He no answer* anari. *Not even simple* anari.*

He can't hear anari,* Tae explained. *We can't hear* anari.* He attempted to portray a concept of oneness that included at least everyone on the ship other than Mistri. He did not know how well he managed to do so. When he communicated in any mental language, pictures, emotions and impressions often accompanied the words he received. However, he had no idea if the speakers sent these things on purpose or if it happened as an unintentional aside. *But we are still . . .* He did not know a comprehensive word for "people" in *usaro* or *anari*, as Mistri had referred to the languages, so he used the common term and tried to focus on the inclusiveness of its meaning.

Mistri pursed her lips, which made her appear pouty rather than thoughtful. *I don't know this word "people."*

Tae was afraid of that. He still hoped to include Arturo, so he switched back to speech. "It's a word we use to refer to all living things that walk on two legs, have two arms, and are intelligent enough to make things and talk to one another. Do you have a word for that in your language?"

Mistri chewed her lower lip and clung to the mental language. *Kjempemagiska are masters. Alsona are servants. Both walk on two legs, have two arms, make things, and talk. Very different. We have no word for both together.*

Tae had suspected as much. The *Kjempemagiska* considered the *alsona* a lesser species and showed no qualms about killing them, often in vicious fashion.

For a youngster, Mistri had good focusing skills. She managed to remain on subject longer than most her age. *Pretty birds walk on two legs, have two wings, and talk a little bit. Usaro only. Are they people, too?*

Tae could not help smiling. He would hardly refer to crows as "pretty birds," but some did mimic human speech. He imagined Heimstadr had different animals, including colorful crows, but did not want to get into that right now. He also did not want to spend time explaining the difference between real communication and repetition, so he took the easy way out. *Wings do not count as arms. Arms have hands, which can hold things. Wings do not.*

Pretty birds hold things with their feet. Mistri simulated picking up an object with her foot and sticking it into her mouth.

Tae had never seen crows do more than pick up a twig or shiny object in their beaks and carry it to their nests. Still, he did not wish to discuss birds. *"People" would include Kjempemagiska, alsona, elves, us and maybe some other beings we don't yet know about.* He suddenly realized the gods also fell into his description, but he doubted they would appreciate it. Having no idea of *Kjempemagiska* religion, he avoided the subject.

Mistri did not seem to notice. *Elves?*

Another type of people. Our captain is one of them.

Realizing they had lapsed back into mind communication, Tae spoke aloud. "This word 'people' is important to us. It reminds us that, even though we come in various shapes and sizes, and a range of colors and types; even though we may live in different parts of the world or even on different worlds; even though we speak different . . ." Tae found another word that did not translate. ". . . 'languages,' we are all basically the same."

Mistri held her head in her hands and shook it broadly back and forth. She was wildly confused. "No understand. We same? No." She shook her head harder. "No." She pointed at Arturo. "Animal." She embraced him. "Love animal mine."

Arturo allowed her to hold him without any sign of objection, though it hampered his ability to protect her. It seemed futile, but Tae knew he needed to at least try to get through to Arturo. "To us, animals are creatures with limited ability to think. They may be able to communicate on a basic level with sounds and body movements, but they can't create or string together words to make a point. They don't use their mouths to talk. Do you understand?"

Mistri released Arturo, but her head continued shaking. "Bobbin say words, not many. You talk . . . good. They . . ." The young giantess indicated Subikahn and Matrinka. "They . . . say words? Talk?"

Tae sighed and looked at Arturo, who only glared back. At the moment, he truly did resemble an animal. "They do talk, Mistri. Very well. But it's a different . . . 'language.' "

"Lan-widge," Mistri repeated slowly. "What mean?"

Tae was not sure he could explain. Even the adults of Mistri's world did not seem capable of understanding a concept that had no logic to them. All dogs barked, no matter their birthplace. All cats meowed. To them, *usaro* and *anari* were equally innate and universal. Anyone who did not understand it was considered unintelligent and, by definition, animal. "Let me show you. I'm going to tell Arturo's mother to sit on the floor using words that will make sense to her but not to you." He turned to face Matrinka. "Sit on the floor."

Matrinka looked startled. "Why?"

"Just do it, please."

Matrinka sat.

Tae looked triumphantly at Mistri, who seemed strangely unimpressed. "You say to me *usaro*. She hear."

"What?" It took a moment for understanding to seep into Tae's brain. *She thinks Matrinka heard what I told Mistri in the language of Heimstadr. The Common Trading instructions could just as well have been idle whistling.* Mistri had vast experience with Arturo, who understood a lot of *usaro* words, even if he could only speak a few. Tae attempted to explain, "They don't understand what I'm saying to you or what you're saying to me because they don't know *usaro*. They can't even hear *anari*, let alone speak it. Our world has several languages. All of them you have to speak aloud. I asked Matrinka to sit using our Common Trading language, but she also knows 'Béarnese.'"

Tae pointed out Subikahn. "He speaks Common Trading, Eastern, Renshai, and Northern."

Mistri shook her head more slowly.

Tae sighed again. If they hoped to use her kidnapping for any positive purpose, she had to understand. "Let's take a single word as example." He picked something Mistri would certainly know. "*Aldrnari.*"

"Aldrnari," Mistri repeated, pronouncing it old-NAR-ee.

"In Common Trading, the same word is 'fire.' In Northern, it's *bruni*. In Béarnese, it's *feuer*. In Elvish, it's *hyrr*."

Captain called through the hatch in Common Trading, "Unless you're referring to the Great Fire, in which case it's *villieldr*."

Tae jerked his head upward. He had not heard the hatch open. "You speak their language?"

Matrinka scrambled to her feet.

Captain descended. "No, but I know enough of the human languages to figure out what you're doing. I'm just not sure why."

Tae did not want to become sidelined by a discussion of his intentions and techniques. The longer he talked to Mistri, the more he learned about the *Kjempemagiska* and how to communicate with them. "Are we still being pursued?"

Captain hopped down the last stair into the hold. "We've either lost them, or they've decided not to chase us any farther. Either way, we're safe for the moment."

"Who's steering the ship?" Subikahn addressed Captain but kept his gaze on Arturo.

"I am." Captain did not explain how he did so while be-lowdecks.

Though he wanted to join them, Tae withdrew from the discussion. He needed to continue his conversation with Mistri before she either tired of it or decided to stop coop-erating for some other reason. "What I'm trying to tell you is that Arturo does talk. He was fluent in Common Trading and Béarnese, like his mother."

Mistri seemed more focused on the exchange between Tae and the captain. *Those sounds you made at each other. Those sounds can mean . . . words?*

The intention of his thoughts came through. Mistri was trying hard to understand, and that boded well. Her mind seemed to be likening it to a substitution code, the type a child might employ with another to keep parents from un-derstanding their conversation. *Yes.* Tae still fumbled for the best way to build on that explanation.

Why don't they just use words? Are they trying to keep me from knowing what they said?

It's not a matter of privacy, Mistri. The idea seemed so simple to Tae, so obvious. Exposed to many languages since birth, the people of the continent accepted the concept as part of the normal way of the world. The Islanders had no such experience to draw upon. *I don't think I can explain it in a way you'll understand. All you really need to know: Bobbin and I are the only ones here who can understand you. None of us even hears* anari, *except me; but even I can't hear it all the time.* Tae continued to shield Imorelda and their bond. He also realized he could not expect the cat to remain silent at Mistri's mental level at all times. *If I don't respond, switch to* usaro.*

Once again, Tae tried to address Arturo. He used *usaro*, as Arturo seemed intent on remaining loyal only to Mistri. "Bobbin, I don't know how much you remember, but I told Mistri the truth. You were born a prince and given the name Arturo as an infant. That woman, Queen Matrinka . . ." He waved in the general direction of Matrinka, ". . . is your mother. Your father is King Griff of Béarn."

Arturo merely stared.

"You have two full sisters. Marisole is older, and Halika

is younger. Halika, by the way, is the only one who continued to believe you might have survived the pirates' attack after everyone else had given up hope. You also have four half siblings: your brother, Barrindar, and three sisters named Ivana, Calitha, and Eldorin. Ivana's mother is an elf." Tae studied Arturo, looking for any sign of recognition. Although he noticed none, at least the young prince appeared to be listening.

Matrinka had glided closer as Tae spoke. "You're telling him about his family, aren't you?"

Tae nodded. Names always translated one-to-one; and, to Tae's knowledge, elves did not exist on Heimstadr, so he used the common word for them as well. He was not wholly certain he was using the royal titles correctly, either. He had gleaned those from overheard *anari* and its accompanying concepts. They seemed to refer to highest ranking *Kjempe-magiska* and their offspring.

"I tried that already. In common and in Béarnese."

Tae reluctantly plucked his gaze from Arturo to turn it on Matrinka. "The repetition won't hurt, and it may allow him to realize it's true. We have no reason to make up a history for him; but, even if we did, we'd have a hard time coordinating such details." He swung his head back to Arturo, catching a hint of reaction. "Unlike Mistri, he can also understand every word we say in Common Trading, even if he doesn't want to acknowledge it." Tae turned his attention back to Arturo in time to see something flicker through the silent man's eyes in response to a conversation he pretended not to understand.

Tae ignored the subtle response to continue.

Matrinka's eyes blurred, and she closed them. Her attempt to fight the tears came out in a quaver in her voice, "Tae, tell him we all love and desperately miss him. Remind him how happy we used to be, how much he enjoyed his life, how determined he was to serve Béarn to the best of his ability."

Tae tried to cut Matrinka off with a gesture.

With her eyes tightly shut, Matrinka could not see him. "I didn't want him to go on that ship, but he begged his father, Darris, me—"

Tae seized Matrinka's arm. "Matrinka, you need some air."

The queen's eyes jerked open, and a tear spiraled down her cheek. She opened her mouth to say something, looked at Tae, and closed it. Turning away before another tear could fall, she headed quietly above decks.

Why did you do that? Imorelda demanded.

Mistri gave Tae an intense look. She was probably using *anari*, which he could not hear because Imorelda had switched levels to communicate.

I'll explain later. Tae worried Matrinka's emotion might prove too much for Arturo's fragile state. If they pressed too intently, he might withdraw or grow suspicious; a truly good life did not require a hard sell. *Please keep me with Mistri.*

You owe me.

Hugely, Tae agreed.

CHAPTER 22

*Most humans wouldn't know quality if it scratched their
eyes out and batted them around the floor.*

— *Imorelda*

THE RAIN THAT HAD PLAGUED much of the trip to
Elves' Island had abated, but the weather had grown significantly colder overall. The travelers' breaths emerged in
puffs of smoke, and frost rimed the horses' whiskers. More
for show than warmth, Ra-khir's leather gloves seemed
woefully inadequate, and he flexed his fingers repeatedly to
keep them from stiffening on the reins.

Tem'aree'ay and Ivana had remained behind with the
elves, and that decision, made without King Griff's input,
nagged at Ra-khir. He did not believe the elves would
harm them, but he worried the two might not find themselves fully welcome among her people. He did not want
them to suffer or to try to blunder home unaccompanied if
things did not work out well on the island. The queen consort's horse now carried Chan'rék'ril and El-brinith, who
had agreed to join the group in order to speak for their
people.

The arrangement had not suited Valr Magnus or Calistin, both of whom would have preferred to bring the entirety of the elfin clan back to Béarn. Only after the elves
had explained their ability to craft a magical portal to Béarn
had the two relented. At the time, Ra-khir had wondered if
the elves might also be capable of transporting the entire

human party back to Béarn, to save them the bother of travel, but he did not request the favor for three reasons.

It seemed impolite to suggest the elves tax themselves magically and impolitic to request such indulgence when the elves were already reluctantly considering a major request. Ra-khir's third reason was more self-serving, and he hoped it had not swayed his decision. He wanted to pass through Keatoville on the return trip to visit Darby's mother and younger sister. In any case, the elves did not offer and no one else had suggested the service. Only after they had ridden for several hours did Ra-khir dimly remember that transport from one part of a world to another required magic at both ends of the voyage.

Since their return to the mainland, the members of the expedition had kept mostly to themselves. The elves had rebuffed Marisole's entreaty to remain with Tem'aree'ay, and it had taken Ra-khir's best arguments, answered with sullen and passionate song, to convince her that her duty lay solely with Béarn and its king rather than with his second wife. Darris was the current bard, which placed him directly at Griff's hand; but, as the bard's heir and recipient of the attendant curse, Marisole had to back him up if Darris was incapacitated or killed. Subsequently, her duty lay with the future ruler of Béarn, whomever the Pica Stone chose. In any event, she had no real obligation to guard Tem'aree'ay.

As they rode toward Keatoville on the main roadway, Ra-khir contemplated the oddity of Marisole's situation. She was the bard's heir by virtue of bloodline but officially a princess of Béarn. That put her in the unique and unenviable position of possibly becoming the ruling queen of Béarn as well as her own bodyguard. He wondered if the fates or gods might inflict that very circumstance upon her. If they did, how would it affect the bardic curse and the monarchy? He wondered if Matrinka, Griff, and Darris had considered the same possibility and supposed they surely must have behind closed doors.

Valr Magnus had mostly avoided Ra-khir since their verbal spar over Calistin's behavior. There was no overt hostility; the general of the Northern tribe of Aerin listened to Ra-khir's suggestions and instructions, responded appropriately and politely, even occasionally put forth an opinion. However, he did not initiate conversations with Ra-khir or

Calistin nor offer unsolicited advice again. Early on, Calistin seemed to make a concerted effort to avoid the Northman. At first mistakenly, then unthinkingly, their interactions were becoming more normal, though they had not yet returned to their previous level of camaraderie.

Ra-khir tried not to think too hard about the situation. Logically, he knew he needed to throw off the yoke of irritation Valr Magnus' presence inspired, but the resentment and deeply seated anger refused to be fully banished. He was, first and foremost, a Knight of Erythane. He had no right to hold personal grudges, to allow such things to temper his judgments or even his manner. Yet his hatred for the Aeri general remained only partially suppressed. The look of glee on Valr Magnus' face as he had struck Kevral the fatal blow remained vivid in Ra-khir's memory. The idea that the Northman intended to steal the loyalty of one of Kevral's sons as well drove him near to madness. It was all Ra-khir could do to mitigate the compulsion to drive his own blade through the bastard's heart.

From moment to moment, Ra-khir found himself torn between cursing the need to suppress his emotions and guilt that those emotions needed suppressing. Valr Magnus had done everything humanly possible to soothe frazzled nerves, to explain his mostly innocent role in the betrayal, to undo the misdeeds of himself and his fellow Northmen. He had apologized at least half a dozen times, every one delivered with unquestionable sincerity.

If someone had asked Ra-khir what he wanted from Magnus, he could not have answered. He could think of nothing further to reasonably demand. His heart felt otherwise, shredded by Kevral's death, squeezed by the realization that, what had seemed like a challenge was actually a cold-blooded murder, driven by vengeance. Ra-khir focused, as he had so many times before, on words his father had spoken: "Revenge is a bull men mistake for a steed. He who attempts to tame it, to ride it, will inevitably be the one broken."

It had never made sense to Ra-khir in the past. Now, he considered the words more carefully, seeking clarity where little previously existed. As a youth, he could scarcely imagine a man blithely attempting to saddle a snorting, pitching bull, blind to the bulging muscles, the gleaming danger of its hooves and horns. He had seen bulls grazing calmly amid the herd, but one only needed to watch the animals half a day to understand the danger beneath their placid exteriors. Ra-khir knew his father subscribed only to fairness, to morality, to justice. Surely, Kedrin had not been telling his son that any attempt to quell the need for vengeance would result in the destruction of the man.

The bull is not the need for vengeance; it's the consequences of the vengeance. It was a strange epiphany that should have hit Ra-khir much earlier in his life. Long ago, he had discarded the saying as something he would never understand; but a few moments of concentrated thought in his adulthood had finally brought realization to light. *He's not saying to avoid all thoughts of vengeance. He's saying that if you take revenge, the consequences of your actions may destroy you instead of your intended target.*

Chan'rék'ril made a soft sound, similar to a baby's coo. Though far different than gruff human throat clearing, Ra-khir recognized it as a plea for attention. He shook off his thoughts to look in the elves' direction. Their horse walked alongside his own, and both of them studied him through gemlike, canted eyes. He wondered how long they had waited for him to break loose from his thoughts and spare them a moment.

Ra-khir forced a smile of welcome. He knew the topic of conversation, the one his elfin companions reverted to as often as possible since joining the group. "How can I assist you, Chan'rék'ril?" As a knight, Ra-khir was honor-bound to use the preferred name of those he addressed. He appreciated that both Chan'rék'ril and El-brinith had never revealed their full elfin names to him. It made it so much simpler to remember.

"Your son," Chan'rék'ril started, and Ra-khir knew exactly where the rest of the sentence would go. "He has the *ejenlyåndel.*" Chan'rék'ril had pointed this out three times now.

Ra-khir nodded. "So you've said. He's acquired a soul."

"Yes. It's not a trick, not a mistake."

Ra-khir had suggested neither, though Chan'rék'ril had obviously considered both possibilities.

"Your son is not . . ." Chan'rék'ril hesitated, struggling for the right word or, perhaps, a careful, non-insulting one.

". . . friendly?" Ra-khir tried.

"Approachable," Chan'rék'ril filled in, while El-brinith silently watched the exchange. Both elves shared the saddle, with El-brinith in front, which seemed exceedingly uncomfortable to Ra-khir. He could not tell which of them steered. They kept the reins neatly tied to the pommel. "When he's not eating or sleeping, he's swinging a blade around. Dangerously."

Ra-khir doubted Calistin would appreciate his practices referred to as "swinging a blade around dangerously." "Calistin's pretty simple to understand that way." Realizing he had said nothing helpful, Ra-khir prodded. "Did you ask him where he had acquired his soul?"

Chan'rék'ril shifted backward, appearing surprised or affronted by the question. "Of course."

Ra-khir listened to the clop of hooves on the roadway, rocked by the familiar, sure movements of Silver Warrior. "What answer did he give you?"

Chan'rék'ril looked at El-brinith who made a foreign gesture. He addressed Ra-khir again. "Calistin said he didn't know what I was talking about. Then rode away. He hasn't said another word to us. When we approach him, he leaves."

Ra-khir nodded thoughtfully. Keatoville was not much farther, and he found it difficult to keep his mind from the small town where Darby was born and lived. They needed supplies, and he felt inexplicably nervous about seeing the boy's mother, Tiega, again. He did not want any distractions, but this matter of Chan'rék'ril's had to be addressed. Ra-khir suspected it had everything to do with why the elves had finally relented, agreeing to examine Ivana and even to entertain the possibility of assisting in the war, depending on the meeting between Chan'rék'ril, El-brinith, and King Griff. It would not do to upset the elfin ambassadors before they even reached Béarn. "Give me some time. I'll talk to him."

Both elves looked visibly relieved, and Ra-khir gave them an upbeat smile. He knew little about souls. Up until Kevral's visit to Valhalla, he had secretly believed them a construct of the human mind. After she had witnessed the *Einherjar* battling in Valhalla, he could no longer question their existence. From the moment Kevral had been bitten by the spirit spider, he had worried incessantly for her; so he appreciated the elves' desperation and insistence on answers.

When Ra-khir had learned that Kevral died with her soul intact, allowing her her place in Valhalla, an enormous weight had lifted from his shoulders. Then, guilt had savaged his first moments of real comfort. It had seemed evil to revel in her wholeness when it meant the same terrible emptiness had been inflicted on their son instead.

The irony was not lost on Ra-khir. The very thing that had stolen all other sources of joy from Calistin had also caused him to dedicate himself entirely to the afterlife he could never attain. Except, Ra-khir realized, if Chan'rék'ril was right, Calistin had regained or acquired a soul. Whatever the process, Chan'rék'ril needed to know it, had to alleviate the anxiety that had to tear at him every moment of every day in the eighteen years since the spirit spiders' attack.

Ra-khir studied Chan'rék'ril. The elf had almost human lines on his face, and his gemlike eyes held a hint of something deeper and darker, an angst Ra-khir had never before read in elfin eyes. Anxieties similar to Kevral's had assailed Chan'rék'ril, not a concern for the eternal warring afterlife promised by Valhalla but for the future of his entire race. One elfin soul contained the knowledge and history of multiple lifetimes; its loss was a tragedy Chan'rék'ril had to bear. The ancient soul that had once inhabited him was gone.

Suddenly wishing he had not waited to address the matter, Ra-khir asked softly, "Knowing what happened with Calistin is vital to the elves, isn't it?"

Chan'rék'ril bowed his head. "You know our great secret, Sir Ra-khir Kedrin's son. The number of elves is finite and dwindling. We lost so many at the *Ragnarok* and can't afford to lose more. Then, there is me . . ."

Ra-khir bobbed his head to let Chan'rék'ril know he understood without the need to articulate. Although many humans had learned of the cycle, the elves still clung to the knowledge, holding it close and dear. "Whether you succumb to natural causes, accident or slaughter, your soul is already lost."

Chan'rék'ril's head sank lower. "If a way exists to regain one's soul, we do not know it. But we need to. What your son did, what he knows, might be the key to elfin survival."

Ra-khir now believed he fully grasped the significance. The hope of the elves, and thus their cooperation, lay in Calistin's experience. "Are you quite sure Calistin even lost his soul? By the time of his birth, the elves had already gone into seclusion."

Chan'rék'ril mumbled something unintelligible into his chest, and El-brinith answered in his stead. "We have pondered the problem of the spirit spiders since the bites occurred. Remember, immediately afterward we examined Kevral and found *ejenlyåndel*, the immortality echo. At the time we did not know much about the human soul, though, and we made some inaccurate assumptions. It was not until Kevral's death that we discovered she had retained a fully developed soul. Only then, I remembered she was pregnant at the time of the bite, and we finally realized what must have happened. We surreptitiously tested the boy and discovered the truth."

"No soul," Ra-khir filled in, then frowned. "Are you the ones who told him?" Calistin had mentioned it during the father-son discussion that had occurred after the Paradisian attack on the Renshai women. Until his proclamation on Elves' Island, Ra-khir had kept his suspicions a secret. He had wondered how Calistin knew.

El-brinith tented her long, slender fingers. "We didn't reveal ourselves in any way. I still worry he would have chopped us into elfin salad had he known we furtively cast magic upon him."

Ra-khir suspected she was right. Kevral had died less than a year ago, which meant however Calistin had obtained his soul, it had happened recently. All three of Kevral's boys had left Ra-khir to join the Renshai diaspora that came as a consequence of her losing the battle. He had not reunited with them until the war. Since then, Ra-khir had noticed significant changes in his youngest son: the willingness to parley with his mother's killer, the sudden and intense emotion when reminded of Valr Magnus' actions, the uncharacteristic questions about love and courtship accompanied by a hint of what appeared like embarrassment.

"And now, he has one," Chan'rék'ril reminded. "And we must know how he obtained it."

For Ra-khir, it meant hope and appeasing curiosity. For the elves, much much more. He wanted to know, nearly as much as Chan'rék'ril, but he also realized that once the elves had an answer, they might lose all desire to assist the human armies against whatever threat the *Kjempemagiska* posed. "I'll get that information," Ra-khir promised, unsure why Calistin had chosen not to share it with his father yet. That did not bode well for Ra-khir's chances, but he felt certain he could get Calistin to open up now that he seemed to have developed a more normal approach to social conventions and people in general. "But it may take some time. For now, I need to focus on Keatoville just around the corner. We need supplies, and I have to present myself properly. The duty to represent the Knights of Erythane is mine, regardless of any desire on my part."

Darby rode up in silence. When all eyes turned to him, and the conversation had clearly finished, he spoke, "Sir Ra-khir. So sorry to interrupt." He gave the elves a formal nod of greeting, as his training required.

"No need for apology, Darby." Ra-khir assured him. "We had finished."

"Thank you, sir." Darby slowed his horse to Silver Warrior's pace. "It's just that you'd said we were stopping in Keatoville, and it's due south now. If we ride any farther, we'll pass it by."

Ra-khir pulled up his steed. "Thank you, Darby." A tiny hamlet a few steps from the beaten path, Keatoville was easy to miss. He would never have noticed it the first time without Darby. "I had forgotten quite how ..." Ra-khir searched for the proper words, "... quaint and diminutive it was."

"Tiny, you mean," Darby supplied helpfully and with a smile that showed he took no offense. "It's this way." He steered his mount through a thin wall of brush to reveal a path more suitable to game than humans.

Ra-khir followed. Almost immediately, the neat rows of cottages appeared, surrounding the village's few businesses and the communal meeting hall at the direct center. The townsfolk looked up from their chores, dropping brooms and rakes to stare at the travelers.

"Do you think we're too large a group?" Ra-khir murmured. The last time, he had come accompanied only by Darby and a donkey cart filled with trinkets from an abandoned battle site where Northmen and Renshai had clashed.

"They'll be fine," Darby returned. "Once they recognize the two of us."

Recalling his last visit, Ra-khir imagined Darby was right. The villagers had seemed thrilled to meet a Knight of Erythane. He recalled the cottage of Darby's family, a dilapidated wooden construct, horrible and leaning. The father had died in an accident that had also claimed the life of a competent and popular leader. The villagers had blamed Darby's father and, subsequently, shunned the widow and her two children. Ra-khir had shamed them into promising to build the family a new cottage and left with the understanding that he would return to see how well they had performed.

By the time the entire party appeared from the woods, the citizens of Keatoville were gathering on the edge of the village. Quietly, they watched until Ra-khir and Darby became fully identifiable. Then, a great cheer arose, and the group surged to meet them. Cries of "Darby!" and "Sir Knight!" wafted from the crowd.

Darby sat up proud and tall, as befit a knight-in-training. Ra-khir glanced behind them to ascertain that the crowd was not unnerving Calistin. The youngest of Kevral's sons had never taken an interest in his father's work, the way his twin brothers had, had never witnessed the adulation of a crowd unaccustomed to a regular presence of knights. Ra-khir worried that a horde of people rushing toward him might rouse the warrior instincts of a Renshai, or even of Valr Magnus.

But if either of the men at the back of the party felt menaced, they did not show it. Schooled to instant action without revealing intention, Calistin always appeared cool and in control, and now proved no exception. However, his features betrayed a trace of surprise and uncharacteristic interest. He seemed more curious than troubled. Valr Magnus' face was also easy to read, though he clearly attempted to school his expression. The corners of his mouth showed the barest hint of a bemused smile.

Ra-khir turned his attention to his other companions. Riding beside him, Darby looked calm aside from a barely visible trembling. In the center of their group, Marisole was the only one who seemed entirely at ease. The oldest of Béarn's princesses and princes, she had been born and raised under constant surveillance and always in the public eye.

The elves studied the humans massing around them. Ra-khir still found their emotions difficult to read; they bore remarkable similarities to humans in some respects and distinct differences in others. He worried more for their comfort than that they would perform any dangerous actions out of distress or fear.

Having assured himself that no one with him was in, or posed, any imminent danger, Ra-khir finally focused on his adoring crowd. He had always preferred to fade into the background, though his knightly education forced him not only to tolerate crowds but to maintain his dignity, respond appropriately to demands and requests and to radiate fairness and justice. Now, the residents of Keatoville barraged him with so many questions and comments, he could not distinguish them, let alone address them all.

Under normal circumstances, few noticed the knights-in-training who had not yet earned their titles or brilliant white steeds; many never made it to knighthood. Here in his hometown, Darby had, apparently, become legend. The crowd called out to him by name, their pleas every bit as eager and loud as the ones they addressed to Ra-khir. Soon, the two men found themselves as enclosed as the relatively small population of Keatoville could make them. Silver Warrior stood stock-still, but Darby's mount rolled its eyes, whickered, and repeatedly pawed the ground. Ra-khir worried someone, probably one of the children weaving through the crowd, might get kicked or stomped.

Ra-khir raised a hand, and the people of Keatoville quieted. Conversations still buzzed through the mass at the rear, and the squeal of excited children pierced the air occasionally, usually followed by a stern look or shushing plea for silence. "Good citizens of Keatoville, thank you for your welcome." Ra-khir bowed grandly, brandishing his hat in a single, fluid motion. "I am Ra-khir Kedrin's son, Knight to the Erythanian and Béarnian kings: His Grace, King Humfreet and His Majesty, King Griff. This is my squire, Darby Emmer's son. And these are our traveling companions." The introduction finished, he replaced his hat without naming the others, allowing them to do so in their own time and fashion.

A murmur rose from the crowd, mostly greetings of various types.

Ra-khir took over again. "We have business with Darby's family, if you will please allow us passage and privacy. Afterward, we intend to purchase supplies for our return journey from anyone who has provisions to sell or barter. At sundown, we will adjourn to the meeting hall to address any issues or questions." Ra-khir hoped that pronouncement would allow them free passage and assure the villagers the group would provide sufficient time for them all before leaving.

"Some of my companions are socially inexperienced and may choose not to join us. I humbly request you allow them their space and bring any issues to me or Darby instead." He hoped including his young apprentice would elevate Darby in the eyes of his hometown villagers as well as help defray the myriad questions certain to come their way. The citizens would expect Ra-khir to adjudicate disputes, beg news of Béarn, Erythane, and the war, as well as satisfy their curiosity about their mission and the knights in general.

Ra-khir addressed his companions next. "Feel free to look around, camp outside the village, or wait for us at the meeting hall." He glanced around at the waiting Keatovillers. "If you need help finding things, I'm sure the good citizens of Keatoville will assist." A settlement this small would not have a market, per se, or organized areas of commerce. Darby had described a village where visitors rarely came and, when they did, stayed at the homes of the family or friends they were visiting. The central meeting hall served as a gathering place, a shelter in times of need, and a tavern at other times.

Ra-khir encouraged Silver Warrior to edge forward carefully. The crowd parted around him to allow the knight and his squire access to the street leading to the edge of town, where Darby's family lived. Marisole rode toward the center of town, surely driven by the intense and inescapable bardic curiosity. The elves turned their mount and headed back the way they had come, clearly preferring the forest. Ra-khir expected Calistin to join the elves; instead, he claimed the space Marisole had vacated, at Silver Warrior's heels. Valr Magnus hesitated, as if to follow as well, then headed toward the center of town and the meeting hall instead.

Taking Ra-khir at his word, many of the villagers dispersed, but more than half remained, walking alongside the three horses headed for Darby's home. Most remained quiet or talked softly amongst themselves, but a group of teens surrounded Darby, ribbing him in what seemed to Ra-khir a good-natured manner. Darby ignored them, for the most part, remaining stiffly in the saddle, his eyes forward, though his mouth twitched into a half-smile in response to their questions and comments.

It did not take long to arrive at the site of Darby's family's cottage. The moment they did, all eyes fixed on the knight and his squire, clearly awaiting a response. One deep male voice rose over the others, "So what do you think, Sir Knight?"

The wilting wooden framework was gone, along with the rotted and leaking thatch roof, the patchwork handfuls of muddy straw, and the haphazard caulking. In its place stood a neat and sturdy cottage that rivaled any along the roadway. Fresh timbers formed a robust scaffolding larger than its predecessor. Neat washings of mud caulk filled every crevice and crack in painstaking lines that followed the grain, for appearances as well as utility. The thatch on the rooftop looked fresh. Smoke curled from its stone chimney, indicating a fire in the hearth. Ra-khir doubted the previous sloppy construction had allowed for such a luxury; they had probably done all their cooking outside.

A grin stretched the knight's face. "You've done a magnificent job." He tried to look at all the men in turn. "Absolutely superb. This must have taken a lot of time and effort from all of you."

The remaining townsfolk cheered.

One of the two front window flaps stirred. An eye appeared briefly, then the door swung open and Tiega emerged. Tall and slender, she wore a dress of blue satin that cascaded over delicate curves no longer lost to hungry gauntness. Milky skin accentuated large, long-lashed eyes that matched the brilliant cyan of her dress. Her cheeks swept high, her nose strong and straight, and honey-brown hair fell in waves to just below her shoulders. Ra-khir stared, incapable of speech, entranced by her beauty.

A moment later, Keva appeared at her mother's side. On Ra-khir's last visit, Darby's sister had appeared to be composed entirely of gathered twigs. Now, she had transformed into a fledgling version of her mother, caught in that mystical twilight between childhood and adolescence and destined to become similarly striking.

Teiga broke the silence that had overtaken the group. "Darby!" She held out her arms.

Darby looked to Ra-khir for guidance. He would not perform any action until his mentor condoned it.

Ra-khir slid from Silver Warrior's back and gestured for Darby to dismount as well. The moment he did, Tiega rushed forward and enfolded him in her arms.

The scene warmed Ra-khir and brought memories flooding back of his sons' younger days. Kevral had never placed much stock in displays of affection. From infancy, she had trained the boys as Renshai: hard, tough, destined for warrior greatness. They always knew she loved them, but she never coddled them. Her lullabies were songs of war, her touches corrections in technique, her praises never followed anything short of perfection. Hugs were scarce and required earning. Swordsmen had to learn to find their own solace, to tend their own wounds.

As a father, Ra-khir had proven a softer target. He remembered several times when the twins displayed the tears for him that they would never allow their mother to see. He recalled the warmth of their little bodies against him, the anguish gradually melting in his loving grip, and wondering how Kevral could bear to let her sons face such pain alone. Saviar, in particular, would come to the Bellenet Fields, where the knights trained, to seek out the sort of parental conversations he could only have with Ra-khir.

Ra-khir could never remember a time when Calistin had sought his succor, every bit as hard and seemingly cold as his mother. Not that Kevral lacked passion. No matter how late she stayed training Renshai, she always returned at night to warm their marital bed. She did not always do a great job of showing it, but he never doubted she loved him as much as he did her. Their boys were a great source of pride to her; and, though she had a hard time demonstrating affection, Ra-khir always knew she felt it deeply.

Calistin studied Tiega and Darby with undisguised interest bordering on awe. He remained on his horse after the others had dismounted, his head tipped to one side, his intent blue gaze fully focused on mother and son. Surely, he had seen mothers embrace their children before; but, this time, it drew his attention in a way it never previously had.

After a long hug, the two separated, but not fully. Tiega kept hold of Darby's hands. "How is the training? Do you still want to become a Knight of Erythane?"

"More than ever!" Darby exclaimed with a measure of enthusiasm the best actor could not feign. "It's hard, but it's amazing." He pulled free of his mother to study the cottage, jaw sagging open. "They've done an incredible job." He turned toward the citizenry, his voice cracking and a tear spilling from his eye. "Thank you. Thank you so much for all you've done for my family." Keva glided forward, and Darby threw his arms around his sister.

Tiega turned to Ra-khir and opened her arms again.

Ra-khir stepped forward, and Tiega scooped him into an embrace, her movements fine and sure, as agile as any dancer. In a moment, they were wrapped together, her body soft and warm against him, the satin gliding along his sleeve and catching on his callused hands. She snuggled into his chest, and her breath on his neck excited him wildly. His heart rate quickened, and blood rushed toward his thighs. He knew he had to pull away before he became irrevocably aroused, before she noticed, but he wanted to hold her in his arms forever.

Disengaging, Ra-khir gazed into Tiega's eyes. His father and blood son had eyes so pale they looked nearly white. Tiega's were darker, bluer, deeper. Like the swirl at the base of a waterfall, they dragged him in, denying escape. They held a wild mixture of love and hope, desire and pain, intelligence and need. He worried he might drown in those eyes.

For a time, she returned his stare. Then, her gaze rolled beyond him to the waiting citizenry of Keatoville. She smiled. "Sir Ra-khir, won't you please join us inside?"

Inside. The word seemed to lack all meaning beyond the context of Tiega's eyes. *Inside Tiega.* Ra-khir could think of nothing he would like better, but he shook the thought away. It was still too soon. "Thank you," he managed, trying to appear casual as he straightened his breeks and tabard to hide his arousal. He hoped no one, especially Tiega, had noticed it. "I'd love to accompany you." Remembering Calistin, he glanced toward his own son, still mounted. "Would it be all right if Calistin came with us?"

Though Tiega had never met Calistin, she could easily deduce to whom Ra-khir referred. "Of course." She gestured broadly toward the Renshai.

Finally reclaiming his bearings, Ra-khir turned to his squire, "Darby?"

As Darby already clutched the cheek pieces of his own bridle and Calistin's, Ra-khir said nothing more. He flicked Silver Warrior's reins over the stallion's head, waited for Calistin to dismount, then followed Darby to a small paddock at the end of the road holding six sheep and a cow browsing on a pile of hay. A trough held clear water, and a small flock of white chickens pecked around the larger animals.

Ordinarily, a squire would handle the knight's charger as well, but Ra-khir had long ago made it a habit to always see to the comfort of his own mount. As Darby had his hands full, Ra-khir tripped the latch and shoved open the gate. They led the three horses inside, then stripped off the tack, leaving it just outside of the paddock. After he finished his business with Darby's family, Ra-khir would return to groom Silver Warrior and would see to it Darby did the same for the other two horses.

With the horses safe, Ra-khir and Darby returned to the cottage. Having seen their reactions to the renovations, the remainder of the townsfolk disbanded, leaving only a few gawkers. These watched the knight and his squire enter the dwelling and shut the door behind them.

A fire burned in the hearth, filling the large common room with warmth and light. A cauldron huddled amid the flames, making steady bubbling noises. Tiega had hauled out the sleeping pallets. Calistin sat uneasily on one, Tiega on another, and Keva on the third. Ra-khir took a position next to Calistin, while Darby claimed the area beside his sister. Bags of foodstuff hung from the rafters, protected from mice and rats. He could make out what appeared to be root vegetables, dried fruit, and cheese as well as a sizable ham.

Tiega spoke first. "I want you to know how much I appreciate everything you've done for me and my children. I don't know why you've taken such keen interest in Darby, but I'm so glad you have."

Ra-khir said what he had to say. "Darby's a good boy, ma'am. Well-raised and polite, bright, competent, dedicated." He glanced over at the young man to find him looking at his hands, his cheeks flushed. "He'll make a fine knight someday."

Tiega took the compliments to her son in stride. "No doubt." She did not press further, but a smile lit up her face, making it appear even more attractive.

Finding himself staring at her again, Ra-khir returned to his study of the cottage. The planking still held its fresh, tannish color, though the muddy odor of the caulking had dissipated and the straw gave off no aroma at all. The fire crackled gaily, and the bubbling sounds of the kettle made him salivate in anticipation. Home-cooked meals had always been a special surprise. Kevral had usually sparred or taught sword forms well into the night, and Ra-khir had grabbed most of his meals on the run. His fondest food memories came from childhood or lazy evenings with his companions in the Knight's Rest Tavern. Now, after weeks of nothing but featureless hard tack, the idea of a fresh meal beckoned.

Tiega broke the uncomfortable hush that had settled back over the group. "Calistin tells us the war in Béarn was won." She added, "He also informed us he's your son."

A pang of guilt assailed Ra-khir. He should have performed a more thorough introduction before inviting the young man into a woman's home. "My youngest of three. The other two boys, Saviar and Subikahn, are twins." He did not get into the details of parentage. It would invariably lead to discussions potentially unsuitable for mixed company. All three boys were born while Kevral was married to him, and he had raised all of them on at least a part-time basis. Though he tried not to tread on Tae's parental claims and time, he did not love Subikahn any less nor believe himself any less committed to Tae's son and his future.

"Your wife must be very proud."

Ra-khir's attention went fully to Tiega. The entirety of Béarn, the North and Erythane knew how Kevral had lost her life. He could scarcely believe he had neglected to mention his widower status to Tiega. "She was, most of the time.

But I lost her last year." Ra-khir tried to keep his response matter-of-fact, steady; but he still choked on the words. He wondered if he would ever be able to speak them without fighting back tears.

"I'm so sorry." Tiega's expression showed appropriate concern, but Ra-khir thought he heard a faint hint of something else in her tone, an emotion he could not quite identify. Neither joy nor relief, which would have been inappropriate, it had a trace of hope or longing. Ra-khir supposed talk of his bereavement brought back memories of her husband's death. "Accident or illness?"

Ra-khir would have rather mumbled something equivocal, but he knew that would upset Calistin who took pride in Kevral's valiant death. "She was a superior warrior slain in combat."

That drew Tiega's attention and Keva's as well, and Ra-khir knew he had to explain. Darby already had most of the details and could fill in any gaps after Ra-khir left the cottage.

"She was Renshai, as are all of my boys."

"Oh." There was clear disappointment in Tiega's tone, which upset Ra-khir. He had not pegged her as the type who held prejudices, though most Westerners and nearly all Northerners did when it came to Renshai. "She must have been a fine warrior, indeed. A very special kind of woman."

The last part did not seem the type of thing a Renshai-hater would say. The combination confused Ra-khir, though clearly not Calistin who came to the immediate defense of his mother.

"She was probably the most talented swordsmistress of our tribe." Calistin spoke with an exuberance he showed for nothing other than battle. "Few, men or women, could best her in spar, and she was an outstanding *torke*."

"Teacher." Ra-khir translated the Renshai word. "It also means sword instructor."

"Very impressive." Tiega's tone fit her words, though there remained the barest undercurrent that now seemed to most favor disappointment. "It's no wonder you haven't re-married. I don't imagine many women could fill your wife's shoes."

Suddenly, it all became clear to Ra-khir. Tiega was not disparaging his choice of a mate; she was comparing herself to Kevral and worried she could never meet the impossibly high standards Ra-khir apparently sought in a wife. *She likes me.* His heart pounded so fast and hard he worried everyone around might hear it. He hastened to reassure her. "I loved Kevral wholly and completely. I was devastated by her death, but given her desire to die in valorous combat, we never really had the option of growing old together." Ra-khir sighed. He had known it all along but never fully internalized it. He missed her terribly.

"I've reached a point in my life where I'm no longer interested in or capable of taming wild horses. The heart wants what it wants when it wants it, but I'm keeping my mind open. A calm and beautiful woman who will love me and my sons, who can prepare a tasty meal, who will dedicate herself to me as I will to her would suit me fine." Ra-khir added carefully, hoping it was not too much, "And I've always wanted a daughter."

Tiega lowered her face, but not before Ra-khir saw her flush, recognized a smile. From the corner of his eye, he could see Darby's expression brighten as well. He knew the boy liked him and already thought of him as a replacement father. Keva's mouth slid open, and she turned to look at her mother. Apparently, Ra-khir had made his point a bit too transparently. He had not intended it to be something children saw through. Only Calistin did not change his expression. He looked around at the others, though, at least recognizing he had missed something they found obvious.

Suddenly uncomfortable, Ra-khir studied his callused hands. "I was wondering . . ." he started, finally getting to his business. He had rehearsed the question, but, in the wake of their current conversation, it no longer seemed casual. ". . . if you would consider moving to Erythane." He added, too quickly, "I mean to be near Darby and all. During his training." It did not come out as smoothly as he had planned.

Tiega chuckled. "We've been discussing that possibility since Darby went off to become a knight. If you remember, we talked about it when the two of you left. You wanted us to wait until after the war."

Ra-khir found himself even more embarrassed. "Well, yes. But I wasn't sure if you remembered. Or if you might have changed your mind."

Tiega glanced at Keva, who nodded. "We've already decided to move. Now, it seems, we have even more reason to go." The mother stared at his face, apparently waiting for him to meet her gaze.

Ra-khir was not ready; but, politely, he did so. Her eyes enraptured him, fiery blue against strikingly long and dark lashes. A surge of something akin to panic slid through him. He had not intended his words as a proposal.

Apparently sensing his discomfort, Tiega continued, "I mean, I'd like to get to know you better. To see if we might ... mesh well enough ... to ... to ..." Her cheeks turned a neat shade of scarlet that only served to complement her milky skin and pale eyes.

Ra-khir cursed himself for making her feel awkward. "... attempt a courtship?" he finished lamely. They were acting like inexperienced adolescents fielding a first crush. He wanted her on a visceral level, propelled by the kind of desire even a manner-driven Knight of Erythane found difficult to control. For all of his life, women had thrust themselves at him, had referred to him as dashing and handsome, a gift his father and Saviar shared and which he often considered more of a curse. He never knew if they craved him only for his looks or his status. Now, he hoped, he was not making the same snap judgments, a terrible mistake. Tiega was beautiful on the outside, but the inside mattered so much more in the choice of a lifelong mate.

Darby whispered something to Keva, and the girl giggled, breaking the spell.

Ra-khir quickly looked away, clearing his throat. "Well, then. Can you ride?"

Tiega sat up straighter and glanced at her children, silencing Keva. "We have the donkey and cart, and I won't have any trouble purchasing a horse. We still have plenty left from the war spoils Darby scavenged."

Soothed by the routine of making travel arrangements, Ra-khir rose. "I told everyone we'd head for the meeting hall tonight. I suppose we should be on our way."

Tiega would not hear of it. "Not until after supper, Sir Ra-khir. I promised a warm stew on your return, and I'm a woman of my word."

Calistin licked his lips. "I'd appreciate a stew, ma'am." He looked askance at Ra-khir who sat back down.

"It sounds delicious, and I never break promises." Ra-khir had not actually vowed to share that stew, but the details did not matter. He wanted to stay, and this gave him good reason. "But I'm afraid we'll need to leave immediately afterward, if only because I'm always, necessarily, a man of my word. We'll meet back here in the morning."

"You and Calistin will spend the night here." It was a command, not a question.

Ra-khir looked up, scandalized. "My dear lady, we can't do that. It's not . . . proper."

Tiega slapped him.

Instinct brought Ra-khir to his feet, but he could do nothing other than look surprised and hurt.

Red circles of anger appeared on Tiega's cheeks, and her eyes blazed. "How dare you suggest I would do anything improper!"

"I wasn't suggesting . . . I mean I wasn't thinking . . ." Realizing he was babbling, Ra-khir started again. "I didn't mean we would do anything improper. Just that people might think—"

"I don't give a damn what some fool chooses to believe. Anyone who knows me or anything about the Knights of Erythane won't make ridiculous assumptions." Tiega indicated a curtain pushed flush against the wall. "I'll bunk with Keva. Darby and Calistin can share, and I'll expect you to act like a gentleman and stay entirely on the men's side of the divider once the lamp goes out."

"Yes, ma'am," Ra-khir said meekly. He touched his stinging cheek with a hand warmed by the hearthfire. "I would never betray my honor or that of the Order." He glanced at Calistin to find his youngest son smirking, evidently enjoying his father's consternation. Darby looked at the ceiling. If the interaction amused him, too, he gave no sign, remaining true to his ongoing training. Keva hid half her face behind her upraised hand, but she couldn't completely conceal her grin. "My only concern is the number of questions and issues the townsfolk raise. We might return quite late."

"We'll leave you the area on the door side. If we're asleep or indecent, we'll have the curtain drawn, of course." Tiega added to Darby, "Stoke the fire when you get in."

"I will, Mama," the boy promised.

"Then it's settled," Tiega said in a voice that made it clear she would brook no debate. "After super, Ra-khir and Darby will head for the meeting hall." She swung her gaze to Calistin. "Are you planning to go with them, Calistin? Because you're welcome to stay."

Ra-khir retook his seat, surprised to find himself inordinately interested in Calistin's reply. Given a choice between listening to villagers regale a Knight of Erythane or joining common womenfolk, a Renshai, especially a consummate one like Calistin, would have to find either excruciatingly boring.

Calistin managed one of his rare genuine smiles. "I'd love some stew; it smells delicious. After supper, I'll need to practice." He patted a hilt affectionately. "When that's finished, I'll be glad to help you out anyway I can while Papa and his squire do . . ." He hesitated, ". . . whatever it is knights do."

Ra-khir shrugged. "I've raised him eighteen years, and he still has no idea to what I, and his grandfather, have dedicated our lives." Not wanting to sound bitter or insulting, he added, "Not that he hasn't dedicated himself at least as passionately to the Renshai. It's not likely you'll see him, or his swords, before moonrise."

Tiega turned Calistin a motherly look. "He's an adult, Ra-khir. He can come and go as he pleases, and he's welcome here anytime." She winked at him. "And if he happens to bring a few spare pieces of firewood with him, it'll be greatly appreciated."

"I'll do that," Calistin promised. He sounded almost happy to be asked, which caught Ra-khir off guard. Back home, no one expected anything of Calistin other than full commitment to his swords. Requesting any chore or favor that might distract him was akin to sacrilege.

Ra-khir could not help wondering if the attainment of a soul had anything to do with the changes he saw in Calistin. He considered them overwhelmingly positive, though whether the Renshai, as a tribe, would agree remained to be seen.

CHAPTER 23

*When hatred is strong, when generation after generation
has distorted history far beyond truth and made it seem as
if aggressors were victims, it can spawn a hatred so intense
that it defies any logic.*

— *Sir Ra-khir Kedrin's son*

THE FIELDS OF WRATH little resembled what Saviar
remembered from his childhood. He rode around the edges,
confused and uncertain, wondering if he had somehow mis-
calculated its location. Repeatedly, he checked his landmarks: the Road of Kings with its weathered rock statues
lay northward, the mountain city of Béarn to the west, and
Erythane directly north of the king's city. The woodlands
surrounding the once-barren plains that had served as the
Renshai's home still looked the same. Only the plains themselves had changed.

Though the Fields of Wrath belonged to Erythane, it was
Béarn's king who paid the Renshai to guard the royal heirs,
to remain at the beck and call of King Griff and King Humfreet should enemies attack either city or the kings face a
difficult situation best solved with violence, or merely its
threat. The Renshai used this money to hire Béarnides to
build and maintain their necessary structures, to commis-
sion the finest blacksmiths to forge the Renshai swords or
to buy necessities such as food, kept in communal stock.

Now, the cottages sagged and crumbled, lacking basic
maintenance. Snot-nosed, barefoot children chased one

another, squealing, along dirt pathways swathed with thistles. Men and women in tattered homespun lounged at open doorways, occasionally shouting at their idle offspring but making no move to physically handle them, even when several hurled stones at Saviar or taunted him in the Erythanian tongue.

Weeds had overgrown the open training areas, and the ones deliberately left wild had become impenetrable. The door to the communal storehouse swung, creaking, in the wind. What little food remained inside it looked fouled and worthless, overcome by mice and rats. The Fields of Wrath reeked of sewage and rot. Having invested nothing in the buildings, the furniture, foodstuffs, the land, the current inhabitants seemed unconcerned about its future. Or, apparently, their own.

Saviar found himself staring, but not for long. The more time he spent unmoving, the bolder the current citizenry grew. The adults joined the stonethrowing, adding sticks, lumps of hardened clay and chunks of broken furniture. Clearly, this was not just a warning; these strangers intended him harm. Soon, Saviar had little choice but to attack or retreat. Slaughtering them seemed far more satisfying, but they clearly wanted him to do so, which made him cautious. From their gibes, they knew he was Renshai, knew he could cut them down like so much chaff, knew he could slaughter all of them and barely break a sweat. If they wanted him to attack, then doing so would somehow serve their interests. Whatever their reasons, he did not intend to oblige them.

Saviar withdrew to the Road of Kings. At his back, he could hear their raucous cheers, their hoots of derision. He did not have a full command of Erythanian, but he knew "Renshai" when he heard it, and he felt reasonably certain they prided themselves on chasing off an armed invader, taunting him with a parade of insults that included the nastiest of all: *fegling*, their word for coward. Imbued with patience, Saviar ignored them. They were baiting him, and he would not allow rage to overcome logic.

For an explanation, Saviar knew he needed to turn toward Béarn or Erythane. In the past, Béarn had shown a greater propensity to welcome Renshai, so he trotted down the Road of Kings, so named because an ancient wizard had taken the route to restore the rightful heir to Béarn's throne long after a coup had put a crown on the head of a usurper. It led to the heart of the mountain kingdom.

Anger finally descended on Saviar, not at the name-calling but at the devastation these worthless strangers had caused to his home, the casual disrespect they heaped upon the stronghold of the Renshai. *Where are they?* He worried for his grandparents, his friends, his brothers. It would only take a handful of Renshai a few moments to dispose of the pathetic band of malcontents who had taken over the Fields of Wrath. To violently displace the Renshai would require the combined armies of the Westlands, and Saviar could not see them leaving willingly a second time. Even if they accepted another challenge like the one that had killed his mother, they would have done it with infinitely more caution. Even an unfair fight was the Renshai's to lose. Nothing short of trickery could win the battle for anyone else.

Other thoughts followed swiftly. Saviar realized his absence might have worsened the situation. Thialnir relied on his judgment in situations requiring finesse, and if someone had banished the Renshai, they needed every member of the tribe to assess the circumstances and assist any move. Even that made little sense. Only the King of Erythane had the authority to expel an entire group of people from his sovereign land.

Ignorant of the current state of the Renshai, Saviar wished he had not left Weile, his followers, and Jeremilan until after they had met with King Griff. At the time, it had seemed logical for him to head to the Fields of Wrath. Weile needed to return the Pica Stone, and the eldest of the Mages of Myrcidë had business that would, hopefully, result in his people assisting the forthcoming war. Now, Saviar's decision to head out alone seemed like folly.

Two men stepped out of the forest onto the road ahead of Saviar, then stopped, as if waiting for him. The Renshai's gait did not waver as he approached. Simple travelers, he supposed, though he would have preferred highwaymen. He would appreciate the opportunity to work out his frustrations in a flurry of swordplay, no matter how short. He assessed them as he drew closer. They sported dark clothing, worn close; it would not hinder them in a fight. Both had straight, black hair. They recognized him the same moment he did them.

"Saviar!" Weile's men called in unison.

Saviar would have liked to return the greeting, but he did not know their names. During their weeks of travel from the middle Westlands, he had learned that Weile's men valued their privacy. They spoke little; and, when they did, they most often used either the Eastern tongue or some sort of personal code Saviar had no basis to decipher. He had not managed to root out their names, personal references or titles. "Hello, there, friends." It took effort to expel the words, let alone sound anything more than vaguely disappointed.

If the men noticed Saviar's discomfort, they gave no sign. Not that he could ever read them. They were all masters of subtlety. "Come with us, please. Weile sent us to find you."

Saviar did not bother to question how they had done so. He had made no effort to hide, and he supposed Weile might have sent others out searching as well. There could be only one reason why the leader of the East's elite guardsmen sought him out so soon after they had separated. *He knows what's happened to the Renshai.*

The two men waited for Saviar to reach them before leading him into the forest. The trees held leaves in a wash of colors: brilliant crimsons mingled with greens that ranged from rich jade to glaring emerald, with every shade of yellow and brown between them. A carpet of leaves from previous winters crunched beneath their feet, hiding roots and fallen branches to trip the unwary. The Easterners moved easily, almost soundlessly. Renshai maneuvers included techniques for moving quietly through any terrain, but Saviar's current mood made him shun the required concentration. He shuffled through the debris, not caring how much noise he made.

One instant, they were traipsing between trunks and clambering over deadfalls, the next Saviar found himself surrounded by olive-skinned, dark-haired men who moved like shadows. Suddenly, Weile appeared beside him, as if wisps of wind had come together to form the man. "I'm sorry, Saviar," Weile said softly. "Had I any idea, I would never have let you go off alone."

Saviar had no patience for riddles. "Idea of what? Where are the Renshai?"

Weile crouched against a deadfall and motioned for Saviar to do the same.

Saviar drifted toward his twin's grandfather but did not wish to waste even the time it would take to settle into a defensible position. He asked as he moved, "Where are they, Weile?"

Weile went straight to the answer. "Many are in Béarn, serving their time as guardians or preparing for their rotations."

Saviar crouched in front of Weile. Normally, only one or two Renshai of the proper gender guarded any particular prince or princess. From Weile's description, it sounded as if several Renshai had come simply to train and wait.

"Others are on special assignments. For example, Subikahn is due back from a spying mission with his father, and Calistin went to Elves' Island with Ra-khir."

That caught Saviar's attention. Calistin was never Rakhir's first choice for a traveling companion. Likely, he would have taken Saviar had his eldest son been available. *I should be with him.* For the second time that day, Saviar realized the discomfort his long absence had caused others, first Thialnir and now Ra-khir. *If I had been here, would the Renshai have gone missing?* Impatience overtook him. "Where are the rest of the Renshai? You've not accounted for a couple of hundred, at least."

Weile sucked air through his nose. "Saviar, they're in Erythane's dungeons. Awaiting trials."

That left Saviar with more questions than it answered. "Trials? How many trials?"

"As many as there are incarcerated Renshai. Or nearly so."

Saviar could only stare, awaiting more information. As always, Weile was even more patient, so Saviar finally pressed. "Trials for . . . what?"

"Murder, mostly. Mayhem. Assault." Weile smiled crookedly. "The usual, Saviar. But you and I know the true crime here is 'breathing while being Renshai.'"

Saviar dropped lower. "So what's going to happen to them?"

"That's up to the king and courts of Erythane."

Saviar did not know what to say.

"Or . . ." Weile added thoughtfully.

Saviar waited for him to continue. When he did not, Saviar prompted. "Or?"

"Well, I hardly think morons should have full say in the disposition of hundreds of the world's most competent warriors." Weile glanced around the silent group, then back at Saviar. "Do you?"

Saviar tried to read Weile's thoughts, always an impossible task. "Morons meaning . . . the king and courts of Erythane."

"Naturally."

Saviar continued to think aloud. "And non-morons meaning . . ." He left a long blank, finally filling in, ". . . me?"

"Us," Weile corrected.

Saviar's mood soared. "You mean you'll help me save the Renshai?"

"My grandson is Renshai," Weile reminded. "And his brothers. And others I consider important." He did not specify, but Saviar suspected he referred to Subikahn's lover, Talamir.

With those details, Saviar had little trouble putting the entire story together. The only thing he could not fathom was why the Renshai had not slaughtered every one of the lazy slobs currently occupying the Fields of Wrath. "This isn't going to be easy, is it?"

Weile shrugged. "I'd be disappointed if it were."

"And dangerous."

"With any luck."

Saviar's appreciation for his twin's grandfather, already immense, rose to new and dizzying heights. "When can we start?"

Weile glanced at the angling sun, then at the few of his men in plain sight, then back at Saviar. "Right now works for me."

Saviar could think of no better time.

Between the blazing hearthfire and the usual lot of guardsmen, Erythane's courtroom felt uncomfortably hot to Knight-Captain Kedrin. The spectators had rolled up the sleeves of their light satins and silks, and a few of the women had sneaked off their wood-soled, velvet shoes, laying their bared feet delicately on top so they could quietly slip them back on with no one the wiser.

At times like this, Kedrin appreciated the finely woven linen of his uniform, its cooling properties and its ability to absorb copious quantities of perspiration before staining. Security and advising, not comfort, remained his priorities, but he found it easier to concentrate on those without sweat trickling down his forehead and beading beneath his clothing.

The current case, a minor property dispute, had finished. The litigants trod up the central carpet, one behind the other with a guard between them. The heads of both men drooped, a sure sign neither was wholly happy with the king's decision, the hallmark of a successful and fairly arbitrated case.

The double doors burst open. A guard thundered around the litigants and bowed. He held his position, as protocol demanded, though he could not quite keep still. He shifted his weight from foot to foot, and his hands trembled.

King Humfreet did not leave him in this state. "What is it, Mandell?"

The guard replied so quickly, he nearly trampled on the king's words. "Forgive me for interrupting, Your Majesty, but there's a man who just arrived and I think we need to see him next."

King Humfreet scowled, stroking his beard. His gaze swept the spectators in the center of the massive room, their ranks split into two rows by the long central carpet up which every citizen, noble or common, walked in order to gain audience with the king. Myriad torches lining the walls lit the room like day, assisted by hearthfires on the right- and left-hand walls. A chandelier in the exact center of the chamber held hundreds of unlit candles, their wicks blackened from previous use. Elevated on an elongated dais sat two thrones, the higher one holding the king and the slightly smaller one beside it Crown Prince Humbert, eleven years old and just learning protocol.

Currently, nine guardsmen stood on the dais with Knight-Captain Kedrin, one on either side of the thrones, three behind each, an extra at Humfreet's right hand and Kedrin standing between prince and king. Others took up various posts around the periphery of the massive room.

Mindful of his son's education, King Humfreet said carefully, "This is most irregular. We have protocols for a reason, and the order of audience is usually inviolate." It was not wholly true, but nearly enough to school young Humbert.

Mandell glanced at the boy, then cleared his throat and addressed the king again. "Apologies, Your Majesty. I wouldn't bother you if I didn't believe it absolutely necessary." He glanced behind him, as if worried he was being chased. His tone held an edge that made it clear to Kedrin he considered "no" a dangerous answer. "Captain Callan is in agreement, Your Majesty."

Though the youngest of several Erythanian captains, Callan would not have authorized the deviation from procedure if it did not have merit. No group was more wedded to rigid rules than the Knights of Erythane, but Kedrin believed it wisest to follow the wishes of the guard. When the king looked in his direction for advice, Kedrin gave him a single solid nod of approval.

"Very well," King Humfreet said. "Bring him in."

Despite his insistence, Mandell made no move to obey. "Your Majesty, the man has an entourage."

This, in itself, was not unusual. There were rules regarding the number of people who could approach the king at once, though. "How many?"

"Three."

Kedrin's brow furrowed, as did the king's. It was not outside the established allowance.

"Very well," Humfreet said, with a touch of impatience.

Mandell explained, "Two have no weapons to declare, but the third is Renshai, Your Majesty."

No further explanation was necessary. A Renshai would sooner give up a limb than his sword, even on a temporary basis. At the present time, also, the tribe was not kindly disposed toward the rulers of Erythane. King Humfreet beckoned for Kedrin to approach.

The Knight-Captain immediately did as the king bade, bowing with a formal flourish, then kneeling to place his head closer to the king's. He understood the conversation was to remain confidential.

As soon as the knight was in place, the king whispered, "Do you suppose they've found counsel?"

It was possible, though not the normal way of Renshai to rely on anything but their own training and skill. As they all specialized in swordcraft and war, they had no one to turn to among their own. Kedrin imagined an advocate who enjoyed a challenge might take the case, although he was not wholly certain the generally despised Renshai could find one. He had anticipated the cases becoming the province of the knights, who would assure fair adjudication. He did not know if the hiring of a professional advocate would ultimately help or harm their case. "Perhaps, Your Majesty, though one would expect him to wait for the first trial rather than interrupting court proceedings. If we knew the identity of this particular Renshai, it might give us a clue to his intentions."

King Humfreet sat up straight to address the guard again. "Who are these people?"

The guardsman grew even more fidgety, if possible. "The leader says he will introduce himself only to you, Your Majesty." He gestured toward Kedrin. "The Renshai, I believe, is the Knight-Captain's grandson." He turned his attention fully on Kedrin. "The one who resembles you."

Kedrin could not imagine Saviar becoming involved in anything untoward. Of the three, he was the most levelheaded. *Usually.* He leaned back in toward the king. "Under the circumstances, I see no reason to worry over weapons." Renshai rarely came before the kings, but when they did, Griff and Humfreet routinely allowed them to keep their swords.

Humfreet's features were bunched. He seemed not to notice Kedrin's words, focused on the more obvious affront. "Their leader refuses to abide by our rules? By what right?"

Mandell quailed beneath the king's mighty stare, but he still managed to reply. "Your Majesty, their leader is obviously a man of great power and breeding. Using only the politest of words, the sort you might hear from a Knight of Erythane, he made his needs unquestionably clear." He swallowed hard. "Your Majesty, he wishes to see you at once. If denied, he stated, in the most gracious terms, that he would be regretfully forced to seize the castle—"

Humfreet sprang to his feet, his features purpling. "What!?"

Mandell took several backward steps but managed to finish. "—Neither I, nor Captain Callan, doubted for a moment that he could do exactly as he stated." The guard's brows dipped lower, as if confused by his own actions.

Clearly, he wondered why he had so fully believed a statement that would normally seem outlandish.

The courtroom erupted into simultaneous conversations.

King Humfreet gripped Kedrin's arm painfully tightly, as if to drag the knight into his lap. He spoke through tightly pursed lips. "What sort of scum does your grandson consort with?"

Trained to think before he spoke, Kedrin discarded the flippant and defensive replies before honing in on truth. "Saviar is an adult, Your Majesty. I have no control over his associations, though he's always shown reasonably good judgment in the past." Only then, the possible identity of the so-called leader who accompanied Saviar came to his mind. Kedrin turned on the guard. "Mandell, this leader you speak of. Is he a mature man of Eastern origin?"

The guard froze in position, mouth partially open. He clearly would have preferred to flee. "I . . ." he started, then stopped. "He . . ." Again, he paused, brows drawing even further downward, lips twitching into a frown.

The difficulty describing a man with whom he had had such a serious confrontation clinched the identification. Not wishing to further discomfort Mandell, especially in front of the king, Kedrin dismissed his own question. "Thank you, Mandell. That's all I needed to know."

The guard's mouth snapped shut.

Kedrin addressed King Humfreet again, still pitching his voice below the din of conversation. "Your Majesty, I would highly recommend you see this leader and his entourage at once. And I would take him at his word. He has commandeered larger kingdoms than Erythane."

Humfreet's fingers gouged Kedrin's flesh. His eyes widened, and he turned this expression on the Knight-Captain. "He has taken over entire kingdoms?" He shook his leonine head, then belched out a laugh. "He and his three men?"

"Not the same three men, certainly. It was before Saviar's birth." Kedrin knew if anyone else had spoken to the king as he had, they would have been laughed out of the courtroom. Only because of his status as a knight, quite possibly only because he was the captain of the knights, the king was still listening. "If this man is who I think he is, we see three men because he wants us to see three men. He leads a vast network of the type of quiet, competent followers who operate in shadows. He not only seized the high Eastern kingdom, he erased the previous royal family from sight, mind, and history. Think back, Your Majesty. Who ruled the Eastlands prior to King Tae?"

King Humfreet's expression suggested Kedrin had gone raving mad. "Why it was . . ." He paused abruptly, nostrils flaring. ". . . you know. That Easterner." It clearly bothered him he could not dredge the name from memory. "I haven't forgotten. We exchanged some communications. Trading issues. He was not unreasonable. Far better than the swinish, dimwitted scoundrel before him."

Kedrin's arm had gone numb below the king's grasp. "I'm not suggesting he magically destroyed the collective ability to remember him or his predecessors, Your Majesty. I'm not even saying it wasn't an improvement. I'm just pointing out that, for better or worse, the prior royal line vanished practically overnight." He added carefully, to make his point but not overly boldly, "Your Majesty."

Apparently, it worked, because the king's fingers clamped on even more tightly. The pain grew excruciating.

Only his training allowed Kedrin to maintain his composure enough to ask, "Your Majesty, if it pleases you, could you release my arm?"

King Humfreet's gaze went to his gripping fingers as if they belonged to someone else, but he did release Kedrin. The abrupt restoration of blood flow felt nearly as painful as the hold. Though he schooled his features well, the king could not wholly keep discomfort from his tone. "Guard, see the man and his entourage in." He glanced at Kedrin for reassurance. "The Renshai may keep his weapons, so long as they remain sheathed."

Biting his lip against pain, Kedrin nodded his approval. He doubted anyone could stop Saviar from drawing and killing whomever he pleased, but the point needed making. Other than with the guards, weapons did not belong in a king's courtroom.

Mandell made the appropriate gestures of obeisance before heading back to the double doors. Kedrin expected him to scramble, but the guard demonstrated impressive decorum. Either he had recovered from his initial discomfort or he fretted as much for interacting with Weile and his band as he did over upsetting his king.

When the doors closed behind Mandell, the courtroom fell into an abrupt and eerie silence. Apparently, the spectators had finished with their speculations, now awaiting the reality of what might follow. Kedrin noted that, despite the opening in procedure, no one chose to take his or her leave. If they feared the upcoming confrontation, they gave no sign of it, only the tense anticipation of coiled springs.

They did not have long to wait. The doors swung open, held in place by two of Erythane's guardsmen. A moment later, four men entered the courtroom. Saviar was the largest, his copper-colored hair in its usual snarl, his linens unpatched but rumpled and travel-stained, a sword sheathed at each hip. The other three had silky black hair, olive-toned skin, and dark eyes; but, there, all likeness ended. The one who caught and held Kedrin's eye was the slightest of the group, though third in height. He recognized Weile Kahn at once, more from his bearing than appearance. He dressed simply, in dark linens and a hooded cloak, but that took nothing away from a grandeur that seemed to radiate from him. He moved like water and, though he said nothing, everything about him projected confidence and unspoken danger. One of his entourage stood only two finger's breadths shorter than Saviar and was nearly as broad, the other squat and barely as tall as the Renshai's shoulder.

Saviar executed a bow befitting a knight, clearly taught by his father or learned, perhaps, while watching Ra-khir or Kedrin interact with the court of Béarn. Weile also bowed, though less formally and with fluid grace. The other two men remained in place at Weile's either hand. Though they stood silent and mostly still, their eyes never stopped moving, taking in everything. Kedrin doubted a spider could slip past their notice.

King Humfreet raised his head in an aloof manner. "Introduce yourself and state your purpose."

Weile kept his head level as if he, not the king, had the higher position. He seemed not to notice that this left him gazing at the king's knees. "My name is Weile Kahn, and I've come to reclaim the land belonging to my people."

Kedrin looked at Saviar, who returned a mild stare and expression. Whatever the plan, he intended to allow Weile to reveal it.

King Humfreet glanced at Kedrin, who could only shrug.

He had no idea to which land Weile Kahn referred. In a clear attempt to regain the upper hand, Humfreet used the information Kedrin had given him earlier. "Weile Kahn. Weren't you once the high king of the Eastlands?"

If the revelation startled Weile, he gave no sign. He continued to look straight ahead, at the king's legs still seated on the throne. "I am *that* Weile Kahn." They were simple words, spoken without malice, yet they had the effect of making the king look a bit silly for the question. It was highly unlikely another Weile Kahn existed. And a king, it seemed, ought to recognize another, even after he passed the title to his son.

An artery throbbed in King Humfreet's temple, but he gave no other sign the exchange had bothered him. He cleared his throat. "Which lands are you asking to reclaim?"

"I am not asking, Sire. I am merely informing."

They were fighting words, of a sort, yet so mildly spoken they seemed benign. Humfreet amended his question. "Which lands are you claiming?"

Weile tipped his head ever so slightly. It allowed him to meet the king's gaze without raising his head. "These lands of course, Sire. The ones beneath this castle."

A collective gasp passed through the courtroom. Kedrin expected conversation to erupt, but it did not. Instead, they grew even more quiet, as if afraid to miss a single word of the inevitable exchange. He felt certain Humfreet wanted to shout, to find a swift and horrible punishment, to set his guards on this would-be usurper and drive him from the courtroom. But, mindful of Kedrin's warning, he humored the demand, at least for the moment. "Are you asking me to relocate my palace?"

"No, Sire." Weile's tone never changed; and, if he realized he played a dangerous game, he gave no indication. He stood his ground as if he had asked for nothing more substantial than the air he was breathing. "By convention, the castle comes with the land."

Humfreet silently beseeched Kedrin again, but the Knight-Captain still had no answers. He had no idea where Weile was taking the conversation, but he felt certain the Easterner knew exactly what he was doing. Every syllable, every gesture, accomplished something. Weile had faced off with more kings in one lifetime than most men could name.

This situation had the potential to turn catastrophic for someone; and, if he had been the betting type, Kedrin would have put his money on Weile. That placed him in the impossible position of keeping King Humfreet and the people of Erythane safe without losing face or fairness. Weile Kahn had made demands they could not possibly indulge.

Kedrin made a subtle gesture for the king to continue the discussion. For now, it seemed the only prudent course of action.

King Humfreet obliged his adviser, though the expression he turned on the knight suggested he would not continue to do so for long. "On what grounds are you claiming ownership of this land?"

Kedrin thought he saw a ghost of a smile flit across Weile's face before he responded, "Obviously, Sire, on the same grounds the Paradisians have laid claim to the Fields of Wrath."

Those words birthed Kedrin's epiphany. He knew exactly where the conversation had to go from that point onward. And, to his surprise, he wanted to hear it. Thus far, he and the other knights had preached a fairness that had led them to this point; and something about the whole situation seemed wrong. Ra-khir had explained Tae's past and, along with it, Weile Kahn's. Even knowing the Easterner's ties to scoundrels and rogues, even hearing that his power came from his odd and uncanny ability to organize the lawless, Kedrin could not help but respect him. He would sooner attempt to tame the world's most poisonous reptiles.

The king did not catch on quite as quickly. "But Erythane's kings have dwelt in this palace, at this exact spot, since long before either of us was born."

As always, Weile had an answer. "The same can be said for the Renshai and the Fields of Wrath." He added, as if in distant afterthought, "Sire."

Kedrin studied Saviar, who could no longer keep the smile wholly from his face, though he tried valiantly.

Humfreet shook his head. "But Erythane has sovereignty over the Paradisian Plains. The Paradisians are the original owners."

Weile cocked his head further, as if confused by the king's statement. "As a scholar of history, I reject that claim. However, for the purposes of the current conversation, let us consider it gospel." It was the most words he had spoken at one time; and, by the time he finished, the attention of every spectator had latched onto him. Only the hearthfire dared to make any noise. Without it, Kedrin suspected he could have heard a beetle scurry.

"All right," the king said cautiously, clearly seeking a verbal trap. "Easterners never occupied Castle Erythane."

"Before the Erythanians settled here, who owned this land?"

"No one," Humfreet shot back. "It was barbarian land."

Weile nodded. "And Easterners are the direct descendants of those very barbarians."

King Humfreet jerked his attention to Kedrin, who had absolutely no idea whether or not Easterners and barbarians bore any blood kinship. He had also never located a map that labeled the disputed territory the Paradisian Plains nor found a mention of Paradisians in scrolls that predated the current decade.

"Straight black hair, swarthy, dark-eyed . . . isn't it obvious?"

Kedrin had never met a barbarian; he could not refute the description.

For all his education, King Humfreet's grasp of history, in this regard, was no match for Weile Kahn's. He dropped the argument and went directly to the point. "Surely, Weile Kahn, you don't think I'm going to hand over my entire city to you because sometime in the unspecified past people who resembled you, and may or may not be distantly related, once owned the land it stands on."

Weile shrugged, as if the answer was indisputable. "Sire, if you follow your own rules and laws, you have no choice."

"What!" the king roared.

Kedrin made a crisp gesture, a plea for tolerance followed by a request to speak.

King Humfreet responded with a series of flighty movements that meant nothing in particular. "You have the floor, Sir Kedrin."

Kedrin executed a formal bow. "Thank you, Your Majesty." He sprang from the dais to place himself nearer eye level with Weile Kahn. He wanted the ability to catch and hold his gaze, to try to read his intentions. "With all due respect to all parties involved, Weile Kahn, the Fields of

Wrath were not taken from the Renshai nor given to the Paradisians. They were asked to find a workable compromise."

Weile made a wordless noise that conveyed contempt. "And whenever the Renshai attempt that 'workable compromise,' your men arrest them."

Kedrin wished he could read the Easterner's mind. "Because the Renshai's idea of a 'workable compromise' is to slaughter the Paradisians."

Weile pursed his lips, obviously fighting a spontaneous emotion. Unsuccessfully, apparently, because a snort worked its way out of his nose.

That set off Saviar who started laughing so hard, so genuinely, it became contagious. Many of the spectators joined him, although most of them likely had no idea what he found so hilarious. Weile joined the mirth until it seemed like everyone in the room, aside from the king and his guards, was laughing.

Though thrown off his stride, Kedrin tried not to show it. His hands clamped to his hips. "I see nothing funny about innocents dying."

Weile sobered in an instant. "With all respect, Knight-Captain, that's because in order to prevent yourself from appearing to favor your grandsons, you are feeding into the popular bigotry. Which, in my opinion, is far worse."

Kedrin fought down anger. It did not do for a Knight of Erythane to demonstrate negative emotions. "Are you saying I'm prejudiced against Renshai?"

Weile's dark gaze flicked to Kedrin's so swiftly, the knight could not have avoided the judgment in them even had he wished to do so. "You will find, Knight-Captain, my words convey precisely what I mean. Rephrasing is never necessary . . ." He added dangerously, ". . . nor prudent." He continued, "You stated 'the Renshai's idea of a "workable compromise" is to slaughter the Paradisians.' "

It was, Kedrin felt certain, verbatim. He could hardly deny it. Even if he weren't scrupulously honest, every man and woman in the courtroom had heard him.

"No one here would entertain the notion, for even a moment, that, if the Renshai truly wished to slaughter the renegade Erythanians laying claim to the Fields of Wrath a single one would still be breathing."

Kedrin could not deny the truth in Weile's statement. "You have a valid point, Weile Kahn." He used Weile's full name, aware that Easterners considered shortening an insult. "But my point is still valid, even if my phrasing wasn't properly handled."

Weile made a concessionary gesture indicating Kedrin now had the opportunity to correct his error without any argumentative penalty.

"I would better have said . . ." Kedrin paused a moment, looking away from Weile's pointed stare. The gaze unnerved him more than he wished to admit. For an instant the idea of punching the Easterner in the mouth had flitted through his thoughts, something his knightly manners should never have allowed, even as a brief notion. ". . . the Renshai have responded to all of the Paradisian advances with violence."

Weile pursed his lips, nodding thoughtfully. "And these 'Paradisian advances' have consisted of . . ." He paused dramatically. ". . . sweet tea and welcome cakes?"

Even the fires seemed to grow silent in the wake of Weile's suggestion. "In fact, wasn't the first Paradisian proclamation: 'We do not acknowledge the existence of the Fields of Wrath, and every man, woman, and child with Renshai heritage or blood must be purged from the world.'?"

"I'm not aware of any such proclamation."

Weile pulled a strip of parchment from a pocket inside his cloak and passed it to Kedrin.

The knight accepted the parchment, scrolling it open to reveal multiple lines of flowery, Erythanian script and labeled, "The Proclamation of the United Paradisian People." The first item on the list stated exactly what Weile had said it did, translated perfectly into the Common Trading tongue. Kedrin considered arguing the origins of the parchment but suspected he would lose. He had no idea where it came from but had no evidence Weile was lying, either. "Assuming this is exactly what you claim, it's somewhat understandable that people who feel demoralized by occupiers might create such a document."

Weile blinked. "So you would be equally understanding if the first line of the proclamation of the Eastlands was 'We do not accept the existence of Erythane. Its kingdom must be forfeit; and every man, woman, and child with Erythanian blood slaughtered.'?"

A collective gasp went up from the spectators, and they muttered darkly.

Silent too long, King Humfreet pointed out. "But we are not occupying you. You've not laid claim to any part of Erythane."

"We have, Sire," Weile Kahn reminded him. "The first words I spoke in this courtroom were: My name is Weile Kahn, and I've come to reclaim the land belonging to my people."

The spectators continued to speak out amongst one another as the main players now became quiet.

"But you know what you're seeking is patently ridiculous," the king continued. "Erythane won't surrender its palace without a fight."

"Yet," Weile pointed out, "you expect the Renshai to give up their entire city and arrest them when they try to fight."

"That's different!" Humfreet shouted. "Anyone who can't see that is an imbecile not worth reaching."

The king's raised voice quailed the spectators, and even Kedrin cringed. But Weile Kahn appeared unaffected, even by the intensity of an insult clearly aimed at him. "Sire, rare is the time I'm not among the cleverest in any room; and when it happens, I'm wise enough to hold my tongue. I could count on my tails the number of times I've been wrong."

Even Kedrin found his gaze falling to the seat of Weile's britches, though he knew he would find nothing wagging there. Weile Kahn was not a man with whom he cared to trifle. Kedrin turned his attention fully on his king, his expression strained, his head shaking ever so slightly in warning. Unaccustomed to questioning, the king was growing angry, and Kedrin felt certain that the moment he lost his composure, he lost the battle of wills at least, and probably far worse. "I think we should hear what he has to say." He added emphatically, "So long as he gets to the point."

"My point," Weile said softly, and the entire room went deathly quiet again in an attempt to catch every nuance, every syllable. Only the fires continued to flicker and crackle noisily, their shadows dancing over the aging Easterner and igniting fiery highlights through his jet-black hair. "My point is that the world treats Renshai differently than any other people, denying them the same basic rights automatically afforded others by virtue of birth, even those who contribute nothing of value to society. The Fields of Wrath have belonged to the Renshai for centuries, yet—suddenly—they are occupiers. The dregs of Erythanian society band together to steal the homes paid for by Renshai, the food stored by Renshai, the practice grounds built by Renshai, and the world coos sympathetically. They rain stones on the Renshai, steal from them, slaughter their infants in the dead of night, and the West remains silent, noticing only when the Renshai undertake their sovereign right to defend themselves, at which point the Renshai are condemned as the aggressors."

Weile Kahn took a step in Kedrin's direction, and the two men locked gazes for a second time. As he was clearly expected to speak, Kedrin did so, "It's a matter of fairness, Weile Kahn. Of proportion. The Paradisians throw a few rocks, but the Renshai cut them down with swords."

Weile turned to Saviar. "Young man, you recently visited the Fields of Wrath?"

Saviar stared straight ahead, like a soldier in ranks. "I did so."

"How many rocks were thrown at you?"

Saviar did not miss a beat, "Sixty-seven."

"And how many Erythanians did you cut down."

"None." Saviar continued to stare straight ahead. "I merely circled the fields." He swiveled his head to meet Kedrin's gaze, and the knight found his own strangely white-blue eyes reflected back at him. "As a citizen of Erythane, the law grants me every right to kill my attackers. But as a Renshai, I'd have been arrested."

Kedrin's brows beetled. "He coached you, didn't he?"

"Not a single word," Saviar shot back. "You see, the half of me that descends from Renshai wanted to defend myself, but the half of me that descends from Knights of Erythane knew I had to allow myself to get stoned to death out of 'fairness.' At that point, self-preservation took over, and I fled like a worthless coward."

Kedrin said softly, "You're allowed to defend yourselves, Saviar. Just at a proportionate level."

"A proportionate level." Saviar tipped his head, then started to pace, demonstrating all the humanity Weile seemed to lack. "What, exactly, does that mean, Granpapa?

We're supposed to sheathe our swords and throw the same rocks back at them? To make it exactly fair, I suppose, we could match our rock throws one to one. But what if we're better rock throwers than they are? Would we have to hit or miss by the exact margins they did?"

Kedrin leaped in, "We're not saying you can't use—"

Saviar talked over him. "Or do you mean we can kill one of them for every one of us they murder? That's fair, I suppose, but hardly proportionate. I mean, there are tens of thousands of Erythanians and only about three hundred Renshai. So a truly proportionate response would mean killing a hundred squatters for every Renshai." His own words, clearly spontaneously spoken, made him smile. "A hundred to one sounds about fair to me." His brow wrinkled in mock confusion. "Is that why you're arresting Renshai? We haven't killed enough Erythanians to make the response proportionate?"

Kedrin could scarcely believe what he was hearing. He had allowed the proceedings to get out of control, and he could not blame King Humfreet. The king was only following his advice. "That's madness, Saviar. There may be tens of thousands of Erythanians, but only a small number consider themselves Paradisians."

Again, Weile laughed loudly, which restored the spectators' attention to him.

Kedrin jerked his head to glare at the Easterner. "I don't see anything remotely funny about this situation."

Weile sobered so quickly, it caused a sudden and intense shift in the demeanor of the entire courtroom. Somehow, he seemed even more dangerous for it. "That's because you're still looking at it with the bias of the world behind you. You have to because, when you put anyone else into the position of the Renshai, it exposes the worst in all of us. And the joke becomes horribly, painfully obvious." His words fell like lead. No one dared interrupt what came next. "We're currently preparing for a war with the *Kjempemagiska*. Let us say those magical giants arrived on our shores this very afternoon. Would you rein in our warriors? Would you tell them not to attack until the *Kjempemagiska* killed one of us, then to make certain the response was proportionate?"

"I might," Kedrin defended. "So long as the chance for parley still existed."

Weile stared at him with withering disdain. "Very well, Knight-Captain. Clearly, rhetorical questions are not your strong suit, so I will use an actual example. When the pirates invaded Béarn, did we temper our response? Or did we obliterate them?"

Kedrin sensed a trap, but he would never lie. "We obliterated them, thank the gods. But they had killed several of us first and made it clear their sole intention was to destroy each and every one of us."

Weile lifted the Paradisian charter. "And how is that different from what the squatters intend for the Renshai?"

"But," Kedrin started and stopped. "It . . ." He shook his head, suddenly realizing Weile had a point worthy of long consideration. To argue now meant clinging to a side from stubbornness rather than its veracity, value or fairness; and that was something no knight, especially a captain, could do and still maintain his honor.

The king picked up where Kedrin left off. "But that's a different situation. The pirates weren't throwing rocks at us. They had weapons at least as good as our own, an organized government intent on destroying us and stealing our land, and they refused to compromise."

Weile turned his attention back to Humfreet, still clutching the Paradisian charter. "Would you have compromised, Sire?"

"Of course."

"You would have given up land to the servants of the *Kjempemagiska*?"

"We would have worked something out."

"Would you have given up . . . Erythane?"

Kedrin could practically hear every head in the room turn in the king's direction. Though accustomed to his subjects' attention, the suddenness and intentness of it appeared to unnerve even him. Sweat beaded on his upper lip, and his dark gaze pinned Kedrin. "Of course not!"

"So, Sire, you would have compromised with some other country's land and resources? Left the Pudarians homeless, perhaps? Cleared sectors of the Eastlands?"

Kedrin tried to look casual as he climbed back on the dais. His king needed him at his side.

King Humfreet watched Kedrin's every movement. "You can't expect me to voice the details of a prospective plan that would have taken weeks or months to hammer out, with the input of all of the kings and leaders and advisers involved."

Weile did not back down. "And yet, Sire, we demand that each individual Renshai understand what a 'proportionate' response is to being beaten by sticks, shoved over cliffs, and stoned to death? I can only speak for myself, Sire, but if someone had, as his charter, the intent to murder me and every member of my family, I wouldn't wait until he attempted to kill me, no matter what weapon he used. I'd come at him with every lethal trick at my disposal. And, if I may be so bold, I believe with every fiber in my being that you would do nothing different if a killer came after you or your son." Weile gestured at Humbert, who shrank under the sudden attention. Humfreet jerked his gaze to his son, and Kedrin felt certain he had wholly forgotten the boy was there, watching the proceedings unfold in this most unusual manner.

King Humfreet sat up straighter on his throne. "Is that a threat, Weile Kahn?"

The guards, always attentive, became even more so. The ones in the back of the courtroom moved a step or two forward. The ones on the dais closed in on their king.

Weile's expression suggested the king's question had taken him aback. Kedrin almost expected him to stagger in exaggerated surprise. "Certainly not, Sire. You've already agreed to compromise."

Humfreet leaned forward in his seat. His voice became almost a snarl. "When did I do that?"

Weile glanced at the spectators as if to channel their disbelief as well as his own. "Well, Sire, you've stated that, in the same situation, the Renshai must do so. And you've said you would have compromised with the pirates given the opportunity."

The king shook his head. Kedrin saw the same loophole but felt certain Weile had the plug, which he would deliver as an inescapable coup de grace. Kedrin tried to stop him, whispering, "Your Majesty—"

Humfreet did not wait for the advice. "But I haven't agreed that I'm in the same situation as the Renshai. You have no real claim to my lands. You're an Easterner and, thus, have your own sovereign lands."

Kedrin forced himself not to cringe.

"The Erythanian squatters also have their own sovereign lands."

"The Paradisian Plains." King Humfreet fairly crowed.

"Erythane," Weile corrected. "These so-called Paradisians are, and have always been, Erythanian. They did not become Paradisians until the enemies of Renshai named them such as an excuse to drive the Renshai from their homeland. History makes no mention of any Paradisian Plains; and, believe me, I've read every archive in Béarn."

Now King Humfreet implored Kedrin with his gaze.

Weile added, "If that's all it takes to claim a historical homeland, I hearby decree that, from this point onward, my followers shall use the name Harkonians. And we claim the land beneath my feet as Hark, our homeland and birthright." He looked up with sure and terrible calm. "We await our fair compromise."

King Humfreet sprang to his feet, face purpling, finger extended to point at Weile Kahn. "Guards! Seize him!"

Before the guards could move, Saviar had both swords in hand; and long, black daggers seemed to magically appear in the fists of Weile's men.

"Your Majesty!" Kedrin shouted. "I beg you, no!"

Screams erupted from the spectators, and they broke for the double doors in a panicked rush. The guardsmen in the back were swept away, while those on the dais ran to the fight. Four guards bundled up the king and prince, herding them toward the secret exit designed for their protection. The remaining five Erythanian regulars from the dais approached with obvious reluctance. As they drew their weapons, they looked to Kedrin for guidance, clearly in no hurry to impale themselves on a Renshai sword.

Kedrin leaped to the floor between them without pulling a weapon, keeping his back to the Erythanians. He wanted to quell the situation, not ignite it; and Saviar, at least, would see a turned back as a grave insult to his skill. "Please, stop. No one's going to arrest anyone."

One of the men at Kedrin's back protested. "But the king decreed . . ."

Without taking his eyes from Saviar, Weile, and the bodyguards, Kedrin spoke over his shoulder. "Fine, Netan. Do as you've been ordered. The rest of us will watch and learn." Sarcasm rarely entered the knightly repertoire; but, at the moment, Kedrin was not feeling particularly chivalrous. The guard had a better chance of getting them all killed than arresting Weile Kahn.

"Not necessary," Netan sneered. "The alarm's been sounded. In a moment, a whole phalanx will be bursting in here to arrest all of you, including a traitorous knight."

"I'll wait," Weile said, without a hint of concern. Kedrin almost expected him to yawn.

Kedrin examined his grandson, already strapping at nineteen years. He held a warrior's stance, crouched, with both swords at the ready. Nothing but determination filled his eyes. Like any Renshai, he would relish the opportunity to die in combat. Weile's bodyguards' expressions were well-schooled, wholly unreadable. As for Weile, Kedrin was reminded of the morning he watched a feral cat deliberately wander into the center of a circled pack of dogs. The tabby had glanced around aloofly, sat on its haunches and proceeded to extend one leg, licking the length of it. Apparently convinced of its might by that simple display, not one of the dogs had dared to challenge the cat, instead slinking off into the shadows to find less confident prey.

Kedrin had pledged his life and honor to the kings of Béarn and Erythane. Now, he hoped, he would not have to choose between Humfreet's wishes and his interests. Just as he would ignore an order to leave the king's side during battle, he would not start a fight that might, ultimately, result in unnecessary deaths. The Knight-Captain knew Weile had no real designs against the throne of Erythane; he had given up a grander title. He had merely found a uniquely dangerous way to make a point he considered vital.

Kedrin addressed Weile. "No phalanx is coming through those doors, is it?"

Weile smiled. "No, sir."

Kedrin closed his eyes briefly and sighed. Worried for missing anything, he reopened them swiftly. "You haven't done anything ... irreversible?"

Weile said, "No casualities." He added menacingly, "Yet."

"I don't like your methods."

Weile crooked an eyebrow. "No one's asked you to like them, Sir Kedrin. Nor, for that matter, to critique them." He kept his attention wholly on Kedrin, as if the guards were beneath his notice. "Just because we share twin grandsons does not mean we're cut from remotely similar cloth." The eyebrow fell, and both beetled down together. "Although I did once believe the Knights of Erythane, especially yourself, eschewed prejudice and always embraced honor and morality."

Kedrin refused to take offense or act out of reflexive anger. "We do our best, but we're human. We make mistakes. Whether our stance on the Fields of Wrath is one of them, I'm not yet wholly convinced; but I'm certainly openminded enough to consider the possibility."

Another of the guards spoke next. "Captain, what do you want us to do?"

They were not technically under his command, but their last order placed them in a tenuous position. As the highest ranking official remaining in the room, Kedrin did have the authority to determine their next action. If he said nothing, they would have no choice but to carry out the king's decree, a maneuver that would surely result in their deaths. If Kedrin countermanded that command, they were free to ignore it, but it placed the sole burden for disobedience on Kedrin's head. Though he did not know how the king would react, Kedrin accepted the responsibility. "Stand down and await further instructions."

Kedrin heard the shifting of weapons, the rustling of clothing. He backed up, attention still on Weile and his companions. "If you all agree to wait here peacefully, I'm going to have a discussion with King Humfreet."

"With what purpose?" Weile demanded. "I can't vouch for the safety of Erythane's guard force much longer."

Kedrin had no real idea how Weile was managing to keep the castle guards occupied, but he knew of no longterm way of holding men unconscious that did not also threaten their lives. Weile might, but Kedrin had no intention of relying on that possibility. "I'm just going to explain the full and current situation to the king in the hope of convincing him to continue negotiations or, at least, give someone the authority to make a decision in his absence."

Kedrin knew who that someone was likely to be. If the king did not feel safe, he would not risk any other member of the royal line. More than anyone else, he trusted the judgment of his knights, especially their captain. Kedrin, however, did not currently share the king's confidence in his top adviser. *Weile's good, too good. Am I really coming around to his point of view or is he dragging me there by trickery?* Kedrin knew he had to figure it out . . . and quickly.

"Go, then," Weile said. "But realize none of us has the luxury of infinite patience." His gaze finally swept the guards. Blandly. "And if these guards are foolish enough to attack in your absence, we will have no choice but to dispatch them."

Kedrin felt certain the guards knew their limits. "You have my word that I will accomplish this as swiftly as possible." He knew he should use the regular doors, sweep around, and locate the king, but he could not afford to risk capture by Weile's men. Instead, he slipped out the secret passageway through which the guards had evacuated their king.

Designed for quick egress, the passage took Kedrin safely through an empty corridor to a massive iron portal he knew was currently barricaded to protect the king and his prince. Kedrin tapped out the coded sequence that revealed his identity. The door cracked cautiously, several guards peered out, then it opened suddenly, spilling Kedrin to the floor in front of a pair of anxious guardsmen. They slammed the door behind him.

Kedrin regained his footing in the most dignified manner he could muster, readjusted his uniform, and took in the small, empty room. "I need to speak with His Majesty."

The guards glanced at one another uneasily. "Now, Knight-Captain?"

"Any other time will be too late," Kedrin explained.

The other added, "He is not in proper mood for receiving, Sir Kedrin."

Though trained in them to a fault, Kedrin did not have time for formalities. "He will see me. There is no other way."

"Very well, Knight-Captain," the guards said, almost in unison. They rapped out the proper sequence on another hidden door, then opened it cautiously to reveal the last two guards standing at attention in front of Prince Humbert, who was huddled in miserable silence. Nearby, King Humfreet paced like a wild animal in a cage, his cheeks a feverish scarlet, his eyes rolling, his hair wild.

Kedrin ignored the king's disheveled state. At the moment he had attention for nothing but his duty. "Your Majesty, forgive my intrusion, but it's essential that we speak immediately."

The guards cringed, almost imperceptibly. Prince Humbert tipped his head in evident curiosity. The king froze in mid-pace. "What!" he roared.

It was not the response Kedrin expected. King Humfreet relied on his counsel and, in the current circumstances, should have hungered for it. Whatever other talents he might have, Weile Kahn had a knack for enraging royalty beyond reason. Though Kedrin knew the king had heard him, he dutifully repeated, "It's essential that we speak immediately, Your Majesty."

Humfreet continued to look in the direction he had been pacing. "This cannot wait?"

"Not one more moment, Your Majesty." Kedrin regulated his voice to a slow and monotonous calm. He could not risk further sparking the king's temper. It might make him volatile or, worse, foolishly impulsive. "Please." He motioned toward the empty room.

Humfreet finally turned to face Kedrin and his escort, eyes flashing. "You two," he commanded his guards. "In with the others."

Though surely uncomfortable, the guardsmen scurried to obey. The king had essentially left his security solely in the hands of Knight-Captain Kedrin. And, while they had every reason to trust the knight's loyalty and competence, they had to worry whether he could handle such a serious threat alone. Soon, the door slammed shut, with the guards and prince on the inside, leaving Kedrin and Humfreet alone.

The king's features sagged, the color drained from his cheeks, and he turned Kedrin a weary look. "What is it, Kedrin? What's the situation? And, please, no flowery speeches or minced words. Is that horrid little man in custody?"

Kedrin swallowed hard. The king was not going to like what he had to say. If anyone else said it, they would probably be joining the fate of "that horrid little man." "No, Your Majesty. I'm afraid . . . that's not going to happen."

Rage snapped through the king's eyes, replaced much more swiftly than Kedrin expected by tired resignation. "How many casualties?"

Good news had never seemed more difficult to speak. "None, Your Majesty."

The king's head snapped up. "What? How can that be?"

Kedrin could not recall having seen someone simultaneously appreciative and angry before. "It's a four-to-five standoff in the courtroom, Your Majesty. I left it that way to discuss the situation with you." Kedrin knew he walked a fine line. He could not tell the king what he wanted to hear, nor could he lie. Finding the proper phraseology to inform, compose, and advise without sparking unreasoning rage seemed nearly impossible.

"How . . . ?" the king started.

As commanded, Kedrin did not mince words. "Your Majesty, I'm afraid I countermanded your order." He waited for the ax to fall. Netan was right; it was a form of treason.

But the king remained silent, awaiting an explanation.

"I thought it best, Your Majesty. Better you execute me than doom all but these four guardsmen." Kedrin made a motion to indicate the last of Humfreet's guardians, now enclosed with the prince. "Saviar alone could handle three or four. Weile Kahn's bodyguards are trained killers; and I've heard he's no slouch as a fighter, either."

King Humfreet blinked, staring at Kedrin as if he had gone mad. "Knight-Captain, are you suggesting four interlopers could best my entire guard force? Even my army?"

"No, Your Majesty. However, I have no doubt they would have undone the five guards you sent against them. And me as well."

Humfreet still did not understand. "You speak as if I have only these nine dais guardsmen."

Kedrin sighed deeply. He lowered his head. "At the moment, Your Majesty, you do."

"What?!"

Kedrin understood why his every pronouncement seemed to elicit the same one word response from Erythane's king. "I'm afraid it's true, Your Majesty. It appears Weile Kahn has neutralized the entirety of Erythane's castle guard force, quite possibly her military as well."

"That's impossible!"

Kedrin could only shrug. "He makes this claim. I don't currently have the wherewithal to substantiate it, but I can assure you no backup units responded to the alarm."

"He's bluffing." King Humfreet dismissed Kedrin's concerns with an off-handed wave. "No one man could destroy my entire army."

"Not destroyed. Neutralized, Your Majesty. He says he hasn't harmed a single man."

"That's preposterous!" Humfreet pinned Kedrin with his gaze. "Why would you entertain such an assertion? You know it's not possible."

"No response," Kedrin reminded, "to Erythane's highest level alarm, Your Majesty." He added carefully, "And Weile Kahn is not precisely 'one man.'"

"He's triplets?" Humfreet broke in sarcastically. "With a single body?"

Kedrin had to remain calm, though he felt nearer to explosion. He was not angry, particularly at King Humfreet. He felt bombarded by ideas and emotions. Nothing seemed right or real, and he could not afford to give shoddy advice or to make a bad decision from pressure, fear, or uncertainty. "He's the face and voice of a multi-country conglomerate of treacherous individuals. As I understand it, he has spent decades organizing the most dangerous and terrifying among us: assassins and killers, thieves and con men, traitors and villains of every description. Men who would shiv their mothers for a copper follow him with the devotion of a priest. One might argue that he is the most powerful, and yet one of the least known, rulers in current existence."

The king studied the highest-ranking Knight of Erythane as if seeing him for the first time. "And we should concede to someone of dubious repute simply because of his ties? His power?"

The idea itself rankled, but the king's suggestion that Kedrin ascribed to such a notion was the direst of insults. "Certainly not, Your Majesty. I would die in the worst agony rather than bow to corruption or injustice."

The king upraised both palms in question. "So what makes this case different? Why are we even listening to this bounder?"

"Because, Your Majesty, what makes Weile Kahn so powerful is not only his connections. It's his uncanny ability to be . . ."

The king's brows rose in anticipation.

Kedrin hated to fill in the last, necessary word. ". . . right.

I'm afraid his immodest suggestion that he's nearly always the wisest man in the room, that he never makes mistakes, is exasperating, irritating, and vexing. But, also, true."

"Are you saying you believe his assertion that we're all favoring the Paradisians because we're biased against Renshai?"

Kedrin was not yet ready to admit that. "He has managed to convince me we hold Renshai to a different standard than any other group of people."

The king's features crinkled. He shook his head, but he questioned rather than denying the accusation outright. "How so?"

Kedrin deliberately chose an example Weile and Saviar had not addressed, since those had, apparently, not convinced the king. "You know the Knights of Erythane have moderated many duels, Your Majesty. We've often been asked to assure the weapons are fairly distributed."

Humfreet nodded. He seemed calmer, more open to listening to disparate viewpoints.

Encouraged, Kedrin continued, "But in their duel with the Renshai, the Northmen added a condition we had never before considered, and we went right along with it. They refused to pit their best warrior against the Renshai's best, instead insisting the competence of the warriors themselves must be evenly matched."

The king clearly missed the point. "So? Doesn't that make it a more fair battle?"

"A more even battle, certainly, Your Majesty," Kedrin conceded. "But that begs the point. We're discussing whether or not we hold Renshai to a different standard than others, and we definitely did so in this case."

"Thus making it a fairer fight." Humfreet pointed out again.

"Maybe." Kedrin could not forget Saviar's argument in the courtroom. Whatever he felt about Weile Kahn, he knew his oldest grandson had a good head on his shoulders. "But it sets a strange precedent I had not previously considered. Are we now obligated to judge students only against others of equal intelligence or ability? How can we justify racing horses of varying speeds against one another? Are we now doomed to assuring that every battle, every race, every contest ends in a perfect tie?"

"That's just stupid."

"Stupid, certainly. But it's what we demanded of the Renshai. And it resulted in the unnecessary death of a good woman."

"You mean the Renshai's champion?"

"I do." Kedrin saw no need to remind the king that the woman they discussed had been his in-law daughter, Kevral.

The king pointed out the obvious. "But it was a fight to the death. Someone was going to die: if not the Renshai champion, then the Northmen's."

"Agreed." Kedrin dropped that particular argument; it was not, ultimately, germaine. "We went along with the Northmen's argument that a fight between their best man and the Renshai's was not a fair one because the Renshai man was more competent."

"True," King Humfreet said carefully, clearly anticipating a trap.

"Yet, isn't that the whole point of training? Of experience? Of battle? The side with the most competent warriors, with the shrewdest generals, sometimes only with the largest numbers wins?"

King Humfreet was the one who delivered a coup de grace first. "But wars aren't fair. They can't be."

Unwittingly, delivering that line also proved Kedrin's point. "Because fairness is not the end all and be all. It does not, in and of itself, define morality." It was a profound and complicated lesson Kedrin had not considered until that moment, and the realization frightened him. Knights were supposed to be the ultimate authority on world ethics. How horrible, how dangerous that it had taken him this long to learn what suddenly seemed like a difficult, but basic, lesson. "In war, when the side of right wins, it's not because they are righteous. It is solely because they have the best-trained army or the most experience or the wisest strategy."

The king clearly also realized the significance of the revelation. "What are you saying, Kedrin? It's all right to treat people unfairly, so long as the end result is . . . righteous?"

Kedrin did not like the king's summation. "Your Majesty, I believe I'm saying that we need to be more careful how we define and apply the concept of fairness lest we risk punishing practice, work, success, and achievement." Once started, he would not stop until his thoughts solidified for both of them. "I'm saying the race should more often be won by the swiftest, the contest by the wisest, the debate by the most educated. When consenting humans are pitted against one another, our job is to assure the rules apply to both sides, that the terrain or equipment is reasonably equal but not to handicap the individual contestants, whether their skills arise from natural wits or athleticism, repetition, preparedness, or strength of will. The gods, in their infinite wisdom chose to bless each of us with brawn or cleverness, looks or speed, artistic skills or lightning reflexes. What we do with these god-given gifts is up to each of us, but no one should be punished for being competent, whether it stems from natural talents, hard work, or a combination of both."

King Humfreet blew air through his lips. "Kedrin, I ... understand what you're saying. I just don't see how it applies to Renshai. Or ..." He spat out the name as if it burned his tongue. "Weile Kahn."

Kedrin knew he no longer had time for deep consideration. By now, he suspected, the men in the courtroom were growing restless. "Until the challenge against the Renshai by the united Northlands, we had never considered it necessary to weigh the relative skill levels of opponents prior to a duel. And, until the Renshai versus Paradisians conflict, we never treated a group of people without a country as if they were a sovereign entity."

King Humfreet interrupted, "Now, wait a moment. The only reason the Paradisians don't have a country is because the Renshai took it from them."

Kedrin was no longer wholly certain that was true. Until Weile Kahn stated otherwise, he had accepted the Northlands insistence, and their documentation, because it came from royal sources. Kedrin still had not personally uncovered any independent evidence that the Fields of Wrath had ever borne the name Paradisian Plains, and Weile's confident assertion that such validation did not exist was making him suspicious. The Northlands had a longstanding and avowed hatred for Renshai. "Assuming that's true, Your Majesty ..."

"Assuming?" King Humfreet slammed his hands to his hips. "Assuming it's true. It's common knowledge."

"Information is common," Kedrin reminded, "only because it's oft repeated. That does not, by definition, make it truth." Seeing no need to argue this particular point, Kedrin hurried on, "But even if it's true, Your Majesty, it's a bad precedent to set. Because if we decree that conquered lands are equally owned by conquered and conquerer, that having once lived on a piece of land gives descendants full right to return to it even decades or centuries later, fairness dictates that you must share Erythane Castle with Weile Kahn and his . . ." Kedrin tried to recall the name Weile Kahn had taken, ". . . Harkonians."

"What?" Same word, less emphatically.

Kedrin continued, "In addition, as we have limited the Renshai to proportionate responses, fairness dictates we respond to attacks in kind. So, if these Harkonians hit us with sticks and fists, we cannot bring arms to bear."

King Humfreet's entire body seemed to vibrate, and Kedrin thought he might explode. The captain of the Knights of Erythane took an involuntary backward step. But when the king finally spoke, his voice was soft, almost perplexed. "Knight-Captain Kedrin, I've trusted your judgment for decades. I know you to be a moral man, highly intelligent and principled almost to a fault. Surely, you're not advising us to welcome a band of criminals permanently into Castle Erythane."

Kedrin managed a smile despite the burdens crushing down on him. In addition to his king's wrath, he was facing a crisis of conscience simultaneous with the real life drama still unfolding in the courtroom. "No, Your Majesty. I'm advising just the opposite. I'm advising we vacate all arrests pertaining to the ongoing dispute between the Renshai and the Paradisians. Only then, we can try to negotiate a peaceful solution to the ongoing problem of two peoples claiming the same piece of land."

King Humfreet stroked his beard, sighed deeply, then lowered his head in apparent defeat. "It's just as well. King Griff is still convinced we're about to face another massive war, and he's reminded me we might well have lost the previous one without . . . certain Renshai. Griff would never interfere with Erythanian politics, but I know he's sure we'll need them in the upcoming conflict." He sighed again. "But it's not that easy, Kedrin. There are other things to consider.

We also need the Northmen, both as soldiers and for their ore; and they support the Paradisians. The Renshai may be better soldiers, but the sheer number of Northmen makes them far more necessary."

Kedrin nodded. Morality, not politics, was his priority and his area of expertise. Unfortunately, clear-cut lines did not exist in reality, and he had to work each one within the constraints of the other.

"And is setting the stage for negotiations going to appease ..." King Humfreet jerked a thumb toward the passageway into the court.

Kedrin had no idea how far Weile Kahn would push, but just the fact that the Easterner had confronted many kings and survived suggested he knew where to draw lines. He might fan a spark into a campfire, but he was wise enough to stop before it became a conflagration. Conversely, the Paradisians did not seem to know when to prod and when to retreat. They relied upon the law, the knighthood, and the Northerners to protect them. Left wholly to their own devices, the Paradisians would provoke the Renshai until every Paradisian lost his or her life. Long before that happened, however, Kedrin felt certain every Renshai enemy would find a way to support the Paradisians, directly or indirectly, against the Renshai, dragging more countries, more rulers, and more civilians into the fray. "We need to negotiate with the understanding that, in this circumstance, peace is not a possibility."

"It's not?"

Kedrin shook his head but did not explain further.

"What if we designated half the land to each of them? And built a sturdy fence between them?"

Kedrin's head shake grew faster as several realizations came to light at once. He could scarcely believe he had not seen the plot earlier, had not previously realized the devious complexity of what had once seemed so simple. "It won't work, Your Majesty. This is not a dispute over land."

"Not a ..." The king trailed off, his head cocked, eyes narrowed. He seemed to be trying to read Kedrin's mind. When that failed, he asked, "What do you mean it's not a dispute over land? Never has any conflict been more obviously a dispute over land." He added cautiously, "Has it?"

Kedrin knew they had to return to the courtroom now.

He had stayed away too long already and did not want Weile Kahn concerned that they were plotting a way to entrap him. That might force his hand against Erythane's guards and soldiers. "Your Majesty, it would take too long to explain. Do you trust me?"

To Kedrin's relief, Humfreet never wavered. "More than anyone else in the world."

"Then please, Your Majesty, either come with me now and talk to Weile Kahn or grant me the authority to bargain for you." Kedrin looked up, worried he had crossed another line himself.

Humfreet hesitated while Kedrin held his breath. That the king did not immediately dismiss the matter brought hope. "You're sure it's safe."

Kedrin would not lie. "I don't believe Weile Kahn is foolish enough to harm you." He added with the utmost caution, trying to sound matter-of-fact and not remind the king of his previous error. "So long as no one threatens him."

Humfreet took another long breath, releasing it in what seemed like his hundredth sigh since Weile Kahn had entered the courtroom. "You're sure we can handle this man?"

Kedrin was not, but one thing seemed certain. "Your Majesty, I'm not sure anyone can. But I truly believe we're more likely than anyone outside of Asgard to succeed."

"Very well," King Humfreet said. "And let us hope the gods are with us."

CHAPTER 24

My people have obligations to the kingdom, but I have at least as many obligations to them. Not the least of those is protecting them from injustice, not just as a group, but as individuals. I cannot abandon that obligation, even facing the threat of war.

—*King Griff of Béarn*

THE MAP-COVERED, windowless walls of Béarn's Strategy Room, and its single long table still impressed Saviar Ra-khirsson, who had come here only once before, to discuss the Northmen's initial proposition. At that time, they had agreed to aid Béarn in the war, and to supply the necessary iron ore, but only if Griff agreed to dismiss the Renshai from battle.

As always, the head seat was occupied by the high king of the Westlands, Griff, the one to his right by his adviser, Darris, and the one to his left by Prime Minister Davian. King Humfreet of Erythane took a place at the farthest end, currently referred to as the second head in deference to his title.

Knight-Captain Kedrin sat at King Humfreet's right hand, always pristine in his uniform. His hat, politely removed after a magnificent bow, perched jauntily on the back of his chair. Saviar sat along the far side of the table, his back near the wall. The Renshai's official representative, Thialnir Thrudazisson, had passed the mantle of leadership to Saviar for this particular negotiation and had chosen not to attend.

Béarn's minister of local affairs, tiny Chaveeshia, sat to Humfreet's left. It was her job to shepherd and represent visiting neighboring allies, usually Kedrin and Thialnir but, this day more importantly, the king of Erythane. Both Thialnir and Weile had requested Saviar, the former as his replacement-in-training and the latter for reasons all his own. The Easterner sat beside Saviar, his two bodyguards so quiet and unobtrusive behind him that Saviar kept forgetting they were present. Guard Captain Seiryn stood attentively behind King Griff. As always, a page crouched on the floor in the corner, recording every word for posterity.

The door opened to admit the remaining representatives invited to the gathering. Minister of Foreign Affairs, Richar, guided two Northmen and a ragged Erythanian into the room. Saviar knew one of the Northmen, Erik, an avowed hater of Renshai. Saviar had befriended Erik's son, Verdondi, a relationship that had lasted only as long as his ignorance of Saviar's heritage. The other Northman, and the Erythanian, were strangers.

Richar bowed to his king, then introduced his guests. "Erik Leifsson, Captain of the *Sea Dragon* and highest ranking Northman currently in Béarn." The man Saviar knew bowed to each king in turn, glared at Saviar, then took one of the three seats on the opposite side of the table from Saviar and as far from the Renshai as possible. He resembled Thialnir in many respects, though at least a decade younger: large-boned and -framed, broad-faced and wearing multiple braids in his golden hair.

Richar continued, "Geirrodr of the Gelshni tribe, Captain of the *Silver Serpent*, second highest ranking Northman in Béarn." Also a large man, Geirrodr repeated the same motions as his companion before taking his seat. Richar waited until both Northmen settled into chairs before making the last introduction: "And Perry Arner's son of the Paradisians." The Erythanian bowed low and awkwardly, clearly unaccustomed to royalty. He had a long, narrow face, smeared with dirt, a haphazardly shaven chin, and wore homespun with several obvious holes. His sandy hair was brushed to a sheen, and he kept flicking at it and missing, as if accustomed to it being longer and dangling in his face.

Richar waited until Perry sat between the Northmen before performing his own well-rehearsed gestures of respect. No chairs remained, so he stood behind his charges as the bodyguards did, though he frowned at what he probably saw as an outrage. Custom dictated that he have a seat at the table, but those higher ranking than him had no reason to move and those lower, including Saviar, chose not to.

At a gesture from King Griff, Knight-Captain Kedrin recited the age-old formalities that preceded such a meeting, long-winded details that seemed to bore every other person in the room. Saviar had never attended a session that did not include a knight, but he suspected the simple king would prefer to forgo this procedure and probably did so whenever he could. At last, Kedrin finished and King Griff took over. "Friends and colleagues, as you know, we have gathered here to barter peace between two groups of people, the Renshai and the Paradisians, as well as to decide the disposition of a disputed piece of land known by most recent decree as the Fields of Wrath."

Most of the faces in the room remained neutral throughout the recitation, aside from the Northmen who frowned deeply at the names "Renshai" and "Fields of Wrath."

No one interrupted the king's description of purpose; however, the moment he finished speaking, Erik impatiently gestured for the floor. The king yielded it to him. "So long as there are Renshai involved, there can never be peace."

The insult grated on Saviar, but he schooled his features. His time with Ra-khir and Kedrin had made him patient, and he knew Weile Kahn had a reason for convincing Saviar to come in his leader's place. Thialnir would have pounded the table and spat out an angry retort to the Northman's challenge. He was strong and dangerous, always speaking his mind with direct and forceful honesty; but, for once, the Renshai would win this negotiation with guile or not at all.

King Griff encouraged Saviar. "Do the Renshai have a response to that?"

Saviar looked at the king of Béarn as if he were the only man in the room. "Your Majesty, I'm afraid Erik's right. So long as there are Renshai involved, there can never be peace." Saviar could feel every eye on him, and it made him want to squirm. He resisted the urge, however, and looked serenely back at every curious face.

Griff encouraged, as Saviar knew he would. "Would you like to further explain yourself, Saviar Ra-khirsson?" Though phrased as a question, everyone in the room, with the possible exception of Perry, knew it was a gentle command.

Saviar obliged, "The enemies of the Renshai are many and powerful, in some cases united only by their hatred. Despising Renshai has become the focus of their lives, their children's only education, their very religion. It's not enough for them to torment us; they will never rest until we are all killed. It is because of these enemies that anything involving Renshai will always be violent. They will always attack us, and we will always defend ourselves from their attacks."

It was Erik who pounded the table in Thialnir's absence. "Lies and nonsense! It is the Renshai whose lives revolve around hatred and violence; they dedicate every moment to their swords and love nothing else. The enemies of the Renshai come by their enmity honestly, through having been slaughtered, their lands occupied, their children threatened."

Perry said nothing but bobbed his head vigorously.

Weile pointed out calmly, "It is the Paradisians who are hurling rocks."

Erik turned on Weile Kahn. "Of course they're hurling rocks! What would you do if vermin flooded into your homeland and demanded you tolerate their presences? Live by their rules?"

Saviar tried not to smile. He had experienced enough of Weile's tactics to know he would have an answer.

The Easterner did not disappoint. "I would do what any sensible person would do. I would exterminate those vermin with tools created to perform the task. I would do exactly what the Renshai haven't done . . . but should have."

"Exactly my point!" Erik crowed. "You exterminate . . ." Only then, he realized Weile Kahn had reflected the argument backward. ". . . the vermin."

Geirrodr stepped in to help. "The Renshai being the vermin in question. Not the Paradisians."

King Griff grabbed back his authority. "Except here we're dealing with human beings on both sides, not rats and mice. In order to broker a peace, it's inherent that both sides acknowledge the other's humanity, their right to exist as people."

Saviar nodded his agreement, but Erik muttered, "Never."

Saviar expected conversations to ensue, but they did not. Nearly everyone in the room was schooled in protocol and propriety, and those with lesser experience wisely remained silent. King Griff took the responses in stride. "Well, then. It's clear we cannot yet broker a peace. For now, we can focus only on the land dispute." His attention went to Perry, who had not yet spoken. "Representative of the Paradisians, please speak your piece."

Saviar sat back, curious. His arms tried to cross themselves over his chest, but he resisted. He did not want words or gestures to suggest contempt, and he preferred to keep his hands free in case violence erupted. He did not expect it in Béarn's Strategy Room, but he was trained to always be prepared for it, especially in the presence of Northmen.

Perry rose and cleared his throat. He spoke with a lower-class Erythanian accent, the type Saviar associated with street thugs and orphans. His Common Trading tongue was barely passable. "Welp, we's simple folk. All's we want's our lans an' homes wit'out them Renshais thret'nin' us an' killin' us an' takin' us's stuff. We's jus' wanns 'em killers off our beootaful Paradize Playins." Glancing swiftly around the table, he plunked back down in his chair.

Taking that as a cue he had finished, King Griff turned his attention to Saviar with the same request. "Representative of the Renshai, please speak your piece."

Saviar rose. "Quite simply, and with all due respect, Your Majesty, we want only to do our job, which is to protect the heirs of Béarn and come to her aid in times of war." He had one further line to add, the one on which Weile Kahn had insisted.

Before he could speak it, however, Erik interrupted, "Naturally, the Renshai cannot request anything without demanding war. What chance do the simple Paradisians have against people who worship confrontation?" It was disingenuous at best. Nearly all male Northmen, including

Erik, trained for battle; and every Northern warrior yearned for his place in Valhalla just as the Renshai did.

Saviar went silent, patiently standing. As he had not yet relinquished the floor, protocol dictated he had not finished speaking.

But Erik clearly would not yield. He also stood up, his voice much louder than Saviar's had been. "Your Majesties, if you please, it's all quite simple. The Paradisians were living on the land quite peacefully before the Renshai arrived and took it by force. It's true the Paradisians throw rocks, but the Renshai react with swords. Many more Paradisians than Renshai have died in this one-sided conflict. How could anyone consider that fair?" Erik looked from king to king. Apparently, he wanted an answer, but Griff did not indulge his rudeness.

"I believe," the king of Béarn said, "the representative of the Renshai has the floor."

"Thank you, Your Majesty." Saviar resisted the urge to gloat. He would not stoop to Erik's tactics. "As I was saying, we want only to fulfill our duty, the one our greatest ancestor arranged: we are the protectors of Béarn's royal heirs and we serve the kingdom in times of war. In order to do so competently, we need housing and sustenance for which we are only too happy to pay with our due wages." He finally had a chance to add Weile's portion, "Our only additional request is for equal treatment under the law as full-fledged Westerners and citizens of the country of Erythane."

Saviar wanted to remind those present that the Fields of Wrath had belonged to the Renshai long before the Paradisians had taken it over, wrecked their homes and stolen their stores, but he knew when to finish speaking. With a short bow to each king, he sat down again.

Griff nodded sagely but said nothing in regard to what he had heard thus far. Instead, he asked another question. "Representative of the Paradisians, what is your tie to the land in dispute?"

Perry leaned over to Erik, whispering.

Saviar wondered which word he had not understood. It suddenly made sense how easily the Northmen had manipulated these Erythanians. If Perry was a sterling example of his kind, the Paradisians did not have much room for bragging.

He supposed they had selected him for other reasons, perhaps to play on the sympathies of all parties involved.

Erik spoke into Perry's ear for some moments, then the Paradisian stood again. He made a sloppy bow in King Griff's direction. "You Majesties. For hunnerds a years, Paradezians live on dem playins. They's kilt by Renshais, what taked our lan', an' we go live in a slums a Erythane. Then, the Renshais get sended away—"

"—banished," Erik corrected.

". . . yeah, bannicht. We comed back an' live good agin. Then they comed back an' kilt us. S'our lan' 'cause we has it first an' last." Perry sat down.

Before King Griff could turn his attention to Saviar, Erik popped up. "Excuse me, Your Majesty, but Perry's not a good speaker. He's having trouble expressing himself, and I'd like to add some things for him, if you'll allow it."

King Griff glanced at Saviar, who nodded. He did not want anyone claiming the Renshai had taken unfair advantage. Again. It occurred to him the Northmen would make the allegation regardless, but he was not appealing to them. Nothing he said or did, short of suicide, would appease the Renshai's enemies.

Erik rose, bowed appropriately, and cleared his throat. "Your Majesties, as anyone can plainly see, the Paradisians are simple people who want the same things anyone else does: the right to live in peace on their own lands without constant threat of death or enslavement. As you can see by Perry's dress, even the highest born among the Paradisians lives in squalor because the Renshai have stolen their lands, their homes, their possessions, and refuse to allow them any dignity. It's true we hate Renshai, but not without cause. For what they've done to the Paradisians alone, we should feel justified in banishing, if not eliminating, them." Erik sat back down without a trace of discomfort, despite having made the case for genocide.

King Griff managed to repeat his question for Saviar. "Representative for the Renshai, what do you claim as your tie to the land in dispute?"

Saviar rose and accorded the necessary bows. "You mean, besides the fact that, unlike Perry or Erik, I was born and raised there?"

Weile touched Saviar's foot beneath the table, in warning.

Saviar lowered his head, as if in consideration but actually to control his emotions. "I contend that the Renshai are the ones who have lived on the Fields of Wrath for hundreds of years, having displaced no one. These Erythanians . . ." He refused to use the term Paradisians. ". . . merely took over what remained of our personal possessions in homes we commissioned and paid for, that were built to our specifications on our land, while we were temporarily banished."

The Northmen leaned across Perry to whisper furiously.

Saviar ignored the rudeness. "During that brief time, spanning only months, these Erythanians gave the land a new name and also concocted a history. However, our banishment was lifted, our name was restored, and we were given official right to return to our homes by Your Majesties and a representative of the Northmen in the presence of Captain Erik."

At the sound of his name, Erik looked up and glowered at Saviar.

"The Renshai do not feel that a few months of squatting in our homes gives them the right to lay permanent claim to our land." Saviar took his seat.

Immediately, Weile Kahn popped up to take the floor. He bowed nimbly. "Excuse me, Your Majesties, but Renshai aren't known for their speaking ability." His comment mimicked Erik's without insulting Saviar as Erik had Perry. "Saviar is having trouble expressing himself, and I'd like to add some things for him, if you'll allow it."

Erik shot up. "That's preposterous! Saviar's father is a Knight of Erythane, and he clearly has no trouble at all expressing himself."

Weile turned Erik a look of withering disdain. "If Saviar has expressed himself adequately, what could I possibly add that you might find objectionable?"

Erik had an answer, "You called the Paradisians vermin!"

Weile pointed out calmly, "You called them simple people incapable of expressing themselves. And, if I recall correctly, and I always do, 'vermin' came out of your mouth, not mine."

King Griff broke in, "I have no problem listening to friends of the court on either side." He gestured for Weile to continue.

Weile obliged. "As this page can affirm . . ." He gestured toward the page in the corner, who turned beet red. His quill stilled, and he studied his feet nervously. The pages of the Sage were trained to go unnoticed. They were sworn to secrecy, recording the goings on accurately and without making a sound. ". . . I've spent enormous amounts of time reading every historical text and reference the Sage would allow me to peruse." The Sage was known for being over-protective of his charges: the chronicles of Béarn, the books and scrolls of history, the finest trove of information in the world. "I've done the same in every corner of the world. And, I assure you, I am the foremost authority on the history of the Fields of Wrath."

"I object!" Erik hollered. "No man has the right to claim himself the foremost authority on anything. And, just because he does, it does not make him so."

Until now, Knight-Captain Kedrin had remained a silent spectator. He stood up and made a grand gesture that commanded the attention of every eye.

King Griff obliged. "Knight-Captain Kedrin has the floor."

Kedrin made a flourishing bow. "I apologize deeply, Your Majesties, but I have tolerated as much rudeness in the presence of royalty as I can stand." He rounded on the Northman. "Captain Erik, I can forgive your speaking out of turn, especially as this is a subject for which you have strong feelings. However, when you suggest that the High King of the Westlands is too guileless to make his own assessments of a man's claims and competence, I will always draw the line."

"I never said—" Erik started, but Kedrin silenced him with a cutting motion.

"Your implication was clear to every man and woman at this table, and it was not appreciated. You have had multiple opportunities to speak; if His Majesty wills it, you will have more. At the moment, however, Weile Kahn has the floor as acknowledged by King Griff. He has not yet relinquished it; until he does, you shall remain silent."

It was not a request, and even Captain Erik of Nordmir

knew it. He obeyed, sitting on the edge of his chair, his expression grim, almost vengeful.

Saviar knew Kedrin's motivation had nothing to do with the subject of the proceedings or any promise he had made to Weile Kahn. The Easterner had demanded few concessions, though his capture of the guard force of Erythane had given him enormous leverage. He had asked for the matter to come before King Griff, with the king of Béarn becoming the final arbiter. Weile admitted he had already released the jailed Renshai under the pretext that he had needed all the cells for Erythane's guardsmen, and he requested that all Renshai crimes and any sentences be commuted, to which King Humfreet had agreed. The king had seemed relieved, probably knowing the Renshai, having spent time in the dungeons, would not prove as cooperative the second time. Weile's only other request was that Humfreet and Kedrin be present at the negotiations.

Kedrin made an archaic gesture, and King Griff spoke, "Weile Kahn, please continue."

"Any true scholar of the Fields of Wrath knows it was a barren plain considered uninhabitable. It was first colonized, some four centuries ago, by a few Renshai who chose to remain in the West after the bulk of them had returned to their home in the Northlands. These settlers, initially considered traitors, became the Renshai's salvation after the tribes of the North banded together and slaughtered all the Northern Renshai. The tribe was reborn from these Western Renshai and continued to inhabit the Fields of Wrath until a few months ago. No text older than a toddler so much as mentions Paradisians or the Paradisian Plains."

Erik could not contain himself. Once again, he leaped to his feet. "But that's a lie! We've presented plenty of evidence."

Weile's gaze flicked to Erik, as if he found him beneath contempt. He adopted the voice of a weary parent trying to explain something a child was simply too young to understand. "Evidence that exists only in the North and contradicts every Western source. That's strange, given the land at odds is part of Erythane."

Erik glared, indignant. "Are you calling us liars?"

Weile Kahn's eyebrow cinched. "Once again, you are

proscribing to me things that you proclaimed. Quite loudly. At this very meeting."

Erik could scarcely deny it. At a warning gesture from Kedrin, he sat back down, fuming.

Weile Kahn remained a study in calm, expressionless despite his personal victory. "For point of argument, let us say that everything Erik has presented is correct, that the Renshai defeated the Paradisians in order to possess the Fields of Wrath."

Saviar watched the slightest of grins break through Erik's rage and knew, from experience, the Northern captain was in for a fall.

"I doubt there's a piece of land in any part of the world that hasn't, at some point in its history, changed hands through violence." Weile stared at the ceiling momentarily. "Let us start, say, with . . ." Abruptly, he turned his attention back to Erik. ". . . Nordmir."

Clearly startled, Erik met Weile Kahn's dark gaze with eyes like blue chips of ice.

Weile continued, "It's a well-known fact that the boundaries in the North are . . . let us say . . . a bit fluid. If a contingent from the former Blathe claimed the strip of Nordmir on which your family currently resides, Erik Leifsson, would you give them your home and those of your neighbors?"

Erik turned his gaze to Kedrin, as if requesting permission to reply to the question. It seemed ludicrous given the Northman's previous outbursts. Kedrin nodded once, and Erik obliged, "If their claim was legitimate, I'd have no choice."

A grin appeared on Weile's face so suddenly it could have been a perfect mask. "I'm so glad to hear that. Because, I have here in my pocket . . ." He removed a scroll from the folds of his cloak. ". . . a document stating that I am a direct descendant of Blathe settlers driven from their homeland by Nordmirians. And look, my forefathers came from the exact area of Nordmir where your family currently dwells." He shoved the scroll toward Perry and the Northmen.

Erik did not reach for it. "You, sir, are far too dark to be the descendant of any type of Northman."

Weile did not hesitate. "My great-grandfather on my mother's side fled from Blathe after the war. I resemble my father's side of the family."

Saviar hid his amusement behind a neutral expression; but, inside, he was laughing. He doubted a single word of what Weile was currently saying was true, but he would have an answer for any objection Erik could raise.

Erik put a hand on the scroll but did not open it. "Your documents are forged."

Weile touched the other end of the scroll and placed his opposite palm in the air. "I swear upon the souls of my ancestors, upon my honor, and to any living god that my document is every bit as authentic as the ones you've used to claim the Fields of Wrath for the Paradisians."

Unable to control his laughter another moment, Saviar faked a coughing spell. He folded his face into his hands. He only hoped King Humfreet and Kedrin would keep quiet about Weile's equally emphatic claim of descendancy from barbarians driven from Erythane in the spot where the castle now stood.

Cornered, Erik flicked the scroll back toward Weile. "It's a forgery, and you're a scoundrel. Nordmir won the land from Blathe in fair combat."

"Fair combat meaning you slaughtered them out of existence and took their land?"

"They were willing combatants."

"Were they?"

"And, had they triumphed, they would have taken our land."

"The fact that they were smaller, less fortified, and had inferior training and weaponry be damned."

The remainder of the negotiators remained silent as Weile and Erik argued.

Erik shook his head. "The superior force in a war should win. What's the point of this discussion?"

"To demonstrate the hypocrisy of your claim, Erik Leifsson. When the idea of displacing your family was rhetorical and you could see the analogy to the current situation between Renshai and Paradisians, you had no problem handing over your home. When you thought it might actually happen, you instantly changed your allegiance."

"I changed nothing." Caught in a lie, Erik chose denial, then obfuscation. "There is no parallel between Blathe and the Paradisian Plains. It's an entirely different set of circumstances."

Saviar expected Weile Kahn to press, but he did not. He had made his point and chose to sit back down in silence, leaving only Erik standing.

Erik appealed to King Griff. "Your Majesty, I know you're wise enough to see what this miscreant is missing, to see how he's twisting unlike situations to make them seem similar when they're not. Every war, every condition, every cause is different and must be examined with its own particulars in mind." Only then did he take his seat, hands clenched beneath the table and attention fixed on the high king.

Weile reclaimed his scroll, and it disappeared back beneath his cloak.

As before, Griff made no reply. He merely directed another question at Perry. "Representative of the Paradisians, if we divided the territory into two equal parts, naming one the Fields of Wrath and the other the Paradisian Plains, would this solution satisfy your people?"

As before, Perry consulted Erik. This time, Erik did not whisper a reply. "Your Majesties, Perry is having difficulty finding his words. May I answer in his stead?"

Saviar wondered if Erik was regretting his decision to make the Paradisians appear as helpless and weak as possible. Or, perhaps, he had done so specifically to allow himself to become their speaker.

King Griff said his first words since his opening statement that did not constitute an inquiry. "Only if it pleases Perry Arner's son. He has first right to speak for himself and his people."

Perry did not seem to know what to do. Finally, he rose, gave another awkward bow and said, "Thass fine wit' me fo' Erik ta do th' talkin' fo' us." He dropped back down to his chair.

Erik rose again. "Your Majesties, the invaders did not steal half the land from the Paradisians, they took it all. Perry's people already tried sharing with the Renshai, and we saw the result. The Renshai slaughtered dozens of Paradisians without a bare hint of remorse. And now that they have, apparently, gone free without punishment ... in fact, rewarded with half of the Paradisians' lands, why would they hesitate to massacre Paradisians again?" This time, Erik seemed to realize he had said enough and sat.

Saviar took a deep breath and waited for King Griff to, inevitably, address him next.

The high king did not disappoint. "And you, Representative of the Renshai. How would you react to a division of the land with side-by-side residency with the Paradisians?"

Saviar caught the leg of his chair as he prepared to rise, sending it toppling backward. Appreciating the delay this gained him, he placed it back into proper position and apologized, still trying to determine what to say. Finally, he had no choice but to speak, not entirely certain what would emerge from his mouth. "Your Majesties, if that is what came out of these negotiations, we would do our best to make it work. We have never barred any Erythanian, any *ganim* for that matter, from living among us, though few choose to do so. So long as they mean us no harm, they are welcome, and we will happily pay them for any services they provide. However, if attacked in any manner, we demand the full right of any Western citizen to defend ourselves with whatever force is necessary." He sat.

Erik rolled his eyes but did not attempt to reclaim the floor. As Erik took the role of spokesman, Geirrodr apparently felt the need to fill in for Erik. He murmured loud enough for everyone to hear. "We have seen how the Renshai 'defend themselves.' "

Saviar did not rise to the bait, and Weile acted as if he had not heard. Kedrin frowned his displeasure but did not rebuke the Northman. Either he did not want to be seen as taking sides or he had decided to lecture selectively, perhaps only when the slight might offend royalty.

King Griff took charge again, as he must. "Before I make my decision, does any party to these negotiations wish to add anything more?"

Saviar remained in place. He believed Griff had all the information he needed and trusted the high king of Béarn to make the right decision, whether or not anyone else liked or agreed with it. However, Saviar did not formalize his intention to remain silent, wanting the opportunity to change his mind should anyone on the other side make a point that required disputing.

Perry shook his head. "I gots nothin' lefta say, ya Majesties."

To no one's surprise, Erik rose. "I'm afraid that as

Representative of the Northmen, I must add one important detail." He sighed deeply, the first indication he was dealing with significant concerns of his own beyond simple rabble-rousing. "The Northmen do have a stake in this decision and will not be a party to what we consider a grave injustice. If the innocent Paradisians don't get their due, we will have no choice but to withdraw our alliances and support for any nation involved, including military backup and trading authority."

It was a veiled threat; and, though it did not surprise Saviar, several of the king's ministers showed obvious signs of disapproval and discomfort. Nostrils flared, upper lips quirked upward, eyebrows bunched. Saviar studied his grandfather. Though well-schooled in remaining nonjudgmental and keeping his thoughts to himself, Kedrin was clearly struggling. His left eye twitched and his lower lip slipped into his mouth, presumably so he could bite it back along with the angry words he surely longed to speak.

In this situation, only a king had the authority to intervene, and neither seemed inclined to do so. Humfreet looked more relieved than agitated. Saviar suspected he was glad he had turned the matter over to King Griff. Griff wore the same innocent expression he always did. The Renshai had never heard anyone disparage the sweet and simple-seeming king, but he suspected the gravest insult would roll neatly off the Béarnide's enormous back. Griff found the best in every person, in each situation, and no one ever seemed to find a reason to speak ill of him.

Experience told Saviar it ought to take a room full of advisers arguing for months to find a potential resolution to a problem this dangerous and complex. He also knew Griff did not have the luxury of time. Between the menace of the Northmen, the demands of Weile Kahn, and the imminent confrontation between the Paradisians and the released Renshai, every moment counted. The looming possibility of war added more urgency, especially with shifting alliances and impatience among the diverse peoples. Unlike the Knights of Erythane, justice was not Griff's only priority. In fact, it might not even rank near the top of his concerns.

Wise men had much to say about compromise, most of it as conflicting as the situations that demanded it. It seemed to Saviar that it mostly consisted of a decision that left adversaries believing they had gained only what they did not want in exchange for sacrificing what they justly deserved. He braced himself, knowing he would not like much of what King Griff had to say, yet also that the Renshai would get no better deal from anyone. Whatever the result, the Renshai would find a way to live with it. They always did.

King Griff cleared his throat. He shifted his weight as if to rise, then noticed the entire room scrambling to do the same, and stopped mid-movement. Instead, he spoke from his seat. "I have listened to all sides of this quarrel, as well as to the underlying subtext that makes this far more than a dispute over a piece of land."

Saviar caught himself staring. According to stories, when Griff had first arrived in Béarn, he had had no training, no royal upbringing, the unsophistication of a commoner. He still did not use the archaic and flowery language of the more staid and traditional ministers and Knights of Erythane, but he had developed a much stronger command of language and no longer sounded like the unschooled adolescent he had been when he first took the throne.

"While there is never a perfect solution, I believe I have one that will satisfy the spoken claims of the disputants."

No one murmured or coughed. They barely breathed. King Griff had a strong and deep voice that carried, but not a single person in the room dared to miss a syllable of his judgment. Most of them had heard him render rulings many times. They had become accustomed to his logic, strangely overlooked by purportedly wiser heads, that solved the most complex of problems in a way that seemed to define justice. Spectators raved about the competence and neutrality of his pronouncements, but Saviar knew that did not always translate to satisfaction for those involved in the conflict.

"Let us start with the land dispute." To Saviar's surprise, King Griff went straight to the heart of the matter. "It appears both parties believe they have strong, historical roots in the area currently referred to as the Fields of Wrath. However, it's equally clear that sharing the land is not a practical compromise. Erythane has far more important things to do than police one tiny piece of ground in her territory."

Humfreet lowered and raised his head once in tacit agreement.

Griff looked at his Erythanian counterpart. "With the permission of King Humfreet, ruler of Erythane, I intend to grant the Fields of Wrath its sovereignty, thereby relieving Erythane from the burden of protecting, ruling, indulging, and otherwise engaging with this small but troublesome piece of property. As the Renshai have been pardoned from any crimes in this dispute, they will be allowed to return to the area long enough to gather any and all personal property left at the time of their arrests. Béarn and Erythane will oversee the process, assuring a safe and orderly transfer of such portable property, after which time the Fields of Wrath, and its current buildings, will become the sole property of the Paradisian people."

Saviar's heart pounded, but he kept his mouth shut, certain the king would add much more before the proclamation ended. It could not possibly end this way, with the entirety of the land, as well as the homes paid for with Renshai blood, belonging to the Paradisians. And the Renshai, once again, left homeless.

"As a sovereign territory, it could be renamed and ruled at the discretion of the Paradisians. However, it should be noted that no aid, monetarily or militarily, will come to the Paradisian people from Béarn or Erythane unless and until actions occurring there infringe on the rights of our citizens or endanger our sovereignty or those of our people."

Saviar glanced at Perry, trying to discern his reaction without appearing to stare. The Paradisian wore a smile that also revealed uncertainty, stroking his stubble while Erik whispered furiously into his ear.

King Griff cleared his throat again. His attention went to the opposite side of the table. "There is a piece of Béarnian land along the boundary between our country and Erythane. Currently, it holds a thriving forest, but I've often thought of clearing it and now have reason to do so. Once that's done, it can remain a part of Béarn or I am willing to concede it to Erythane to replace the land lost by the disaffiliation of the Fields of Wrath."

King Humfreet made a gesture Saviar did not recognize, but Kedrin surely did. From context, the Renshai guessed Humfreet wanted to hear the entire ruling before making his decision on the matter of which country presided over the newly cleared land.

Griff signaled agreement before continuing, "The wood from the forest will be used to erect multiple homes and necessary buildings on the freshly cleared land." He glanced around the gathering. "I am certain that, no matter who presides over the land, all of the people gathered here will happily split any costs given the common goal of restoring peace."

Saviar bit back his own smile. King Griff had effectively trapped the Northmen in their own lie. By hiding behind a claim of protecting the Paradisians, rather than their true aim of obliterating the Renshai, the Northmen would have no choice but to assist.

There were nods all around, though some were far more vigorous than others.

"Though it will remain a part of Béarn . . ." Griff's gaze flicked to Humfreet. ". . . or Erythane, this new territory will be home to the Renshai who will become full-fledged citizens of Béarn or Erythane accordingly, entitled to all the same rights and . . ." He added, with emphasis, ". . . protections as any Béarnide or Erythanian. Naturally, the homes and buildings will be built to their specifications."

In the wake of the high king's speech, the room remained just as quiet. Saviar could almost hear the thoughts spinning through every mind as they considered the ramifications that went far beyond the words. The Renshai would lose the Fields of Wrath but would gain a homeland, legitimacy, and the full support of strong allies. It was not the result he would have chosen, but he knew the Renshai could live with the decision.

Perry shook his head, and Erik's whispering became an audible hiss. If the two had been alone, the Northman would probably be shouting at his undereducated charge.

King Griff added one final piece. "One thing I want to make clear to the residents of the newly-independent Fields of Wrath: while neither Erythane nor Béarn will lay claim to or defend your homeland, we will not sit idly by if interlopers whose alliances with us are not solid attempt to usurp sovereignty or place arms and warriors in dangerous proximity to Béarn or Erythane."

Saviar could no longer wholly suppress his grin. Once

again, Erik had done himself in with his own veiled threat. By stating the Northmen would impose military and trade sanctions against Béarn should the bargaining not go their way, he could hardly object to the king of Béarn characterizing the North as a territory "whose alliances with us are not solid." Erik had effectively barred the Northlands from assisting the Paradisians with anything other than direct humanitarian aid: food, clothing, money, all things the Northmen had no real interest in providing. Furthermore, Erik could not deny that the ruling had gone their way, as the Paradisians had gotten exactly what they had asked for: the Fields of Wrath, free and clear, and the right to rename it Paradise Plains.

Philosophers could debate the guileless brilliance of Griff's decision for years and not catch all of its subtleties, Saviar suspected. The military ramifications alone seemed legion. If the Paradisians or the Northmen went after the Renshai, it would require a direct attack on lands and citizens of the mighty kingdoms of Erythane or Béarn. The Renshai had no reason to attack the Paradisians; however, if it ever became necessary, the Renshai had the full power of the West behind them while the Paradisians had only themselves.

A frown scored Erik's features. Perry leaped to his feet with an abbreviated and agitated bow. "Please, Your Majesty." His homespun accent disappeared; it had been an act. "Can't we have the brand-new houses and the protection of Erythane or Béarn?"

Before Griff could answer, Erik broke in. "Your Majesty, with all due respect." Apparently realizing he was acting inappropriately again, Erik rose and bowed before continuing. "This can hardly be considered fair. While the Paradisians appreciate retaining their homeland, you've left them utterly defenseless against a Renshai attack."

King Griff stroked his beard, as if in deep consideration. "Captain, are you saying whoever retains the disputed land should have the right and means to defend themselves?"

"Of course," Erik shot back. Then, apparently remembering his manners again, he added, "Your Majesty. If not, the Renshai will simply retake Paradise Plains the way they did the first time. With violence."

Saviar's brows winched upward. He wondered if anyone

else noticed the blatant hypocrisy. Still, he said nothing, trusting King Griff to handle the situation.

The king clearly needed no assistance. "Captain Erik, is it your contention that my ruling was one-sided?" There was no malice in the question, only curiosity, which emboldened Erik, though he was still wise enough to criticize the king's decision in a circumspect manner.

"Your Majesty, I hope you understand I mean no disrespect when I agree with your statement. The Paradisians do get the land in dispute, but it does them no good if it's indefensible. Meanwhile, the Renshai get every other advantage: free new homes, full citizenship, and extraordinary protection against a group of people who could never truly menace them." Saviar noted the conspicuous silence on the real threat to the Renshai: the people of the North. Sandwiched between Erythane and Béarn, granted full citizenship and protection, the Renshai would become entirely safe from the Northmen as well. Not that the Renshai wanted or needed such security.

Kedrin made an almost imperceptible gesture. Saviar would have missed it had he not happened to glance in Humfreet's direction. Even then, it caught only the corner of his vision.

King Griff's response was a spare nod, and Kedrin rose with another flourishing bow. "Your Majesty, I merely wish to point out that compromise, by its definition, requires both sides to make concessions. The land is the item in dispute. If one side gets the entire prize, the other must receive proper recompense."

Erik did not guard his speech with Kedrin as he had the king. "With emphasis on the word 'proper,' I maintain that nearly all the advantages go to one side."

"The Renshai?" King Griff said, as if guessing.

"Yes, Your Majesty," Erik affirmed.

Griff continued to stroke his beard. "What if we added a condition requiring the new citizens of Béarn or Erythane to relinquish any or all claims to the disputed land?"

Erik made a dismissive gesture. "A fine gesture, Your Majesty, but ultimately only words. The Renshai do not honor promises as others do."

Saviar found his hand on his sword hilt and deliberately pulled it away. Responding violently to insults, no matter how fallacious and inflammatory, would only vindicate Erik's slurs.

King Griff's brows rose, and his hand left his beard. "The Renshai have always honored their promises to Béarn. Are you suggesting the Renshai would not honor the condition? That they would attack the Fields of Wrath despite it and reclaim that land?"

"I am, Your Majesty."

"But, in the same position, the Northmen and the Paradisians would abide by it?"

Erik straightened proudly to his full height. "We are men of honor, Your Majesty. We keep our word." He glared at Saviar. "The world would be a far better place if the Renshai had never existed."

Saviar felt certain he could draw and strike Erik's insolent head from his shoulders before anyone could stop him.

Apparently reading his mind, Weile leaned in toward Saviar to whisper, "Trust Griff. He knows what he's doing."

Unaware of the exchange, King Griff nodded thoughtfully. "Captain Erik, representative of the peoples of the North for these negotiations, let us consider a fair compromise to be 50% concessions per party. Where would you say we are right now?"

Erik seemed surprised by the question. "With the relinquish condition, Your Majesty, I'd say we'd moved from 80% in the Renshai's favor to 75%." He added quickly, "But that's still a long way from parity."

Saviar suspected that parity, to Erik, meant giving both pieces of ground to the Paradisians and brutally slaughtering every Renshai. He could see Erik's strategy. Finding a halfway point between Erik's vision and the current compromise could only work to the disadvantage of the Renshai, placing them in a position that would allow the Northmen to strike in numbers.

King Griff laced his enormous hands on the tabletop. He bobbed his head, staring at his own fingers for several moments.

Erik and Perry retook their seats while the king of Béarn considered.

For a long time, Griff said nothing. In deference, no one else spoke either, not even in directed whispers.

Finally Griff looked up, pinning Saviar with his dark, wise gaze. "Representative of Renshai."

At a nudge from Weile, Saviar sprang to his feet. "Yes, Your Majesty."

"The North and the Paradisians have declared the pro-claimed deal unbalanced against the side granted sover-eignty over the land in dispute."

Saviar did not know what to say. The king had only re-peated the events that had transpired, as if Renshai were too inexperienced and ignorant to understand from con-text. Realizing Griff was accustomed to working with Thi-alnir, he chose not to take offense. "So I heard, Your Majesty."

Griff's gaze was intent and provocative. Suddenly, Saviar realized the king was not rehashing the conversation out of any disrespect for Saviar, or for Renshai in general, but to encourage him to say something clever. Under the table, Weile touched his leg again, this time with encouragement.

The wisest men at the table had put the onus on Saviar, and he did not know what they wanted. It seemed urgent, though, and exceptionally important. His thoughts ran in frantic circles, seeking the common thread, the significant factor. When it finally came to him, it seemed so clear and obvious he could not believe it took him so long to figure it out. "Your Majesty, in the cause of peace and to make all sides happy in this dispute, the Renshai will agree to take what has been amply and vigorously designated the lesser side of the bargain. That is to say, we will give up all the responsibilities and benefits offered to us so you can bestow them upon the Paradisians instead. In exchange, we will ac-cept the responsibilities and benefits Your Majesty offered to them."

Weile squeezed Saviar's leg again and offered him a cocksure smile. The corners of the king's mouth twitched, but he otherwise gave no indication he had anticipated or encouraged Saviar's suggestion. Erik's nostrils flared. A frown scored his features, and his eyes narrowed; but there was nothing he could do or say. Bitten by his own words, he could hardly claim the deal was biased against his side.

Only then, Saviar realized this was the deal King Griff had been intending from the start. The only way the king could grant the Renshai the Fields of Wrath, without incurring the ire of the North, was to convince them that the winner of the land was the loser of the bargain. There was still one hurdle left.

Griff's head swung toward Perry. "Representative of the Paradisians."

Perry jumped up like a frightened rabbit. "Yes, Your Majesty."

"Does it suit the Paradisians to relinquish all rights and title to the Fields of Wrath in exchange for land, homes, and full citizenship to either Béarn or Erythane?"

Perry did not even glance at Erik for support this time. Saviar realized the Paradisians had everything to gain from the arrangement: free homes, free land, and the protection of a great kingdom, whether Erythane or Béarn. For them, it had never been about their self-proclaimed homeland. They had been pawns of the North, used as symbols of Renshai evil and oppression, whipped to a frenzy and willing to murder and die for the promise of money, land, and homes. Now, they had all of it, minus the constant killing, their ties to the North no longer useful or necessary, at least to the Paradisians. "We will sign this agreement and consider ourselves satisfied with the result."

Erik made a garbled noise. Though seething, there was nothing he could do or say. After his proclamation that the deal favored the side that received the new land, with both groups happy, he could hardly deny that the terms were satisfactory. The North would have no right or reason to call a foul, to exert trading or military sanctions against Béarn.

King Humfreet waved for the floor. "Thank you, Sire, for handling this difficult situation. If it pleases you, Erythane will claim the new land only with the understanding that all citizens of Erythane are Erythanians regardless of prior affiliation. Whoever settles there will have the full rights and responsibilities of Erythanian citizens, including taxes; and, henceforth, will be known only as Erythanians."

King Griff motioned toward Perry. "Do you understand the condition my colleague has placed upon you?"

Perry glanced worriedly at Erik but got nothing in return. "I'm not sure, Your Majesty."

Griff explained, "When you give up all rights and claims to the land officially known as the Fields of Wrath, there are no Paradise Plains. Your people are no longer Paradisians; you are Erythanians."

Saviar considered that information. He doubted he could have gotten the Renshai to accept such a condition in the Paradisians' place. He also realized it was different for them than for his people. Until a few months ago, the Paradisians were Erythanians and had been so their entire lives.

Saviar knew Erik had to argue. Without the Paradisians, the North had no claim to the Renshai land, no wedge to declare the Renshai evil occupiers of innocents' territory.

As expected, Erik cut in, "Your Majesty, you're asking them to give up more than their land. You're asking them to sacrifice their very identity."

For the first time, Griff actually looked as if the words might have offended him. "Captain, that was not a condition of the compromise. The people represented by Perry were promised full citizenship, with all its rights and responsibilities. King Humfreet makes and enforces the laws pertaining to Erythanian citizenship." Griff studied Perry who seemed bored with the conversation. The need to maintain the title of Paradisian interested him far less than it did the Northmen.

Griff continued, "There is also the option of maintaining the cleared land as a piece of Béarn. We have no requirement that our citizens refer to themselves as Béarnides. They could still call themselves Paradisians, though to what purpose? The agreement calls for full relinquishment of any rights or claims to the disputed land. And, as you've pointed out, the North and Perry's people will honor that promise."

Perry apparently followed enough of the conversation to insert, "Your Majesties, we have no problem becoming Erythanians again."

Erik whispered furiously into Perry's ear. Though louder than usual, it came to Saviar only as a pointed buzzing. He could only imagine the berating Perry was receiving but suspected the significant part was a promise of monetary rewards for keeping the name the North had given them.

For a moment, Saviar considered the possibility that the Paradisians would take the noble path. They had gained so much in the deal, and it did not harm them a bit to retake their former name. Having lived beneath the laws of Erythane for most of their lives, they would find them familiar, comfortable. Then, Saviar remembered the type of people Perry represented: the type whose loyalty went to whoever paid them, whipped to a hatred that made them willing to sacrifice the lives of their elders and children. Thus far, the Northmen's promises had gained them sympathy, support, land, homes, money.

Perry continued as if he had never paused, ". . . or living on Béarnian land. But we'd like to keep our name, so we prefer Béarn."

There was only one reason the Northlands would offer strong incentive for the Paradisians to keep their name. Clearly, they intended to reassert their "right" to the Fields of Wrath at a later date. Saviar smelled future trouble; but, for the moment, he reveled in the Renshai's many victories. They had their land back, their long-time homes, and the Renshai were no longer prisoners awaiting sentencing. He caught Weile Kahn's hand beneath the table and gave it a squeeze he hoped conveyed his thanks. For now, at least, the nightmare had ended.

CHAPTER 25

You can't become worldwise without facing the world.
        —*King Tae Kahn Weile's son*

THE PRIVATE ROOM in Béarn Castle had been outfitted
to Tae Kahn's suggestions: a few benches along the farthest
walls from the door and a dining table in the center of the
room with a few chairs around it. Situated on the fifth floor,
also at his request, it usually served as a family dining room.
Everything potentially dangerous had been removed, including lanterns and torches, the only light streaming
through the single small window.

Upon docking, Tae had sent Matrinka ahead to alert
King Griff and instruct the servants to set up the room,
while Captain tended the ship. After careful explanation,
Tae and Subikahn had covered the heads of their guests
and steered them, blindly, to the prepared room. Tae had
done so for their own security. The ship had arrived in
broad daylight, and many curious dockworkers, sailors, and
soldiers had already mobbed him, begging news. Tae could
just imagine them recognizing Arturo and swarming him in
his confused state, and Mistri would prove a curiosity certain to draw even more scrutiny. Tae had no way of knowing
how either of his charges would react, and King Griff had
every right to make any decisions regarding who knew of
Arturo's return and the arrangements for their unexpected,
young prisoner.

Matrinka arrived before Griff accompanied, to Tae's

surprise, by a prince and two princesses. Barrindar, the oldest offspring of Griff and his third wife, held Marisole's hand. Halika, Matrinka's youngest, skipped in alone, scanning the room with curious dark eyes. Still shrouded, Mistri sat quietly beside Tae on one of the benches, stroking Imorelda who had settled into the little girl's enormous lap. Arturo sat in a chair at the table, his covered head bowed, Subikahn standing behind him.

Hoping Imorelda was still tuned to Mistri, Tae sent, *Give me a moment. I need to talk to Matrinka.* Rising, he took Matrinka's arm and steered her to a corner to whisper, "You brought the children?" He added doubtfully, "Matrinka, I don't think that's a good idea. How will they feel when Arturo doesn't know them? Did you prepare them for that possibility?" On the ship, they had discussed revealing Arturo and Mistri to Griff alone, seeing their reactions, and allowing the king the right to make any decisions regarding the situation before involving anyone else.

Matrinka eyed Tae coolly. She had clearly considered the options and made her decision. "Marisole is the bard's heir. She's supposed to be learning how to handle difficult situations with grace, and she just returned a day ago from an equally difficult journey."

Tae's gaze rolled to the youngest of Matrinka's children. "And the others?"

"Barrindar insisted on accompanying Marisole, and I saw no reason to stop him. He's calm in a crisis and will support the girls, if needed. Halika is the only one who believed he was still alive, and she deserves to be one of the first ones present for his unveiling."

Tae could read a lot into Matrinka's reply. Clearly, she had not yet told the prince and princesses why she had summoned them, which seemed appropriate. No one should have that information ahead of the king. It also substantiated what he had overheard months earlier outside Matrinka's window. Seeing Marisole and Barrindar together confirmed them as the objects of Darris' and Matrinka's dispute over a prince and princess involved in an illicit love affair. Matrinka had not yet chosen to discuss the situation with Tae, and this certainly was not the moment for such a conversation. "Griff is all right with them being here?"

"Griff," Matrinka said stiffly, "is negotiating with elves at the moment. I am the queen of Béarn, and I have chosen to have these three present."

This was obviously important to Matrinka. She rarely invoked her title and spent far more time berating her friends for doing so. Tae could not resist reminding her of that fact. He bowed deeply. "As you wish, Your Majesty."

Matrinka glared, then curtsied. "It *is* as I wish, *Your* Majesty." It was the perfect stalemate. Tae smiled. "Point taken." Then, he sighed. "I'm mostly worried about security. We don't know how either of them will react. It might be dangerous for young royalty."

Apparently, Matrinka did not share Tae's concern. "I hardly think a three year old is a threat to any of them."

"Three-year-old giant," Tae reminded. "Frightened and capable of unknown magic."

Matrinka talked over him. "No matter what he can or can't remember, Arturo is still Arturo. He's studied and careful by nature. Even if he does something crazy, we have a Renshai who can overpower him. When Griff arrives, Darris will accompany him, and he's also trained as a royal bodyguard."

Practically instinctively, Tae realized. The bard bloodline seemed to assure reasonable ability with a sword as well as spectacular musical ability, with or without formal training, at least for the firstborn child. Matrinka had not spoken the words, but Tae knew she also trusted him to pacify Mistri. With his young charge safe, Arturo had little reason to act out violently.

Tae's thoughts returned to the sea voyage. It had taken days to leave the *Kjempemagiska* far enough behind that Captain could no longer spot them with his Box of Farseeing. Perhaps they had given up and returned to Heimstadr, but Tae doubted it. More likely, they had gathered their warships and were, at this moment, speeding toward Béarn only a few days or weeks behind them.

But the journey had given him time to win Mistri's trust and, ultimately, glean some information about the *Kjempemagiska* culture, if only on a very basic level and through the eyes of a young child. He had also spent significant time with Arturo. Though the Béarnide spoke little and seemed suspicious of any information presented, he did appear to be listening and considering. Mistri spoke for him frequently, and Tae had a low level understanding of how the two had met and bonded as well as how the *Kjempemagiska* thought of Arturo/Bobbin, their *alsona* servants, and the people of the continent. He had also picked up an enormous understanding of the island languages, verbal and mental. Though Mistri had a young child's understanding of spoken syntax, her mental abilities, and the information accompanying the sendings, filled in the gaps. Knowing children, Tae had little difficulty adjusting his perception.

Realizing he had gone silent too long, Tae pursed his lips and nodded. "As long as you know the risks, I have no right to countermand you."

"I know the risks," Matrinka assured him.

Tae returned to his seat beside Mistri.

Imorelda yawned and stretched; the last remnants of a purr rumbled away. *She fluffed my fur all the wrong way. And she folded my tail. And she pulled my whiskers.*

Tae looked at the cat. Despite her complaints, her move from Mistri's lap to his appeared casual and unhurried. The silver-and-black stripes lay in their regular soft array. *If that's the worst that happens to you, you're one lucky cat.*

You're the worst that happens to me. You beat me and squash me and drown me and burn me . . .

And yet, Tae pointed out, *you're still with me.*

Only because you need me. Imorelda lashed her tail but settled into Tae's lap. *Without me, you'd have been dead a long time ago.*

Tae could scarcely argue. *So true, my love. So true.* He had missed their conversations, even if they did tend to consist mostly of her complaints and denigration. She clearly meant them all with love.

Mistri groped blindly for Tae and caught his thigh, then his arm. She squeezed, the cover muffling her voice. "Can't you hear me?"

Reluctantly, Tae pointed out, *And I'm afraid I still need you to translate, Imorelda. This will be stressful for everyone, but especially for Mistri. She may well be our key to winning this war, to saving us all from dying horribly. She has to trust me, and to do that, she has to be able to communicate with me.*

Tae had already explained this to Mistri several times on the ship, but he dutifully did so again. "When I'm close enough, I can always hear *usaro*. But I'm the only one on the continent who can hear *anari*, and even I'm sometimes deaf to it." An analogy occurred to him. "Don't you have deaf people at home? People who can't hear anything?"

Mistri shook her head, then stopped mid-movement. "Some *alsona* old or head-hurt or no ear, can't hear *usaro*. Everyone hear *anari*." She touched the covered sides of her head. "Don't need ear."

Tae was certain he did not want to know how *alsona* became "head-hurt" or lost their ears entirely. He switched to *anari*, for Mistri's sake. As they used the Heimstadr languages, no one could overhear them either way. *I'm not sure what's going to happen here. Matrinka's bringing Bobbin's father, the king, and his bodyguard, Bobbin's sisters and one half-brother. None of them know he's still alive. I don't know how they'll react.*

Happy? Mistri suggested.

Definitely, Tae confirmed the innocent assertion. *But also confused and, possibly, suspicious. He's lost weight, and he's not acting like himself. Matrinka doesn't have any doubts; she's his mother. But others may not feel as secure about his identity.*

Are you sure Bobbin is this prince man?

It was a legitimate question, one Tae had already pondered several times. Imorelda's insistence that every human had a unique smell had clinched it for him. *Bobbin can't hear* anari, *can he?*

Mental silence followed. Hidden, Mistri's features gave Tae no clue. Finally, she spoke, *No.* Another hesitation. *Is that why he's so . . . animally?*

Tae knew he had reached a breakthrough. For the first time, he dared to wonder if Matrinka might be right, if the *Kjempemagiska* response to them would change if they understood their assault involved intelligent beings. Tae shook the idealistic thought from his head, sheer madness. The *alsona* closely resembled the people of the continent, spoke both of the *Kjempemagiska* languages, and lived among them, yet the magical giants still had no qualms about enslaving and torturing them. *It's certainly why he doesn't understand a lot of what you say to him—he only hears what you say in* usaro. *And until he'd heard it for a while, he didn't understand what you said aloud, either.* Once again, Tae sent a concept of differing languages with his words. It might take Mistri several repetitions and explanations to understand an idea that did not exist in her culture.

Despite Tae's ability with languages, the island peoples' had mystified him until he discovered the mental component. It was amazing Arturo had managed to pick up anything at all and probably had everything to do with his spending all of his time with a young child who was also still learning to speak.

Matrinka, Barrindar, Marisole, and Halika had seated themselves at the table. Barrindar and Marisole chatted mostly with one another, staring deeply into one another's eyes and smiling too much. Tae made a silent note to bring the issue to Matrinka's attention. He was more observant than most, but she could scarce afford for the royalty of Béarn to become suspicious of the unholy relationship between the siblings. Halika studied the figure beneath the shroud with fanatical interest, responding distractedly to her mother.

Finally, Darris and Griff swept in. The king's black locks were a mass of tangled curls, and sweat trickled down his beefy face, yet he still managed a weary smile for Matrinka and his children. A head and a half shorter, Darris looked all business. He glanced from Tae and his mysterious companion, to the shrouded figure at the table, before settling his gaze on Matrinka. Only then, he finally showed a hint of contentment looking upon the woman he had loved for so many years.

From training, the prince and princesses rose at the sight of their father. Matrinka gestured for the men to sit, which they did, and the others followed suit without the formality of bows or curtsies. Aside from Mistri, who was hooded, and Darris and Subikahn, who were working, every person in the room was royalty.

Matrinka got right to the point. "I'm so sorry to pull you from negotiations, but this is extremely important."

Griff nodded broadly. If Matrinka labeled a situation "extremely important," he would not question it. She tipped her head toward Subikahn, who pulled the shroud from Arturo's head. At the same time, Tae quietly revealed Mistri.

A moment of stunned silence followed, then Halika flung herself over the table at Arturo.

Startled, Arturo sprang to his feet, overturning his chair. Subikahn had his weapon out before the chair hit the floor with a clatter. Disregarding all danger, Halika wrapped her arms around as much of Arturo as she could. "I knew it! I knew it! I TOLD YOU!" His massive chest muffled her words. "You all said I was crazy, but I knew Arturo was still alive."

Arturo struggled only a moment before returning the embrace. He lowered his head to her ear and whispered something Tae could not hear.

That's his littlest sister, right?

Right, Tae sent back. He took Mistri's hand, a gesture intended to keep her in place as much as comfort. With all attention on Arturo, no one even seemed to notice her.

Marisole looked at Matrinka. "Is it really . . . ?"

"Yes," Matrinka said. "But he doesn't remember. He washed up on the island of the enemy nearly dead and without his memory. A little girl found him, convinced them to heal him with magic, and kept him as a . . . for want of a better word . . . a pet."

In response to Matrinka's words, Arturo glanced around the room until his gaze fell on Mistri. His arms winched around Halika.

Griff rose. "Arturo. My son." He asked the practical question no one else had. "Were there . . . any other survivors?"

Only one in the room could answer that question. Tae sent to Mistri, *He wants to know if any of the others on the ship with Bobbin were saved.*

Mistri shrugged her thick shoulders. *We found one other body. Alsona, we thought. Then, some . . . parts.*

Tae did not need the details. "There were no other survivors."

Halika finally released Arturo, then whirled to confront her siblings. "You owe me about six hundred apologies. I was right about Arturo."

Barrindar bowed deeply. "I humbly apologize and admit my error."

"Not you, Barri." Halika jabbed a finger toward Marisole. "Her! And Mama and Papa!"

"I'm sorry," Marisole said, studying Arturo's face. "It really is Arturo." She could not help adding, "Isn't it?"

"Of course it is." Halika seized his hand. "Tell them, Arturo. Tell them, you're Arturo."

Tae found himself wincing. Since his kidnap, Arturo had barely spoken and, then, only in *usaro*.

"Darling," Matrinka started but never finished.

Arturo spoke over her. "I am Arturo," he said in rusty Common Trading. The words seemed to surprise even him. "I remember . . . my sisters. Marisole, Halika." He placed a massive hand on her slender shoulder, engulfing it. "My brother, Barrindar."

Tae's heart pounded, and he watched the man's every movement. Suspicious by nature, he needed to know for certain whether Arturo had actually regained some of his memory or was playing them, seeking an opening. Subikahn, too, remained crouched and ready, his sword in his hand.

Arturo seemed to take no notice of them. He did not even glance toward the Renshai. Instead, he studied Matrinka as if seeing her for the first time. "Mama."

Tears dribbled from Matrinka's eyes. "My baby boy." She came around the table and caught Arturo into her arms.

It suddenly occurred to Tae he had not heard from Mistri at a time when he should have. Neither had Imorelda made any sarcastic comments, which suggested she still held the connection. Tae whirled to face Mistri. The young giantess, too, was crying. *What's wrong?* he sent.

Bobbin's not my Bobbin anymore. Mistri sobbed. *He's never coming home, is he?*

Tae did not know how to answer. Given the fluency *anari* granted her, as well as her size, he sometimes forgot her tender age and what she might truly grasp of situations. *Bobbin has come home, Mistri. This is his home.*

No, she said petulantly, clutching her arms to her chest. *My Bobbin! Mine!*

Tae sighed. It was a long time since Subikahn was young; and, given his son's proclivities, Tae doubted he would ever have grandchildren. *Mistri.* He allowed disapproval to flow through the contact. *You wouldn't want Bobbin to keep you here against your wishes, would you? It's not fair to take him away from his family.*

Mistri rubbed her eyes with her fists. *But he's my Bobbin, my best friend. And he saved my life, too.*

Tae said the only thing he could. Any promises were not his to make. He had no idea when or if she would ever see her parents again. *All the more reason why you need to grant him his freedom.*

Mistri rubbed her eyes harder, gulped in a couple of breaths, and managed a brave nod.

Tae tried to listen to the ongoing conversation between the royals even as he handled the little girl's heartbreak. He needed to know what information Arturo was giving them, could give them. When coupled with the knowledge Tae had gathered from Mistri, Captain, and the minimal spying he had managed, it might add up to something useful. Tidbits of fact could sway the tide of entire wars.

Tae gathered Mistri in his arms, though she was nearly as tall and heavy as him. He hoped nonverbal comforting would suffice, turning his mind and ears toward the other conversations. From what he could overhear, the reuniting had brought back a significant number of Arturo's memories from his childhood, though they stopped abruptly at the moment he had boarded the Béarnian warship. He remembered nothing about the attack. His life had ended when he stepped onto the ship and began again when he awakened in Mistri's doll crib.

When Arturo mentioned the little girl, all eyes finally went to the young giantess, wrapped in Tae's embrace. He warned them away with a stiff headshake and a gesture from behind her back. Curious, hostile or welcoming, their attention would confuse, perhaps even frighten, her.

Darris asked the all-important question. "What do you want us to do, Your Majesty?"

The question encompassed everything from how many people should know about the situation to Mistri's disposition.

Griff sighed, clearly considering his options. "We need to make a pronouncement regarding Arturo's return, but we shouldn't turn it into a celebration. Family, staff, the populace needs and deserves to know, but Arturo must have time to recover the gaps in his memory at his own pace." He addressed the young prince. "Does that work for you?"

Arturo nodded. He looked contemplative and confused. He would need to put both of his recent lives into context. No doubt, he would have behaved differently on Heimstadr had he known his identity, in ways that probably would have gotten him killed. His glance strayed back to Mistri, concern etched on his features, and Tae knew the prince's commitment to the child would not waver no matter his thoughts and epiphanies. "What about Mistri? She must be terribly frightened."

To Tae, Mistri seemed more curious than afraid. She appeared to take the situation in stride, and Tae gave grudging credit to her parents. Clearly, they had maintained a household that never drove Mistri to ponder the possibility of danger, at least not from other intelligent beings. He suspected she possessed the normal fear of darkness, falling, wild animals, and, of course, drowning; but a young child who had never witnessed or suffered violence could remain trusting and innocent for many years.

Tae stopped himself from laughing. He wondered how any race with such capacity for cruelty kept the brutality so well hidden from their offspring. Perhaps only the males engaged in such behavior or, maybe, Mistri's parents shielded her specifically. For whatever reason, the indulgence of Mistri's parents was probably the sole reason Arturo had survived his ordeal. Mistri loved him, so they allowed Arturo to live much as a continental parent might humor a child's insistence on clinging to a runty pig or a songbird with a broken wing.

Mistri pulled free and retook her seat on the bench. She smiled at Arturo and gave him a shy little wave.

"Hello, Mistri," Arturo said, using the island tongue. He strode to her, catching her into a wholehearted hug, and she melted into his arms. For several moments they clung, looking for all the world like father and overgrown daughter. There was evident love in their embrace, but Tae knew their relationship would have to change, their priorities would shuffle, and he hoped they would find a new and better way to relate to one another.

Griff took a step toward them, then stopped, perhaps afraid his presence might overwhelm Mistri. "Does she understand our language?"

"Not a word," Tae assured him. "Speak freely. She'll probably want to know what you're saying, but I'll only translate what you want her to hear."

Arturo disengaged from Mistri gently to return to his mother and sisters. As Tae anticipated, Mistri contacted him again. *What's happening now?*

We're still explaining the situation. Arturo's father, the king, is trying to decide what to do next.

With me? Mistri guessed.

So far, just with Bobbin. He's suddenly remembered a lot and has to get it all sorted out in his mind. His father wants to keep things quiet around him so he can ... get better.

Mistri squeezed her lower jaw between her hands. *Bobbin's sick?*

In a manner, yes. Tae did not want to go into unnecessary detail. *He remembered lots of things today he had forgotten, but there are holes in his memory and he's having trouble putting the two phases of his life together.*

Mistri looked stricken, so Tae attempted to reassure her, though he doubted the girl could truly grasp the enormity of the circumstances.

His mother's a healer, so she can help him. He just needs time with his family to think things through.

Unaware of the conversation between man and girl, Griff announced, "The girl will stay here, at the castle, in the Blue Room." He chose a bedroom dedicated to the children of visiting dignitaries.

Tae silenced Mistri with a gesture so he could focus on the king's words. Though Imorelda had accustomed him to simultaneous conversations, he still preferred them one at a time.

"She'll have a personal maid. Female, of course. And younger is better."

Tae knew little girls tended to bond well with adolescent females, perhaps because they emulated them.

Tae explained, *He's offering you a room in the castle and a maid servant.*

Mistri nodded, clearly unaware of the honor bestowed upon her.

King Griff stopped there and looked at Tae quizzically. After several moments of silence, the Easterner finally realized something was expected of him.

"I have nothing to add," Tae assured the king.

Creases appeared at the corners of Griff's eyes. "Don't you want to translate for her?"

Tae smiled. "Done. We're talking, just not out loud."

"Ah," Griff said, though his features suggested he did not fully understand. "Well, then, I'll continue. I think it best we keep her close, in the castle and courtyard areas. Tae, I'm assuming you've already gotten as much information as you can from her."

Tae's grin broadened. "Naturally."

"I have no right to ask you to stay; but, so far, you're the only one who can communicate with her other than Arturo." Griff's gaze strayed to his long-lost son. Clearly, he worried about Arturo's alliances as well as putting him to work before he was ready.

Griff needed to know, so Tae explained, "Arturo's limited to nonverbal, nonmental communication and the vocabulary of a toddler, unfortunately."

Mistri's gaze flitted between Tae and Griff as they alternated speaking. *What's he saying?*

Tae touched Mistri's arm in a plea for more time. "I need to organize my armies, but I'll donate as much time as I can spare." He wrapped his fingers around Mistri's broad arm. "Immersed in our language, she'll probably learn quickly. Just be aware of that when you talk around her. She's not a dog."

Griff sifted out the most pertinent details. "You think the war is imminent." It was not a question.

"I'm afraid so. They're going to come for Mistri. Sooner than later and probably much more swiftly then they originally intended."

"You're sure?"

"As sure as anyone can be." Knowing Matrinka had not had the opportunity to explain the situation to Griff, Tae did so in shortened form. "Their warships were stocked and ready, so any delay up to the point Mistri joined us was due to strategy and training. That may work to our advantage. Driven to war early by what they see as need, they may not have as well-prepared warriors or tactics as they would have given more time." Tae realized that worked both ways, but defensive fighting did not rely as much on preparation.

Matrinka explained the part Tae had skipped. "We didn't mean to capture Mistri. We had to grab Arturo because he didn't recognize us, and she tried to defend him. It was either save her or let her drown."

Tae forced himself not to consider the possibility he had made the wrong decision. If Mistri had died, it might have fueled anger; but the *Kjempemagiska* would not feel the pressing need to liberate her. Of course, as he had just stated, that might actually work to the continent's advantage. Realizing he had left Mistri hanging, he addressed her, *We're just discussing how you came to be with us. And how much time I can spare translating for you.*

Mistri hugged Tae's arm with both of hers. *I need you.*

Tae could scarcely argue. *You'll do fine with or without me, Mistri. I'll give you as much time as I can, but I do have other responsibilities. Béarn's royal family and their staff are good people, and Arturo loves you. No harm will come to you here.*

Tears welled in Mistri's eyes. *I want to go home. I want to see Mummy and Poppy again.*

Tae did not bother to respond. They had already discussed the situation; and, while he had not gotten into the violent aspects of the relationship between the *Kjempe-magiska* and the peoples of the continent, she knew enough to realize they could not safely sail her home. On his own, and in discussions with Subikahn and Matrinka, Tae had given grave consideration to the issue. Children were not supposed to be casualties or pawns of war, and he had every intention of returning her to her parents. At the current time, he had no idea how, or even if, such a thing were possible.

Tae returned to the other conversation. "They may well have planned to attack from one or several different points of the continent this time, but following Mistri will force them to come here again. Not great news for Béarn but, at least, we have a familiar battlefield, set supply lines and many of the armies still have presences. We should be able to recall them fairly quickly."

"Whittled down and battle-weary," Griff pointed out.

Tae only nodded.

"You're sure they'll come for her?"

The mental conversations that had occurred while the giants chased Captain's ship left Tae without any doubt. "The ones chasing us returned to their island, but only for reinforcements. They won't arrive tomorrow, but they will be here probably not long after and in full force."

Griff's jaw clamped shut. Tae suspected he stopped himself from swearing. "How fast can you and Weile recall your troops?"

The Eastlands were the farthest territory from Béarn, but Tae had anticipated this attack and had instructed his generals appropriately. He latched onto a different part of the question, the one that actually surprised him. His father was supposed to be in Stalmize, the royal city, and he had relinquished any claim to his title or connection to the Eastern army. "Weile?" he pressed carefully.

Griff did not leave Tae in suspense. "He's here in Béarn. Or, at least he was as of a week ago and a few weeks prior as well. He borrowed something from me, went off on some sort of mission, and returned with a representative of a group that calls themselves the Mages of Myrcidë. Chymmerlee is one of them."

Subikahn appeared beside them as if summoned. "Was Saviar with them?"

Griff nodded, "As a matter of fact . . ." He broke into a smile. "He and Weile gave King Humfreet fits, and they brokered a deal between the Renshai and the Paradisians."

Tae's brows shot up. "My, you have been busy!"

Griff shrugged off the impossible. "Despite assurances to the contrary, the feud will likely surface again. Hatred for Renshai is too ingrained in certain societies to let something as trivial as peace get in their way."

Gaze still on his charge, Subikahn nodded vigorously. "So my brother is . . . well?"

Tae and Griff turned their attention to the young Renshai. It seemed like a trifling question amid so many weighty issues. Nevertheless, Griff responded to it. "He seemed so. Weile, too. As far as I know, they're helping the Renshai put the Fields of Wrath back together. I'm afraid I haven't had time to notice. I'm dealing with the elves and the mages now, trying to get them to work with us, and together, to assist against the giants' magic. Given what your father just told me, it would seem my current project has become urgent."

As was often the case, Tae fixated on the oddities rather than the meat of the conversation. He could not help wondering why Subikahn had expected to find Saviar with Weile. Most remarkably, Subikahn had been correct, which suggested he knew something significant he had not discussed with this own father. Now was not the time to wheedle that information out of Subikahn, however.

"Would you like my help?" Tae offered, uncertain what he might add. He knew some Elvish, but not enough to become conversational yet. And many of the elves spoke the human common trading tongue. When it came to sword skill, Béarn had more than its share of Renshai, while Griff and Weile and, probably, Saviar bested him in diplomacy. Tae knew the time constraints better, but as he had been spouting these to little avail since the first war ended, everyone would hear it better from the king of Béarn's mouth than his.

If Griff weighed those same considerations, he did so swiftly. "Thank you, Tae. For now, it's more important for you to muster the armies of the Eastlands and keep her happy." He tipped his head toward Mistri who squirmed in her chair, waiting impatiently for the conversation to finish.

Darris stepped up to the king's side. "Your Majesty, it's time you got back to those negotiations. Even elfin patience is finite."

After his time spent with Captain, the least elflike of the elves, Tae was not so certain Darris was correct; but the need for King Griff's presence in this discussion seemed to have run its course. The massive Béarnide caught Arturo into an embrace, whispered something into his ear, thumped his back with a meaty hand, then lumbered from the room. The others continued their reunion, and Tae did his best to comfort the giant's child in preparation for imminent war.

CHAPTER 26

A Knight of Erythane always chooses the right way, not the easy way.

—Sir Ra-khir Kedrin's son

THE COMMON ROOM of the Knight's Rest Inn seemed particularly quiet, as it had for the past week. Erythane's upscale drinking establishment, frequented by her knights, was never a rowdy, boisterous place, but now it seemed more like a tomb. People conversed quietly at the tables while barmaids slipped around them like ghosts. Kedrin worked his men even harder than usual, and those knights still at the tables looked world-weary and exhausted. Most had already retired for the night, and nearly all the current patrons were merchants.

Ra-khir sat across the table from Tiega, drinking in her beauty with far more enthusiasm than his ale. The Knight's Rest had the best and most expensive food in town, but it all tasted like ash in his mouth. Tiega, however, remained the highlight of his evenings. The long and dirty ride home had done nothing to dull his ardor. Whether windswept, casually tousled or combed to a sheen, her honey-brown hair fell in luxuriant waves around her delicate features. Smudges on her nose and cheeks only made her loveliness realer. The brilliant blue of her eyes drew his gaze away from any imperfections, if they existed. Kevral had also had blue eyes, but they had always appeared steely and strong. Tiega's showed a strange vulnerability that brought out every protective instinct in Ra-khir. They were two very different women. And, yet, the attraction he felt for both was remarkably similar. Once again, and too soon for his liking, he was falling in love.

The timing could not have been worse. Scouts of every variety had fled into the darkness the same day Tae and Matrinka had returned to Béarn, their job to alert the varied peoples of the continent that the next war was essentially upon them. Once again, they needed to mass on Béarn's shores, to set up their supply lines through the high kingdom, to conscript every arm, to hone and bring every weapon. They had less than a month, Tae estimated. And now, only nine days later, Tae announced a single week till doomsday based on objects viewed through a magical box belonging to Captain the elf.

Ra-khir did not realize his head was sagging until Tiega's hand fell onto it, smoothing his hair. "You need sleep, my darling. Why don't you take our room? Keva and I can find a place by the fire."

Though noble, the suggestion was ridiculous. "No, Tiega, there's no need for me to put you and Keva out. If I'm too tired to go home to the Fields of Wrath, I can bunk with one of the other knights. Several of the bachelors live here full-time." Ra-khir did not mention his father. Though close, Kedrin did not seem in the kind of mood that invited anyone, especially his son. Ra-khir could imagine his father drilling him in his sleep.

Not that Ra-khir's own home seemed any more welcoming. The Renshai took battle as seriously as any human could, practicing at all times of the day and night, in every terrain. The chime of steel was constant there, and his sons seemed to relish battles inside the confines of their home, dashing around and over the furniture, in and out the windows. To them, he was just another obstacle to overcome; if he chided them, he found himself drawn into their battle.

The boys conversed gaily of death in combat, which made Ra-khir uncomfortable in a way it never had before. The memory of Kevral's slaying was still fresh and raw, an agony he did not need continuously rekindled. He did not want to lose his sons but knew he probably would or, more likely, they would lose him. Though their enthusiasm and audacity far exceeded his own, so did their skill and training. Though not nearly as brash, the knights followed a code of honor that often resulted in lethal sacrifices. To save others, Ra-khir would not hesitate to die.

Ra-khir lowered his head fully to the tabletop and reveled in Tiega's gentle touch. "I'm sorry I brought you here. To this."

Tiega's hand stilled in his red-blond hair. "Don't talk like that, Ra-khir. It was my choice, mine and Keva's, and I'm happy we made it. If these are my last days, I'm glad to have spent them in your company and with my son. I've always wanted to see the great cities of Béarn and Erythane. If they fall, what chance does a hamlet like Keatoville have?"

Had he more energy, Ra-khir might have argued. It would take the *Kjempemagiska* time to get to all the small Westland villages. Some people might escape and hide, even beyond whatever magic these giants might possess to find them. He kept Tae's stories of their cruelty to their servants to himself. He did not wish to consider the fate that might prove worse for the survivors than those who succumbed to the war. One thing seemed absolutely certain; they could not afford to fail.

"Béarn and Erythane will not fall." Ra-khir attempted to reassure Tiega, though he found it difficult to convince himself. Even if Béarn could call back every army that had assisted with the first war in time to face the *Kjempemagiska*, so many people had already died. Their forces were smaller, even less organized, weary of war, and facing a much greater threat. He only hoped the addition, even reluctantly, of Myrcidians and elves would make the difference. Ra-khir sat up straight and reached a hand across the table. "Béarn and Erythane will always stand strong. We will repel these invaders."

Tiega took his hand, clasping it in both of hers. "Of course, we will. And I'll be nearby, beseeching the gods, lending whatever emotional or physical support you and the others need."

Ra-khir managed a smile. "I know you will, and thoughts of you will guide my lance, speed my sword, and serve as an anchor of comfort in the best and worst of times."

"I love you, Ra-khir," Tiega whispered so softly, he was not entirely sure he heard her. But the words that followed were clear, "Come back to me, my love. Alive and well."

"I'll do my best." Ra-khir stopped short of a promise and avoided the one topic he knew might destroy her. This time, they would need every man. Darby would be joining the war.

Queen Matrinka wound through a dining hall packed with elves and humans, flashing back nearly two decades to the time when many of these same elves had gathered to whisk her friends from world to world, seeking the pieces of the once-shattered Pica Stone. Now, the enormous sapphire glowed a fiery blue on the center table while the oldest of the elves ran his hands over its sleek surface.

Servants scurried through the masses, bringing food and drink for the busy elves, who mostly ignored it, gathering and sorting weapons across the many tables. These ran the gamut from finely worked broadswords to Béarnian spears to arrowheads of myriad shapes and sizes. The Renshai swords occupied a table to themselves, toward the center of the room and nearest the Pica Stone, surrounded by anxious warriors of both genders who would sooner leave their eyes than their weapons. No one dared to touch these, not even the elves who stood with heads lowered and hands raised, chanting in dull monotones that seemed more vibration than sound.

A few of the elves, including Captain, uttered harsh strings of syllables in a language even Tae Kahn could not master, filled with diphthongs, ululations, guttural stops, and other sounds that seemed impossible for human mouths and throats to form. Many of the words incorporated letters that did not exist, blends that should not, and a tone that simulated waves crashing onto rocks, wind through summer leaves, or the wavering cries of insects and animals in the night. She knew the name for the background noises that strengthened the spells: *jovinay arythanik*, a combining of elfin magical strength to enhance the magic of one.

A dozen Myrcidians sat in one corner of the room, watching with an intensity that seemed almost painful. They were like statues, so focused on the ritual unfolding in front of them, and Matrinka could not even catch them blinking. The oldest looked as if he might collapse into dust.

The idea of exposing their weapons to waves of elfin

magic had seemed logical and necessary. In the first war, they had faced a single *Kjempemagiska*, and most of their weapons had bounced harmlessly from its clothing and its flesh. Since the day Matrinka and her friends had faced their first demon, a being formed of raw chaos, she had learned that plain steel could not harm magical beings. When imbued with magic, however, weapons affected such targets as they normally did. Unfortunately, few items imbued with magic existed.

Spotting Tae at a small table in a dark corner, Matrinka headed toward him. He appeared to be sitting alone, which surprised her. She could not remember the last time Imorelda had allowed him out of her sight. Winding between the rows of tables and chanting elves, careful not to nudge them and risk ruining the magic, Matrinka approached Tae. "Mind if I join you?"

Rising, Tae gestured toward a chair across from him, and Matrinka perched on it. She leaned across the table. "I never expected to find you here." Not wanting to suggest he did not belong, she added hastily, "Though I'm glad to find a friendly face, especially yours. Nothing seems right or normal anymore."

Tae grinned. "Well, if it's right and normal you're looking for, you've come to the wrong person."

Matrinka chuckled. It felt good to laugh.

"Mistri's napping, and I arranged a meal fit for a visiting princess for Imorelda."

Matrinka nodded, appreciating the information. "She deserves it, Tae. She's worked very hard."

"For a cat." Tae glanced around furtively, clearly not fully comfortable talking about the situation in a room full of others, even if no one could overhear them.

Matrinka changed the subject to one that had worried her since she had learned of the project. "Do you think this is the right way to handle this?" She made a broad gesture to indicate the elfin magic. "Wouldn't it make more sense to try to place spells on each weapon to make sure it takes? Even if they couldn't get to quite as many, in the hands of the best warriors, they should prove far more devastating."

"It's not that simple," Tae took the time to explain what Griff had not. "Remember our conversation with Captain? The elves aren't actually imbuing the magic into the weapons because they don't have the power or capacity to do that. To my knowledge, the Pica Stone is the only surviving true magical item."

A male voice floated from the close darkness. "That is . . . incorrect."

Startled, Matrinka leaped to her feet. It was all she could do not to skitter away from the table. Only then, she noticed Weile Kahn and his two ever-attendant bodyguards in the farthest part of the corner. "H-how long have you been there?"

Weile rose and bowed. "Since before you arrived, Your Majesty." The bodyguards did not speak. Nor did they stand.

Matrinka hated formality. It slowed down the conversation and made people far too careful. "Just call me Matrinka, please. Tae and I are like sister and brother."

Weile tipped his head. "Which would make me . . . your father? I'd be honored."

Matrinka sat down again, and Weile followed suit. "If you don't mind three more grandchildren, I'll take you up on the offer. My father died years ago."

"Yes," Weile said. Matrinka doubted there was much history Tae's father did not already know. "Midgard has the Pica Stone, the Sword of Mitrian, the ship of the elfin Captain, and the ruins of the dwellings of the four Cardinal Mages."

Matrinka blinked. It took her a moment to realize he had returned to the previous conversation.

Tae caught on more quickly. "According to Captain, the *Sea Skimmer* contains only trace, not true, magic like the Pica. The Sword of Mitrian is stripped. Even if we could find where the Cardinal Wizards used to have their homes, those places now have cities built on them or have languished into dust and forest."

Weile shook his head. "At least one of the Cardinal Wizard's homes is still in use."

Suddenly, Weile had their full attention. Matrinka worried the secretive man might end the discussion there; people who spouted everything they knew at every opportunity could not maintain the air of superiority and mystery that Weile did.

However, Weile continued without hesitation, "The

Myrcidians built their communal living place on top of the ancient ruins of the Western Wizard's abode, and it still contains some powerful magic."

Matrinka wanted more, but Tae seemed unconvinced. "How could you possibly know that?"

Weile shrugged, as if he had spoken common knowledge. "I'd tell you to ask your son, but he's sworn to secrecy."

"And yet," Tae pointed out, "he told you. And you've not been discreet at all."

Weile chuckled. "Subikahn is sworn to secrecy, not me. He gave me just enough information to figure things out on my own. He knows I can't resist a puzzle."

Matrinka was appalled, "Are you saying Subikahn broke a vow of honor?"

Tae studied her as if she had gone mad. "Are you mistaking Subikahn for Ra-khir?"

Weile's point was gentler, "His brother's sanity and life were in danger. In those circumstances, I believe most decent people would make the same choice." He pinned her with his dark stare. "Most especially you, Matrinka."

Though a bit taken aback, Matrinka considered and realized the truth. If the life of one of her children hung in the balance, she would break a vow to strangers in an instant. "You're right, of course."

Weile grinned evilly. "I never tire of hearing that."

Matrinka had not received an answer to her original question. "I still don't understand what the purpose of all this is." She made a broad gesture to encompass the entire room. "Don't we have better ways to prepare for battle?"

Tae pointed out the obvious. "It's not as if this is the only thing we're doing. We have armies massing near the docks and on the beaches, and battleships readying for the arrival of the *Kjempemagiska*. Scouts have scattered everywhere, recalling warriors and armies, sending out the word, and watching for spies and trickery, crafting the best lines for supplies. The Eastlands, for example, has much to contribute once our fighting men reach Béarn. Again."

Matrinka waved him off. She had attended enough meetings with Griff to understand all of that. "But surely we can do something more significant with our only magical beings. Something more . . . preparatory."

Tae sighed deeply, and Matrinka suddenly thought that

he considered her foolish. "The problem, as I understand it, is that elfin magic is . . . mostly peaceful. Almost, well, frivolous."

Matrinka appreciated that he seemed to understand her frustration. "We're not asking for explosions, are we? I mean, couldn't they . . ." She searched her imagination. ". . . make the beaches slippery?"

"To what end?" Tae easily found the flaw. "That would impede us as much or more than the giants who probably have magic that would allow them to counteract it. Imagine them hovering over the battlefield while our troops are desperately trying to wield swords while they're slipping and sliding."

"Not if we stay off the beach."

Tae shook his head. "A battle of distance would not be in our best interests. Magic travels farther than sword strokes. If we rely solely on bowmen, we're at a distinct disadvantage. Not only are their arrows superior to ours, they're sure to have spells that outrange us, and we will, eventually, run out of ammunition. Also, magic can affect large swaths compared to our one-at-a-time bolts and arrows."

Matrinka had another idea. "What if we were the ones flying?"

Tae nodded. "The elves could, almost certainly, do that. But how many warriors do you know who could handle aerial combat? Especially with only a week or two of training."

"Some of the Renshai, maybe?"

Tae shrugged. "I don't think so. The Renshai maneuvers rely too much on quickness and split-second timing to work without a single foot on the ground. It seems safer to rely on familiarity."

Matrinka felt certain the elves could come up with something useful. "What about changing the terrain only as the giants step on it?"

"Maybe," Tae returned. "However, the small amount of experience we have suggests we can better use our limited magical access to tie up the *Kjempemagiska*'s war magic, which requires the elves to work as a cohesive group. That would limit the giants to mundane tactics familiar to our soldiers and generals."

Matrinka saw the obvious flaw. "Except we can't possibly win in regular hand-to-hand combat. Even if we have superior numbers, and that's not certain . . ."

"That *is* certain."

Matrinka studied Tae.

"We know they're overpopulated, but the descriptions provided by Mistri and Arturo don't suggest they're to the point of literally living on top of one another. You've seen the size of their island. It's big, but only a twentieth the size of our continent at best."

Matrinka knew Tae was not stupid, but he seemed to be missing something obvious. "True, but it's not as if we're standing on top of one another, either. There's plenty of space between most of our cities and still more forests than inhabited areas overall."

"Maybe."

"And we won't manage to gather every male on the continent in time for the war."

"Yes," Tae agreed. Then he continued, "But we certainly cover far more than a twentieth of the land here. And we're much smaller, so we can fit a lot more of us in the same area without noticing it. I'm willing to bet we'll outnumber the *Kjempemagiska* a hundred to one on the battlefield."

Matrinka bobbed her head, realizing she had gotten sidetracked again. "Fine. Even if we have superior numbers, our weapons can't harm the giants. So what's the point of close fighting?"

Tae mimicked Matrinka's gesture, indicating the entire room. "That's what we're trying to rectify, Matrinka."

Matrinka felt as if the argument had come full circle. "But, Tae, isn't that exactly the problem? We know elves don't have the power to make objects magical one by one. How can they possibly do it with a whole bunch of weapons all at the same time?"

Tae tossed his head, then laughed. "I guess I thought you already knew this part. Otherwise, we could have avoided a lot of words when you first asked the questions."

Matrinka put her chin in her hands and leaned toward Tae to express her full interest in whatever he had to say.

Tae obliged. "We know that the few true magical items in the world can harm Outworlders. For example, Thor's hammer could flatten the *Kjempemagiska*, demons, and elves. When Colbey wielded the Sword of Balance, legend states the gods themselves ran scared." Tae's eyes narrowed. "Don't you remember Captain's treatise after I had scouted the *Kjempemagiska* warship and brought back the rope and the knives?"

Matrinka recalled having a conversation on the *Sea Skimmer*, filled with strange elfin terms, but the details had not stuck with her. "Vaguely."

Tae refreshed her memory. "Objects prized by and long-exposed to creatures of chaos gain some minor magical properties the elves call *skyggefrodleikr* or shadow magic. For example, Kevral's sword, previously wielded by Colbey, could cleave demons. In Calistin's hands, that same sword killed the only *Kjempemagiska* we faced in the last war. We have a few weapons we already know are effective against Outworlders. There's Saviar's sword, used for centuries by an *Einherjar* in Valhalla; Rantire's sword, given to her by Ravn; the six utility knives I acquired, and Valr Magnus' weapon, also previously Colbey Calistinsson's. They weren't deliberately given magic. They acquired it through sacrifice and exposure."

Finally, Matrinka understood. "So, the hope is, if we pummel our weapons with random elfin magic, they may get enough exposure in a short time to acquire the magical properties that usually require . . . much longer exposure."

Tae bobbed his head with a taut grin. "Basically. It's a little more complicated than that, I'm told. Captain also mentioned *reipfrodleikr*, trace magic." He gave Matrinka a sideways glance.

Though uncertain what her friend wished to convey, Matrinka realized his explanation had jogged her memory. Captain had said this "trace magic" was a side effect of his specialty, which if she remembered correctly, was adding magical strength to structures. She nodded. "That's right. I remember." She tried to put it all together. "That's a little more active and deliberate than shadow magic, but it's not . . ." She did not know how to finish. ". . . real and permanent?"

Encouraged, Tae finished, "As I picture it, probably badly, it's kind of like soaking our weapons in a magical bath. It's not random, though. They're emphasizing the type of magic that strengthens solid objects."

Matrinka had to ask, though she knew she might not like the answer. "What do the elves think about this? Do they believe it will work?"

"Cautiously optimistic."

Matrinka pressed. "Meaning specifically?"

"They don't know." Tae leaned back in his chair. "Captain hopes the magic will stay on the blades for a couple of weeks, long enough to fight the war before it dissipates. It's apparently futile to hope for anything more."

"Except," Matrinka started, "couldn't we just have the elves hand out their personal weapons? They've been exposed to elves every day, so shouldn't they have the same properties as the giants' rope-cutting blades?"

"Weapons?" Tae asked mildly, brows cocked. "Elves?"

"Not a single weapon?" Matrinka had spent enough time chatting with Tem'aree'ay to know Tae spoke truth. "What about utility knives?"

"They don't build," Tae reminded. "They come from a world without weather, and they're impervious to cold."

Matrinka grasped for straws. "What about the trees on Elves' Island? They've been long-exposed to magic. Maybe if we carved out clubs . . ."

Tae laughed. "Even true magical items don't retain their properties if their shape and intention is altered." He added quickly, "Or so I'm told."

Matrinka realized others had clearly given the situation at least as much consideration as she had. They were all equally desperate. "Well, then. I suppose this really is the best the elves can do."

Weile finally spoke again, and Matrinka stiffened. She idly wondered how she could possibly have forgotten him a second time. "I'd rather say it's the best the elves are willing to do."

That seized Matrinka's attention, and she could not help staring at Tae's father. His swarthy skin and black hair helped him blend into the darkness of the corner, and the whites of his eyes contrasted starkly with irises that seemed merely an extension of his pupils. "You think they can do more?"

"Probably not, but I can't help wondering. As Outworlders themselves, they have everything to fear from weapons that can strike creatures of magic. Especially in the hands of humans."

The words sparked outrage. Matrinka leaped to her feet. "We would never harm them. They have to know that."

Tae waved at her to sit.

Weile looked blandly amused by Matrinka's outburst. "Even if they believe it, they know how short-lived we are compared to them. They have no way to extract promises from our unborn grandchildren and great-grandchildren. Once armed, we will not be easily disarmed."

Agitated, Matrinka remained standing. It pained her to believe the elves hesitated to trust them. "What if we drew up some sort of treaty?"

Tae rolled his eyes. "Matrinka, if the elves are really holding back because they don't trust us, no piece of paper will make any difference." He turned a stormy glare on his father. "But I don't believe that's what's happening. And even if it were, what could we possibly do about it? A week ago, the elves refused to assist us at all. How can we complain about how they choose to do so now?"

Tae was right, of course. Desperation could not allow them to appear ungrateful at the risk of losing the magical support they had won only with great effort. The negotiating between Béarn and the elves, Béarn and the Myrcidians, had gone on behind doors closed even to Matrinka. She had no idea of the true cost of their allegiance, but their magic had become priceless and they could have asked for nearly anything. She made a mental note to demand the information from her husband, then put the idea aside. She was not at all certain she wanted to know.

CHAPTER 27

Your enemies will not give you quarter for weakness, and the worst of them will target those most-vulnerable moments.

— *Kyntiri, a Renshai torke*

ALONE IN A TINY, seldom-used study on Béarn Castle's highest floor, Barrindar and Marisole clutched one another tightly, fiercely, jealously. They sat on the floor; piece by piece, the furniture that had once filled this room had been plundered by family members to replace older, more put-upon furnishings. Marisole, herself, had scooted out the last plush chair a year ago to place it into her own room in front of her dressing table. Nothing remained but four gray walls and a plush carpet spanning the entire floor. Woven from the sheared hair of Eastern fiber goats, it had a luxurious texture finer than anything manufactured in the West. And, though more than several years old, it still maintained the faint hint of exotic spices that had traveled in the same merchant's wagon.

Over the last several months, this room had become the young lovers' favorite place. Here they sat for hours in the warm beam of sunlight streaming through the only window, fingers entwined, talking about their likes and dislikes, complaints and triumphs, their hopes and dreams for the future. Sometimes, they could catch only a few minutes between lessons and practices: him with weapons and politics, her with music, and both with academics. Marisole was the only female who attended sword training by the Béarnian masters, and they granted her no quarter. Many times, the two had compared bruises or nursed sore muscles in the deep pile and softness of the carpet.

Now clenched in Barrindar's strong embrace, Marisole felt whole for the first time in many months. She had missed him terribly during her journey to visit the elves, her dreams of him starry. Often, she had found her hand drifting habitually toward one of her male companions, only to remember she was far from home and the one hand she wished to hold. She had worried her absence would grant him the opportunity to find a younger woman to love. Given time alone to think, he might consider the couple of years between her birth and his. More likely, he would realize the folly of their forbidden pairing. To the populace, they were brother and sister, though only distant cousins by blood. Béarnian law strictly regulated who heirs to the throne could marry.

"Kiss me," Marisole said.

Barrindar happily complied, his lips and tongue as eager as her own. His mouth tasted of honey bread and grapes; his arms gripped her protectively. Against her thigh, she could feel the first stirrings of his arousal, and a fire grew in her own loins. She wanted him, every part and thought and mood of him. Gripping his firm, warrior's buttocks in both hands, she pulled him even more tightly against her.

Barrindar grunted into her mouth. He released the kiss long enough to say, "Stop, Marisole. If you don't, I'll—" He seemed suddenly incapable of finishing the thought.

Marisole laughed sweetly. "You'll what, Barri? Rape me?"

Barrinadar disengaged completely, a look of horror etched on his features. "You know I couldn't harm a hair on your beautiful head."

Marisole refused to let him go. "But I want it, Barrindar. I want you more than anything in my life." She added in a small voice that sounded more frightened than she intended, "How can I have found the match to my very soul and still die a virgin?"

"You're not going to die, Marisole." Barrindar clearly tried to sound certain, but under the circumstances no one could. Barrindar intended to fight beneath Béarn's banner, assuming King Griff would allow another young prince to risk his life at war. His life was more at stake than Marisole's, but he could not honestly declare her safe. Based on the actions of their servants, if the giants won the war, they would slaughter every human, no matter their age or gender.

"No one is safe," Marisole pointed out, drawing him close again. "Especially the royal line of Béarn." She gazed into dark eyes radiating warmth and intelligence. "Do you want to die a virgin?"

Barrindar managed a laugh. "No man does. But I'd rather die a virgin than sleep with any woman who isn't you. I love you, Marisole. I always will."

His words were as sweet as any music in Marisole's ears. "I love you, too, Barri. That's why I want to surrender my virginity . . . to you and only you."

Barrindar closed his eyes. "We can't, Marisole. You know we can't. If we're caught . . ."

Marisole's longing had become desperate need. She whispered, "Who's going to catch us?"

"But what if we . . . ?"

When Barrindar did not complete the thought, Marisole tried to. ". . . enjoy it? . . . hate it? . . . make too much noise?"

"No." Barrindar stopped her with a finger to her lips. "What if we . . . make a baby? You promised your mother we wouldn't do that, we'd be careful."

Marisole kissed him again, slowly and tenderly. She could feel him stirring again. Whatever his doubts, his body wanted hers. "We're both virgins, right?" She paused a moment, suddenly worried he had not told her something.

Barrindar did not hesitate. "Yes, Marisole. Of course."

"Well, everyone knows two virgins can't make a baby."

Barrindar tipped his head and studied her in the beam of sunlight. "I . . . didn't know that." He acquired a hungry look that only made Marisole adore him more.

In the entirety of her life, Marisole could not imagine loving anyone as much as she did Barrindar, with such raw and real intensity. He was her world, her life, her every desire lay with him. And she suddenly knew, without need to question, he was the rightful heir to Béarn's throne. They would remain together forever, her protecting him and him her, as the gods ordained.

Unless the war killed them first.

A chill wind blew across the castle rooftop. Miserably huddled in her cloak, Matrinka allowed her gaze to sweep the Béarnian beaches, once again swarming with warriors in patches that revealed their origins. She easily picked out the blue-and-gold flags and uniforms of Béarn as well as the black-and-orange banners of Erythane. She found the aqua and bronze of the Northman's Aeri, led by the famed and formidable General Valr Magnus. He had remained at the service of Béarn even after the other Northmen had gone home, accompanying Marisole, Ra-khir, and others on their quest to convince the elves to assist. At his call, his men had been among the first to arrive, disheveled and wearied by their fast march but immediately prepared to serve him.

Matrinka picked out other continental armies, including the famed silver and green of the Northern high kingdom of Nordmir, a contingent from the Eastlands bearing black and gold, and others in colors she did not recognize. These were mixed with bands of disorganized farmers in well-worn homespun, citizens of every variety in street clothes and clutching trade tools or rusty weapons, and several banded groups from various Western towns, most of whom comprised town guards or vigilantes lovingly wearing the retired weapons, shields and, occasionally, armor of their forebears.

As always, the Renshai chose a position front and center. Like most of the peasant classes, they sported no armor or helmets, no shields or even jewelry that might accidentally foil a blow. They neither bore nor wore any colors to define them, fought under no banners, and their functional garb spanned the rainbow and beyond. They did not even have an obvious leader. Unlike the other units, which contained no female warriors Matrinka could spot, the Renshai had about equal numbers of each gender. And, of course, every one carried a sword or two and no other visible weapons.

As with the last war, for the most part, the archers took the lead, the infantry at their heels, and the cavalry behind the beachhead. The strategy had worked well during the last war, and it seemed foolish to change it, especially since not a single member of the enemy forces had escaped alive to report it to superiors. Of course, this was a very different type of war, Matrinka realized, and multiple reminders of it accompanied her on the roof.

In one corner, Mistri, Tae, and Imorelda crouched in apparent silence, carrying on a mental conversation she longed to hear, if only to have catspeak, once again, in her mind. Some twenty-five or thirty elves joined them, appearing almost human except for a propensity toward fragility, lean angularity, and reddish highlights, their eyes slanted and colored like gemstones. Silent as ghosts, they took their unobtrusive places around her and did not even whisper amongst themselves. Matrinka suspected they communicated regularly with one another, using direct *khohlar* so no one else could hear them. Accustomed to that form of communication, they gave no outward sign, not even a gesture or twitch, an eye roll, a look toward the recipient of their mental language.

Griff stood in the middle of it all, surveying the battlefield, his hands clasped and his brow furrowed. He also did not speak, his head low, studying the battlefield until he must have memorized every detail. Like Matrinka, he clearly despised the danger into which he placed so many lives, yet he could do nothing other than to try to play the game with cunning and logic. Experienced generals and their appointed captains and lieutenants commanded those armies. Griff could do nothing useful from the front. He had learned strategy but never warcraft due to a sheltered upbringing as a farmer's stepson in the shadow of his father's death. And the combined forces needed his guileless wisdom and neutrality alive and intact as long as possible to keep their world from shattering.

Matrinka appreciated that all of the princesses and princes of Béarn were safely installed on the upper floor of Béarn Castle instructed to go nowhere else other than the rooftop. Arturo had argued he belonged on the battle lines, only to be rebuffed by the healers who proclaimed him medically unstable. He had aspired to become a naval commander before fate had intervened.

Barrindar had not progressed far enough in his weapons training. Though he tried hard to focus and learn, even putting in additional time, he had no natural grace or talent. A much better swordsman, Marisole was trained specifically as a bodyguard, and she felt duty-bound to remain with the other heirs of Béarn, watching over them as the curse demanded while Darris attended the king. No one expected her to answer to any general.

Matrinka recognized other things separating this war from the previous one. Friendly warships prowled the shore, some Béarnian, others the dragon-prowed creations of the Northmen, a few from other Western countries and even one single-masted Eastern craft that appeared clunky and out-of-place. Goods and services tended to move in a westerly direction, and overland travel worked better for the Eastlanders.

Though she could not spot them, Matrinka also knew several more elves had secreted themselves on either side of the beachhead, beyond the armies, along with the dozen Myrcidians who had agreed to help. Those had argued bitterly with the elves regarding the safety and security of various positions before finally, reluctantly, agreeing to the current arrangement.

Matrinka understood the first stage of the plan. Using his Box of Farseeing, and probably some additional magic, Captain had pinpointed the arrival of the enemy ships to this day. The first line of the continent's defense involved the warships, and Matrinka found her gaze repeatedly drawn to the ocean. She had overheard one of the Béarnian captains telling her husband that the western winds, blowing toward the east, gave the enemy a decided advantage in naval warfare. It would speed their arrows and obviate the need to shoot against nature. Matrinka wondered whether chance or the gods favored the giants, or if the *Kjempemagiska* controlled the direction of the wind through magic.

Thinking of Ra-khir and Darby, Matrinka searched for the Knights of Erythane, finding them among the cavalry flanking the Erythanian army. Even from this great distance, she recognized the knights as a group, resplendent, precision in their every movement, their white steeds like beacons amid the many browns, chestnuts, and bays.

Another gust of wind tore down Matrinka's hood, spilling her coarse black hair and sending it flying in tendrils. She grasped for the errant fabric with both hands, hauling the hood back over her head with such force it shadowed her face, momentarily blinding her. Bleak thoughts emerged in this manufactured darkness. The seething mass of humanity on the beach disappeared from her sight, and she could only see them, still and lifeless on scarlet-stained sand. Of the thousands of warriors, how many would return to their families intact? How many would have families to return to?

Suddenly driven to gather her friends and children close, Matrinka resisted the urge. Even if she could find them all amid the preparations, she had no right to do so. Everyone made sacrifices, even the queen of Béarn, and she would only be interfering with the strategies and tactics of generals far more skilled than herself. In a war of this type, there was no real safety, neither for the soldiers nor the civilians. For all their size and strength, the *Kjempemagiska*'s most formidable weapon was their magic, and that was still mostly unknown. A single giant might have the power to take down Béarn Castle with an incantation, sending those atop her tumbling helplessly through the air to die on the shattered remnants of her stonework.

Once in Matrinka's mind, the idea would not be banished. Repeatedly, she imagined herself falling, screaming, entangled with the bodies of elves and heirs, buffeted by hunks of granite, landing with skull-shattering force on the rubble of the once great castle and knowing nothing more. Flicking the cloth from her eyes, she looked upon the massed armies once more, reveling in their movements, in every indication they still lived. She plucked individuals from among the groups: this one pacing, that one resting, another addressing his troops. Every one represented a human being loved by a mother, a wife, a child. So many would not come home. *If they even have homes to come back to.*

Matrinka despised herself for nearly falling prey to despair. She had to believe they would win because, to do otherwise meant surrendering to hopelessness. To survive, they had to keep morale up, to find every positive in a bleak situation. In that, at least, she could play a role. So long as they believed in the possibility of victory, it still existed; and she could keep her mind, and others', busy finding fresh ideas and solutions. No matter how low she felt, no matter how much the images dizzied her, she had to at least pretend to believe the continent would triumph, even in her darkest hours. Not because their survival was an inevitable gift of the gods, but because they had the strength and cleverness to make it happen.

Matrinka's thoughts did not buoy her, but she knew they would in time, if she forced her focus onto them. Whether or not she succeeded in steeling her own resolve, she promised to maintain this aura of positive assurance. If it helped just one other, allowed him or her to find the path to enlightenment, it was worth any amount of effort. With this in mind, she turned to face Griff, only to find him in frenzied conversation with Weile Kahn. She had not seen Tae's father arrive, nor heard the trapdoor open to admit him, and could not help wondering if he had the same strange and dangerous habit of clambering up walls as his son.

However Weile Kahn had arrived, Griff appeared agitated by their conversation. His hands flailed wildly, his usually friendly features oddly grim. Matrinka headed toward them. Then, Weile pointed suddenly toward the ocean, and she stopped dead in her tracks to look.

A horde of enormous ships streamed toward them. Matrinka had seen them before, through Captain's device on the *Sea Skimmer*, but that had scarcely prepared her for their size and breadth. Though nearer to shore and with the benefit of perspective, the continental ships looked like toys compared to the massive objects floating toward them. When she had last seen the *Kjempemagiska* warships, the sails were furled and the triple masts rose like skeletal arms beseeching the sky. Now, they held sheets dyed a deep purple-red. At the center of each one, someone had painted a creature Matrinka could not recognize, at least from that distance. It appeared furry and compact, patchy black and white or gray.

Griff dashed to the edge of the roof, Weile at his heels. For one sickening moment, Matrinka thought he might forget to stop, charging into empty air and falling to his death on the crags below. But Griff halted a safe distance from the edge, a hand shielding his eyes from the sun, the wind tearing at his hair, beard, and cloak. Far below, the armies fell into alert ranks as, one by one, the commanders saw or received word of the impending battle.

The elves edged forward, just far enough to gain an unimpeded look at the Western Sea and the troops massing on

Béarn's beach. The world went oddly still, as if everyone had stopped breathing simultaneously. Then, a hint of dizziness touched Matrinka's senses and she realized she, at least, had done so. She forced herself to suck in a deep breath. She could not afford to turn lightheaded or stagger while she stood on the palace roof.

Moments dragged into hours, or so it seemed to Matrinka, as the massive ships glided toward the shore and the lined-up warships belonging to the continent. Smaller and more streamlined, the Northern ships had superior maneuverability. These could have easily left the Béarnian ships behind to engage the enemy first, but they did not. They joined the ranks of the larger warships, waiting for the giants to arrive.

Finally, they drew within range of one another's arrows. By then, Matrinka's heart was hammering; she had expected some grand magical display by the *Kjempemagiska*, something that would blow the Béarnian warships sky high or render them into matchsticks in a moment. But nothing of that sort happened. She could scarcely see the volley of arrows arching from their own ships, made visible only because several of them were flaming. These appeared to land on the lead ship of the invaders.

For a moment, nothing happened. Uncertain what to expect, Matrinka found herself holding her breath again. A myriad of thoughts flooded her mind. Perhaps the enemy ships also required magical weapons to strike them, and the continental arrows bounced off like so many harmless twigs. Perhaps some magical shield sent the arrows flinging back toward their archers or, maybe, deflected them harmlessly into the sea. Then, just as Matrinka thought nothing at all would happen, the lead ship of the *Kjempemagiska* disappeared. More arrows flew, and two more massive warships winked out as if they had never existed.

As one, the elves gasped.

"What!" the king shouted. Matrinka could not recall the last time she had seen him so agitated. He whirled suddenly on the elves. "What just happened? What did I see?" His gaze sought Captain among the others. "Did those ships just turn transparent?"

Captain stared out over the scene, yellow eyes flashing. "No, Sire. They're not invisible; they're gone."

"How?" Griff demanded. He spun back toward the ocean. Several more of the giants' ships had disappeared. "Where are they going?"

Captain turned toward the other elves, but no one said anything aloud. "They're not going anywhere, Your Majesty. They never existed. These ships . . . aren't real. They're illusions."

"Illusions," Griff repeated.

"To fool us, Majesty. They have no other purpose."

Once again, Griff whirled to face the elf. "Can they harm us?"

"No," Captain assured him. "No matter how real they appear, they have no corporeal form, nothing legitimate or solid. The moment something unnatural touches them, the magic breaks and the image dissipates." He pointed at them. "Watch."

"It's a trick, Your Majesty," Weile said suddenly. "The real ships docked near the twin cities. As we speak, the enemy is overtaking Corpa Schaul and Frist."

Griff released a moan of deep pain. Matrinka suddenly realized Weile had come specifically to bring news of the attack on the twin cities. That was, most likely, what he had been discussing with Griff when the illusory ships arrived. She bit her lip to keep from shouting what the men already knew. Unless they did something quick and desperate, Frist and Corpa Schaul would fall. Any troops they had were currently in Béarn, leaving their civilians and, perhaps, a skeletal force that had no hope against the advance of an army.

Images sprang into Matrinka's mind, women and children pleading for their lives, then chopped to pieces, their bodies strewn through city streets like broken toys. She pictured the faces of loved ones: her children, her lover, her friends. Fires consuming the once-great cities of the continent. Giants crushing homes and shops and parks beneath their massive feet, kicking aside bloody, half-charred bodies with stoved-in faces and empty eye sockets. Tears flooded Matrinka's eyes. "We have to save them! We have to get there!"

Griff said nothing; it would not do for the great king of Béarn to become desperate or sob like a child.

Weile said softly, "It's too late for the twin cities, but we may still save the rest of the world."

When Griff finally spoke, he addressed Captain again. "Can you move us there quickly?"

"No, Sire." Captain shook his head while the other elves looked on in silence. "We would need at least a couple of elves at the arrival spot, and those could only travel by conventional means. Even then, to open the way would take extensive magic that would surely draw the full attention of the *Kjempemagiska* and put every elfin life at simultaneous risk. Your men would also be entirely vulnerable as they emerged from the portal."

Matrinka glanced toward the ocean. As the illusory ships drew nearer, she could imagine the captains of the continental ships desperately preparing for ramming. "Captain, can your *khohlar* reach the ships?"

Captain's gaze flicked to Matrinka. "The beach, at least, Your Majesty."

Griff caught on. "Tell them about the ships, Captain, please."

The call went out immediately, *These enemy ships aren't real; they can't hurt you. When they touch you, they'll vanish.* He looked at Griff. "Good, Sire?"

Griff looked out to sea. The first of the giant's ships reached the Béarnian warships and disappeared in a rain of arrows. "Tell them to conserve their ammunition but stay alert." He paused. "Wait. Is it possible some of those ships are real?"

Elfin heads bobbed; but, standing in front of them, Captain was not in a position to see them. "It's not *im*possible, Your Majesty." He grew notably thoughtful, canted eyes narrowing, a finger stroking his cheek.

Matrinka expected more and, from their silence, she knew the men around her did as well. When Captain said nothing further, Griff prodded, "Would there be some way to tell real from illusion?"

"With magic? Easily. But it would waste some energy better used for other things."

Matrinka understood the details beyond Captain's point. Strictly by body count, they outnumbered the *Kjempemagiska*, probably a hundred-to-one according to Tae. However, when it came to magic, the giants were all able to use it, while the defenders were limited to fewer than seventy elves and twelve Myrcidians. They could not squander a bit. "What about by sight?"

Captain had an answer for that as well. "An experienced seaman might notice something. Whoever created the illusionary ships couldn't account for all the subtleties of the weather. If someone with sea eyes studied the flotilla, they might see tiny differences that could reveal an imposter hidden among them. It's even possible someone has to remain nearby to keep the illusion alive, which would necessitate one actual ship or, at least, someone hidden on the beach."

A shiver racked Matrinka at the thought a giant magician might have sneaked into Béarnian territory without notice.

"Possible?" Griff pressed. "Or necessary?"

Captain lifted his lithe shoulders, then dropped them. "I couldn't say, Sire. We would need to do that, but the *Kjempemagiska* may not. It depends on how their magic works."

Weile sighed. "Doesn't magic have any rules that apply to everyone?"

It was clearly a rhetorical question, but Captain took it literally. "Of course, but you have to keep in mind the basis of magic is chaos. Or, rather, the harnessing of it. And the gods emphasized different aspects for their own creations. We are what Frey made us."

Now was not the time for lectures on gods and creation. As the images of crumpled bodies and rivers of blood descended on Matrinka again, she reminded softly, "The longer we take, the more lives are lost."

That galvanized Griff. "Captain, please inform the men of the possibility of a real ship and also what to look for. I'm going to gather the generals. We need to quickly mobilize the armies." He headed toward the trapdoor opening into the castle.

Weile caught up to him in two quick strides. "Your Majesty, I have another idea, if you'll indulge me."

Griff nodded as he walked. Matrinka chased after them, needing to hear what they said. Likely, they would leave her behind; the more knowledge she had, the better she could assist in preventing panic, in keeping the kingdom and its most vulnerable citizens safe.

Weile glanced at her but continued speaking. "We'll need a battlefield. It's best to pick somewhere between Béarn and the twin cities."

Griff did not speculate but gestured for the Easterner to continue as Darris trotted ahead and reached for the latch.

Weile continued, "My men and I move a lot faster than any army." He did not have to demonstrate; his ability to bring Griff knowledge of the battle quicker than Corpa Schaul could send a messenger spoke volumes. "We can empty the towns and cities next in line for attack, especially Pudar, lead the nonmilitary citizenry away and toward the East. We can slow the giants with traps and trickery, steer them toward your chosen site of battle without them even knowing it."

Griff made a noise of consideration. "What's to stop them from chasing the women and children? From destroying the empty villages?"

"Nothing," Weile admitted, "but I don't think they will."

Darris stopped with the hatch partway open. Weile had his attention as well.

"Smashing buildings takes unnecessary time and effort they can't afford to waste. They're probably relying on the fact that we're not expecting them to come overland. They might even have managed to flank our armies before we knew they were coming, if not for my . . . sources. But even if the giants didn't expect to catch us unaware, they don't want to give us any extra time to prepare. Once they've defeated our front line combat troops, they figure they can wipe out whoever remains with relative ease."

Darris threw open the hatchway, and the men funneled through it. The moment they did, Captain sent the promised mental message to everyone, followed by a request. *Please let us know how the generals choose to handle this.*

Griff could not reply by the same means; only elves used *khohlar*. Matrinka suggested in his stead, "Captain, you or any representative you choose is welcome to join the meeting. We must keep the elves informed."

A moment later, the head of a young page appeared through the trapdoor. "Lord elf, King Griff has requested you attend the General's meeting."

In less horrific circumstances, Matrinka would have laughed. She watched Captain hurry toward the young man, disappear through the opening, and let the panel fall behind him. A gust stole her hood again, and the wind blasted through her ears, sharply painful. Out on the vast, sapphire expanse of the Western Ocean, illusory ships popped and disappeared like wayward bubbles.

CHAPTER 28

The best defense is a dead enemy.
—*Calistin Ra-khirsson*

WIND RIFFLED THE WILD GRASSES of the empty
prairie adjacent to the Bellenet Fields of Erythane, where
the Knights of Erythane held their jousts and practices. A
haven to Saviar in his youth, the land now felt tainted by the
heavy threat of war and death. That, in itself, seemed a
strange paradox. Saviar reveled in the familiar exhilaration
that thrilled every Renshai anticipating a great and worthy
battle. Still, he had come here, in his youth and adolescence,
to visit his father, usually when the demands of his mother,
his brothers, and his *torke* had become too great to bear.
Watching Ra-khir and the other knights had served as a
comfortable escape and left him with fond memories of his
interactions with his father.

The surrounding woodlands hid the elves so well that
nothing revealed them to Saviar. Trained for stealth and
alertness as well as the sword, he looked and listened intently; only the natural noises inherent in wind and nature
touched his ears, and the swaying branches gave no hint of
the intelligent creatures hidden within the confines. Of the
twenty-six Myrcidians, Jeremilan had spared just under half.
Though he was among them, Chymmerlee was not. Saviar
could understand that decision. She was with child. Though
she had gotten into that state in a most vulgar fashion, he
understood the hopes of the Myrcidians rested upon that

tiny life and Chymmerlee's as well. The crime that had resulted in its existence revolted Saviar, but the child and its unwitting mother were blameless.

Though Renshai milled about Saviar, and the armies of myriad cities readied all around the plains, Subikahn's approach still caught him by surprise. It was all he could do not to draw, whirl, and impale his twin. "You of all people should know it's unwise to sneak up on a Renshai."

Subikahn turned his brother a withering look. "I didn't sneak. I came openly."

Saviar did not believe it. "Then you need to learn to walk louder. I didn't hear you, and I wasn't so absorbed in thought that I didn't notice Calistin." He gestured toward their younger brother who perched on a large stone and examined the edges of his blades with an intensity that suggested he had not already done so dozens of times. Saviar understood Calistin's consternation. They were used to keeping their weapons pristine, but the sword his mother had given him, like the one she willed to Calistin, contained what the elves referred to as shadow magic. Their edges rarely dulled and never notched, no matter the intensity of their use. Each of the brothers also had a sword recently exposed to elfin magic.

These had bothered Calistin more. The Renshai had thought long and hard before allowing their blades to become anointed. First, they had had to agree to release the swords to strangers, something Renshai never did because it would leave them essentially naked. A few had refused to allow it, though most had agreed, and those remained beside their swords throughout the long procedure. Even then, the Renshai had required reassurance from the elves that this magic would only negate the *Kjempemagiska*'s unfair and unnatural defenses, allowing the Renshai to cleave what they otherwise could not, and it would not assist in their own defense.

On the plain, the soldiers seemed tight as coiled snakes. Saviar heard none of the usual joking and laughter, no spontaneous games, and fights broke out at intervals. The captains did not wait for things to worsen but intervened much more quickly than usual, and Saviar noticed some of the farmers quietly sneaked away when they thought no one was watching.

Only the Renshai looked eager, and nearly all of them had come. Griff had invited the youngest Renshai children to Béarn Castle in order to free up as many of their parents as possible. The servants of Béarn watched the youngsters while those Renshai serving their time as guardians of Béarn's heirs remained at the castle as well. That pleased everyone involved except, perhaps, Béarn's servants who had to tend a band of tiny, active risk takers who carried swords and had no appreciation for courtly manners or royal furnishings. The older Renshai children enthusiastically joined the war preparations, hoping to become blooded, which would grant them instant status as adults no matter their ages. Saviar could scarcely begrudge them; he had won his own adulthood less than a year previously in the same manner.

"Saviar, Subikahn!" It was Calistin who called, which startled Saviar. Their younger brother rarely deigned to recognize them.

With a questioning glance at one another, the twins trotted over to their brother. Calistin had sheathed his swords and crouched in ready position on the boulder. As they approached, he waved them closer. "Here."

Suspicious of his brother's motives, Saviar leaned against the rock, trying to appear casual but capable of moving in any direction in an instant. Calistin had created many of the Renshai maneuvers, and he seemed to relish trying them out on his brothers, often without warning.

If Calistin noticed his brothers' discomfort, he gave no sign. "Subi, I've been asked to give you something, at least for the duration of the war."

Subikahn pressed his fingers against the rock, as wary as his twin. "Oh?" he said carefully. "What would that be, Calistin? A skull fracture?"

Calistin lowered his head, clearly reluctant. He sighed, then released the sword Kevral had given him from his belt and held it out to Subikahn, still in its familiar and well-worn sheath.

Struck speechless, Saviar could only stare. It was rare for any Renshai to hand his sword to another, but Calistin was known for being not only the consummate Renshai but also an unfeeling bastard. It seemed impossible he would hand over any sword, especially one with such physical and sentimental value. Especially to a brother.

Subikahn was understandably dubious. "So what happens now? I reach for the sword, and you slice off my hands?"

A frown scored Calistin's youthful features. He appeared more like a child approaching puberty than a man of eighteen, yet the coiled irritation bespoke the mind of an unrepentant killer. "If you wait too long, I'll retract my offer, no matter that the order came from Colbey himself."

No name could have galvanized the twins more. "Colbey spoke to you?" Saviar wondered why it surprised him. Of all the Renshai warriors, Calistin was the most skilled, and Saviar could think of no one more likely to draw Colbey's attention. He asked the question that surprised him more. "And he told you to give your sword to Subikahn?"

Calistin tipped his head, looking even more annoyed. "Isn't that exactly what I just told you?"

Subikahn accepted the sword with proper reverence and studied it in the dappled shadows. "We believe you." He kept his eyes firmly planted on the weapon he now held across both hands, instinctively testing its balance. "We're just having trouble grasping why the world's greatest Renshai would disarm our best warrior mere hours before entering the most important battle of our lives."

"Because he gave me this." Calistin drew the sword from his other sheath so swiftly it seemed to materialize in his hand. Highlights danced from its edges, dizzying, almost blinding in their intensity. The hilt was different than the standard Renshai sword: the guard broader and shorter, less suited for the special disarming maneuvers; the grip split-wrapped; the pommel shaped like the head of a wolf with diamond eyes that seemed to writhe. The gemstones put the blade glimmers to shame, shining as if the light itself originated from them, like stars in a cloudless sky.

Subikahn recognized it first. "That's the Sword of Mitrian!"

When he realized his brother was right, Saviar all but swallowed his tongue. The Renshai's only artifact, the Sword of Mitrian maintained a place of honor in the common house on the Fields of Wrath. No one had the right to wield it. Legend stated the Eastern Wizard had created the item in exchange for the Pica Stone, using yellow gemstones that held the captured soul of a great warrior as the wolf's eyes. Eventually, the gems were shattered, the soul freed to its proper afterlife, and the last shred of magic used to resurrect the great king of Béarn at the time. Since then, the sword contained no magic and had become a symbol of Renshai greatness.

Calistin explained, "The diamonds belong to Colbey's wife, apparently, and he borrowed them without her permission. The sword, we all know. When the war has ended, both need to be returned to their rightful owners." His gaze went to the sword in Subikahn's hand. "And my property as well."

It was a warning, not a request, Saviar noted. If Subikahn attempted to keep the sword, Calistin would have no qualms about retrieving it, even if it meant hunting down and killing his own brother. It would prove an interesting dilemma. Calistin would win in a straight fight between them, but he would have to find Subikahn first. All made moot, Saviar realized, by the fact that Subikahn would surely return the sword just as he had given Saviar back his weapon when they met up in Béarn.

"Of course," Subikahn said simply. If he felt any jealousy toward his brothers for their inheritances, he never verbalized or demonstrated it. "And thank you. There's no way to know whether or not the swords the elves' worked on will strike, and we need usable weapons in as many hands as possible." He laced the sheath to his sword belt, shoving aside the weapon currently residing on his left hip. Renshai always carried at least one sword but often as many as three.

Saviar mulled Subikahn's words. The generals had led the troops to believe exposure to the elf's magic was a sure thing. The reason for their deception became instantly clear. If the leaders displayed their doubts, pessimists among the troops would assume the worst, others might panic, and still more might see defeat where none existed. Whether or not the magic succeeded, they needed the men present, fired up and hopeful.

Saviar considered. "So . . . the three of us and Valr Magnus may have the only usable weapons?" He left out Rantire who he knew was at the castle guarding Griff, as always.

Even Calistin seemed rattled by the realization. "Four? Against an army of thousands?"

"A bit more than that." Subikahn glanced around to assure no one could overhear. Elves filled the forest, quieter than mice, but the possible lack of useful weapons was information they already knew. "My father took six utility knives from the giants' ships, and they also contain shadow magic. He kept one; Weile has another. He gave one each to Ra-khir and Kedrin. The last two were given to Darris and Marisole."

"Who aren't even here," Calistin pointed out.

Saviar understood Tae's decision. "But who are charged with guarding the king and his heirs."

Subikahn continued, "At first, he suggested Renshai should wield them, but I couldn't find any takers. They're giant utility knives, by Modi. Their balance is . . ." He shook his head. ". . . inferior is understatement. They thought it better to take their chances with elfin magical exposure."

Saviar nodded carefully. If he did not already have a sword with special properties, he wondered if he would have made the same decision. "So what's our strategy?" It was a dangerous question. Renshai fought without pattern or leadership by design. "Do we cluster together to try to bring enemies down quickly or spread out to take on as many as possible?"

To Saviar's surprise, even Calistin did not rebuke him, though Subikahn spoke first. "My father says the giants won't hesitate to kill those they consider inferior but have little experience with violent deaths of their own kind. Few things can harm them in their own world, so, like elves, they surely have extended lifespans."

Calistin was not only listening, he was giving due consideration to his brothers' words. That, in and of itself, struck Saviar as a small miracle. "I had trouble killing one, even with the assistance of a warrior who could pass for Renshai."

Subikahn made a strangled noise. Saviar could only stare. Calistin had just confessed to having difficulty vanquishing a foe. Then, he had praised the skill of a *ganim*. Three surprises at once on the heels of Calistin passing a sword to a brother, was more than they could handle.

As usual, Calistin did not seem to notice his brothers' consternation. "I think we should work together, at least until we've killed one and have a feel for how much effort it takes and see their reaction to losing one of their own."

Only then did he realize his brothers were gawking at him, utterly speechless. "What?"

Saviar found his voice. "We're just wondering who you are."

Subikahn added, "We seem to have misplaced our brother, Calistin."

Calistin's features hardened into their usual iron. "Yes, I've changed. Don't think it doesn't bother the piss out of me." His blue-gray eyes narrowed. "And don't think, for one moment, I can't still best both of you with a broken leg and an eyepatch."

"Found him!" Subikahn said, pointing at Calistin.

Saviar stifled a chuckle, trying not to think too hard about the coming war. Renshai relished a challenge, no matter how one-sided. In the coming hours, so many of them would find their rightful places in Valhalla. Nothing else truly mattered.

On the opposite side of the battlefield, Ra-khir waited with the rest of the Knights of Erythane. During the last battle, a strange series of events had placed him at the head of a Renshai army. His position had been more titular than real. Unaccustomed to strategy, the Renshai had ignored nearly all of his commands; but they had needed him simply to become a part of the combined armies. He had presented them only as outcasts in the command of a Knight of Erythane, bypassing the inevitable complaints from the Northern armies. At least, it had allowed him to fight at the sides of two of his sons as well as help protect Chymmerlee.

Knight-Captain Kedrin had given a long motivational speech to prepare the twenty-four knights and two squires for battle. The battle plan called for as many volleys as possible from the bowmen, followed by an attack by the infantry. Cavalry remained at the back to catch whoever plowed through the armies or attempted escape. Mounted on their snow-white chargers, the Knights of Erythane had to remain toward the rear by order of King Humfreet.

Ra-khir understood the decision of his monarch, though it niggled at his honor and made him feel unworthy. He wondered how much that had to do with nearly two decades of living with four Renshai on the Fields of Wrath.

They would dismiss anyone not eagerly plunging toward the fray as a coward.

Ra-khir also knew both kings had tasked the Knights of Erythane with the safety of their magical brethren. He knew the effort it had taken to convince the elves to assist, not to mention the many rewards King Griff had promised to them once the war was won. The Myrcidians, he understood, had been even more difficult to convince. Neither had sent a full contingent, and Ra-khir knew, if they lost a single life, their cooperation could disappear in an instant.

The reports of the earliest scouts were sobering. Ra-khir learned only what his father had passed along, and he doubted even Kedrin knew the full extent of the damage. Survivors described an enormous wall of water that enfolded the twin cities, pouring over cottages, shops, and solid stone buildings, collapsing them like toys. Then the water sucked back into the ocean, dragging debris and bodies, live and dead, helplessly out to sea. All that remained of Corpa Schaul and Frist were barren hunks of land littered with wood and straw, bits of stone, and bodies of humans and animals. Bleating sheep and goats kicked furiously in the swirling water, sobbing people clung to flotsam and the tops of trees, dogs pawed through the rubble.

Then, the giants came. The tsunami seemed not to have affected them at all, and they poured in from ships anchored well off-shore. Like children hunting fish, they casually speared the clinging and floating survivors, not seeming to notice or care about gender or age. Infant or adult, man or woman, struggling mightily or barely clinging to life, the giants left them mangled and lifeless. Often, they did not bother to clear the body from their spears before stabbing the next, collecting impaled children along their hafts like gruesome trophies.

By the time the giants made landfall, the surf roiled with scarlet froth and sharks feasted on the carnage. The giants shoved the gore from their spears and fell upon the wreckage. Anyone who had not already run, whether because of shock or terrible curiosity or injury, was slaughtered. If the giants heard or understood the human prayers and pleas, they paid them no heed and afforded them no mercy. The *Kjempemagiska* picked through the wreckage of the cities, pocketing anything that took their fancy and destroying whatever did not.

Apparently satisfied, they created enormous bonfires over which they roasted scores of animals, some of the witnesses swore humans as well, and consumed them, tearing off entire cow legs with the ease of a human removing drumsticks from a well-cooked chicken. In the evening, they smoked pipes, cleaned weapons, and chortled to one another. They played weird and horrific games on the rubble, using human heads as balls, intestines as ropes, or hurling planks and logs great distances, cheering the results.

Ra-khir glanced around at the gathered men of the continent and knew it all came down to this standoff. If the *Kjempemagiska* triumphed, no human could hide for long; the giants' superior might or magic would find them. Small pockets of resistance would prove hopeless against such a threat. It was here and now, now . . . or never. Anyone who hid, any coward who ran, only prolonged his death. They needed every capable soldier, every usable weapon. Every lethal trick at their disposal.

Scouts came charging in, their horses lathered and rolling their eyes in terror. "They're here!" The message ran through the ranks. "To arms! To arms!"

Then, the commanders took over, shouting instructions to their men in strident voices devoid of any fear. Ra-khir heard more than saw the preparations: the whisk of swords from sheaths, the clanking of those few lucky enough to have armor, including the Knights of Erythane, and a faint buzz that grew louder by the moment. Soon, only that one noise filled his ears and, then, his entire being. His heart rate seemed to slow to its cadence, the ground hummed under his feet, even the trees rattled in time to the rising and falling beat. *They're coming*, Ra-khir realized, and fear welled up inside him. He forced it down with all his will; he could not afford to succumb to it, to let it slow or stop or even inconvenience him.

"It's the elves," someone whispered near him, and Ra-khir realized it was true. The vibration that seemed to shake the earth itself was not the marching feet of the *Kjempemagiska* but the sheltering rise of *jovinay arythanik*. To Ra-khir's surprise, the simple realization that they had power on their own side buoyed his mood. Suddenly, success became not just a desperate need against great odds but a rallying force.

As the Renshai had no archers, they stood on the front line. The sight of the *Kjempemagiska* marching toward them in lockstep brought the urge to charge, but Saviar resisted. Doing so would make them a target for the continent's bowmen, and King Griff had chosen the battlefield well. It stood on higher ground than the approaching army so the giants appeared slightly smaller than they would have otherwise. Along with the other infantries, the Renshai remained at the top of the slope, watching, waiting.

The woodlands rang with *jovinay arythanik* in the voices of several dozen elves. Other elfin cries rose over the steady drone, speaking guttural syllables Saviar had come to associate with magic. Below and ahead, several of the giants raised weaponless arms, as if to throw invisible boulders. Right hand clamped to *Motfrabelonning*'s hilt, left on the sword touched by elfin magic, Saviar saw glimmering auras appear around nearly all of the giants' forms. *Magic*, he realized. He also knew only beings of chaos, such as Myrcidians and elves, and people clutching imbued items, such as himself and his brothers, could see the glow.

Saviar crouched, trying to prepare for anything. He had no idea what the giants might be capable of doing with magic, only that he needed to tend to his defense. The elfin chanting became impossible to ignore. It seemed to quake the ground, joined and interwoven not only with one another but with the grasses of the plain, the trees of the forest, the clouds in the sky. It felt like a cold, strange wind rushing through and past him to gather around the *Kjempemagiska*. Saviar saw no result from the magic the giants attempted. Their auras fluttered, warped together, then disappeared entirely. Whatever the elves and Myrcidians were doing, it was, for the time being, thwarting the *Kjempemagiska*'s magic.

Several shouts went up from the giants; then, abruptly, they charged with a coordination too precise for random guessing. Saviar had heard nothing from them, yet they sprang forward in a wave, swords drawn and sweeping, as though signaled and directed.

The command to fire came from many directions. The bowmen let loose a volley that showered down on the *Kjempemagiska* like a rain of narrow sticks. If any hit their mark, the giants gave no sign. Not one stumbled or even hesitated, and the only cries Saviar heard were the kind made by eager men charging into battle. A second volley flew through the air, the shafts clicking against stone and grasses. Again, the *Kjempemagiska* appeared to take no notice, their headlong charge unslowed and unsullied. A third round of arrows, quarrels and bolts took flight. Then, the swordsmen of the continent raced forward, and the bowmen fell back to trade bows for swords and knives, hammers and axes.

Now the Renshai charged forward, swords ready, battle-screaming. Other armies rushed in as well. It appeared the Northern warriors led the way, as eager for Valhalla as the Renshai. Cries ululated in ringing echoes, steel thudded against wood and bodies, sang against other steel. Then, Saviar engaged a *Kjempemagiska*, and the rest of the world faded around him. He led with his off-sword, as much to test it as to surprise his opponent.

Saviar's sword dragged along the straps of the *Kjempemagiska*'s sandals, slicing one but hanging up on a second. The giant swept a massive, curved sword in Saviar's general direction, his movement far quicker than the Renshai expected, yet poorly aimed. Saviar dodged easily, driving *Motfrabelonning* across the giant's knee. This blade penetrated more easily, slicing open his leggings and shaving a line of skin. Blood welled from the injury, and the giant bellowed in rage. This time, the curved sword sped for Saviar at lightning speed. It was all Saviar could do to spring aside, and the breeze of its passage staggered him. Apparently, the last strike was not intended wholly for him. More likely, the *Kjempemagiska* believed he could easily take down multiple humans with a single strike.

A golden blur whipped past Saviar to draw a gaping hole in the giant's legging and calf. Muscle bulged through the opening, and the giant kicked at his new threat, missing Calistin by less than a finger's breadth. Saviar plunged in, burying both swords in the *Kjempemagiska*'s thigh. *Motfrabelonning* parted flesh like honey, but the other jarred Saviar's arm to the elbow, as if he had stabbed a tree trunk. Flesh parted, but with grinding slowness. The giant jerked, tearing the inferior sword from Saviar's hand and sending it flying. Saviar's first thought, to rescue his weapon, passed quickly. He could not afford to lose *Motfrabelonning*, so he clung to the hilt with both hands.

The giant flailed. Saviar lost touch with the ground, his body swaying wildly with every motion of the enraged *Kjempemagiska*. Air surged around him, threatening to sunder his hold. If his grip faltered, Saviar knew he would not only lose one of the few weapons that could fight these monsters, but also his life. Whatever he struck, whether rocks, trees or solid ground, would surely kill him if the giant did not.

The giant's free hand raced toward Saviar, seeking to crush him in an enormous fist. Subikahn dove in, severing the thumb before it reached its target. The giant howled, his injured hand whipping to his face. His sword continued its downward slash. Calistin avoided it, threaded between steel and wielder to bury the Sword of Mitrian into the *Kjempemagiska*'s groin. The hesitation allowed Saviar to wrap his legs around the giant's bleeding knee and Subikahn to jab for the other. Braced, Saviar dragged *Motfrabelonning* downward, felt flesh part under the blade, then blood geysered into his face. The force drove him backward, his fingers still clenched to the hilt. The sword came free, and he tumbled to the ground in a scarlet fountain of *Kjempemagiska* blood.

The giant let out a haunting scream, like a dying rabbit magnified a thousand times. He collapsed so suddenly, it was all Saviar could do to scramble out of the way. The enormous body thundered to the ground, quaking it, then went still. Steeped in blood, salt in his nose and mouth, Saviar crouched and reassessed the situation. To his left, the forest still trembled with elfin magic. To his right, the *Kjempemagiska* had made headway, carving through the middle of the continent's main infantry, leaving raggedly piled bodies in their wake. At least two hundred men had fallen in the first few moments of battle.

It seemed hopeless, yet Saviar did not allow despair to take root. He was Renshai, his lot to die in glorious battle, taking as many of the enemy with him as possible. No matter the situation, no matter the odds, he would fight until his last dying breath; and he knew his brothers would do the same. If the giants had to fall one by one, triple-teamed by the last three humans in the world, Saviar would never stop. Not bothering to look for his lost and dishonored sword, he raced back into battle.

As Saviar, Subikahn, and Calistin launched themselves at their next opponent, it suddenly occurred to Saviar this one did not come at them with the same exuberance as the one they had killed. The giant hesitated, an error that cost him a gash across one arm from Saviar and a hip tear from Calistin. In that moment, Saviar realized the noises of the battle had changed. He could hear the shrieks and sobs of the dying, but the clang of weapons diminished, as did the triumphant deep roars of the *Kjempemagiska*. The one they fought now had to tear his gaze from his fallen companion and, even then, only after the Renshai had wounded him as well.

Cries of "Modi!" filled the air around them, the Renshai battle cry that beeseeched the god of wrath. As always, it spurred Saviar. Most often used by critically injured Renshai charging into their last battles, it also had a place as a rallying cry for those who simply needed to recharge their excitement for war. Like blackflies, Saviar and Subikahn nipped here and there at their opponent, never in one place longer than an instant. The giant's great sword swept around them with a speed that belied his enormous bulk, but the need to hold all three brothers at bay simultaneously prevented a well-directed swipe at any of them.

Again, the sons of Kevral worked together, dancing around their opponent, driving in whenever they could, always keeping him enough off-balance to create openings for one another. Slashes appeared on the giant's legs, tearing his leggings to scarlet-stained ribbons. And, although none of the Renshai had yet scored a blow deep enough to threaten life, they also had not taken a single wound themselves. The winds generated by passes of the *Kjempemagiska*'s huge blade stole many opportunities, forcing the brothers to regain their balance before slashing in again.

Around them, the pace of the war slowed notably, as if something invisible had demoralized the attackers at a time when they should be bellowing in triumph. The tying up of their magic clearly bothered the *Kjempemagiska*, but not enough to keep them from diving into physical battle. Several *Kjempemagiska* gathered around their fallen comrade.

When they realized they could no longer help him, their cries of dismay rose over the screams of the injured humans. They had clearly believed they could win this war without a single casualty, and Saviar drove in for a deeper strike, determined to prove them as wrong as possible.

The *Kjempemagiska* defended the furious attack on his thigh with a strong chop at Saviar's body. Forced to change direction in an instant, Saviar dropped. The sword whistled over his head, slicing fine red hair, and buffeting him with a whirlwind of air that sent him tumbling. He scrambled for purchase, not quickly enough. The sword screamed down on him, destined to pin him to the plains.

But the giant's focus on Saviar forced him to take his attention from Calistin. The younger brother plunged the Sword of Mitrian through his back, severing the left kidney. Blood boiled from the wound, and the giant's attack on Saviar wobbled. The sword missed the Renshai by a finger; the giant managed one step, then collapsed. Saviar eeled aside to avoid the growing shadow, but he could not move far enough fast enough. The massive body slammed down on his legs, sending agony shooting up his spine, knocking all breath from his lungs, and leaving him gasping for air.

"Modi!" Saviar gasped out. He struggled to free himself, the movement sending waves of pain through every part. He could not afford to remain trapped more than a moment. Soon, the giants would come to tend their fallen brethren, and their revenge would be swift and horrific.

Calistin appeared around the massive body, wiping blood from his sword with a filthy rag.

"Help me," Saviar called, writhing and shoving but doubting Calistin would lend a hand. The youngest of the brothers had shown nothing but disdain for warriors who could not save themselves.

But, this time, Calistin did not hesitate. Seizing a spear from the giant, he levered it over a rock and under the body, shoving downward with all the strength his sinewy body could muster. Nothing visible happened, but Saviar could feel a tiny shift. Desperate, he wriggled and pulled, jerking his legs free but leaving his boots behind.

"Thanks, Calistin!" Barefoot, he leaped to his feet and prepared for the next attack.

CHAPTER 29

The best laid plans are more often thwarted by inexperienced allies than enemies.

— *General Valr Magnus*

IN A BEDROOM on the highest floor of Béarn Castle, Tae Kahn kept his eyes shut and regulated his breathing to maintain what passed for normal sleep, uncertain what had awakened him. Then, Imorelda's plushy paws batted his face, and her voice impaled his head. *Wake up! Someone's talking to Mistri.*

Tae sat up, taking in the room in an instant. Mistri was sitting in her adult-sized bed, the covers drawn around her. Afternoon light streamed through the window. She had gone down for a nap, and Tae had chosen to accompany her, grabbing some sleep while he could on the floor at the foot of her bed. *Put me on their level, Imorelda. Hurry.*

Tae's brusque delivery earned him an aura of lingering disapproval, but Imorelda did as he bade. A male voice full of desperate hope filled his mind in an instant. *Mistri? Mistri, where are you?*

I'm here, Poppy! she sent.

Where's here, Mistri? Are you well?

Tae waited for her answer with the same anticipation as her father.

I'm fine, Poppy. I'm well.

Tae hesitated, torn between two approaches. If he only listened in on the conversation, Mistri's father would not know of his presence unless and until she told him. He could learn a lot before the *Kjempemagiska* discovered him. On the other hand, Mistri liked him and would, probably, reveal him early. Once she did, the father would wonder how long and why he had eavesdropped, which would make it difficult to develop a trusting relationship. *Sir, no one has, or will, harm your daughter.*

The *Kjempemagiska*'s suspicion was tangible. *Who are you?*

Mistri clutched her blankets tighter and studied Tae. *That's my friend, Poppy. Tae. He takes good care of me and Bobbin.* Smiling, she crawled across the bed and reached for him.

Tae gave Mistri his hand. Hers was larger and softer than his own.

The reply came back, *Is he ... alsona?*

Mistri squeezed Tae's hand. *No, Poppy. Not alsona.* She clearly struggled with the concept. *More ... alsona-like.*

"Human," Tae supplied the preferred word. He knew the *Kjempemagiska* term for the people of the continent; but, as far as he could tell, it translated into something more akin to "wild pigs."

Hyoomin, Mistri attempted a literal translation. *He's alsona size, but with hair like ink. And skin like mehiar.* As she spoke the word, she pictured a drink that resembled tea strongly flavored with honey and milk.

Confusion floated through the contact. Tae waited. If emotion that strong came to him, it indicated the man intended to communicate it. *Tae?*

I'm here, sir. Again, Tae addressed Mistri's father with the honorific he knew the *alsona* used when speaking to *Kjempemagiska*. He had assumed it akin to "sir," but he suddenly realized it probably meant "master." He did not mean to imply inferiority in any way, nor that the people of the continent intended to enslave themselves to these giants.

You're yonha?

Tae sighed, hoping his explanation made sense. *You call us that, yes; but it's not accurate. We'd prefer you thought of humans as smaller* Kjempemagiska.*

Alsona? the giant suggested.

Tae knew the world literally meant "people," but sharing connotation with the men of the island was dangerous. *No, because we're not slaves. We're free, and we intend to remain that way.* He did not care if his words conveyed threat. As much as he intended to befriend this giant, he did not want any misunderstandings about the conditions of such a relationship. *May I have your name, Mistri's Poppy?*

Amusement crept through the contact. *I'm called Kentt, and I recognize your name, Tae. You're the one who came to Heimstadr and abducted my daughter.* Fresh emotion accompanied the words. Though Tae could not quite place it, it did not seem friendly.

Mistri released Tae's hand, headed for the window, and looked out over the Béarnian courtyard.

Tae followed her, wondering if she could spot Kentt. If so, the guardian Renshai ought to have noticed him as well. *Mistri's capture was accidental. We were intending only to rescue Prince Arturo, the one you call Bobbin. Mistri chased after him and nearly drowned. We rescued her. As you know, however, it wasn't safe for us to return her at that time.*

The reply was ice. *We would have rescued her.*

Tae did not believe that to have been the case. *You could not have reached her in time. We believed our only choices were to pull her aboard or let her drown.*

A short silence followed. Tae imagined Kentt rehashing the scenario in his head, surely not for the first time. Tae now suspected Kentt was the *Kjempemagiska* with whom he had exchanged *anari* from Captain's ship. At length, Kentt sent, *We would have let one of yours drown.*

It was not the response Tae expected. He countered with, *Apparently not. You saved Prince Arturo.*

Bobbin was nothing more than a plaything for Mistri. A pet.

Mistri intervened, her expression one of a child affronted. *Bobbin is my friend, Poppy! I love Bobbin, and you did, too. You know you did!*

Tae did not allow himself to laugh. He did not know how much of his emotion, if any, came through the mental communication. He did not have the kind of experience with it the others did, and his sendings were buffered by Imorelda. *We see all intelligent life as equally valuable, whether* Kjempemagiska, alsona, *human, or elfin. If attacked, we won't hesitate to kill those who try to harm us; but we do not visit those sins upon their children.*★ Tae put his hands on Mistri's shoulders. "Is he out there?"

Mistri shook her head. "Can't see. He near enough to *anari*."

Tae already knew that.

Kentt said quietly, ★*Bobbin showed small signs of . . . intelligence. He managed a few simple words in* usaro.★

★*We're all highly intelligent,*★ Tae insisted, trying not to think of Ivana. He knew his share of stupid people, but other than the half-breed human, they still fell well above the level of animals.

★*Then why are you the first to talk?*★

Tae sucked in a deep breath, uncertain how much to reveal to Mistri's father. The *Kjempemagiska* might be playing Tae, pretending to go along for the sake of information.

Mistri proved less patient and circumspect. ★*Tae's the only one who hears* anari. *They can't answer what they can't hear. They do* usaro, *but they use different . . . words.*★

Tae winced, hoping she had not revealed too much.

★*Different . . . words?*★ Kentt prodded.

The explanation tumbled from Mistri, accompanied by a childish understanding that suited the situation well. ★*When they say "apple," they mean* lasat. *When they say bed, they mean* bassana. *And when they say Arturo, they mean Bobbin.*★

Confusion radiated in waves. ★*But why? Why not just say* lasat? *Or* bassana?★

Again, Mistri's basic, childlike understanding accompanied her words. ★*The gods didn't give them the real words, so they named things with other sounds. They all used the same sounds for a long time, and these became their words. Like naming Bobbin Arturo, they name a* bassana *bed. They can talk as good as we can, but each word sounds . . . different.*★

The simplicity of a three-year-old sank in to Kentt's mind as Tae knew no explanation of his own would. He did not bother to correct her misconception that all the peoples of the continent spoke a common language. The trading tongue was common enough.

★*Is that true, Tae?*★ A hint of awe came through the sending.

Tae imagined that, to beings who believed language a

gift from the gods, a group of people inventing it on their own, even incorrectly, had to seem brilliant. *A bit simplified, but near enough.*

And you're the only one of your kind who hears anari? *Why is that?*

Tae believed he and Mistri had shared more than enough information to demand reciprocation. *I can't say for sure I'm the only one who hears* anari, *but I know most of us don't. I've found that humans are more unique in their individuality than Outworlders:* Kjempemagiska, *elves, and also* sona.* Tae avoided lumping in some of the monsters they had met during their travel to other worlds, such as spirit spiders and also gods. He did not wish to risk offense to the gods or to the *Kjempemagiska.*

To himself, Tae ascribed the many variations of humans to shorter lifespans and lack of magic, which put larger distances between the various peoples and did not give them the extended time together necessary to develop in a uniform manner; but he believed it best not to bring these particular issues to Kentt's notice. *We deserve to know why you're invading us, murdering our people—our men, women, and children—indiscriminately when we've done nothing to justify such brutality.*

Silence prevailed. Other noises reached Tae's ears: the indecipherable buzz of conversations in other rooms of the palace, the distant clatter of dishware in the private kitchen, the purr of Imorelda in the center of the empty bed. Curtains flapped in the wind, clamps banged against masts at the docks, and voices wafted up from the guardians in the courtyard.

Mistri broke the hush, *Are you doing what Tae said, Poppy?*

It was an innocent question, full of curiosity and sorrow, shock and disappointment.

Kentt's response was pure outrage. *This is not a topic to discuss in front of a child.*

The horrible irony did not escape Tae Kahn. *So, if I'm to understand you, it's fine to torture and murder our children but not to speak of it in front of yours?*

Mistri is innocent!

Tae could not back down. *As are our children, Kentt. Their mothers, even our men. We have done nothing to harm *you or your people, aside from defend ourselves under un-precedented and unwarranted attack.*

Kentt said nothing, but irritation came through the contact loud and clear. *We do not have to defend our motives to animals, any more than you do to the calves and lambs, kids and piglets, deer and coneys you butcher.*

So you require our flesh . . . as food?

We require your land. Ours has become too crowded to support us, and our continued survival obliges us to take yours.

But not to slaughter us. Our kings and queens are reasonable. If you asked, they could find places for your people to settle peacefully among us. Tae studied Mistri to see how the conversation affected her. She stood stock-still, clearly focused on the words, her expression unreadable.

We are superior beings. We cannot and will not settle for those places you have declared unsuitable for your own habitation.

Tae would have liked to keep the conversation to the pertinent but knew he had to correct the misconception. If he did not, he tacitly accepted it and set the stage for their continued negotiations. *We accept the premise that you're superior to animals in the same way that humans and elves are. However, we reject the premise that you're superior to us.*

Surprise akin to shock came from the other side. *You would dispute our supremacy?*

Without doubt or hesitation.

But we have magic . . .

We are not wholly without it. Tae did not specify the source of that magic. He would play no part in the targeting of elves and Myrcidians.

And we have size.

Tae could hardly dispute that fact. *We also reject the premise that size bears any relation to status. In fact, we have a saying that goes "the larger the enemy, the longer and more jarring his fall."* It was not a real quotation; Tae had just made it up for illustrative purposes. *We value intelligence and cunning over height, compassion over beauty, skill and strength over bulk.*

Kentt started and stopped speaking several times, like mental hiccups, before finally sending, *Today, in battle, our superiority will be proven when we destroy your armies without a casualty of our own. We have no choice but to kill. You* yonha *are too foolish and defiant to serve us as the* al-sona *do.**

As soon as possible, Tae needed to let King Griff know that the battle on the field had, apparently, begun. **If you truly believe you will war with us and not lose many of your own, you will be sorely disappointed.**

Kentt repeated forcefully, **We will not lose a single man.**

Tae did not argue. It made no difference what he said, the *Kjempemagiska* would not believe him. Disabusing him would only harm the peoples of the continent. The longer the giants clung to that belief, the worse the shock of the first casualty would prove. Once demoralized, they would be more likely to make foolish mistakes that might cost them the entire war.

You speak of compassion, little Tae. When will you release my daughter?

Mistri looked up at Tae, her features crumpled, pained. She was about to cry. He put a reassuring hand on her shoulder. **Mistri will tell you she's been free to come and go since we arrived in Béarn. She is not a prisoner.** He nodded encouragingly to the massive girl.

Mistri spoke her first words in a long time. **I'm here, Poppy. In a room in the castle. Where are you?**

Kentt hesitated before addressing Tae again. **You know, I can use magic to bring down that castle. I can leave it a heap of useless rubble.**

Tae knew Firuz, the only *Kjempemagiska* present at the first war, had nearly managed to create a tsunami before being stopped by the combined effort of Tem'aree'ay, Ivana, and Chymmerlee. **You would kill your own daughter?** Tae tried to sound incredulous, his hands winching on Mistri's tensed shoulders.

Don't listen to the* yonha, *Mistri, my love. I would never harm you.

Tae is not a yonha, Mistri defended them. **Not Bobbin, either. They're hyoomins, Poppy.** She demonstrated uncommon understanding by adding. **I told you I'm inside the castle. If you knock it down, Tae's right. You'll kill all of us.**

Kentt's response was quick and sweet. **I wouldn't knock it down with you inside, my love.**

Mistri turned to face Tae, and he caught her in his arms.

He did not know if he needed to coach her, but worried her unusual circumstances and young age might render her incapable of making the necessary connections and decisions. "Mistri, he's just essentially said he's going to collapse the castle with magic after you leave us. You'll be fine, but we'll all die."

Mistri turned her head to look at Imorelda, purring contentedly on the bed, then gave the right answer. *I won't come out, then, Poppy.*

Why not? Kentt shot back.

If I do, you'll kill my friends. If I stay, you won't do that because it would kill me, too.

The exasperation of a father thwarted came through the mental contact. Tae knew the feeling well. Under other circumstances, he might have felt sorry for Kentt. *Mistri, come to me!*

Mistri folded her arms over her chest in the sullen posture toddlers and adolescents perfected. *No.*

*Mistri . . . *

No!

If you're safely returned, I won't collapse the castle. I won't hurt . . . anyone. You're worth more to me than the world itself. You're my special little girl, my one and only.

Tae jumped in, *Kentt, I have only one child also, a boy on the battlefield. I want him safely returned every bit as much as you do Mistri.* He had spoken more for Mistri than Kentt, so it surprised him when the giant answered.

I . . . have no control over your son's fate, Tae. The implication was obvious. Kentt knew Tae could kill Mistri and had, thus far, chosen not to do so. He also seemed to be acknowledging Tae's influence over his little girl. *I believe . . . the fighting has already begun, and I doubt it will last long.* He added words that surprised Tae, mostly because they seemed sincere, *I'm sorry.*

Tae resisted the urge to describe Subikahn as an exceptional warrior less likely to die in the battle than other soldiers. Not the sort to brag, he also did not wish to single out his own son for enemy attention.

Still focused on her own interaction, Mistri spoke instead, *Promise, Poppy. Promise on Mummy's hair.*

Distracted by the intervening conversation, Kentt asked, *Promise what, baby girl?*

I'm not a baby! Mistri pointed out, with more of the young child stubbornness. *I'm a big girl.*

I'm sorry, big girl. What promise are you asking for? Suspicion entered his tone again. Clearly, he believed Tae was behind whatever demand followed.

Promise you won't knock down the castle. You won't hurt Tae or Bobbin or Imorda. Mistri could not get the cat's name out properly. *Promise, Poppy. Or I'm not coming out.*

Kentt's emotion was unusually difficult to read. Tae suspected he tried to adopt the same sincerity as his daughter while, at the same time, wishing he did not have to deal with childish games. *I promise to—*

On Mummy's hair, Mistri reminded.

On Mummy's hair, Kentt added dutifully. *That I won't make the castle fall and I won't harm Tae or Bobbin or . . . that other one you named, unless they try to harm you or me.* He paused a moment. *Is that satisfactory?*

Tae wanted to add a number of names and conditions, but he doubted Kentt would respect a vow to any human as he would one to his daughter. *Kentt, I'm happy to return your daughter to you safely, but I will have to accompany her. She's not known to others at the castle. Because of her size, they may not realize she's a child. Given the current state of things, any stranger will be met with understandable mistrust. I can make certain no one harms her before she reunites with you.*

Kentt hesitated. *And what would you demand of me?*

Tae sucked in a deep breath and let it out slowly. He had not anticipated a one-on-one discussion with any *Kjempemagiska*. He had fully expected them to storm the castle and take Mistri by force. *I ask only that you make an effort to understand our situation. We are intelligent sovereign beings, not the animals you name us.* Tae could scarcely believe he was making the argument Matrinka had fostered and he had dismissed. He suspected the *Kjempemagiska* used the animal argument only as an excuse. Like *alsona*, they saw humans as something above beasts but inferior to themselves, creatures to enslave and destroy at will. Kentt's cooperation had everything to do with recovering Mistri alive. Most parents would say anything, do almost anything, to rescue their child.

Nonetheless, Kentt hesitated, at least appearing to consider Tae's demand. *I . . . will do my best to see you as you see yourselves, but I cannot promise others of my kind can or will do so. Most could not understand why we allowed Mistri to keep Bobbin. They thought us foolish and him . . . dangerous.*

Tae found himself remembering when an Eastern child had insisted on keeping a *wisule* as a pet. The mother had resisted having the foul-smelling rodent in the house; but, seeing no harm in it, the father had built it a pen in the yard where the boy had spent hours playing with it. Frightened by a dog, the *wisule* had bitten the child. Within days, the boy had contracted a fiery fever and died.

Elves did not worry about diseases; they seemed entirely unaffected by them. Given their magical nature, *Kjempemagiska* probably never got sick, either, thus assuring they, like elves, died only of age or violence. It certainly explained why they had population issues as well as why they focused so intently on preventing even a single casualty.

Knowing he could learn much about the culture with a single question, Tae asked, *Dangerous? In what way?*

They worried Bobbin might turn on her viciously. The answer seemed startled from Kentt. *What other way is there?* He answered his own question before Tae could. *Unless you consider the possibility she might come to love her pet like a family member, thus putting her in danger of losing perspective.*

Tae could not help turning his gaze to Imorelda again. Given a choice between rescuing her and most humans, he would pick the cat. *Of course, Imorelda is more intelligent than most humans.* He addressed the point instead. *Or gaining perspective. I would maintain that learning to extend compassion beyond one's personal household is a virtue that could only improve most societies. Imagine what new endeavors and inventions those* alsona *could bring to you if you allowed them to think and act freely.* It was a dangerous and unnecessary comment that Tae immediately regretted making.

Kentt sent a huff through the contact that Tae interpreted as laughter. *Do you suppose they would use that creativity to find ways of irritating their masters?*

Not if the masters graciously granted that freedom and

vowed to protect it. Tae intended to add only to himself, *An apology wouldn't hurt, either.*

An apology? Tae could imagine Kentt doubled up in laughter. *Apologize for allowing them to live rather than trampling them into the dust they came from? Apologize for protecting them? Apologize for granting them the privilege of interacting with the god's chosen ones?*

Tae made a mental note to keep his personal thoughts in a language other than *anari.* However, now that he had broached the subject, he needed to address it. *I've been inside the minds of the* alsona. *They serve faithfully from fear and custom, not because they believe it a privilege to do so.*

Slavery does not exist here?

Tae thought it better not to mention how recently that ban had come about. The West had outlawed it centuries earlier, but the East had not done so until Weile Kahn had taken possession of the throne. From what Tae had read about the North, slavery was not officially sanctioned, although neighboring tribes often took captives and forced them to work as unpaid labor, usually for relatively short periods of time. *Not anymore. We came to realize the value of every intelligent creature, no matter their differences from ourselves.*

Kentt put the conversation back on track. *So, in return for the safe return of my daughter, you ask only that I consider your point of view.*

Tae knew he could not really leave the agreement as spoken. There was still nothing to keep Kentt from destroying the castle the moment Mistri left it. *That . . . and your promise you won't harm us or our dwellings, even after you've reunited with Mistri.*

I can only promise for myself, Kentt pointed out. *My rank is high, but I don't have the authority to end a war that's already started.*

Obviously.

Another pause ensued. Mistri took Tae's hand, and he squeezed reassuringly.

Kentt finally spoke, *I can promise you I won't harm any humans or dwellings. However, I reserve the right to protect myself, and my daughter, should either of us be attacked.*

Tae could not keep his suspicions from becoming

aroused. He always worried for the wording as well as the intention of any agreement. He could hardly argue anyone's right to self-defense, but he would not allow a single breach to result in carte blanche for destruction. *So long as any defensive violence is directed solely at the attackers and not used as an excuse to violate all the terms of this agreement.*

Tae realized that, once he returned Mistri, he could not stop Kentt from doing anything he pleased. The feelings wafting through their mental contact seemed genuine, yet Tae had little enough dealings with such communication to know if they could be feigned. Hiding duplicity would prove far more difficult than disguising tone of voice and body language, but Tae imagined people who had used mental communication all their lives might know how to do it.

Kentt spoke with calm assurance, *If Mistri is given over to me unharmed, and we are not attacked, I agree to spare your people, and all of their constructions, from physical or magical harm performed by myself. If any such attack does occur, I will limit my response to those responsible. I also promise to consider the war from your human standpoint. Is that satisfactory, Tae?*

Tae liked when the giant used his name. It suggested the *Kjempemagiska* saw him as an individual worthy of direct communication. *Thank you. For my part, I promise to return Mistri safely to you and will do what I can to assure no one attempts to harm you or Mistri until such time as you have rejoined your people.* Tae realized he did not have full authority in this situation. He needed to consult King Griff. *This will take a bit of time, Kentt. We have only spoken language, and we have to spread the information thoroughly and accurately. I also need to know your location.*

I believe it best to keep my location secret until you've spread the word.

Tae could understand Kentt's point. Once he gave up his position, humans could quietly surround him while he waited. That left Tae wondering how Kentt had arrived on the continent without their knowledge. He doubted Mistri's father would tell him, although it probably had something to do with the illusory fleet that the navy was currently dispatching. The *Kjempemagiska* had either sneaked among the fakes with a real ship or, more likely, used the distraction to swim, unnoticed, to shore. *That's fine. I'm going to set things in motion now. Be sure to stay out of sight until I've explained the situation.*

Tae turned his attention back to the cat, gently freeing his hand from Mistri's. "Please accompany me, Imorelda. As usual, I'm going to need you."

Imorelda turned her head in his general direction with slow disdain.

"Please?" Tae repeated.

Imorelda sent, *Carry me.* She made no move to assist, curled up in the same position she had chosen to relax.

Tae indulged her. He had little choice, and he owed her a lot more. First, he petted the length of her several times, enjoying the velvety feel of her fur beneath his callused fingers. He had stroked her for her comfort, but he found his own heart rate and breathing slowing and some of the tension leaving his shoulders. Despite the urgency of the situation, he took the time to say, *You're beautiful and a friend beyond friends. I don't know what I'd do without you.*

Imorelda rolled onto her side. *Press your fingers against my belly.*

Imorelda had directed his ministrations before, but never asked for such a thing. Tae did as she bade, sinking his touch into the bulge of her abdomen. He waited a few moments, feeling nothing. Then, something tiny twitched against his index finger. *What are you doing?*

I'm not doing anything, you moron. The kittens are moving.

Imorelda's words made no sense. *What kittens?* It all came together in an instant. *You're . . . with child?*

Children, Imorelda pointed out. *At least three, perhaps as many as five. I'm not sure yet.*

But I thought you . . . Tae caught himself. The last thing he wanted to do was discourage her, even at this difficult time. He burrowed his fingers deeper, feeling another diminutive kick. *By the gods, Imorelda. That's wonderful news!*

Is it? Despite her words, Imorelda did not sound nearly as unhappy as when Matrinka had first suggested the pregnancy. *And stop poking me.* She rolled to her feet. *It's uncomfortable enough having the little nuisances squirming around internally. I have to have someone squeezing me from the outside, too?*

Tae cradled the cat in his arms, suddenly afraid she might break. *Matrinka is going to celebrate!* He headed for the door, Mistri trailing.

"You not listening." Mistri tugged on Tae's tunic. "Why you not listening?"

You can't tell Matrinka! Imorelda vied for Tae's attention as well.

What? How can we keep this from Matrinka? She'll go mad with excitement. Still carrying Imorelda, Tae looked at Mistri. "Remember, Mistri? When I'm concentrating on other things, I can't hear *anari*. I need you to use *usaro* for a bit. Please."

Imorelda could obviously tell Tae was speaking to Mistri, but that did not stop her from talking over and around the conversation. *That's exactly why we can't tell her. She'll hover all over me. And poke me, like you did.*

Tae knew it was useless to point out Imorelda had instructed him to feel her abdomen. He saw other reasons to keep Matrinka ignorant that Imorelda would never verbalize, even if they occurred to her. With pregnancies, too much could go wrong, especially in a time of war. Tae needed Imorelda with him, even at the most dangerous of times, and the loss of the cat or her future progeny would plunge Matrinka deeper into grief. The queen had enough to worry about without focusing on an animal's life in addition to her subjects'.

"What about Poppy?"

Wanting to take some of the burden from Imorelda, Tae faced Mistri. For an instant, he started to crouch, then remembered the youngster stood at his eye level. "Can you let me know if he says anything before I contact him again?"

Mistri nodded, and Tae smiled.

"Thank you," he said.

Imorelda seemed content to purr in his arms. Despite her previous protestations, she looked unusually happy.

The threesome headed toward the king's private quarters.

CHAPTER 30

A short sword can easily beat an extra-long sword. The extra length hinders the warrior's resolve and makes it easy to close in on and defeat him.

—*Colbey Calistinsson*

WAR CRIES, THREATS, SCREAMS, and the din of clashing steel gave way to the moans of the injured, conversation and sobs of sorrow, hopelessness, and outrage. Saviar, Subikahn, and Calistin examined the two enormous casualties they had forced the *Kjempemagiska* to abandon. Lying still, they did not seem quite so large, perhaps half again Saviar's height and double his weight. Their boots looked like enormous replicas, the fabric of their jerkins woven with a closeness and skill that obviated the need for armor. The continental clothiers could never have matched the precision. An enormous, curved sword lay near one's outflung hand and a second sword was half-buried beneath the other's body.

Calistin had eyes only for the weapons. He hefted one of the swords, and it overbalanced him, forcing him to take several uncoordinated sidesteps to regain his equilibrium. Saviar stifled the urge to laugh. He had never seen his agile brother appear so graceless.

Subikahn tugged the other sword free, then liberated a utility knife from each of the dead *Kjempemagiska*. "We need to find someone who can wield these."

"These?" Calistin examined the weapon in his own hands. "Who could? A solid sweep would put the wielder on his ass. The only way it could kill an enemy is if he died laughing."

Saviar grinned. It was the closest he could remember Calistin coming to a joke.

But Subikahn did not, apparently, appreciate the humor. "They were forged by and kept with magical beings, which means they probably contain shadow magic. Like our special weapons . . ." He patted the hilt of the sword Calistin had given him. ". . . they will work against the giants. We need as many magic weapons in as many hands as possible." He glanced around, brightening suddenly. "There's Thialnir. He's the biggest Renshai I know."

Saviar knew he rivaled the leader of the Renshai for size, and his youth probably made him the stronger, but he kept the thought to himself. He already had a sword that functioned against the *Kjempemagiska*. He set to freeing his boots from beneath the body that had pinned him earlier.

The giant corpses had drawn many curious onlookers from every part of the combined armies, but the other Renshai arrived first as they were already close at hand from the battle. Subikahn scrambled toward Thialnir, but Calistin beat him, offering his prize to the leader of the Renshai.

"What's this?" Thialnir asked suspiciously, though he surely knew the source of the weapon.

"Can you wield it?" Subikahn asked as Thialnir accepted it from Calistin's hand.

Thialnir gave the curved sword a mighty swing as others dashed out of his way, granting him a wide berth. "Not as well as my own. Why would I want to?"

Subikahn repeated his explanation as Thialnir lowered the blade, testing the balance in both hands, ending with, "The weapons sanctified by the elves can cut the giants, but only with great difficulty. These . . ." With effort, he raised the massive sword in his own hand. ". . . work like regular weapons on them."

Thialnir reached for the other *Kjempemagiska* sword. "Do you mind if I take them both? I'm headed to the commanders' meeting, and I imagine Captain Galastad can find an unusually large Béarnide who might find use for the other one."

As he pulled on his boots, feet and legs restoring the crushed leather to its proper shape, Saviar nodded agreement. No people on the continent came naturally bigger than Béarnides, and they had to have a few who made even Griff and himself look small. "You might consider my father, too. Tae gave him a giant's utility knife; but, knowing him, he probably handed it off to someone he considered more skilled with a sword."

Saviar hopped to his feet, appreciating that he no longer had to fight barefooted with sticks, rocks, and debris stabbing and bruising his soles. "Give him one of these, and he'll have no one to pass it off to. Meanwhile, we'll see if we can find some takers for their knives . . ." He jerked his thumb toward the bodies, now being swarmed with examiners. ". . . among the Renshai. They refused previously when Subikahn's father offered similar ones; but, now that they've had a chance to notch their current weapons against our enemies' iron hides, they may change their minds."

Thialnir juggled the enormous swords, then headed into the thick of the armies. Unlike most of the commanders, he did not need to assess the situation or rally his troops with promises or sanguine speeches. Renshai gave their all to every battle; they knew no other way. They would eagerly plunge into any war, no matter their odds, and fight to their dying breaths. Thialnir knew his people would handle any casualties with proper dignity, would tend the salvageably wounded and dispatch any Renshai who sustained fatal injuries in a way that allowed them the glory of Valhalla. At the moment, nothing else mattered.

By the time Knight-Captain Kedrin arrived, nearly all the other officers were already gathered in a selected clearing at the edge of the woodlands, beyond the infantry and cavalry. They had learned to treat one another with distinction and respect, no matter the title. Some places had multiple generals, others a single general with lieutenants or captains beneath him, while still more, like Béarn and Erythane, reserved the title of general for their kings, regardless of whether or not they served in combat.

Though only titled captain, Galastad of Béarn's infantry took the lead role in Griff's absence. He was an enormous man with a tight-cut mop of curly black hair and a bristling beard. Only Kedrin, Valr Magnus, and Thialnir came close to him for height, but he carried significantly more weight than any of them. Kedrin noted that only eight of the nine tribes of Northmen were represented. General Elgar of the Erdai was notably missing.

For the Westlands, Erythane had Kedrin as well as Hansah, ranking lieutenant over the infantry and regular cavalry. General Sutton of Santagithi had gathered several smaller towns under his command, nearly all the ones spanning the area between his own city and massive Pudar, which was under the authority of the experienced and skilled General Markanyan. Nearly all the other villages and hamlets of the West had added soldiers to the armies of Béarn, Erythane, Pudar, or Santagithi rather than attempt to form a command structure of their own. Notably absent from the West was a representative for the twin cities. They had come to the war outraged and insistent on taking the front and center positions. Now, it appeared, few if any remained.

The entire Eastlands had united under a single general, Halcone. Kedrin knew the East divided their army into multiple units under several lieutenants, including a Renshai named Talamir who had served as Subikahn's *torke* while he lived with his father. Only General Halcone attended this meeting, and Kedrin felt sure the other officers were handling the necessities: the dead, the injured, the dispirited. Weile Kahn also hovered in the background. He claimed no title, yet no one suggested he did not belong.

The oldest of the elves, known simply as Captain, came to the meeting as well, accompanied by an elderly mage from Myrcidë called Jeremilan. Rumor claimed the elf was as old as the gods themselves, though the mage looked more the part. He walked without assistance, yet he appeared terribly frail, his skin grotesquely wrinkled, his gray eyes faded, his fingers gnarled. It appeared as if a strong wind might scatter him into dust, swirling away the bits until nothing remained. Captain, on the other hand, seemed as ageless and timeless as most elves, his amber eyes canted and strange but also clear and bright.

Captain Galastad of Béarn took command, as the

situation warranted. "It appears we are all in attendance. Having spoken with each and every one of you, aside from Knight-Captain Kedrin . . ." There was a bare hint of displeasure that Kedrin might have missed if it had not referenced his own conduct. He had been the last to arrive, but only because his position required certain formalities the others did not. Although he had experienced no casualties, he had assisted the other units with their own. He considered claiming the floor for an apology but saw the irony of such a thing. Doing so would only waste more time, presumably the reason Galastad was rebuking him in the first place.

Galastad continued, "I regret to inform you that we have taken significant casualties, upward of a tenth of our warriors. There has been a near devastation of the Erdai, including General Elgar, and of the army of the twin cities of the West which had already suffered the full loss of its home force and civilians."

Murmurs followed. Several whispered fervent prayers, although Kedrin was not one of them. He had never turned to the gods before, and it seemed hypocritical to start doing so now.

"The enemy has also taken some losses, which we estimate at one tenth of a percent of their total force."

Kedrin did some quick math. There were two dead *Kjempemagiska*, which meant the general estimated them at two thousand strong, about the same number as the casualties on their own side.

"Obviously, we need to deviate somewhat from our present strategy. We have some new facts to facilitate that process. First, we now know that, though the enemy considers us wholly expendable, they don't have the stomach to tolerate casualties of their own. The first death caused them to stop fighting. The second came as a result of trying to retrieve the body, and it sent them into retreat."

"Are they gone?" asked General Sutton of Santagithi, with small hope in his tone.

Captain Galastad of Béarn responded, "Unfortunately, no. Captain of the elves assures me they have not gone far. They're regrouping and, probably, changing their tactics as well."

General Markanyan of Pudar demanded, "Do our scouts have anything to report?"

Galastad glanced at Weile, who currently seemed to control most of the worthwhile spying information.

Weile stepped from the shadows. "They could come at us again at any moment. I can guarantee us only a half of an hour of warning. They are conversing aloud but in a tongue no one knows, and as I understand it, they have a mind-language as well."

Galastad now acknowledged Captain with a wave. "Can you decipher that?"

Captain remained close to the woodlands, as if he might flee at any moment. "We can't hear it, either, General. We might have magic that could make it audible, but we barely have the numbers and strength to contain their offense. If we start throwing chaos around, we risk not having it when it's urgently needed. As it is, we're not preventing the small, healing magics they're using right now in order to conserve our strength."

Thialnir of the Renshai stepped in. "Can we afford to allow them to heal their injuries? Doesn't it mean they can keep coming at us full force?"

The general of the Northern Gelshni spoke next, though Kedrin could not recall his name. "As it is, the elfin magic isn't working. Our weapons are worthless against them."

"Not worthless," Thialnir argued. "They cut. It just takes a lot more force than one might expect. You have to sweep hard and true, put weight and muscle behind the potentially lethal targets, drive in and don't give up until the job's done."

General Sutton shook his head. A clever strategist, he saw the problems immediately. "That's fine for large, experienced warriors, but I've got an awful lot of citizen soldiers who are becoming tired and discouraged. Does anyone have a problem with moving up the cavalry before the next strike? I don't think hunting down men who break through the ranks will be the issue here, especially considering the thickness of the forest and brush surrounding the battlefield." He turned toward the elfin Captain, though this put his back to Captain Galastad. "Given the giants' reaction to casualties, it's my considered opinion that we need to put our strongest forces at the edges of the forest. They surely know it's the elves keeping them from standing a safe distance from our weapons and wiping us out with magic."

Galastad nodded sagely. "As you must realize, the battlefield was well-chosen to keep our users of magic safe. We're all but surrounded by dense woodlands, leaving our enemy only one opening for attack. The elves don't have the same difficulties the giants, or even we, would have moving around the forest."

"Understood," General Sutton replied. "But I'm still concerned the giants might focus attacks on the front edges of the forest. With their enormous swords, they might take down enough trees to make some headway. We need to slow them down so our users of magic have time to safely retreat without losing control. If the elves and mages drop their spell negating the enemy's magic, we're all doomed."

Galastad took the information under advisement. "Are we all agreed on moving the cavalries to the fore and fortifying the edges of the forest?"

Several "ayes" and no "nays" greeted the proposal, so he continued, "To that end, I'd like to put the Renshai on the southwest corner at the forest edge, Béarn's army beside them, then Santagithi and allies, with Pudar toward the center. On the northwest corner at the forest edge the Knights of Erythane, then Erythane's main forces, and the various Northern armies in whatever order they please. The Eastland armies will fill the second rank, along with the citizen soldiers and smaller armies I might have missed."

Valr Magnus stepped up. "The Aeri will take the central position, beside Pudar." It was a brave stance given that, during the previous assault, the forces in the middle had been all but destroyed.

No one, including Kedrin, argued with the suggested positions. He considered Santagithi the greatest general in history, and Sutton seemed to have all the strategic instincts of the man for whom his town was named. The Knights of Erythane would have a difficult time, and he prepared himself for the inevitable loss of men.

As the fighting forces seemed settled, Captain Galastad of Béarn turned his attention to Captain and Jeremilan. "Are we still strong on the magical front?"

Jeremilan spoke first. "I'm afraid the Mages of Myrcidë

must withdraw from the battle. It's become far too dangerous, and we can't spare a single life."

The words sparked immediate outrage. Every eye went to Jeremilan, who seemed to further whither under the intense scrutiny.

Jeremilan had no choice but to explain, "For centuries, I have kept our presence secret from the world, yet our numbers have still remained dangerously low. Our bloodline is priceless and unique. We should never have come."

Captain Galastad approached the situation with remarkable control and caution, given that Jeremilan had just announced his intention to commit wholesale treason, a betrayal that probably condemned the entire continent to quick and brutal murder. "Do you not understand that this is the last, best hope for all of us, including your people? Have you heard what happened to Corpa Schaul? To Frist? Standing together, we may still lose, but failure is certain standing alone. Not only will you render our situation more difficult, probably impossible, you will doom yourselves as well."

Jeremilan drew himself up as well as he could, though it did little more than stress the huge difference between the captain's height and his own. "We successfully hid for centuries. We can do so again."

"No." Weile Kahn's single word, though soft, was emphatic. "You have a contract to honor."

Jeremilan jerked his attention to the Easterner. "What good is a contract if we're all dead? The agreement included a promise that we would be fully protected. We had the right to terminate the contract if any mages came to serious harm."

Galastad asked the obvious question. "Have they?"

"No," Jeremilan admitted. "But it is inevitable."

Weile stepped in again, "You were unfound for centuries because you hid yourselves in magic and we had no reason to look for you. These *Kjempemagiska* are magical beings. If you leave, and we fall, they will hunt you down and destroy you to a man, woman or child."

"I believe we can stay hidden."

"I hadn't finished." Weile's voice remained calm, steady. "If you leave, and I survive, I will hunt you down and destroy you to a man, woman, or child."

A chill spiraled through Kedrin. He suspected that, if Weile Kahn wanted a man dead, his life was as good as forfeit.

Jeremilan whirled to face Weile. Even as he moved, he was suddenly surrounded by dark men in black who seemed to materialize from the shadows.

Though his gemlike eyes seemed to take in everything, the elves' Captain demonstrated no fear. He spoke gently, as if the threat, both real and verbal, had not occurred. "I'm afraid we need every being with magical abilities to assist. It's taxing us to the limit already. I've called for elfin backup, but I don't know how many more elves we can enlist. Even if I could get all of us, and that's unlikely nearly to the point of impossibility, we'd still be outnumbered ten to one." He paused, allowing the effect of his words to sink in before heaping on more dire information.

No one else spoke while waiting for Captain to continue, though Weile's men did fade back out of sight. "It's only the *Kjempemagiska's* decision to focus on physical as well as magical combat that's allowed us to keep them in check thus far. If they focused solely on magic, hit us with one mighty blast, it's possible . . ." Captain stood still for several moments, showing no inclination to finish his sentence.

At length, Galastad prodded. "What's possible, Captain? What would happen?"

A hint of something entered Captain's voice. Though he could not pinpoint it exactly, Kedrin compared it to awe. "I'm not entirely sure. Two great and desperate forces of chaos slamming into one another . . . the backlash would be tremendous . . . it could . . . it might . . ." He shook his head, then lowered it in deep consideration. Kedrin wondered how long it took someone as old as the world to locate specific memories for comparison. Captain started again. "It's liable to cause a cataclysmic explosion."

Galastad asked the question on everyone's mind. "How . . . cataclysmic?"

In answer, Captain only shrugged. "Difficult to predict."

General Sutton asked the question on every mind. "What can we do to prevent it? And if not prevent it, survive it?"

Captain sucked in a deep breath. "The best thing you can do is win this war. The fewer the *Kjempemagiska*, the weaker their combined magic and the less chaos we need to call forth to counteract it, the safer we all become." He looked around and, apparently noting the horror on nearly every commander's face, he added, "We're working on it, trying to find ways to redirect the excess energy and mitigate the damage. Believe me, the elves have more to fear from losing lives than anyone else here." He added pointedly, "Including Jeremilan."

Although most of the commanders did not know what Captain meant, Kedrin did. Humans, including the Myrcidians, could repopulate so long as one of each gender survived. The Knight of Erythane saw the danger in plying Captain with too many questions. "Please, accept our thanks for everything you've done so far as well as anything you might do to save as many human lives as possible." Kedrin made certain to include Jeremilan with his attention and gestures. "I admit to knowing little more about magic than most humans, but I certainly know that the two of you and your followers are our only means of preventing the enemy from wiping us out with a catastrophic spell. But if you're here speaking with us, who is monitoring the *Kjempemagiska?*"

"We're fine at the moment," Captain reassured Kedrin and the many others who had surely considered the same question. "Right now, the *Kjempemagiska* are using minor magics, mostly of the healing variety. If they attempt offensive types of magic, we can throw the shield up in an instant."

General Markanyan of Pudar tossed out, "Given the difficulty we're having, shouldn't we reconsider blocking their healing as well?"

Sutton added, "Do we have access to healing magic, too?"

"Yes." Captain looked at Markanyan, then Sutton, "and yes. There's a balance, however. We're tying our chaos energy to theirs. If we prevent them from any castings, we deprive ourselves of the same ability; and, right now, attempting to recruit more elves and securing an escape route take precedence. As for healing, many of us have that capability. However, every elf or mage we spare for healing is one less weaving the defensive net."

Kedrin could not help running with the information. It

seemed immoral to allow men to suffer and die when others
might heal them. If any of his two dozen knights became
injured, he would want them to get the best care possible.
The agony of knowing the elves could have saved a brave
warrior who died or became permanently damaged would
haunt him for eternity, yet he would not risk everyone in
order to demand the magical ministrations of elves or
mages.

Weile called out suddenly, "The enemy's on the move."
Kedrin turned, but the Easterner had already disappeared
from sight.

Galastad raised an arm. "Meeting adjourned. Set up
your forces as discussed, and may all the gods go with us."

In the king's quarters on the topmost floor of Béarn Castle,
Tae relayed the information he had received from Mistri's
father to the king and queen of Béarn, Darris, and Seiryn,
the captain of the castle guards. Imorelda perched on Tae's
shoulders, and Mistri ran around the exquisite antique furnishings squealing with delight at the sight of the carved
bears. No one argued Tae's need to return the girl to her
father, only the means of doing so.

Matrinka paced, knotting her fingers in front of her.
"Tae, it's just too risky for you to go alone."

"I won't be alone," Tae reassured her for what felt like
the fifth or sixth time. "I'll have Mistri and Imorelda."

"And a Renshai," Griff inserted for what was, definitely,
the first time.

Tae's gaze flicked back to the king. His first instinct, to
argue, passed quickly. It seemed like the perfect compromise. The presence of a warrior would ease Matrinka's concerns, and Tae could explain away a single companion as
opposed to a band of guardsmen. "Fine," Tae said, then
added quickly, "so long as it isn't—"

"Rantire," Griff asserted. "You will take Rantire."

Tae glanced at Darris who was smiling so broadly he was
practically laughing. "Sire, please. Name any other Renshai."

"Rantire," Griff explained as if Tae had not spoken, "is
the only Renshai in Béarn with a weapon capable of inflict-
ing damage on those giants. As a Renshai would rather loan

out his eyes than his sword, there's no choice in the matter. Promise you will take Rantire with you."

Tae knew trickery would not save him this time. He sighed and nodded. Rantire was fierce, intense, and loyal in the extreme, but she was not stupid. She would not act impulsively, and her extreme dedication arose from a promise to the son of Colbey and Freya that she would keep Griff safe, not Tae. "Fine. I will take Rantire with me."

Mistri tugged at Tae's sleeve. "Poppy talking. Want to know if we coming."

Imorelda, please. Take me back to Kjempemagiska *level.*

Imorelda dug a claw into the top of Tae's shoulder but gave no other sign of reluctance. A moment later, Kentt's mind-voice filled his head. *How much longer?*

Tae understood his impatience. *We're leaving now.* He said aloud in Common Trading, "I need to get going. Call Rantire and have her meet me at the door."

Matrinka seized both of Tae's wrists and stared into his eyes. "You won't leave without her." It was not a question.

They both knew Tae could slip away, through any window, before Rantire could think to look for him. He looked into Matrinka's dark eyes, so soft and kind, and knew he could never lie to her. "I will not leave without Rantire."

Matrinka released him, and he turned his mind back to his inaudible conversation. *I'll have a woman with me as well as Mistri and my . . .* He did not know the *Kjempemagiska's* word for "cat." *. . . pet. It's furry, striped, and small enough to sit on my shoulders.* Tae appreciated that Imorelda did not speak the foreign tongue. Though neutral, she would not have liked his description of her. *Are you accompanied?* Tae could not believe he had not considered such a significant question sooner.

Again, Kentt hesitated. Tae wondered if he was composing a lie or simply did not wish to give away more information than necessary.

Tae pressed, *I'm coming to you in good faith, without an army at my back, though you could probably crush me with one hand. I'm returning your daughter unharmed and in good spirits after saving her from drowning. Surely, that earns me some basic honesty, perhaps even a bit of respect.*

I'm alone, Kentt sent.

Tae believed him. Spying often required it, even in the most dangerous situation. Even with the illusory ships as cover, Tae doubted two giants could have sneaked ashore. He took Mistri's hand and headed out the door.

Matrinka's voice floated through the crack before it disappeared, "Good luck, Tae. And, for once in your life, be careful."

CHAPTER 31

Warriors make their decisions on the battlefield, faster than an eyeblink; and they rarely get a second chance to be wrong.

— *Colbey Calistinsson*

AS THIALNIR HAD WARNED, the *Kjempemagiska*'s second charge focused strongly on the edges, where the plains met the forest. This suited Saviar and the other Renshai, who found themselves under unremitting assault. Flinging themselves into combat, they had nothing to lose. They either became live heroes or dead *Einherjar*, equally valued goals.

No longer locked with his two brothers, Subikahn drove in to attack as if born for this precise moment. His sword was a blur as he slashed, dodged, and flew in again. The disproportionate strength and enormity of the *Kjempemagiska* and their weapons rendered most of the disarming and parrying Renshai maneuvers unworkable, but that still left Subikahn with a repertoire of hundreds. Cut and evade, jab and spin, his body did his bidding with a speed that the massive giants could not hope to match. Many times, the curved sword swished near enough to buffet him with wind, to steal control and balance, but always he recovered swiftly, a nonstop nuisance covering his opponent with rents and tears, drawing blood in small but significant assaults.

A flash of light caught Subikahn's attention. Though short-lived, its presence jarred. It was either something the

giants had managed despite the elves' containing magic, or
an elf or mage had blundered from the cover of the forest
and onto an area that currently belonged to the *Kjempemagiska*. Either way, Subikahn knew, it spelled trouble.

Ducking under a massive sword strike, threading between his opponent's legs, Subikahn found himself on open
ground and racing toward a second flash of light. It took
more than a dozen running strides; then, suddenly, he was
upon it. A single *Kjempemagiska* held a group of Myrcidians pinned against the brush, his curved blade speeding
toward them. In a moment, it would mow down all five in
one slash.

With no time to yell or even to think, Subikahn charged
the monster at full speed. Strangely, as he moved faster, the
world seemed to slow. The blade rushed toward the mages.
Subikahn could see them flinching, their eyes closing as they
prepared to die. Then, Subikahn was airborne, hurling himself at the giant without thought to his own safety or survival.
His sword swept in a perfect arc, slashing through the giant's
wrist. The *Kjempemagiska* bellowed, changing the course of
his attack in an instant, driven solely by adrenaline and instinct. With no part of his body touching ground, Subikahn
became a slave to momentum. The curved sword ripped
across the Renshai's abdomen, then flew free, one of the giant's massive hands still clutching the hilt. Blood gushed
from the stump of his wrist, splashing Subikahn like an errant wave and boiling out over the cowering Myrcidians.

It was not until Subikahn hit the ground, rolling from
training, that the pain caught him. The landing shot discomfort through every part, but the agony concentrated in his
midsection. He clutched at the tear in his gut, only to find
wet loops of intestine falling into his hands. *Fatal,* he realized, as if in a dream. He managed to scream out a single
"Modi!" before darkness overtook him.

Saviar also saw the flash of light that indicated magic.
Locked in mortal combat, he redoubled his efforts, gash-
ing and retreating, seizing every opening and denying the
same to his enemy. Though he no longer had the support
of Calistin and Subikahn, two other Renshai assisted him.
They left far fewer marks on their target, but they helped

distract the *Kjempemagiska* long enough for Saviar to get in additional shots. Their elfin-exposed weapons did just enough damage to confuse the giant, who had, apparently, not yet figured out which of them was using the full-fledged weapon.

When the second flash came, Saviar was wedging his blade between two of the *Kjempemagiska*'s vertebrae. Spine-shocked, the giant collapsed. Saviar ripped his sword free and ran toward where he had seen the errant magic. To his left were the trees. To the right, he could see the distant mountains and the edge of the *Kjempemagiska* army. Behind him, he heard the shouts and slams of the battle over the roaring of the wind through his ears. Then, a single giant hove into sight, bellowing and staggering, sword flying from his hand. A moment later, he heard Subikahn's cry and knew his twin desperately needed his assistance.

Saviar would not have believed he could increase his frantic pace; but, suddenly, the world seemed to gallop past him at racehorse speed. Soon, he could see a human form on the ground. Blood geysered from the giant's stump, and the *Kjempemagiska* furiously waved his remaining hand at it. Whatever magic he attempted failed. His eyes widened until they seemed to encompass his entire face, and he collapsed to the ground, lifeblood pulsing into the saw grass.

It occurred to Saviar that, had the giant thought to staunch the flow with more mundane means, he might have survived the wound, terrible as it was. Now, Saviar changed his focus entirely to Subikahn; the giant was no longer a threat. He would not regain consciousness before dying from loss of blood.

Saviar hurled himself on the still body on the ground. Grabbing Subikahn by the shoulders, he shook. Once, twice, then the dark eyes flickered open and looked squarely at Saviar. *Alive, thank the gods.* "Subi! Subi!"

Subikahn opened his mouth to speak, but Saviar put his finger to his brother's lips.

"Don't try to say anything. I'm getting help."

Subikahn ignored the advice. "Listen . . ."

"No!" Saviar put his three middle fingers firmly on Subikahn's mouth. "Save your energy."

"Fatal," Subikahn gasped. "Let me . . . speak . . . or I'll . . . bite you."

Saviar withdrew his hand. Only then he noticed the pale
loops of bowel between Subikahn's clutching fingers. Blood
appeared to coat every part of him, though how much was
his and how much the giant's Saviar could not guess.

"Must know . . ." Subikahn's nostrils flared as he sucked
in enough breath to speak more than a few words at a time.
". . . your injury . . ." He made a feeble gesture toward where
Saviar's crouched legs straddled him.

Saviar could not understand why Subikahn felt the need
to discuss old struggles now. "My injury? You mean the one
that festered? The one that caused us to meet the mages?"

Subikahn managed a slight nod.

Saviar remembered awakening from a months-long
coma caused by the septic wound and the blood poisoning
that resulted. His prior memory went back to when he and
Subikahn had left the other Renshai, a week or so after a
battle against Northmen. He could not recall the source of
his own injury, the intervening time before infection overcame him, or anything during his time unconscious. He had
asked Subikahn about it numerous times but never got a
worthwhile answer. Uncertain he wanted to know the truth
anymore, Saviar asked guardedly, "What happened, Subikahn?"

"We . . . were . . . angry. Sparring . . ."

The words made no sense. The twins had exchanged
practice blows since infancy, but they had never harmed
one another. Renshai learned control before all else. Nevertheless, Saviar believed he knew what Subikahn was trying to say. "You? You cut me?" His brother had always led
him to believe he had received the wound during the
Northmen's attack.

"Accident," Subikahn huffed out.

Saviar felt as if icy hands clutched his heart. Infections
never happened quickly. Wounds took time to fester, and
even longer to pollute the blood and body. Any Renshai with
significant fever would furiously attack someone certain to
kill him, to assure his death in combat and his place in Valhalla. The Renshai even had a name for it: *tåphresëlmordat*.

For nearly a year, Saviar had wondered why he had not
done as any Renshai would, worried he had fallen prey to
unspeakable cowardice. Subikahn seemed to be protecting
Saviar, deliberately hiding the fact that, when it came to end-

ing his own life, Saviar had showed himself to be a worthless craven. Many times, Saviar had plied Subikahn with questions, to no avail. Still, if Saviar had not had the wherewithal to initiate a battle, Subikahn should have forced him to attack. At the least, Subikahn should have ended Saviar's suffering with a *nådenal*, a needle-shaped, guardless dagger subjected to rigorous ceremony, its purpose to end the life of a suffering ally too weak to perform a proper *tåphresëlmordat*.

The oft-repeated question arose again. *Why didn't I attack before the fever took me?* The words stuck in Saviar's throat. This time, he knew, he would get the truth; and the answer would change the world forever. Either Saviar was a coward unworthy of the Renshai or Subikahn was. Either way, Saviar did not want to know.

But Subikahn did not need the question spoken aloud. In this situation, the Renshai mind was transparent. "My ... fault," Subikahn said, staring at Saviar, who found it impossible to meet his brother's gaze. "You ... challenged. I ... refused ... you. Lied. Told you ... you ... all right."

Saviar clenched his teeth but let his brother speak. Subikahn's actions were unforgivable.

"If ..." Subikahn's tongue flicked across his lips. "If ... mages hadn't saved you ... I ..." He licked his mouth again. "I ... condemned your soul to ..."

"No!" Saviar shouted. He would not allow his brother to speak the word "Hel," could not, at this moment, contemplate the possibility. The mere idea was blasphemy. "No!" The Renshai had no written laws, only a strict code adhered to for as long as the tribe existed. There was honor, and there was condemnation. It was the way of Renshai. Honor was given to one's swords, the swords and person of allies, even the swords and person of enemies who had proven themselves worthy through honest combat, no matter how reviled. "No!" Dishonor to a weapon could be arduously atoned. Dishonor of a warrior was inexcusable, and even inadvertent condemnation of a deserving ally's soul to Hel was an immorality beyond contemplation. "No." Saviar leaped to his feet, needing to sate his rage on something other than Subikahn.

Only as he lurched away, mind numb with incomprehension, anger, and horror, did Saviar notice five people moving cautiously toward them. Under other circumstances, he would have recognized them immediately as Mages of Myr-cidë. Now, lost in a fog of disbelief, grief, and rage, he felt driven only to destroy.

"By the gods," one mage shouted, "he's still alive!" He slammed past Saviar in his headlong rush to Subikahn. "Jer-emilan, everyone, come quickly! He's alive!"

It was nearly beyond Saviar's control to clutch his weapon in hopeless rage rather than cut the mages down as they raced past him to kneel at Subikahn's side. They spoke amongst themselves in a language Saviar did not know, their auras flaring around them.

A fire churned inside Saviar. His head pounded, his gut seethed, and his knuckles whited around *Motfrabelonning*. Instead of the mages, he turned his sword on the giant lying still on the ground. The blood intermittently spurting from his stump suggested he still maintained the last vestiges of life. Saviar leaped onto his face, driving his blade through one eye, then the other, ending with a slice that opened the *Kjempemagiska*'s throat nearly from ear to ear. Little blood emerged, most of it already on the ground, and even less satisfaction accompanied the mutilation. Light reflected from the giant's bloodless skin. Saviar whirled to see the mages swarming over his twin, their auras flashing and light blossoming around the Renshai's still form.

Once again, Saviar checked the urge to plow through the mages, sword leading. He had not forgotten his promise to protect them. It took all his effort not to attack, so he found it impossible to keep offense and suspicion from his tone. "What in coldest Hel are you doing?"

Fully focused on Subikahn, the mages did not respond, but Saviar discovered his own answers. There could be only one reason the Mages of Myrcidë had come to this spot; they had planned to secretly desert the battle. Apparently, the *Kjempemagiska* had found them first and nearly slaugh-tered them before Subikahn arrived. He had saved their lives and now, Renshai or not, they were doing whatever they could to save his.

The Myrcidians blocked Saviar's view, but he could still picture the slash in Subikahn's tunic and abdomen in his mind's eye, the glistening loops of bowel freed from their confinement. No one could survive such an injury. And yet, Saviar realized, these same users of magic had nursed him from the brink of certain death as well. *A coward's death. A sure commitment to Hel because my own brother thought too little of me to grant me the opportunity—the right—to earn Valhalla.*

Without the ministrations of the mages, Subikahn would die in minutes or hours. The manner of his death, succumbing on the battlefield to wounds sustained in valiant combat against an opponent who would also die from his injuries, would surely win Subikahn the rewards of Valhalla. *An eternity of blissful combat. A place among the* Einherjar *heroes. The greatest rewards of the universe, the same ones he would have withheld from me.*

Under other circumstances, Saviar would have driven the mages away, preventing them from stealing the ultimate honor any man could receive from the brother he loved, until a moment ago, without conditions. Now, Saviar hesitated, horribly conflicted. He loved Subikahn without reservation, had for as long as he could remember. They shared a closeness he had always believed only twins could understand. But Subikahn's actions as Saviar had grown more helpless were abomination, the supreme demonstration of dishonor, the epitome of degradation. If he stopped the mages, Saviar allowed Subikahn the honor all Renshai had strived for for eternity, one he had always before believed they both deserved. But, clearly, his brother did not find him worthy of the same.

Had the other Renshai known of Subikahn's prior actions, they would have inflicted punishment upon him that Saviar could only imagine. He had never heard of any Renshai abandoning his honor in such an appalling manner. Banishment seemed the least of the possibilities. More likely, they would have forced him to die in some lingering and dishonorable way, his soul condemned to Hel, his mind forced to contemplate his crime and his eternal damnation for all eternity. Perhaps they would have deliberately infected him with disease or, worse, locked him up until he gradually starved.

Saviar loved his twin too much to allow it to happen. He would never tell anyone what Subikahn had told him. If he died now, Subikahn would go to his pyre a casualty of the war, a hero in every mind but Saviar's. Yet, Saviar saw an end more just, in its way, more horrible. If the Mages of Myrcidë healed Subikahn, he would have to suffer not only the knowledge of what he had done to Saviar but also live with the realization that his deathbed confession was no longer a secret. In some ways, it seemed the perfect punishment for his crime. Subikahn would have to confront his dishonor and also the condemnation of his brother, things he had, thus far, managed to avoid.

Not wanting to dwell on the situation a moment longer, Saviar steeled himself and charged back toward the battle.

As Tae Kahn walked through Béarn's courtyard with Mistri and Rantire by his side and Imorelda perched on his shoulders, the guardsmen stepped aside without comment. The flower beds that bore a brilliant array of blossoms in spring and summer now lay fallow. The statuary and benches looked strangely worn and haggard, as if displaying the mood of the men chosen to remain behind and keep the city of Béarn.

Tae knew he might never see even the gardens again, let alone the Eastlands he loved and ruled. The petty arguments and differences between the peoples of the continent seemed long ago and far away. Nothing seemed good or wholesome or right anymore. This day, the world would either end or continue wholly changed. The war would take its casualties, mostly at random, leaving them sorrowful and broken, a tattered group of loose societies unbalanced and unhinged by death, grief, and destruction.

Tae had little to say to his companions. Ignorant of the coming storm, Mistri fairly skipped, and Tae found himself jogging to keep up with her. Griff and Matrinka had briefed Rantire and assured him she knew when to remain watchful and when to attack. Since she did not speak a word of Heimstadr, and Kentt knew none of the continental languages, Tae had no concern she might verbally antagonize him into a hostile action simply to sate her hatred, bloodlust, or desire for battle.

We're coming, Tae sent randomly as the guards ushered them into the outer courtyard. *We need to know where to find you.*

When no reply came at some length, Mistri added, *Poppy?*

Mistri, he sent back. *My beloved. Are you truly a group of only three?*

Mistri did not hesitate, *Tae, a lady, and me. And Imorda.*

Imorda? He echoed the childishly incorrect pronunciation, then added, *That's Tae's pet?*

Yes.

The giant continued to address his daughter, which Tae understood. Mistri would not lie to him. *What kind of animal is Imorda?*

Mistri looked at Tae.

"Do you not have cats?"

Mistri shook her head.

"Describe her to him." Tae did not want to put words in the child's mouth. Kentt would know at once if she sounded coached. "Just be sure to include her size. I suspect he's worried about his safety and wants to make sure she isn't a . . ." He did not know the island animals, so he had to resort to description himself. ". . . huge and vicious brute."

Mistri tried. *She's little and furry. She's nice, and she can't hurt anyone, Poppy.*

Kentt reminded, *Jarfr are little and furry, too.*

Mistri laughed out loud. *Poppy, jarfr are big. Imorda's more like . . .* She studied the cat on Tae's shoulder's. * . . . mermelr.*

Tae got the mental image of an oversized, squat squirrel with a less flexible tail.

But with stripes like yessha . . . *

This time, Tae saw something horselike with alternating bands of brown and white.

* . . . and a longer, thinner tail.*

Tae wondered if Mistri could simply focus on Imorelda, sending that picture to her father the same way he received ones of the animals she mentioned. He supposed the way they received *anari* might differ from his own. Or, perhaps, she did send Kentt the image of a cat, one Tae did not see because he already had his own ideas of how they should and did look.

Sounds like a strange beast indeed.

Having left Béarn proper, Tae headed toward the shore, though he had no particular reason for choosing that direction. It made sense given that Kentt had arrived by sea and no one had yet spotted him. *Kentt,* he reminded. *We *don't know how to find you.* Only then, Tae realized the giant was stalling not because he had a plan to ambush them but because he worried they might harm him. Given his size and abilities compared to theirs, his threat to bring down the entire castle, it seemed impossible, yet the emotions slipping through the contact made it clear. Tae realized the giant might not be a warrior at all, just a concerned father who had begged to join the assault for the sole purpose of rescuing his missing child.

Tae tested his theory, *Kentt, you're not a soldier, are you?*

Another pause, this one shorter, then a gentle, *No.* Had he spoken aloud, the word would have emerged in a whisper. *I begged to come along. No one believed I would find my daughter alive. Or, if I did, she would serve as the bait in a colossal trap. Nevertheless, they indulged me, let me swim alone to shore to spy under cover of the illusionary ships. They promised that, once the main battle ended, they would help me rescue Mistri.*

Most of that explanation had to go over Mistri's head, but she caught enough to become concerned. She studied Tae with the wide-eyed innocence of any child. "You not gonna hurt Poppy?"

Tae said the only thing he could, "Of course not." He had no particular intention of or reason to do so; if the *Kjempe-magiska* attacked, however, he would defend himself. He saw no sense in trying to explain war or trust or danger to a child nor did he feel knight-bound to any agreement, whether or not he considered it an oath. "And I hope you'll see to it your father doesn't harm us, either."

Mistri gave him a look that suggested he had said something particularly stupid. "Lots said he shouldn't fix Bobbin. But Poppy fixed him. Twice. Poppy's . . ." She searched for the right word. ". . . nice."

Tae put a reassuring hand on Mistri's arm. "He sounds good-hearted, your Poppy." It suddenly occurred to him that, in her own innocent way, Mistri had made a significant point. The *Kjempemagiska* must have figured out that Arturo had originated from the continent, yet Kentt had chosen to allow him to live. Love for his daughter explained some of it, but he had likely developed some affection for Arturo as well. Tae switched to the trading tongue for

Rantire. "Kentt's not a soldier. He only came to get his daughter back, and he's promised not to attack."

Rantire bobbed her head once. "If he's a civilian, and he doesn't do anything aggressive, he has nothing to fear from me."

Mistri had to know, "What she say?"

Tae smiled at the girl. "She said she's not going to hurt him, either." He squeezed her arm gently, "Mistri, you need to get your father to tell us where he is."

Mistri nodded vigorously, and Tae released his hold. *Poppy, where are you?*

I'll give you a signal. Follow.

Tae cocked his head, then stroked Imorelda's rump, the only place he could reach. She curled her tail around his throat but otherwise gave no reply. This was something new, and he needed her to focus.

A hum sounded through the link.

Mistri took Tae's hand. "Come on!"

"Where?" Tae had no idea how to act on the noise.

"Follow," Mistri pointed south of the docks.

Tae wondered if he could learn to pinpoint a mind-signal the way Mistri did. For now, he followed her. Though her legs were short and pudgy for her size, she moved swiftly; he found himself jogging again to keep up with her. Imorelda buried her claws into his shoulders for balance, and he tried to smooth his pace.

Down the beach they headed, around sand dunes that blocked their view of the docks and, eventually, the ocean as well. Mistri's pace quickened until sand scattered beneath her feet, forcing Tae and Rantire to run along with her. At length, she slowed, winding around a tight collection of dunes, then stopped entirely. *Poppy?*

The hum stopped. *You're close, I think. Look for a circle of sand hills, and you'll find me in the center.*

Tae scanned the beach. Between high dunes, he caught spare glimpses of Béarnian warships just offshore, along with an occasional dragon-prowed Northern vessel. No sign of the gigantic, illusory fleet remained, at least that he could see. He thought he saw a natural formation that might fit Kentt's description and pointed. "There?"

Mistri looked in the direction of Tae's extended finger, then plodded toward the indicated dunes. Her breaths emerged quick and hard, which allowed Tae and Rantire to move up beside her. Tae could hear his heart pounding in his ears, at least twice as fast as normal. Then, they stepped around the dunes and saw him.

Kentt sat in the sand. Had he stood, he probably could have peered over dunes that seemed more like tiny mountains to Tae. His sodden clothing was exquisitely crafted, the stitching small, straight, and even, the dyed colors steady enough to withstand his swim through salt and waves. Tightly woven, his sleeved, short-skirted coat and loose trousers might turn away a sword nearly as well as mail. His cloak was open, except at the throat, where a silver clasp pinned it. Wavy hair the color of tea spilled down his back, his features finer than Tae had expected, and his eyes a pale mixture of blue, gray, and green. Clean-shaven, he sported a lantern chin and a large mouth by human standards with lips to match.

"Poppy!" Mistri hurled herself into his arms.

Kentt seized his daughter, enfolding her into his enormous embrace. His body shuddered repeatedly, and it took Tae inordinately long to realize he was sobbing. "Mistri, oh, Mistri." He grasped her so hard, he seemed certain to crush her.

Mistri squirmed in his grip.

Despite the danger, Tae found himself smiling. Their differences seemed vast and insurmountable; but, at least, they had one thing in common. The *Kjempemagiska*, apparently, also loved their children.

CHAPTER 32

Legendary? Is that how the common man denies hard-won skills these days? In my time, they credited it to lies or magic.

— Colbey Calistinsson

THE GROUND SEEMED TO QUAKE under the feet of the advancing *Kjempemagiska*. Well-trained, the white steeds of the Knights of Erythane held their ground, but Darby's horse bolted. Worried the panicked animal might harm the infantry, Ra-khir broke ranks to catch the fleeing animal. Seizing its bridle, he reeled the small chestnut against Silver Warrior's flank. The stallion held firm, pinning the other horse between itself and the trunks of the forest, while Ra-khir held its head high and tight until it could no longer buck.

The remainder of the knights charged as the *Kjempemagiska* screamed down upon the armies, en masse. One sweep sent Sir Garvin, Sir Thessilus, and Knight-Captain Kedrin airborne, their horses toppling like tenpins. Garvin fell in two places, cleaved in half. Thessilus landed in an awkward position and went still. Apparently, the giant's blade had lost some of its momentum by the time it struck Kedrin, because his roll appeared deliberate. Garvin's mount went straight down, Thessilus' head over tail, and Snow Stormer fell sideways, a gash in his side.

"Dismount, if you can't control him," Ra-khir instructed Darby. Tasked with the oversized sword his sons had insisted Thialnir and Kedrin give him, he could not follow his own advice. On foot, he could barely handle the weapon. He wheeled Silver Warrior and galloped toward the fray, sword held out in front of him, lancelike.

Six of the knights managed to surround one giant, and the battle appeared promising until another *Kjempe-magiska* struck from behind his companion, taking down two more knights and tramping onward as if it had taken no effort whatsoever. At full gallop, Ra-khir rammed him, impaling him. The impact sent Ra-khir floundering backward, unseating him. Silver Warrior skidded to a stop, too late. Still embedded in the giant, the huge sword was wrenched from Ra-khir's grip. He slammed to the ground, contact jarring through his spine, in time to see a booted *Kjempe-magiska* foot speeding toward his head.

Desperate, Ra-khir dove between two deadfalls. The foot crashed onto both trunks, splintering them but saving Ra-khir from crushing. Seeming not to notice him, the *Kjempe-magiska* moved onward. Ra-khir scrambled to a crouch between the shattered deadfalls, reassessing the battle. He could hear Silver Warrior whinnying wildly, seeking him. Nearer, he found his head-struck father staggering purposelessly. Ra-khir seized Kedrin's arm and pulled him down into the hollow of the deadfalls. "Captain, listen to me."

Silver Warrior's distress brought the memory of another horse that could pass for its identical twin. When Colbey had descended into the abyss to battle demons, he had believed it a suicide mission and had given his steed, Frost Reaver, to Ra-khir. The stallion had called frantically for its centuries-old master, its own life prolonged by a steady diet of Idunn's golden apples of youth. That gave Ra-khir an idea, and he blurted it aloud before he could consider it further. "Call *all* the Knights of Erythane to battle, Captain. We can't spare a single one."

Kedrin's white-blue eyes seemed incapable of focusing on Ra-khir, but his reply suggested his ears still functioned. "What are you babbling about? The Knights are here, Ra-khir. They're all right here."

Ra-khir grabbed his father's shoulders, then ducked to avoid another blow, pinning Kedrin to the ground. A massive sword hissed over the deadfalls. "No. One's missing.

One's *always* missing. Captain, you need to call Sir Colbey to active duty."

An Erythanian infantryman tripped over the deadfalls and nearly collapsed onto the knights.

For a moment Kedrin stared at Ra-khir in disbelief. Humans prayed to gods, humans begged gods, humans beseeched the gods; but humans did not demand the service of gods, even one who did not claim the title. Whatever he was, the immortal Renshai lived and married among the gods; and, even in his mortal time, no one had ever dared tell Colbey what to do.

Kedrin's pupils dilated until they threatened to take over his irises. "I can't do that!"

Ra-khir studied the battle. Piles of human bodies littered the ground, but only one *Kjempemagiska* lay still, the one he had skewered before he lost his mount and his weapon. This war required every man. As soon as his father regained his wits, they both had to return to it for however short their lives might last. "You have to, Captain. If you don't, we're all doomed."

Kedrin sat up just as a *Kjempemagiska* sword lunged toward them. Ra-khir drew and parried with his regular sword, enhanced only by exposure to elfin magic. The massive blade hammered his own, shocking agony through both arms all the way to his shoulders. He bit back a scream and threw himself at his opponent, trying to protect his father as long as possible, to give him the opportunity to do what had to be done. Only the Knight-Captain might have the authority to do what Ra-khir had suggested.

Ra-khir raised his sword again, prepared to meet the next assault but hoping he could dodge rather than needing to deflect again. He doubted his arms could take another hit. He flew at the giant, ducking under the curved blade, cutting in to score a slash that barely grazed the giant's ankle. The huge sword came at him again. Ra-khir spun away, using all his strength to score a line of scarlet across the *Kjempemagiska*'s wrist. Unlike the oversized sword, his blade required great strength just to leave a mark.

Frustration seized Ra-khir. In a fair fight, he had a chance. With his weapons curtailed, he doubted he could last much longer. "For Erythane and Béarn!" Ra-khir raced for the giant, leaping into the air and putting every bit of body weight behind the attack. It was sheer desperation. If he aimed right, hit hard enough, he might cut open the chest or abdomen with enough force to cause lethal damage. Whether he hit or missed, Ra-khir doubted he would have a second chance.

Ra-khir's blade struck true, driving through the giant's finely woven coat and plunging into his belly. Ra-khir sagged, trying to rip the sword downward, to open the wound enough to assure his opponent's death. The curved sword dropped from the giant's grip. He roared, catching Ra-khir in both hands and squeezing.

Air rushed from Ra-khir's lungs. His bones creaked, and an agony beyond any he had known raced through every part. He opened his mouth to scream, but nothing emerged. No air remained in his body, forced out by the strength of those crushing fingers. The world faded into swirling spots of black and white. Ra-khir's consciousness faded.

Then, something swift and silver streaked past Ra-khir's head, severing both of the giant's wrists. Helpless, Ra-khir fell like a stone, the crash of his body against the ground reigniting the anguish and sending it spiraling through his entire being. Air rushed into his lungs so suddenly, it seemed to fill every part of him. He fought his way back to consciousness just in time to see the giant tumble backward. A golden blur of movement whisked toward the giants, lightning incarnate.

Colbey! Ra-khir realized. Though his whole body screamed with pain, he staggered to his feet. The tide of the battle turned in that moment, and—somehow—everyone knew it. One by one, the giants fell like trees before a relentless ax. Humans rallied behind the immortal Renshai, finishing off his kills, dragging aside the injured humans, driving in to attack with renewed and hopeful vigor. The cries of the hurt and dying were usurped by cheers. Dispirited men came to life, and Ra-khir could see the wave of confident expectation flying down the front line as if carried on a lateral wind.

Colbey seemed unstoppable, his blades never still. It appeared as if he killed a giant with each stroke, though Ra-khir knew better. It took five or six, all well-aimed, to down each opponent. He just did so with extraordinary quickness, his weapons swift-moving blurs, his exuberance and energy apparently unwaning.

But Ra-khir understood Colbey better than most, knew the immortal Renshai relied on the human combatants to finish the jobs he started, knew his endurance had limits that would not allow him to plow through more than a hundred *Kjempemagiska*, at best. For all his ability, the immortal Renshai was fallible; and, the longer he fought, the sooner he would make that inevitable and fatal mistake.

Ra-khir had to rally every possible combatant, to drive them all at the giants simultaneously, in order to break the *Kjempemagiska's* spirit and send them into awkward and desperate retreat before Colbey made that lethal error and the giants, once again, took the upper hand. He did his best to spur everyone around him into action, raced down the lines with his optimism seething, whipped the humans into a frenzy that could last beyond whatever Colbey could manage. The war was definitely not over, and the more they accomplished before the fall of their would-be savior, the better chance they had of winning this war.

It soon seemed to Ra-khir that he need not have done anything. Each unit saw the wild warrior and gave him their own interpretation. The silver-striped blond hair gave away a Northern heritage that every tribe claimed as one of its own. He was a god to others, a hero from their ancient legends, a magical being unleashed by the elves. Ra-khir made no effort to disabuse them of any notion that caused them to rise up and fight, especially since the truth might dishearten them. Too many peoples of the continent hated Renshai without reservation and, quite often, without reason.

By the time Ra-khir reached the opposite front of the battlefield, the Renshai had already identified their leader. They hooted and howled, leaving bloody corpses in their wake with the same fervor as Colbey, without need of his help. Calistin and Saviar formed the leading edge of another onslaught, equally bloody; Ra-khir knew that, if they survived this battle, the legends would surely merge. He saw no sign of Subikahn but did not let that worry him. It was unreasonable to believe he could find any individual soldier in a war this large.

Ra-khir ached in every part. Sharp pain stabbed through him with every breath. Each movement sparked a fresh

wave of anguish he was finding it increasingly difficult to
cast aside, even in the name of desperation. He had made it
across the entire front solely on the strength of a pure and
absolute need, but even that seemed no longer enough. His
consciousness wavered. Reality closed in tight. For the moment, the troops had rallied; but it lasted only so long as
Colbey Calistinsson and Calistin Ra-khirsson remained
alive to lead. Soon, fatigue would increase the likelihood of
a misstep. Their luck could not hold up forever. And, once
they fell, the tide of the war would turn again. Then, nothing
could stop the *Kjempemagiska*.

Bodies littered the battlefield, the vast majority of them
human but a growing number the enormous forms of *Kjempemagiska*, killed not only by Colbey, Calistin, and Saviar
but by their encouraged followers. Ra-khir estimated a
dozen *Kjempemagiska* bodies mingled with the smaller
corpses, then another dozen, a third. Aggrieved roaring
filled the air, sounds as mournful as a lone and anxious wolf
seeking the comfort of its pack. It occurred to Ra-khir that
the loss of only two of their own had caused them to retreat
the first time. With a jolt that sent anguish coursing through
him, Ra-khir realized they were about to do something hys-
terical and enormous, something the peoples of the continent had no means to handle.

Waves of nausea passed through Ra-khir, and he cursed
the injuries that made him feel so fragile. He did not know
who to turn to, what to shout; but he suspected the elves
needed to know and probably already did. He could almost
feel the giants withdrawing, a physical retreat of such force it
seemed to suck him into it as well, like an undertow. A warning speared his head, laced with panic, **Stay low. Hang on!**

The message did not seem personal. Ra-khir did not believe someone had sent it directly to him, but it galvanized
him. Despite his own wounds, he needed to find a way to
assist the battle, whatever it took. And, at the moment, it
took the right weapon.

The enemy's retreat incited the others as well. Warriors
surged around Ra-khir, pounding toward the front, prepared
to follow their golden leaders into what had finally become
a two-sided battle. Finding a *Kjempemagiska* corpse, mangled nearly beyond recognition, Ra-khir grabbed for the
vanquished sword. Mounted, he had found their weapons

unwieldy. Grounded and aching, the weight nearly undid him. He seized the hilt at a dead run, but his arms failed him. Still gripping the weapon, he toppled to the ground, and the pounding feet of the soldiers behind him smashed his left ankle and slammed against his head. Like an anchor, his grip on the sword kept him from moving, but he did draw himself in, attempted to leave as small an area as possible for others to trample.

The world turned dazzlingly white. At first, Ra-khir thought the blow to his head had ruined his vision. Then, he remembered during the previous war, when Saviar had thrust *Motfrabelonning*'s hilt into his hand and allowed him to see the flashing auras that accompanied the use of magic. Someone kicked Ra-khir's fingers as he passed, and the knight lost his grip on the sword. The light disappeared. Ra-khir lunged forward, seized the hilt again, and the world seemed to ignite into blinding brilliance.

Ra-khir wobbled to a stand, the sword a sagging burden in his fist. The pain in his left ankle surpassed the myriad aches of the rest of his body, refusing to take any of his weight. Gradually, the lights took form: a massive horse-shoe around the battlefield perfectly defining the woods, a separate mass toward the northwest comprised of giants, a few stragglers here and there who Ra-khir had no means to identify. The air became thick, heavy with expectation. It seemed as if the entire world, and every living thing in it, paused for the barest moment.

Then, an explosion shattered Ra-khir's hearing, stole the last of his deteriorating vision, and flung him effortlessly into the sky. Wind rushed around him with such force it threatened to tear out his lungs and violate every part of him. Even his organs felt abruptly cold. All senses failed him, and he knew nothing but a terrible force that hurled him like a wet and boneless doll. The pain coalesced into an agony beyond bearing. Position lost all meaning, and not a single sense remained to anchor him. Merciful, empty darkness settled over Ra-khir, and he knew no more.

Gradually, the sky turned a sickly shade of green, heralding an upcoming storm of tremendous magnitude. Abruptly, Kentt shoved Mistri from his grasp and, for the first time, rose fully to his feet, towering over the others hidden amidst the dunes.

The instant he did so, Rantire drew, crouching. Tae's heart pounded. The *Kjempemagiska* did not carry any obvious weaponry and seemed too focused on the horizon to mean them any threat. He only hoped Rantire would not read his lack of reaction to her aggressive stance as a grave and personal insult. "He's not a warrior," Tae reminded her. "He's concentrating on something far away, something bigger than you or me or even Mistri."

Taking a cue from her father, Mistri also turned in the direction of his stare. The sky was darkening far too swiftly, as if something menaced the sun itself. Tae doubted their decision to look toward the distant battlefield was random. Tae prodded softly in *usaro*, "What is it?"

Kentt seemed so utterly focused, even beyond his own safety, Tae did not expect an answer. "Magic. It's magic."

"Yours?" Tae prodded.

"No." Kentt finally spared his human companions a glance. "I have nothing to do with it, but it's bad. Very bad."

Tae glanced at Rantire who remained in a crouched and armed position, though she made no move to attack. "Please, you need to tell us. What's happening? What can we do to stop it?"

Kentt seized Mistri with both hands, pulling her against him and folding his arms across her. "We cannot stop it. We can only hope to survive it."

Tae looked toward Béarn. So many people inhabited the castle, including the royal family. Without Griff or his heir, without the focal point of all neutrality, the world was doomed whether or not the *Kjempemagiska* lost the war. "Can we protect the castle?" Imorelda's claws sank into Tae's neck. He could feel her fur bristling. He attempted to pull her into his arms, but she shoved her head through the neck of his tunic. The cloth tightened dangerously, and he swiftly undid the clasp, worried she would throttle both of them to death.

Kentt glanced at the sky, now so dark Tae could barely make out the dune in front of him. Sand started to swirl.

"Not necessary. It's carved from the mountains. If anything can withstand the force of this backlash, it can." He dropped back to a crouch, pulling Mistri with him. "It's us you have to worry about. Those on the beach, the ocean, the flatland."

Something akin to lightning cleaved the sky. The wind screamed toward them, flinging sand with a violence that drove it deeply into Tae's face. He slammed his lids shut, scratching grainy trenches across his eyes. The pain was overwhelming. Screams wrenched from his throat, unbidden, and opened the way for fine dust to fill his nose and mouth. Choking, he dropped to the ground, clutching his tunic, with Imorelda beneath it, against his chest. Her claws gouged through his undergarments and into his flesh. "Can you help them?" Tae gasped out, swallowing salt and grit as the wind threw the words back into his face. Only then, he remembered he could communicate without opening his mouth. *Please, help us! Help them!*

Gales tore at Tae's clothes. Imorelda hunkered against him, snuggled between the layers. The exposed skin of his hands and feet, his face and neckline seemed suddenly on fire. He could feel the wind-driven sand tearing, dared to wonder how fast the wind must be blowing to lend the sand such power. The pain rose to raw agony. He found himself screaming. Then, something enormous covered him, shielding him from the bulk of the storm.

I'm trying, Tae. The grief of the world seemed to accompany the sending, buffeting Tae with waves of hopeless agony. *Two enormous and opposite magical forces have collided. Devastatingly! Explosively! We're suffering only the distant backlash. No one at the site could possibly have survived.* The *Kjempemagiska*'s mental sending became a head-filling howl of misery. The intensity of Kentt's despair nearly overwhelmed Tae. He, too, lost all will to live.

We're going to die, Imorelda moaned. The instant she broke the contact between human and Kjempemagiska, the intolerable depression lifted and Tae found himself capable of mustering courage again.

We're going to live, Tae assured her, now realizing Kentt's own body cocooned them nearly as fully as he shielded Imorelda. *We've survived worse.* He did not mention the fate of all their relatives, their acquaintances, their friends on the battlefield. Imorelda did not understand the language of Heimstadt, and Tae had to believe Kentt was wrong to keep himself from becoming paralyzed with heartache, too.

There's nothing worse.

Tae knew he needed to keep in contact with Kentt, regardless of the discomfort. Now fully assured the bottomless angst eminated from the *Kjempemagiska*, Tae believed he could keep his own emotions stable. *Imorelda, I'm sorry. If we're going to live through this, I have to be able to communicate with them.*

Imorelda shifted beneath him, but she said nothing more. Soon, her wild but familiar discomfort was replaced by the searing agony of Kentt's misery.

Tae sent, *Kentt, I'm sorry. I'm so sorry. But you can't surrender. You have to survive for Mistri.* Only then, he realized Mistri had not been silent. Her screams and sobs had formed a continuous noise in his mind, one so consistent he had blocked it out entirely. *We need you, and you need us. Both of you.* Tae had no idea of the truth of his words. Kentt's belief that all the *Kjempemagiska* soldiers had died was unwavering. It was not a supposition; somehow, he knew. Tae had to assume the giants had some sort of magical connection, but it could not extend to humans and elves. It was still possible that some of the peoples of the continent, or the elves, were alive.

Then, as suddenly as it had come, the storm was over. The sand settled back into its place, the sun reappeared, and daylight bathed the shores of Béarn again. Silence assailed them, as if all hearing had ceased to exist. Tae scrambled free of Kentt to look at the castle. After the near-total darkness, the sunlight blinded him. He shielded his eyes, desperate to see, and the familiar mountains filled his vision. The castle looked the same as it always did, gray and welcoming, as stunning a piece of stonework art as human tools could master.

Kentt's anguish had turned to a numb hush, letting Tae's own emotions emerge. He savored the sight of Béarn Castle, still standing. He turned to assist Rantire but found her already beside him, her posture defensive, her face flayed raw, sword still clenched in her bloody fist. Tae loosened his hold on Imorelda, lowering her gently to the ground. The effort of shoving through his neck hole had scraped some fur from the top of her head; otherwise, she looked none the worse for wear. Her feeble meow of welcome was the first physical sound he heard.

Kentt rose. Apparently, he had used magic to shield them, because he appeared entirely unruffled. The sand and wind had left him unscathed. He released Mistri and spun her around, looking for injuries. Her clothing was badly wrinkled, imprints of the dunes temporarily impressed on them, but she also appeared fine. Finally, Tae turned his attention to the open shore. A few of the warships remained, most of those listing. Others had vanished, leaving only scraps floating on the sea. Debris riddled the beach: wood, straw, metal. Clothing and bodies.

Tae resisted the urge to flop onto the ground and sob. Now was not the time to grieve or even to demand answers. There were still lives that might be saved. And, Tae realized, for once he was not among the critically wounded.

Saviar could not recall the last time he felt so physically battered and exhausted. Lungs smoky, head still dizzy from the swirling winds that had pummeled the battlefield and beyond, he staggered toward the center of the field. The elves had used *khohlar* to assure the disoriented survivors that no danger remained. Even the Renshai instincts, pounded into him since birth, could not override the emptiness he felt. Had a demon dropped from the sky, he doubted he could raise enough energy to care, let alone defend himself.

Bodies and body parts littered the grasslands, chunks of armor and broken swords, bark and limbs as big as cottages. The forest trees, once wreathed in multicolored leaves, now stood or leaned like shattered skeletons, their tops charred. The grasslands smoldered in several places. Dazed humans walked in crazy circles or made their shuffling way, like things half dead, toward the center of the battlefield. Saviar saw the corpses, too. They hung in trees, carried by the gale. They lay buried beneath fallen trunks, smashed in trampled piles, flung across open terrain as if prostrated before demanding gods.

A snort caught Saviar's attention. To his right, at the edge of the forest, a white stallion nuzzled a human form dressed in the familiar blue-and-gold tunic of the Knights of Erythane. Saviar might have ignored the scene, one more casualty in a war that had claimed thousands, but it struck him odd to find a knight on the Renshai side of the battle-grounds. The generals had placed them at opposite ends of the front; and, while the winds might have dragged flotsam from anywhere, Saviar thought he recognized the horse as well. "Silver?"

The horse lifted its head and turned to look at Saviar. It trumpeted out a shrill whinny, and its forehooves beat the ground in a frantic tattoo.

With a sigh of resignation, Saviar walked toward the horse. The last thing he wanted to find now were the bodies of his family members, but he owed Silver Warrior that much. The horse had served his father well for many years, and Ra-khir had shown equal dedication to the animal, in-sisting on tending it himself instead of trusting it to the min-istrations of groomsmen.

As Saviar expected, he discovered Ra-khir on the ground in front of Silver Warrior. Though still, he seemed intact, red-blond hair obscuring his features but his power-ful body, and knightly garb, unmistakable. Saviar closed his eyes and knelt. His father had never sought a place in Val-halla, at least not before Kevral's soul had gone there, yet Saviar wished it upon him anyway. Death in the flurry of swordplay would earn him that honor, but Saviar doubted the *Valkyries* would choose souls stolen in the mayhem of a magical storm. The means of his death mattered.

Tentatively, Saviar reached out a hand and gently brushed away the errant locks to reveal his father's familiar features. The purple stars of broken blood vessels marred his handsome cheeks, the look of someone squashed be-neath a heavy object while still alive. Perhaps a tree had fallen on him, taking his life, then the powerful winds had whisked the trunk away to drop it harmlessly aside or onto another. Tears stung Saviar's eyes. The means of his father's death allowed him to mourn. He laid a hand on a ravaged cheek, surprised to find it warm. He touched Ra-khir's lips, feeling a soft rush of air. Shocked, he pressed fingers to his father's neck, rewarded by the throb of a living artery.

Silver Warrior stuck his head over Ra-khir's, watching.

Afraid to shake Ra-khir and risk further injuring him, Saviar put his mouth close to his father's ear. "Papa, wake up. Wake up! Wake! Up!"

The green eyes shot open. For a moment, Ra-khir stared uncomprehendingly. Then, suddenly, he sprang to a crouch. His eyes told Saviar he regretted the motion. His entire body seemed to spasm, and he released an involuntary moan of pain.

The abrupt movement startled Silver Warrior, who jumped back with a whicker of alarm.

Saviar seized Ra-khir's arm. "Papa. Are you hurt?"

"Not . . . fatally," Ra-khir managed. He added sullenly, "Though, for a while, I might wish it so."

Saviar remained still, allowing his father to rise at his own pace. Pretending not to watch Ra-khir move like a man twice his age, Saviar caught Silver Warrior's flopping reins and held them near the stallion's mouth. "I got tossed around a bit, too." It was gross understatement. The gale had flung him like a toy, slamming him against a tree before he managed to wrap his arms and legs around a sturdy branch and cling until it passed.

"One of the giants got hold of me," Ra-khir explained, his breathing quick and shallow, a sure sign of broken ribs. "He nearly crushed me. I suspect I was out for most of the . . ." He seemed at a loss for words. ". . . tossing." Though fully standing, he clutched at Silver Warrior's saddle for support. "Magic, I believe."

Saviar harbored little doubt. He, too, had seen the surging auras prior to the explosion and killer winds. Fires had ignited in the tops of the trees and all along the plain, extinguished by the gale that had seemed determined to leave nothing living in its path. Yet, somehow, hundreds had survived. *Hundreds out of tens of thousands.* Saviar scanned the battlefield again, confused. Though an appalling number of bodies littered the ground, there were not nearly enough to account for all the dead. Surely, the winds had carried away some, but that could not justify the sparseness of the casualties. He estimated a thousand human corpses, but he doubted that number would more than double once those crushed beneath trees, driven into the forest, torn apart or blown away were added to the total.

Elfin *khohlar* touched Saviar's mind again. *All survivors come to the center of the field for counting and sorting. Assist the wounded to accompany you, if possible, but don't delay. Do not attend the corpses at this time. All will be accorded proper honors, but it is imperative we identify them first. You have nothing to fear from giants; they have all perished.**

Saviar wondered how the elves could possibly know the status of the *Kjempemagiska*, but he had no way to question.

Ra-khir looked at Silver Warrior's saddle but made no effort to mount. "Your brothers, Savi. Have you seen them?"

Saviar stepped to his father's side. "Want me to help you up?"

"No," Ra-khir responded, too quickly. Then, apparently trying to hide the extent of his discomfort, he covered badly, "We'll leave Silver Warrior open in case we come upon wounded needing our assistance." He took the reins from Saviar and allowed the horse to support part of his weight. "Your brothers?" he reminded.

Saviar wanted to talk about anything other than Subikahn. "Calistin was beside me, at the front, last I saw him. The giants hadn't touched him, but I don't know about the storm."

They headed toward the middle of the plain. Others joined them as they walked, most appearing dazed and confused. Saviar steered several in the right direction, looking for anyone who needed extra assistance. "And Subikahn," Ra-khir pressed, studying Saviar over the horse's neck.

Saviar realized he had made a mistake by mentioning Calistin first. He had always considered Subikahn a sibling and Calistin a plague the gods had forced him to endure. "When I last saw him, he had suffered a critical injury. He had mages all around him, though, attempting to fix it. I don't know if they succeeded or what happened afterward."

"Oh." Ra-khir continued to examine him over Silver Warrior. Though separated for months at a time growing up, the twins remained closely linked emotionally. It surely seemed odd Saviar had not waited to assure Subikahn's survival before returning to battle.

Saviar did wish he had remained long enough to know whether or not the healers believed they could save Subikahn. Ambivalent about his brother and their future, he still wanted to know whether Subikahn had found Valhalla or if he would see his twin alive again. At the time, he could think of nothing to say. Now, he had a million questions that begged answers before he lost Subikahn's earthly presence forever.

As Ra-khir still prompted him with silence and an anticipatory expression, Saviar explained, "There wasn't time for conversation."

Ra-khir accepted that. "No, I suppose not."

They stopped to help an unconscious Western teen whose legs splayed at awkward angles. Saviar hefted him onto Silver Warrior's back, arranging him sideways across the saddle, then they continued to the center of the battlefield. Knight-Captain Kedrin arrived at nearly the same time, supported between two other Knights of Erythane. Filthy and sodden, they had all lost their hats and, apparently, their mounts. At the sight of his son and eldest grandson, Kedrin smiled tiredly.

A group of men who appeared war-weary but otherwise well greeted each straggler as he or she arrived, directing them to various places. Saviar lowered his head and awaited their turn. Fatigue pressed him until he thought he would fall asleep on his feet, then a young Erythanian approached them. "Sir Ra-khir, glad to see you." He executed an awkward bow, then glanced at Saviar who resembled Kedrin more than anyone. "This must be your son."

"Saviar," the Renshai introduced himself.

The Erythanian pointed to himself. "Rayvonn. I'm supposed to inform everyone that the healers are overtaxed and taking only the most severely injured. Those bleeding heavily or unconscious." He gestured toward a makeshift series of tents. One of the plains fires had been coaxed into life in the middle of the grouping, and people raced around assisting those most in need. He looked at the man dangling from Silver Warrior's saddle. "That would include him."

Rayvonn continued, "We're asking the able-bodied to assist in the sorting process. Everyone else is supposed to go there ..." he pointed southward, "... if they're Eastern. There ..." He turned westward, "... if they're Northern." He gestured over his shoulder. "Or there if they're Western." He added, somewhat conspiratorially, "If they don't remember, I'm sending them to the healers."

Saviar grinned at the feeble joke. "Thank you. Let me get these two sorted and I'll see if I can muster the energy to join you." He would have preferred to sleep, but he supposed he fit the definition of able-bodied. Before Ra-khir could stop him, he hoisted the unconscious teen from the saddle and into his arms. He did not want to try separating the steed from his knight, and Ra-khir could use the animal's support, emotionally as well as physically. "I'll meet you in the Western camp." Ignoring Ra-khir's protests, he carried his limp burden toward the healers.

The deadweight on his shoulders proved more of a burden than Saviar expected. He staggered into the healers' camp, and it took extraordinary effort to ease the teen to the ground rather than dropping him unceremoniously at the healers' feet. He knew nothing about the young man he had delivered, so he said nothing, simply tottered off to rejoin his father. He had taken only a few steps when Calistin appeared at his right elbow. "Been drinking, brother?"

Saviar wanted to turn Calistin a withering look, but that would take too much effort. Instead, he went still, waiting for his younger brother to catch up. In a moment, they were walking side by side. "The Western camp is over here." Saviar inclined his head in the proper direction, his arms aching. He glanced at Calistin, surprised to find every part of him covered in gore. Torn nearly in half, his tunic hung in long tatters, revealing his sinewy, hairless chest, also caked in blood. "Is any of that yours?"

Calistin walked in the indicated direction, at Saviar's side. "Is any of what mine?"

Saviar could scarcely believe Calistin needed clarification. "The blood, the guts, the bits of . . . stuff."

"Oh." Calistin looked himself over. "Not much, I don't think."

Saviar did not envy the healers' task. Everyone surely had bruises and gashes from the tremendous force of the wind. Exhaustion and shock affected them all. Broken bones and crushed organs would prove common enough, but he doubted many who tasted the giants' curved swords had survived. The power behind those deadly blades could cut through trees, and the *Kjempemagiska* often mowed down several men with a single strike. He hoped the elves still had some magic to assist, assuming many had survived.

Calistin's voice jarred Saviar from his thoughts. "Where's Subikahn?"

Saviar did not wish to repeat the conversation he had had with Ra-khir. "He hasn't shown up yet. Papa and Granpapa are at the Western camp, though. They'll be glad to see you."

"What about Darby?"

The name did not immediately register. "Who?"

"Papa's shadow."

Saviar had forgotten about Ra-khir's squire. "Haven't seen him, either." *Not that I was looking.* He hated himself for harboring resentment against the youngster, but he still felt as if Darby had stolen the life and attention rightly his. More so since Ra-khir had started spending all his off-time with Darby's mother. He did not go so far as to wish the boy ill. Surviving one's first battle was always a challenge, especially for someone inexperienced and constrained by a burdensome sense of honor. *Hopefully, he was smart enough to run away and hide.*

The Western camp seemed remarkably sparse, consisting of a couple of hundred men and a few well-tended fires. Apparently, the storm had carried or chased the game away. The odor of roasting meat was conspicuously absent, and the men gnawed on hard tack. They had crudely sorted themselves by representative country, those officers who had survived and arrived hovering over them, counting and recounting as more battered warriors arrived.

Saviar spotted Thialnir, his arm bound against his chest, a long line of crusted blood where something sharp had opened his cheek. The Renshai had started with nearly three hundred warriors. Now, Saviar estimated between seventy-five and ninety remained, plus an additional twenty-seven, mostly children, in Béarn. On a percentage basis, they had clearly done better than most, especially given their placement on the front line. Some countries and tribes, it seemed, had lost the entirety of their armies. Still, the number of survivors was too small to fully explain the dearth of bodies on the battlefield.

Calistin joined the Renshai, his welcome hardy and secure. Saviar paused only long enough to make his presence known and ascertain Subikahn's absence before seeking out Ra-khir and Kedrin. He discovered them just beyond the Erythanian gathering. Seven additional knights had joined them as well as Darby, who appeared windswept and sported an enormous bruise across his forehead. Seated on the root ball of a freshly toppled tree, Kedrin was in deep discussion with the elf known as Captain while Ra-khir stood by, watching and listening.

Saviar sidled up beside his father and whispered, "What have we learned?"

Reluctantly, Ra-khir turned from Kedrin and Captain to address his son. "They're discussing how best to inform everyone what happened."

"What happened?" Saviar pressed.

Ra-khir shrugged. "I'm not exactly sure, but Captain seems to know. Your brothers?"

The abrupt change of subject nearly defeated Saviar. He cursed the exhaustion that made every little thing difficult. "Calistin has joined the other Renshai. Still no sign of Subikahn."

"Or, apparently, the Mages of Myrcidë."

That intrigued Saviar. "You think they're still together?"

Ra-khir shrugged. "They were when you last saw them. How long ago was that?"

Saviar considered. It seemed as if days had passed since the start of the magical storm. "Not sure, exactly. Shortly before some crazed Knight of Erythane cleaved his way through the giants, spurring the troops to follow." He studied his father. "That's what I heard, anyway. Is it true?" Working together, he and Calistin had cut a similar swath; but Calistin was the most talented human swordsman alive, and Saviar was no slouch, either. Whoever it was must have wielded a significantly magicked sword, and he knew of only one knight who had one. "Was it . . . you?"

Ra-khir put his hands on his hips, turning Saviar a mockstern look. "Thanks for sounding so incredulous." He smiled, glancing toward the ongoing conversation between Kedrin and Captain. The ranking commander of Béarn's troops, Captain Galastad, had joined them. "But, no, it wasn't me."

Saviar looked over the remaining knights but did not see anyone who looked the part. He ran through their names in his head. The people of Erythane always knew and revered the current two-dozen Erythanian heroes, weaving their names into poetry, rhymes, and songs. He caught himself humming the familiar tune aloud and, apparently, so did Ra-khir.

"Think less conventionally, Saviar. Most people don't know that, at any time, there are actually a maximum of twenty-five knights. But you do."

Saviar's gaze went instinctively to Darby, then stopped abruptly as he realized the truth. "Colbey Calistinsson."

Ra-khir did not confirm Saviar's guess; his smile did it for him.

Though Saviar had figured it out himself, he still did not believe it. "A lot of the Renshai were saying it was Colbey, but I dismissed them. I mean, every group out there was trying to claim the mystery warrior as one of their own, and I figured that, if Colbey had joined us, he'd be at the Renshai end of the battle."

Ra-khir shrugged. "He came when we called him, and it's a lucky thing he did. Without him, I don't believe any of us would have survived."

Saviar did not know whether his father meant any of the knights or any of the people of the continent. Ultimately, it did not matter. Even with Colbey's assistance, they would have eventually been overpowered if not for the magical intervention. *Whose?* Saviar suspected he would not find out until he learned what the elfin Captain was telling the ranking officers of Béarn and Erythane.

Suddenly, *khohlar* filled Saviar's mind in a voice he somehow knew belonged to Captain. ⋆*I apologize for the intrusion into your minds, but it's the nature of* khohlar *to reach everyone within range. Your leaders have requested you not leave your camps at this time and feel it's best for all of you to listen while I explain the magical events that ended the war.*⋆

Saviar doubted, given the opportunity, any man would choose to leave. Though odd, *khohlar* was not uncomfortable or painful, and curiosity had to plague every man and woman who had taken part in the war. The luxury of denying the existence of sorcery no longer remained. Before the arrival of the elves on Midgard, the majority of humans believed in it only as mythology and timeworn legend. The reality of it had become undeniable to those few who had had dealings with the elves, and their experiences had radiated outward. Reactions toward it differed greatly: from appreciation to suspicion, skepticism to distrust, excitement to hatred. No one on the field could dismiss it anymore, but many might still find it terrifying or abhorrent.

⋆They have chosen to have me communicate in this form in order to reach all of you at one time with consistent information rather than allow rampant miscommunication, speculation, and rumor.⋆

Saviar appreciated the point. With each telling, stories changed, often vitally. *Better for everyone to experience the same description and draw simultaneous conclusions, whether similar or differing.* He sat on a deadfall and waited for Captain to continue. It helped that he could see the elf, where many of the men could not. Captain still verbally discussed the situation with Kedrin and Galastad, as well as several other world leaders, including Valr Magnus, who had joined them. Ra-khir took a seat beside his oldest son, the slow caution of his movements revealing his aches had worsened.

Captain's presence returned to Saviar's mind, but this time no specific words accompanied the *khohlar*. Instead, he showed an image of the familiar battlefield, the long stretch of plains grass surrounded by a horseshoe-shaped, dense forest which had hidden the elves. In the projection, the area that had once contained the many human armies seemed strangely empty, and Saviar came to realize the *khohlar* was mapping only the areas of magical activity.

The entire forest glowed faintly blue, highlighting the location of the elves, hiding amidst the foliage and between the tightly packed trunks of myriad trees. Saviar could also make out a tiny patch of aqua near one edge, which he felt certain represented the Mages of Myrcidë, though nothing in Captain's sending gave him this impression. He suspected anyone who did not know about the mages would unconsciously blend the patch into the vaster expanse of blue.

Sparks of glaring red defined the location of the *Kjempemagiska*. Unlike the steadily pulsating glow of the elves, crimson bursts appeared sporadically or in larger patches. These radiated outward in stabbing spurts; and, where they appeared, they became swiftly smothered by blue, like water rolling over sparks of fire, killing it wherever it ignited.

This time, understanding did accompany the sending. Captain wished them to recognize the situation: the elves kept alive a fused and relatively steady bunker of magic on which they remained fully focused while the giants used their magic periodically and singly, which allowed them the freedom to physically fight as well as cast occasional spells. These spells did them little good, however, as the elfin wash of unremitting protection overcame the smaller, individual magics.

As Saviar watched the pictures forming in his head, he noticed the red flashes gradually disappeared as the *Kjempemagiska* realized the futility of their magic. The flares never stopped entirely, though. Either the giants cast from habit or to test the longevity of the elves' shielding; but the *Kjempemagiska* spells never materialized, forcing the giants into an exclusively physical fight.

Though the *Kjempemagiska* had seemed unstoppable, Saviar realized the enormous and unsung role the elves had played in a war in which they had remained essentially invisible. To men watching their ranks cut down around them, desperately trying to inflict some sort of damage on creatures too large and too invulnerable to best, it had seemed as if the elves had done little to assist. Now, Saviar realized, they would all have fallen in moments had the *Kjempemagiska* retained their battle magic.

When Saviar looked closely at the map Captain created in his mind, he could see a rare figure of white light. From their locations, it dawned on him that he was seeing the shadow magic from the few weapons on their own side that carried it. The brightest light, he felt certain, represented the Sword of Mitrian in Calistin's hand, bolstered by the diamonds Colbey had secured from his wife. Saviar picked out himself and Subikahn nearby, the three forms a ceaseless blur of motion, sometimes near and other times separated by battle. He could see the moment when Subikahn dashed off on his own, headed toward the aqua glow of the Mages of Myrcidë.

Focused on that precise location, Saviar saw the white light representing Subikahn fly in a wild arc. Soon after, a brilliant flare of quickly-snuffed red appeared in front of Subikahn, then the glow that represented him became still. Even then, it continued to burn, though whether because Subikahn remained alive or because the glow would highlight the weapon with or without a wielder, he could not know.

Apparently, Captain sped up the images of war because

it seemed like no time at all before the glow representing Saviar arrived near Subikahn. Soon afterward, it departed, and the white wash of Subikahn's sword became lost beneath flashes of aqua magic.

On the opposite side of the battlefield, a golden glow winked into existence, so intense he found himself unwittingly riveted. This new addition surged forward as if unhampered, and Saviar imagined Colbey Calistinsson slicing down giants with an ease and fervor no mortal could match. Saviar found himself coveting the centuries the immortal Renshai had had to hone his craft, to perfect every one of the Renshai maneuvers and create so many new ones of his own.

Captain sped through most of that time as well. Then, dizzily, he slowed the action nearly to a crawl. At the far edge of the war front, away from the sapphirine glow representing the position of the elves, a new light was rising. It started as pinpoints of crimson, dying out beneath the rush of elfin magic. Then, gradually and awkwardly, the spots of red light began to fuse. Through Captain's *khohlar*, Saviar came to understand that the *Kjempemagiska* had had little previous experience with shared magic, that they had nothing precisely like the elfin concept of *jovinay arythanik*. Still, they were learning as they went, consolidating power, dragging it all together.

The sensations Captain sent were ones Saviar had never experienced before. It felt as if something sucked him toward the gathering magic, compelling him forward. He clutched the Pica Stone, drawing its expansive energy into his being, using it as a focal anchor even as he warned the other elves to hold their voices, their spells, their very beings. At the moment when the elves became uncertain whether they could continue to fight the force that hauled them inexorably closer and into the battle, the tide reversed in an instant, hurling them backward in a frenzied explosion that seemed to rip through the fabric of the universe.

Blinded, deafened, jolted with a bolt of intense pain, the elves collapsed and the storm raged in. Captain sent desperate callings to his followers, urging them to stay on task, not to lose the cadence of their magical song at the risk of surrendering every elfin and human life. Saviar could feel their group resolve wavering as they contemplated the horror of the forthcoming cataclysm, the agony they would suffer when magic collided. One by one, they disappeared from the *jovinay arythanik* in despair.

But one voice remained strong, a tiny point of sound that never hesitated, never surrendered. Incapable of contemplating the future, this one elfin spirit remained wholly dedicated to the cause, a beacon for the others, an anchor on which to recreate the *jovinay arythanik*. Bit by bit, it swelled back to life, resolve and need replacing panic. The elves rebuilt their strength around it, gave their all, and made it even more powerful. And now, Captain added one piece that, at the time, the elves had not known, the identity of that one small soul: Ivana. Her simplicity had been their salvation.

Then, the conflicting magics struck one another like thunder, shaking the ground, roiling the air, rendering the world itself unstable. Unable to succeed in their intended purposes, the magics backlashed like whipcracks instead, the red smashing into the giants and the blue encompassing the elves. Struck down by their own destructive spells, the giants knew nothing more.

More defensive in nature, the elfin spells did not immediately kill its masters, though it reverted to the raw chaos of its origins. For the humans, this manifested as a brutal, unstoppable tempest. To the elves, it went far deeper. It entered their very beings, ripping at their organs, ravaging their souls, threatening to shatter every bone to splinters. Though Saviar could tell Captain now attempted to mute the extent of his pain, some slipped through the *khohlar*. He could hear soldiers gasping at the enormity of Captain's sending and found himself gritting his teeth against the inevitable fragmentation of his body, an agony beyond bearing.

Captain's desperation came through clearly. He knew he had to do something to lessen the storm, or sacrifice the lives of every elf and human within furlongs of the battlefield. He fought through excruciating pain, seeking anything on which to ground his reason, to lessen the impact of the backlash. Hopelessness swam down over him, and he fought it with a grit and determination that any Renshai would admire. At long last, he noticed one detail that had, previously, eluded him: the opening they had created to bring in more elves. It vented a bit of the wind, though only temporarily. Since they still existed on the same plain, the magic only looped around and returned.

Gates! Captain realized and sent the word in *khohlar* to every one of his followers. Saviar supposed the message must have touched the human minds as well, but the ferocity of the storm had stolen any means or desire to focus on a stranger's voice in their heads. **Open gates! Any kind! Anywhere!**

Somehow, the elves found the wherewithal to respond to the command. Saviar came to realize that only some of the elves had the ability to create these openings to other worlds, other plains of existence. Usually, they required the combined magical forces of many elves, but the swirling chaos that threatened to destroy every living thing provided the necessary power as well. Gradually, gates winked into existence, openings in Midgard that mitigated the storm by venting power off of their world, sucking it into indefinable elsewheres.

It was this venting, Saviar realized, that had allowed any of them to survive the massive collision of magics. By rights, it should have killed all of them, quite possibly the entirety of Midgard. But the venting itself had unintended consequences. The catastrophic winds had picked up any elf or human near an opening like insignificant flotsam, dragging them through the gate along with the banished chaos.

Captain returned to words, **There are thousands of worlds of which our kind has explored only a few. We know some are not compatible with life, but most do harbor living creatures of one form or another. It is possible that we can find and return many of the unfortunates carried from our world through the gates, but it will take enormous planning, careful magic, and brave volunteers willing to make several dangerous journeys to restore our loved ones. I believe there are some among you able and ready to take on these challenges.**

Exhausted as he felt, Saviar found himself intrigued, almost eager. He knew his parents had undertaken a similar mission in his infancy, though it had involved retrieving only shards of the then-broken Pica Stone rather than living beings.

Someone seized Saviar's arm. He whirled and crouched, ready for a fight, and found himself looking into Calistin's familiar face. "That's where Subikahn is. And my sword."

Suddenly, wholly engaged with his brother, Saviar stared. "Where?"

"Through one of those gate-things. He and the mages got pulled through together."

Saviar considered asking how Calistin knew but thought better of the question. At the time, Calistin had been holding the only true magical item in the area. Even Saviar's shadow-magicked sword allowed him to see auras and, once, a *Valkyrie* when he held it in his hand. It would not surprise him if Calistin had also figured out the magical code of Captain's *khohlar* and did a more complete job of focusing on Subikahn in the chaos of the storm. "You're sure?"

Calistin nodded.

Saviar could feel his heart rate quicken, his breath catch in his throat. His twin had confessed to an unforgivable crime, had all but damned Saviar's soul to Hel. Still, he wanted to hear exactly why Subikahn had done it, wanted to force his twin to stare directly into his eyes and explain. "Was he still . . ." Saviar paused, waiting for Calistin to fill in the obvious blank. When he did not, Saviar reminded himself he was dealing with Calistin. Though brutally competent, his youngest brother had the social skills of a stone. ". . . alive?"

"Alive, yes, of course. Do you think I'd forget to mention Valhalla?"

Calistin had an undeniable point that made Saviar feel stupid. Calistin had a knack for that but rarely outside of swordplay.

Compassion entered Calistin's tone, appearing even more out-of-place because, for once, Saviar did not share it. He was not ready to forgive his twin, not sure he ever could. "Subikahn's alive on another world, and he needs our help to come home. We have to go after him, Savi. He's our brother."

Saviar could not help wondering if a stranger had replaced his youngest brother. Again. But before he could say a word, Captain resumed his *khohlar*.

*Your commanders have asked me to inform you we need as accurate an accounting as possible to avoid stranding anyone, dishonoring them, or putting our heroic volunteers at unnecessary risk. To that end, they have asked me to tell you that no one is to leave his camp until every individual

*has met with his commanding officer to assist with making a
complete list of survivors and missing soldiers. Only then,
each commander will make arrangements for how to handle
and account for those killed. They say you should feel free to
sleep, eat, or converse while you're waiting for your turn at
your encampment.**

Calistin headed toward the Renshai camp, and Saviar
reluctantly followed. He would have preferred to remain
with their father and grandfather, to discuss the future and
his role in it, but he did not want to make the situation any
more difficult for Thialnir. They would celebrate, not mourn,
their brethren lost in combat, but they would all find some
secretive comfort in seeing a significant number of living,
breathing Renshai remained.

The moment Calistin reached the Renshai camp, Valira
flung herself into his arms. Shocked, Saviar could only
watch as Calistin tensed. For a moment, he thought his little
brother might cut her down from instinct. He had never
shown his family more than the barest hint of empathy, and
he seemed not to understand affection.

To Saviar's surprise, Calistin raised his arms and wrapped
Valira into his own, almost tender, embrace. It looked
clumsy, lacking Calistin's usual inhuman grace, but the near-
normalcy of the exchange held Saviar spellbound. There
was real affection in their interplay; and, if it currently all
came from Valira's side, Calistin at least appeared to be trying.

Valira's hands slipped surreptitiously to Calistin's sinewy
rump, and Saviar thought his eyeballs might pop out of
their sockets. Equally surprised by the impropriety, Calistin
stiffened, then laughed. He caught Valira fully in his arms,
hefted her over one shoulder, and carried her the last few
steps into camp.

Saviar knew he ought to look away, but he found it impossible. A strange smile glued itself onto his face. Even in
the wake of brutal war, with the bodies of brave warriors
still cooling on the ground, maybe, just maybe, they would
all find joy where they could.

<hr/>

While King Griff and his entourage prepared to visit the
battlefield, Tae Kahn sat with Kentt and Arturo on a match-

ing set of plush chairs while Mistri napped in her bed. The *Kjempemagiska* had to squash his ample bottom between the armrests, but he made no complaints as he studied Tae and the cat curled contentedly in his lap. Tae's hands stroked and scratched her intently, eliciting a nonstop and contented purring. Rantire crouched near the door, looking bored.

"Will we accompany them?" Kentt addressed Tae, but his gaze remained on Imorelda. Everything about her seemed to fascinate him. He found it particularly interesting that the growl-like sound she made was actually a joyful noise.

Tae considered Kentt's interest in Imorelda a positive sign. He could see parallels between his relationship with the super-intelligent cat and Kentt's with Arturo. "I don't think it's wise." He gave extra attention to the area behind Imorelda's ears and under her chin. "The warriors know your people only as lethal enemies. We need to give the king a chance to explain you before you come walking onto the battlefield."

"I would be noticed," Kentt admitted, tipping his head to study Imorelda from a different angle. "And they won't know I mean them no harm."

Though he had insisted on being present, Arturo watched the conversation without speaking. Tae suspected he understood most of the exchange but worried his pidgin *usaro* could add little to it or would make him look stupid. Tae made a mental note to help the young prince learn the language so he could take a greater role in any future negotiations. Hopefully, Kentt, and maybe others among the *Kjempemagiska*, had a soft spot for their former pet.

Tae tried the direct approach. "Do you?" He realized it was a nebulous question. "Mean us no harm, I mean. Your people did come here to annihilate us, after all."

"Yes," Kentt said thoughtfully, though it seemed an extreme and dangerous admission. "But that's no longer an issue. You won the war, and we'd be foolish to attack again. It will take several generations, many centuries, before we could possibly begin to forget our losses. And, having lost so many, we no longer have need for your land."

Tae attempted humor. "Is that an apology?"

Kentt laughed. "No, but I will grant one if you want it

and believe it will make any difference. Mistri and I are at
your mercy. You have not imprisoned us behind bars, but
we are just as surely trapped. We have no way to get ourselves home." His gaze went to Arturo, and the smile forming on his lips convinced Tae he correctly understood their
relationship.

Tae thought back to what the lost prince had told him.
While Arturo did not have a full understanding of the
Kjempemagiska hierarchy, he believed Kentt held some
sort of nonmilitary leadership position. Kentt's job, apparently, had something to do with studying the plants, animals,
and minerals of Heimstadr and its surrounding ocean. Arturo believed he was alive because of Kentt's curiosity
about him as much as Mistri's desire to keep him; over time,
that had grown into real affection. While the other *Kjempemagiska* had treated him like a worthless animal, Kentt had
taken a particular interest in his ability to learn spoken language alongside his daughter. Tae knew their relationship
would have to change, but he hoped they could maintain
their mutual affection for Mistri, and for one another, as
Kentt learned to see Arturo as an equal.

"Your magic won't take you home?" Tae asked.

Kentt tipped his head. "If it could, would we have arrived by ship?"

"I suppose not."

Imorelda rolled onto her back. *Pet me.*

I was sure that was what I was doing, my love.

*Oh, is that what you were doing? I thought you were
using me as a hand rest.*

Tae increased the rate of his ministrations, though he
doubted anything would fully satisfy Imorelda. He knew the
conversation bored her. She did not understand a word of it,
and, thus, could not chime in as she usually did. "I imagine
your ships are still where your bretheren left them."

Kentt's brows shot up. "Could you singlehandedly sail to
Heimstadr?"

"No," Tae admitted, then realized he knew someone who
could. "We have some sensational sailors, though. I'm sure
they could get you home."

Kentt sat up straighter. "Would they?" His tone betrayed
only a bare hint of hope. In the reverse situation, Tae

doubted the *Kjempemagiska* would consider assisting one of the people of the continent.

But we are not them. The *Kjempemagiska* had lost all of their warriors, which might make them more amenable to treaties and cooperation, perhaps even to sharing their magic and technology with the peoples of the continent. The royal family of Béarn had every right to execute Kentt and Mistri, but Tae knew the giants were in no danger. Matrinka would insist on helping anyone in need, no matter their loyalties or proclivities. Before Griff could even speak, Arturo had decreed that no harm would come to either of them, but especially to Mistri. His love for her was clear and genuine, and Tae could not help wondering if Imorelda felt the same way about him.

"I believe it's a real possibility, Kentt. Of course, you'll need to give them a reason to risk their lives bringing the two of you home."

Kentt studied the ceiling for several moments, then met Tae's gaze with an earnest smile. "Consider us unusually tall humans. And name your price."

EPILOGUE

TWILIGHT BATHED THE battlefield, lulling the soldiers, warriors, and civilians into a well-deserved sleep. To General Valr Magnus, the broken trees looked like skeletal arms clutching at the moon. The stars winked in, one by one, in a vast expanse of cloudless sky. The Aeri general had finally finished chronicling his survivors and casualties, bid the living and wounded a good night, and set up his infantry and cavalry captains to handle guard rotations and pyre preparations for the morning.

The necessities finished, Valr Magnus found his thoughts straying in an unlikely direction: to Ra-khir and his sons. Gradually, he had come to recognize and understand Ra-khir's enduring hatred. The intensity of love between the Knight of Erythane and his lady went beyond anything Magnus had known or experienced. He could only imagine what such a unique and special bond felt like, the agony of having it torn asunder for, as it turned out, no legitimate reason. Nothing had been gained by Kevral's death. Those involved in the deceit had dishonored not only themselves, but Kevral and Magnus as well. Magnus had rightfully vacated the contract, nullifying his win and returning the Fields of Wrath to the Renshai.

Magnus had apologized repeatedly for the ignoble way he had won that battle. But, though Ra-khir had tolerated him throughout the mission, he had never truly forgiven. The Knight of Erythane surely understood that Magnus had been an unwitting pawn, but he was still the instrument of Kevral's destruction. *It's not as if I can bring her back to life.* Magnus knew Kevral would not have wanted that anyway; she had found her rightful place in Valhalla.

War had a way of redefining perspective, and Valr Magnus finally realized his mistake. He now knew he needed to give Ra-khir a different sort of apology, one that focused less on the means of Kevral's death and more on the effect it had had on her family. Unintentionally or not, he had destroyed something rare and beautiful, an affair the world might never see again, two of the world's most unlikely lovers creating a family of great character and talent. Then, he had destroyed it with a single act of violence. The next time he and Ra-khir came together, no matter the reason, he would give the proper apology and hope that, this time, Ra-khir would find it in his heart to forgive.

A voice touched Magnus' mind. Although he had little experience with such things, he felt certain it was not the elfin Captain's this time. *We need to talk.*

Magnus knew of no way to respond. Instead, he looked around, trying to spot the source of the contact. He did not attempt a verbal response. It would only make him appear crazy to anyone watching or listening.

The other continued as if Valr Magnus had voiced the question in his mind. *It's Colbey, Valr. I can read your thoughts as well as send mine.*

Valr Magnus shivered. Even the magical elves could not get into his head. At least, they did not address his thoughts as Colbey had just done. He tried focusing on a question. *Where are you?*

Just beyond sight, in the forest. Go straight southwest from your current position. If you don't find me, I'll find you.

Though weary, Magnus complied. It seemed foolish to show disrespect to a mind-reading Renshai, especially one fabled to have lived for centuries. Carrying nothing but his two sheathed swords, one of which Colbey had personally given him, he headed in the indicated direction.

As Magnus passed the camps and neared the trees, a hand emerged from the brush to wave him to the indicated spot. The general shoved through dangling branches, most displaced by the storm, to find himself in a tiny clearing. Colbey Calistinsson stood near a massive, pure-white stallion regarding Magnus with one strangely wise eye. Patches and flecks of bloody gore covered the wizened Renshai, except for his swords' sheaths and hilts, which were meticulously clean.

Realization dawned on Magnus, and he found himself speaking before he could think. "So you're the one who spurred the troops! Many mistook you for a Knight of Erythane."

Colbey replied simply, "I am a Knight of Erythane."

Magnus laughed. Then, realizing Colbey had not joined him, he said dubiously, "Really."

"Really." Not a hint of mirth entered Colbey's tone. "It's a long story, and I don't wish to tell it now. But I am a Knight of Erythane, and I came at the call of my commanding officer."

Believing himself tricked, Magnus furrowed his brow. "So how come your name isn't mentioned with the other twenty-four? And I've never seen you drill with them?"

Colbey clearly did not wish to discuss the matter further. "I've never been invited before." His blue-gray eyes turned searching. It was the first time Magnus looked long enough to notice scarred lines across the Renshai's cheek. It appeared something enormous had clawed him long ago. "But that's not why I called you here."

Magnus guessed the immortal Renshai's purpose. "I imagine you wanted this." He unclipped the scabbard from his belt and cautiously offered the borrowed sword back to its owner.

Colbey made no move to take it. "No, Valr. I want you to keep the sword. A gift from me."

Valr Magnus bowed. "You honor me." Suddenly suspicious, he added, "And I'm guessing you want something equally valuable in return."

Colbey did not deny the accusation. "It's time, Valr Magnus. Time to mend the rift between the Renshai and the other Northmen."

Magnus stared, surprised by the Renshai's words. It took him several moments to find his voice. "You might just as well ask the sun to remain in the sky after dark, water to flow upward, cows to fly. Renshai and Northmen have hated one another for centuries. It's ancient, primal, ingrained."

"It is ancient," Colbey confirmed. "And ingrained, but never primal. Hatred is not natural; it is taught."

Valr Magnus saw no reason to argue. His gaze swept the hulking shadows of the trees. The broken canopies admitted wide swaths of stars. "Well and deeply taught. No one man can change that."

"One man," Colbey pointed out, "can change the tide of war."

Magnus could scarcely deny it. "The Renshai would argue you're no mere man. And, now, I would have to agree."

"I'm not talking about me," Colbey said softly. "You killed some of those giants, too, inspiring the warriors at the center of the combat front. Calistin and Saviar did the same at the farthest end. I merely did my part here." He gestured toward the side of the forest they currently occupied.

Magnus shook his head. "Neither of us could have inspired anyone without the magical swords you gave us."

"Swords are only tools. It's what you do with them that matters."

Once again, Magnus studied the immortal Renshai, from the gold-and-silver hair that fell around his face in feathers to the boots on his feet. Magnus towered over the older man, yet he still could not help feeling intimidated by the slight, sinewy figure. "You speak sacrilege by Renshai standards."

Finally, Colbey laughed. "Perhaps, but it's true. The bards will write songs about the Slayer Magnus, not the weapon he wielded."

Magnus returned to the original point. "As near impossibility as it was, defeating magical giants was easier than brokering peace between two factions who insist on hating one another."

Colbey said the last thing Magnus expected, "The Renshai do not hate the Northmen as a group."

Valr Magnus took a step backward, guarded. "Colbey, surely you've lived long enough to know every dispute has two sides."

"Always," Colbey confirmed. "But we oftentimes make the mistake of believing both sides are inherently equal in a moral sense and, thus, the solution lies always in the middle. That, my friend, is a dangerous assumption."

Magnus did not like the turn of the conversation. "You're saying the Renshai are superior."

"Not superior," Colbey said. "Merely better directed. For the last three hundred and twenty years or so, I've seen to it personally. Unlike the other Northmen, we don't teach our children that people we dislike are the spawn of demons or animals, that their mere existence is anathema. The Renshai aren't clamoring for the other Northmen to be wiped from the face of the world. They will gladly end a war, but they will never start one."

Magnus' training told him differently. "But the Renshai were banished from the North because of their savagery against the other Northmen. They started wars all the time, and they butchered those they killed to prevent them from reaching Valhalla." He trained his gaze fiercely on Colbey. He could scarcely deny it.

"We did that," Colbey admitted. "And we were rightly banished."

Magnus could not help noticing that Colbey had adopted the pronoun "we" to refer to the ancient Renshai, while he had previously used "they" for the living tribe. "You can't be saying you were there at the time."

"I was."

"How old do you claim to be?"

"We don't count birthdays on Asgard." Colbey grinned. "I think the goddesses prefer not to know how old they are. I believe my four hundredth is imminent, though." He took over the narrative. "And after our banishment, we sowed a path of destruction all across the West. By the time the year was out, however, we regretted our ferocity, our mistakes. We returned to the North to reclaim our homeland. The Northmen finally agreed to a duel: we got the island now known as Devil's Island if we won; permanent banishment if we lost."

"And you lost." Magnus stated history as he had learned it.

"We won," Colbey corrected. Then, in response to Magnus' dubious expression, added, "I was there, remember? We settled on Devil's Island and lived there several years in peace. Then, one night when I was away assisting a seafaring band of Nordmirians, the Northmen banded together, sneaked onto Devil's Island, and slaughtered as many Renshai as possible in their sleep. Eventually, the Renshai rallied, but they were outnumbered more than ten to one. Even our youngest infants were not spared."

Magnus had heard the lie. "That's a story the Renshai made up."

"I was there," Colbey repeated for the third time. "I cleaned up the mess, recreated the tribe. If you doubt me, you merely need to read the true histories recorded by the scribes of Béarn at the time. Denial of the sneak attack, the mass killing of Renshai, is a revision the Northern tribes have made to history."

Valr Magnus had no proof of his assertion and, thus, no right to argue. Neither was he ready to accept the unverified word of a Renshai, even one whom the gods had, apparently, accepted as a near equal. "Let us assume everything you say is true. What can I do to change the situation? I have no control over what others teach their children, and I have none of my own."

Colbey sighed deeply. Clearly, the years weighed heavily upon him. "I've dedicated several lifetimes to this issue, not wholly without success. I've redefined the Renshai from the most savage tribe of the North to a group still dedicated to swordwork but using it only in the employ of rightful causes. Imagine what you could accomplish by steering the time, energy, and passion of the Northmen from destruction of the Renshai to the construction of something positive, something better. As long as they remain mired in hatred and revenge, the Northmen can never advance, never become more than what they used to be three hundred and twenty years ago."

Magnus dared to consider the possibility. Colbey had an undeniable point, in theory. In practice, he had no idea where to begin. "I don't have three hundred years." Not knowing how Colbey had gotten them, he added cautiously, "Do I?"

"Probably not." Colbey did not rise to the bait. "But you can do as much as you can with the years you do have. You've shown yourself to be decent and honorable. Your people revere you for your skills, your dedication, and your kindness. Lead by example, always, by explanation when necessary. Right now, the Northern tribes have no choice but to work together; they have lost too many men not to do so. This seems like the perfect opportunity to reclaim the Renshai as your own as well."

Valr Magnus glanced at his hands, where he still proffered the borrowed sword.

Colbey's gaze followed his. "It needs a name."

Magnus clipped the scabbard back onto his belt. "The sword?"

"Circumstances suggest so."

Magnus considered a moment. "How about *Handelegg-colbeyr*?"

"The arm of Colbey." The Renshai laughed. "I suppose that's apt enough, assuming a general of Aerin is willing to carry a weapon named for a Renshai legend."

That raised a sudden flurry of questions. "Is it true what the Renshai claim about you? That the *Ragnarok* has already occurred and your interference saved mankind? That you married Freya?" Once, Valr Magnus would have dismissed the whole thing as Renshai mythology, but Colbey's ability, his knowledge, his instant comings and goings, his incursions into others' minds proved at least some of the Renshai's claims were truth.

Colbey yawned and stretched, then patted the horse still standing calmly at his side. "Let's just say I don't take kindly to exaggeration." He mounted, smiling. "And I like to keep most of my achievements to myself."

Is he saying he's done even more than what the Renshai claim? Magnus drew breath to ask. But, before he could speak, the immortal Renshai and his horse had vanished as if they had never been.

With a sigh of his own, Valr Magnus headed back toward his army, prepared to pick up as many pieces as possible. And start again.

Appendices

WESTERNERS

Béarnides

Aerean (AIR-ee-an): Minister of Internal Affairs

Aranal (Ar-an-ALL): a former king (deceased)

Aron (AHR-inn): the current Sage

Arturo (Ahr-TOOR-oh): a prince; second child of Griff and Matrinka

Barrindar (BAA-rinn-dar): a prince; first child of Griff and Xoraida

Calitha (Kuh-LEE-thuh): a princess; second child of Griff and Xoraida

Chaveeshia (Sha-VEE-shuh): Minister of Local Affairs

Davian (DAY-vee-in): Prime Minister

Eldorin (Ell-DOOR-in): a princess; third child of Griff and Xoraida

Franstaine (FRAN-stayn): Minister of Household Affairs; in-law uncle of Helana

Galastad (GAL-uh-stad): highest ranking infantry officer; a captain of the army

Griff (GRIFF): the king

Halika (Huh-LEE-kuh): a princess; third child of Griff and Matrinka

Helana (Hell-AHN-uh): Griff's mother; Petrostan's wife

Ivana Shorith'na Cha-tella Tir Hya'sellirian Albar (Ee-

VAH-nah): a princess; half-elfin, only child of Griff and Tem'aree'ay (see Outworlders)

Jhirban (JEER-bonn): captain of the flagship Seven (deceased)

Kohleran (KOLL-er-inn): a previous king of Béarn (deceased); Matrinka's grandfather

Lazwald (LAHZ-wald): a guardsman

Marisole (MAA-rih-soll): a princess; first child of Griff and Matrinka; the bard's heir

Matrinka (Ma-TRINK-uh): the queen; Griff's senior wife; mother of Marisole, Arturo, and Halika

Morhane (MOOR-hahn): an ancient king who usurped the throne from his twin brother, Valar

Myrenex (My-RINN-ix): a former king (deceased)

Petrostan (Peh-TROSS-tin): King Kohleran's youngest son; Griff's father (deceased)

Richar (REE-shar): Minister of Foreign Affairs

Ruther (RUH-ther): a guardsman

The Sage: chronicler and keeper of Béarn's history and tomes

Saxanar (SAX-uh-nar): Minister of Courtroom Procedure and Affairs

Seiryn (SAYR-inn): captain of the guards

Sterrane (Stir-RAYN): best-known ancient king (deceased)

Talamaine (TAL-uh-mayn): Matrinka's father (deceased)

Valar (VAY-lar): Morhane's twin borther; Sterrane's father; a previous king murdered during his reign

Walfron (WALL-fron): supervisor of the kitchen staff

Xanranis (Zan-RAN-iss): Sterrane's son; a former king (deceased)

Xoraida (Zor-AY-duh): Griff's junior wife (third); mother of Barrindar, Calitha, and Eldorin

Yvalane (IV-uh-layn): Kohleran's father; a previous king (deceased)

Zapara (Zuh-PAR-uh): a guard

Zaysharn (ZAY-sharn): Overseer of the Caretakers of Livestock, Gardens, and Food

Zelshia (ZELL-shuh): a head maid

Zoenya (Zoh-ENN-yuh): a previous queen (deceased)

Erythanians

Alquantae (Al-KWAN-tay): a knight

Arduwyn (AR-dwinn): a legendary archer and friend of King Sterrane (deceased)

Arner (ARR-ner): Perry's father

Avra (AHV-rah): a street tough

Braison (BRAY-son): a knight

Callan (CAL-in): a captain of palace guards

Edwin (ED-winn): a knight; the armsman

Esatoric (ee-sah-TOR-ik): a knight

Eshwin (ESH-winn): a horse breeder; Tirro's neighbor

Frendon (FRENN-dinn): interrupted battle between Kevral and Valr Magnus by jumping from a tree (deceased)

Garvin (GAR-vinn): a knight

Georan (JOR-inn): brother to Harveki; uncle to Frendon

Hansah (HAN-suh): ranking lieutenant over infantry and regular cavalry

Harritin (HARR-ih-tinn): a knight

Harveki (Harr-VECK-ee): father of Frendon; brother of Georan (deceased)

Humbert (HUM-bert): crown prince; Humfreet's son

Humfreet (HUM-freet): the king

Jakrusan (Jah-KROO-sinn): a knight

Kedrin (KEH-drinn): captain of the knights; Ra-khir's father

Khirwith (KEER-with): Ra-khir's stepfather (deceased)

Lakamorn (LACK-uh-morn): a knight

Mandell (Man-DELL): a palace guard

Netan (NAYT-en): a palace guard

Oridan (OR-ih-den): Shavasiay's father

Parmille (Par-MEEL): a street tough

Perry (PEH-ree): a spokesman for the Paradisians

Ra-khir (Rah-KEER): a knight; Kedrin's son; father of Saviar and Calistin (see Renshai)

Ramytan (RAM-ih-tinn): Kedrin's father (deceased)

Rayvonn (RAY-vonn): a soldier

Shavasiay (Shah-VASS-ee-ay): a knight

Thessilus (THESS-ih-luss): a knight

Tirro (TEER-oh): a farmer; Eshwin's neighbor

Treysind (TRAY-sind): an orphan (deceased)

Vincelin (VINN-sell-in): a knight

Pudarians

Alenna (A-LENN-uh): Prince Leondis' wife; mother of second Severin

Boshkin (BAHSH-kinn): Prince Leondis' steward and adviser

Cenna (SEH-nuh): an ancient queen (deceased)

Chethid (CHETH-id): one of three lieutenants

Cymion (KIGH-mee-on): the king

Daizar (DIGH-zahr): Minister of Visiting Dignitaries

Darian (DAYR-ee-an): one of three lieutenants

Darris (DAYR-iss): the bard; Linndar's son; blood father of Marisole, Arturo, and Halika (see Béarnides)

DeShane (Dih-SHAYN): a captain of the guards

Eudora (Yoo-DOOR-uh): the late queen; Severin and Leondis' mother (deceased)

Harlton (HAR-all-ton): a captain of the guards

Horatiannon (Hor-ay-shee-AH-nun): an ancient king (deceased)

Jahiran (Jah-HEER-in): the first Bard (deceased); initiated the bardic curse

Javonzir (Juh-VON-zeer): the king's cousin and adviser

Larrin (LARR-inn): a captain of the guards

Leondis (Lee-ON-diss): the crown prince; second son of Cymion and Eudora

Linndar (LINN-dar): a previous bard; Darris' mother (deceased)

Mar Lon (MAR-LONN): a previous bard in the age of King Sterrane (deceased)

Markanyin (Marr-KANN-yinn): the general of the army

Nellkoris (Nell-KORR-iss): one of three lieutenants

Severin (SEV-rinn): first son of Cymion and Eudora; previous heir to the throne (deceased)

Severin (SEV-rinn): Leondis' son; named for his deceased uncle

Renshai

Alvida (Al-VEE-duh): a young woman

Arsvid (ARS-vid): a man

Ashavir (AH-shuh-veer): a boy

Asmiri (Az-MEER-ee): a guardian of Prince Barrindar

Calistin the Bold (Kuh-LEES-tinn): Colbey's father (deceased)

Calistin Ra-khirsson (Kuh-LEES-tinn): youngest son of Ra-khir and Kevral

Colbey Calistinsson (KULL-bay): legendary immortal Renshai now living among the gods

Elbirine (Ell-burr-EE-neh): a guardian of Princess Halika; trained with Kevral

Episte Rachesson (Ep-PISS-teh): an orphan raised by Colbey; later killed by Colbey after being driven mad by chaos

Erlse (EARL-seh): a man

Gareth Lasirsson (GARR-ith): tested the worthiness of Ra-khir and Tae to sire Renshai; Kristel's father

Gunnhar (GUN-her): a guardian of Arturo (deceased)

Kevralyn Balmirsdatter (KEV-ruh-linn): Kevralyn Tainharsdatter's namesake (deceased)

Kevralyn Tainharsdatter (KEV-ruh-linn): aka Kevral; Ra-khir's wife; mother of Saviar, Subikahn, and Calistin (deceased)

Kwavirse (Kwah-VEER-seh): a man

Kristel Garethsdatter (KRISS-tal): a previous guardian of Queen Matrinka

Kyndig (KAWN-dee): another name for Colbey Calistinsson; "Skilled One"

Kyntiri (Kawn-TEER-ee): a *torke* of Saviar and Subikahn

Mitrian Santagithisdatter (MIH-tree-in): foremother of the tribe of Tannin; Santagithi's daughter (deceased)

Modrey (MOH-dray): forefather of the tribe of Modrey (deceased)

Navali (Nuh-VAWL-ee): a *torke*

Nirvina (Ner-VEE-nah): a *torke* of Saviar

Nisse Nelsdatter (NEE-sah): a previous guardian of Queen Matrinka

Pseubicon (Soo-bih-kahn): an ancient Renshai; half-barbarian by blood (deceased)

Rache Garnsson (RACK-ee): forefather of the tribe of Rache; son of Mitrian (deceased)

Rache Kallmirsson (RACK-ee): Rache Garnsson's namesake; Episte's father (deceased)

Ranilda Battlemad (Ran-HEEL-duh): Colbey's mother (deceased)

Rantire Ulfinsdatter (Ran-TEER-ee): Griff's bodyguard in
    Darris' absence; a dedicated guardian
Raska "Ravn" Colbeysson (RASS-kuh; RAY-vinn): only son
    of Colbey and Freya
Saviar Ra-khirsson (SAV-ee-ahr): first son of Ra-khir and
    Kevral; Subikahn's twin
Sitari (Sih-TARR-ee): Calistin's secret crush (deceased)
Subikahn Taesson (SOO-bih-kahn): only son of Tae and
    Kevral; Saviar's twin
Sylva (SILL-vuh): foremother of the tribe of Rache; an
    Erythanian; daughter of Arduwyn (deceased)
Tainhar (TAYN-har): Kevral's father (deceased)
Talamir Edminsson (TAL-uh-meer): a *torke* of Subikahn
    and his lover
Tannin Randilsson (TAN-inn): forefather of the tribe of
    Tannin; Tarah's brother; Mitrian's husband (deceased)
Tanvard (TAN-vayrd): a man
Tarah Randilsdatter (TAIR-uh): foremother of the tribe of
    Modrey; sister of Tannin (deceased)
Thialnir Thrudazisson (Thee-AHL-neer): the chieftain
Trygg (TRIG): a guardian of Arturo (deceased)
Tygbiar (TIG-beer): a man; veteran warrior
Valira (Vuh-LEER-uh): a young woman

Santagithians

Herwin (HER-winn): King Griff's stepfather
Mitrian (MIH-tree-inn): Santagithi's daughter (see Ren-
    shai) (deceased)
Santagithi (San-TAG-ih-thigh): legendary general for whom
    the town was named; main strategist of the Great War
    (deceased)
Sutton (SUTT-inn): general of the army; current leader

Mages of Myrcidë

Archille (Arr-KEE-lee): a man
Arinosta (Air-in-OSS-tah): an elderly woman
Blenford (BLENN-ford): a man
Chestinar (CHESS-tin-ahr): a sickly man
Chymmerlee (KIM-er-lee): a young woman; youngest of
    the mages

Dilphin (DILL-fin): a man
Eldebar (ELL-dih-bar): older man
Giddion (GID-ee-inn): a middle-aged man
Hevnard (HEV-nard): a middle-aged man
Janecos (JAN-ih-kohs): a middle-aged woman
Jeremilan (Jerr-ih-MY-lan): the leader; oldest of the mages
Lycros (LIGH-krohs): a man
Netheron (NEH-ther-on): a middle-aged man
Paultan (PAUL-tinn): a man
Roby (ROH-bee): an elder
Shadimar (SHAD-ih-mar): legendary Eastern Wizard who returned King Sterrane to his throne (deceased)

Ainsvillers

Burnold (Burn-OLD): the blacksmith
Karruno (Kuh-ROON-oh): a farmer
Oscore (OSS-ker): the bartender

Keatovillers

Darby (DAR-bee): Ra-khir's squire
Emmer (EM-er): Darby's father; Tiega's husband (deceased)
Keva (KEY-vuh): Darby's younger sister
Tiega (Tee-AY-guh): Darby's mother
Tiego (Tee-AY-goh): Tiega's father (deceased)

Other Westlanders

Howall (HOW-ell): Sheatonian; the guardsman (deceased)
Khalen (KAY-linn): New Lovénian; a fabric-seller
Lenn (LENN): Dunforder; owner and barkeeper of only inn
Nat (NAT): a highwayman
The Savage: New Lovénian; a brawly (deceased)

EASTERNERS

Alneezah (Al-NEE-zah): a castle maid
Alsrusett (Al-RUSS-it): one of Weile Kahn's bodyguards (with Daxan)

Chayl (SHAYL): a follower of Weile Kahn; commander of Nighthawk sector

Curdeis (KER-tuss): Weile Kahn's brother (deceased)

Daxan (DICK-sunn): one of Weile Kahn's bodyguards (with Alsrusett)

Halcone (Hell-KAHN): high general of the Eastern armies

Jeffrin (JEFF-rinn): an informant working for Weile Kahn

Kinya (KEN-yah): a long-time member of Weile Kahn's organization

Leightar (LAY-tar): a follower of Weile Kahn

Midonner (May-DONN-er): previous king of Stalmize; high king of the Eastlands (deceased)

Nacoma (Nah-KAH-mah): a follower of Weile Kahn

Saydee (SAY-dee): a server at the Dancing Dog

Shavoor (Shah-VOOR): an informant working for Weile Kahn

Shaxcharal (SHACKS-krawl): the last king of LaZar

Tae Kahn (TIGH KAHN): the king of Stalmize; high king of the Eastlands; Weile Kahn's only son

Tisharo (Tuh-SHAR-oh): a con man working for Weile Kahn

Usyris (Yoo-SIGH-russ): a follower of Weile Kahn; commander of Sparrowhawk sector

Weile Kahn (WAY-lee KAHN): Tae's father; father of organized crime

NORTHERNERS

Alsmir (ALS-meer): AERI; captain of Aerin's infantry

Andvari (And-VARR-ee): NORDMIRIAN; warrior and diplomat

Avard (AV-ahrd): AERI; a bartender in Aerin

Elgar (ELL-gar): ERDAI; general of Erd's army

Erik Leifsson (EH-rik): NORDMIRIAN; captain of the Sea Dragon, a warship

Geirrodr (Gay-EER-odd): GILSHNI; captain of the Silver Serpent

Griselda (Gree-ZELL-duh): AERI; a server in the tavern in Aerin

Mundilnarvi (Munn-dill-NAR-vee): NORDMIRIAN; *Einherjar* killed in the war against the Renshai

Olvaerr (OHL-eh-vayr): NORDMIRIAN; Valr Kirin's son (deceased)

Olvirn (OHL-eh-veern): AERI; captain of Aerin's cavalry

Sivaird (SEE-vayrd): AERI; captain of Aerin's archers

Tyrion (TEER-ee-on): ASCAI; an inner court guard of Pudar

Valr Kirin (Vawl-KEER-inn): NORDMIRIAN; an ancient enemy of Colbey's; Rache Kallmirsson's blood brother (deceased)

Valr Magnus (Vawl-MAG-nuss): AERI; general of Aerin's army; the best swordsman in the North

Verdondi Eriksson (Ver-DONN-dee): NORDMIRIAN; Erik's son

HEIMSTADERS

Bobbin (BOB-inn): Mistri's pet human

Dillion (DILL-ee-yon): an *alsona* (deceased)

Fallon (FOUL-in): a general of the *alsona*

Firuz (Fa-ROOZ): one of the *Kjempemagiska* (deceased)

Floralyn (FLOOR-a-linn): a *Kjempemagiska*; Mistri's aunt and Hortens' sister

Hortens (HOHR-tense): a *Kjempemagiska*; Mistri's mother

Jaxon (JACKS-onn): an *alsona* (deceased)

Kalka (KOWL-kah): a general of the *alsona* (deceased)

Kentt (KENT): a *Kjempemagiska*; Mistri's father

Mistri (MISS-tree): a *Kjempemagiska* child

OUTWORLDERS

Arak'bar Tulamii Dhor (AHR-ok-bar Too-LAHM-ee-igh ZHOOR): eldest of the elves; aka He Who Has Forgotten His Name; aka Captain

Arith'tinir Khy-loh'Shinaris Bal-ishi Sjörmann'taé Or (ARR-ith-tin-eer KIGH-loh-shin-ahr-iss Bal-EE-shee Syorr-mahn-TIGH Orr): Captain's given name

Captain: the common name for Arak'bar Tulamii Dhor

Chan'rék'ril (Shawn-RAYK-rill): an artistic elf

Dh'arlo'mé'aftris'ter Te'meer Braylth'ryn Amareth Fel-Krin (ZHAR-loh-may-aff-triss-ter Te-MEER Brawl-THRINN

Ah-MAR-eth Fell-krinn): former leader of the *svartalf* (deceased)

El-brinith (El-BRINN-ith): an elf with a good feel for magic

Khy'barreth Y'vrintae Shabeerah El-borin Morbonos (Kigh-BAYR-eth eev-RINN-tigh Shah-BEER-ah ELL-boor-in Moor-BOH-nos): a brain-damaged elf

Tem'aree'ay Donnev'ra Amal-yah Krish-anda Mal-satorian (Teh-MAR-ee-ay Donn-EV-er-a Ah-MAL-yah Kreesh-AND-ah Mahl-sah-TOR-ee-an): an elfin healer; King Griff's junior wife (second)

ANIMALS

Clydin (KLY-dinn): Darby's chestnut gelding

Frost Reaver: Colbey's white stallion

Imorelda (Ih-moor-ELL-dah): Tae's silver tabby cat

Mior (Mee-ORR): Matrinka's calico cat (deceased)

Silver Warrior: Ra-khir's white stallion

Snow Stormer: Kedrin's white stallion, replacement for the previous horse of the same name

GODS, WORLDS & LEGENDARY OBJECTS

Northern

Aegir (AHJ-eer): Northern god of the sea; killed at the *Ragnarok* (deceased)

Alfheim (ALF-highm): the world of elves; destroyed during the *Ragnarok*

Asgard (AHSS-gard): the world of the gods

Baldur (BALL-der): Northern god of beauty and gentleness who rose from the dead after the *Ragnarok*

Beyla (BAY-lah): Frey's human servant; wife of Byggvir

The Bifrost Bridge (BEE-frost): the bridge between Asgard and man's world

Bragi (BRAH-gee): Northern god of poetry; killed at the *Ragnarok* (deceased)

Brysombolig (Briss-om-BOH-leeg): Troublesome House; Loki's long-abandoned citadel

Byggvir (BEWGG-veer): Frey's human servant; husband of Beyla

Colbey Calistinsson (KULL-bay): legendary immortal Renshai; blood son of Thor and a mortal Renshai; husband of Freya

Einherjar (Ighn-HER-yar): the immortal souls of dead warriors chosen from the battlefield who dwell in Valhalla

The Fenris Wolf (FEN-ris): the Great Wolf; the evil son of Loki; also called Fenrir; killed at the *Ragnarok* (deceased)

Frey (FRAY): Northern god of rain, sunshine and fortune; father of the elves

Freya (FRAY-uh): Frey's sister; Northern goddess of battle

Frigg (FRIGG): Odin's wife; Northern goddess of fate

Geirönul (Gay-EER-awn-ull): Spear-bearer; a *Valkyrie*

Gladsheim (GLAD-shighm): "Place of Joy"; sanctuary of the gods

Göll (GAWL): Screaming; a *Valkyrie*

Hel (HEHL): Northern goddess of the cold underrealm for those who do not die in valorous combat; killed at the *Ragnarok* (deceased)

Hel (HEHL): the underrealm ruled by the goddess Hel

Heimdall (HIGHM-dahl): Northern god of vigilance and father of mankind; killed at the *Ragnarok* (deceased)

Herfjötur (Herf-YOH-terr): Host Fetter; a *Valkyrie*

Hildr (HEELD): Warrior; a *Valkyrie*

Hlidskjalf (HLID-skyalf): Odin's high seat from which he could survey the worlds

Hlökk (HLAWK): Shrieking; a *Valkyrie*

Hod (HAHD): Blind god, a son of Odin; returned with Baldur after the *Ragnarok*

Honir (HOHN-eer): an indecisive god who survived the *Ragnarok*

Hrist (HRIST): Shaker; a *Valkyrie*

Idunn (EE-dun): Bragi's wife; keeper of the golden apples of youth

Ìfing (IFF-ing): river between Asgard and Jötunheim

Jötunheim (YOH-tun-highm): the world of the giants; destroyed during the *Ragnarok*

Kvasir (KWAH-seer): a wise god, murdered by dwarves, whose blood was brewed into the mead of poetry (deceased)

Loki (LOH-kee): Northern god of fire and guile; a traitor to the gods and a champion of chaos; killed at the *Ragnarok* (deceased)

Magni (MAG-nee): Thor's and Sif's son; Northern god of might

Mana-garmr (MAH-nah garm): Northern wolf destined to extinguish the sun with the blood of men at *Ragnarok*; killed in the *Ragnarok* (deceased)

Midgard (MID-gard): the world of humans

The Midgard Serpent: a massive, poisonous serpent destined to kill and be killed by Thor at the *Ragnarok*; Loki's son; killed in the *Ragnarok* (deceased)

Mimir (MIM-eer): wise god who was killed by gods; Odin preserved his head and used it as an adviser (deceased)

Mist: Mist; a *Valkyrie*

Modi: (MOH-dee): Thor's and Sif's son; Northern god of blood wrath

Nanna (NAH-nah): Baldur's wife

Nidhogg (NID-hogg): dragon who gnaws at the root of the World Tree in Niflheim

Niflheim (NIFF-uhl-highm): Misty Hel; the coldest part of Hel to which the worst of the dead are committed

Njord (NYORR): Frey's and Freya's father; died in the *Ragnarok* (deceased)

Norns: the keepers of past (Urdr), present (Verdandi), and future (Skuld)

Odin: (OH-dinn): Northern leader of the pantheon; father of the gods; killed in the *Ragnarok*; resurrected self by placing his soul in the empty Staff of Law prior to his slaying, then overtaking the leader of the elves (deceased)

Odrorir (ODD-dror-eer): the cauldron containing the mead of poetry brewed from Kvasir's blood

The Ragnarok (RAG-nuh-rock): the massive war prophesied to destroy the gods, humans, and elves; partially thwarted by Colbey Calistinsson and Odin

Ran (RAHN): wife of Aegir; killed in the *Ragnarok* (deceased)

Randgrithr (RAWND-greeth): Shield-bearer; a *Valkyrie*

Raska Colbeysson (RASS-kuh): son of Colbey and Freya; aka Ravn (RAY-vinn); see Renshai

Ratatosk (Rah-tah-TOSK): a squirrel who relays insults between Nidhogg and the eagle at the top of Yggdrasill

Rathgrithr (RATH-greeth): Plan-Destroyer; a *Valkyrie*

Reginleif (REGG-inn-leef): God's Kin; a *Valkyrie*

Sif (SIFF): Thor's wife; Northern goddess of fertility and fidelity

Sigyn (SEE-gihn): Loki's wife

Skeggjöld (SKEG-yawld): Axe Time; a *Valkyrie*

Skögul (SKOH-gull): Raging; a *Valkyrie*

Skoll (SKOHWL): Northern wolf who was to swallow the sun at the *Ragnarok* (deceased)

Skuld (SKULLD): Being; the Norn who represents the future

Spring of Mimir: spring under the second root of Yggdrasill

Surtr (SURT): the king of fire giants; destined to kill Frey and destroy the worlds of elves and men with fire at the *Ragnarok*; killed in the *Ragnarok* (deceased)

Syn (SIN): Northern goddess of justice and innocence

Thor: Northern god of storms, farmers, and law; killed in the *Ragnarok* (deceased)

Thrudr (THRUD): Thor's daughter; goddess of power

Tyr (TEER): Northern one-handed god of war and faith; killed in the *Ragnarok* (deceased)

Ugagnevangar (Oo-gag-nih-VANG-ahr): Dark Plain of Misfortune; Loki's world on which sits Brysombolig

Urdr (ERD): Fate; the Norn who represents the past

Valaskjalf (Vahl-AS-skyalf): Shelf of the Slain; Odin's citadel

Valhalla (Vawl-HOLL-uh): the heaven for the souls of dead warriors killed in valiant combat; at the *Ragnarok*, the souls in Valhalla (*Einherjar*) assisted the gods in battle

Vali (VAHL-ee): Odin's son; survived the *Ragnarok*

The Valkyries (VAWL-ker-ees): the Choosers of the Slain; warrior women who choose which souls got to Valhalla on the battlefield

Verdandi (Ver-DAN-dee): Necessity; the Norn who represents the present

Vidar (VEE-dar): son of Odin destined to avenge his father's death at the *Ragnarok* by slaying the Fenris Wolf; current leader of the gods

The Well of Urdr: body of water at the base of the first root of Yggdrasill

The Wolf Age: the sequence of events immediately preceding the *Ragnarok* during which Skoll swallows the sun, Hati mangles the moon, and the Fenris Wolf runs free

Yggdrasill (IGG-druh-zill): the World Tree

Western

(now considered essentially defunct;
mostly studied for its historical significance)

Aphrikelle (Ah-frih-KELL): Western goddess of spring

Cathan (KAY-than): Western goddess of war, specifically hand-to-hand combat; twin to Kadrak

Dakoi (Dah-KOY): Western god of death

The Faceless God: Western god of winter

Firfan (FEER-fan): Western god of archers and hunters

Itu (EE-too): Western goddess of knowledge and truth

Kadrak (KAD-drak): Western god of war; twin to Cathan

Ruaidhri (Roo-AY-dree): Western leader of the pantheon

Suman (SOO-mon): Western god of farmers and peasants

Weese (WEESSS): Western god of winds

Yvesen (IV-eh-sen): Western god of steel and women

Zera'im (ZAYR-uh-eem): Western god of honor

Eastern

(though more common than the Western religion,
it is also considered essentially defunct)

Sheriva (Shuh-REE-vah): omnipotent, only god of the Eastlands

Outworld Gods

Ciacera (See-uh-SAYR-uh): goddess of life on the sea floor who takes the form of an octopus

Mahaj (Muh-HAJ): the god of dolphins

Morista (Moor-EES-tah): the god of swimming creatures who takes the form of a seahorse

FOREIGN WORDS

a (AH): EASTERN; "from"

ailar (IGH-lar): EASTERN; "to bring"

al (AIL): EASTERN; the first person singular pronoun

aldrnari (old-NAHR-ee): HEIMSTADER; "fire"

alfen (ALF-in): BÉARNIAN; "elves"; term created by elves to refer to themselves alsona (al-SOH-na): HEIMSTADER; "person" or "people"; "the servants"

alsonese (al-soh-NEEZ): TRADING; Tae's made-up name for usaro

amythest-weed: TRADING; a specific type of wildflower

anari (uh-NAHR-ee): HEIMSTADER; the mind-language of Heimstadr

anem (ON-um): BARBARIAN; "enemy"; usually used in reference to a specific race or tribe with whom the barbarian's tribe is at war

åndelig mannhimmel (AWN-deh-lee mahn-hee-MELL): RENSHAI; "spirit man of the sky"; an advanced Renshai sword maneuver

aristiri (ah-riss-TEER-ee): TRADING; a breed of singing hawk

årvåkir (awr-vaw-KEER): NORTHERN; "vigilant one"

baronshei (buh-RON-shigh): TRADING; "bald"

bassana (ba-SAW-nah): HEIMSTADER; "bed"

bein (BAYN): NORTHERN; "legs"

berserks (BAYR-sayr): NORTHERN; soldiers who fight without emotion, ignoring the safety of self and companions because of drugs or mental isolation; "crazy"

bha'fraktii (bhah-FROCK-tee-igh): ELVISH; "those who court their doom"; a *lysalf* term for *svartalf*

binyal (BIN-yall): TRADING; a type of spindly tree

bleffy (BLEFF-ee): WESTERN/TRADING; a child's euphemism for nauseating

bolboda (bawl-BOH-duh): NORTHERN; "evilbringer"

bonta (BONN-tah): EASTERN; vulgar term for a male homosexual

brawly (BRAWL-ee): WESTERN; street slang for gang-level protection racketeers

brigshigsa weed (brih-SHIG-sah): WESTERN; a specific leafy weed with a translucent, red stem; a universal antidote to several common poisons

brorin (BROHR-inn): RENSHAI; "brother"

bruni (brew-NEE): NORTHERN; "fire"

brunstil (BRUNN-steel): NORTHERN; a stealth maneuver learned from barbarians by the Renshai; literally "brown and still"

butterflower: TRADING; a specific type of wild flower with a brilliant, yellow hue chrisshius (KRISS-ee-us): WESTERN; a specific type of wildflower

chroams (krohms): WESTERN; a specific coinage of copper, silver, or gold

corpa (KOR-pah): WESTERN; "brotherhood", "town"; literally "body"

cringers: EASTERN; gang slang for people who show fear

daimo (DIGH-moh): EASTERN; slang term for Renshai

demon (DEE-mun): ANCIENT TONGUE; a creature of magic

dero (DAYR-oh): EASTERN; a type of winter fruit

djem (dee-YEM): NORTHERN; "demon"

djevgullinhåri (dee-YEV-gull-inn-HAHR-ee): NORTHERN; "golden-haired devils"

djevskulka (dee-yev-SKOHL-ka): NORTHERN; an expletive that essentially means "devil's play"

doranga (door-ANG-uh): TRADING; a type of tropical tree with serrated leaves and jutting rings of bark

drilstin (DRILL-stinn): TRADING; an herb used by healers

dwar-freytii (dwar-FRAY-tee-igh): ELVISH; "the chosen ones of Frey"; a *svartalf* name for themselves

Einherjar (Ighn-HER-yar): NORTHERN; "the dead warriors' souls in Vahalla"

ejenlyåndel (ay-YEN-lee-ON-dell): ELVISH; "immortality echo"; a sense of infinality that is a part of every human and elf; the soul

eksil (EHK-seel): NORTHERN; "exile"

erenspice (EH-ren-spighs): EASTERN; a type of hot spice used in cooking

ernontris (err-NON-triss): OUTWORLD; a specific gruesome and magical type of torture

fafra (FAH-fruh): TRADING; "to eat"

feflin (FEF-linn): TRADING; "to hunt"

fegling (FEGG-ling): ERYTHANIAN; "coward"

feuer (fee-YORE): BEARNESE; "fire"

floyetsverd (floy-ETTS-wayrd): RENSHAI; a disarming maneuver

formynder (for-MEWN-derr): NORTHERN; "guardian", "teacher"

forrader (foh-RAY-der): NORTHERN; "traitor"

forraderi (foh-reh-derr-EE): NORTHERN; "treason"

forsvarir (fors-var-EER): RENSHAI; a specific disarming maneuver

frey (FRAY): NORTHERN; "lord"

freya (FRAY-uh): NORTHERN; "lady"

frichen-karboh (FRATCH-inn kayr-BOH): EASTERN; widow; literally "manless woman, past usefulness"

frilka (FRAIL-kah): EASTERN; the most formal title for a woman, elevating her nearly to the level of a man

fussling (FUSS-ling): TRADING; slang for bothering

galn (GAHLN): NORTHERN; "ferociously crazy"

ganim (GAH-neem): RENSHAI; "a non-Renshai"

garlet (GAR-let): WESTERN; a specific type of wildflower believed to have healing properties

garn (GARN): NORTHERN; "yarn"

gerlinr (gerr-LEEN): RENSHAI; a specific aesthetic and difficult sword maneuver

gloik (GLOYK): TRADING; slang term for oaf

granshy (GRANN-shigh): WESTERN; "plump"

gullin (GULL-inn): NORTHERN; "golden"

gynurith (ga-NAR-ayth): EASTERN; "excrement"

hacantha (ha-CAN-thah): TRADING; a specific type of cultivated flower that comes in various hues

hadongo (hah-DONG-oh): WESTERN; a twisted, hard-wood tree

handelegg (HON-dell-egg): NORTHERN; "arm"

HandeleggColbyr (HON-dell-egg-KULL-bayr): NORTH-ERN; "the arm of Colbey"; Valr Magnus' sword

harval (harr-VALL): ANCIENT TONGUE; "the gray blade"

hastivillr (has-tih-VEEL): RENSHAI; a sword maneuver

herbont (HER-bont): TRADING; a specific type of gnarly tree that tends to grow with multiple trunks

hervani arwawn telis braiforn (her-VONN-ee ar-WAN tell-EES bray-FORN): ELVISH; "joining together that which normally has no true focus"; adding magical strength to solid objects

hyrr (HIGH-er): ELVISH; "fire"

ivana (ee-VONN-nah): ELVISH; negative slang term for "half-human/half-elfin creature"; named for Ivana (see Béarnides)

jarfr (YAR-far): HEIMSTADER; a specific, ferocious predator (akin to a wolverine)

jeconia (jah-KOHN-yah): TRADING; a specific type of venomous snake

jovinay arithanik (joh-VIN-ay ar-ih-THAN-ik): ELVISH; "a joining of magic"; a gathering of elves for the purpose of amplifying and casting spells

jufinar (JOO-fin-ar): TRADING; a specific type of bush-like tree that produces berries

kadlach (KOD-lok; the ch has a guttural sound): TRADING; a vulgar term for a disobedient child; akin to brat

kathkral (KATH-krall): ELVISH; a specific type of broad-leafed tree

kenya (KEN-yuh): WESTERN; "bird"

khohlar (KOH-lahr): ELVISH; a mental magical concept that involves transmitting several words in an instantaneous concept

khohlar, direct: ELVISH; khohlar sent to an individual; aka singular khohlar

khohlar, indirect: ELVISH; khohlar sent to everyone

kirstal (KEER-stahl): HEIMSTADER; a specific type of towering, thickly-branched tree that grows on Heimstadr

kjaelnabnir (kyahl-NAHB-neer): RENSHAI; temporary name for a child until a hero's name becomes available

Kjempemagiska (Kee-YEM-pay-muh-JEES-kah): HEIMSTADR; "magical giants"; "the masters"

Kjempese (kee-YEM-peez): TRADING; Tae's made-up word for anari

kinesthe (kin-ESS-teh): NORTHERN; "strength"

kolbladnir (kol-BLAW-neer): NORTHERN; "the cold-bladed"

krabbe (krab-EH): NORTHERN; "the crab"; a Renshai sword maneuver

kraell (kray-ELL): ANCIENT TONGUE; a type of demon dwelling in the deepest region of chaos' realm

kyndig (KAWN-dee): NORTHERN; "skilled one"

lasat (lih-SAHT): HEIMSTADER; "apple"

latense (lah-TEN-seh): RENSHAI; a sword maneuver

lav'rintii (lahv-RINN-tee-igh): ELVISH; "the followers of Lav'rintir"

lav'rintir (lahv-rinn-TEER): ELVISH; "destroyer of the peace"

lessakit (LAYS-eh-kight): EASTERN; "a message"

leuk (LUKE): WESTERN; "white"

loki (LOH-kee): NORTHERN; "fire"

lonriset (LON-rih-set): WESTERN; a ten-stringed instrument

lynstriek (LEEN-strayk): RENSHAI; a sword maneuver

lysalf (LEES-alf): ELVISH; "light elf"

magni (MAG-nee): NORTHERN; "might"

mehiar (mih-HIGH-er): HEIMSTADER; a tea-like drink flavored with milk and honey

meirtrin (MAYR-trinn): TRADING; a specific breed of nocturnal rodent

menneskelik (men-ESS-ka-leek): ELVISH; "humanized"

mermelr (MERR-mell): HEIMSTADER; a specific squirrel-like animal with a flat tail (akin to marmot)

minkelik (min-KELL-ik): ELVISH; "human"

mirack (merr-AK): WESTERN; a specific type of hardwood tree with white bark

missy beetle: TRADING; a type of harmless, black beetle

mjollnir (MYOLL-neer): NORTHERN; "mullicrusher"

modi (MOE-dee): NORTHERN; "wrath"

Morshoch (MOOR-shok): ANCIENT TONGUE; "sword of darkness"

Motfrabelonning (mot-frah-bell-ONN-ee): NORTHERN; "reward of courage"

muldyrein (MULL-dih-rayn): ELVISH; "mule"

mulesl om natten (MYOO-sill-ohm-NOT-in): RENSHAI; "the night mule"; a Renshai sword maneuver

musserënde (myoo-ser-EN-deh): RENSHAI; "sparkling"; a Renshai sword maneuver

mynten (MIN-tin): NORTHERN; a specific type of coin

nådenal (naw-deh-NAHL): RENSHAI; "needle of mercy"; a silver, guardless, needle-shaped dagger constructed during a meticulous religious ceremony and used to end the life of an honored, suffering ally or enemy, then melted in the victim's pyre

nålogtråd (naw-LOG-trawd): RENSHAI; "needle and thread"; a Renshai sword maneuver

noca (NOH-kuh): BEARNESE; "grandfather"

Nualfheim (Noo-ALF-highm): ELVISH; "new elf home"

odelhurtig (od-ehl-HEWT-ih): RENSHAI; a sword maneuver

oopey (OO-pee): WESTERN/TRADING; a child's euphemism for an injury orlorner (oor-LEERN-ar): EASTERN; "to deliver to"

pen-fruit: WESTERN; an edible fruit that is the seed of the pen-fruit tree

perfrans (PURR-franz): WESTERN; a specific scarlet wild-flower

pike: NORTHERN; "mountain"

placeling (PLAYS-ling): ANCIENT TONGUE; a creature with Outworld blood placed magically into a human womb

prins (PRINS): NORTHERN; "prince"

ranweed: WESTERN; a specific type of wild plant

raynshee (RAYN-shee): TRADING; "elder"

reipfrodleikr (righp-FROHD-lighk): ELVISH; "trace magic"; an impression of magic on an object that is not magical but has had magic cast directly upon it

rexin (RAYKS-inn): EASTERN; "king"

rhinsheh (ran-SHAY): EASTERN; "morning"

richi (REE-chee): WESTERN; a specific type of songbird

rintsha (RINT-shah): WESTERN; "cat"

Ristoril (RISS-tor-rill): ANCIENT TONGUE; "sword of tranquillity"

sannrfrodleikr (san-FROHD-lighk): ELVISH; "true magic"; an item that is inherently magical

sangrit (SAN-grit): BARBARIAN; "to form a blood bond"

sarvenna (sar-VENN-uh): TRADING; a specific type of plant that has anesthetic properties

saw grass: WESTERN; a specific type of grass

shucara: (shoo-KAHR-uh): TRADING; a specific type of medicinal root

skjald (SKYAWLD): NORTHERN; "musician chronicler"

skulkë i djevlir (SKOOLK-eh ee dyev-LEER): NORTH-ERN; "devils' brutal fun"

skulkë i djevgullinhari (SKOOLK-eh ee dyev-gull-inn-HAHR-ee): NORTHERN; "golden-haired devils' bru-tal fun"

skyggefrodleikr (skigg-eh-FROHD-lighk): ELVISH; "shadow magic"; an impression or echo of magic on an object that has been in long and close proximity to, and/or greatly treasured by, one or more powerfully magical be-ings (or to raw chaos)

stjerne skytedel (STYARN-eh skih-TED-ell): RENSHAI; "the shooting star"; a Renshai sword maneuver sugarberries: TRADING; a specific type of edible berry with green and orange striped skin

svartalf (SWART-alf): ELVISH; "dark elf"

svergelse (sverr-GELL-seh): RENSHAI; "sword figures practiced alone"; katas

take: TRADING; a game children play

takudan (TOCK-oo-don): OUTWORLD; "sewer rat"

talvus (TAL-vuss): WESTERN; "midday"

tåphresëlmordat (taw-FRESS-al-MOOR-dah): RENSHAI; "brave suicide"; leaping into an unwinnable battle for the sole purpose of dying in glory for Valhalla rather than of illness or old age

thrudr (THRUDD): NORTHERN; "power," "might"

tisis (TISS-iss): NORTHERN; "retaliation"

torke (TOR-keh): RENSHAI; "teacher," "sword instructor"

tre-ved-en (TREH-ved-enn): RENSHAI; "Loki's cross"; a Renshai sword maneuver designed for battling three against one

trithray (TRITH-ray): TRADING; a specific type of purple wildflower

tvinfri (TWINN-free): RENSHAI; a specific disarming maneuver

ulvstikk (EWLV-steek): RENSHAI; a specific sword maneuver

usaro (oo-SARR-oh): HEIMSTADER; spoken language

uvakt (oo-VAKT): RENSHAI; "the unguarded"; a term for children whose *kjaelnabnir* becomes a permanent name

Valhalla (vawl-HOLL-uh): NORTHERN; "hall of the slain"

valkyrie (VAWL-kerr-ee): NORTHERN; "chooser of the slain"

valr (VAWL): NORTHERN; "slayer"

vesell argalfr (vih-SELL AR-galf): ELVISH; "wretched woman-elf hybrid"

Vestan (VAYST-inn): EASTERN; "The Westlands"

vethrleikr (VETH-er-lighk): HEIMSTADER; "weather magic"

villieldr (VILL-ee-eld): ELVISH; "the great fire"; the *Ragnarok* fire that destroyed Alfheim

vitanhvergi (veet-ehn-HVER-gee): ELVISH; "understand a nowhere"; a "nonconcept" beyond elfin understanding that does not translate from another language or culture

waterroot: TRADING; a specific edible sea plant

wertell (wer-TELL): TRADING; a specific plant with an acid seed used for medicinal purposes

wisule (WISS-ool): TRADING; a foul-smelling, disease-carrying breed of rodents that has many offspring because the adults will abandon them when threatened

yarshimyan (yar-SHIM-yan): ELVISH; a type of tree with bubblelike fruit

yessha (YEH-shuh): HEIMSTADER; a type of animal that resembles a brown-and-white striped horse

yonha (YON-uh): HEIMSTADER; "wild animal"; refers to humans

yrtventrig (ihrt-VENN-tree): RENSHAI; a specific sword maneuver

PLACES

Northlands

The area north of the Weathered Mountains and west of the Great Frenum Range. The Northmen live in nine tribes, each with its own town surrounded by forest and farmland. The boundaries change.

Aerin (Ah-REEN): home of the Aeri; Patron god: Aegir

Asci (ASS-kee): home of the Ascai; Patron god: Bragi

Devil's Island: an island in the Amirannak. A home to the Renshai after their exile. Currently part of Nordmir

Erd (URD): home of the Erdai; Patron god: Freya

Gelshnir (GEELSH-neer): home of the Gelshni; Patron god: Tyr

Gjar (GYAR): home of the Gyar; Patron god: Heimdall

Nordmir (NORD-meer): the Northlands high kingdom, home of the Nordmirians; Patron god: Odin

Shamir (Sha-MEER): home of the Shamirians; Patron god: Freya

Skrytil (SKRY-teel): home of the Skrytila; Patron god: Thor

Talmir (TAHL-meer): home of the Talmirians; Patron god: Frey

Westlands

The Westlands are bounded by the Great Frenum Mountains to the east, the Weathered Mountains to the north, and the sea to the west and south. In general, the cities become larger and more civilized as the land sweeps westward. The central area is packed with tiny farm towns dwarfed by lush farm fields that, over time, have nearly coalesced. This area is known as the Fertile Oval. The easternmost portions of the Westlands are forested, with sparse towns and rare barbarian tribes. To the south lies an uninhabited tidal plain.

Almische (Ahl-mish-AY): a small city

Béarn (Bay-ARN): the high kingdom; a large mountain city

Bellenet Fields (Bell-eh-NAY): a tourney field in Erythane

Corpa Bickat (KOR-pah Bih-KAY): a large city

Corpa Schaull (KOR-pah SHAWL): a medium-sized city; one of the "twin cities" (see Frist)

Dunford (DUNN-ferd): a small village east of Erythane

Erythane (AIR-eh-thayn): a large city closely allied with Béarn; famous for its knights

The Fields of Wrath: plains on the outskirts of Erythane; home to the Renshai

Frist (FRIST): a medium-sized city; one of the "twin cities" (see Corpa Schaull)

Granite Hills: a small, low range of mountains

Great Frenum Mountains (FRENN-um): towering, impassable mountains that divide the Eastlands from the Westlands and Northlands

Greentree: a small town

Hark: a mythical town created by Weile Kahn located at the site of Erythane Castle

Hopewell: a small town

Keatoville (KEY-toh-vill): a small town east and south of Dunford

The Knight's Rest: a pricy tavern in Erythane

Myrcidë (Meer-see-DAY): a town near the Weathered Mountains that consists entirely of magically hidden caves

New Lovén: (Low-VENN): a medium-sized city

Nualfheim (Noo-ALF-highm): the elves' name for their island

The Off-Duty Tavern: a Pudarian tavern frequented by guardsmen

Oshtan (OSH-tan): a small town

Paradise Plains: an Erythanian name for the Fields of Wrath

Porvada (Poor-VAH-duh): a medium-sized city

Pudar (Poo-DAR): the largest city of the West; the great trade center

The Red Horse Inn: an inn in Pudar

The Road of Kings: the legendary route by which the Eastern Wizard is believed to have rescued the high king's heir after a bloody coup

Santagithi (San-TAG-ih-thigh): a medium-sized town

Sheaton (SHAY-ton): a small town northeast of Dunford

The Western Plains: a barren salt flat

Wynix (Wigh-NIX): a medium-sized town

Eastlands

The area east of the Great Frenum Mountains, it is a vast, overpopulated area filled with crowded cities and eroded fields. Little forest remains.

Dunchart (DOON-shayrt): a small city

Ixaphant (IGHCKS-font): a large city

Gihabortch (GIGH-hah-bortch): a city

LaZar (LAH-zar): a small city

Lemnock (LAYM-nok): a large city

Osporivat (As-poor-IGH-vet): a large city

Prohathra (Pree-HAHTH-ruh): a large city

Rozmath (ROZZ-mith): a medium-sized city

Stalmize (STAHL-meez): the Eastern high kingdom

Bodies of Water

Amirannak Sea (A-MEER-an-nak): the northernmost ocean

Brunn River (BRUN): a muddy river in the Northlands

Conus River (KOHN-uss): a shared river of the Eastlands and Westlands

Icy River: a cold, northern river

Jewel River: one of the rivers that flows to Trader's Lake

Mahajian Ocean (Muh-HAJ-ee-en): distant extension of

the Amirannak Sea southward; surrounds the island of Heimstadr

Perionyx River (Peh-ree-ON-ix): a Western river

Southern Sea: the southernmost ocean

Trader's Lake: a harbor for trading boats in Pudar

Trader's River: the main route for overwater trade

Objects/Systems/Events

Bards, the: a familial curse passed to the oldest child, male or female, of one specific family. The curse condemns the current bard to obsessive curiosity but allows him to impart his learning only in song. A condition added by the Eastern Wizards compels each bard to serve as the personal bodyguard to the current king of Béarn as well.

Cardinal Wizards, the: a system of balance created by Odin in the beginning of time consisting of four, near-immortal, opposing guards of evil, neutrality, and goodness who were tightly constrained by Odin's laws. Obsolete.

Great War, the: a massive war fought between the Eastland army and the combined forces of the Westlands.

Harval: "the Gray Blade"; the sword of balance imbued with the forces of law, chaos, good, and evil. Obsolete.

Knights of Erythane, the: an elite guardian unit for the king of Erythane that also serves the high king in Béarn in shifts. Steeped in rigid codes of dress, manner, conduct, and chivalry, they are famed throughout the world.

Kolbladnir: "the Cold-Bladed"; a magic sword commissioned by Frey to combat Surtr at the *Ragnarok*.

Mages of Myrcidë: a society of genetic human mages once feared and revered. The greatest and strongest of the Cardinal Wizards came from this society before the Renshai killed them all and left their dwellings in ruins. Always reclusive, after their destruction, they were all but erased from human memory.

Mjollnir: "Mullicrusher"; Thor's gold, short-handled hammer so heavy only he can lift it.

Necklace of the Brisings, the: a necklace worn by the goddess Freya and forged by dwarves from "living gold."

Pica Stone, the: a clairsentient sapphire. One of the rare items with magical power. Once the province of the

Mages of Myrcidë, it became the totem of Renshai, was returned to the "last" Myrcidian by the "last" Renshai, then was shattered. The shards were regathered, the stone remade, and it now tests the heirs of Béarn to select the one worthy of rulership.

Ragnarok (RAN-yer-rok): "the Destruction of the Powers" the prophesied time when men, elves, and nearly all the gods would die. Because of actions by Colbey Calistinsson and Odin, things did not go exactly as fated. The current flashpoint of religious differences comes in the form of those who believe the *Ragnarok* has already occurred and those who believe it is still to come.

Sea Seraph, the: a ship once owned by an elf known only as Captain and used to transport the Cardinal Wizards. Obsolete.

Sea Skimmer, the: replacement for the Sea Seraph.

Seven Tasks of Wizardry, the: a series of tasks designed by gods to test the power and worth of the Cardinal Wizards' chosen successors. Obsolete.

Trobok, the: "the Book of the Faithful" a scripture that guides the lives of Northmen. It is believed that daily reading from the book assists Odin in holding chaos at bay from the world of law.

The Knights of Erythane

(in child's rhyme order)

Kedrin (captain)	Edwin (armsman)
Garvin	Bennardin
Harritin	Vincelin
Kovian	Braison
Jakrusan	Tellbastian
Ra-khir	Vellassir
Aromay	Alquantae
Shavasiay	Yoneté
Esatoric	Ashtonik
Tylan	Castillon
Lakamorn	Petrone
Thessilius	Leicinder

Fiona Patton

The Warriors of Estavia

"In this bold first of a new fantasy series... Court intrigues enrich the story, as do many made-up words that lend color. The smashing climax neatly sets up events for volume two." —*Publishers Weekly*

"The best aspect of this explosive series opener is Patton's take on relations between gods and men."
—*Booklist*

"Fresh and interesting...I look forward to the next."
—*Science Fiction Chronicle*

THE SILVER LAKE
978-0-7564-0366-9

THE GOLDEN TOWER
978-0-7564-0577-9

THE SHINING CITY
978-0-7564-0717-9

To Order Call: 1-800-788-6262
www.dawbooks.com

Melanie Rawn

"Rawn's talent for lush descriptions and complex characterizations provides a broad range of drama, intrigue, romance and adventure."
—*Library Journal*

THE GOLDEN KEY UNIVERSE
THE GOLDEN KEY	978-0-7564-0671-4
THE DIVINER	978-0-7564-0681-3

EXILES
THE RUINS OF AMBRAI	0-88677-668-6
THE MAGEBORN TRAITOR	0-88677-731-3

DRAGON PRINCE
DRAGON PRINCE	0-88677-450-0
THE STAR SCROLL	0-88677-349-0
SUNRUNNER'S FIRE	0-88677-403-9

DRAGON STAR
STRONGHOLD	0-88677-482-9
THE DRAGON TOKEN	0-88677-542-6
SKYBOWL	0-88677-595-7

To Order Call: 1-800-788-6262
www.dawbooks.com

Julie E. Czerneda

A TURN OF LIGHT

"An enchanting and gentle fable, rich with detail and characters you will love."   —Charles de Lint

"A gorgeous creation. Julie Czerneda's world and characters are richly layered and wonderful—full of mystery, hope and, most of all, heart."   —Anne Bishop

"I was captivated.... Many fantasy novels out there are *about* magic. Few, like Julie's, embody it."

—Kristen Britain

"*A Turn of Light* is deft, beautiful storytelling. Marrowdell is real, and full of 'the country folks' so often overlooked in favor of princes and knights in armor. This book shines, and I want sequels. Many sequels. One can never have too many classics."   —Ed Greenwood

978-0-7564-0952-4

To Order Call: 1-800-788-6262
www.dawbooks.com

E. C. Blake
The Masks of Aygrima

"Brilliant world-building combined with can't-put-down storytelling, *Masks* reveals its dark truths through the eyes of a girl who must learn to wield unthinkable power or watch her people succumb to evil. Bring on the next in this highly original series!"

—Julie E. Czerneda

"Mara's personal growth is a delight to follow. Sharp characterization, a fast-moving plot, and a steady unveiling of a bigger picture make this a welcome addition to the genre."

—*Publishers Weekly*

"*Masks* is simply impossible to put down."

—*RT Book Reviews*

MASKS
978-0-7564-0947-0

SHADOWS
978-0-7564-0963-0

FACES
978-0-7564-0939-5

To Order Call: 1-800-788-6262
www.dawbooks.com

Tad Williams

SHADOWMARCH

SHADOWMARCH
978-0-7564-0359-1

SHADOWPLAY
978-0-7564-0544-1

SHADOWRISE
978-0-7564-0645-5

SHADOWHEART
978-0-7564-0765-0

"Bestseller Williams once again delivers a sweeping spell-
binder full of mystical wonder."—*Publishers Weekly*

"Tad Williams is already regarded as one of fantasy's
most skilled practitioners, and this latest work
more than confirms that status."—*Amazing Stories*

"Williams creates an endlessly fascinating and magic-
filled realm filled with a profusion of memorable
characters and just as many intriguing plots and subplots....
Arguably his most accomplished work to date."
—*The Barnes & Noble Review*

To Order Call: 1-800-788-6262
www.dawbooks.com

Joshua Palmatier
Shattering the Ley

"Palmatier brilliantly shatters genre conventions. . . . An innovative fantasy novel with a very modern feel. . . . For readers who are willing to tackle a more challenging fantasy, without clear heroes and obvious conflicts, *Shattering the Ley* is an excellent read."   —SFRevu

"*Shattering the Ley*, the terrific new fantasy from Joshua Palmatier, is built of equal parts innocence, politics, and treachery. It features a highly original magic system, and may well be the only fantasy ever written where some of the most exciting scenes take place in a power plant. I couldn't put it down."   —S. C. Butler, author of *Reiffen's Choice*

ISBN: 978-0-7564-0991-3

And don't miss the *Throne of Amenkor* trilogy!

THE SKEWED THRONE   978-0-7564-0382-9
THE CRACKED THRONE   978-0-7564-0447-5
THE VACANT THRONE   978-0-7564-0531-1

To Order Call: 1-800-788-6262
www.dawbooks.com

DAW 153